PENGUIN MODERN CLASSICS
Shekhar: A Life

AGYEYA (1911–87) was the pen name of S.H. Vatsyayan, regarded as one of the foremost figures of Hindi literature who was instrumental in pioneering modern trends in the realm of poetry, fiction, criticism and journalism. As a young man, he joined the movement for India's independence alongside Bhagat Singh and Chandrashekhar Azad, and was even arrested by the British authorities. His monumental novel *Shekhar: Ek Jeevani*, widely regarded as his masterpiece, was drawn from his own experiences in prison and has now been published in Penguin Classics as *Shekhar: A Life. Prison Days and Other Poems*, a collection of his verses, has also been published in Penguin Classics. He has also been awarded the Sahitya Akademi Award and the Jnanpith Award for his poetry.

SNEHAL SHINGAVI is associate professor of English at the University of Texas, Austin, where he specializes in teaching South Asian literatures in English, Hindi and Urdu. He is the author of *The Mahatma Misunderstood*, and has translated to wide acclaim the iconic short-story collection *Angaaray* as well as Bhisham Sahni's memoir, *Today's Pasts*. He is currently translating Joginder Paul's novel *Ek Boond Lahu Ki* (One Drop of Blood).

VASUDHA DALMIA is professor emerita of Hindi and Modern South Asian Studies at the University of California, Berkeley. Her monograph, *The Nationalization of Hindu Traditions: Bharatendu Harischandra and Nineteenth Century Banaras* (1997), studies the life and writings of a major Hindi writer of the nineteenth century as the focal point for an examination of the intricate links between politics, language, culture, religion and nationality. She has edited and co-edited several works. Her book on the Hindi novel, *Fiction as History: The Novel and the City in Modern North India*, appeared in 2017.

'In the 1940s, Agyeya's biographical novel, the two-part *Shekhar: Ek Jeevani*, took the Hindi literary world by storm. It challenged the moral universe of the Hindi world, and attracted approbation and severe criticism in equal measure. It is a travesty that *Shekhar*, among the most iconic Hindi novels of the twentieth century, has been unknown to the non-Hindi–reading public. Justice has been done by two remarkable scholars, veteran Vasudha Dalmia and young Snehal Shingavi, in a masterful translation that recreates *Shekhar*'s magic—its passion and restraint, its conflicts, currents, undercurrents and emotions. A must-read for everyone. A publishing landmark.'

AKSHAYA MUKUL

AGYEYA

Shekhar: A Life

Translated by Snehal Shingavi and Vasudha Dalmia

PENGUIN BOOKS

An imprint of Penguin Random House

PENGUIN BOOKS

USA | Canada | UK | Ireland | Australia
New Zealand | India | South Africa | China | Singapore

Penguin Books is part of the Penguin Random House group of companies
whose addresses can be found at global.penguinrandomhouse.com

Published by Penguin Random House India Pvt. Ltd
4th Floor, Capital Tower 1, MG Road,
Gurugram 122 002, Haryana, India

First published in Hindi as *Shekhar: Ek Jeevani* by Saraswati Press,
Allahabad 1941 (Part 1), 1944 (Part 2)
First published in English in Penguin Books by Penguin Random House India 2018

ISBN 9780143426356

Typeset in Adobe Caslon Pro by Manipal Digital Systems, Manipal
Printed at Manipal Technologies Limited, India

Contents

Translator's Note

Translating Agyeya's monumental novel *Shekhar* poses certain interesting challenges, pleasures and impossibilities.

First and foremost, *Shekhar* is a watershed moment in the development of the Hindi novel. Not only is it one of the first formally experimental novels but it has also been an exceedingly important one to so many people. Perhaps no other novel other than Premchand's *Godan* has produced so much secondary critical work, with dozens of monographs devoted to the singular innovations that *Shekhar* produced. As a result, being attentive to both the formally innovative aspects of the work as well as the long tradition of scholarship on it meant juggling quite a few things in the air at the same time.

Secondly, and unsurprisingly, *Shekhar* is the product of a polyglot imagination. The novel freely relies on allusions to English, Sanskrit, Bengali and other languages. Part of this is because the main character travels the length and breadth of colonial India, but part of it is also due to Agyeya's own multilingual interests. Moreover, despite the fact that the main character insists on retaining and even building upon Hindi and its attendant cultural traditions (usually because they are being encroached upon by a colonial English), the novel does not hold on to the same political impulse. It was one thing to be able to work in what is already a highly challenging Hindi that Agyeya so deftly deploys, but quite another to be able to track down all of the other literary traditions that he was utilizing. This was made even more difficult by the fact that in a number of places, Agyeya's narrator (perhaps Agyeya himself) incorrectly remembered certain poems. It was something of a translator's dilemma whether to retain the errors in memory that were likely the result of the novel's composition in prison or to clean them up. In most places, I have opted for correcting Agyeya's lapses in memory as I could not find any literary reason to retain the errors. Wherever possible, these emendations have been noted in an endnote for any enterprising scholar.

Thirdly, Agyeya and his critics all refer to the 'missing' third volume of the *Shekhar* series. Two volumes have been translated here, but the third was never published. As Agyeya hints in his own preface to the novel, he believed that the purpose of the third volume had evaporated. Drafts of this third volume probably exist somewhere, but it seemed to me a mistake to try and track them down for the purposes of this project for a few reasons. Notwithstanding the author's own desires that the volume not be published (which is important enough), the third volume was never an event in Hindi literature. No one saw it and clearly no one read it. Thus, to have it translated into English and brought in that form for the first time did not seem warranted.

Fourth, as the endnotes will demonstrate, I worked from two different editions of the novel: the Mayur edition and the Saraswati edition. Having both was useful because errors in one would often be resolved in the other.

Fifth, I have tried as much as possible not to rely on transliteration of Hindi nouns for which there are no good English equivalents. While there are clearly cultural and historical values to retaining some words, there is also the danger that this shirks the responsibility of a translator to try to take one world view and make it stretch to accommodate another. In this, I have been guided by Walter Benjamin's essay 'The Task of the Translator'. Benjamin makes a rather novel argument that what good translations are doing is not flattening out the perspectives of another language or culture but rather pointing always to the places where the destination language (in this case, English) has to grow, evolve and change to be able to understand another. In that sense, a good translation ought to be able to defamiliarize the familiar language. That's only really possible, in my opinion, if one tries (and fails, inevitably) to find new ways of making English evolve to deal with experimental Hindi fiction.

Finally, this translation would not have been possible were it not for the tireless work of Vasudha Dalmia. Vasudha was not only a marvellous collaborator in this translation project, but in many ways its inspiration. I discovered *Shekhar* in one of the many Hindi seminars I took with her at the University of California, Berkeley, and ever since then she has gently nudged this project along. She has also been over each inch of this translation, editing and emending it, noting all of the text's infelicities, until it was polished. It bears underlining that while no translation is the work of a single person, this translation in particular bears her imprint on it in a marked way.

In saying all of this, I mean to point to the places where I faced the most challenges; these were not always the moments of my successes. In those places where my language skills (especially in Sanskrit and Bengali) were not adequate, I relied on the work of other scholars and translators to help me out. Those have also been indicated in the endnotes. This work has been years in the making and several people have given feedback and support for which I am ever grateful; the mistakes in this text, it bears repeating, are, of course, my own.

Austin, Texas   Snehal Shingavi
March 2018

Author's Introduction

1

There is a power in pain that gives sight. A person in torment can be a visionary.

'Shekhar: A Biography', which is the product of ten years of my effort—it's actually not quite ten years yet, but then again the 'Biography' isn't finished either! An attempt to put into words a *vision* seen in merely one night of intense pain.[1]

You might think this arrogance. I'm not trying to say that I completed this massive manuscript in a single night. No, read my words again carefully—'Shekhar' is an attempt to put into words a *vision* seen in merely one night of intense pain.[2]

It's possible that you might want to know what that night was like. But it's not possible to explain such intimate details, nor would it be of any use to you. The only thing that could have an explanation and a meaning for you is that I saw this particular *vision*. All I can tell you about how I came to regard that night is that when the police hauled me away in the middle of the night, like bandits, and made me a prisoner, and then shortly thereafter—after I had spoken to, and then yelled at, and then got beaten up by senior police officials—it seemed to me that my life was quickly coming to its end.

I didn't think of myself as someone deserving to be hanged, and I still don't; but it didn't seem impossible on account of the circumstances then and my state of mind. Rather, I was firmly convinced that I was staring directly at my fate. I said earlier that serious torment can make someone a visionary; I can say here that grave hopelessness makes one dispassionate and thereby readies one to be a visionary. It was as if my condition escaped the bounds of feelings and presented itself to me in the form of a problem—if this was going to be the end of my life, then what was the value of that life, what was its meaning, what did it accomplish—for the individual, for society, for humanity? . . . My life slowly opened up to the dispassionate heartlessness of this curiosity and the omniscience of torment, not in the shape of a personal and irrelevant anomaly, but in the shape of a phenomenon, in the shape of a social fact; and gradually the formulas of cause-and-effect disentangled themselves and began to come to hand . . .

As dawn broke, the picture had changed entirely. I had a hold of several meaningful truths, but it was as if my body was spent, had turned to dust. I fell asleep exhausted but having found peace and remained asleep for two or three days.

That's all I can tell you about that night. For a month after that, nothing happened. A month later when I was transferred from Lahore Fort to Amritsar Jail, and I obtained things to write with, I wrote down in four or five days the meaning and purpose of life that I had understood on that night. The three hundred or so pages written in pencil are the foundation of 'Shekhar: A Biography'. I've spent more than nine years forming a body for that life-spark. To form a body—because that kind of intensity[3] cannot be reproduced solely in the imagination, and when it is found in life, the imagination can only restrain it, straitjacket it.

*

If you have studied the lives of revolutionaries, you will notice that a hard determinism lies hidden beneath all of the works of those tireless, energetic souls. Revolutionaries, ultimately, are a breed of determinists. But this determinism is not the sterile fatalism that makes one powerless or useless, rather it makes them more dispassionate and inspires them to action. In this, it is one step ahead of the karma yoga—or the dispassionate fulfilment of one's duties—of the *Bhagavad Gita*, because it does not reduce the actor to a mere instrument. And if you think of it this way, that a revolutionary's determinism is not satisfied with an unchanging destiny, that he has a firm (but amorphous) faith in the scientific chain of cause-and-effect that governs life, I believe that the majority of the scientists today are determinists in a similar way.

So the hero of 'Shekhar: A Biography' has attempted to understand the formulas of this destiny in his life. Because to understand them is to understand life itself, to understand its meaning. Whatever God does is good, and so each event is its own purpose—that's one way to see things; but this can be another solution to make life bearable for the individual who cannot accept this line of reasoning. So you will find in the first part of 'A Biography' that Shekhar also recalls small episodes from his childhood. The study of childhood has its own importance, and several foreign artists have studied and sketched portraits of childhood, but a study is not feasible in 'A Biography'. It is only the means to discover the formulas, which exist in every life, but which we never have the ability to see—which is only possible when life is illuminated from the wound of some event, or when a person becomes all-seeing through the intensity of suffering . . . I don't have the right to speak about my composition, but bearing in mind the relation between 'Shekhar' and me, it seems to me that this is what is great in his life and at the same time what is wretched. Great because his curiosity possesses passion, faith; wretched because this intensity keeps him from becoming a true seeker and leaves him a mere sophist and his sophistry (rationalization)[4] begins to seem pitiful and pathetic . . . *

---

* [Agyeya's note] After the explanation above, it shouldn't be necessary to add that although Shekhar's world view is ordinarily the same as the writer's world view, still wherever Shekhar depends on certain rationalizations or fallacies, they are Shekhar's and not the writer's. Everyone makes such pathetic misidentifications in logic, but it is a mistake to assume that the defects of a character in a story also belong to its writer. It is necessary to say this because readers of Hindi often make this mistake, and I know this from experience.

So in a nutshell, this is the story of the origin of 'Shekhar: A Biography'. You might say that this is not a vision, it's a system of logic, a philosophy. But I believe that philosophy is ultimately a revelation, a vision—and to strengthen my case I will take recourse to the Hindi name for philosophy—darshan, or vision!

2

Is this 'Biography' an autobiography? This question will certainly be asked. Or perhaps it won't even be asked, since a reader will march ahead with the notion fully formed. In Hindi, where every poet apparently uses his wife as inspiration for his writing, where a poem about separation seems to provide incontrovertible proof that so-and-so wrote it after his wife's death, it seems pointless to hope that 'Shekhar', which is not only a biography, but a biography delivered orally by an individual, will not be seen as the autobiography of its writer. I remember, three years ago when I had published a poem 'Second', several readers wrote me sympathetic letters and one went so far as to write, 'I am totally sympathetic to you; as someone in the same situation, I can completely understand what you are going through.' The editor of the paper, too (although as a joke), asked me, 'You have never been married, so how could you quarrel with your second wife so?' If such people are offered proof that I have written about a second marriage without ever having been married a first time, they will think that they have been deceived. It pains me to say it—but it is still true—that the majority of Hindi literature and criticism is built on a misconception; that the narration of self-formation (and not self-realization, because you can have realization without formation) is the best and truest kind. Few writers in Hindi seem to understand or accept that the proof of a writer's power is to be able to use the imagination or sensibility to enter into another's experiences, and while doing so, to be able to suspend the assumptions and ideologies of self-formation, to be

objective. On the contrary, you will find several such writers who
will call such realization (and I repeat that self-formation alone
is not self-realization but that formation can be self-realization if
we are able to be open to the possibility) foreign, second-hand,
and therefore, shoddy and untrue. For such people, T.S. Eliot's
phrase, which is really the only response, would have no meaning:
There is always a separation between the man who suffers and
the artist who creates; and the greater the artist the greater the
separation.[5]

*

But this has become a long digression, and I have to admit that
I could become an important artist by relying on the things Eliot
has said. There is not a single character in 'Shekhar' who is not by
and large a composite character,[6] although my experiences and my
pain are irrigating Shekhar. And the irrigation is such that saying,
'ultimately, all literary fiction is at its root autobiographical, if not
a sketch of one's own life then a projection,[7] the story of one's own
possibility' will not free it from the charge. There is too much of
me in 'Shekhar'; I was unable to follow Eliot's example (whose
importance I concede). 'Shekhar' is doubtlessly one individual's
record of personal suffering,[8] although it is simultaneously a
reflection of that individual's life struggles. It is not so personal
or peculiar that you could dismiss its claims by saying 'this is
the personal matter of a single man'; it is my insistence that my
society and my age speak through it and announce that it is a
symbol of mine and Shekhar's age. But even after all of that I
know that if the beginnings of this novel had happened under
different circumstances and in a different way (and perhaps by
different, more capable hands!), then this introduction would be
unnecessary . . . Nor could a reader completely disregard it and
have the occasion to say: forget about the events that happen in
'Shekhar', even the settings are uncannily similar to the writer's
own journeys (although to say that, a reader would have to be
especially familiar with me).

Let me say something about this last equation. In order to preserve the truth of the picture of the child-man, I took scenes from my own life for the early parts of 'Shekhar', and then gradually the life and emotional world of a maturing Shekhar drifted apart from my life and emotional world, so much so that I felt as if I were the witness and chronicler of an independent human being, I had absolutely no power over him. Whether it is appropriate for the creator of a character to say that or not, whether a character can really have that much of an independent existence or not, whether a character can ever not be a puppet in a writer's hands but also make a writer dependent on him or not, those who are interested in such esoteric questions can consult Pirandello.[9]

3

I have already said what I needed to propose about the origins of 'A Biography' and how a reader should approach it. But perhaps there is still more that remains to be said, since the reader will receive this introduction with only the first part of the biography, and what about the other two?

'Shekhar: A Biography' is divided into three parts.[10] Even though all three parts are woven together with the same narrative threads, they remain complete works independent of each other. It could be said that the biography is really the sequence of three independent novels. But even if this weren't the case, it would still be possible to publish them separately, but since it is the case, there is no need to offer a defence. It is not necessary for those who do not wish to read the second part after completing the first to believe that they have wasted their time on an unfinished story. They could consider the first part to be a complete novel, and they could justifiably base their judgement on the first part alone. I won't complain about biases.

But it wouldn't be a digression to offer a defence here to those readers who want to know why they should read the remaining parts while reading the first or want to know what assumptions they should make about the other parts. For those readers I want to say that if you look at the three parts of 'Shekhar' from the perspective of purpose—and if I can be so arrogant as to say from the perspective of meaning!—there is a singular solitariness; a monochromatic warp holds together and bears the fat and strong individual strands of yarn from a multihued weft to form a carpet, and similarly the multicoloured verses of the three parts of life form a single fibre of my desires and my words, which is singular, indivisible, and which to me is both a criticism and a worship of a life. In forging 'A Life' I have tried to forge a plot; as a result, no matter how it turns out I cannot approach the reader as a supplicant, but I will say this: if you have the daring to sit in judgement, at least have the decency to read the whole thing first.

Having introduced you to Shekhar, I now step away—then you can familiarize yourself with him directly. Shekhar is not an important man, nor is he a good man. But he is trying honestly to find himself in the light of humanity's collective experience. He might not even be a good companion, but you won't harbour him any ill will after walking with him to the end, I have full faith in that. And who knows, when we are all composite characters in the world today, then you might discover that somewhere within you, too, is a Shekhar, who is not important, nor good, but awake and independent and honest—deeply honest!

Prologue

The gallows!

The rareness of life—it can neither be reproduced by any of the forces in this world, our progress, our science, nor by any of the tools and techniques developed by our civilization—and yet a simple heartlessness is all it takes to snuff out that same life, to ensure its destruction—the gallows!

But why the gallows? To punish a criminal. But will this rehabilitate him? Will this erase the effects of his crimes? The indelible line which has been drawn by his hands—will that be erased when he is gone? The gallows: a lesson to teach others. But what kind of education is this supposed to be which orchestrates a display of cruel, heartless contempt towards life in order to teach respect for it? And has this ever taught anyone anything? The idea of the gallows has always gripped me strangely—it has something of the power of a cobra's eyes: bone chilling and yet unfalteringly hypnotic . . . A hypnotizing summons that turns even this machinery of vengeance into something poetic, as the unfortunate—or should I say most fortunate!—person who is sacrificed on its altar is rewarded with one of life's realizations, so his untimely end is simultaneously a kind of completion of his life . . .

The gallows!

The high tide of youth in a dried-up ocean. The tresses of darkness cascading, thick with shadows, over the dawn. A monstrous, dark raincloud athwart the beauty of the autumnal sky. Its realization is precisely in this opposition, in this sudden juxtaposition and in the implied, unprecedented poetry of terror that it produces . . .

What kind of realization—to what end? What will my death realize—and what realization did my life produce?

The curtain rises and falls. The scenes drop and are raised. But with the curtain's every fall, and every transformation of the scene, transfixed even in death, another drop falls into the stream of the play; another drop which is nothing in itself but without which the stream lacks movement—without which it doesn't even exist.

I am performing my life's retrospective, I am living the life I have already lived a second time. I, who had always looked ahead, have come to the final stretch of my life's journey and am now looking back to see where I came from and how I drifted, and the curious experiences that have brought me here. Which is why it seems to me that there had been a plan in my drifting, containing the germ of my ultimate objective. My psychological idiosyncrasies contained a unique hedonism that was turning into my guiding principle. And the mountains, valleys, rivers and streams, trees and forests, storms and rains that came across the path of my life all possessed for me and me alone a unity, whose purpose was to give the particular shape of my life completion at a specific time, in specific circumstances in a specific place, after specific preparations and means, in which it would find its own realization, its own fruition and its own coherence . . . as of now I am unfinished but I am not lacking; I am incomplete, but there are no more places to affix things that could complete me.

Except for this retrospective. Perhaps it is the provision for the final stretch of my life's journey, because this, and only this, brings me contentment.

*

Before everyone else, I turn to you, Shashi.

Not because you came into my life first or because you are the freshest memory. But because the core of my being depends on you—exactly like the blade of a sword depends on the whetstone's dream. You are the whetstone that has sharpened my life's blade again and again, that has scraped and ground me and turned me into something that is not ashamed to stand exposed before the world—that knows no reason to feel ashamed.

You aren't alive any more. You were broken along the way as I created Shekhar, perhaps you were even broken by Shekhar's own hands. And I've been repeating it over and over in my mind—'Shashi is gone, Shashi is dead, Shashi is gone'—but I still can't fathom what has happened exactly. No one can accurately assess the damages he has caused, or feel it fully.

Why? Why . . . how does a sharp sword know that the whetstone is broken as long as the sword isn't dull or doesn't break? And I'm still alive. I'm still burning, still 'am'.

But then why do I say that you don't exist any more? The whetstone that sharpens a sword doesn't break until the sword breaks. I have to die, swinging from the gallows, but for now I'm still alive.

Give me permission to remember you. To speak of you and use the word 'memory' is to desecrate a prayer, but I'll still ask it of you. Give me this right. You've died, you've become the essential 'nothing'. Let me explain this to myself, but in order to do that, I have to bring forth a thing which is 'something' for me—your shadows, which I used to believe were real . . .

No, it's not the one where I was scared and so I asked you, 'What happens, Shashi?' And you replied hoarsely, drifting off into unconsciousness, 'Happiness, Shekhar. Happiness . . .' I don't have the strength to bear that moment for anything more than an instant.

I can remember how we used to meet and talk effortlessly. We felt affection; we felt attraction; but not the kind of affection that flows by holding on to hardship, not the kind of attraction that builds its home only on a foundation of pain . . .

This realization hit me hard when I got out of jail and saw you for the first time. That's why I said, 'I've lost so much now that I'm out. While I was in jail I thought you and I were one, but now it seems that I have to learn who you are all over again.' You cried . . .

Suddenly, you said, 'Won't you come and see my home?' Because you were married now, you had a home . . .

I saw your home and the man who was the reason that the house was now your home. And it seemed to me that you were content and your life had now been set firmly on its tracks and there was no one else anywhere near those tracks. So I became even more afraid that I had to learn who you were all over again—because you weren't familiar any more . . .

I said, 'Shashi, sing something for me.'

'I don't do that sort of thing any more.'

'Why, are you too old now?'

You laughed. And as a result of the sound of your laughter I had a vision, the kind that only seldom occurs. I saw unwaveringly and with perfect clarity, the cloud-capped sky, the dimmed twilight, the settled winds, the invisible lightning and a solitary bird falling helplessly as its wings suddenly broke in mid-flight, which while it was falling tried to find its flight, find its place by writhing in pain, writhing in pain . . .

Then I suddenly knew who you were . . . and I couldn't bear to be there any longer. I asked for your leave and left.

You came to the door to see me off.

'Got a good look at my house?'

'Yes, I saw. I saw quite a bit,' I said and left hurriedly, and you stood there encircled by the perimeter of your home.

The ruins of the buildings that were built at the time of Banda Veer[1] and others built around that time, and some more recent than those, but still very old buildings. Shekhar sits in one such building. He's sitting in his 'room', but in reality it's just the sill of an old-fashioned window on one side of the granary. Wide and misshapen, blackened with antiquity, but functional. He's sitting on that sill, his arms hanging to his side and his head is bent to his right, leaning out.

There are several bullet holes on the walls of the room and on the window. There are a few emplacements in the walls that were designed for returning fire from the inside. The bullet holes and the emplacements comprised a chapter in the history of that house that no one reads any more. He's sitting there, in the window, and also not noticing them, nor can he see anything beyond the scene that is before his eyes.

A small courtyard enclosed by falling walls. In one corner, a small jujube tree casting a shadow over a dilapidated, dried-up well. A pile of old-fashioned bricks next to the well, and some yellowed, wind-scattered, peepul leaves on the right side of the courtyard. Outside the walls, a peepul tree and a cow that is tied to it, the vaulted rooftop of a tiny little temple nearby and the drooping pods of a tamarind tree complete the tableau. And all of this in the tranquil quiet of the afternoon.

That's what he's looking at as he sits. Shashi's father lies ill with a heart condition, and so the whole family is anxiously expecting a calamity. A dark shadow hovers over the house, and it seems as if the silences of the rooms in the house are whispering to each other in muffled voices.

It's to escape from that strange, pulsating silence that he comes to sit here, and tries to forget the smell of the air in that house by watching this scene instead. Because he loves each member of that family but can't bear that taunting muteness.

Shashi is the queen of that household, and his sister. It's on account of Shashi that he abandons the vital and unfettered atmosphere of college and comes here, finding consolation even in these shadows.

She's not really his sister. But in that context, even if he feels a difference, it's not of distance, but of deep closeness, of an unobstructed friendship. A feeling like the early morning sun in autumn that not only lays to rest the shadows of that house but dissolves the shades of his differences, too.

She's not a relative. That's why Shekhar doesn't 'remember' her, doesn't 'look in' on her. He hasn't earned the right. He's only been allowed to worship. He sits there and dreams, dreams in which Shashi does not appear like a portrait but like the light which illuminates the portrait—a feeling remains rather than a thought.

That feeling arises sometimes in a terrible shudder. Shashi sings. Her voice lacks sophistication, she lacks the nuance of a trained artist and the attraction that radiates, but it has a stormy brilliance, the sweet warmth of fire in autumn. Her voice has the richness of a violin, the taut pain of a lute playing on some distant mountain at sunrise, the precise urgency of a flute heard in a pitch-black night of the monsoon, and on top of all of that, the marvellous daring of a voice, with the depth of youth, which pushes itself to the limits of breaking but doesn't break.

And she sings—what? A song that Shekhar has heard several times, from many different voices, several times from thousands of individuals singing collectively, but whose meaning, whose rising flame he has never felt.

What was it that awoke within me when I heard that song? Love, or anguish, or aggression, or all three? Whatever it was it came over me like a trance and showed me wild dreams of heroism and battlefields, where I could clearly hear myself telling the story of my own strength, my own sacrifices, my own fire-smelted soul—a story whose premise, whose internal force was Shashi. And it would awaken in me the awareness of a very sacred object, for which I was ready to go on jihad, and it would overpower me, this enigmatic feeling.

This call of Shashi's personality, this 'appeal',[2] was for the part of my mind that spills over from the ferment of life's activities, the part that is a rebel. But there was another part of my mind that could only reflect the beauty of creation, which really is my brain's heart, and therefore is a poet, and that part would wake at the sound of Shashi's laughter. There was something in that laughter that thrilled, but would steal the power of speech from you. It was a laugh beyond poetry; you would have to fall silent when you heard it. My imagination could show me visions of rivers, of waterfalls, of moonrises, of oceans, the Milky Way, but then quietly it would return to recall the sound of that laughter.

The cloud-capped sky, the lightless evening, the settled winds, the invisible lightning, and today there is no solitary bird falling

helplessly as its wings suddenly break in mid-flight, who while it
was falling tried to find its flight, find its place by at least writhing
in pain, at least writhing in pain . . .

In this tiny hell, the voice of an ascetic points me to a sacred
hermitage and reduces my vast delusion by an iota, forgetting that
it in no way was appropriate in this situation, and with a godly
sympathy, says, 'O Sheldrake bride, bid your mate farewell. The
night is come!'[3]

Oh night!

I can no longer recall from which faraway land we departed
and arrived here! Our houseboat has only taken us a mile away
from Srinagar yet, but it seems as if it has taken ages, as if it has
been going for countless years and will go on for countless more,
as if the travellers have been stricken with Narad's curse and can
never stop anywhere.[4]

The houseboat has passed through the Jhelum canal and is
now entering Manasbal Lake. It has already crossed the filthy
waters of the Jhelum, and it has long since passed the dense shade
of the chinar trees. Now the lake's limpid waters reflect the sky's
cloudlessness, and the long grasses that undulate in the lake,
reflecting the brilliance of the sun, sparkling and prismatic—
sometimes golden, red, sometimes taking on a dazzling green.
And sometimes a ray of light will cut through their tangles and
make glisten a rock lying at the bottom.

The houseboat isn't moving quickly. It's drifting. The current
is so weak that it's as if the power which set it in motion gave it
a push and then exhausted itself, and the boat is pulling along
in the stupor of that single push it hasn't been able to stop yet.
Its other bow—it's as if it has just awoken from a nap, seen the
lattice of light dancing before it and is extending its still-drowsy
arm to catch it.

Two people sit on its stern. The boy is wearing knickers, but
the rest of his body is naked, his hair scattered and tousled, and he
holds a long staff that he's turned into a fishing pole by attaching
a hook to one end. He plucks white lotus blossoms from the lake
and drops them into a pile in front him, but he's not satisfied. He's

only plucking the half-opened blossoms; for some reason, the fully opened ones don't interest him.

A girl sits nearby. But mentally, she is hundreds of thousands of miles away. She has several landscape paintings of Kashmir made by an English painter, and in her lap, she has a book—Kalidasa's *Raghuvansha*. But she isn't looking at the paintings, nor is she reading the book. She's looking at the boy blankly, humming something to herself. Who knows what she's thinking.

The boy is about eight years old, the girl about thirteen. The boy is me and the girl is my sister.

There are other people on the houseboat. But in the world of this afternoon there are no others deriving pleasure from the sun of this affection. They are separate, lost. And the houseboat is advancing patiently, chasing their dreams.

The boy exhausts himself plucking flowers and now there are no more bunches of flowers; and now it's only after a long stretch that he finds the occasional flower. And now they're reaching the deep parts of the lake. The boy tears the long stems of the flowers into pieces and makes a garland out of them. The stems are torn in half to make a link, and at the bottom of each chain dangles a flowery pendant. He goes on making garlands and each time he finishes one he sneaks over to his sister and gently puts it around her neck. She sits unfazed. Each time she smiles a dreamy smile at him and then drifts away. Her brother has piled her up with flowers, but he's not satisfied, and she doesn't stop him either.

The flowers are almost gone—the few that remain have broken petals. The boy thinks that these might not be suitable for garlands. But at the same time, he realizes that there aren't enough garlands—there is still room for many more . . . but then, perplexed, he goes to his sister and says guiltily, 'The rest weren't any good.'

His sister sees his disappointment and laughs. She says, 'There are plenty. Do you want to crush me?'

And then she drifts away again. The boy sits next to her and listens to her humming like a devotee, almost as if a goddess were giving him a blessing.

I still haven't forgotten those words. In those days, I didn't know what they meant, but I do now. But I haven't been able to decipher the dreams that I saw in those days, and the feelings they evoked—they're beyond meaning . . .

> If this garland can rob one of life, why did it not kill me when it fell on my heart?[5]

Listening to his sister sing, a sudden, unknown feeling rises in the boy's mind. It wasn't produced all at once, it's been germinating slowly for several days in his heart, but its rich fullness is new, and it has surfaced on his mental horizon for the first time today while putting the garlands around her neck and listening to her sing. Very gently he brushes his sister's cheek and says, 'You look so good.'

His dictionary doesn't have entries for beauty and ugliness, good and evil, truth and falsity. He's an innocent child but he fully appreciates the fact that 'truth is eternal and good'.[6] And so to express the unknown feeling in his heart, he says, 'You look so beautiful.'

And the sister understands him. She laughs again, and the slightest blush comes over her and makes her look even more beautiful and she turns away to stare at the water.

To find her imperceptible reflection? I don't know, and she only maybe knows herself. And now she is undergoing a secret transformation. I still tell her all of my secrets, but she's beginning to understand that she has claim to an independent reserve of mysteries—her own heart?

*

The order of my memories has come undone, like when a necklace of pearls falls apart and the spilt pearls are rethreaded haphazardly. I see another scene at the same time that I see this one. It has the same characters, the setting is the same, but its essential theme is completely different. This scene has the same point of view as the other, but in the course of my life it seems as if this scene bears no relation to the other, and if there is a connection then it is that the two scenes are symbols of the simultaneous development of very different feelings . . .

The same lake, the same houseboat, the same day. Evening has fallen, everyone has gone inside. I am alone on the roof of the houseboat. The light from the turbid and complex colours of the sky is reflected on the lake and has turned it into something like the guileless eye of nature, still drowsy from sleep, and like eyelashes around it, the long grasses are cutting into the horizon wildly. Despite being entranced I'm watching the inky shadow-images that the grass makes. It's black, itself devoid of beauty, but still encircling such beauty!

But even more than that, I'm sitting here waiting for something. Towards the east, the grassy eyelashes look even darker, because a clean white light falls on them from the sky. I'm trying to imagine it, the kinds of changes that will be produced in the various elements when the moon rises, the kinds of patterns that will develop. I had not realized that reality can outstrip my imagination . . .

Below, inside the houseboat, someone is singing. I am trying hard to listen. Two voices are singing together—one of them belongs to my sister and the other to our aunt. I don't remember the words to that song, but both voices still ring in my ears . . .

I imagine that the voices are two powerful swimmers riding the invisible waves on the lake and vanishing into the horizon, into the moonrise, to meet the rays of moonlight, because the rays of moonlight are their sisters, and they will adorn them with garlands of lotuses . . .

Ah! Those rays of moonlight draw nearer—the black eyelashes of the lake have now turned into lines of mascara in the eyelids of the horizon, and above them the moon has risen like an enormous, petrified eye . . .

A strange thought wells up in my mind. The moon is a virgin, and the dark beauty of the earth is its cloak. But the moon is so beautiful that the cloak has no right to cover it and so the moon has shed and discarded it and, naked, it now walks the horizon. Its radiating beauty makes even the abandoned covering beautiful.

I can't definitely say that these thoughts actually arose in my heart at that moment in this very form. But in the images that appear in my memory, that child is filled with these thoughts as he stands there. If these thoughts were not in his head in precisely this form, then their germ definitely was. It was definitely true that he had acquired an indirect knowledge of the fact that beauty was completely naked and that nakedness was completely beautiful . . .

A voice enters, tearing through the child's dream. 'Shekhar, come down now!' This, too, is his sister's voice. Ever since then, whenever I forget myself in a metaphysical frenzy while looking at an extremely beautiful scene, a sharp voice calls to me and says, 'Shekhar, come down now!'

> Dead, long dead;
> Long dead!
> And my heart is a handful of dust,
> And the wheels go over my head,
> And my bones are shaken with pain,
> For into a shallow grave they are thrust,
> Only a yard beneath the street.
> And the hoofs of the horses beat, beat,[7]

Under the cover of a grove of eucalyptus trees stands a half-hidden bungalow called 'Eagle's Nest'. This was the bungalow where she was living on the day Shekhar had buried her under flowers and abandoned her, filled with an irrepressible spirit, unable to bear the shadow that Sharda cast over him. Today, after so many days, Shekhar was running towards that very same grove, and memories of the past were racing through his mind . . . and the first wave of adolescence was crashing inside him.

> The hoofs of the horses beat . . .[8]

The same Sharda who used to make him laugh. Sharda, who played music on the veena that he could lose himself in, who had teased him so much that she had become his friend. Who had become everything for him, who didn't have her own home, who filled him with an urge today . . . which he also could not bear.

He came right up to the grove and stopped. Did he hope that he would find Sharda waiting for him at her doorstep and that she would start when she saw him? Because that didn't happen. She wasn't at the door. The door was closed. And even the smoke wasn't there today, the smoke that used to rise from the chimney of 'Eagle's Nest', the smoke he used to spend his days watching from a distance . . .

Timidly, Shekhar went to the door of the house. There was a lock on the door. He looked in through the window—the house was completely empty.

For a while he couldn't make sense of what was directly in front of him. And then slowly it dawned on him, and

The hoofs of the horses beat, beat,
The hoofs of the horses beat . . .

He stumbled and sat down on the steps.

When he got up and left, his mind was completely blank. After that he just never had occasion to be hurt by this wound or even try to understand it.

*

Just as a creature that lives inside its shell will only go outside it when it is hungry or when it is seeking a mate, and once it is satisfied it will return to the safety of its shell, similarly unsatisfied and discontented, Shekhar, too, emerged. Wretched and wounded, even if he had wanted to go back, the hunger inside him wouldn't let him return. He was vulnerable to injury, armourless, and life was leading him farther and farther away from the safety of his home . . .

He was quietly eating his roti. And, at the same time, he was thinking. Mother was sitting next to him in the kitchen; Father was talking to her. A letter had just arrived carrying news about his brother who had dropped out of college. It said that he was in Calcutta trying to find work as a policeman. That's what Father was explaining to Mother, and Shekhar was eavesdropping absent-mindedly.

His brother had told people in Calcutta the name of the college he had attended but had lied about the names of his parents. When the college was asked to verify his identity they sent a telegram to Father.

Father was hurt most by the fact that his son had lied about his parents. That's the sort of thing he was saying.

Mother said, 'I always used to say, how in the world could anyone trust such a son?'

Father said, 'Humph.'

Then Mother said, 'And if you ask me in all honesty'—and then her voice suddenly got softer—'ask me in all honesty, I'll say that I don't trust this one either.'

This one?

Shekhar didn't see anything, but sitting there it didn't take him long to imagine the whole scene, that agitated, stony visage and that thumb pointing towards Shekhar—'This one!'

He sat like that, stonily, until night fell. He didn't eat or drink anything. Mother came and scolded him, then she cursed her own fate, cried and left. Father came, yelled at him and left. Night fell, everyone was asleep, and it was perfectly quiet. Shekhar went into his room, closed the door and bolted it, blew out the candle and sat down on his charpoy and smouldered . . .

Much of the night had passed before he picked up his diary and tried to relieve his turmoil . . .

'It would have been better if I had been a dog, or a mouse, or some stinking insect or worm—better than being the kind of man whom no one can trust.'

He got up. He stared at the wall, agitatedly, and said in English, 'I hate her, I hate her!'[9] Then he got dressed, jumped out of the window and started walking.

As he neared a park some miles away he vowed that he wouldn't listen to his mother, he wouldn't communicate with her, he would never do the kind of thing that would compel his mother to put even an ounce of trust in him . . .

He didn't make this promise out loud, he wrote it down on a piece of paper. But immediately something inside him changed again. He tore the paper to shreds, threw the pieces on the wet ground and began grinding them with his feet—until they were invisible, covered with mud and buried.

'I am trustworthy, will stay trustworthy. Why should it be my defeat that she doesn't know how to trust?'

He came home just as dawn was breaking.

I see a disconnected scene. It's very vibrant; I can often see it perfectly clearly, but I don't always get the order right. I use the image that I have seen of myself in the scene to estimate my age, but my memory doesn't help me be any surer of that estimate.

I am bringing back Father's monthly wages after cashing his cheque at the bank. Father is at the office, and I am taking the money out of my pocket to give to Mother. There are several denominations and a lot of banknotes, and several silver rupees, and that's why, when I see Mother's extended hands, I say, 'Mother, take them in your *anchal*, there's too much.'

Mother slowly spreads her anchal, but laughs as she says, 'I'll spread my anchal only when you bring home your own earnings; why bother for this?'

I am about to hand over the money but I stop. I look at Mother with a strange look in my eyes, which she doesn't seem to understand—perhaps I don't understand it either. Then ignoring her outspread anchal, I pull out the side table and deposit the money there—'Count it.' And I leave the room.

*

When I think about how this is possibly among the reasons that I am here—as a reaction to this distrust—I don't know why I refuse to give Mother credit for this immense change, for this incredible influence. I don't know why my heart wants to deny her even this much gratitude, to be indebted to her for this undesired but good impact.

Ever since that day, no other image has haunted me—while sleeping or awake, conscious or unconscious, in fight or flight—as often as the image of the terrible, unexpected knowledge of her distrust. I remember, after I was arrested, when my thoughts first turned to home, I thought that when Mother heard the news of what happened, her first reaction would have been one of victory, something like 'I knew it. I never trusted him!' Then she would be sad, might even cry, or get angry, but her first thought, no matter how fleeting, and even if she immediately regretted it, her first thought would be that she should have seen this coming . . . and I don't know why, but this thought gave me much consolation, made me perfectly calm and made me completely indifferent to the police's excesses.

Forgiveness is the soul's religion, but I am unable to do it. It's not the case that I've become angry because of the things that have happened to me here. At least it isn't any more.

I know that even if this hadn't happened, I'd still have evolved into this state, become the person that I am today. There was some force inside me ever since I was born, or the germ of a force, which had been propelling me here undeterred, and still would be, even if Mother never spoke to me or said a word about me. This knowledge, on the one hand, prevents me from getting angry, but on the other hand, it also keeps me from being grateful . . .

I believe that revolutionaries aren't made; they're born. A revolutionary disposition isn't fashioned from the power of struggle against material conditions, from the activities of life, from the action–reaction response to circumstances. It's not something external that attaches to the spirit; it's an innate part of it. I don't believe in God because if we suffer from helplessness or powerlessness, these are not external factors, but internal ones. If they were external, they would be characteristics of another, and then we could call that 'God', but it's inside us, it's our own, even if it takes an external influence to make it solid. We could call it a 'personal destiny'.[10]

It's not my argument that Karl Marx was simply born or that Shelley didn't learn anything from the world or that Trotsky wasn't as affected by his world as much as he affected the world. What's unique about a revolutionary's spirit is that it remains revolutionary even when it embraces the modern ideas that are flying around as part of its development since it is more advanced than the most advanced sections of its times. That's why Einstein is a revolutionary despite being born in reactionary Germany, and despite being cradled in the womb of the world's greatest, fieriest, most intense world-historic event of the Russian Revolution, Stalin never became a revolutionary. He simply remained to pick up the scraps . . .

If this is the case, is it pointless to propagate revolutionary ideas? No, but if the ideas are being disseminated in the hope that they will produce new revolutionaries or that they will give rise to revolutionary possibilities, then they will prove fruitless. But if the objective is to recruit existing revolutionary forces, collect the existing will to revolution, to give it a line of march, then this objective will come to fruition.

After all, the revolutionary is a natural leader. Why should all of his followers be revolutionaries? If I am a carpenter, if I make things with adzes and planes, why do the adzes and planes need to be self-motivated and self-directed? Why is this necessary?

I've seen countless such individuals who say, and think, that a particular mental reaction to something made them revolutionaries, like Tilak's funeral,[11] the images of martial law or Jatin Das's hunger strike.[12] They lie! Or perhaps they lack the self-awareness that would allow them to see their own revolutionary instincts lurking behind these external causes, or then maybe they don't have the instinct, and they aren't revolutionaries.

Those are elements of a revolution, external manifestations of a rebel's plan and reflective abilities, but not the necessary, fiery, inner drive that gives them substance and endurance. Under duress, they fall naked, their internal vacuousness, their bankruptcy, becomes transparent; these people, who trumpet the power and influence of eminence, hide a secret in their depths which escapes and bleats its presence.

These days our leaders repeatedly proclaim that ours is only an economic revolt. We have no bread in our homes, we aren't paid our wages, we're hungry, and that's why we're rebels. I think that this is ignoble, an immense insult to the self.

There was a time when 'religion' was the dominant force. Then, our hypocritical leaders tried to demean the idea of revolution by saying, the people's revolt is not religious, but social, so we should have the right to reform our society. When 'society' began to become more important, those same hypocrites became nervous when they confronted it, and then they argued that they wanted full political control, and when 'politics' became important, they then claimed, we aren't interested in challenging politics, we are rebelling against financial mismanagement. Vile, vile, vile! I say, O revolutionaries, come, first rid yourself of this vanity! Learn, understand, declare that we are not against misadministration, but we are rebels against homogeneity, against conformity; we want to change everything; ours is a revolution driven by our opposition to religion, to politics, to economics, and in the end even against our personalities.

Idols can be built from the earth, but the earth cannot be built. An even better idol can be made from the same clay or even clay of a lesser quality, but if there isn't any clay, no amount of propaganda, no amount of education, no amount of burning sacrifice can create an idol.

A revolutionary heart needs a revolutionary-maker, in the same way that the touch of an artist can transform the clay. To complete a revolutionary, to create a quintessential man, one needs mental power, immense control, unceasing toil, just like one needs when making a work of art from clay.

But even after being fully trained, acquiring all the necessary abilities artificially, a person without that inner force can only become a revolutionary up to a point just like a picture with all the ornamentation and decoration but lacking inspiration can only be a work of art up to a point . . .

That's why I say, I believe that just as a thousand years' worth of effort is insufficient to create a Leonardo da Vinci or a Rabindranath Tagore, similarly, the generation of a complete and model revolutionary is a precondition for successfully bringing about a new century, a new culture.

The most important thing for an artist, after mastering
a working knowledge of art's internal force, is to have a pure
reverence for art itself. Similarly, the most important thing for
a revolutionary is to have a devotional attachment to revolution.
That's the only way he acquires the ability to lose himself in his
work, to devote his entire subjectivity to it, and still have the power
to judge it objectively. It's the only means by which his drifting is
intentional drifting—if he dies it's because he wants to sacrifice his
soul, if he loses himself in the world, it's because he has understood
his personality . . .

It's on account of this, and exclusively on account of this, that
he can perform any number of 'immoral' acts, but they won't taint
him; he can 'sin' and still remain pure.

Amongst these pure sins, one very important sin worth
committing for a revolutionary is hate.

The capacity for an immense, comprehensive love is
certainly within the repertoire of the revolutionary, but another
element is also necessary, essential, alongside it—the ability to
hate. An enduring, burning, terrible affliction, but despite being
all of these things an objective, pure hatred, by which I mean
the kind of hate you can experience with an attentive mind,
not the kind that completely destroys us or drives us crazy and
enslaves us.

This is something that the Nihilists understood. Hatred
played a central role in their all-consuming, fiery passion, and they
drank it like strong liquor and lost their personalities in it and used
it as a model. This was the mistake they made, it came from the
flood of their passion, carried in on a wave, a flood which initially
rises high on a shore and slowly, hiding itself in a spray of foam,
returns to its natural boundary. But still, they had taken this fierce,
intellectual hatred to have significance, and made full use of its
driving force, took full advantage of it.

The world still doesn't understand this; the everyday ethical
order of ordinary society considers this quite despicable. That's
why they think hatred is an unnatural tendency which destroys
humanity, which prevents everything else. They don't understand

the power of this feeling, this epoch-changing power, if it can be used properly and rationally!

I fantasize about the day when our nation's—our world's—people who call themselves revolutionaries will be filled with a fierce but calm, rational hatred and they won't be afraid of it, and will accept its inspiration and place their stamp on the world, and then plant yet another seed for an epoch-altering revolution . . .

Because revolutions are endless, permanent, because amongst their mechanisms, the most productive tool after love is this rational hatred.

Except for suffering—terrible suffering. Because suffering is also a high quality and very pure weapon.

But why write about suffering?

To describe a house and the specific landscape[13] around it one has to survey it. Not by simply standing outside close at hand, but from quite a distance . . . so where can I go to talk about suffering, from what vantage should I weigh and measure it, determine its worth and significance?

*

Since then, I've felt as if my mind has been cleft into two parts. Sometimes it feels like more than two, but there are at least two parts. And as far as I can tell, the cause of this unbreachable rift is that imaginary image which my mind saw as it penetrated the walls of that kitchen, at the moment when Mother said—'I don't trust this one, either.'

This rift could have a reason, a cause, but only a psychologist could really know. At a minimum, though, I know that it exists. Because sometimes I myself have felt those two parts of my mind at war with each other, fighting for control over my conscience. And sometimes one has more influence than the other, sometimes the other, and the result is that there is a contradiction in my work, an incoherence that manifests itself, which people who only know me from the outside fail to understand, but which has entered into my personality and become one with it, dissolved in it like a solution. Sometimes it happens that neither side has priority, at which point they lay claim to the various centres of my brain, and so if one controls my hands, the other controls my mouth, or one will have the reins of my consciousness and the bodily apparatus will be run by the other. At such moments I must appear like a machine whose wires have got crossed but which is still in motion.

I'm not crazy! But sometimes I think that the line which keeps me on this side of insanity, the line which prevents crossing over, is extremely thin!

Perhaps it is just as thin as the line separating love from hate, cruelty from suffering, affection from renunciation.

Because these cannot be separated, everywhere that love is strong, hate is just as sharp. Suffering is not merely the result of cruelty, it is a manifestation of it, and the lover not only loses himself in love, but also loses the object of affection.

Love is such a slippery and sweeping emotion that individual personality ceases to exist. The lover never 'remembers' the object of his affection because he never forgets her. He becomes so accustomed to the idea of her that he never thinks 'I should see her', that I should make a separate, special effort to see her. When we look at a very well-lit scene we won't notice the light, but when looking at a dark scene, we will involuntarily ask, 'What part of this is supposed to be lit?'

*

Someone has sent me flowers.

If sunlight and shade complete one another, then shouldn't a feeling well up when I look at these flowers? In this cell five paces long and three paces wide, in this piece of darkness enclosed by iron bars, why don't I feel the glory of realization when I look at these flowers? Why do I feel entirely incomplete, totally empty, when I look at their scattered white beauty and their wide yellow eyes? Is there an overly zealous rebel, a destructive desire arising in me?

Break break break the prison,
strike upon strike.
Hey, what song have the birds sung today,
The rays of the sun have arrived.[14]

What must the person who sent me these flowers be thinking about these things she has sent me—what is it that scorches me for which I am nevertheless grateful?

She was a student of mine, but I wasn't her teacher. I simply used to teach her, but she never thought of me as her teacher. I was like an older brother to her—but the kind of brother that could be loved, who could be leaned on, on whose support dreams could be woven . . .

And who could wreck them with indifference!

I need to teach her, work hard at teaching her. But she was never able to learn a thing! I used to ask her, 'Do you remember the last lesson?' That's when she'd hang her head, meaninglessly smile and grow silent.

At that point, I would question her over and over, and then reprimand her, 'You won't learn anything this way.' Then I'd sit her down to recite the last lesson again.

And she would completely refuse to read. She'd place the book in front of her and stare at it intently. Her eyes would fill with large tears and she couldn't see anything.

Then I would say lovingly (but with only the slightest amount of love), 'All right, I'll do today's lesson with you. Tomorrow, make sure you've learned both lessons!' And then she'd read. And the next day, it was the same problem all over again.

Once I got really angry. When I looked at her tearful eyes I got irritated and said, 'You don't read or write anything, and then when I say something you start crying! I give up. I'm not coming back any more.'

I got up to go. Then she said, pathetically, 'Where am I supposed to find the time? Mother works me to the bone every day.'

How could a teacher tolerate this? Her mother came out. I asked her, 'How much time does she get to study?'

'She spends the whole day with her nose in that book. I never say anything to her for fear that it will disturb her studies. Why, is she not studying properly?'

I should have told her the truth, but I said, 'No, she studies, but if she got a little more time, then perhaps . . .'

She left. So I asked her again, 'So?' What could she say? There should be a limit to how long one can daydream while staring at a book!

I said in a sterner voice, 'So now?'

'I'll study harder from now on.' I started teaching her again.

Then one day I didn't go to teach her. Missed the next day and the next. On the fourth day I wrote a letter to her father saying I couldn't teach her any more. He sent me a cheque with my name on it the next day.

The story was finished. But the next day their servant, a young boy, came to me and said, 'The mistress wants to know whether you'll come and teach her.'

I barked back, 'What mistress?'

'The young mistress. She called for you.'

I asked again, 'Sheela?'

'Yes.'

She probably didn't know that her lessons had been cancelled. I said, 'Tell her I can't come. Her father has cancelled her lessons.'

He left. I didn't think for a second about what kind of a coward I had been for lying. I just kept thinking that I had won.

That victory was in fact my defeat. Had I told her the truth about my refusing to come, perhaps she would have considered herself the victim of injustice and found some consolation in that notion—I didn't even leave her that possibility. Ever since then, her accusing spectre has been following me, crying, saying, 'Liar! Liar!'

I run away, avoiding her. I've been running ever since. And now looking at these flowers I think, where will I run from these wilting blossoms?

But why should I run?

Sheela, I didn't lie to you. I have, for sure, been lying to myself all these years. The lie that I told you didn't mislead you; it misled me. But I understand my mistake now. Today, I, the brother who caused you pain, who gratefully acknowledges your devotion, who forgets his embarrassment and says that I didn't lie to hide myself from you, ended up hiding from myself. This is the settling of that account whose payment you haven't received yet, which perhaps you will never receive, but which has been settled and redeemed.

*

As long as the flowers were fresh, it never seemed as if they were bound. I had tied them to the iron bars of my cell, but the piece of cord that I used to bind them can't be seen. Soft, white flowers tied to rods of black iron, a pleasant way to remember a very unpleasant truth . . .

Today, the rods remain. The dried flowers remain in their unceasing grip, leaving their own memorial, and hanging there helplessly. They are trying to make me remember something— who knows what! They say lust is fleeting, it wilts and then the fibres of love provide constancy in life . . . or perhaps it's the other way around! They're saying that when love dies, then lust carries its corpse around, hoping to hide itself in deception . . . they say, and they're reminding me of something, they're hinting at something . . .

On one of 'the charming banks of the Ravi'—but whatever it is it isn't charming—is a dense forest of small shrubs and stumps of trees. Like a long, drawn-out sigh, the warm, dead night. Above, a few stars, tangled in the dried branches of the trees, below, the vapours of the dried moans of dead and disintegrating leaves. And in front . . .

The scattered remains of a corpse. Both of its arms have been cut off. One of its feet has been cut off. The belly has been sliced open and the entrails are spilling out. Eyes wide open, piercing into the web of branches above, they're looking, at some star. The mouth is smiling a warped, agonized smile.

He's been dead for some time. There were a few witnesses present at the precise moment when that specimen of humanity fell like a broken column from a terrible explosion, but when he died, there was no one to help him disentangle the knotty turmoil of his life. They went to get help—leaving him behind. But it was getting dark, and the waiting one could bear it no longer . . . so he began searching for the last night watchman.

And when he returned with him, when everyone regrouped to pick him up and carry him away, had they lost him? He had gone away, leaving his distorted smile, a symbol of his pain and suffering, his hopes and works.

Those four or five men are standing over that body. They aren't crying, they aren't shedding tears. They are shedding their long-held ambitions because their goal had dissipated like the smoke after an explosion. He escaped, slowly finding his way through the tangled web of the branches of the dense jungle, writhing but quietly, leaving a full smile behind in that impervious solitude, and when the last night watchman left him behind, his own internal anguish had turned into a solitary watchman and was aimlessly watching over the dead lump of isolated hopelessness.

If we could ever uncover what the blindness of his wide eyes made out in that wilderness . . .

Those four or five men are standing over him. Standing in a line, at attention, heads bowed. With a feeling of respect, they all raise their hands in salutation and stand like that for quite some time.

They are all silent, the morning raag (Bhairavi) that would complete the scene is echoing in a mute voice from some place inside them . . .

These are the last rites of this soldier with a poet's heart; the last shudder of that revolutionary's revolution.

The scene fades out. The only thing left behind in that boundless white sky is that body left in a pool of clotting blood . . .

On either side of him are two figures—a woman and a man. They are looking at each other. Their eyes do not look down to see the corpse, their hearts do not feel as if they are desecrating the grave of some beautiful sacredness. They meet, wrap each other in their arms and copulate out of some bestial hunger, all right next to that corpse. And then . . .

Illusions! I am looking at the bouquets of narcissus flowers hanging on the iron bars and the pieces of cord that are binding them together.

For humans, lying, fraud and deception come extremely naturally because God made them in his image and according to our wisdom God is the biggest liar, fraud and con artist . . .

Otherwise, what other explanation could there be for the image that I see? Can humans sink this low—and so low right in front of such glorious self-abandon?

When I recall the circumstances in which that explosion and that death occurred and when I think about how at that moment that person was desperately blowing at the dying embers of his life to try and keep his nearly dead dreams alive a little longer, and how there were conspiracies plotted around him, and how wildly nakedness was dancing while taking cover in the lowest weaknesses of the human heart, then suddenly I no longer have faith in myself or the things that I've done . . . was this the stream of inspiration feeding everything?

I think that although conventional wisdom seems ready to accept the idea that every human impulse stems from a material need, I believe instead that humans have a metaphysical force within them, some kind of natural, genuine inspiration. Our biggest problem is to resolve these two mutually opposed principles. After this is resolved a thousand other questions. But this question is so big, obscure and sweeping that you can find examples of it at each step, and so we could spend our entire lives trying to resolve it, but the problem remains just as it was before.

*

Alas for all the loves that youth lets fall
Like the beads of a told rosary[15]

But why don't I feel any sadness in recalling all of these scattered loves?[16] Why don't I feel feelings of failure or deceptiveness welling up? An angry rebellion wells up in me not because I've lost something or because I've borne so many burdens, but because I've inflicted so much suffering, so cruelly wounded so many innocent hearts . . .

What is my life's realization? What is its purpose? All lies—nothing, nothing, nothing! Actually, less than nothing, a negative debt that I mistook for a treasure.

But what am I doing? Am I not making their affliction worse by offering up such base excuses for such immense wounds? Because there is really only one salve for the deepest cuts and that is the indifference of the cutter; mercy scrapes at the wound and reopens it . . .

What am I? What sense do I have of myself? What is the truth of a life on which so much energy has been spent, so much effort expended, in order to destroy it? A line drawn across dust flying through the wind, was that it?

It can't be! All of my dreams cannot be worthless even if my life was worthless. I may be nothing, my works nothing, my life nothing, but how can my revolutionary impulse vanish? I have brought about a record of deep transformation, the ideal of a radical revolution in every object in the world—or at least as far as my reach went in the world—tirelessly. Will they be choked to death by the gallows? I may not survive, and no sign of me may remain, but will this force also be wiped out? Will the thrill of its illumination also be lost?

Science tells us that nothing happens, nothing will happen. Whatever has happened will remain until the end of the future and what is yet to happen was there at the onset of the past because the past and the future are nothing, because time is nothing, like height, width and length. It's just a vector of motion, a form of it. And so even when I die I will be alive, but even as I live I am already dead . . .

I shouldn't be so attached to life. But how am I being attached to life? Attachment happens when life has a realization. And I've been thinking that death is its realization!

But what? Science also says that you only get one life, that there is no part of human existence that is eternal. It is completely destroyed in death, nothing remains to be reincarnated . . .

And energy? Can energy also be destroyed? No, energy cannot be destroyed. It merely changes form. But energy is impersonal, and energy and matter are not separate—they are two aspects of the same thing. What today is my revolutionary energy will turn into a chain of irons to bind someone else tomorrow—some revolutionary who, like me, wanted to change the future, and who will be chained for the rest of his future.[17]

Alas, the small minds of men and, alas! The immense truths of existence!

But isn't there some solace in this thought? Doesn't it contain the essence, truth and success of all our activity and our evolution? In this utter destructibility are infinite reincarnations, limitless transformation—under the principle that no two moments can ever be the same and that in the tiniest fraction of time he can die and in the immediate next fraction of time is the possibility of his birth . . . I die because my life is merely an introduction to my death, in which reside thousands and millions of future lives.

I am the concentrated essence of my innumerable past lives. Beginning with the dead comet that produced life on this planet, and created a multitude of basic life forms, and from those developed countless different species of vegetation, reptiles, insects and mammals, I bear the imprint of this legacy on me. I am also in the many characterizations of the best paragon of a humanity that has ceaselessly evolved for tens of millions of years. From this perspective, whatever I am, I am not my own, nor am I anything new. I am a new edition of an incredibly old volume, an expanded and corrected and annotated edition whose original author is unknown.

And I am new, and rare. Not a single moment of my life has happened before. I am a new thing, a new promise that the future will keep, a lesson that will remain for posterity.

Permanence belongs to moments, but moments are desperately fragile. I, too, am, and whatever novelty exists in me, I want to finish speaking of it in a moment because it belongs to the future. I can't stop without speaking it and there is no time to think—what is the life of a moment?

Let me speak my inner story, let me shed my inner anguish,
let me scatter my inner light, let me allow my private experiences
to be looted, let me give away my long-collected lessons of inner
strength, the ecstasy of my inner being.

So that I may go. I am exhausted, so that I may sleep. But
first, let me reveal my one secret, which is the race of man's legacy
to me and my legacy to the race of man—the story of my will to
revolution . . .

What sorts of memories occur to me in my silence.

> You are made anxious today, O Poet!
> By the jangling of earth's ornaments
> The aimless, unceasing movements of unseen feet
> Pulsating, throbbing the sound of your wandering footsteps
> From your heart arises a clamour.
> Who knows why your blood
> Dances like the waves of the ocean
> Today the impatient forest quivers
> I am reminded of that tale
> Proceeding through ages
> Drunkenly, unsteadily
> Silently, quietly
> From form to form
> From soul to soul
> In the morning, at night
> Whatever I have acquired
> I have merely passed on
> From song to song.[18]

I'll speak.

As I consider the story of my life, as I consider its importance
in the life of a revolutionary by evaluating and weighing and
measuring each individual argument, I begin to hold it in higher
esteem. There is something in this life. An energy, a celestial glow,
which if it isn't the will to revolution, it is definitely the capacity to
worship the will to revolution.

I just remembered something from a long time ago, some ten or eleven years back. I was about fourteen years old then, maybe fifteen. This revolutionary sentiment was smouldering within me and I had wandered to many places before coming back home. I had tried very hard to lead a revolt against my own home and each time I would end up grinding my teeth in helplessness and insignificance.

One day, I don't know why, I left home. I don't remember how I came to this decision, or what compelled me, but I still remember today the feeling I had when I left. It is still boiling within me as if it will break through the external pressure and explode. I'm thinking with a wounded pride that there is no place for me in this enormous world, and I keep looking back towards my home as if to destroy it.

Beaming with pride and full of hope, I left my home. What were my worldly possessions? In addition to a small package of biscuits, one loaf of bread and the clothes on my back, an old overcoat into whose pockets I put both of these things.

I have left home to wander, and I'm standing on a hill thinking, where should I go? 'Where to go' doesn't yet produce a clear feeling in me because it hasn't occurred to me that sometimes you have no place to go. I didn't feel compelled to go to any particular place; I am voluntarily choosing between many attractive directions . . .

My feet set off in one direction—I kept moving in the direction they propelled me. For the first seven or eight miles I had no idea where I was going; I never even thought about it as my mind was still fixed on vexing thoughts of home. But after about ten miles, my home became too remote for my thoughts. Then I looked at the road, and the part of the road that went off into the distance made me aware that they were taking me towards a waterfall that I had seen many times on a map and in my dreams.

I had decided to leave home for the rest of my life when I set out, but I hadn't considered how I would survive for the rest of my life on a package of biscuits and a loaf of bread. And the sun was beating down hard, and I was very hungry . . .

I took my clothes off on the banks of the first stream that I came to and lay down. When my body had cooled off a bit I turned over on my stomach and dipped the biscuits in the water and started eating, and that's how I polished off half of my life savings. Afterwards, I started to dream about a time when no one would have to suffer humiliation, whether in the home or in the world.

I got out of the water and put my clothes on and lay down with my loaf as a pillow so I could rest for a while.

When I woke up it was dark; the stars were shining. I looked around. I was walking through a coffee plantation, but there was no sign of the waterfall that I was walking towards . . .

I walked another mile. I was still in the plantation. When I came to a small brook, I decided to stop there for the night and at the same time remembered that I had a loaf of bread.

All of my savings were gone. I spread my overcoat on the ground and tried to sleep, using the protruding root of a coffee tree as a pillow, listening to the din of the cicadas.

I don't know if the din ended first or if I fell asleep before it did. But I awoke in the middle of the night. I was shivering. I picked up the coat and wrapped myself in it, and tried to go back to sleep. The cicadas were silent. I listened. From a distance came a deep, oceanic sound. It was the sound of a waterfall.

Wrapping myself up in the coat made me feel even colder. So I put half of it on the ground and wrapped myself up in the rest and, in my endless attempts to keep this arrangement balanced, it somehow turned into morning.

When I could see the waterfall from afar, I sat down on the road and watched it for a long while. I thought that life should be like this, resplendent, limpid, filled with music, free, always alert and endlessly progressive, free from the chains of households and always rebellious . . . I got up slowly and walked towards it.

I don't know how much of the waterfall's frothy water I drank that day because water doesn't alleviate hunger, and whenever I got hungry, I drank.

I passed the night under that waterfall. I found a clean and flat ledge that had been baking all day in the sun to sleep on, and at night when the ledge deceived me and turned cold, I fought with that geezer of an overcoat, trying to make it longer until night turned to daylight. Even after daybreak I didn't wake up. I remained curled up until the sun came and spread its loving warmth across my cramped form.

My anger had subsided by then; the prior tumult inside me had calmed. I was sitting thoughtfully and observing the waterfall, noticing emptiness in its life . . . I thought that I could feel a stubborn monotony in its volatility, a subservience in its unrestricted freedom, a hunger . . . and I was drinking the water over and over again in order to hide from myself!

By the afternoon, that thoughtfulness had abandoned me. I was depressed and irritated. The feeling that I had was not unlike the feeling I had when I was leaving home. But now it was leading me back home.

It was a feeling of frustration and defeat and I couldn't keep it from myself—my hunger wouldn't let me ignore it. I got up and turned back! I passed the night on the road, and by morning I was back home. I had even forgotten my frustration and defeat and had a new respect for life, one that had become hardened and recast through pain and experience.

There had been a wide search conducted for me—but no one had thought to go near that waterfall. Father didn't say anything to me, nor did he ask me where I went.

He quietly accepted my return. He possessed a generosity which allowed him to endure not only his own but the defeat of others—it took me a long time to recognize this in him . . .

I will tell my story with the newly acquired respect I discovered that day. That feeling of respect, which contains the equanimity of experience, the purity of pain and, perhaps, a little bit of the rage of defeat . . . because although my life has found a kind of realization, it is not quite complete. It's almost like the feeling when someone has eaten and extinguished his hunger but hasn't had anything to drink and is still thirsty. It is this story of the agony of completion and incompleteness that I will tell.

Oh light, oh flames! Endow that feeling of respect, that purity and that rage with durability so that I can centre my energies

completely on that message which I have retrieved from the dark
past of evolution, which I will leave behind for the bright future . . .

Sometimes I think, what can I leave aside from that terrible
curse—because my life has been a curse.

> Cursed be the social wants that sin against
> The strengths of youth!
> Cursed be the social lies that warp us
> From the living truth![19]

                                        *

How should I write it?

Shall I compose my story by pouring all of the will power of my
personality in it, using all of the analytical powers of subjectivity,
and shout out a challenge full of pain and fire, or

Shall I step outside of my ego and examine my actions and
the drives that inspired them from an external, objective vantage
point, and speak a calm, dispassionate and intellectual message, or

Shall I think of it as a loan from some natural force, and then
like a debtor paying off his entire debt when he returns it, make
redress for some wrong committed and offer up a detailed, contrite
confession?

Shall I think of my personality as 'me', 'he' or 'you'?

I've come from a feeling of duty; there is a responsibility on
my shoulders. So it is only right that I am like a criminal standing
before a judge taking responsibility for his actions, one who hears
the unbiased evaluation of his weighed and measured character in
the form of a charge sheet from the judge's mouth, and that's why
I think it's best if I put myself in the form of 'you' and conduct an
evaluation of it. Or in order to leave behind a memorial of myself,
to leave behind the stamp of my personality and my prowess, I will
call myself 'me' and express myself.

But I don't want to do either of these things. I have accepted
my responsibility, and so if I am 'you' then only for myself. Besides
I have no selfhood, and the stamp that I want to leave—I am

merely the art of the flow of life which will be reabsorbed in the flow—I am myself a stamp!

I have brought a message, which is not my own, but which I have received from the evolution of my race, which I say under pressure from an external compulsion. All of my actions are the result of a compulsion which is external to me, separate from me. I want to gesture to the future of that compulsion—consider it a force separate from my personality, something supernatural.

Therefore the story in which the message inheres will belong to 'him'. His name is Shekhar. He is currently awaiting death. In this waiting he is revealing his selfhood to himself, and after reading the truth of his life, drawing out its essence and transcribing it, I will also be leaving.

I am leaving. Where? The same place he is going—where we are both strangers. Because we are indivisible, ultimately one. And our unity is awaiting its death . . .

*

I will say everything with an excited, all-consuming faith. I will say it all. Even if his life is destroyed in the process of making his brilliance manifest, even if it runs into nothingness and is lost, even if he reaches no one.

> Destructibility!
> When the thorns will be ravished by cruel storms of wind
> Who will hear the words of the blossoms, trapped therein
> When my selfhood will be mute in its final repose
> The silence within me how will anyone disclose
> Who, destructibility!

VOLUME 1

DEVELOPMENT

Part 1

Dawn and Divinity

Life's most profound occurrences always happen in unacknowledged moments.

It's hard to pin down the exact moment when pain sets in; the feeling is obvious enough, but it's almost impossible to know when, where and how the infection took hold because we were not paying heed to it then.

His birth happened, too, in one such unacknowledged moment. He was born in a tent, pitched next to scattered ruins in a desolate land, far beyond inhabited country. His father wasn't present at the time; his mother was unconscious, too, at the time.

There was a midwife present. But there is always someone, somewhere, who witnesses the beginning of every pain, one person or other who understands the secret to the turbulent motion of development, but since we don't know that 'someone', since we can't perceive the received information, we claim that the 'someone' doesn't exist . . .

No one really knows whether this newborn perceived his own birth. No one could tell you whether he was alert or not because there is no definitive account of his first moments. We have hearsay evidence, of course, that tells us that it was approximately twilight. The birds had finished chirping and had retreated to their nests, where in some meditative contemplation, some inert curiosity, they fell silent, and the watchman who made his rounds through the ruins began his circuit, walking back and forth, singing some off-key tune . . .

But just as ways to heal can only be prescribed after a distinct stab of pain, similarly, as soon as his mother woke up exhausted and said, 'Hai!' there was a commotion all around. The newborn was washed and cleaned and made to look like a proper Brahmin boy; the four or five occupants of the tent began running around, here and there and back again, pointlessly, purposelessly . . .

In the meantime, his father returned. After he made sure his son was all right, the anxious tension in his body dissipated, and the wrinkles on his forehead, furrowed out of some hope of preventing misfortune, relaxed and disappeared, and he stood there quietly with his thoughts, half-happy, half-satisfied. Then the local pundit arrived, and a Buddhist mendicant, too, and all present turned to forging a new link for the newborn in the chains of their personal life philosophies in order to bind the infant to a fixed spot in their own worlds . . .

The ruins he was born in were the ruins of a Buddhist temple. On that very day, a casket containing the remains of Gautama Buddha had been brought out for viewing, and the mendicant had come to the child's father as his guest in order to worship it. When he saw that an infant had been born on the same day, he said to his father, 'This child is an incarnation of the Buddha. Make sure that he is initiated into a Buddhist order.'

Father said, 'Yes.'

The Brahmin priest who was in attendance said, 'This child has been born into a line of Brahmins and his upbringing should be in accordance with that lineage, and because of the influence of the Buddha on his birth, he will be a devotee of non-violence and will bring glory to Brahminism.'

Mother said, 'That's good.'

Father thought for a moment and said, 'We should call him "Buddhadev".'

Mother thought to herself, 'No matter what, I'm going to call him "Tau".' And then out loud, she said, 'I vow on his behalf that he will be a vegetarian for his entire life.'

Father had decided to himself, 'I'm going to make him an engineer so that he can build new cities.'

Mother thought to herself, 'My Tau will be a barrister and will help the downtrodden.'

And so, before he was even aware, the child's life had been shackled by custom and many palpable but powerful bonds cast a shadow over his life; he had been sold off.

They say that a human being makes his own bonds, but then who is responsible for the shackles that are on his feet from the moment he is born, shackles that take an entire lifetime to cut away?

Ask the priests and the mendicants, because no one has been able to determine what bonds they, too, had fixed in their own minds.

*

A voice asks, *how did you come to learn all of this*?

We seldom notice the moment that a complete, human consciousness begins to dawn in a newborn; so certainly no one would have noticed the moment when an order of experience less developed than human consciousness—which merely makes marks, but neither understands writing nor desires—was born.

But perhaps as soon as a child becomes a formless lump of flesh, he bears an indelible stamp, which belongs not only to the contemporary forces that produced him but also to those innumerable events that preceded his birth and the countless transformations that will succeed it. The stamp is placed and remains affixed there; it never becomes clearly manifest, never enters our consciousness—until it overwhelms us like the echo from an incomprehensible shock at the blow of an unexpected revelation.

These matters about the moment of his birth are most likely not scripted by his own brain. And he can't tell you where he experienced any of this, how he experienced it and whether or not he even really experienced it. Because these recollections are probably aggregates of the mental images generated by collecting and hearing various, disconnected narratives on countless different occasions, observing half-finished gestures and perceiving half-formed, invisible thoughts through some synthesizing internal force.

But there are also some things that don't come to light this way—that no one ever speaks out loud, that no one ever considers. How did these things enter his brain? How did these images appear on the screen of his memory?

Sometimes he thinks about it to himself, but he is unable to find a satisfying answer that way. Are these images the result of things he's overheard, or products of his own memory, or has he, by thinking about them over and over again, convinced himself through some self-hypnotizing force that he's actually seen these events, really had these experiences?

The question remains a question and will remain a question. But those images and those scenes are real for him, he can still feel them today . . .

Small hands filled with a tender warmth . . . eyes, swimming in an ocean, filled with adoration, like dark stars . . . breasts . . . a gentle, soft, warm glow on the tip of the nose . . . the course of a long breath on which he slowly rises and falls, like something rising and falling, floating on the waves of the ocean . . . What are all of these? Stories? Memories? Or self-deceiving desires which contain no truth?

*

There are so many of these sorts of memories or half memories, but it's strange that he remembers his impressions of the first few events of his life well; they are depictions of the three great drives that govern every human being—pride, fear and *sex*.[1]

Why? The rapid development of these three drives, their presence in the earliest memories of life, demonstrates how significant they are, that human beings acquire them at the same time as their humanity, not from future circumstances or actions . . .

It's difficult to determine which of these memories came first and which later because they are of roughly the same time, and so it's best to treat them as if they are like two screens in the same memory theatre, because together they reveal something . . .

His naming ceremony has already happened.[2] He's already witnessed the sacrificial fire with his wide eyes, and his innocent ears have already heard the mantras someone whispered into them. He's about three years old, but his unalloyed, overconfident ego is greater than the one Napoleon would have had had he remained undefeated for 1,00,000 years!

He's begun to think of himself as a responsible child and he's always serious, so his elders treat him with respect and he's earned a reputation for being quite mature. He's often given chores to do which he does with a cheerful pride. He's even been sent out today on an errand—his brother is ill, so he's been told to go and fetch the doctor. And that's the reason why he's come so far from his home to the street in front of the doctor's house.

But his feeling of responsibility only lasts as long as he has been entrusted with some important task. He doesn't think that he is obligated to complete the task. Often he forgets to do the work he's been entrusted with in his excitement—like today. He's come this far, but he's no longer a dutiful messenger. He has turned back into a child, and the laughter begins to rise inside him and calls him out to play in a voice that no self-respecting child (and what child isn't self-respecting?) could refuse . . .

The round, red letter box[3] that sits facing the street has captured the boy's imagination. Somehow, he's climbed on top of it, straddling it as if he were riding on the back of a horse, and he's swinging back and forth with one hand on the stump at the top as if he's holding on to the reins. The other hand is patting the neck of the 'horse' like he has seen his father do . . .

He's the emperor. He's sitting on his victorious horse and challenging the world. Whenever a pedestrian passes near him, he scowls and yells at them and says whatever comes to his head. He's an emperor in his imagination but to the pedestrians he's merely a rude child, which is why no one says anything to him, no one gets offended. They just look at him and walk on.

In his world, he's as tall as the letter box. From his throne he can look on at the entire world and laugh at it insignificance.

That's when the postman—an insignificant postman from an insignificant world!—comes and destroys his dream, tells him to get down from there, and when he doesn't immediately obey, gets angry and says it again. That's when the crestfallen child-emperor takes his revenge—he jumps down, lands directly on the postman's toes, grinds them with his heel and then runs away, stopping for breath only when he gets home, and after catching his breath, he convinces himself that he really has won.

And then the sudden slap from his father reminds him that he is a small, dependent child who had been sent to get the doctor and who has come back home without him, wasting a full hour in the process.

The second memory. He is wandering through a museum by himself, in the gallery where the wild and savage animals are on display. Suddenly he's face-to-face with a terrifying lion. One paw raised to strike . . . frightening teeth . . . that tongue . . . those bloodshot eyes . . . and he screams, overtaken with fear, and he runs.

The child does not realize that the lion is filled with straw. He runs. It feels as if the lion is chasing him, will catch him any second. He does not even turn around to look because he never wants to see those teeth, that tongue and those eyes again.

And he's by himself. There's no one around to ward away his fear. Somehow he manages to get outside and then continues running on the street. A peon recognizes him and grabs him, lifts him in his arms, and realizing that he is unable to run, the boy lets out a panicked wail as if the lion is about to get him!

But it doesn't get him. It doesn't for a long time. Then the boy nervously turns around and, when he sees that the lion isn't following him, breathes a sigh of relief.

The fear was suppressed for now, but it found a new home in the child's imagination. Ever since that day, he had begun having terrible nightmares. He would wake up in the middle of the night screaming. And if he woke up and saw that the room was dark, then the darkness would come alive for him with not one, but innumerable lions. Ever since that day, the lights in his room stayed on all night long, but no one had any idea what had happened to him, why he was having nightmares or why he was becoming so thin and irritable . . .

The fear went away by itself. One day, a similar lion was brought home. After much trepidation and watching his brothers do it first, he went up to the lion and sat on its back. And when he discovered that it was lifeless, he screwed up his courage and tried to see what would happen when he put his hand in its mouth. That's when the fear suddenly vanished, that's when the child picked up a knife and tore through the skin, scattered the grass and straw that was filled inside and began to laugh . . .

This had another serious consequence. The child learned that fear comes from being afraid. All of the scary things in the world are merely lifeless hides filled with grass and straw and it's folly to be afraid of them.

It's a lesson that he's kept with him ever since. He still believes that whenever one sees something frightening, one shouldn't be afraid, one should cut through its hide and remove the grass stuffing inside and scatter it about, and then laugh. It has made him overconfident, some say destructive and cruel, but he knows . . .

He was punished for cutting through that hide. And afterwards, on several other occasions, he was punished for destroying these artificial fears, because society cannot exist without fear. Today, too, he is in prison for the crime of proving the hollowness of one such exaggerated, terrifying fear, and he's awaiting his punishment. Because he has laid siege to the world's biggest fear—the fear of the law—his crime calls out for the worst punishment . . .

But he laughs because he's already tasted victory . . .

And a third memory . . .

It's vulgar and revolting. Its exact shape and its root cause are not things that I remember. All I remember is his state of mind, his feelings while he was standing there.

I—that child—am observing a scene. I don't remember what, but I do remember that it is something inappropriate, something forbidden, something repulsive, something vile and that these are the apposite feelings that enter his mind while watching it.

It is inappropriate. Only those who have turned back after having been tempted by lust to the very shores of sin can understand—they turned back not because of some external prohibition or law or their own inability or fear but because of an internal, self-generated guilt . . .

And they are the only ones who live life. It's easy to follow the customary path, and the world praises those who live according to custom. But there is no reason that life should be easy or inspire respect. Life is greater than that; it's not bound by custom and it flies higher than the desire for fame . . .

Life truly belongs to those who don't follow the rules but understand the basic impulse behind the rules and create rules for themselves accordingly . . .

Love has made man a man!

Fear turned him into a social being!

And pride assembled him into a nation!

*

The world thinks that education is its highest obligation, but only the kind of education it desires, not the one that the student wants. And that's because society's 'respectable man' is not a man at all, he's a 'type',[4] and society wants to beat and pummel every individual from the start, to grind down his personality and turn him into a replica of that type, to destroy his inherent make-up and make him a mere facsimile . . .

How is such an education provided? The poor are beaten and pummelled from childhood, not just in their homes, not just in the streets, but everywhere and by everyone. The entire world becomes a schoolhouse for them where they are given their education with dry heartlessness. Since those who are better off are not educated in these abrupt ways, their education begins at home or at school, and their real-world education is deferred for as long as possible.

To make iron chains, iron is first melted in a furnace and then immediately poured into moulds. But to make a chain of gold, the gold is first softened and then stretched into a fine wire and then rounded and cut, after which it can be worked upon. In the end, it's polished, and that's when it's done. These are the differences between the educations of poor and rich children.

Shall we call this fortune or misfortune? He was born in a well-to-do family, and accordingly he was educated at a convent[5] school.

A cluster of boys and girls in a tiny little garden surrounded by the vine-covered walls of a European convent school.

On one side of the cluster stands a nun—the cluster's teacher. Her face is full of affection, her hair is silvering and her eyes shine with a sort of amusement. She also has a childish lisp, but this only happens when she tries to speak Hindi.

The cluster is planted in the centre of the garden and the boys and girls are playing very seriously. A boy stands in the middle, holding a wooden mallet, and in front of him is an anvil made out of wood, too! The other boys and girls have formed a ring around him. The boy is pretending to be an ironsmith, and each time he brings the mallet down on the anvil, the boys and girls sing out in unison, 'Hit it! Hit it! The iron wants the mallet!' And the ring circles around . . .

The nun is quite pleased since the children seem so taken by this game. Their faces are serious, sure, but that may be the result of her presence. If she were to leave, they would be less restrained and happier. She thinks this to herself and quietly leaves the garden.

Quietly, but not so quietly that the children don't notice. As soon as she left, all of them realized that they were free. And they immediately began taking advantage of their freedom. It took less than a minute for two boys to start arguing, and then fighting, and the others quickly took sides. The battle went on for about ten minutes, and then suddenly peace descended. Because the door had opened and the nun had returned. And now her face no longer had an affectionate expression nor did her eyes sparkle playfully.

Students were not beaten in that convent school.

That day, Shekhar was returning home at approximately
4 p.m. Slowly, engrossed in some thought. A typewritten card had
been attached to a button of his jacket. He couldn't read what was
written on it but he could guess because the Sister had told him to
be sure to show it to his father and bring back a response, and then
she added, 'You've been very wicked.'

He was as serious as he was because he was trying to come
to a decision. He had certainly been 'wicked' in the nun's words,
but that was no reason for him to be sent home to be beaten. His
sense of fairness spoke to him, 'I've beaten up others, been beaten
up myself. Why should I be punished again at home?'

He came to a decision. He took off the card and tore it to
shreds. Threw it away. When he got home he told his father, 'I
now want to go to a boys' school. I'm grown up now. I won't go
back to that convent school to learn with girls.' His father laughed
and said, 'Good.' He kept thinking of the nun's playful eyes, eyes
that would be waiting for him and for a reply to her card. That
thought made him giddy. He began shouting at the top of his
lungs, 'Let her wait! I'm going to school—to school!'

But he didn't go directly to school.

Described earlier: the process by which gold is slowly softened
and not immediately cast in a mould. When Shekhar left the
convent school, his parents were thinking of other arrangements
for his education. And until that had been found, he had his
freedom . . .

When a child is getting 'educated' he rebels, but when the rebel
is left alone his natural curiosity gets the better of him. Whenever
his older brother sat with his teacher to study, Shekhar would go
and stand next to the table because no one ever prevented him
from standing there. He was so short that he couldn't reach the
top of the table, so he would stand on his toes and hold on to the
corner of the table and use it as a support to listen in. His brother
and his teacher would laugh, but they didn't say anything to him.
They didn't pay him any attention.

Several days passed in the same manner. One day, Father came
to see how his brothers' studies were going. He saw them learning

Panini's *Sanskrit Grammar* and said, 'Recite today's lesson for me. Do you remember it?' His brothers started off well enough, but they forgot it halfway through, got nervous and stopped. Father laughed affectionately and said, 'Study, study, pay attention and study hard' and got up to go. That's when he said, in a voice bubbling over with eagerness, trembling from excitement, 'I'll recite it.'

Everyone laughed, but Father smiled with what appeared to be bemused consent when he looked at him.

It didn't last long. Soon all of their faces wore awestruck expressions. That young child had perfectly recited not only the day's lesson but the lessons from the day before and the day before that and a day from quite a while back. Without pausing for even a second!

His father was overjoyed and said, as if he were rewarding him, 'Starting tomorrow, you'll also get lessons. We'll get another teacher just for you.'

Some reward!

Yes, so the next day his new teacher arrived. But he really only arrived since he didn't stay for very long. A mere three or four days after they started, the teacher found his student holding on to the back of a chair and banging his head against it like a thunderbolt, over and over. The teacher asked, 'What are you doing?'

'I'm toughening myself up,' he said and went back to what he was doing.

The teacher didn't surmise that the child had possibly heard someone say something like that before, like 'He turned out to be tough', and hearing a note of praise in the utterance, he had decided that he wanted to be tough, too. The teacher laughed and said, 'Let's see how tough you are! Will you butt heads with me?'

A summons? He said, 'Let's go.'

They only butted heads once. When the boy readied himself to butt heads again, he saw that the teacher was no longer amused. He had his hand on his forehead as if he needed help standing, and then he got up and left.

And he never came back. Because every teacher knows that education is possible only so long as a teacher still intimidates a student.

A few days later another teacher arrived from Lucknow. Every part of his body announced that it was from Lucknow. He sat down to teach with paan in his mouth, and when the child started taking dictation, he repeatedly spat on the ground and ruined the boy's concentration.

Impudently, the boy said, 'Teacher, are you planning on teaching or merely spitting all day?'

The teacher lodged a complaint with his father. Father scolded the child, 'Why are you always getting into trouble? Do you want to learn or not?'

The boy responded in the same tone as before, 'How am I supposed to learn? Is this teaching? All the teacher does is spit.'

Father felt that the child had a point. But he wasn't accustomed to being spoken to in this manner by a child. Angrily, he said, 'Don't talk nonsense. Go and study. And if I hear one more complaint about you . . .'

The child went away. He felt as if there were no justice in the world. But he also wasn't ready to suffer injustice. He hung his head while he went back to the study room, but when he got there and saw his teacher, he said audaciously and haughtily, 'Spitting-teacher!'

Shocked, the teacher said, 'What?'

'Spitting-teacher! Spitting-teacher! Spitting-teacher!' The child went on repeating it over and over as if he were banging on something with a hammer.

That was all the studying that happened that day—at least in front of the teacher. When the teacher left, they locked him in that room, without his dinner, and made him promise never to do it again.

But no. The child was exhausted and went to sleep. He stayed there until the next day when it was once more time to study and when he was brought before the teacher, he started again, 'Spitting-teacher! Spitting-teacher! Spitting—'

He was taken away and given a different kind of education, but the teacher never returned.

This was how the first act of his education ended.

After this, his sister started teaching him. But she had a different technique altogether. And the child discovered that education could be worthwhile. And a student could also be worthy. He began worshipping his sister, and began to learn, without anyone's knowledge . . .

But that happened later. It'll be discussed at the appropriate time . . .

That's how his mind used to work. He had no shortage of natural intellect. But there was no force in the world capable of directing the course of that intellect. His intellect was his, for him to use, and he could exercise it at will. He knew that whenever he accepted the orders of his natural intellect, he did well, and when his intellect was under the command of others, he tripped and faltered . . .

If this mind could be tamed, everything was possible! But could his mind be tamed?

*

Such was his education, and he learned—what? Contempt for education, disgust . . . !

But even in those days he learned quite a lot, and he learned it with such serious mental discipline that the education left its mark on every fibre of his mental screen, and it can't be erased. The threads of his education have become woven into the warp and weft of his life, and they shine just like a line of some precious mineral in a slab of rock.

What was the secret of his autodidacticism?

Shekhar was standing on the balcony of his house. Everyone was busy with their own work. His brothers were absorbed in their own studies, his father was taking care of work at the office and Mother was making rotis while his younger brother slept in her lap.

He was alone. He felt that he was alone. And he was also feeling that he was alone because he thought, 'I am not the kind whom people called "good". I don't study, I don't do what is asked of me, I'm impudent, argumentative, devilish. Otherwise I would be enjoying myself with Father right now, or I would be eating sweets with Mother, or reading a good picture book with my brothers. Instead, I stand here alone, forgotten by everyone . . .'

While he was standing up there one of his father's friends came for a visit and he asked him, 'Is your father home?' When he didn't get a response and was unable to attract his attention, he went inside musing over the possibility that there were children who were not in the least bit curious about strangers. More than an hour later, the child was standing there in the exact same manner, deliberating on a tiny idea seriously . . .

That was when Father's friend emerged, and when he saw him standing there just as he was, he went back in and came back out with his father. He had no idea that they had been watching him for a few minutes. How was it possible that a body filled with wonder and designed to be full of playful activity could stand so still, and how could this boy who was more difficult to restrain than other boys his age be so perfectly calm?

Suddenly, he jumped when he heard his father's question, 'Shekhar, what are you thinking about?' Flabbergasted, he responded, 'Nothing.'

But perhaps because his father felt worried about seeing him stand so still or perhaps because he felt sorry for him, his father didn't get angry; he proceeded to ask with concern.

And he couldn't suppress it—it was such a new thing. He said, 'I was thinking that without evil, it's impossible for good to exist.'

His father didn't catch his meaning right away. He said, 'What do you mean?'

'It's only when people see evil that they understand what good is! If we didn't have evil, how would we know what good is!'

The two of them were stupefied for a minute, staring at each other. And then Father, perhaps because he thought that it wasn't a good idea for small heads to be preoccupied with big matters, said to him, 'Go, go inside and play. There will be plenty of time to think about these things when you're older.' Not as a reprimand, but rather with a touch of admiration.

But the child began to think, 'But if I have to think about these things when I get older, then why not think about these things now and grow up sooner?'

Afterwards, his father became increasingly watchful with him. Whenever he found him alone or preoccupied, he would get him to play something or distract him with something else. He now found that he was by himself less often, but he also knew that he was still alone since all of this unaccustomed attention made his isolation even more palpable . . .

Four or five days later the same kind of thing happened. He was standing in the same place, in the same manner. He was staring at the arches in front and thinking about a new topic that had come to him that morning while he was being taught his prayers. He was looking at the houses and thinking, 'Why did God make all of these? How did he make them all?'

That's when his father came again and asked, 'What are you thinking about now?' His mother was behind him, she was waiting for his answer, too.

Seriously, he said, 'Who made all these houses?'

His mother laughed. She said, 'People, who else?' She probably thought that he was eccentric, but thought it best to humour him.

'Then, God couldn't have made them, right?' The child asked it like a question, but there was a doubt in it, as if it were the answer to some question already asked . . .

Mother and Father looked at each other anxiously—the child also saw their expressions. Then Father said, 'Come down here, I'll explain it to you. God himself made them.'

The child followed him but at the same time he was thinking about the fact that if the answer to the question was so clear and easy, then what was the reason for the anxious expressions? Why . . .

Birds were purchased to entertain him, to keep him busy. A pair of geese, a pair of partridges and a parrot. The care of these birds was divided amongst the boys—his older brother got the geese, his second brother got the partridges and, in his share, he got the parrot.

He began teaching the parrot with great earnestness. He was told that he should teach the parrot to say 'Sita-Ram'. And whenever his mother and father were near the parrot they would say, 'Say it: Sita-Ram.' And he said the same thing in front of them. But whenever he was by himself, he would stand in front of the parrot and laugh, over and over, stopping in between—a forced laugh in the hope that he could teach the parrot to laugh . . .

But the parrot learned neither to say 'Sita-Ram' nor to laugh. One day his father took the parrot from its cage and took it in his hand and started feeding it chillies. The child asked, 'Why?' He explained that when the parrot tastes something spicy, it speaks.

The child said, 'Give it to me. I'll feed it.' Father gave him the parrot.

The parrot didn't eat the chilli from his hand; it was squirming, trying to get its wings free of his grip.

The child was losing patience and was trying to force the chilli into his beak.

The parrot bit his finger and wouldn't let go.

The child let go of the parrot and violently shook his hand until the parrot released him.

The boy kept worrying his hurt finger, while the bird flew out of the house and perched on the peepul tree out front.

When the boy remembered the bird, he began looking for it. He found it after a few minutes, and stared at it in wonder.

The boy was no longer angry with the parrot. He extended his arm and started calling to it, 'Miya Mitthu!'[6] The parrot ignored him.

The boy watched as the parrot, slowly and nervously, flew from one branch of the peepul tree to another, and then another. It seemed as though its wings were fluttering in fear of hitting the bars of his cage and getting hurt. And when it realized that it didn't hit the cage even when it moved around, it flew off the tree and landed on an electric pole that was a little farther away from the house, and from there to another pole. The boy understood that the bird was trying to convince itself that it wasn't trapped by the bars of the cage, that it was outside, free. And then suddenly, filled with exultation and pride, it flew and flew beyond the boundaries of sight.

The child sighed deeply and in a serious tone said to his father, 'The parrot flew away.'

His father appreciated the sound of seriousness in his voice and said, 'No matter, we'll get another for you.'

But he said, 'No, I don't want another parrot.'

Father laughed and said, 'Because your finger got bitten, eh? There are all kinds of birds, pick any of them. Come with me and pick one out. We'll buy . . . .'

'No, I don't want another bird.'

Sometimes he would think that he should try to free the geese and the partridges. But he'd stop himself, perhaps because he thought that since they didn't live in cages and could fly away they wanted to stay.

Once, his middle brother fell ill, and then became very seriously ill. Often, during the day, he'd begin ranting because of the fever and then call out, 'My partridges! Bring me my partridges! Where are my partridges?' The partridges would then be brought and placed near him, and he'd stroke them and calm down, even fall asleep.

He'd lost quite a bit of weight. One day his fever got so bad that he even stopped ranting and vacantly, in half-consciousness, just lay there and stared at the ceiling and didn't ask for his partridges.

But they came by themselves. His mother and father were next to him keeping watch, worried, and they saw one of the partridges get up and sit at the head of the bed, and the other began pacing at the foot of the bed. They felt as if the partridges were also feeling the strange tension in the room's atmosphere and were sad because their needs were unmet . . .

The partridge that was pacing at the foot of the invalid's bed, his path was getting increasingly confused and his legs were wobbling under him. And his mate, the female partridge, watched him with concern, but didn't move from her place at the head of the bed.

The partridge sat down at the foot of the invalid's bed, exhausted. His neck bent as if he were drowsy, and his body went limp.

After a little while, everyone saw that his body had collapsed to one side and gone stiff.

After a little longer, the invalid emerged from unconsciousness into a state of delirium and said, 'My partridge?'

After a few days, the invalid recovered. Who knows why, but until then he had been content with one partridge, hadn't even thought about the other one. But as soon as he got up from the cot he asked, 'Where's the other partridge?'

No one had the courage to tell him. A few days later, the female partridge was removed, given away to someone.

Sometimes he'd remember and ask, 'My partridges?' He'd even get depressed. But slowly he forgot about them, and eventually realized what had really happened to them . . .

Shekhar had no consoling answers. Nor could he come up with any explanations. He only knew that he had learned something and learned it deeply. He couldn't tell you what he learned. Maybe it was faith, maybe belief, maybe . . . who knows . . .

He doesn't remember what happened to the geese. Perhaps they were given away because they were reminders of the partridges . . .

The birds had all left Shekhar's life. Birds were no longer brought home. But had they also left Shekhar's mind?

Shekhar recognized that there was another world outside of his world in which there were birds, in which there was freedom, in which there was faith, in which there was love, in which there was unparalleled independence to play and think, whose solitary principle was, 'Only be what you are' . . . and that world was like heaven to him, a much-sought-after dream, the door to freedom from his familial shackles, a comfort in his isolation.

So what if all of his beliefs were false? So what if this other world also possessed all of those cruelties, all of those torments, all of those falsehoods which were the reasons that he flew from the first world? So what if those things that were barely dreams in his world did not even exist as dreams in the other world, did not exist at all? He needed solace, and he found it in this imaginary world, and that's why his dream was real, true, that's why that world exists and will remain . . .

One evening, he went to a park. At the time, it seemed as if it were filling up with birds, and they were all delighting in their lives unrestrainedly—such melodious joy! The child asked, 'Is this a jungle?' Because he had heard that birds lived in the jungle. He got an answer, 'No, this is a park.'

'What is a jungle?'

'They are similar, like very big parks. But see how the trees and flowers here are all planted with a plan? It's not like that in a jungle—they grow wherever they want, in any which way.' The child thought, how free a place like that must be where everything is independent, where these saplings could grow-flower-fruit as they desired . . . and then the heaven of his dreams took on a solid form and got a name, too—jungle . . .

To this day, the forests are to him things that the city never could be, never will be . . . Today that early dream has come down a notch from its exalted status, jungles are no longer heavens, but still many things had happened to make his love for forests grow stronger. And today, too, bound in this cage he thinks of forests, where . . .

Like that parrot, he doesn't flap his wings for fear that they will get hurt from hitting the cage. Because he's also learned from experience that it hurts. But is his soul also imprisoned, can it also be wounded, is it also unable to flap its wings?

*

That soul wanders about in those forests, where its heaven lies, free . . .

But of all of his lessons—self-taught lessons—this was just one aspect. His education was happening in another, much vaster region. You could say that this first aspect was the root of his education; it was the part that lay underground, invisible. It gave his character a foundation, but the education which formed his character, the part of his education which was above the ground and visible and worked its influence, that was something else . . . If his early education gave him stability, then this education gave him movement. The first gave him gravity and the second established the direction of motion . . .

There was also a girl among his playmates whose name no one knew. Everyone called her 'Phula' when they talked to her. She was the daughter of a widow who lived next door. Phula took part in all of his games, and sometimes while playing the two of them would also enter each other's homes. There was a complete childlike freedom there . . . But one day, he was warned by the people at home that if he were to go over to the neighbour's house, he shouldn't eat or drink anything there, he shouldn't touch anything, because they were of a low caste. He asked, not with impudence, but with curiosity, 'Are there other people who don't eat with them, too?' And he got an answer, 'No, no one from a decent caste eats with them.' 'Then why do we play with them or talk to them?' This time he didn't get an answer. He asked again and got an answer, 'Don't bother me. Just accept the things you are told. Don't make everything into an issue.'

The child left. From that day on he mostly stayed away from the games, especially when Phula was around. It wasn't because he had become obedient, but because he wanted to come up with a solution first, a decision. As a result he kept thinking even when he did play, and especially when he played because the issue would take shape right in front of his eyes.

The solution to the issue hasn't been found in more than 4000 or 5000 years, but what are 4000 or 5000 years to a child's confident soul? He had no conception of the flow of time. All he had were two states, light and dark, consciousness and sleep. So for him the flow of time had no meaning; all he had was the struggle between light and dark . . .

He used to sleep indoors. But ever since the summer began he had started sleeping out on the roof. Their roof was connected to the roof of the widow's home, and the wall that separated the two wasn't very tall, so things spoken on one side could be heard on the other. When the child would go to sleep, he would occasionally hear the sounds of Phula's playful laughter, and the issue would be raised for him again . . . Sometimes when he heard her mother call out, 'Phula, time to eat,' he would think to himself, 'They must be very hurt when they sit down to eat because no one is ready to eat with them.' He felt, 'They must be sneaking around, eating in secret, because they don't have the right to eat in front of anyone else.' He thought, 'How could she bring herself to eat?'

Often he heard the mother and daughter laughing and playing after they were done eating. And one of their games included a part where the mother would ask the daughter, 'Phula, what caste are we?' And when she laughed or when she said, 'I don't know,' her mother would explain, 'You should say, we are_____.'

One day the child asked his mother, 'What are _____?' Mother explained that it was the name of a lower caste, and with her thumb she pointed at the house next door. 'Those people, you know.' After that day, the child thought, 'If they are of a lower caste, why don't they try to hide it? Why does the mother try to make her daughter remember this fact over and over? And there is even pride in her mother's voice.'

The question remained unanswered in the boy's mind. From afar, he began worshipping this woman who could take pride in this fact, and Phula, too, became like a downtrodden goddess. But he never went over to their place. Every night he would hear them laugh and think to himself, 'I could play with them, too.' But during the day he would stop outside their house and turn back, who knows why!

Today he's come to terms with that feeling, today he can almost feel something of that terrible torture, which after having suffered, that widow-mother filled their lives with that pride, like a defensive armour for the soul. He also understands the feeling of contempt for insult which drives Phula's mother to teach her this pride. And today he knows that this won't solve the issue, that pride is inadequate, but despite knowing this he feels sympathy and compassion for her helplessness! Today he understands how the Jews are the most insulted and oppressed race in the world, and how they derive their life force from those insults and oppressions. They bend defiantly and are never vanquished . . . But the fruit that he is plucking from the tree of knowledge today planted its poisonous seed, on that very day . . . .

*

I remember something from long after that—from twenty years ago. From back when I used to run around in self-protection. One day, in the intense heat of June, I had walked twenty miles with another person. We were very thirsty; we couldn't find water anywhere. We were silently walking along the road.

All of a sudden, we saw a person coming towards us. I asked him, 'Hey brother, where can we find some water around here?'

'Nowhere near here. You'll find some near the river over there.'

'How far is it?'

'About three miles.'

I thought of something, so I asked, 'Where do you live?'

He pointed in one direction and said, 'My house is pretty close—behind that thicket.'

'So there must be water over there, right?'

'No, sir.'

'Huh? No water at home? How do you manage?'

He was silent.

I said again, 'Come on, give us some water. We're very thirsty.'

He was silent again.

I said, 'It's fine if you don't want to come. We'll go there and ask for it. Is there someone at home?'

He was silent again. After a little while he asked, 'Sir, what caste do you belong to?'

'We don't care about caste, but if you are worried, we're Brahmins. So your utensils won't be polluted.'

'No, that's not it,' he said and became quiet. Then he said, 'You should go elsewhere and find water.'

We had been hopeful, but those hopes were now dashed. I asked, 'But why won't you offer us some water?'

Then out of helplessness he said, 'Sir, we're of a lower caste . . .'

I started laughing all of a sudden. 'Is that all? We don't care about caste; we're equals.'

'No, sir, it can't be.'

'All right, if you won't offer us water, we'll drink it ourselves. How do we get to your house?'

'No, sir, this . . .'

My companion got upset—perhaps he was really thirsty. He asked, 'What kind of man are you? You carry shit all day, and now you're too proud to offer us water!'

I was about to stop him when that man suddenly stood upright and said, 'Sir, you can think whatever you want about me, but please don't insult my job. I earn an honest wage . . .'

I wondered at the combination of the humility of the wretched and his pride! And I thought that it was right . . .

We didn't get any water. We kept going.

Wouldn't it be something if this happened everywhere? I know that it doesn't; there are many places where you can't find this pride, this dignity. There you only find wretchedness, complete servitude. There, mothers and fathers teach their children not to be proud but to be obedient; they teach them to bow not out of dignity but servility. These souls have been so tightly bound that they can't tell you how they were shackled and they don't realize that they helped the chains grow stronger . . .

That prideful dignity is not the ultimate solution to the issue, but it is a solution, certainly, and natural, too . . .

*

One more lesson.

They didn't have a cook at their house although they had been looking for one for many days. One day a man came and asked if there was a need for a cook.

After making a few inquiries, the man was hired.

Shekhar and his brothers went to the kitchen to see the new order of things. They saw that the kitchen and the stove had been freshly washed, and the cook was sitting near the stove and drawing a line with a fistful of lime. The pots that crossed the line had to be newly washed, and whenever the cook went out he washed his feet again before going back across it. He would hop across on one foot so that the pollution wouldn't follow him. Every once in a while, the cook would say to the children, 'Don't come here. Don't come here.'

The children saw their fill and left. When they went outside, they drew a line and began jumping over it on one foot, just as they had seen the cook do, and started laughing.

Well. When it came time to eat, a new problem arose. If the cook came to serve dinner, he would have to wash his feet ten times a minute. It took a minute to wash his feet at any rate, so who would roll out the bread? Who would butter it? Who would serve it? It was decided that the cook wouldn't leave the kitchen, and that one of the brothers would serve the food. But the plates that left the kitchen couldn't go back into the kitchen! When seven or eight plates had been polluted in this way, the child came up with a plan. He took his plate and placed it on the other side of the line.

'Dear God! What have you done! You've polluted the entire kitchen!' the cook said as he jumped to his feet. The child fell into a fit of laughter.

A complaint was made. It was decided that the cook would serve everyone and then cook for himself.

After everyone had been served, the kitchen was cleaned again. The cook then bathed and cooked his own meal.

The child went back to the kitchen. He put a pot outside the line and then pushed it across to the other side and said, 'Cook, can you put a little salt and pepper in this?'

Another round of complaints. The child was questioned, so he responded, 'I didn't put the pot inside the kitchen. I put it down on the outside and pushed it in. How could this have spoiled the kitchen?'

The cook decided that his meal would have to be prepared for the third time. It was already 2 p.m. Mother had ordered that tea be served at 3. And with tea, snacks.

The cook sighed deeply.

In the evening, the cook made his own meal first. After he had eaten, he went to Father and said, 'Sir, I won't be able to work here.'

Everyone let out a deep sigh of relief. The cook departed.

*

Iron or gold, neither is forged with just one blow. They have to be beaten, blow upon blow, blow upon blow . . .

That's how education works. It doesn't make do with just a blow or two; there are countless blows. But they aren't that different; they appear as repeated marks of a single blow . . .

Except sometimes, when the metal gets misshapen, it receives its blows in crooked ways. All construction, the entirety of education, is composed of merely two or three basic kinds of blows, and their limitless forms. And by examining those two or three kinds of blows, you can get a sense of the whole method . . .

There is a third lesson . . .

The Gomti was flooding—flooding badly . . .

Shekhar had gone out with his father. Out, meaning on a little boat, manoeuvring it here and there with bamboo poles because the water on the roads was more than a foot high, and the way was blocked. If it was traversable then only for boats.

The boat was on the major thoroughfares. The view was so lively that it was as if a little part of Venice was in India because vendors were going around in their boats selling all kinds of foodstuffs—grains, vegetables, cooked meats, fruits and the like. Some were making the rounds selling books and newspapers, others were selling pictures of the flood—yes, even toys were being sold. The boats were going up to the doors of houses as if they were docking on riverbanks and the vendors called out the names of their wares and their prices.

But that was on the bigger roads, which they had already passed. Now they were headed into the poor parts of the city—to observe. This part of the city was lower than the rest (like they always are), so there was much more water here, and the boat was moving at an exciting pace. Exciting! What fun! The streets here were completely deserted, and it stank, and a funereal shadow fell over most of the houses—and if there was anything which pierced its silence then it was the sound of some child wailing. He asks his father, 'Why don't the vendors come here?'

'What would they do here? Nothing gets sold here.'

'Why?'

'These are poor people, they can't afford it.'

Filled with a wave of compassion, the child thinks about those children whose parents are 'poor people' and can't afford toys for them. Nor fruits.

The child asks, 'Where do their children play?'

'They don't play.'

'Why?'

'. . .'

What could anyone say, that they didn't even have the strength to play? These are the ones who don't play, who are themselves playthings, whom fate plays with.

Calling these memories 'memories' requires stretching the meaning of the word. After all, I don't remember things exactly like this, or more precisely I don't remember the facts. When I look to the past these things don't appear like images before my eyes. I only remember the feelings that I experienced, that special state of mind I was in when I took part in a certain scene. These images that I sketch are the phantasmal impressions left on the screen erected by that state of mind. If these are memories then they are the free associative memories of the mind, not the kind of memories for which we use our eyes to fix the original impressions . . .

But what is education? Not a series of images. It's a series of feelings—feelings whose gradual development we can observe; that grow wider and deeper, on top of which these images are suspended. These images are in one sense the funerary remains of those feelings, and life is a wide expanse of such memorials . . .

*

Stability and ability.

The source of these two qualities in his education is clear. But he believes that there is another virtue, a drive, an impulse, a powerful attraction—where did that come from?

He thinks that it is something. Like a bubble in the stream of progress, perfectly fragile but still a little independent, a little dynamic, a little catalytic, a little exalted, a little immortal. What?

It's a strange fact that the ideas and events that determine a life's direction, that turn it in one direction and show it the permanent course to its future destination, those same events and ideas are impenetrable and imperceptible, and no one can determine their root impulse, the source of their decision-making powers.

So when I ponder where I found this ceaseless, upward-looking impulse—what is it which always sets the course of my life, and kept elevating it, in the direction of some summit that can't be seen, that can't even be imagined, hidden somewhere beyond the highest clouds—I never arrive at a clear answer . . .

I can see several disconnected images . . .

The past several events had unsettled Shekhar, whatever firm convictions he had, his certainties, all were dashed.

Now everything seemed fraudulent. He couldn't bring himself to get attached to anything for fear that it, too, might turn out to be a lie, and slip through his fingers. So he began more and more to be alone, to wander off on his own.

The most noteworthy thing about all of the images that he can recall from this period of his life is their tranquillity. It's possible that he was in such a desperate quest to find peace in those days that wherever he found it, even if only for a moment, the spot became fixed in his memory. That's why these memories are so pleasant . . .

The bank of the Gomti River. Evening. Shekhar is walking by himself, slowly, noticing the trees. Some of the trees are covered by lattice upon lattice of yellowed dodder, mounds and mounds of them—that's what he was looking at, and he was thinking about why these were the only organisms given the ability not to need the soil, never have their feet touch the ground, remaining elevated always, and drawing their life juices from the earth by using others as their support. But he couldn't think about this for too long; his mind would wander to the coppery light that trembled on the waves of the Gomti and stay there. He felt as if there were something in the light that was calling out to him, drawing him in, offering comfort, but he couldn't name it. The word 'beauty' was not yet part of his mental landscape . . .

Shekhar was sitting by himself in the colonnade in Lucknow.

An extremely beautiful horse passes in front of him at a rapid speed. There was no effort to his motion, no hesitation, as if there were no command of will. The motion was self-complete, beautiful, like a wonderful song with its own unique rhythm.

Shekhar gets up all of a sudden. This was a new thing in his life—and it jolted his mind like electricity.

Rhythm[7] . . . tempo . . .

He sat back down. Clear as the sky, as a mountain stream.

Perhaps, ever since then, his life has been spent searching everywhere for that. Perhaps he even found it; because many years later, even in the darkest days of his life, when he was troubled by the oppositions around him, a sudden ray of moonlight would pierce the darkness and those same oppositions and problems would be resolved and they would seem to be the diverse parts of a great unity . . .

One day, his father took him to the museum, left him in the room with the statues and went to work.

Shekhar looked around nervously. There were statues all around him, some intact, some broken, some bodiless heads, some headless bodies, some black, some white, some made of stone, some made of clay, some of sparkling metal and some eaten by rust.

His gaze fell on one statue and stopped.

Or rather, his gaze stopped at the statue's feet, because the statue was quite large. And his line of sight only reached its feet.

He slowly looked up. His gaze reached the ceiling where the statue's head was.

Shekhar looked at it again, from head to toe. All the way to the wooden platform underneath the feet where in big letters was written, 'Mahavir Jain'.

A thought arose in Shekhar's mind and said, 'The statue is completely naked.'

It was naked. Shekhar didn't understand how, while sketching its massive, terrifying, expansive nudity, the sculptor's hands didn't tremble, his mind didn't shrink back. The truth of nudity, naked like truth, was not a part of his world, was never allowed to be a part of his world; for him, nudity was a lie, vulgar, loathsome and ugly. Still, or perhaps because, he kept looking at it with fixed and unwavering eyes, looked at it for a long time.

As if his mind had accepted that nudity, in his eyes it was not to be forsaken; it was natural and beautiful.

He went back home slowly. The sweet and cool breath of peace had spread a light perfume across his mind.

A few days later, when his father had taken him to Sarnath and they had stopped in Bodh Gaya, he sneaked out when he had the chance and made his way towards the museum in Sarnath, passing next to the edge of a large pond. Some people were gathering water chestnuts in the pond, and at the edge and in the mud several half-naked boys were causing a commotion; he didn't even lift his eyes to look at them. The imaginative resources that he drew on while away (so many moments spent recalling delightful, forgotten scenes) no longer existed, because today he was going to the museum . . .

Very few people went to the museum in Sarnath. And when Shekhar got there, it was closing time.

He noticed that there was no peon at the door or at the gate. He quietly went under the gate and made his way inside.

The statues were on the right. Shekhar walked around for a while looking at them, and then sat down on a wide pedestal for a statue of the goddess Tara.

Suddenly it seemed to him as if a durable silence had descended there. So deep that he strained to hear if there was even the slightest sound, but there wasn't. It was complete.

He quickly got up and went outside.

The door was locked; he was alone inside the museum. He slowly went back. Eventually he sat back down in the same place.

When we long for company, want sound, silence terrifies us; we listen to it and it appears to speak back to us. It speaks to us in words that in older times a writer who knew the human mind would have written, 'It hissed.' It didn't seem to Shekhar that the silence was hissing at him, that it was coming to bite him. It didn't occur to him to think, 'I will be locked up all night, I won't be able to eat or sleep, and Father will be looking for me.' He was sitting there in a grand, beautiful, tranquil, thrillingly peaceful moment. He had forgotten knowledge. He sat there and kept sitting there . . .

Now when he thinks back at that episode, it makes him nervous. The peace was all-encompassing, and that silence! But at the time nothing seemed strange to him. What was strange was the word made by a door opening that dashed the silence . . . A word that he couldn't bring himself to believe—that's how far gone he was! The call of his own name seemed foreign to him— 'Shekhar!'

He got up with a start, and quickly got away from the statue of the goddess Tara. He couldn't bear the idea that people would discover where he had been, where he was for so long, what he had been doing; he thought that if people learned of the particular spot where he had been sitting, he would die of embarrassment . . .

Just like the spot where Buddha gained enlightenment, the spot was as pure to him as it was hidden to the world . . .

He was asked how he got there, what he'd been doing—why, where, when—the questions that always get asked, but whose answers hold no meaning, except for the fact that the questions are always just as mandatory as the replies are identical!

Shekhar's embarrassed silence was his reply.

When he tells himself that it is a bit of the world's peace, the world's soul in him, is he lying, is he deluding himself?

He is surrounded by suffering, poverty; injury, disease, death, all of it is present. The architects of the religions of the world have made use of the inventive powers of their class and brought forth the worst and most terrifying anguishes of hell into the world, into his world, and he doesn't accept them, wages an adversarial rebellion against them, fights them. But isn't this because his soul can imagine or feel a place where none of this exists, because his soul has obtained a glimpse of some otherworldly peace? Despite living in this hell, he is connected not to the hell but to a global peace.

Delusion? Can a delusion give life to a complete biography, an entire society? Can delusion give you power? You can die for a delusion, but can you live for a mere delusion?

People say that a revolutionary is narrow-minded, that his mind is weak, his heart is off. People also say that his dreams are hollow, idealistic and impossible. They might be right. But he is able to look at the marginalized and the helpless with respect, his heart can lift the downfallen, his mind can run an entire nation. And for his dreams he can fight with truth and tenacity, and his dreams can come true.

Is this also a delusion?

*

I see myself as a five-year-old child who is running on the grass barefoot wearing only a pair of blue knickers. The boy is carrying many lotuses on his shoulder, some in full bloom, some half-opened and some still closed. The path that he is on passes by the shade of the chinars and is almost completely covered by the leaves and flowers of the trees. The shaggy-leafed stinging nettle grows in a few of the dark and cold corners, but the child isn't scared of them because he knows the treatment for it.

This scene appears clearly before my eyes, but I still can't place it properly—I can't remember its position in the order of life. It definitely happened in Kashmir, but I don't understand why it's been etched into the tablet of my memory in such deep letters, especially because I can't remember any reason for it or any consequences either.

Shekhar's father had been suddenly transferred, and after auctioning off the things he no longer needed one day, he said goodbye to his friends and brought his entire family to a bungalow they bought on the banks of the Jhelum River and began living there.

It was the time of the Great War when prices were high, but property values had come down.

Shekhar was around six years old when he decided that it was time for him to write a book and become famous.

He knew that his father wrote books. One day he had asked his father what he was writing page after page. His father told him that he was writing a book. He also explained that the book would have pictures in it, and also that the papers would be fed into a press so that this book could be made into hundreds and thousands of books, and each of them would have the same pictures. This idea captivated him and he decided that he, too, would produce a picture-filled book.

But where would he get the pictures? He didn't want to ask his father for help since he was worried that he might try to stop him out of envy. But after thinking about it for a while, he had an idea—flowers! He collected flowers from all kinds of places and placed them in books to dry. He asked the gardener for their names. And now that he had acquired all of his materials he resolved to start his book.

The first problem was paper. One day, when his father had gone to the office, he stole his keys and opened the drawer to his desk and took his father's best stationery, paper thicker than card stock, which was clean and glossy and decorated with the red government insignia of the lion in the corner. Shekhar had remembered that all books have thick and glossy paper for their pictures.

He took twenty or so sheets and had his sister sew them into a book. She was an assistant and a companion in all of his efforts— although for the labour of sewing the pages into a book she took five pages for herself. Now Shekhar was worried about the cover for his book and the solution that he came up with was so daring that he had to calm his pounding heart as he opened the bookcase and took out the gold-trimmed, leather-bound Bible, and with a single motion he separated the book from its cover. He hid the book in the pile of buckets behind the kitchen and placed his book inside the cover. All of this happened in a matter of mere moments.

When everyone returned home in the evening his sister spied him alone and the first thing she asked him was, 'What did you do today?' Shekhar's guilty soul told her everything—he didn't have it in him to lie. Then in order to keep his secret safe Shekhar had to forgo his share of the next day's sweets and in this exchange he got his sister to sew and fit his book into the cover.

The next day brother and sister sat down to write the book. Shekhar fixed the different flowers to each page with glue. Sister brought her botany book and Shekhar looked through it and tried to describe his flowers in the same way that they were described in the book—first a description of the flower's colour and shape, then its uses and then—what was this thing called 'habitat'?

Sister said, 'I don't know. They didn't teach this in school; they skipped it.'

Shekhar went and asked his father, 'What does "habitat" mean?'

'Habitat is a place where something resides or is found. Why?'

'No reason—sister sent me to find out,' he said and nervously ran out. Behind him he could hear his father's voice, 'Why doesn't she come and ask herself?'

After a month's worth of work, Shekhar had finished his book. When his sister had looked at it and given it her approval, Shekhar had decided that he would put his book into the press, too, and make hundreds and thousands of copies. So one day when he found his father especially happy, he went up to him and put the book in his hands.

But almost instantly, he turned red and ran out. He was there long enough to notice that his father's expression had changed, and that he had opened the book.

After a few minutes his curiosity got the better of his embarrassment and his fear. The sounds of the echoing laughter of his mother and father drew him back, and when his father saw him, his laughter doubled. He caught him by the waist and picked him up and said, 'I haven't laughed this much in ages. It's a marvellous thing, your book.'

This made Shekhar nervous because he wasn't sure if this was praise or something else. To him it seemed an object of praise— the book was written in beautiful letters and the pictures were also quite beautiful, and their names were written in red. What better descriptions of fuchsias and violets were there than this:

Fushia, Vylet flower with fore red small leeves vary prety Kashmiri
girls put it in there hare nurse zinnia puts it in her ears to dance in
the kitchen.
Habitat, Shalamar gardens and Chashma Shahi.
Iris, very butiful some are bloo some red and some white there is a
yellow stick inside the flower.
Habitat, Mr. Chatterjis house near gupkar the best were in our house
but the flud took them away.[8]

But for some reason, no one liked it any more than something to laugh at. Shekhar was downcast, and his father's indulging words—'Don't worry, son, you'll write something better next time. But don't ruin my books!'—depressed him.

This was the end of his first literary endeavour—or you could say that it was the beginning of the end because the real end took place two years later when it was eaten up by the white ants and various other insects in the rubbish heap.

The production of literature is like a call to a living death. The writer earns little in producing literature, he derives no satisfaction from his creativity because as soon as he finishes he realizes, 'Wait, this isn't what I intended to make.' As if he were the messenger of energy, he never intends to stop anywhere—he has to wander continuously, provoke agitation, set things on fire and never be at peace—he never intends to stop anywhere. Perhaps that is the reason that Providence stops him at the beginning of his journey and says, 'Look, don't go this way. This path isn't made for your feet.' If he stubbornly advances, it reminds him, 'All right, but understand—you're responsible for what happens.' Then cruelly, it cuts his name from its ledger, from the list of its nurtured and protected children.

Shekhar tried again six months later. This time it was poetry.

It was spring and Shekhar was in Jammu. The streets in Kashmir were blocked off. It was getting quite warm, but Shekhar still went around barefoot and bareheaded. After a while, when his feet couldn't bear the heat any more, he would run back into the room where his classes were about to start in a few minutes. He wanted to spend whatever time was remaining in physical activity. That's when his brother came in with the news that the teacher had arrived.

The teacher was an American named John Gass and Shekhar always called him 'Mister Gass'. Today, though, when he saw that his leisure time was going to be disturbed, he got angry at his teacher.

As he walked towards the room, he came up with a plan. In other words, he was inspired by the muse of poetry.

Ever since Shekhar's book had been derided, the humiliation and the laughter were eating away at him, and he had decided that if he ever got the opportunity he would reclaim his lost pride with a supreme poetic gesture. Today it suddenly dawned on him that this was his opportunity, and he realized that he was a poet.

He stepped up to the teacher and like a trained parrot meekly said, 'Good morning, Mister Gass.'

The teacher said, 'Good morning,' and sat down. Shekhar's eyes, which had been dazzled by the bright sun outside, seemed to have darkness within. He slowly meandered to his stool and as he sat down he said, 'Mister Gass, I wrote a poem for you.'

Mister Gass smiled and said, 'Really? Let's hear it.'

Shekhar responded immediately in a sing-song voice:

> My teacher's name is Mister Gass,
> If G is gone then he is an ass.[9]

Approximately half an hour later, Shekhar was rubbing his reddened cheeks, sitting in a garden of bulletwood trees a mile away from his house, and bemoaning the injustice of the world. His father had chased him to this spot beating him all the way, and when he had gone back, Shekhar sat there thinking.

Between moments of frustrated rage he would remember where he was and then pluck a blossom or two and sniff and then lose himself in thought again.

*

Brother and sister, even though they are brother-and-sister, can remain unfamiliar for a long time—can even remain strangers their whole lives. Shekhar, too, came to see his sister as his sister only when he was six years old and only when a childhood girlfriend explained to him what sisterly affection was. That friend was Shashi.

Shekhar first saw Shashi when he was around four years old, when Shashi was a little more than three. Shashi's mother, Vidyavati, was like a sister to Shekhar's mother and so she had come with her daughter to see her and stay with them for a while.

Shekhar was asleep when she arrived. When he got up in the morning, he saw that there was a bed not too far from his bed and a girl was sitting on it and looking at him with curiosity.

That's when his mother came and told him, 'Shekhar, this is your sister.'

Shekhar wouldn't accept it, even though he didn't say anything. It didn't make sense that someone could just say, 'This is your sister' and make someone your sister. There was Saraswati who was his sister. She had been living in the same house ever since he had known her. She played with him and got scolded by Father. And when she got angry she would beat him up.

And her? Shekhar tried to imagine getting beaten up by Shashi and immediately thought to himself, 'No way.'

He realized that even if someone said it a million times, Shashi was Shashi and not his sister.

After a little while, Shekhar's mother said, 'Come, the two of you need to take a bath.' The two of them were taken to the bathroom and made to sit.

Shekhar's normal method of bathing was as follows: he would use a towel to plug the gutter that would drain the water from the bathroom and when water got to the top of the gutter, he would splash around in it. He started repeating the same procedure today. Shashi stood in one corner and watched him; Shekhar ignored her.

The water filled to the top. Shekhar began to bathe. Shashi stood where she was.

Then Shekhar's mother returned and gave Shashi a small brass mug and said, 'Use this to take a bath.' And then she left.

Shashi started to fill up her mug at the faucet with her small hands when Shekhar went up to her and said angrily, 'That mug is mine.'

Shashi kept looking at him with her big eyes wide open, not speaking or moving, letting the mug fill.

Shekhar came closer and said, 'It's mine. Give it.'

Shashi stepped back and said, 'No. I'm going to take a bath.'

'Give it!' Shekhar screamed as he lunged at her. He took the mug and at the same time hit her on the head with it. Shashi shouted, 'Ma!' and started crying.

Shashi's mother came and immediately understood what had happened. She asked Shekhar, 'Did you hit her?'

When Shekhar saw the blood on Shashi's forehead he immediately put the mug on the ground and stood there frightened.

Shekhar's mother ran in with a rod in her hand and said, 'He hit you, didn't he?'

It wasn't clear if it was because she looked at Shekhar's face or at the rod or for some other reason, but Shashi pointed to the mug and said, 'The mug fell on me.'

'How? Did Shekhar hit you?'

'It fell on me by itself,' she said and resumed crying.

Shekhar's mother gave him an angry look as she showed him the rod before she left. Vidyavati checked Shashi once more. Then she started washing her forehead gently.

Shekhar didn't wash any more. He quietly put on his clothes and stood there for a minute. He looked at Shashi for a second before he jumped up, snatched the mug and walked out.

He didn't talk to Shashi afterwards. But when it was time to eat, he quietly filled the mug with water and put it next to her plate before he started eating.

When Shekhar saw her pick up the mug and take a drink from it without giving him a look, he felt as though he had acquired something better than all the mugs in the world.

Shashi left that evening and then Shekhar didn't see her again for another ten years.

*

Shekhar's sister was named Saraswati. She was five years older than him, and after her were Shekhar's two older brothers, Ishwardutt and Prabhudutt. Shekhar was named 'Buddhadev' at birth, but for some reason, when Vidyavati saw Shekhar for the first time she went to his mother and said, 'Sister, you should call him Chandrashekhar.' Despite the arguments she got from others, she kept calling him Shekhar, and because of her persistence, everyone eventually started doing the same.

Saraswati and Shekhar used to play together, but Saraswati's hands and Shekhar's cheeks played together more often than the two of them did. And ever since Shekhar's father had given her the directive to teach him, Shekhar came to believe that 'sister' was the name of that creature who argues while playing, beats you even when she's wrong, annoys you, teaches you compound consonants immediately after teaching the single characters (though Shekhar didn't call them compound consonants at the time), tells Father when you didn't study and, in the middle of an argument, obtains a fatwa from Mother that says because she is older, Shekhar has to listen to her. When they were in Kashmir, Shekhar got immense pleasure from quietly leaving the window open on a rainy night so that his sleeping-next-to-the-window sister, Saraswati, would get drenched. (Shekhar had insisted that he sleep next to the window because he liked to look at the moon, but his mother had said no to this because he was little and would catch a cold.) But suddenly, one day in that same Kashmir, in that same rainy season, 'Saraswati' turned into 'sister' and sister turned into 'Saras'—although he never uttered that last intimate name, keeping it hidden in his own mind.

It rained continuously for eight days. The melodious ripple of the Jhelum River gave way to an unremitting, deep roar. Shekhar's father ordered that all of the expensive things in the home be carried up to the second storey of the bungalow. That's where they were staying now, and Father often sat by the window, looking out with worry. A cigar hung from his mouth. Occasionally, when he remembered to, he would take a drag or two from it and then get lost in some thought or another.

The bungalow was on the riverbank in the midst of an orchard which was surrounded on all four sides by a ten-foot-high mud wall. To get inside, there were stairs at the centre of both sides of all four walls. The walls were thirteen or fourteen feet wide at the bottom and quite thin at the top. The water level of the river had reached up to the ground and water began spreading everywhere—it was slowly rising above the level of the ground inside the walls. The roar of the angry river could be heard clearly, leaping across the flowers near the bungalow inside, as if it were running wild with freedom.

Tense anticipation fell over the bungalow. Shekhar stared at his father and thought, 'Why is he looking at the wall closest to the river with that fixed, unblinking, thoughtful look?' He couldn't figure it out. Nor could he understand why his mother sometimes looked at him, or at his brothers, or at Saraswati with those tearful eyes. But even though he didn't understand, it seemed as if the electric atmosphere had swallowed him up as well and he, too, was looking around at everyone with the same unvoiced, shapeless worry.

Suddenly he saw the worry of something happening outside spread clearly across his sister's face. He slowly slid up next to her and softly asked, 'What is it?' With her finger, Saraswati gestured to him to follow her and they quietly went towards the stairs. The two of them went down silently—no one saw them.

As soon as they got to the bottom, Shekhar asked, 'What is it?'

Saraswati angrily said to him, 'Mouse holes.'

'What mouse holes? I don't understand.'

'You're an idiot. The water is rising outside. It's going to start coming in through the holes—and then? They have to be closed up.'

Shekhar understood. The two of them went to the closest wall and started to pack the holes with mud. They even pulled up their beloved iris plants and packed them into the holes with the mud.

Shekhar lifted his head to look at Saraswati. She was at that moment standing there indecisively with an iris plant in her hand. In an instant, she broke off one of its big, beautiful blossoms and tucked it in her braid and then stuffed the plant in the hole. Shekhar thought it was strange that this curious girl could be thinking the exact same thing he was—but in a moment he forgot all of this and went back to work. It was clear to him, and to Saraswati, that they would only be able to work as long as no one inside discovered their absence. They also felt as if something was going to happen any second now (they didn't know what) and Father would never let them remain outside. And so they were working very fast. Not out of fear of some impending disaster, but out of a fear of being called inside.

Their backs began to ache, but they seemed to make no progress. Each time they almost finished closing one hole another would burst open and keep getting bigger—it was as if a fountain had erupted inside. And from the height of the fountains, Shekhar estimated that the water was four feet high on the other side of the wall. He had yet to consider what would happen when the water level reached the top of the wall . . .

Above the roar of the water they heard their father call out in a new, strange voice. They stopped and looked at each other—they couldn't immediately decide whether they should go inside or keep at their work (without understanding the danger they were in, they could tell that the work they were doing was a matter of pride). Before they could make up their minds they heard a splash as if something had fallen into the water. They saw some uprooted irises and a breach in the wall through which flooded out dirty, thirsty waters . . .

They made up their minds. The two of them ran to the house together. They hadn't reached the door when the roar of the water became unbearable and they saw that they were running through knee-high waters.

And then—the door! Father was standing there. They looked at his face once and went inside. There was something on his face that no one saw twice—and one hopes no one ever does.

After a moment, everyone gathered upstairs. After a few minutes, water began flooding into the rooms downstairs. The water had risen twenty-five feet above its natural level . . .

That's how high it was now. But afterwards, Shekhar kept thinking about that moment when his eyes met Saraswati's after hearing their father shout out to them, when the wall was breached, when they ran together towards the door in some mute understanding—because in reality it was only one moment, an indivisible portion of the flow of time, a gust of felling, a single pulse of the heart—and it seemed to him as if Saraswati communicated something to him, taught him something—but what?

He remembers that much. Afterwards she wasn't Saraswati any more; she became his sister. He doesn't remember when he started calling her 'Saras' with love, in his own mind.

A boat was slowly moving across the still, tranquil lake. The lake was so quiet that it seemed as if the boat was also standing still; no evidence of its movement was discernible. Shekhar and his brothers were going to explore the island of 'dreams'.

When they got there, his brothers proposed they swim, which was immediately passed, since Shekhar didn't have voting privileges. They took off their clothes and got in the water.

Ishwar and Prabhudutt began swimming. Shekhar didn't know how to swim, so he watched his brothers with wonder. How gently his brothers' movements sliced through the water! How unbearably irresistible was their progress like a quivering arrow! Shekhar's fascination had just reached that stage where the prohibitions stopped governing his actions, where his heart had become so entranced that imitation became a reflexive action . . . He jumped farther into the water and began moving his hands just as he had seen his brothers' hands move . . .

But it only took a moment for him to sink. He came up for air with great difficulty, but before he could take a breath, sank again. His hands were still moving with the same amazed imitation . . .

He saw a beautiful dream of immense darkness, and then it seemed to him that he was so thirsty. Then he was gasping for breath, and then nothing . . .

When he regained consciousness, he was lying flat on his stomach and his brother was pressing down on his back. The boatman who had pulled him up from the water was standing nearby.

When they reached home, before he could even draw a breath, his brothers had told the story in their own manner. Father scolded him, 'What got into your head? If you didn't know how to swim why did you try to show off? You could have listened to your brothers' warning!'

His brothers told the story, so 'the brothers' warning' had been added by them. Shekhar didn't say anything. He quietly looked at his father. Father spoke again, 'What are you looking at? You should be ashamed of yourself. What if you had drowned?'

Shekhar didn't think that being saved from drowning should be a cause for embarrassment, nor did he think that drowning was such a terrible thing.

In reality, fearing death is something that only adults do.

A few days later, when all three brothers were playing with some boys from the neighbourhood, Shekhar could tell that they were all impressed when they heard about his close call. It gave him a little touch of arrogance. Because he was younger than all of them he was usually overlooked, but now that he had the opportunity to impress them he wasn't going to let it go. He said, 'So it wasn't such a terrible thing. I'm going to do it again some day. See what it's like to drown, what it means to die. I most certainly will die like that one of these days.'

The boys all looked at him in shock. Then they left without saying anything.

The feeling that his father's words were unable to produce in him, this did. Shekhar became grave and thought, 'Is death really something to be afraid of?'

One day, overcome by the invisible shadow that this thought had cast over him, he asked his mother, 'Mother, when will you die?'

Mother was coming down the stairs with a bottle in her hands when she heard the question. The bottle slipped from her hands and fell, and she asked, flabbergasted, 'What?'

When he heard the sound of the bottle crashing, Father came. When he heard what had happened, he was stunned for a moment. Then he added one after the other three or four slaps to Shekhar's collection. Then he took Mother and went upstairs.

After a little while Shekhar peeped in through the window and saw the two of them sitting quietly, seriously, and not looking at anything, not even at each other, even though their eyes were trained . . .

And then quite seriously, quite uncertainly, he asked, 'Is death that terrifying?'

One day, Shekhar went to the market with his father and saw that the grocer was wrapping his merchandise in paper that had pictures on it. They were colourful images—blue, green and brown. And the pictures were of soldiers, ships, planes, cannons and smoke. You could say they were topsy-turvy, and these days he had a special proclivity for topsy-turvy matters. He tugged at his father's shirt and said, 'Get that for me.'

'What?'

'Those papers.'

Father laughed and said, 'All right.' Then he said to the shopkeeper, 'Brother, can you give him a few of your old newspapers?'

Shekhar added, 'Only the good ones. I don't want the torn or messed-up ones.' When he noticed that the shopkeeper wasn't giving his request any special attention, he went and picked out eight to ten of them himself.

When he got home, he got his brothers and sister together and laid the newspapers out separately on the floor. He looked at them and began reading the descriptions underneath the pictures.

'We declare victory in _____: countless enemy soldiers killed. We are advancing.'

'Bullets rain down from our plane _____.'

'_____'

Shekhar asked, 'Who is this "we"?'

Ishwardutt said, 'The British are fighting the Germans.'

Then Shekhar saw a picture of Sikh soldiers advancing with bayonets on their rifles. Next to it was written, 'We charged _____ with bayonets; _____ enemy soldiers killed, some of our men also died and were wounded.'

Shekhar said, 'But these aren't British.'

His brother explained that the Sikh soldiers were fighting for the British. The British ruled over India, so Indian soldiers were sent to fight for them. And Father had said that about 1,00,000 Indians had died.

Shekhar asked, 'How do they die?'

'They die, that's all.'

'What happens when you die?'

'Idiot! You aren't alive, can't walk or speak, and then they take you and burn you.'

'If you drown, is that how you die?'

'Yes.'

'How?'

'You stop breathing and then life goes out of you.'

Shekhar thought about this for a while. Then he suddenly asked, 'What is life?'

'It just is, all right!'

He was persistent, 'What is it?'

'I don't know. Go ask Father!'

After a little while, Shekhar asked, 'Where does life come from?'

'From God.'

'Where does it go?'

'Back to God.'

'God takes them?'

'Yes.'

Shekhar wasn't convinced, 'Humph.'

After a little while, he asked again, 'Are all these lives with God?'

'Yes.'

'Even the Germans?'

'Yes.'

'And God makes all the bodies, too?'

'Yes.'

'God does everything?'

'Then did God cause war?'

'Yes.'

'Then—' he started to speak but then stopped. He recalled that he had read in the newspaper that the Germans were very cruel. They beat their prisoners, they starved people, they whipped women, dragged them through the streets, etc. Does all of this happen just because God wills it?

*

Shekhar was sitting in a tonga with his brothers and going for an outing. On the way, he saw a half-dead horse tied to a broken-down cart coming towards them. The cart was full, and the horse couldn't pull the weight but the driver kept whipping him, cursing him.

Shekhar thought to himself, 'Our tonga is so splendid.'

The driver put down his whip and took out a rod. He struck the horse repeatedly and hard across the back. The horse picked up his head somehow and jerked, and then dropped his head like before. The blows kept coming, his body trembled, but he didn't move forward.

Once, he made a serious effort—and Shekhar watched as his knees buckled and he fell—and then never got up.

The *tonga-wallah* explained that this sort of thing happened quite often. When there is no grain for the horse, and it grows weak from hunger, it is fed cannabis and jaggery, and more work is extracted from it. He pointed to the horse that was pulling the tonga and said with a tone of pride, 'Once, I made this one go forty miles that way pulling the tonga.'

Ishwardutt asked, 'Doesn't that kill the horse?'

'How could it kill the horse? This is how it gets stronger. That horse died because it was starving.'

The tonga kept moving.

On the way back, when they passed the same spot, Shekhar asked 'Do men who die from hunger also die like this?'

No one gave him an answer.

*

Shekhar had picked up a terrible habit—he would sit for long periods of time by himself and think.

And it seemed to him that he could remember things that he hadn't seen with his own eyes. He remembered . . .

One day, Father came back home from the office at an odd hour. As soon as he got home, he spied Shekhar's mother sunning herself in the courtyard. And he said in an annoyed voice, 'So it's begun.' And then he went inside. Mother got up and left, too. Shekhar couldn't work out whom to ask the question that was eating him up inside—what has begun?

He remembered . . .

One day, a letter arrived addressed to Mother. Mother read it, was stunned after she finished reading it, and her eyes soon filled with tears. With a concerned tone, Father asked, 'What's the matter?' She handed the letter to him. Father read it and fell silent. Then, while still thinking, he started reading it aloud, 'Ramachandra has enlisted and is being deployed.' Shekhar didn't understand anything.

It was a full year later that Shekhar learned what 'enlisted' meant, when some unconscious chain of thought led him to remember his uncle Ramachandra and he asked his mother, 'When is uncle Ramachandra coming?'

His mother looked at him as if afflicted, but couldn't answer him.

His uncle was, at that time, lying in some hospital in France— blind, having lost one arm and unconscious.

One day, when Shekhar came inside the house after playing, he saw his mother crying softly. He turned around and left. When he came back an hour later, she was still crying. She was doing her chores while crying, and when her eyes would fill with tears, she would wipe them away.

Shekhar timidly asked, 'Mother—'

His mother looked at him. She wiped her tears. Then she turned away and said, 'Son, your uncle won't be coming any more.'

Shekhar couldn't bring himself to ask why.

One day, when Father delivered the news that the war was over and that we had won, that a treaty had been signed, and that now things were good again, the first question on Shekhar's lips was one that he couldn't bring himself to ask, 'So will Uncle be coming back?'

Shekhar had heard that there were riots in Punjab, that people had been fired upon, that many people had been killed, and that the military was being sent in. Some police stations had been set on fire, railway lines had been torn up . . . He disentangled these things, put them back together and went to his father and said, 'There's going to be a war in Punjab, too.'

His father said, 'One doesn't say such things. Let's at least end the first one.'

'The first one is long done.'

'But we still have the consequences to deal with. Prices are so high these days, and—'

Shekhar responded haughtily, 'And what of it? If God wills it, they will go even higher.'

His father glared at him and said, 'Get out!'

*

Father began to notice that Shekhar was asking a lot of questions, and being home-schooled hadn't rid him of this habit. After all, what authority could Saraswati's teaching exercise have? He called Shekhar to him and said, 'Shekhar, you will have to go to school. You'll go with the servant tomorrow and get enrolled.'

What his education was like at school is a matter for another time. The first thing that happened was that Shekhar was informed that the Viceroy of India was coming in a few days and the students would have to learn drills for his welcome ceremony.

Shekhar had a uniform made for the drills. He decided that he would stay at school his whole life. He had been studying with Saraswati for eons and no Viceroy had ever come, nor had he ever had a uniform to wear.

The Viceroy was coming on a steamboat. It was led by two riverboats from Shekhar's school rowed by his schoolmates—their white uniforms with red borders looked quite striking.

Shekhar was standing at the edge of the water—he was among those assigned to guard the spot where the Viceroy would dock. The boat was still far. Even with a great deal of effort it was impossible to get a glimpse of His Excellency the Viceroy, and so Shekhar was observing the masses of Kashmiris that had gathered on both sides of the river.

Both sides of the river were crammed with Kashmiris wearing long robes and scarves. Some had gleaming white robes and white turbans on their heads; in some places there were dense throngs of women wearing red hats that looked like turbans.

Suddenly both sides of the river erupted as if the heavens thundered, and the thunder developed a rhythm of its own. Shocked, Shekhar saw the assembled masses on both sides of the river, men and women (except for those Pandits wearing white turbans) beating their chests in unison and saying something as if they were gasping for breath, something which he could only understand after much concentration.

'Increase food aid! Increase food aid!'

The steamboat came close. Shekhar tried to locate the Viceroy but that terrifying scream had cast a shadow over the atmosphere. It weighed so heavily on everything that he couldn't find the Viceroy. If he saw anything it was those countless faces and the wailing with raised arms . . .

When he came home, he asked his father, 'Why were those people screaming?'

Father explained that prices had gone up because of the war and those people were starving. The Viceroy was the representative of the Emperor, who could do anything, and so these people had come to plead with him for rice.

'What did the Viceroy say?'

'The Viceroy can't listen to everyone.'

'But the war is over, so why are the prices still high?'

'. . .'

'Did the Germans raise the prices?'

'No.'

'Why doesn't the Viceroy bring prices down?'

'How can the Viceroy do that?'

Shekhar didn't care for his question being answered with another question. But the poor fellow was powerless. He asked again, 'Can God do it?'

'Yes, God can do anything.'

'Did he also raise the prices?'

'Yes, now run along. Don't you have studying to do?'

The question on Shekhar's lips ran off with him—'Why?'

*

The war was over but its best friend had arrived. People started being confined to their cots everywhere and one day, Shekhar's cot was placed next to the ones for his father, mother and brothers. Saraswati was the only one saved from this fate.

Saraswati was ordered to stay away from everyone as much as possible. If she ever sat with Shekhar after giving everyone their medicine, a voice would immediately reprimand her from inside, 'Go, don't sit there, otherwise you'll get sick.' Shekhar grumbled to himself about this order and thought, 'What's the big thing if she gets sick? She'll just lie here with us.' Or he would get angry at the war which kept him confined to his cot. Whenever Mother would say, 'Son, don't worry, God will take care of everything' it would make him want to burst, to explode, and ask whether this war was worth it? Was hunger worth it? Was it worth Uncle not coming home? Was it worth that horse dying? Was it worth it, all of these people falling ill? Was it worth it, all the death? That God did everything wasn't something he had a problem with, but he couldn't stand the notion that everything he did was worth it. This lie was outrageous to him . . .

Everyone got better. Father started going back to work. Shekhar was the only one still confined to his cot. This didn't bother him too much since he got his own room, and Saraswati could come and go without any restrictions.

One day, a sitting-by-the-headboard Saraswati said, 'My head hurts a lot today.'

Shekhar said, 'Now you'll get sick.'

'No, not today. First, you need to get better. Then even if I get sick it won't be a big thing.'

'I don't want to get better,' Shekhar said for some unknown reason. Maybe to get some sympathy. 'I'm going to die soon.'

'Stupid boy! Don't say things like that!'

Shekhar could tell that Saraswati was saying the same things that the others had been saying, but he didn't have the same feeling, the same anxiety, that same paralysing fear. He liked it; he felt as if he could ask Saraswati things that he couldn't ask anyone else. He asked, 'You're not afraid of dying, are you?'

'No.'

'Is dying scary?'

'No.'

'Why is everyone so afraid?'

'The reason they're afraid is not because death is so bad. They're afraid because they like to live.'

Why hadn't anyone else provided such a straightforward, honest answer to him?

After a little while, Shekhar extended his arm to Saraswati and said, 'I won't die.'

Saraswati took his hand and placed it on her chest, and then she gently slapped him by the ear and left.

By evening, there was another cot in the room for Saraswati.

*

Father said, 'Now that everyone is better, let's go on a trip. And we can make a pilgrimage, too—to the temple at Kheer Bhawani.'[10]

The next day, a houseboat passed Amira Kadal with the entire family on it.[11]

Life's routine changed. Every evening, after dinner, there would be a family meeting, either in the sitting room of the houseboat or on the deck, during which the boys would sometimes be asked to tell stories. More often Father or Mother would tell stories. The stories were the kind that were told to children in India—stories from the Puranas about gods, something which always has a moral attached to the end. Small examples of God's greatness, lengthy lectures explaining the importance of honesty, various proverbs on frugality, an unnecessarily protracted complaint about the wickedness of the boy (whoever he was) who had stolen jam one morning and didn't confess . . . Sometimes these stories were entertaining, but whenever it was time for the moral of the story, Shekhar got bored. He had come up with a name for himself for these daily meetings—'Mother's rebukes'.

While listening to the stories, Shekhar would occasionally think, 'If God exists, then why doesn't he appear to me?' Sometimes he would be so racked with doubt that he would think, 'Maybe it's because I am so weak and unworthy that I can't experience

God.' And sometimes his tiny personality would gather together all of its force at once and ask, 'It isn't the case that there is no God, is it?'

This continuously suppressed doubt or the absence of doubt, this continuous vigilance lest someone discover an iota of his scepticism, was eating him up, and the weight was too much for his underdeveloped brain to bear.

He felt as though the moment was imminent when his suppressed doubts would burst forth, and who could tell in what shape . . . but he was calm on the outside and, yes, happy, too.

The bosom of the lake, night.

On the roof of the houseboat, in the moonlight, sits Shekhar, tired. What hasn't he done all day today! He doesn't understand beauty fully, but for some reason he is drawn to it whenever it is in front of him. Something quickens inside him and he sets about doing some work or another with a demonic energy. Looking at beauty doesn't completely absorb him, but it makes the energy of life flow through his every activity a little more . . .

He's broken off countless lotus blossoms today and turned them into necklaces for his sister, made her into a goddess and worshipped her, said goodbye to the rosy-fingered sun in the evening and, most of all, he remembered Saraswati forgetting herself singing . . . He doesn't remember the words of the song, they don't even matter, and the sentiment doesn't matter; all that matters is the ineffable musicality of that featureless song . . .

The bosom of the lake, night. On the roof of the houseboat, in the moonlight, sits Shekhar, tired.

Below, his sister's voice calls to him, 'Shekhar, come down from there.' But he doesn't go down, can't go down. He knows that he doesn't need to worry about going down; his sister will get him herself.

She comes. Comes to him and looks around in every direction and then decides to sit down in silence, too.

We measure time with lifeless clocks—we're such fools. Can clocks measure the eons that pass in a second and the moments that last for eons?

The pair is silent. Still. Life stands still, and while standing still it races on so rapidly, not forward, not backward, but in some nameless, immeasurable direction . . .

The night is so exceedingly beautiful that Shekhar can think of nothing else. Its inexpressible beauty, its characterless nocturnality, proved that there was no God, because what kind of God could make hunger and war and also produce such beauty? And if God didn't make it, why should the rest of the world be his creation?

Saraswati was perhaps also thinking something similar. Perhaps she was also asking the night a question without an answer—'God, do you exist?'

Dawn breaks.

Breaking because Shekhar, upon waking, could tell that the light was scratching and clawing to root out that beauty from every crack and crevasse that had enveloped the night everywhere, that was alive, and the assault that was taking place against it was so great that he could look at nothing else . . . The lake is long behind them, the houseboat stands in some polluted stream near the temple of Kheer Bhavani, the dugouts are all in line and giving off smoke . . .

Shekhar and his brothers are dressed in white clothes, and everyone is going towards the temple. Father has a few wood apple leaves and fresh lotus blossoms in his hands and Mother is holding sandalwood and some other things. Shekhar is walking ahead of everyone.

Shekhar is standing at some distance from the temple and admiring it with curiosity. The others are circumambulating the temple together in ritual. On seeing him standing by himself, Father gestures for him to join them, but he doesn't move from his spot. Father doesn't call him again but Shekhar knows that the matter is not settled.

As soon as they get back to the houseboat, Father asks him in a stern voice, 'Shekhar, why didn't you do as I asked?'

Shekhar remains silent for a moment—draws a long breath. Then, he himself doesn't know what is happening or what he is saying, but the force that has been building up for several days finds a path and breaks free:

'I don't believe in God! I don't believe in prayer! Bhavani is a lie! God is a lie! There is no God!'

*

Non-existence.

Shekhar was beaten with a switch in front of everyone for saying this, but oh, the pride of being able to say this, the peace that comes with dead certainty, the wave of self-satisfaction! The radiant bliss of being beaten for his faith! And that total victory that came when his brothers whispered to him in secret that they didn't believe in God either!

Does God exist or not? The God whose existence or non-existence we can comprehend, whom we call featureless, formless and infinite, and yet our brains try to grasp His existence in our fists, to be able to say with meaning that he exists—what difference does the existence or non-existence of such a God make?

If God exists, then He is one about whom it cannot be said that He exists, who is beyond the orbit of our faith . . .

But it can also be said that God is that about which we can say with complete certainty, 'He does not exist.'

*

God had another gambit to play.

It would have been sheer impertinence to use such expressions about God had Shekhar not considered God an equal adversary but thought him to be something more. But as long as he was not impressed by God's omnipotence or his omnipotence over humanity, how could he think God was doing anything other than employing stratagems?

So God played another gambit—in order to manifest Himself to Shekhar.

One evening, Shekhar felt as if the entire mood in the house had changed—as if it were being pressed down by some weight. And even though everything was being done in the same way, that there was nothing new going on, it still seemed like there was quite a commotion . . .

Shekhar asked the ayah, Jinniya, 'What's going on today?'

'Where?'

Shekhar said reflexively, 'Inside.'

Jinniya laughed and said, 'You'll find out tomorrow. God works wonders.'

She didn't say anything more. When Shekhar threatened her that he would tell his mother that she sneaks into the kitchen and dances in front of the cook, she said without concern, 'Humph,' and then left.

Somehow, Shekhar fell asleep thinking about it over and over. But as soon as he got up in the morning, he remembered it and ran to Mother's room—the room where she had been confined to bed rest for several days. Seeing his father from the door made him stop in his tracks. He only went closer after Father left. That was when Jinniya was leaving the room with something bundled up and said, 'Shekhar, look, it's your new brother—'

And that was exactly when from inside that bundle that thing called 'new brother' began to scream with all the might in his tiny body . . .

Shekhar stood stunned for a few moments, reeling from the terror of that stupefying cry. Then he timidly touched the bundle and said, 'Show me.'

Jinniya showed him. Shekhar looked a little disappointed. He said, 'Enough.'

Because he couldn't even open his fists and didn't know how to see . . .

The stupefaction passed, then came the deluge of questions.

'How did he get here?'

'Where did he come from?'

'When did he get here?'

'Who brought him?'

'Did Ravi come the same way? Does everyone come the same way?'

Jinniya had been answering all of his questions and Shekhar had believed all her answers. But when he asked, 'Why are babies born?' and he got the answer, 'Whatever God wills, happens,' that's when he realized that everything he had been told from beginning to end was a lie, and he gave Jinniya an angry look and went outside.

Mother, Father, sister, the servants still to arrive, none would explain anything to him. He wouldn't understand the animals or the birds either. Had he been a bird he might have believed this secret since birds don't lie and birds don't have a God . . .

But whose God is He? Pridefully, Shekhar said, 'There is no God—there isn't! There isn't!'

*

His own questions, his own single utterance, changed the course of his life.

He observed—understood—that no one was anything to anyone, which is to say there was no one worthy enough to be his master, instructor or ordainer of faith. There was no one that one could depend on, count on, to be completely reliable in every matter. If he could count on anything, then it was his own intellect. Man had to rely on it to get along, to survive in the world, and there are definitely moments when the intellect can provide clear answers, but it also has enough honesty that when it doesn't know something, it remains quiet and doesn't give a false answer.

It didn't have a good effect on him, at least in the opinion of others. He became a wilful, arrogant, obstinate and aloof ass. And the remedies that were implemented to straighten him out had the opposite effect.

He was already going to school, but he began to change in school, too. He had been made the class monitor because of his calm disposition, but now he was constantly on the lookout for some mischief. He was quite smart, so even when he didn't pay attention, he never came second to anyone in class, and there was no special difficulty in coming up with ideas for causing trouble all the time.

The bell rang. The boys all gathered in the classroom. Shekhar had set out the attendance book, the chalk, the duster and other things on the table, but the teacher had not yet arrived.

In the absence of the teacher, it was Shekhar's responsibility as monitor to keep the class under control. His method of choice was to have the boys get together and sing a vulgar Kashmiri song. He was the one in charge, so what did the boys have to fear? The song began. They hadn't finished two verses when the teacher showed up. In the suddenly descended silence his shrill voice rang, 'Where is the monitor?'

The monitor went to the front.

'What is this?'

'Nothing. We thought you might be late, so we—'

'Who started this commotion?'

Everyone was silent. At such moments there was a natural, wordless understanding amongst the boys.

The teacher asked in an even harsher voice, 'Who started it?'

The silence continued for another moment. Then an ungainly Muslim boy—whom the entire class hated—came forward and said, 'The monitor told everyone to sing. I didn't sing.'

Shekhar and two of his close friends were made to stand in a corner like 'roosters'—which meant they had to put their arms under their legs and grab their ears and try to stand up. The teacher is standing right in front of Shekhar and saying, 'Stand higher—higher!'

Shekhar was stripped of his role as monitor which was then handed over to that Muslim boy. This wasn't a big thing, but being humiliated like this before the whole class was not something he could bear. Would he be their laughing stock? Never! And the blazing anger that flared up within him showed him how he could get his revenge. As ordered by the teacher, he 'stood higher', and as he did this he intentionally did a flip. His acrobatic manoeuvre landed him on the floor, and his heavy boots flew and hit the teacher on his back. The teacher let out an 'Ouch!' and fell on the chalkboard as the entire class erupted in laughter.

The whole episode seemed so improbable that for a moment the teacher was stunned. When he saw Shekhar get up and stare at him, he regained his lost voice. Grinding his teeth together, he said, 'I'm going to teach you a lesson.'

But his threats turned out to be empty. Shekhar spoke in a voice that he might have used in speaking to a bug, 'You're an ass!' And he darted out of the class like an arrow. He could hear the sound of the class laughing behind him, and he felt as if he had won.

After that day, Shekhar didn't go to school. There were several flaws in his character, but he did acquire a strength seldom found in school; he acquired the ability to remain alone. Schools produce 'types'; he became an individual.

*

But no one is so isolated, so alone that the world outside disappears. In Shekhar's life, animals, birds, insects, snakes, flowers, trees, grass, rocks and stones took the place formerly occupied by humans. The throne that had been vacated by the God of human society was now filled by the goddess of the life-world, nature.

Saraswati was still teaching Shekhar. A moulvi had been hired to teach him as well. But Shekhar's day began when the moulvi left and ended when he arrived . . . The moulvi was like a bad dream. The rest of the day Shekhar wandered wherever his feet took him. That's where he went and saw whatever he saw. Sometimes he harassed the snakes, sometimes he sat perfectly still next to them and waited for them to crawl across him so that he could see how they move forward (he had heard that snakes used the membrane in their bellies to push themselves forward and this is what he wanted to observe). Sometimes he caught butterflies, looked at their colours and then let them go. Sometimes when he heard a ringdove's voice, he tried to imitate it, and for hours he would watch how it got irritated and modulated its voice differently each time and then fell silent after hearing its own echo. Sometimes he would climb trees, notice the architecture of a nest and make note of the various types of eggs in it. He would wait for days in the hope that the eggs would crack so that he could see the babies and learn what the eggs of various birds look like . . . Sometimes he would notice the male kite soar quite high in spring, while the female kept calling out to him, and after hours of anticipation, finally descend. Once he listened to an owl for hours and wondered, 'Does he speak through his mouth or his nose!' The first time he heard a cuckoo's 'coo-coo', he inexplicably felt that the cuckoo was probably blue and his breast was most likely red. A few days later when he saw a bird that looked like that, he sat in anxious anticipation waiting for it to speak, and wherever the bird went, he chased after it. Eventually his patience paid off. At sunset the bird settled on a fig tree and opened its mouth and let out a shrill call, 'che-oo'. Shekhar's heart skipped a beat . . . A few days later he learned that it wasn't a cuckoo but a magpie . . .

Once, while wandering in the forest, he got lost. He did not get nervous as a result of his splendid isolation—because of his contempt for dependency; he didn't run here and there wildly (those who have been lost in the woods are the only ones who will understand what it means not to be afraid in such moments!). He pushed down the grass that came up to his chest, made a place for himself to sit and began to watch the clouds. Whenever a wild fly buzzed nearby, he would watch it; he'd make notes in his mind about the blue and green metallic sheen of its belly, its mud-red head, its black antennae, all of it.

The jungle was state-protected land; hunting was prohibited. While Shekhar was sitting a deer came near him and stood completely still in nervousness for a while. Then it raced, bounding with all four legs, and vanished in an instant. The beauty of its form, the melody of its movement! Shekhar had seen it in pictures and read many descriptions—but the real thing!

Shekhar got up in enthusiasm. A misshapen beast passed next to him through the grass and ran off panting; Shekhar couldn't tell if it was a horse or a buffalo. It was like both yet different from the two . . .

Shekhar went off in one direction, lost in thought. He wasn't worried about getting back home yet—it was only afternoon.

Walking through the grass, he came to a clearing. A girl was running around here and there with a butterfly net, her hair tousled over her face—with no sense of the rest of the world. Shekhar stopped to watch her, watched her for quite a long time. Suddenly, the girl gasped and turned around to look at him—in exactly the same way as the deer had looked at him—and kept looking at him, the butterfly net dangling to her side.

Shekhar went up to her and asked gently, 'Who are you?'

'I'm me.'

Shekhar couldn't think of how to press this point further. He switched tracks, 'I'm just wandering through.'

The girl didn't answer and threw her net over a passing butterfly. It escaped. Shekhar started laughing and said, 'Not like that, let me show you.'

The girl said, 'No, I'll catch it myself,' but as she was talking Shekhar took the net from her and pounced and caught the butterfly.

Offended, the girl looked at him and took the butterfly. She said nothing.

Shekhar asked, 'Shall I catch more for you?'

'No, that's enough. I'm tired.'

She went off in one direction. Shekhar asked, 'Where are you going?'

'Home.'

'Where is it?'

She pointed with her chin, 'There.' It wasn't clear exactly where she meant. Shekhar followed her.

'Where are you going?'

'Your home.'

'Why?' she asked and kept walking on. Shekhar followed, too.

'How far is it?'

'A little way from here. Didn't you see?'

'No.'

'Then how did you get here?'

Shekhar responded a little hesitatingly, 'I forgot the way.'

She laughed out loud. 'So that's it.'

They got to her home. Shekhar asked, 'Where will you put the butterflies?'

'Don't know. Maybe I'll put them in a basket and let them out . . .'

'No, I'll show you,' he said and took her to the door of the house. Every door had two shutters, one made of wood and outside it a mesh, and there was a space between them. Shekhar said, 'Trap them between these.'

The girl said with awe, 'I never thought about that.'

Shekhar spoke as if he hadn't noticed the awe in her voice, 'And leave them a few leaves so that they won't die.'

Shekhar asked, 'Where's the road?'

'Over there. Walk straight ahead and there will be a lake. Turn right and you'll get to the school. You know the way from there, right?'

'Yes,' he said and then started walking.

The girl may have hoped that he would say something else. She watched him walk for quite some time, and then she shouted, 'You'll come again, won't you?'

Shekhar didn't turn around as he asked, 'What's your name?'

'Pratibha—Miss Pratibha Lal.'

'All right.'

Shekhar deliberately gave no indication whether his 'All right' was in response to coming again or her name.

She was friendly, but she was odd. The two would walk through the grass in the forest. Shekhar would lie down somewhere and Pratibha would chase after butterflies. Sometimes she'd gather flowers, sometimes she'd collect bamboo blossoms and then one by one she'd drink their nectar, sometimes she'd just stand there and laugh different kinds of laughs . . . Occasionally she'd look over to see if he was still there, that he hadn't left, and feeling reassured she'd go back to playing. She really only talked to him when she couldn't catch a butterfly after trying very hard or when a flower was just beyond her reach . . . Then she'd ask him for help, and he would get up immediately, do what she asked and go back to the same spot and lie back down. Or sometimes she would set aside the big bamboo blossoms for him and go up to him and ask, 'Don't you want some nectar?' He would take the flower that she stretched out to him and instead of drinking the nectar he would eat the whole flower. That made her laugh out loud. She would say, 'Goodness, you don't even know how to drink nectar!' Despite repeating this several times, it never got old; she would burst out laughing with the same joy each time . . .

Shekhar would laugh and play with Pratibha, he'd listen to everything she asked of him and would faithfully carry it out, but still their friendship never seemed to deepen. Despite being Pratibha's companion, he never emerged from his armour; he was, just as before, a separate, solitary individual. Children are so adept at noticing any kind of distance or aloofness and had it been any other girl, she would have immediately sensed this and been hurt. But Pratibha was so self-absorbed, a butterfly basking in the warmth of Shekhar's company, that she didn't notice anything. She was completely self-involved, and their friendship continued for the reason that he didn't ask anything of her, he was happy with her exactly as she was. It wasn't that he was especially generous; he had never felt close enough to Pratibha to ask anything of her.

One day Pratibha asked, 'Is your father's name Haridutt?'

Shekhar responded in surprise, 'Yes, why?'

'My father knows him. You'll have to come over today.'

Shekhar had been going there every day and today, on hearing that he had to go there specially, said, 'But I come over every day.'

'Silly, not like that. You'll have to meet Father, eat dinner.'

After a while, Shekhar asked, 'Why?'

'What do you mean by why? My father knows your father, so now we don't have to meet like this. Now we can ask permission and meet.'

Shekhar thought about this for a while. It struck him that he didn't live in a world of fathers. He also felt that it was not a problem if his father never entered his world. Pratibha plays . . . he stays in the shade of her play . . . that was enough. But if things were to change, then perhaps . . .

Shekhar said again, 'Why?'

The context of this 'why' wasn't immediately clear to Pratibha. She responded like an arrogant queen, 'What do you mean by why? Because I said so.' Then, insistently, 'Won't you do what I ask?'

Shekhar said, 'Humph.'

Mister Lal pointed to the chair next to him and said, 'Sit down, Shekhar.'

Shekhar sat down. Pratibha was sitting in front of him and her older sister was beside her. On the dining table knives, forks, plates and the like had all been laid out in the English fashion.

Mister Lal was an 'England-returned' doctor. When he came back, he brought a part of England with him which he planted in the fertile soil of India, and he now lived in its shade. At this moment, preparations for dinner are under way and everyone is waiting in anticipation.

Shekhar doesn't know how to eat with a knife and fork. This is what he's thinking about as he's sitting there. But he doesn't want to say anything about it either. It was in the midst of this dilemma that dinner was served. Soup arrives and everyone partakes. The second course is served.

Shekhar picks up the knife and fork copying everyone else. But he finds that he can't use the fork with his left hand. So he switches the knife and fork. Even though he can't cut anything with his left hand either, still, somehow, he gets a piece on to the fork and lifts it to his mouth, but an empty fork reaches his mouth and the bite of food falls off.

Pratibha laughs out loud. 'Hey, don't you even know how to eat?'

The older sister says, 'Hush!'

Shekhar puts down the knife and fork. Mister Lal sees this and tries to make sure that he isn't more upset.

The vegetables are served. Meat is served for Mister Lal. The salad is served. Then ice cream.

Shekhar doesn't eat; just sits there watching. When everything is finished he notices that the ice cream sitting in front of him has melted.

The others are eating it with spoons but despite knowing how to use a spoon, he picks up the bowl and drinks it down.

Pratibha says, 'Look, Father, look at how he's eating.'

When he was drinking the nectar Shekhar had eaten the flower, too, and Pratibha had laughed then as well. Shekhar hadn't smiled but he'd been content. But now . . .

Shekhar stood up. He threw his napkin on the table and, without looking up, quickly walked out.

The next day, he was wandering along the edge of the river. There was no forest and Pratibha—was dead.

*

In the middle of the river was an island which housed a temple of the goddess. Shekhar began to while away his time there.

He would sit outside the temple and watch the devotees as they came and went. As he saw the expressions of faith on their faces those same old questions welled and ebbed within him, and even though he didn't believe it, he found the atmosphere near the temple charming and came back regularly . . .

There were snakes in the river. Shekhar always used the bridge to get to the island, but the devotees waded through the river.

One day, as Shekhar watched, one of them was bitten by a snake. He leaped from the waters and exclaimed, 'Hail to the goddess!' and then went inside the temple. It was only after he had finished praying and come back outside that he began treating the snakebite.

After an hour, again right in front of Shekhar, he repeated, 'Hail to the goddess,' and then went silent. After a few minutes . . . People carried him away.

Shekhar's lack of faith, his faith in doubt, was shaken. When he got home he asked himself over and over, 'God, do you really exist?'

*

Beyond the Chashma Shahi gardens in Srinagar lay the ruins of an old palace. They say that it was built by Princess Zeb-un-Nissa,[12] and that she used to go into seclusion there and write poetry. The palace may have been made by anyone, but whoever picked that spot was definitely a poet . . .

There were snakes there, too. The first time Shekhar went there, he had already heard lots of stories—that ghosts lived there; that the rooms in the palace had no roofs and so the spirits of the dead could descend there; that fairies danced there . . .

The palace was called 'Fairy-Palace' . . .

When he was leaving, Shekhar decided that he would come back again sometime when he was by himself and in a few days an opportunity presented itself.

He got there in the afternoon. The rooms of the palace indeed had no roofs; he climbed the walls and went to the front and looked at the vista created by the Dal Lake below.

He was looking at the Dal, looking at much more than the Dal. Gradually, something of a hypnotic state came upon him, as if he were about to faint. He felt that near him, not near him, inside him, all around him, something had arrived, something which he couldn't describe. But something which was so beautiful, so magnificent, so expansive, so pure . . . so pure that Shekhar felt that he wasn't worthy of touching it, that he was dirty, covered in filth, obscured by it . . . In that hypnotic state, Shekhar took off all of his clothes, one by one, and threw them down, and he stood there with his eyes closed, completely naked, before the sky and that purity, completely enveloped by that purity, shuddering from its touch . . .

After a long while, he opened his eyes with a start, put his clothes quickly back on and, without looking back, ran straight home . . .

What was that? God? Nature? Beauty? The devil? Suppressed desire? God?

He didn't know. But he never experienced that unity, that oneness with the divine, again . . .

He never returned to that spot. The Buddha, too, perhaps never returned to the Bodhi tree.

*

A lot of snow has fallen and continues to fall. Shekhar's father and the rest of the family are going in their car down a snow-covered street. Occasionally, some of the snow gets inside, at which point someone gets upset and everyone else laughs . . .

Everyone was carsick. Shekhar's brothers had even stuck their heads out the window and thrown up, and the stench was seeping inside. Shekhar is sitting upfront so he isn't bothered by it. He keeps watching the falling snow . . .

Shekhar's father was transferred again. That's why they had stayed in Kashmir for as long as they did, otherwise they would have long since left for Jammu. And now they are heading for Bihar . . .

Once, when the road curved, Father said, 'Look there, that's where we came from.'

Shekhar looked up. He could see the road that they had come down on and a broad, white curtain which hid so much behind it . . .

Shekhar remembered that a few days earlier he had made a snowman and kept it a secret from everyone. He had lifted it and taken it up to his room. He put it there and fell asleep. When he woke up the next day, he saw that his sculpture was not there and the floor was wet. In a frenzy, he asked, 'Mother, where's my snowman? Sister, who took my snowman? Brothers, who took my snowman?' And no one could tell him; everyone said they hadn't seen it. He never understood where it really went . . .

While looking at that curtain of snow, the same question dawned in his mind—'God?'

Part 2

Seeds and Sprouts

Shekhar's life became so vacant, which was why he wanted to wring out the last drop of pleasure from everything that came into his life. If it was laughter, he would laugh more than was necessary; when he went out for a walk, he'd run around like a mad dog; when he fought, he would remain hostile even when he forgot why he was fighting . . . As a result his life acquired a false freshness, the delusion of progress, when in reality he was standing absolutely still.

Shekhar is standing on top of a hill, surrounded by ruins, and his dog is at his feet. Fields of pulses spread out in all four directions. Sometimes a gust of wind blows and the stalks of pulse bend and then straighten themselves out, like scores of soldiers on watch dozing off simultaneously and then standing back up at attention when they wake up.

The dog was called Taimur. Shekhar didn't care for him especially, but the dog still followed him everywhere; he had made Shekhar his master for some unknown reason.

Shekhar was just standing there, but Taimur must have seen something in the distance because he ran straight down into the fields of pulse. Shekhar ran off after him, too. He had no inner impulse to do anything, but the push that he got externally was enough to make him flow forward . . .

Shekhar made a path for himself through the pulse with his hands and then discovered what had made the dog run. Several quails were running about in all directions, and Taimur chased after one and then after another, but couldn't catch any of them.

Wherever Taimur ran, Shekhar followed. Gradually, the stalks of pulse became denser. Shekhar pushed his shoulders forward and bent down and sliced through the pulse with his hands, advancing like a crazed bull, and still he couldn't catch Taimur. His shirt was torn, his arms and legs were scraped up and his face was scratched all over, but he couldn't catch a single quail. Shekhar went on even more fearlessly than his dog; his naked feet left bloodied prints as he went forward, but still he couldn't catch a single quail . . .

Taimur grew bored and abandoned the game—accepted defeat. Shekhar had to do the same.

The sun rained down gold over the tops of the ruins as it set. Shekhar was headed back on the road home, covered in blood, exhausted, head hanging; Taimur, who was always in front, was coming behind him, head drooping . . .

They caught no quails, but the game was over and the day had ended.

*

Again, the fields of pulse. Again, Shekhar in front and behind him his dog, Taimur. Now Taimur is Shekhar's brother, his teacher, his companion and servant. Shekhar's mother has gone to her father's village with Saraswati, and he is under no one's jurisdiction.

Shekhar is wandering aimlessly, but his aimlessness is not without suspense. He's waiting for Ganesi.

Ganesi is a Dalit weaver by caste. He works as a coolie in Shekhar's father's employ. Whenever he gets free time, he makes fireworks. That's why he's Shekhar's friend, because he usually takes Shekhar along and puts things together while he watches. He makes gunpowder, fills it into firecrackers, wraps them, all the while explaining to Shekhar how the saltpetre, sulphur and charcoal all have to be ground separately; how you need to use wooden tools when mixing them together so that they don't ignite; and how the paper you use to wrap 'the musk rat' has to be doused with a solution of saltpetre and vinegar and then dried . . . Sometimes when Shekhar insists he lets him grind the gunpowder, and sometimes he gives him a few firecrackers. Their friendship has grown so much that sometimes Shekhar asks his father to give Ganesi the day off and then goes out with him.

Today Shekhar is waiting for Ganesi because he has sent him to get an iguana. It was Ganesi who had told him that iguanas can climb any kind of wall and stick to it. Even if someone grabs it by its tail it wouldn't let go, and in the olden days, people used to scale walls by tying ropes to their tails and using them for support. After he heard this, it was only natural that Shekhar wanted to see one. When Ganesi told him that he couldn't bring back one alive because its bite was poisonous, Shekhar demanded that he kill one and bring it.

Shekhar crossed through the fields of pulse and saw Ganesi coming towards him—a skinny, black ghost with a staff in one hand and a chameleon-like thing in the other. As soon as he came to him he said, 'Young master, here, take this iguana.'

Shekhar looked at him for a while. He was a little disappointed. This is an iguana! Then he said, 'Skin it. I'll keep that.'

Ganesi laughed and told him that an iguana's skin is so thin it couldn't be skinned. But Shekhar wasn't going to take his word for it. If you could skin a cheetah, and he regularly sat on a cheetah skin, then why not an iguana! He said, 'I am telling you, skin it!'

Ganesi realized that he'd have to do it. He took out a knife and sliced open the iguana's belly. Shekhar caught hold of his dog and stood there.

It took half an hour for the skin to be peeled off completely. Shekhar said, 'Set it in the sun to dry. After it's dry, we'll wash it.'

Ganesi didn't say anything and smiled as he spread it out to dry.

What Shekhar saw there three days later doesn't have to be said. That was when Ganesi laughed and asked, 'Young master, now you can see for yourself whether or not the iguana's skin has dried.' Then he said in dismay, 'What skin? What iguana?' The wise Ganesi smiled and stayed quiet.

Shekhar noted that everyone had a skin, but a cheetah was a cheetah, and an iguana was an iguana.

*

The house that Shekhar lived in had a mango orchard. The mangoes were local and of poor quality; there was only one tree that bore hybrid mangoes.

The fruits were just about to ripen. Shekhar would go there every day and look longingly and dream of the day when they wouldn't be on the trees but in his hands . . .

One day, when he saw a few ripe mangoes on a solitary tree, he said to the gardener, 'Give me a mango.'

But the gardener was unsympathetic to this completely reasonable request. He said, 'Young master, I'll pick those mangoes tomorrow and send a basket of them as a present to the master.'

To the master! Shekhar thought it completely unfair that the mangoes be snatched from him, who actually wanted the mangoes, and given to his father who didn't care about them. He said, 'Will you give them to me or not?'

'No, young master.'

Shekhar started to climb the tree himself. The gardener stood back and laughed because he knew that this child couldn't climb the tree.

But Shekhar's hands and feet had the strength of his anger. He got to the top, comfortably sat on a branch, picked out the ripe mangoes and started eating.

The gardener's smile turned into worry. Watching Shekhar, he was even more convinced that the boy would eat up all the mangoes.

But his stomach gave up on him. So he started picking all kinds of mangoes—the unripe, half-rotten and ripe ones—and throwing them around after spoiling them by biting into them. With each mango he threw, he yelled to the gardener, 'Take that! And take that! And take that!'

The gardener couldn't take that, and he began to climb the tree to get a hold of Shekhar. Shekhar looked at him and said,

'Come on, yes, come on!' and he climbed further up and sat at the end of a branch which would clearly break if there was even the slightest increase in weight on it. The gardener shouted, 'Come down or you'll fall!'

'No, come and get me. Let's see.' And he climbed further up.

The gardener was scared. He left. Shekhar gradually got down. He hadn't touched the ground when he saw the gardener return with Father.

He became philosophical. He gave his plucked mangoes a once-over and then stood ready. He did a calculation in his head about how many slaps per mango or how many mangoes per slap he'd get. That he might not get slapped was not a thought that entered his head.

But he didn't get slapped. Father laughed after he heard the whole tale. He said to Shekhar, 'It was fine if you wanted to eat them, but why did you throw them?' And then to the gardener he asked, 'Why did you tell him he couldn't have them because you were giving them to me as a present?'

This was the only time Shekhar expected a slap and got laughter instead. Normally, the opposite used to happen. Still, he had boundless love in his heart for his father.

*

Shekhar's father bought a new house—in Patna, on the banks of the Ganga. Now Shekhar's chief occupation was to cut down the banana trees in their orchard and use their trunks to float in the river (one has to call it 'floating' because he still hadn't learned how to swim). Often, he would slip off the trunk and struggle in the water, but each time someone would see him and drag him out. Despite Father's prohibitions he never gave up this habit because the idea of floating down such a big river without using his arms and legs was so attractive that he couldn't shake it from his head.

He tied three trunks together and made a raft. He took it to the Ganga, laid down flat on it and used his arms to row it into the moving stream. Then he brought his hands in and lay still as he looked sometimes to one side and sometimes to the other.

The slower movements on either riverbank made it seem to him like they were going backwards. After he had looked at both sides for a long time, he started looking up at the sky. It had rained and small bits of clouds were running around every which way. Sometimes they would run into each other and become one. And he watched the vastness of the sky dissolve into azure. Oh, how beautiful it would be to melt into that vast azure sky and become nothing . . . Absent-mindedly, Shekhar thought, 'This is how I will die, where there will be no obstacles . . .'

Obstacles . . . he felt as if the life he was living was nothing more than an obstacle. Today he got the chance to escape from its clutches. Today, with the help of three felled trees, he was going to that distant land where the Ganga flows, where it merges with the ocean, where there is an island of sunset-gold and where there lived a princess dressed in clothes made from clouds that had dissolved into the very same azure expanse . . . Shekhar would go to her and say, 'I'm Shekhar. I've come from the land of attachments,' and she would seat him next to her and say, 'You are free here. You will live in that palace of sirissa flowers and you can do whatever you want . . .'

But maybe the princess wouldn't notice him. Why would she waste her time on an insignificant boy from the land of attachment?

But there would be others there and other girls. Wasn't everyone a princess in the land without attachments?

Shekhar closed his eyes . . .

Then he realized, 'Goodness, that place is really far away. It will take days to get there, and the Ganga flows so slowly . . .'

But he had already passed beyond the point where worry had any power over him. The sky, the liberated atmosphere, the unobstructed vastness had all filled his veins. He was unobstructed, too, vast, liberated and reality was far behind . . .

He thought of a line of poetry in English:

O mother Ganges, vast and slow!

And slowly, with great concentration, he began to add lines to complete the poem . . .

The moment he realized the poem was finished was the moment he realized that his back had grown stiff from the cold and his hands were white and numb. He knew he had come very far from home.

Fear lives in the world of reality, not on the way to that island of sunset-gold. Shekhar slowly and unwillingly rowed himself to the riverbank. He somehow got on to dry land and lay face down in the sun.

When he awoke from his sleep, the sun had already set. He got up and dragged his tired body home. As he neared home, the moon was rising, and the house was completely quiet, even though the lights were on. As soon as he went inside, he saw his mother and father standing in the courtyard, looking outside with fixed gazes, as if they had suddenly grown old—there were so many lines on their faces . . . As soon as they saw Shekhar, their anxiety-ridden faces relaxed. There were tears in Mother's eyes; Father turned right around and went upstairs.

Shekhar followed them and saw that the house was completely empty. The next day he learned that people had taken lanterns and gone quite far down the side of the river looking for him . . . Somehow, his parents learned that he had gone down the river on a raft of banana trees and everyone panicked. When he heard the news, Shekhar forgot himself to such an extent that even after a great effort he couldn't remember the poem he had composed on the bosom of the Ganga, only the trace of the first line remained in his memory:

O mother Ganges, vast and slow!

*

How did one get to the island of sunset-gold when it was far away, when it took so many days to get there, so many days like the first one where in the first few hours your back grows stiff and hands go numb? How did one manage to see the princess who would put you up in a palace of sirissa flowers and sit next to you?

Shekhar knows that it will never happen, but he also knows that it has to happen, inevitably, something would have to happen to fill the emptiness in his life. And helplessly he'd think, why doesn't something happen which would get me closer to that island? When he'd go out for a walk, when so many cars passed right next to him, why didn't a princess peep out from one of them and say, 'Shekhar, come with me to my island where there are no obstacles.' All right, maybe not a princess. When he was walking in the field where there were so many girls playing, why didn't some island-loving girl hidden in their midst come up to him and say, 'Come. Why don't you play in our carefree game?' All right, maybe not even that. But how about when he bumped into something while walking, why then didn't a girl from this very world come up to him and say lovingly, 'Come, Shekhar. I can't do much but I can bring something new into your monotonous world.' Or if only she just asked, 'You aren't hurt too badly, are you?'

Secretly, he would draw colourful flowers and leaves on pretty paper and in the space in between he'd write a letter. To whom? He didn't know. But he poured out the hunger in his heart into that letter, and the anxiety of being able to welcome that stranger . . . He wrote, 'O imaginary one, O stranger, whom I can't even see in my mind, will you read this letter and understand? I am Shekhar, I'm alone and I've been searching for you for I don't know how long, waiting for you, only for you. You are on a heavenly plane, but does that heavenly plane want you as much as I do? O unknowable, O unimaginable!'

Then he would seal the letter in an envelope, put his full address in one of the corners and tie it to a stick before he placed it into the Ganga so that it wouldn't sink as it travelled down. And wait expectantly for several days in the hope that someone would read it, they'd read it—and then he'd get a reply. Even if it wasn't from a girl in the dreamland, at least it would be from someone he didn't know! And when nothing happened for the next several days, he wrote another letter and tied it to another raft in case the first one sank . . .

But nothing ever happened, and he never lost faith . . .

Sometimes a butterfly would get trapped in his room. At first it would crash into the glass of the window or the door because light was coming in through them and it thought it was the way out, and then crash into it some more. Then, admitting defeat, it would make a few circuits around the room and then come back to the same spot and again crash its head against the glass and flail its wings helplessly, and even though falling wouldn't completely fall . . .

Shekhar was in an identical situation. In his search for freedom, first he tried dealing with material things, things that he could see, and when he failed there, he tried to work in the realm of imagination, and when that frustrated him he came back to reality, to material and visible things.

*

Shekhar's father is ill from typhus, and sometimes Ishwardutt gets on the phone to call the doctor. That's how Shekhar came to learn a few things about the telephone. He realized that things that he couldn't find elsewhere could probably be found by using a telephone—because it was new, mysterious.

Father was sick, and so the offices were closed. The watchman would lock everything up and give the keys to Shekhar to take to his father. But those were not keys to the office, but keys to Shekhar's secret world.

It was about 5 p.m. The office was closed and the key was in Shekhar's hand. The watchman had left.

Shekhar opened the door to the office and went straight to his father's room. He picked up the telephone receiver and put it to his ear.

Those days they didn't have an automatic exchange. From the receiver came a voice, 'Number?'

Shekhar gave the number of a pharmacy.

'How can I help you?'

'Do you have thermometers? How much are they?'

'___'

'Tell me the prices of all of them.'

'___'

'And what about medical gloves?'

'___'

'Do you have a catalogue?'

'Yes, sir. Should I send you one?'

'Yes.'

'What address should I send it to?'

Shekhar hadn't expected—or feared—this question. He had been told that the person being called didn't know the number of the caller until the caller himself revealed it, and it was on the basis of this belief that he had the courage to make a phone call. As soon as he heard the question, he panicked and didn't know what to say. He said, 'Send it to the office,' and ran away leaving the receiver dangling.

Second time.

Shekhar again used the keys to unlock the office and sat next to the telephone. This time he called the fire station. He wanted to know whether what his brother had told him was true or not, that a fire engine could get there within five minutes of being called.

He screamed into the phone, 'Fire! Come at once!'

A deep voice asked, 'Where?'

As soon as he realized the consequence of his prank, he got scared. He put the receiver down on the table and quickly locked up the office and returned the key.

The next day, a report arrived from the exchange that someone had been misusing the telephone. Father questioned everyone, but got no answers save silence. That's as far as things went. From that day on, the guard brought the keys to Father himself.

*

Shekhar started flying kites.

He didn't know how to fly kites. But that wasn't an obstacle in his path; it actually made it even more attractive. And besides, there was another pleasure in flying kites—he had been told not to. His father used to say that it was a dangerous game, that while flying kites several boys had fallen off the rooftops.

The way Shekhar would fly his kite was that he would go out into the garden by his house and call someone and ask them to launch it for him, and when it was soaring high in the sky, he would take the kite reel into his own hands and tug the string to make the kite dance and to convince himself that he was flying the kite (or rather, that he had launched it).

One of his chores was to sit next to his father and give him his medicine at the proper time. Not because he was particularly good at this job, but because his father wanted to keep him close by. But when he was flying his kite he forgot about everything else.

Father's peon came and created an obstacle.

'Master Shekhar, you're wanted upstairs.'

'Just wait, let me finish flying this kite,' he said and then forgot.

'Let's go, Master Shekhar!' the peon said after about a minute.

'I already told you, wait!'

The peon kept nagging him.

'Go, go and tell him that I will come once I've brought the kite down.'

The peon left, but came back in a short time.

'Master Shekhar, the master has ordered that I'm to carry you if you don't come by yourself. Let's go.'

The peon called another servant to take hold of the kite string and bring the kite down, and then he carried Shekhar away. Only Shekhar's legs were free; he began kicking them but they only struck air. Then with all his might, he tried to free his arm from the peon's grasp, and when it came free, it struck the peon across the nose. The peon dropped him on the ground quickly, as if stung by a wasp, and ran upstairs because his nose was bloody.

Halfway up the stairs, Shekhar grabbed hold of the banister. He stood there, petrified, thinking about the consequences of that accident.

Father was quite ill, couldn't get up from his cot, but his anger . . .

That's when Shekhar saw his father coming down the stairs. A cane in his hand. His hands are trembling. He was bracing himself with his elbows against the wall and carefully stepping down. How thin he's become! His eyes were not looking here or there, not at the ceiling or at the stairs, but were fixed on Shekhar. Behind him, Saraswati was standing at the top of the stairs, and she had an expression on her face that was making her unrecognizable. Her wide eyes were staring straight into Shekhar's trying to tell him something, something that she couldn't say with her lips. Shekhar understood that he had to stand there, not move, not raise his head, not talk back and not save himself.

He stood there. Six times the cane rose and fell, six times a shock went through his body, but he didn't move. The cane stopped. Father cast an angry look at Shekhar's face. The peon was the only one standing there who didn't understand what it meant but who for some reason was embarrassed.

Shekhar couldn't go upstairs. A little later, when Saraswati said, 'Shekhar, tell the peon to get the doctor,' he was unable to ask her what had happened . . .

Two hours later, his father called Shekhar upstairs. To make peace. He never forgave; one only forgave one's lessers. When he was angry, he didn't consider his inferiors to be inferior, and when the anger subsided he still didn't . . . His generosity was so pure, free from any hint of mercy, so expansive and all-encompassing! That's why Shekhar worshipped him even when he got beaten, just as he never worshipped his mother. She never beat him, but when she forgave it always came mixed up with guilt or obligation or debt . . .

*

Shekhar got permission to go and see a play.

There was a troupe of actors in the village who put on performances twice a year—for Holi and for Dussehra. Shekhar's father was an important man, the most important man who lived near that village, and so it was natural that the play would only commence after receiving his blessings and his permission. He wasn't going himself, but because the play was 'Harishchandra the Honest' the boys were able to go.

In a theatre hall made of thatched walls, Shekhar sat next to his brothers in the front row. When the curtain rises and reveals a twenty-foot-by-ten-feet backdrop of heaven (Indralok) Shekhar was certain that it was close to his island . . .

Scenes come and go. And they take Shekhar's critical abilities, his powers of judgement, with them. Enchanted, gullible and absorbed, Shekhar sits and keeps watching. Somewhere beyond this world where the drama of life is more realistic than life. A great conflict lies before him, an original opposition, and a mother's lamentation for her dying son . . . When a dying Rohit tells his friends:

Tell Mother what happened—
A snake bit me, O tyranny, outrageous tyranny!

He isn't indifferent at that moment. He doesn't laugh, but he chokes up and begins to cry—very softly, so that no one can see his defeat . . .

The play ends, and they set off for home. But Shekhar can't bear to be with his brothers. He walks separately, without paying attention, heavy and dissatisfied . . .

*

In those dark times, several of those scenes flashed like fireflies, but they were all only scenes. They all came and went; nothing remained fixed, except for that dissatisfaction which appeared and grew, and even when repressed, kept growing . . .

The butterfly made another round . . . But where was that open window, where was that path to freedom?

A tide of non-cooperation welled and the entire nation was swept up in it. Shekhar, too, tried to get carried away by it and when he couldn't he began to paddle with his own arms and float . . .

He took out all of his foreign-made clothes and threw them out, and began to wear the few coarse swadeshi clothes that he owned. He stopped going out and meeting people because he didn't have enough swadeshi clothes to wear. Every afternoon he would go and stand by one of the windows upstairs and look out. And sometimes from a distance the call of hundreds of voices in unison reached him:

'Victory to Gandhi! Down with the enemy!'

And then, with every fibre of him being thrilled, he also called out from his window:

'Victory to Gandhi! Down with the enemy!'

He couldn't go any farther; he didn't have permission to leave the house. But the lack of permission was a kind of prod that constantly compelled him to try and find a way . . .

Except for Mother, everyone had gone out. Mother was upstairs, sitting in the rooftop. Shekhar gathered up all of the foreign clothes from all of the rooms in the house and made a pile of them in an open area downstairs. He brought out the lanterns and poured the kerosene from them over the pile (the containers of oil were with the servants, and he didn't have the courage to get them) and set it on fire.

The fire flared up immediately. Shekhar's joy similarly flared up. He danced all around the fire and sang at the top of his lungs:

'Victory to Gandhi! Down with the enemy!'

Mother came down a short while later. And soon after, it was as if Shekhar's cheeks were also foreign—burning . . .

But the whole pile had turned to ash . . .

*

Shekhar began to hate all foreign things. He saw that it was not only the influence of foreigners that flowed through every vein of their bodies, but their terror, too. He remembered old things and some new things, too. He began to see. He began to notice that Father asked him to speak to his brothers in English at home, and that he could speak in English from a young age, but he was still learning Hindi. His first ayah was Christian and only spoke English; and his first teacher, with whom he had to spend all his days, was an American missionary, who may not have taught him to read anything, but taught him English all day long. Shekhar thought that if one's mother tongue was the first language one learned, then his mother tongue was English and his mother was a foreigner . . . His self-respect took a heavy blow—*I am obliged to call maternal the very foreigners I hate.* From that day on, he began to study Hindi with a deep affection, and he tried to eliminate all English words from his vocabulary. He started to remove foreign practices from his habits . . .

In order to prove his knowledge of Hindi, and to show his devotion to Gandhi—which he had no other means to make apparent—he began to write a nationalist play. The memory of the only play that he had seen was still fresh in his mind and so he didn't have any particular problem writing one. The prologue was lifted verbatim, though he had to make a few small changes. And then the play started—a beautiful dream of a free, democratic India whose President was Gandhi. The way to win it was unceasing spinning and weaving, the repudiation of foreign goods and men and turning the other cheek at each opportunity. And the heaven that was at the beginning of 'Harishchandra the Honest' was moved to the end—bearing the imprint of Shekhar's sunset-golden island.

The last scene of Shekhar's play had a free and unoppressed India—a material and visible dream . . .

The play was complete. Shekhar made a clean copy with beautiful swadeshi ink and hid it under the rest of his books. He could still remember what had happened after his first literary endeavour, and that was why he didn't show the play, that priceless gem, to anyone—not even Saraswati! And all the time, wherever he went, a voice echoed in his head—*I am Shekhar, the author of a novel play, 'Chandrashekhar'. And I created it by myself, without anyone's help, with my own hands, this picture of a free, unoppressed India, I did.*

*

Shekhar's father was on tour for a day, and Shekhar was going with him. They locked their luggage up at the station at Bankipur and father and son were strolling outside the waiting room—Shekhar a little ahead, Father following him.

A boy appeared next to them and he looked up at Shekhar and said to him in English, 'What's your name?'

Shekhar looked him over head-to-toe. The boy was wearing a nice suit, with a British hat on his head. His voice had a tone of arrogance in it, perhaps because he wanted to show off his knowledge of English.

Shekhar found the question mean and insulting. He didn't respond. Partly, also, because his father was right there behind him, and he was nervous about speaking in his presence.

The boy thought that there was no one to challenge him, that this boy probably doesn't know English at all. With a little more haughtiness he said, 'My name is _____. Do you go to school?'

Had Shekhar's father not been there, he would have definitely responded (in Hindi), though he might not have answered that question. He also suspected that the boy was repeating some memorized lesson, that he didn't know English that well. He simply stared at the boy hatefully, and didn't say anything.

His father's angry voice boomed—perhaps to prove to that boy that his son knows English—'Why don't you answer him!'

Shekhar became even more upset, even quieter. The boy smiled and walked on.

Father said, 'Come here.' Shekhar followed him into the waiting room where his father caught him by the ears and asked, 'Why didn't you answer him? Has your mouth stopped working?'

And the train arrived just in time to save Shekhar from giving a reply—or from the impishness of not giving a reply.

The next day, at home, Father said to Mother, 'All our boys are idiots. They don't know how to speak to anyone.'

Shekhar heard him.

*

No, nowhere was it to be found, that unrestraint, that release, that freedom! Neither in intelligence nor in stupidity; neither in isolation nor in companionship; neither in poetry nor in drama; neither in work nor in idleness; neither in hate nor in love—not even in the love of his immense, oppressive, generous father . . .

Shekhar's father was tall, fair-skinned, well built and able-bodied. His keen eyes, crooked nose and fat but pressed lower lip were all markers of his proud and angry Aryanness that was carried by a greedy and thieving race of barbarians, in some ancient past, when it entered India and stayed on after it had established its mastery over it. He was generous by nature, but after getting hurt once or twice he developed a suspicious disposition. And when someone becomes suspicious after being hurt, then nothing in the world escapes his suspicion. So despite being honest himself, he considered the rest of the world to be dishonest and thieving—as if he were saying to himself again and again, 'See, you were honest, and that's why you were tricked. The whole world is dishonest. Don't trust anyone!' So despite being a pure-hearted person, he became bent on believing in the faults of others at each turn. When he became older, Shekhar used to say to him, 'Look, human nature is trusting. And since it's trusting, it takes sides and acquires prejudices. So why not believe the world is good? It's not a matter of judgement at all, and when one side makes us happy, we can at least live in peace. We are not forced to spend our days lying in bed.' But Father would respond, 'You're a child. What do you know! You were the one who bought a ten-paisa whistle for half a rupee!' Shekhar would say, 'Let's say that I did, but I am still happy. Thinking about that whistle makes me happy to this day. Even though you weren't the one who lost half a rupee, you still remember that fact today because you can't trust anyone, right?' And Father would cut the argument by saying, 'You are too idealistic. When will you learn?'

He was an Aryan, and so he admired strength and ability. Perhaps that's why he liked to be called 'Sahib', although his pride had never allowed him to put on a hat; he always tied a turban. Shekhar remembers several such incidents, like once when his father beat a coolie who had deigned to address him as 'Babu' instead of 'Sahib'. This was the same father who had on another occasion refused to meet with an officer because his invitation letter carried the stench of something like, 'You can come meet me, although I may or may not meet with you, depending on my wishes.'

One form his worship of ability took was that he liked to feel as though he were powerful. This was the sentiment that led him to intervene in his children's play. It wasn't that he wanted his children not to play or not to study, or that they not do this or that; he wanted them to play or study only because he told them to. Spontaneity—that the only reason that something was happening was that it was happening, or because the person doing it was doing it—had no value for him. Consequently, whenever he arrived, the child would become silent in terror, the game would end, the book would be set aside, the legs would be brought underneath and beds and chairs would be immediately abandoned . . . No one ever knew when something would be outlawed. It wasn't a matter of them being good or bad, proper or improper; rather it was a matter of two other criteria, namely, whether he liked it or not. And that was that. Neither reason nor argument held any sway before them.

'These boys are mine, and only mine, and so I have complete authority over them'—that was his fixed standpoint. And partly for this reason, he named his children in the foreign fashion (to him), in which the father's name is joined to the child's name. If Shekhar had to write his full name, then he would write, 'Chandrashekhar Haridutt Pandit', or in English, 'C.H. Pandit'. Shekhar first saw this fact come to light when he saw that his father had taken a red pen to his book on which he had written his name, completely naturally, 'Chandrashekhar Pandit'. His father had drawn a caret between the two names and written 'Haridutt' above them . . . And another time, when he saw the cover page of a compilation of poems that he had written himself, on which in a moment of ecstasy he had signed 'Shekhar, son of nature', 'nature' had been crossed out and 'Pandit Haridutt' written in its place. On that day

Shekhar felt as if his father had destroyed a pure moment and, unable to bear the tyranny, he destroyed the notebook . . .

It's not clear whether he derived pride from the demonstrations of his boys' successes or because he had an unbiased interest in the progress of his boys, but whenever he was pleased by something one of the boys had done, it would make him enthusiastic. He would praise his son more than necessary, would boast about him to everyone, just as his anger would take his opposite feelings to an extreme point . . .

But just as it is natural for some people to flare up in anger quickly, he was naturally a generous man. He didn't hold on to grudges or ill will for very long. And even two minutes after he had beaten his boys hard he could say, 'No matter what, my boys are a thousand times better than the rest.'

It was over this last point that Shekhar's parents fought repeatedly. Shekhar's mother held strongly to the idea that her children were much worse than other children. Whenever the boys did anything that could be criticized, she was always ready to say, 'Other people's children behave much better.' What she meant by 'better' could be that they enjoyed themselves while playing peacefully; or that they sat obediently; or that they got up in the mornings, washed themselves and started on their chores without being asked; or that they didn't complain about unfairness when they did their work, and they each did the work that was assigned to them . . . Father would argue, 'You always say such things,' and that would make Mother even angrier, 'Yes, I'm coming to you, too—you have spoiled them. Do you know anything about your boys? I am the one that has to deal with them night and day! Look at so-and-so's sons.' And then the catalogue of all the sons of all of the families in the neighbourhood would begin, and poor Saraswati and her three brothers knew that there were no virtues left in the world for them to claim as their own—all had already been seized by other people's children . . .

Shekhar's mother was of average height, heavyset and somewhat lazy by nature. A short forehead, eyes placed too close to her nose and bulging out of their sockets, a straight but small nose, beautifully shaped lips, a mouth that was a bit big and ears that were rubbery, small and set a little far back. Her whole face had been designed to show vivacity and loquacity, but because there was no seriousness or generosity in it, it couldn't be called beautiful. And this deficiency of character and grace was visible in every gesture, in every mannerism, in her whole personality . . .

Mother wasn't well educated. Nor did she have any great admiration for education. After all, women are more practical and realistic. But Shekhar's mother had more than a special love for hands over heads. Anybody could tell you in less than three seconds how many paisas there are in 871 rupees and thirteen annas. That was not as impressive to her as, for instance, a person who could feed a family of three on four and a quarter annas and still have two paisas left . . .

This was another source of debate between Mother and Father. Mother wanted the boys to be energetic, clever and fit while Father thought all of that was pointless . . .

Mother wanted her boys to meet people, learn about their doings, keep track of how much so-and-so makes, what so-and-so is cooking and what so-and-so's sister-in-law's uncle's son does for a living; Father said, 'Don't go to anyone's home and don't talk to anyone. What is all this nonsense to you?' Sometimes Mother would send one of them secretly to a neighbour's house saying, 'Go do this one thing' or 'Go find this out'; if Father ever got wind of this he'd subject them to a lengthy interrogation: 'Why did you go there? What did you go to do? Who gave you permission to go? Why couldn't you send one of the servants?'

Mother wasn't generous. She wasn't wrathful. No one ever saw her beside herself with anger. But she also never forgot a transgression. Her disposition wasn't expansive enough to become excessively angry, and for the same reason she wasn't that compassionate either. Father would even 'reconcile' with the wrongdoer after he got angry with him, but Mother wouldn't even do that when she was in the wrong, and would remain angry with the person she scolded.

Mother held appearances to be very important. Sometimes, the boys would be taught how to perform their dawn and dusk prayers. Father realized that it was impossible for them to concentrate on the rituals in their current state, so he eventually stopped forcing them to perform them. He got quite angry and said, 'What's the point if your heart's not in it? Don't do it.' And after the boys heard him out and stopped doing their rituals, he didn't ask them to perform them again. Then it was Mother who began to force the boys to sit as prescribed in the proper place for prayer and perform the appropriate rites.

Father was emotionally excessive; Mother was cruel because of a lack of emotion. When Father's anger rained down on him, Shekhar felt as though they were friends again; when his mother said nothing, Shekhar felt as if he were being baked by a sweet flame.

And from the union and friction between these two divergent temperaments were born six offspring: Saraswati, Ishwardutt, Prabhudutt, Shekhar, Ravidutt and Chandra. These were the products of that friction, and the playground of its evolution.

*

Life is another name for strangeness. Those whose lives have been crushed into nothingness by the weight of conformity also endure enough challenges to make a beautiful novel. If every human being were to write his own autobiography the world would have no shortage of beautiful books.

But only when everyone has learned to write.

We learned in college that the reason that there are so many stories written these days is because the material for them is readily available. I can still picture it, my skinny English professor, his wide frog-eyes splayed open behind the lenses of his thick horn-rimmed glasses, and the way his voice used his nose more than his mouth when he spoke: 'Each and every one of you has had at least one important challenge in your life that is different from everyone else's, which stands apart and is special. And that's why each one of you has at least one good story in him. Few people have life stories that are thrilling enough, heavy enough, and special enough to produce a good novel . . .'

But it seems to me that all the challenges that I could remember in my life were mine, were original, were complete stories in themselves, and my life was a brilliant novel. I may have been the only one who felt this way; fascination with one's own life turns it into something unique. But at the same time I realize that it wasn't so unique, so idiosyncratic that others couldn't derive pleasure from it; my private experience contained enough of a germ of collective experience that the collectivity would be able to understand it and see a glimpse of itself in it. My life is a solution in which individuality and 'type' are mixed together, without which art is impossible, and without which the novel is impossible.

It's completely possible that even with the right material I might not be able to produce a novel. But when do I intend to write a novel? I only want to rid myself of this weight on my shoulders; I don't want to give my life over to anyone else. I want to realize it myself because I want to offer it up such that after it's been offered I won't get it back. It will be completely destroyed—nothing will be left . . . Then there won't be a Shekhar; there will only be me. This Shekhar, who dreams of being an artist, a fool chasing the fame of poets, will have ended, and what will be left over will be me who will go to the gallows; it will be me, who I call 'me', and even while I say it I don't know what 'me' means.

*

People, generally speaking, forget what their lives were like. That's how society finds it possible to lay down laws such as 'Those mothers and fathers are best who teach their children to live like adults.' The blow that this single sentiment delivers to youth is possibly greater than what any other law or custom or order has ever done. When they teach their children to behave like adults they forget what their own lives were like, that they were once children, too, that they also had the same innocent mischief in them and that they embarrassed their parents, too, with their tricks. If parents could remember their childhoods their whole lives, their children, and they would be so happy!

Parents generally think that childhood is a very happy time because it is free of all responsibilities. And this notion makes them commit so many injustices towards childhood. And because of this notion, they keep telling themselves, 'If only those days would come again!' If only their wish could be granted for a few days—they might learn an extremely useful lesson.

Sometimes, in your helplessness, you have to ask what they think children are. Because on the one hand they say that children are all imps and rascals, but on the other hand they act as if children are lumps of clay. They act in such ways in front of children, which if they understood them at all, they would be embarrassed to even imagine! Who hasn't heard, 'It doesn't matter, say what you want in front of him, he's a child!' or 'What does she understand? She's a kid!' But how could they understand that this 'free-of-all-responsibilities' child bears the heavy responsibility of honesty. That malleable, underdeveloped brain is on account of its malleability very dangerous. When we walk on paved roads our feet don't leave prints, but when we walk on wet dirt, or dust, or sand, our feet leave deep marks. Water flows off paved surfaces, but on unpaved roads the marks left by deep footprints turn the road to mud . . .

Sometimes I wish these pages would reach my father! What would he feel seeing his son happy this way? What would he think now of all of those moments when he didn't understand his son's heart and so he ripped him to pieces and pushed him away? And those moments where on account of being a son he was unable to understand his father's fatherliness and he traded in hurt?

And Mother . . . a mother who thinks of him as a burden, and a very prickly burden at that . . .

It's for the best that they won't see him. I am now separated from the world. Who am I to steal away another person's happiness? For millions of years, humans have had only one desire—either to find happiness or to give up the desire for it; and they've been unsuccessful in both . . .

Shekhar worshipped his father.

People often talk about a mother's influence on her children. Most people believe that exceptional individuals are particularly influenced by their mothers. But as far as I can tell, a mother's influence over her boys and a father's influence over his daughters are of a negative kind. It gives a stability and constancy which is just as much a hindrance in times of rise as in times of fall. It would be better to say that boys who are attached to their mothers and girls who are attached to their fathers tend towards conformity and ordinariness, while boys attached to their fathers and girls attached to their mothers are exceptional.

In the first group you will find law-abiding, gentle people, ordinary women, who have no special faults, who are generally happy and content, who grow up, live and die; in the second group you will find influential writers and poets, reformers who change the nation and the world, revolutionaries, bandits, gamblers, the ghosts of the worst of the worst sinners . . . good or bad, ordinariness is not for them. They don't smoulder, they only explode . . .

Who is the arbiter of good and evil? Shekhar isn't ordinary.

And he worshipped his father.

*

Slowly, Father realized that Gandhian ideals had made a home for themselves in Shekhar's heart. One day he called Shekhar to him and asked, 'Why are you always shouting Gandhi's name?'

'I believe in Gandhi! I am going to follow the path he's set.'

Father laughed and said, 'You're going to follow his path? Do you even understand Gandhi's teachings? If someone slaps you on the cheek, what are you going to do?'

Shekhar responded without hesitation, 'I'll show him the other cheek.'

Hearing an arrogant Shekhar say this made Father quite serious. He said, 'Go and play, this is not the time to get involved with such matters. When you get older, you'll be able to do all of this, but now it's time for you to play!'

Shekhar had heard this refrain many times and knew that there was always some doubt or frustration hidden behind it. He also knew it was pointless to press the matter any further.

One day one of Father's friends was visiting. He was a barrister who always wore fancy clothes, looked like an extremely bloated mountain rat and claimed to be a connoisseur of Indian art. With him were his son and his daughter who wore a short dress.

As soon as they met each other and the instant the two children said, 'Good evening,' Shekhar seethed. But he didn't say anything; he took them to the garden and showed them his pet rabbit. The barrister left with Father.

But they had only come for a short visit. Shekhar and the two children had only been playing with the rabbits for a few minutes when they came back downstairs. Shekhar the Gandhian went to the door to see them all off.

At the door, he folded his hands in the pure swadeshi style, bowed his head a little and said, 'Namaste!'

The boy smirked a little and said, 'Good night, dear.'

Shekhar forgot his Gandhianism. The haughtiness of that smirk was something that Shekhar couldn't stand. And that final 'dear'—this, this nameless organism dares to call me 'dear'! Shekhar lashed out in English, 'You dirty rascal! You sneak!' and many other such things and then slapped him across the face.

He began shrieking like a frightened puppy.

Later Shekhar was beaten, too, beaten a lot. But he said to himself, 'I am no puppy, I don't squeal,' and took his beating.

Since the day Father had Shekhar say the thing about turning the other cheek, he would make him put on a demonstration whenever they had visitors. In front of his own friends, he would call Shekhar and ask him, 'If someone slaps you on the cheek, what are you going to do?' And everyone would laugh when they heard his answer, and then he would be allowed to leave. Partly it was that he wanted to show his son off, but it was also that he hoped Shekhar's arrogance would lessen at having to repeat this over and over, that it might make him humble. At first, Shekhar hated these forced performances, but slowly he acquired a philosophical indifference. He would come, answer the question and leave without looking at anyone. He knew that they didn't need him for anything else; whatever talents he possessed, or the skills that these people wanted to see, they'd been displayed already . . .

One day the barrister returned. This time he was alone. He didn't 'see' Shekhar and Shekhar didn't 'see' him. He went upstairs.

But a little later Shekhar was called for. He went and stood next to his father, and he didn't even look at the barrister.

Father asked, 'Well, Shekhar, if someone slaps you on the cheek, what are you going to do?'

Shekhar saw that the barrister's eyes were fixed on him, as if they were saying, 'I know what you're about to say, but still . . .'

No, not in front of this mountain rat. He's an animal; he should be on display. In front of him? No, Father, no. Don't force me to!

Father repeated the question. And then, especially for Shekhar, he said in a soft voice (the softness didn't mask the anger), 'Speak, you donkey!'

Shekhar stared back at the mountain rat and said, 'I'd slap him on both of his cheeks.'

There was violence in his voice, rage in his eyes, as if he had struck the barrister's puffy cheeks with two imaginary slaps, but as soon as he said it, he let out a deep sigh. Who could detect the deep despair, the overwhelming frustration it contained?

Shekhar descended the staircase. As he had just completed his task his stride should have contained a commensurate pride, but he came down the stairs as if he were weary, broken . . .

Shekhar went to his room, took his books out from his cupboard, threw them on the ground and removed his play from the pile. He thought for a while about what he should do. He saw the cow standing outside the door. He went to it and held the notebook containing the play out to it. The cow seized it in its mouth and wrenched it from Shekhar's grip, and it looked at Shekhar with its enormous, innocent, stupid eyes as it ate it whole . . .

Shekhar went back to his room and sat down, and stared at the wall in front of him and began to cry—without tears, without making a sound, but his whole body, his whole frame, was shaking . . .

It was evening. Shekhar was still sitting there. His shaking frame had become still. Not a single tear had been shed. And he had no idea whether he was still alive or dead.

His despair had grown so deep that he no longer despaired. It was beyond his perception.

Saraswati came into his room with a light. On seeing Shekhar sitting there like that, she left the light outside the room, went to him and lovingly said, 'Shekhar?'

Shekhar didn't hear.

Saraswati placed a gentle hand on his shoulder and said, 'Shekhar?'

Again, he didn't hear.

Saraswati slowly raised his chin with a finger and said, 'Not going to talk, Shekhar?'

Had he been angry he would have brushed her hand away. But he didn't raise his head. He just looked at her with blank eyes.

He didn't see Saraswati.

Saraswati uncertainly said once more, 'Shekhar,' and then moved away. She went and sat in another corner of the room, completely still.

For a long time the two of them sat in opposite corners of the room.

Then a voice called from upstairs, 'Saraswati!'

She didn't move. The voice called again, and still she didn't move. It called again and added, 'Are you dead?'

Shekhar said, 'Sister?'

She didn't speak.

He said again, 'Sister?'

Then he got up and went to her and said, 'Sister?'

'You won't talk, sister?'

'Are you angry? If you won't speak, then I won't speak either. Say something, sister?'

Saraswati got up and went upstairs.

Shekhar got up, too, a little while later. He washed his face and left, and ate his dinner.

In this one little incident something broke inside Shekhar, and whether it also saved him from something, who knows?

But Gandhi was gone, and Gandhianism was gone, too. And Shekhar's godlike father was never a God again.

*

I am looking out at the quiet wall outside my cell. A few lines from Rossetti are echoing inside me:

> Who shall dare to search through what sad maze
> Henceforth their incommunicable ways
> Follow the desultory feet of Death . . .[1]

Death. A calm-inducing event. An unsolvable riddle.

Those who are in pain, who suffer, always cry out for death. They plead for it, but still death remains a horrifying thing for them, they tremble at the mere thought of it. But I think that death is an operation, like having your teeth pulled. You have to sit in a chair, the doctor jerks hard, a sharp pain shoots through you and then there's peace, a release. Death is just like that . . .

But pulling healthy teeth means a lot of blood, and there's swelling. And then, when a life is taken too early . . .

Perhaps the knowledge of death and the desire for life are the same thing. One often hears it said that only those who know what it means to die know what it means to live. You never hear it said that those who know what it means to die love life more than the rest of us. But this is an eternal truth. People think that those who love life fear death. Totally wrong. Those who fear death are incapable of loving life because they don't experience even a moment's peace in life. The real test of whether one loves life or not is if you can give it up without regret; because the best kinds of love can only be silent; those who can speak their love, love emptily . . .

The desultory feet of Death . . .

The wandering, weary feet of death knock at every door, and youth wilts, and life wastes away, and suffering is endless . . . Then a moment of silence descends in which one can hear the fluttering of dark wings, which if seen, mean sleep . . . Everyone dozes off and goes to sleep, every person and everything; except for this never-stilled hunger, this crazed demand for the ultimate end, this involuntary drive for freedom, this never stops . . . The wings of death pass over it, but the shadow doesn't absorb it, leaving it illuminated just as it was . . .

Death's wings harbour the darkness of an endless midnight, but freedom is an incompatibly brilliant light . . .

But I don't want to die. I tell the walls, I tell the bars, I tell the wind, I tell the deaf, heartless indifference, I don't want to die. I love life. I don't want to die!

*

I have been so ground down by the world of hate that love and I have become estranged. But when I look in my mind's eye, and imagine a voice calling to its lover in ripe fields of wheat in the dim moonlight of winter, then a hibernating echo in my heart awakens and says, 'You have also found love!'

I have been so besieged by pain that peace and I have become estranged. But when I imagine I see the image of two entwined bodies on the screen of the dark sky. A wordless voice recognizes itself with a start in my heart of hearts, 'You also knew happiness once!'

Dawn . . .

A divine light in the east, an evaporating mist, a cool breeze, laughing drops of dew, conceited jasmine blossoms, bumblebees buzzing madly, countless birds flying over the woods towards a settlement—I can see all of these things in my mind, in a square shape cast by the scattered red light on my naked walls . . .

It's enough for me that the night is over, and that I can watch this red shape. I build my dreams on its foundation . . .

Jasmine blossoms . . . their sweet fragrance . . . but where is the fragrance of the neem tree—that fragrance that I can never forget, which fills me?

Neem leaves taste bitter but smell sweet. That's how love is, with a beautiful colour and a sharp texture.

But what are life and love to me? They end in the bitter reality of death.

*

By calling God and his life 'non-existent' it was as if Shekhar were stripped naked for all the world around him. As if he had recently emerged from his shell, vulnerable to every wound, every blow, every wound . . . as if he were a mere spectator of life, or not even a spectator, but a machine that makes impressions, is impressionable. Only, he has no strength left, no shield, no armour, no defences; and it's as if he has no sensation left, not even any life left. It was as if he had merely become a vast eye that could see everything, acknowledge everything, but was affected by nothing.

Truth be told, he was exactly as the poet described:

I am a reed through which thy spirit breathes: it cometh and
    it goeth . . .

But there was a sorting office in some dark corner of his brain where each scene, each image, was separated and sorted, named and labelled, and filed accordingly . . .

The spirit's breath came and went, and a new seed planted roots into the untouched earth . . .

Shekhar had turned into what his mother would have called the ideal child—if she had ever been in the habit of giving compliments. He didn't speak much, didn't ask questions; when there wasn't enough to eat, he didn't ask for food; he would uncomplainingly bathe in cold water in the winter; he would finish his studies on time and, moreover, if there was even the slightest delay in studying he would call Saraswati and say, 'Sister, it's time to study'; he performed the twilight rites both times as prescribed—in short, he behaved in such a way that his mother felt that she only had five children, as she never had to worry about Shekhar.

On the slate of his life, Shekhar wanted to erase, just as he had erased mistaken or incorrect letters, himself.

But there were so many things that he wanted to know that he had stopped himself from asking! Whenever a question came to him, he ground his teeth together and when the compulsion still didn't vanish he'd bite his lips—until he bled . . . And then he wouldn't ask the question. Whenever his father saw him biting his lips he'd tell him to stop and when he saw that repeated attempts at asking him to stop had no effect he said, 'Well, shall I fix you then?' and he pinched his lips together and twisted hard. To him, it didn't feel like pain, but afterwards each time he looked at his father it was as if he didn't recognize him at all . . .

First, he wanted to know why Mother would sometimes sit apart from everyone, wouldn't go into the kitchen, would eat from separate dishes and if someone went to her—usually people didn't go to her except for Shekhar's younger brothers—she'd say, 'Don't come near me, go and play!' Who knows who told Shekhar that Mother was ill, but he couldn't see any signs of illness. And then, after a few days, he would get up and see that Mother had bathed and was sitting in the kitchen working. If she was sick last night, what happened this morning?

Second, Shekhar recalled that such things hadn't happened for a long time. But recently, Mother did seem to be ill. Her face was pallid, and she didn't do much work. She was generally depressed and weak.

Third, one day he instinctively asked Saraswati, 'Is Mother sick?' Saraswati gave him an angry look and left without saying a word.

He won't ask—what's it to him?—but he does want to know, like . . .

There's so much he wants to understand. The room that Mother usually stays in has a cupboard with a lock on it.

Shekhar had seen his mother open it occasionally. She kept her jewellery and other things on the bottom shelf. Sometimes tins of biscuits or containers of sweet rose preserve[2] and gooseberry jam[3] and a number of other things that she wanted to protect from her boys were kept there too. But the two shelves above were filled with books—what are those? The whole house is filled with books, the best kinds, priceless, and when the encyclopedias are allowed to be kept in the open, then why are those books kept locked up? If they are good, why aren't others allowed to read them? If they are bad, why are they kept at all?

And where did Shekhar come from? How did he get here? He remembers those days leading up to Chandra's birth. He had asked his mother, 'Mother, where did he come from?' And Mother had said, 'The midwife brought him.' And when he had asked the midwife why she had brought one that was so small, couldn't she have brought a bigger one, she said, 'I didn't bring him. The doctor that was here, he brought him in his bag. And that bag can't hold one that's any bigger than him.' Shekhar didn't believe either of them, but he kept quiet about it. Many days later, when he saw a baby bird hatch from an egg for the first time, he knew that Mother had lied to him. And to test his mother, he went to her and asked, 'Mother, does the doctor visit the birds, too?'

Mother didn't understand his question. She said, 'No, why?'

'Then where do baby birds come from?'

'They hatch from the eggs.'

Mother was telling the truth up to this point! Shekhar pressed on with a renewed hope, 'And where do eggs come from?'

'God sends them.'

That same wall—the biggest obstacle in the way of knowledge—God! Then he asked his sister, 'How does God send eggs?'

'They probably come down when it rains.'

A few days later Shekhar realized that was a lie, too. Rain falls the same way everywhere, but how did eggs end up in specific nests, all different from each other? Then one day he found a nest that was empty, and the next day there was an egg in it, though it hadn't rained the night before . . .

Shekhar knew that everyone was lying to him. And this fuelled his desire to know the truth . . .

*

A special room was sequestered from the rest of the house. It was cleaned, swept with dung patties and its windows were locked. Mother went there to live. A midwife came to stay with her and everyone was prohibited from going there. Remembering what it was like when Chandra was born, Shekhar knew that the midwife, the doctor or some other power was going to grace their household again with another favour. And so he began awaiting the arrival of the doctor.

In the middle of the night, Shekhar awoke with a start. He didn't know why he had woken up, but he knew something had happened; the air was heavy with muffled quiet . . .

He sat up and looked around. He saw that the cot next to his was empty and that Saraswati was gone. He got down from his cot and went to the other room where his father slept.

Father wasn't there. A light was on downstairs.

For some reason, Shekhar didn't have the courage to go downstairs and see what was going on. Any other time, he would have definitely gone downstairs to investigate, but not this time. He wanted to be snuffed out, this time, he didn't want to be seen. If someone had asked him what he was doing there—no, he hadn't the courage to bear the question, let alone give an answer. He no longer had any confidence in himself.

But curiosity . . . He stood there like a drawn bowstring, taut and twitchy . . .

Then a sharp, piercing, but weak, and slightly agitated scream . . .

Shekhar realized that whatever power had been responsible for this had evaded him. And he still didn't have an answer to his question . . .

The staircase creaked from Saraswati's steps. He wasn't afraid of her, but still his heart began racing, and he ran to his cot and lay back down.

Saraswati entered. She sat down on the cot, lifted her feet, wrapped her arms around her shins and leaned her chin on her knees.

Shekhar couldn't keep still. He asked, 'What happened?', as if he had just woken up.

Saraswati was startled. Then she said, 'Shekhar, it happened—you have another sister.'

Sister? Were sisters things that 'happened'? Shekhar asked, 'Like you?'

'Don't be silly. She's tiny at the moment, like a baby bird. When she grows up—'

Gravely, Shekhar said, 'Saraswati!'

Taken aback, Saraswati asked, 'What is it?' Shekhar never called her by her name.

'If I ask you a question will you answer it? You don't have to answer it; just don't lie to me.'

Suspiciously, Saraswati asked, 'What?'

Shekhar steeled himself to ask, 'Where do babies come from?'

Saraswati didn't respond immediately.

As he watched and waited, a flood of words welled up inside him. He said, 'The midwife brings them, the doctors bring them, God gives them—I've heard all of these things, so don't tell me that! I know those are all lies. So tell me, if that was how they came, then why did it have to happen so secretly? Why don't either of us get them? And she said that she didn't want any more children, so why did she get one? Why didn't she send it back? Why does God send them? When I kept asking for a sister, why did he send me a brother? I've seen it with my own eyes how baby birds are hatched from eggs. The mother has to crack the eggs to get them out. Where do the eggs come from? And now we have a sister. But why did she have to come in the middle of the night?

Why couldn't she come during the day? And why can't we go over there? Why does everyone lie about it? Tell me, I know you know.' And then suddenly, out of embarrassment, he stopped. He had, perhaps, never given a monologue of that length . . .

Saraswati tried to be evasive. She said, 'Wait, doesn't God send them?'

'Don't lie to me, sister.'

Somehow, Saraswati managed to say, 'They come from a mother's body.'

Shekhar sat up.

'From where? How?'

'I don't know!' She wrapped her head and face in the blanket and lay down. Shekhar called to her repeatedly, even went to her and shook her, but she didn't speak, didn't say a word.

Shekhar lay back down and stared at the ceiling. It was as if he were willing himself up to the ceiling, hanging from it, so that he could speak to himself, 'Think, Shekhar. Don't ask anyone else, just think. You tell me, where did you come from? How did you get here?'

It was morning and Shekhar was still interrogating that double hanging from the ceiling whom he had pinned there with his eyes.

'Children come from a mother's body.'

Saraswati hadn't lied to him. Otherwise she wouldn't have been so embarrassed. After so much pain and strife, he had finally got hold of one thing that was true, that was and simply was—that couldn't be changed.

'Children come from a mother's body.'

But then what?

Beyond that there is a wall, and for its bricks it has God and society, and family, and mother and father, and tradition, and the substance which binds them all together and gives it significance is fear.

Shekhar looks at every woman who walks in front of that wall and thinks, there must be one hiding in her body somewhere, too. But where?

*

Shekhar has started stealing.

Earlier, it hadn't been possible for him to sneak around doing mischievous things. Because when he was by himself, the principles of his soul, more than others, restrained his actions. But now he was respectable, cultured and noble on the surface—who was described as 'a son who is like a daughter'—while on the inside he was falling.

Increasingly, he was being asked to take on more responsibilities. When he was younger he would be so excited to take on even small tasks and would do them so enthusiastically that more often than not he would make a mess of it, but now he schemed at each opportunity, trying to find ways of spoiling things secretly.

Sometimes he was given the keys to the trunk, and he'd take a few coins for himself. Not because he wanted them, but only because he had the key, and he could abuse the privilege. In the evenings, he was tasked with bringing milk for Ishwardutt and Prabhudutt's teacher (they were currently studying for their exams), and he would drink a few gulps of it along the way. Not because he didn't get milk at home, but because he could do something wrong without anyone seeing him. It got so bad that whenever he'd go into the storeroom, he would spill some ghee behind a box. Every time he did such things it was as if he were thinking, 'You all think that I am good, but I am still rotten. You are fools to call me good, as if it were a boost to my ego.'

No one got wind of any of the things he was doing and his reputation kept improving at home, and with every increase in his reputation, he slid a little closer to his downfall . . .

He was given the keys to the cupboard with the books in it because he had been asked to get almonds or some such thing from it.

He opened the cupboard, took out a few books and hid them under the cupboard, took out the almonds and returned the key.

Later, when he had a chance, he picked up the books and read them in secret.

Shekhar looked over these books printed on cheap yellowed and pink paper with big Lucknow typeface, but he couldn't figure

out what was so important about them that they had to be kept
hidden away.

    *The Gardener's Daughter; The Husband with Two Wives; The
Widow of Baghdad; Three and a Half Lovers; Seven and a Half
Murders; The Beautiful Robber; The Twenty-Five Tales of Baital;
The Tale of the Parrot and the Mynah; Thirty Stories of the Throne;
The Magic Ring; The Mysteries of Egypt.*

He put them into piles of twos and threes as he inspected them
all. They were so cheap, filthy and crude that he felt nauseated and
couldn't read them, but because he knew that they were forbidden
and that by reading them he would be doing something wrong, he
forced himself to read until he finished the last one. And it made
him so happy when he could address his mother in his mind and
say, 'You think that I am good and decent, don't you? But I'm a
scoundrel, corrupted, and I read all of these novels that you were
keeping from me . . .'

Shekhar began tattling.

If ever one of his brothers did the slightest of things they weren't
supposed to, Shekhar would run to his mother and say, 'Mother,
Mother, look at what so-and-so did!' Sometimes he would complain
even when no one had done anything and then when that person
was getting slapped or beaten Shekhar would think to himself,
'That's right. Good, he deserves a beating. I'm bad but everyone
respects me, thinks highly of me. Why are you being good?'

And when his brothers looked at him with apprehension or
suspicion he would feel that he was something, too . . .

One step higher.

Shekhar became a rhymester. Nothing vulgar—Shekhar
hadn't learned what vulgarity was yet—just crude and cruel. He
could never read them to anyone, but when he was by himself he
would read them out loudly. And on such occasions he would even
curse into the air—curses whose meaning he didn't even know,
but which he had overheard and which he knew were bad things
to say . . .

Being good or bad held absolutely no meaning for Shekhar. It
only mattered to him that he was something—and that he could

feel that he was something. This feeling became a very important crutch for him.

*

Chandra had thrown stones and broken the flowerpots outside the house. He ran innocently to his mother and said, breathlessly, 'Mother, Mother, I didn't break the flowerpots.'

Mother asked, 'What flowerpots?'

'I didn't break them.'

That's when Shekhar got there. 'Mother, you know those flowerpots outside, the ones with the blue flowers in them, the ones that Father ordered from the office? Chandra broke them by throwing stones at them.'

Chandra said, 'Mother, I already told you I didn't break them,' as if by saying it first it made his point more credible.

Shekhar turned to leave as if he were content at having finished his obligations and had nothing more to do with the matter.

Mother asked Chandra, 'Are you lying to me? Let me see which flowerpots you broke.'

She took him by the hand and dragged him outside with her.

Chandra was beaten repeatedly. Who knows what kind of things Mother threatened him with to get him to admit that he had broken those flowerpots, but he wouldn't confess. It was intolerable to Mother that someone would flout her authority; in her order of things, he should have confessed even if he hadn't broken the flowerpots because she had determined that he had broken them . . .

For a while Shekhar sat with a book open in front of him and watched the spectacle. He was amazed at his mother who didn't appear angry or sound enraged, but still kept beating the boy, for whom this was a matter of pride, that a child should say what she wanted him to say . . .

When children are beaten by angry parents, they bear the beatings because their spirits aren't wounded by them. But when they are beaten without anger, dispassionately, righteously, a crack opens up in their psyches. Shekhar didn't know this at the time, nor did his mother know it, but this didn't make it any less true.

Mother called out, 'Saraswati! Bring me a live coal with the pincers.'

Saraswati brought it.

Mother took the pincers in her hand and said, 'Tell the truth or else I'll put this on your tongue.'

'I am telling the truth.'

Shekhar thought to himself, 'Will Mother really put the live coal in his mouth?' He couldn't believe it, but that anger-free, expressionless face . . .

'Confess that you broke the flowerpots.'

'I didn't break them.'

Mother pressed Chandra's cheeks together with one hand and forced his mouth open and she brought the coal very close and said, 'Confess!'

Saraswati was standing right there, but she wasn't looking. The coal was so close to Chandra's face that he could feel the heat and his head was shaking like an epileptic's. Mother was still pressing his cheeks together and his mouth was still open, waiting for the coal.

Only children believe completely. Adults have the privilege of distinguishing between pretence and truth. Shekhar, all of a sudden, believed . . .

'Confess!'

Shekhar got up with a jolt, pushed his mother with one hand and slapped the pincers away with the other, and roughly said to Chandra, 'Get away from here.'

And to himself he thought, 'Well done, Chandra. Drown yourself, Shekhar.'

Perhaps something came over Mother. She didn't say anything, not even to Shekhar. She just went inside. The matter was over.

Half an hour later.

Shekhar was trying to concentrate on his studies. He had his pen in his hand. He stared at a line he had written in his notebook and was trying to copy that very same line a second time. But words were echoing in his head, and all he could see was that open mouth, sometimes it was Chandra's, sometimes it was Shekhar's, sometimes it was Mother's, and right next to them was a burning coal . . . Every time Shekhar thought, 'That's Chandra's mouth,' it would suddenly turn into Mother's, and when he thought, 'Mother,' it would turn into Shekhar's. Saraswati was standing there, facing away from him, trying not to look at him . . . And in his ears, 'Confess', 'Well done, Chandra!', 'Drown yourself, Shekhar!', 'I'm telling the truth'. Without any order or connection, they kept coming and going and coming back . . .

Still, Shekhar was trying to write . . .

Chandra came to him and said, 'Give me the pen.'

Shekhar came back to reality and said, 'I'm writing.'

'Give it. I need to write.'

'Take another one.'

'No, I want this one. Give it.'

'Give me a little while and then you can have it. Let me finish writing.'

Chandra went to Saraswati to complain, 'Sister, brother won't give me the pen.'

Saraswati was reading. Without looking up from her book, she said, 'Shekhar, give him the pen!'

Chandra came back and said, 'Give it.'

Shekhar got a little annoyed and said, 'I already told you, let me finish writing.'

Chandra screamed at him from right there, 'Look at him, sister, he won't give it.'

Saraswati responded just as before, 'Give it to him, Shekhar! Don't give me a headache.'

'I've already told him that I'll give it to him once I'm done writing. He won't listen to me. And on top of it, you're scolding me!'

But Saraswati was engrossed in her book, and Chandra had already gone to complain to Mother. No one heard Shekhar's reply.

Mother screamed from somewhere inside the house, 'Shekhar, just give him the pen!'

Shekhar started to say, 'Mother, I've explained to him—'

Mother darted into the room. 'What?'

'I've explained to him—'

'I don't care. First give him the pen.'

'Mother—'

Mother slapped him across the face and said, 'Are you going to give it to him or not?'

'Mother—'

Mother emphasized each word in her sentence this time, 'I said, first give him the pen. Then I'll listen to what you have to say.'

Shekhar, too, emphasized each word in his response, 'I'm not giving it to him.'

Mother gave him three or four slaps across the face in quick succession and said, 'Came just now to save him, didn't you? And now—'

Shekhar felt as if this last argument made his action even more justified, but who would listen to him?

'Where is the pen?'

Chandra quickly chimed in, 'Brother is hiding it in his fist.'

Mother started trying to pry his fist open. She was unsuccessful so she put his hand on the table and began hitting it, first with her fists and then with the edge of a ruler. He didn't give up.

Shekhar couldn't bear the pain or his frustration at his own helplessness.

He said, 'I'm not going to give it to him. I told you I wouldn't, even if you try and kill me!'

Mother let go of his hand all at once, and stared at him, flabbergasted. There was something about his voice, in the way he said 'try', that embarrassed her. She took Chandra by the arm, led him outside and said, 'Come with me. I'll get you a new pen.'

Shekhar got up and went out of the house. He wandered around all day like a stray dog. He came home in the evening, exhausted, and Father said to him, 'So keen on giving up this life, are you?'

Shekhar responded lifelessly, 'Yes, I am.' And he kept walking. Father stared at him bewildered.

Shekhar didn't eat dinner. Nor did anyone worry about him. It was night, everyone was asleep, and he, too, lay down on the cot in exhaustion and then tried to burst the darkness . . .

An uncertain voice spoke to him from the head of his cot, 'Shekhar?' Saraswati came and sat down at the head of the cot.

Shekhar put his head in her lap.

That's when the tears began . . .

Saraswati lifted his head and gently placed it on the pillow. He fell asleep.

*

That night, Shekhar had a dream.

A vast desert. The scorching heat of midday.

Shekhar was racing on the back of a camel, slicing through the desert, racing . . . He had been racing since morning, or was it last night? He was still racing at the same pace.

Someone is chasing him. Shekhar doesn't know who, but he knows that someone is behind him, and each time he looks back, he sees dust being kicked up by the feet of many camels chasing him . . .

Afternoon. It isn't any less hot; it feels worse, in fact. Shekhar is still racing and that 'something' behind him is getting closer.

Suddenly, an orchard of apple trees ahead of him. It's enclosed by a tall mud wall on all four sides. In several places, there are holes in the wall, and also several plants that look like irises. Shekhar gets down from the camel, climbs over the wall and goes into the orchard.

The trees in the orchard are heavy with flowers. So heavy, in fact, that the entire ground is covered with flowers, and it is absolutely gleaming white . . .

Shekhar breathes a tired sigh and lies down on a bed of flowers and goes to sleep . . .

Evening. The entire sky has turned a deep red. The reflection from the scarlet-hued sky makes the whole earth look red, and the apple trees now look like they are wild rose bushes—each flower has taken on a beautiful blush . . .

Shekhar sat up. The terror of danger came over him again. He knows that 'something' has surrounded the orchard and is attempting to enter it. And the dust from its camel's feet is being thrown up in all directions, filling the skies . . .

Shekhar gets up and runs in one direction and leaves the orchard.

A gravelly road, steep. Shekhar keeps on climbing. That 'something' has been left behind, but he still has a long way to go . . . a long way . . . in search of something, although he doesn't know what he's looking for . . .

The evening grows dense. Shekhar is still going. He's thirsty, but there's not a drop of water anywhere. Although there is something in the distance, like the din of a waterfall . . .

He climbs on top of a boulder and looks out ahead of him, and comes to a complete stop.

Thundering below is a mountainous waterfall, brilliant, pure, clear . . .

Shekhar sits on his haunches, rests his arms on the ground in front of him and bends his head forward like a woodland creature about to take a sip of water. But the water is too far down and he can't reach it . . .

Saraswati's hand is on his. She's sitting next to him, in the same way, on her haunches, although she wasn't there a second ago. And the two pairs of thirsty eyes are looking longingly at the water below . . .

Shekhar observes a flower standing up on a thin stalk, somehow completely unaffected by the rapids in the middle of the water. Very big—a single white petal wrapped all around, and a pistil, the colour of hot gold, extending out from the middle.

And as he watches, a mystical peace descends over him and he realizes that this is what he has been looking for, the thing that he was racing towards . . . The peace is so gentle that it makes his hairs stand on end. He squeezes Saraswati's hand tightly . . .

He wakes up. The dream was so vivid, so real, that Shekhar extended his hand to take Saraswati's. He didn't find it.

He got up from his cot. Looked around. Got up and went to Saraswati's cot. She was sleeping. Shekhar tried to look at her face but couldn't. He went back, drew a long, contented sigh and lay down, and became lost in a dreamless sleep.

Part 3

Nature and Man

Shekhar was, and Saraswati was, and no one else was. That which we call the world had ceased to exist.

There was still much to happen. There was that ineffable mood created when Shekhar found Saraswati alone and could talk to her freely. It made him happy to know that even when she didn't respond she at least listened to him. Shekhar was always surprised that though she had much to think about she couldn't tell him though she could tell him so many things that she wouldn't tell other people. And it bothered him to no end when something welled up inside him, when he wanted to tell her something, and he would find her busy with some work in the kitchen, or washing their little sister's—who had been named Kamala—diapers, or sitting by their mother learning how to sew and embroider . . .

And there was Mother . . .

Shekhar felt that the way Saraswati was the embodiment of all that was desirable, that was generally compassionate and sympathetic, his mother was the incarnation of all the concentrated problems he faced, all that was undesirable, generally unsympathetic and cruel. Whenever something did not work out Shekhar discovered after some searching that his mother was the source of the problem . . . She was the one who kept Saraswati working in the kitchen, she was the one who asked her to wash the diapers, she was the one who put her to embroidery. Shekhar didn't understand why 'girls had to learn how to do these things or they were not respected . . .' Whenever Saraswati was with

Shekhar, his mother was the one who always called her away—just
to harass Shekhar, because a number of times she had mockingly
said to him, 'Why are you always hiding behind Saraswati? Why
don't you go to your brothers?'

Father also scolded him. 'Is this a man? He wants to be a girl.
He should just dress up in girls' clothes.'

His brothers teased him, too, 'Sister's tail! Sister's tail!'

But Saraswati never said anything to him. When his brothers
teased him, she would suppress a smile. Sometimes she'd even say
to Shekhar, 'Look how much everyone teases you.' And in those
moments, his heart would stop in fear that she too might laugh
at his expense, make some joke about him, because that would
mean . . .

And don't forget, Shekhar was immensely grateful for
Saraswati.

Shekhar was an atheist and an idol-worshipper. And Saraswati
was his revered idol.

When devotion reaches its limits, the object of devotion is just
as human as the devotee—or rather, for the devotee, the object of
devotion no longer remains a mere projection of what's inside the
devotee, but somehow appears before him and on account of being
before him has for some unknown reason become unattainable,
like one's own reflection in a mirror, though more diffuse and
unbounded . . .

So, too, was Saraswati. Shekhar never felt as if she were
separate from him or that her feelings were separate. When he
was hungry he'd say, 'Sister, will you have some bread?' And when
he was about to go to sleep he'd say, 'Sister, you're tired . . .'

But for Saraswati, this unity, this commingling, was not as
excessive. Of late, she had been worried for some reason—who
knows what was turning around in her head? Shekhar would
ask, and ask, and get irritated, but how long could one remain
irritated with a God . . . He'd think, 'If only my sister weren't
older but a year and a half younger than me. Or let's just say if
I'd been older, and we were the same age, it would have been so
much better . . .' Because he was gravely, but still secretly and

unconsciously, standing at the threshold of a very important truth! That when men are made, they are made for someone to love them, some woman younger than they are who believes in them and to earn whose trust they are willing to risk their lives . . . There are mothers, always, and they have an important place, but they are made by their sisters or other girls like their sisters who on account of being like their sisters are more than sisters . . . Mothers give life, nurturance, fathers offer wisdom, but the strength to tolerate our own personalities—that doesn't come from those sources . . .

Sometimes Shekhar wanted to tell his sister, 'Sister, I don't want so much an idol as an idol-worshipper. There's no one that I want, no one to look at, as much as someone who wants to look at me. It's not that I don't want a perfect person; I want to be the only one capable of making them so. I want someone who worships perfection because that's something I cannot make. I don't have the power to create a God for myself, but someone to worship the divinity in me—but no . . .' These thoughts weren't clear in his mind, he didn't understand them himself, and life kept moving on . . .

For the believer, God is everywhere. And it would be impossible for him to imagine life without God. But God dwells in the sky and even clouds wander in front of it . . .

*

Shekhar's father is on tour. One day, while straightening the letters on his desk, Shekhar read one of the cards, and it left him speechless.

It was about Saraswati's wedding.

'After the wedding, Rama went to live with her husband.' This sentence from some unknown, read long-ago story danced before Shekhar. He felt as if it were a cruel ending—after the wedding, she went to live with her husband. She just went. Her life was over. Everyone had to go in the same way. And in the story, it was written as if it were some ordinary matter—she just left, and then what?

Shekhar threw the card down and ran from the house. At the time, Shekhar's father had been transferred to the south—he was staying in the mountains of the Western Ghats. Shekhar used to wander in the foothills there.

'After the wedding, Rama went to live with her husband.' Shekhar began repeating the sentence over and over in his mind and thought, 'Why am I stuck on this sentence?'

He looked at a tree. It was as if the tree said, 'Rama went to live with her husband.'

Shekhar looked at another tree, and it seemed to smile at him and repeat the same sentence.

And the same thing happened with the third tree, and the fourth tree, with increasing assertiveness . . .

Then one of them said softly, hesitatingly, 'Rama? Are you sure you aren't mistaken?'

And then all of them said in unison, 'Saraswati went to live with her husband.'

Saraswati! Saraswati!

Like a hunted deer, Shekhar began running around wildly in search of refuge. It was evening, but the hunter that was after him hadn't given up the chase, hadn't given up.

It was getting dark, and the prey thought that it had spied a place in the distance where it might be able to hide. It wasn't certain, possibly . . . He ran back home.

When he got home, Shekhar was unable to ask the question. He didn't have to ask anyone else; he only had to ask Saraswati, but he couldn't muster up the courage. He was overcome and couldn't speak. His daily ritual was to report all the things that he had done that day, but still he was silent. Saraswati, too, let the matter rest.

A little before bedtime, Saraswati asked eagerly, 'What's the matter, Shekhar?'

'. . .'

'I know that something is bothering you. Tell me.'

Like jumping quickly into wintry waters, Shekhar blurted out, 'Why don't you marry someone from around here?'

First Saraswati's face turned red and then she became serious. She gave his cheek a light slap and burst out laughing.

And the prey couldn't tell whether it had found refuge or been denied it . . .

*

Two thousand miles to find a husband . . .

Everyone arrived at Lahore. In the hustle and bustle of the preparations, Shekhar fell ill. While he was confined to his cot, he caught wind of what kinds of sweets were being made, what the wedding procession looked like, what the groom looked like (Rama went to live with her husband—no, not Rama, Saraswati!), how the groom's party was made to look stupid, how there weren't enough pakoras and how they had to use their ingenuity to solve that problem, how the groom arrived in a fancy fringed sarong (the name was strange, like 'the camel's horn') and . . . The only thing he didn't hear was where Saraswati was, how she was and what she was doing, feeling . . .

On the day the bride and groom were supposed to circumambulate the fire, Shekhar said, 'I want to go, too.'

He had a fever of 103 degrees Fahrenheit. Everyone told him not to, but he wouldn't listen. 'How could I not go? It's my sister's wedding,' he said. No one understood the seriousness behind his statement, but they had to concede. He was seated in one corner of the wedding pavilion, on a chair, wrapped in a blanket. It was as if he were watching a meaningless circus with eyes that had been clouded over by cataracts.

Shekhar's uncle brought a bundle wrapped in a red embroidered cloth and left it on a spot near the pundit and moved away! It was placed there, joined to the groom (after the wedding, Rama went to live with her husband—not Rama, Saraswati!), and that's how Shekhar surmised that Saraswati was inside the bundle. In a little while, that bundle, without letting its bundle-ness diminish in any way, followed the groom and circled the fire . . .

From somewhere behind Shekhar, a voice called out with impenetrable certainty, 'It's done . . .'

Shekhar turned around to look—it was as if the veil was even more puffed out with delight . . .

And from inside Shekhar, a voice called out with an unflappable certainty, 'After the wedding, Rama went to live with her husband—not Rama, Saraswati! Get it, Saraswati . . .'

He said, 'I've seen it all—now I'm going.'

He was taken from the pavilion.

Saraswati came to see him for a while—at the time, no one else was around. Shekhar wanted to sulk so badly, not to say a word, but how could he sulk at Saraswati who at that very moment looked wan even without the turmeric paste?

Shekhar didn't know what to say. As if he were challenging her to a duel, he said, 'Sister, so you're married now?'

Saraswati looked at him, crushed. Then she said, 'How are you feeling?'

Shekhar turned away and then choked out, 'Saras—'

Saraswati put her hand on his forehead, and as she gently moved it down his face, she closed his eyes, although his face was still turned away. And as she closed his eyes she felt his tears.

It was as if Shekhar were trying to take hold of her hand with his eyelashes. He said, 'I'm fine.' And after a little while, 'You're . . . going away . . . and even then nothing will happen.'

Saraswati said, 'Where is your hand?'

Shekhar clasped her hand with both of his and pressed it down hard over his eyes.

She slowly freed her hand and left.

That night, Shekhar came down with pneumonia.

In Hindi, a wedding is called a 'shaadi'. The word 'shaad' means joyful.

*

A month later, on the day that Shekhar was fit to get out of bed was the day that everyone returned south.

Everyone, and after the wedding Rama went to live with her husband—not Rama, Saraswati . . . And everyone came back . . .

After another month, both of Shekhar's brothers left for college. Left behind were Mother, Father, Shekhar, Ravi, Chandra and Kamala; and the memory of the one who after the wedding went to live with her husband.

While Shekhar's brothers were at home, they wrote Saraswati a letter every third day. They got letters from her. Shekhar would listen in on them reading out the letters, or he'd steal them and read them, but she never wrote him a letter nor had he been able to write her one.

But once they had left for college, Shekhar had no way to get news of his sister. He kept hoping that she would write to him herself, but somewhere deep inside he knew that she wasn't going to just as he wasn't writing to her; she'd only be able to respond after he'd written to her.

So one day he sat down to write a letter.

After taking much trouble to pick out the appropriate kind of paper, he started, 'Revered Sister . . .'

He had been trained always to begin letters this way every time. But on seeing those two words on the paper he began questioning himself, 'What are you doing? Who are you writing to? Who is "Revered Sister"?'

He tore the paper to shreds. Got another. He filled the pen with ink and started to think. Nothing came to him. He began dragging the pen across the paper absent-mindedly. He noticed that it had dried out. He filled it again; it dried out again.

He filled it again and all of a sudden began writing, 'Saras . . .'

'But . . . but . . . I don't even say this to myself without trembling. How can I write in this obscene way on this paper and send it to her husband's house, where she lives now?'

Shekhar tore up that piece of paper as well. And that's when he realized what 'after the wedding, Rama went to live with her husband' really meant . . .

He went and told his mother, 'I don't want to send a letter; you should just send yours.'

Mother responded, 'Why, is it too much trouble to write to
your sister?'

Shekhar sat in a corner of his room and cried.

Who knows what's happened to Shekhar! He never used to
cry and now he cries for no reason at all—sometimes he gets up
in the middle of a meal and goes to his room and cries; sometimes
he eats his meals and wipes away his tears at the same time;
sometimes when his mother asked him, 'Shekhar, have you eaten
anything at all today?' he'd burst into tears; sometimes when his
father said, 'Go and bring the post from the letter box,' he'd open
his window and hang out and cry. He didn't understand why he
was crying. Sometimes his father would ask him, 'What is it,
Shekhar? Missing your brothers?' he'd think *this is the reason why
I'm crying—I miss my brothers*. When his mother asked, 'Do you
want to visit Saraswati?' he'd feel that *the only reason that I'm crying
is because I want to see Saraswati*. And sometimes when Ravidutt
would say, 'Everyone beats me for no reason,' he'd think that *the
reason he was crying was because of all the unfairness . . .* One day he
read a translation of Rabindranath Tagore's 'Vacation' in which
he'd written:

In the world of human matters there is no worse nuisance
than a fourteen-year-old boy. He possesses neither beauty nor
usefulness. He cannot be showered with affection like a child;
nor does he especially desire company. If he speaks with a
childish lisp, then he is called a milk-toothed baby, and if he
speaks like an adult, he's considered impertinent.

It's more precise to say that he's considered arrogant if he
speaks at all. People consider him boorish as he has no regard
for the measurements of his clothes and continues to grow at an
ungainly rate. People think him a criminal in the disappearance
of the charms of childhood and the sweetness of his voice. So
many mistakes of early childhood are easily forgiven but for
a boy of his age even unavoidable errors were unforgiveable.
And he himself is made painfully aware that he doesn't seem
to do anything correctly, so he's constantly embarrassed by

himself and always asking for forgiveness. But it is at this very age that his heart becomes exceedingly desperate for love and respect . . .[1]

When he read it, he realized that this was the reason he was crying . . . One day, he heard someone say that college was the best time of your life, completely carefree. He realized that his brothers must be enjoying themselves, must be completely carefree, and this made him cry . . .

But even though he wasn't able to determine why he was crying, he was slowly coming to the conclusion that the world was full of injustices, and these injustices were especially made for him to suffer! It was as if the world were turning on an axis that he was the centre of, and that everything that existed only existed because he did . . . Simultaneously he became more intolerant—he became furious about these injustices . . .

One day, he knew, for no reason, that he couldn't take it any more. He thought to himself, 'Why should I stay here and tolerate this unfairness? Surely there is a place for me in a world this big.' And he left home with an overcoat, a package of biscuits and a loaf of bread . . .

Where was he going? He didn't know either. All he knew was that he wasn't going to some place, he was going away from some place . . . a place which he had left behind him forever . . .

After walking all day, he went to sleep, exhausted. The next day he came to the base of a waterfall and watched it all day long.

But you can't eat beauty, and he'd eaten his bread . . .

Shekhar observed the waterfall to his heart's content. First he was in awe of it, drawn to it, and then he began to detect unison, a changelessness, and therefore an inadequacy. Then he felt depressed and angry . . .

And he went back, spending the night on the road somewhere, getting back home the next day.

He hadn't assented to the way of life at home, but he had a new-found respect and wonder for it . . .

His father quietly accepted him and the fact that he had run away. He didn't ask where he had gone or why . . .

*

Shekhar was beginning to chafe at his own uneasiness, his unsteadiness. He began to feel he wanted for something, but he didn't know what. And to work out just what he wanted, he endeavoured to do all sorts of things—he began to drift along all sorts of paths at the same time . . .

From a distance, all human development, at least up until now, has looked like this. Humanity wants for something but doesn't know what and in order to find it begins to wander on all sorts of paths at the same time . . . It is as if all humanity, in the course of its life, stands on a vast, empty expanse of time and is caught up in itself; its youth and its days of creativity still lie ahead.

And in a miniature form of that expanse—the uninterrupted soft hum of the ocean concealing itself within a tiny conch—Shekhar was also caught up in himself and wanted to apprehend himself.

He felt that his body was undergoing a change. He felt as if he were ill; he felt as if he had much strength and energy; he felt as if he were about to start a new phase in life . . . He was wild, self-intoxicated, like a musk deer, or like a plague-carrying rat, or a dog chasing its own tail—he made a few circles around himself and then stopped . . .

Shekhar would get up when the darkness was thickest at night and quietly sneak down to the sitting room, take the gramophone and bring it back to his room. He would close the door and play a particular record over and over . . . It was a recording of some English musician playing the violin; he'd never bothered to look at the name, and he couldn't recall the melodies despite having heard them countless times. But at the very beginning, after a rich, deep sound, there was a sudden sharp call, and to him it felt as though that unexpected, bold sharpness had pierced through a shell surrounding him and like a silkworm or a butterfly he was emerging from someone else's custody . . . And he played that very record, sometimes just that part, over and over again and somehow it never got old. He never comes down from that height back to earth . . . He turns the lamp down low and cries sometimes. His dreams race—'O music, where are you from, to whose cry do you give voice?'

Where are you urging me to go? Why do you offer promises of freedom, of liberty, to one in chains?

That's when he stops the record and starts writing poetry . . .

But as soon as he turns it off he feels as though his whole body has come awake and he's stuck back inside that shell. He doesn't understand what his body wants but he knows that it's something illicit, forbidden, sinful. He wants very much to suppress this desire, grind it out, bury it in the dust so that he can't ever find it again—even if that means his body is destroyed with it . . .

He wants to distract himself. He didn't know how he would do that, but he was interested in poetry, and so he hoped that he could lose himself in that. He began reading all sorts of poetry at every opportunity. He read Sanskrit poets, poets translated from Urdu and those that were in his textbooks—Tennyson, Wordsworth, Shelley, Christina Rossetti, Scott—in their entirety. Then he began reading those poets who weren't in his books but whose names he had read and heard—Keats, Byron, Rossetti, Swinburne and even Tasso and Dante in translation . . . He understood some, didn't understand about half. He read the things he didn't understand with even more determination as a way to beat himself up, as punishment.

He became obsessed with some of these poems and they made him restless in the same way . . . Tennyson's 'The Lady of Shalott', 'The May Queen', and these lines from 'The Death of Oenone':[2]

Ah me, my mountain shepherd, that my arms
Were wound about thee, and my hot lips prest
Close, close to thine in that quick-falling dew

Of fruitful kisses, thick as autumn[3] rains
Flash in the pools of whirling Simois.

Reading these lines, his body tautened; his hands began to tremble and his head spun . . . One day he read these two lines from Rossetti:

Beneath the glowing[4] throat the breasts half-globed
Like folded lilies deep-set in the stream

That day he felt as though some unbearable current of energy suddenly coursed through him and it thrilled him . . .

Helplessly he left the room and, unable to make sense of things, picked up an axe, went behind the kitchen and began splitting wood, as much as he could find. When he finished, he went back and read a poem by Lady Norton—'I Do Not Love Thee'—and that seemed to calm him . . .[5]

There were poems that brought him peace when he read them even though he didn't understand them, although it was usually a tormented and unstable peace. Rossetti's 'Blessed Damozel' contained these lines:

Like a vapour wan and mute,
Like a flame, so let it pass;
One low sigh across her lute,
One dull breath against her glass;
And to my sad soul, alas! One salute,
Cold as when Death's foot shall pass.

Or when a lover feels the touch of the tresses of a departed beloved and immediately knows:

Nothing: the autumn fall of leaves.

And a few poems by Swinburne that he would suddenly read out aloud; his words contained a rhythm that compelled him to . . .

And, yes, Kalidasa's 'Ajavilap' which he still remembers and which Saraswati used to sing often:

> If this garland can rob one of life, why did it not kill me when it fell on my heart?[6]

And then his entire will would suddenly be overcome by a death wish and he'd repeat, 'Why did it not kill me?'

*

This was how Shekhar was being carried away by the forces flowing through him. But sometimes there would also be intervening moments when everything became so clear to him, so plain, familiar—moments like the moment Rossetti described in his poem 'Sudden Light'. But then the extraordinary clarity would hurt him . . . One day, while reading Rossetti, he closed the book, closed his eyes and began to hum:

> Such a small lamp illumines[7] on this high way,
> So dimly so few steps in front of my feet,
> Yet shows me that her way is parted from my way;
> Out of sight, beyond light, at what goal may we meet;

And then a moment arrived when a voice from inside him said, 'Shekhar, you are in love!'
Then his whole body tensed and said, 'Yes, yes, I do love.'
But whom?
A few days later he read this poem:

> A lad there is, and I am that poor groom
> That's fallen[8] in love and knows not[9] with whom.

And it made him angry, 'How did my personal experience become someone else's cliché?'
So Shekhar said, 'No, I don't love. I won't.'

And because poetry always reminded him of this fact, he stopped reading it altogether. He began reading the most difficult and dense books he could find. First he read Nietzsche's *Thus Spake Zarathustra*, then Darwin's books on evolution and then he went on to the biographies of Shankara, Vivekananda, Ramakrishna Paramahamsa, medical books, homeopathy books, books on mental illness, anatomy, exercise, yoga and even books on food science—whomever and whatever as long as it was impossible to be excited about reading them, as long as reading them meant beating the brain into submission . . .

And he tried to conduct all the experiments he read in those books on himself . . .

He imposed extreme controls on his daily activities. Getting up at 5 a.m. every day and bathing in cold water (even though no one could bathe with cold water even there in the summer months, and Shekhar had never done it before); scrubbing his skin with a towel; jumping out of the window at 5.30 a.m. to go for a walk (Father woke up at the sound of the door opening, and Shekhar didn't want anyone to know where he was—he was afraid that his father would put an end to his programme and would certainly put a stop to his bathing in cold water which was especially important to him because of all the things in his daily routine it was the least pleasant . . .); skipping breakfast in the morning; eating at 10 a.m., and if food was served even five minutes late, then fasting, no matter what Mother said; not eating anything outside of a prescribed time throughout the day (he had even established times for drinking water); not speaking to anyone; and not playing cards (and not playing anything else that might also be 'useless'). In short, nothing was allowed that was prohibited by his daily routine, and his daily routine, like the British Raj, wouldn't allow even a reasonable interpretation of the restrictions.

There was only one way that changes could be made—if there was something that he particularly found unpleasant, he would have to do it twice. Often, Shekhar would have to bathe twice—and the way he did was to bathe a first time, dry himself off, put on his clothes and then as soon as he warmed up, he'd get undressed and bathe again . . .

When food was a little late in being served, he wouldn't eat anything. Mother would insist, but he still wouldn't listen—he felt it was like being lured to listen. Then she would think that he was angry with her and she wouldn't eat either . . . Once, she didn't eat for three days, but Shekhar didn't budge; he even told his mother that she should eat—it irritated him that she was trying to make him slip up. On the third day, Mother was enraged. She said, 'So no one cares whether I live or die! I can't put up with this nonsense,' and ate. Afterwards she gave up paying any attention to any of Shekhar's activities. At least she didn't utter a single word . . .

*

One day Shekhar overheard Mother talking to Father, 'This boy has gone insane. We need to take him to see someone—he's losing his mind.'

Shekhar went and got Moore's *Family Medicine* down from the shelf and began flipping through the pages from the beginning (he hadn't learned how to use an index yet). Every time he read about a new disease and its symptoms he would conclude that he had it. He managed to diagnose the symptoms of dozens of diseases in himself before he got to the section about mental illnesses, where he discovered that he also had 'melancholia'. Then he got to hypochondria, and in its symptoms he read, 'People suffering from this illness generally read medical books and they mistakenly believe that they have every disease . . .' Shekhar said, 'Hey, that's what I have!'

He put the book down. Immediately all the diseases disappeared and he burst out laughing . . .

But on the inside there was still unease, something sprouting—it hadn't gone away. He still felt like a seed beneath the surface that was about to sprout—as if he was being torn apart by the force of a new life about to be born . . .

He began to look at his mother and father differently. All of his unanswered questions, which he had managed to keep to himself and which he was still continuously trying to repress with double the force and double the strength, began to return and torment him with a bestial, violent joy . . . And they became even more cruel as they fed on the half-answers he received to a few of his questions from the servants or Father's peons, or which he secretly found in the books he read . . .

*

One day, Shekhar's parents fought.

They had fought several times before. It was never a big thing—some thunder, some rain, silence and Mother going without food. Shekhar didn't worry about this overmuch—except for the fact that on such days he had to try constantly to stay away from both of them, and to stay out of sight as much as possible.

But that day, Shekhar knew that this was a different kind of altercation as soon as he heard their muffled tones. He tried to catch the little that he could overhear from where he was standing—he didn't have the courage to get any closer. He didn't hear much, though he would catch something every time they raised their voices . . .

Mother said, 'Then kill me!'

Father said, 'Have some shame! What if someone—'

More was said, certainly, but Shekhar didn't hear any of it. He tiptoed out and went behind the door and, after looking out from its cover, leaped out and ran off.

Father was standing to one side of a small, round table, and in front of him, on the other side, was Mother. Her anchal no longer covered her head, and she bared her chest as she said, 'Then kill me!'

Father immediately left for his office. Shekhar heard a strange sound coming from the room—perhaps Mother was beating her chest . . . She beat her chest a few times and then went off to some other room.

Shekhar was sitting in front of the window. As he stared outside he began running through this incident in his mind . . . He recalled that there had been some tension between his parents for several days.

He hadn't placed too much stock in it at the time, but now he knew that the source of this outburst had been simmering for some time . . .

Mother passed in front of the window. Shekhar saw that she had a determination in her gait that she had never had, and she was walking on straight, quickly. He began to think . . .

It was evening when Father returned from the office. No one came to greet him at the door. He went inside. The servants had tea waiting for him, but there was no one sitting at the table. He went to the bedroom. There was no one there. He went to the kitchen. There was no one there. He looked outside and saw the servant standing there quietly. Shekhar, although he hadn't revealed himself, saw all of this clearly.

His father came over to him and asked, 'Where is your mother?'

'I don't know.'

'Ravidutt, Chandra—come here.'

'Yes?'

'Where is your mother?'

'Don't know. Probably inside.'

'Like hell she is!' Father lashed out. He slapped Chandra across the face with an open palm and then gave one to Ravi, which left their ears ringing. Then he went to Shekhar and shoved his chest so hard that it sent him crashing into a chair and ending up on the floor.

'What is the use of having you around here if you don't even know where your mother is?'

A frustrated anger, at its highest pitch, cries out for respect. Shekhar got up, looked at his father without a trace of vengeance and said, 'You went to the office and that's when she went out.'

Father boxed his ears and asked, 'Why didn't you say so earlier?'

All of a sudden his voice cracked. He said, 'She's gone . . . gone . . .'

The words seemed to drain the life from him. He said, 'She's gone . . . She left after fighting about the slightest thing . . .' It seemed as if he wanted to move but couldn't. He looked at Shekhar like a helpless deer wounded by an arrow and said, 'Shekhar, your mother is gone . . .'

And then suddenly his lifeless anger transformed into a flurry of activity. He caught hold of Shekhar, who had been sitting on the ground after he had fallen, by the hair and dragged him outside and said to him, 'Good for nothing! Go and find her!' He ran outside. Shekhar went off in one direction and he went in the other. The servant who had understood some of what had happened went off in yet another direction . . .

There was a forest two miles from the house, and Mother was wandering back and forth in an open clearing near there.

Shekhar saw her from a distance and simultaneously saw a little farther off, in the other direction, his father coming towards her. He turned around and went back—it didn't matter if it killed him, but he couldn't bear to watch the scene that was going to happen.

It was getting dark as the two of them came home. Father called out to the servant from outside the house, 'We aren't going to eat dinner—Mother isn't feeling well.' They went into the bedroom and locked the door.

The next morning, Shekhar couldn't detect anything. There were no signs of the quarrel; the dark clouds had evaporated. For the first time in Shekhar's life, his father said to his mother after drinking only half of his cup of tea, 'It's really good today. Here, have the rest of this cup.'

Shekhar noticed something else, too. The young female servant in the household—the one who played with Kamala and was always laughing—was acting nervously and keeping her distance, even though no one said anything to her.

*

In the afternoon, Shekhar was standing outside his house.

The telegram man brought a telegram. Shekhar signed for it on behalf of his father and then ran inside with it.

Father was in the bedroom—the door was closed. Shekhar quickly opened the door and said, 'Father—'

Mother and Father quickly separated from each other. Father looked at him angrily and then calmly asked, 'What is it?' Mother was still a little startled and shy and had turned away and hung her head.

Father asked again, 'What is it?'

Shekhar quickly presented his father with the telegram.

He read it and said, 'Listen, Saraswati has had a daughter.'

Mother responded with surprise, 'What? Already?'

Father said, 'Shekhar, you should go.'

Shekhar went outside but his heart was racing. He closed the door behind him so that he could stand at the crack and listen in.

Mother said, 'But it's only been eight months—'

Father seemed surprised as he said, 'Yes, look—'

Shekhar knew that they were coming towards the door. He ran off.

Saraswati had a daughter. Saraswati.

After the wedding, Rama went to live with her husband.

Shekhar wondered, 'So there was a girl hiding inside Saraswati, too?' And that time, Saraswati had said, 'I don't know!' If she were here today, Shekhar would have asked her again; she'd definitely know now even if she hadn't known then. But would she answer him? In the process of this back and forth, Shekhar recalled what had happened when he opened the door to the bedroom. What was it that had scared them? Why was Mother embarrassed?

It was nothing—he had seen everything. Father's arms had embraced Mother, and he was saying something, that's all. Shekhar knew that his own arms sometimes longed to embrace someone, to overpower them, and in his imagination this made him happy, proud and gave him self-respect. So why were they afraid and embarrassed? Why? Arms are arms and strength is strength. What was it that they were hiding, that Shekhar hadn't seen, which was embarrassing?

The question was still swimming in his head when a letter came from Saraswati—her daughter was dead.

Mother read it and said to Father, 'She says that the child was born at eight months.' And then as if she meant 'this was meant to be', she said, 'Yes—Oh!'

The girl died a mere four days and six hours after she was born. Mother says that Saraswati has written that the child was born at eight months. What's this new secret?

When he got a chance, Shekhar asked the cook, 'What does it mean when a child is born at eight months?'

'They are born after eight months.'

'What do you mean? Eight months after what?'

'A baby stays in a mother's belly for nine months.'

As if to corner him, Shekhar asked, 'How does it get in there?'

The cook laughed and said, 'Master Shekhar, you should ask Atti.' He pointed at the young female servant and laughed even louder.

Shekhar was shy around her but he still went up to her. She didn't speak his language, and he was only able to get out a few words in her language somehow, 'Baby—how?'

Atti began to laugh. She didn't understand Shekhar's question. She mocked him and repeated his words back to him, 'Baby—how?' She gestured to indicate that she didn't know what he was talking about . . .

Shekhar wanted to explain his question more clearly but then Mother walked in and asked, 'What are you doing here?'

Shekhar was taken aback; Atti continued with her work. Mother said, even more suspiciously, 'What were you doing here with Atti? Eh, Atti, what was he saying?'

Atti lowered her head and said, 'I don't know.'

Shekhar left.

*

A line appeared like lightning dancing on this screen of darkness—Sharda.

Shekhar's father's bungalow was surrounded by acacia trees and shrubs in the foothills of a mountain. In front of their house, on top of the mountain across the valley, there was a tree whose branches and leaves made the shape of the English letter 'S' against the background of the sky. A little way beneath the summit, the mountain is covered on all sides by cedar, pine and eucalyptus trees. This distant image was the sole source of nourishment for Shekhar's roving eyes, eyes which were hungry for novelty, for change, and which were tired of the monotony cast on everything around them. Shekhar's father was a foreigner in this land. His north Indian provenance was lost on southern provenance and chauvinism; despite being respectable he was still seen as an outcast. And in addition to the loneliness that this created, Shekhar felt that dreadful state of loneliness where all the world's injustices, its courage and fear, its bravery and cowardice, its arrogance and faith and doubt, its affection and anger, its love and hatred all get mixed together and fill one up . . .

Shekhar—hungry from countless hungers; Shekhar—unable to understand his own hunger, unable to find answers to his questions, finding himself surrounded by walls of indifference and frustration. He would go and sit in front of the window of his room and stare out at the sign of that 'S' spread out against the sky and think, 'Has God written my name in that vast emptiness, like the sword of Damocles[10] hanging over my head for all time?'

It was during one of those days that Mother remembered that there were others who lived in the world besides herself, and she resolved to meet them.

Just next door to Shekhar—in that sprawling mountain district, next door meant five miles away!—lived a Madrasi family.[11]

Shekhar had already met the adults of the family—they had been over to visit once or twice. They'd studied abroad and come to learn that even if the world didn't spread over the entire planet it did at least extend beyond the immediate boundary of their home. Mother was going to meet them to 'return' the favour of their visit. Shekhar was asked to accompany her because the people they were going to visit didn't speak Hindi and Shekhar's mother spoke neither their language nor English.

Hungry for novelty, Shekhar cheerfully went with his mother.

They arrived. They crossed through a small grove of eucalyptus trees and have entered their bungalow and the initial introductions and formalities have already taken place. When Shekhar and his mother were entering the bungalow they read on the signs posted outside that the name of the house was 'Eagle's Nest', and at the same time they spied the mistress of the house sitting on the grass in front. There was a young woman with her, and a little farther off, a girl was standing in the middle of a bunch of pea vines picking pea blossoms. When she heard the sound of footsteps she turned with a start to see the newcomers. She then gathered up her open tresses to hide the flowers that were strewn in them and ran inside. That's when the two women who were sitting on the grass got up to welcome them. Introductions were done somehow or other because it wasn't necessary to say too much; an introduction is accomplished easily enough with a smile.

Everyone went inside. They are all seated in a well-decorated room. Mother is sitting on a chair and her son is standing next to her (even though he has been offered a chair and asked to sit with a gesture); the mistress of the house was sitting next to the hearth on the wooden threshold and the young woman—her daughter— was sitting on the floor.

They are all quiet. The mistress of the house in anticipation and the daughter because she has no duty to perform; Mother because she doesn't know any English and because she has put all her hopes on her son; and the son because he cannot find anything to say in the surfeit of novelty in this new world. Sometimes he looked at his feet, which seemed perversely awkward to him, so he tried to hide his left foot with his right and his right foot with his left, and then because he feared that everyone would laugh at his foolishness, he cursed himself. Sometimes he would look at his hands, which seemed unnecessarily coarse and useless to him, so he would clasp one hand with the other and think about hiding them somewhere or cutting them both off. Sometimes he would think about his clothes and feel that no one in the world had ever worn such ridiculous clothes. He then considered the way he stood and felt that he was standing like a giraffe in a circus . . . After he came to that conclusion, he sat down with a thud; the mistress of the house looked at him and all he could think was, 'She must be thinking that this uncivilized boy doesn't even know how to sit down properly.' That unlucky wretch, and that cursed adolescence.

This wouldn't do at all. Since she sees nothing happening, the mistress of the house makes an attempt.

'What class are you in?'

Who can possibly imagine the scale of the mental determination he mustered to answer, 'I study at home'?

'Are you going to sit for any exams?'

A one-word answer, and even then he thinks that the word is too much, 'Matric.'

That's when his mother asks, 'What is she saying?' He explains it to her. He feels alive for a second.

Another voice speaks, 'Can you sit for exams if you haven't been to school?' The question belongs to the young woman.

'Yes.'

A third voice says, 'Wait, how?'

He turns around in surprise. The girl who ran off while she was picking flowers has entered the room. Wide-eyed, he tries to take her in quickly—God forbid their eyes should meet!—and then stares at his feet again—crude feet! At his hands—useless hands!

Her question goes unanswered. Her mother says, 'This is my daughter—Sharda.' But before anyone has a chance to say anything else, she repeats her question, 'How can you sit for exams if you haven't gone to school?'

After a few moments of silence it dawns on him that her question has still gone unanswered. He thinks it was impolite and this makes him even more nervous and he becomes completely incapable of answering the question. So she says, 'What are you thinking? Why won't you give me an answer?'

'This girl is shameless! I'm not responding to her questions, but she keeps asking more questions!' These are his thoughts as he notices that the girl isn't ashamed of the way she appears. Her hair, which was loose outside, is still wet and now tied with a silk ribbon. She's wearing a white kurta and a skirt that exposes her ankles—or was it a petticoat? She's looking at him with an unabashed curiosity, a look that makes him increasingly uneasy and angry, too.

In the meantime, everyone is silent. Mother asks Shekhar, 'What is she saying?' In order to hide his unresponsiveness he tries to put her off by quietly saying, 'Nothing.'

But Mother is a mother, after all. She asks her son, 'How do you say "shy" in English?'

'Shy.'

And as soon as he says it, he understands why she asked and hates himself. His mother smiles and gestures to him with her thumb and says, 'He's "shy".'

They all understand and begin to laugh. But the cup of his shame is still not completely full—he's about to be trampled upon while he's lying in the dirt! Sharda laughs, looks at him and says, 'Good gracious, such a big silly boy like you!'

Mother Earth! Why don't you swallow me! He is unable to bear these insults, so how are you able to endure them? And who knows what else this shameless girl will say?

Oh! He gets a little relief—Sharda's mother is scolding her. As she should. Novelty is one thing, but this shamelessness!

Rebuked, Sharda got up and left.

Then, somehow or another, people began to talk to bring this required-for-the-sake-of-civility meeting to a close.

But the end was still not in sight. Sharda returned, this time carrying her veena over her left shoulder like a bindle stick. She sat on the floor not that far from his feet.

Mother said to her son, 'Ask if anyone plays the veena. It looks beautiful.'

The son turns towards Sharda's mother and says, 'She's asking if anyone plays the veena. It looks beautiful.'

'Yes, Sharda plays it.'

He's speechless. He doesn't think about the obvious next step in the natural flow of the conversation. He is completely unable to do anything—neither can he ask Sharda to play nor can he say anything at all . . .

Sharda laughs. The strings of the veena begin to vibrate.

His pride says, 'She's embarrassed at how brazen she is.' His brain says, 'She's trying to please her mother.'

These were the years of adolescence. Otherwise he would have realized that these were not the only two explanations, the explanation was that mysterious element of a woman's nature, her easily manufactured outward contrariness that hid her beauty and her harmony . . .

What was that secret that burst forth from the resounding strings of that veena?

Like a 'spotlight' in a theatre, gradually the emotions of his heart narrowed from the expanse of the world to focus on one image, and then slowly moved away from even that, lost themselves somewhere in the darkness, washed away. The image is Sharda's half-wet hair, wrapped in a ribbon and tied in a bun, which is slipping down her shoulders and trying to hide behind her ears. As soon as he sees it he feels that the wave of music which is washing him away is like pure, white smoke, like a new cloud that crashes into mountains and runs on; and it melds with a fragrant vapour that rises from Sharda's body and the scent of her wet, earthy locks . . .

He felt as if the two of them had been surrounded by a mass of dense clouds. He felt as if the scent of Sharda's hair was running its fingers all over his body lovingly, but wherever it touches him, it scalds him . . . He's drinking in the fragrance of those unscented locks, with their faint smell of neem blossoms which lights his soul on fire . . . Although he's burning, he is filled with an ineffable joy and flowing away in the sky . . . He's beyond the earth, and now that piece of cloud is moving forward, passing Sharda, beyond the boundary of the sky, into the infinite . . .

He felt as if he were breathing in blades of fire. He felt as though he were suffocating. He's looking straight at that wilful bun of Sharda's hair. Crossing beyond the infinite, at the edge of the infinite . . .

But even the longest journeys come to an end. He's sojourned—who knows where he's arrived! The veena is silent, too. Sharda turns around for a moment and looks right at him, with a laugh that's meant to tease, which disappears as soon as she sees him. Their eyes meet. And that boy who had avoided looking at anyone for too long for fear that they would see him looking at them is now staring at this girl in front of all these people; his eyes aren't even blinking, let alone turning away . . .

But the moments that swing you out into the infinite are not long. The two of them avert their eyes at the same instant . . .

At the same moment Mother says, 'Tell her that she plays very well.'

He would rather die than say that—to Sharda, to anyone else . . .

Mother looks at him once with suppressed rage, but this wasn't the time to say anything, so she says to him again, 'Ask who teaches her.'

He manages to ask—the mistress of the house.

'I teach her.'

Mother instructs him to say, 'So you play as well?'

'A little bit.'

Again, as instructed, 'Some day I'll have to hear you play.' And to himself, 'But not today. Heard enough for one day, couldn't bear to hear any more . . .'

This time without being instructed, 'I have always wanted to learn music, but I've never had the opportunity. I can never find anyone to teach me.' He says this without being instructed because Sharda had risen and gone inside.

Now they are getting ready to end the conversation. Mother has stood up from her chair. He wants to wait until Sharda gets back; he is certain that she will come back. But just as he wasn't asked his opinion before they came here, he isn't going to be asked when they leave.

Until he reached the gate of the bungalow, he could feel someone's mischievous eyes on him—he felt a tingling up and down his spine . . . He turns back to look, but he is mistaken. Then he hears a voice echoing in his mind:

'Such a big silly boy like you!'

In order to explain why he looked back to his mother he says, 'Mother, this place is called Eagle's Nest. It's a strange name, isn't it?'

'Definitely.'

*

When an atheist begins to regain his faith, the most learned pundits can't match wits with him. The all-consuming wave of his blind faith destroys and submerges all of the caves of doubt and the mountains of intellect that stand in its path.

It's exactly like the feeling in adolescence—the age of hatred and disgust at the self—of love!

His house was in the foothills of a mountain from whose summit he could see the grove of eucalyptus trees in front of Sharda's house, but he could see neither the house nor even any other part of the house over the trees but he could certainly see the rising smoke from its chimney . . .

It was the reason he used to sit atop that summit and look down over there. And as he sat there he contemplated this novelty . . .

Because he still doesn't understand what's happened to him or what he wants. Because when he thinks about that house, and about that meeting, he sees the face of the mistress of the house, how she welcomed them, he can't remember a thing about Sharda! But in those rare moments when everything around him becomes perfectly still, he feels as if he can hear from somewhere—from somewhere—the sound of a veena being played. He begins to drift away in its waves, begins to fly, forgets everything, loses himself in the infinite and then becomes nothing. And for two or three minutes at a time he experiences that non-sensory, other-worldly, perfect emptiness which sages and ascetics strive to encounter for

mere seconds, a feeling which brings him into complete unison
with the world and where nothing else remains, and which he only
realizes once the experience is over—when a flutter of a white,
silken ribbon startles him and says, 'Such a big silly boy like you.'

But even after experiencing all that, he cannot connect this
meditative feeling to Sharda! Even when he thought about what
he had learned from novels and would ask himself, 'You aren't
in love, are you?' he would get another question in response to
his question, 'With whom? The mother or Sharda?' He couldn't
answer that—and it irritated him.

He would get lost in that same emptiness, in that unknowable
world that was created by the mystery of the song on the veena.
Then he would wake up.

One day he no longer feels any pleasure watching the smoke
rise from the chimney. He walks away in a daze towards that nest
where all his dreams slept.

He enters the grove of eucalyptus trees and sits in the shade of
a tall tree. The leaves are falling at this time of year so he is able to
sit on a pile of red, brown and yellow leaves at the base of the tree.
And from that spot, he looks over at the nest. It has a big window
in front and a large flower-printed curtain has been drawn across
it from inside.

The room behind the curtain is perhaps empty. But since
nothing can be seen behind the curtain, nothing can disprove his
imaginings. So in his mind's eye he imagines all three women are
sitting in that very room . . .

And then he floats away on the heights of his own poetry set
to the music of the veena, because in adolescence, who isn't a poet!

Something like lightning flashes through him. From
atop another hill in the same eucalyptus grove, someone was
approaching.

The form was new, the clothes were new, the style was new
and the radiance new, but like a jolt of lightning his consciousness
rang out—Sharda!

He melted into his shame, afraid that she might see him in
this condition! He hides behind the tree, then runs off, holds his

breath while he runs and, once he's a good distance away, back home, he comes to a stop.

Then a voice chides him, 'Such a big silly boy like you!' He slowly walks inside.

The unfortunate wretch still has no clue what these changes in his life are, what this novelty that has appeared is, what mark of some incomprehensible power.

He's learned something new. When his father is at the office, around 12 p.m. or 1 p.m., he leaves home and goes and sits a little way from the summit of his mountain at the edge of a path, on some expanse of verdure. His overheated body finds pleasure in its gentle coolness. He sits there waiting for the moment when Sharda will come down the path.

Sharda takes this route on her way to school and when school let out at 1 p.m. she came back home on this very path, alone. He sits there waiting for her and she passes through here around 2 p.m.—the school was about two miles away from that spot and Sharda's house was about a mile in the other direction. He wondered whether Sharda got tired walking that distance—even though he would walk twenty miles easily for no reason at all.

When Sharda gets there, she doesn't stop. He doesn't say anything either. He just sits there quietly and watches her progress—from the first moment that he sees her as she turns the bend with her tired arms carrying her books, until her white clothes and her thin frame disappear behind a big acacia tree, until her footsteps, until the sound of her footsteps falls completely silent . . .

At first he used to watch her from a distance and wouldn't make his presence known. But one day, when he was engrossed in a refreshing nap while waiting for her at the edge of the road, Sharda had seen him, and she quietly walked over to him, and put her bundle of books on his back. He woke with a start, shocked, but then was filled with an instant courage. He takes the books and goes with her and asks her affectionately, 'Don't you get tired carrying such a heavy bundle?' They walked on like that until they got to the thicket of eucalyptus trees a little way from Sharda's house and they halted, at the same time, from the same impulse.

Sharda took the books back, and then to destroy this temporary silence, she laughed mischievously and said, 'The big silly boy is kind,' and then ran off . . .

He stands there staring at his own hand—because his hand has touched the clothes of that running-away Sharda.

They haven't talked since, but they have their silent meetings every day. As she turns that bend—from the darkness of the dense shade—and passes that stretch of verdure, she always looks in his direction and smiles and then keeps walking. She doesn't stop, and he doesn't call to her. Ever since the day that he touched Sharda's clothes, they've reached a mute pact not to repeat the circumstances that brought it about. Although the two of them probably didn't know that they were withholding themselves from each other, hiding their shyness . . .

Shekhar knows that her school is going to be closed for Christmas. He won't be able to see Sharda for two weeks starting today. He thinks, 'These will be two very long weeks,' where he won't be able to see her. He's lost in these thoughts, forgetting about poetry, forgetting his dreams, sitting there, vacantly.

His gaze isn't fixed on that path today. He's filled with anticipation, but perhaps the feeling that the scene might vanish before his eyes at any moment has made him focus in another direction. He's looking at his old friend, the S-shaped tree at the top of the distant mountain, and thinking about old matters . . .

She comes and sees his emptiness and goes over to stand next to him, but he doesn't notice. He only notices when she says, 'What are you looking at, silly?'

But even when he's taken notice, he still responds distantly, 'I'm looking at that tree—on top of that mountain over in the distance.'

'Hmm—why?'

'Because I like it. I used to go there a lot.' He pauses for a second, 'I'm going to go back there for Christmas.'

The thorny path that they've made their mute pact not to tread is quite close to that spot. She moves away. Flatly, she says, 'My school reopens on the 5th.'

'What are you planning on doing?'

'During the holidays? I'll read. And—'

'I've been reading poetry recently.'

Sharda looks at him suspiciously—they aren't heading back towards that path, are they? And she says, 'I like Tennyson's poem.'

He was about to say, 'I've been reading translations of Tasso,' but he recalls one of his poems and it embarrasses him into silence.

She leaves. She says, 'Goodbye!' And then he recites the poem by Tasso to himself, he says 'One long goodbye?'

He wasn't able to hear whether she responded to his question.

He looked through all the books at home until he found a collection by Tennyson, *Maud and Other Poems*. He doesn't remember where Tasso is. He takes this book and goes and sits under his S-shaped tree and reads it disconsolately. His eyes are reading, but his ears are perked in anticipation of certain words, and in his mind, he wonders, 'Will she come?'

He hadn't told her to come, nor had Sharda indicated that she had planned to come. But he's returned here every day for three days and sat here in the hope that she might come . . . Because he had told her that he would be spending his time here—meaning, he'd be waiting here. Was she unable to understand something so simple?

As he's thinking about this, his mind fills with the words that his eyes are reading, and he realizes suddenly that he's singing one of the verses that his intellect hadn't recognized but his heart had known:

Come into the garden, Maud,
For the black bat, Night, has flown,
And the woodbine spices are wafted abroad,
And the musk of the roses blown;
Come into the garden, Maud,
I am here at the gate alone.[12]

And she's come. She comes eagerly, but she hesitates when she sees him sitting there and stops, and showing her surprise, she says, 'Oh my, what are you doing here?'

They begin to wander around—meandering aimlessly here and there. They're talking about frivolous things—although neither is paying any heed to what the other says. They're just happy to be together . . .

They come down from the top of the mountain and climb another nearby peak. Then suddenly, for some unknown reason, he remembers that Sharda's name also starts with an 'S'. He turns around to look—his friend, the S-shaped tree, is only half-visible. He blurts out, 'S for Sharda.'

'What?'

'Your name's written on that mountain.'

'Let me see—where?'

'Over there! Can you see—it's an S?'

'No, it's definitely not an S.'

'You can't see it from here. Wait a second, I'll climb this tree and look.'

He'd seen it several times before; and even if he could see it again from up high in the tree, Sharda still wouldn't be able to see it. He didn't think about any of this. Flush with the bravado of adolescence, only one thought occurs to him: there had to be incontrovertible proof for what he had said.

He quickly climbs a nearby cedar tree. It wasn't an easy tree to climb. He has cuts and scrapes all over, but he doesn't stop, doesn't think about anything else.

He climbs quite far and looks—the S can be clearly seen. And as if he's proclaiming his victory, he cries out, 'It's right there.'

Such were the rewards of his efforts. She says, 'Silly, how am I supposed to see?'

It's unclear why, either because Sharda had mocked him or because of his own silliness or perhaps because of some defect in the tree or because of bad luck, but as he's climbing down, he slips and o-o-o—Crash! And ridiculously, several branches of the cedar tree come crashing on top of him!

Even before he considers his injuries he gets up to make sure that Sharda hasn't seen. She's clutching her belly with both hands and laughing hysterically . . .

He doesn't even realize that his face has been scratched, that he's been cut, that he's twisted his left ankle; he just gets up and starts walking off quickly in one direction like a madman . . .

Sharda stops laughing and asks, 'You aren't hurt, are you?' She gets no answer. 'Come here, show me,' and then, 'I'm not coming.'

'Not coming?'

'Not coming.' He keeps walking.

'You won't come to me?'

'No, never, not even after an eternity!' He walks off. But a little slower than before.

She laughs again—a trembling laugh, but it's still a laugh!—and he begins walking faster again, though it hurts a lot.

Evening.

Shekhar couldn't go back for four days. His feet hurt badly! But today he's determined to go there. He braces himself, tightens his fists and clenches his teeth in determination . . .

He leaves home on the alibi that he's going for a walk. He's hidden a small axe in his coat and somehow he's managed to walk through the house and out the door without a limp. He fixes his stare on that tree and he's walking towards it with a pronounced limp.

He's set out on a terrifying mission. It's not clear whom he is angry with, but he knows exactly what his revenge instinct has planned . . .

He's reached the tree. From this close up, the S-shape can't be made out, and the leaves and the branches all appear different.

He's taken off his coat and removed his shoes. Holding the axe in one hand, he climbs up the tree. He takes a deep breath and clenches his jaw and starts his project . . . He is wounding the tree, cutting off its branches, erasing the relationship between it and Sharda's name . . .

He's now cut off many branches, so he comes down, puts his coat back on, hides the axe and begins walking home like a stumbling drunk, without turning back, very quickly . . .

A little way from the house, near the signboard, his madness leaves him—the curse that weighed heavily on his mind has been lifted. He stops to look at the mountaintop, looking for a sign, while his eyes seemed to be trying to avoid his own gaze . . .

That symbol of his identity, of Sharda's, and of their unity changed from an S-shape into an unfinished cipher, like an overturned, empty bowl, as it stood there looking up at the sky . . .

He lets out a long sigh, swallows his endless stream of tears and says, 'Sharda, I love you so much!'

In adolescence a moment can seem like a vast eternity, and eternity can seem like a mere moment. Seven days from the day that Shekhar had decided that he wouldn't go to meet Sharda he had returned to that very spot.

But she didn't come. A day, two days, three days, a week, three weeks—it's almost been one month now and she still hadn't come . . .

Much has happened in the meantime. It had been decided that Shekhar would take his matriculation exams and prepare to go to college. That was why he was leaving for the north in a few days. But there was something even bigger in his life than his studies and his worries about the changes the future would bring—something that was so personal and serious.

Shekhar's disposition had changed ever since he had cut down that tree. He was steadier, more reasonable. He wasn't tormented any more the way he had been by the face of the mistress of the house and the eldest daughter's voice and the strumming of the veena's strings and Sharda's words that would creep into his thoughts. He had understood the tumult that was taking place inside himself, he had recognized and accepted the truth that was hiding there—that he loved Sharda? He no longer had those mixed-up dreams. He was no longer bothered by that ineffable restlessness that spread through every part of his body. The form of the restlessness was still indescribable, still oppressive and pervasive through his body, but it didn't happen without any provocation or at any time. Shekhar knew that he was completely attached to Sharda and to her thoughts. He no longer tried to deflect attention from the harmony in his life by losing himself in the world of antiquity, no longer reading the Greek myths of Narcissus and Echo, or Hero and Leander, or Daphne and Apollo, or Eros and Psyche, even abandoning Tasso and Tennyson. Whenever he found himself alone now, he would listen to recordings of the violin on the gramophone, or in the extreme isolation of the night, he would listen to a recording of Sheshanna[13] playing the veena and compare the two, which always resulted in a decision in favour of Sheshanna. When he didn't find occasions for this at home, he would go to that pure spot and read Rabindranath Tagore's *Gitanjali*. He now found that mystical poetry to be a pleasure that no other thing had ever given him—he would read one verse and his entire past was washed away like so much dirt on his skin, and he felt as if he stood there, pure of mind, speech and action, ready to worship some God . . .

> I shall ever try to keep my body pure, knowing that thy living touch is upon all my limbs . . .[14]

Sometimes a rapture would course through his veins . . .

> O the Waves, the sky-devouring waves, glistening with light, dancing with life, the waves of eddying joy . . .[15]

After a month and a half of waiting for her she still hadn't come. Shekhar kept waiting for her despite the cruelty of his desire; he wouldn't go towards her house, nor on the road to her school.

Shekhar couldn't bear the thought of waiting that day. He would be heading north in two or three days to take his exams. But it never occurred to him that he should go to Sharda's house and meet her, or at least see her.

She'll come, why won't she come? Why, because Shekhar had said in a moment of anger that he wouldn't come?

Why hadn't she come all of these days?

No one was there to explain to Shekhar that she had come the second day after the incident, and the third, and the fourth, that she had cried for a long time, and that she had taken some leaves from that S-shaped tree and left—without thinking about when she would return.

Shekhar was reading the same verse by Rabindranath Tagore and he was reciting it for a tree, sometimes for the leaves scattered below and sometimes for the sky:

I shall ever try to keep my body pure, knowing that thy living touch is upon all my limbs . . .

The latticed shade of nondescript branches on tall trees; the affectionate spread of soporific sunlight on the cascade of tobacco-red and yellowed leaves; and the deep lentil green of a pine tree in the life-giving environment—all of this filled him up inside, like the lyric-less words of a song by the Toda people, turning into a raag . . .

She came. Wilted and lost. She blossoms in disbelief. The disbelief vanishes but she remains in bloom.

She sits next to Shekhar. The two of them are silent. Shekhar wants to say something, but how can something which can't be expressed in your native tongue, for which silence is a rough expression, be expressed in a foreign language?

Shekhar begins reciting the *Gitanjali* to her. She listens, lost as before.

One day the lotus bloomed, alas, my mind was straying and I knew it not . . .[16]

Then in a voice that cracks, with disconnected and broken sentences, Sharda tells him about the three days that she came to look for him and was disappointed. Shekhar sits there quietly and seriously, hiding the gratitude in his heart . . .

But these were the days of adolescence. How long could he keep up that seriousness?

The pair got up, and Shekhar, holding the book in his hand, ran this way and that trying to catch Sharda, but she was lightning and uncatchable. The running took them far from their familiar favourite spot, to the foot of another mountain, which had a waterfall at its base and on which lilies bloomed in the grass that covered it all over—most of them were perfectly white, but a few had red lines drawn through their petals, making them look like the Sudarshan Chakra.

Breathlessly Sharda collapsed on the grass. Shekhar stood next to her; but even that amount of exertion hadn't overheated his body. The thrill coursing through him hadn't dissipated. Shekhar threw the book into the grass and quickly began plucking the flowers and gathering them up. As soon as his arms were full he would take them and drop them in front of Sharda and then go back to gather more.

Shekhar gathered up all the flowers that could be seen from where Sharda was lying and dropped them all around her and on top of her. She laughed and sat up, and supporting herself with one hand she submerged the other into the flowers and smiled as she thought to herself.

Shekhar was sitting at some distance from her and then lay down in the grass. In that silence, the two of them began repeating their own secrets . . .

A wave of intoxication came over Shekhar, filling his body. He began breathing hard and fast; his entire body was on fire, as if there were molten lead inside his chest. He turned over on to his chest and began pressing his body into the earth with all his strength, gradually pressing both cheeks and his forehead into the cold, wet grass to cool himself . . .

It isn't enough, it isn't, not at all . . . His blood cries out for an even greater feeling.

He thinks about using the entire force of his will to embrace the earth even more tightly, but he gets up, goes up behind Sharda and springs and covers both of her eyes with his hands. She's surprised into silence and Shekhar presses down even harder over her eyes . . .

Why is Sharda's body on fire? Why is she trembling?

An irrepressible desire makes Shekhar bend down, placing his chin on her forehead. He takes in the scent of her dried hair. Then he buries his nose in her hair and draws three, four, five long breaths . . .

The fragrance of neem berries in a new spring month . . . so sweet . . . like the foam on an aged wine, it enters his nostrils and goes straight to his head, and Shekhar becomes exactly like a crazed man who has been given too much to drink—mad from two different madnesses . . .

She is shaking excessively—and the more she trembles the harder Shekhar presses down on her eyes . . . It's as if he thinks that the pressure from his two hands and his chin will calm her tremors, will crush that small, beautiful head of hers . . .

She tries to use one hand to move Shekhar's hands—but where?

What is this—trembling or sobbing? Her breath is being drawn in long, broken gusts and what is this hiccup-like 'Hic! Hic!' sound that she makes?

Shekhar lets her go immediately and sits down on the pile of flowers that is next to her and locks his gaze on her face . . .

An age passes; she stops sobbing-hiccupping. Sharda turns to look at him with big tearful eyes and smiles at him with a grave sadness and in a gentle voice filled with complaint she says, 'You've crushed all the flowers!'

For a long while their eyes are locked on each other and in that moment Sharda stands up. Shekhar can't respond to her charges, nor is he able to get up off the flowers. She slowly turns away and begins walking off, and Shekhar cannot even lift a finger to call her back. She doesn't even leave, but it wouldn't have mattered—Shekhar's tongue lacks even the strength to ask, 'Where are you going?'

The next day, word arrived that the date of the examination had been changed, and Shekhar would have to leave immediately. On the one hand he was eager to get away from the suffocating atmosphere in his home and on the other hand he was dejected by his thoughts of Sharda; Shekhar kept both of those to himself and set out for Lahore the day after next.

*

Shekhar knocked on the door and then waited in the darkness for someone to open the door. After a little while, he could see a light inside, coming towards the door. The door creaked and the chain banged against the door. The door opened. A girl was standing to one side with a light in her hand. Shekhar took a good look at her and walked inside.

But just a little farther inside, he realized that he knew the girl. He stopped and without turning back he said, embarrassed, 'Shashi!'

Shashi joined the hand holding the light with her other hand and said, 'Pranam.'[17] Shekhar immediately remembered the scene with the fight over the mug which was their only thing in common.

He quickly passed her and went upstairs. Shashi stayed by the door.

Shekhar greeted his aunt, Vidyavati, and her husband, Devnath. He inspected his room and immediately began unpacking. He arranged his books on the table and began reading.

His aunt came and said, 'You should rest a little—there's plenty of time to study.'

A little embarrassed, Shekhar said, 'There are only a few days left—I haven't studied much.'

Aunt left. Shekhar opened his book and thought, 'What happened to Sharda that day? Why was she crying?'

Downstairs, there was a peal of laughter. It startled Shekhar, and he picked up his book and began reading aloud.

Shashi laughs a lot . . .

Sharda's laugh was different. That day, when they were talking about the exams . . .

Exams. Studies. The Geometry textbook.

Shashi wasn't that much younger than he was, so why did she greet him formally?

There had to be a scar on her forehead from where the mug hit her.

What was Sharda doing right now? Probably studying . . .

Studies. The Geometry textbook. Exams.

Shashi came upstairs to tell him, 'Brother, Mother is calling you for dinner.'

Shekhar wonders whether it would have been a big thing if Shashi hadn't called him 'brother'. He wasn't that much older than she was. He spoke out loud, 'Let's go, Sisterji. I'll be right there.'

He didn't understand what had led Shashi to say, 'It's not as though I'm older than you.'

Shashi left. Shekhar looked at his Geometry textbook again.

Shekhar generally studied for sixteen hours a day and would only get up when his brain was exhausted and refused to work any more. But even when he lay down on the cot, his mind would fill with so many thoughts, so many images, so many curiosities . . .

There was a girl who lived nearby in his neighbourhood. She was a little crazy, and she was a little squint-eyed, and when the boys from the neighbourhood would pass by her house, they would yell in unison, 'Sumitri, Sumitri—cross-eyed bumblebee.'[18]

Whenever Shekhar heard them or saw her, it would make him laugh. But for some reason, the taunts from the others didn't bother her, but when she saw Shekhar laughing her eyes filled with tears of pain. Having taken note of this a few times, Shekhar stopped laughing.

Whenever Savitri saw him sitting somewhere or reading, she would come up to him and stand there silently. If anyone else came up to them, she would run away, otherwise she would stand there for a full hour. Shekhar never called her over, and she never said anything either; she just watched Shekhar read.

Gradually, Shekhar got used to having her around. Actually, he even began to expect it. If she wasn't there while he was studying, he couldn't concentrate. He would wait for her expectantly and think, 'Why isn't she here yet?'

And then he would remember Sharda—and he'd curse himself. Why am I thinking about anyone else? I love Sharda— and there should be no one else in the world, there is no one else . . . He would grind his teeth and force himself to concentrate on studying—to study and forget about everyone else, so that no one other than Sharda could find a way into his heart . . .

Shashi brought him his meals both times every day. Everyone else ate in the kitchen, but he ate in his room. Shashi had been given the task of making sure that he ate. Shashi never asked him if he wanted her to bring him his meals. Whenever it was time or whenever she thought it best, she'd put his meal on the table and push his books to one side and stand back. Shekhar tried to ignore her presence, kept reading, but after a while, he'd close his book and eat quietly. Whatever he needed, Shashi would bring it up for him, he never had to ask, and moreover his objections went completely unheeded. Shashi would serve him however much she wanted even if he objected a thousand times. But she never spoke. Sometimes to start a conversation, Shekhar would say, 'Sister, can you bring me some of that?' and she would silently do as she had been asked, with not even so much as a yes or a no.

This, too, began disturbing Shekhar's studies. He kept thinking: why, when, how, what; and he would forget that he had to study . . . Irritated, he went to complain to his aunt one day, 'Aunt, Sisterji won't speak to me. Tell her that she should talk to me.'

Aunt laughed. But that evening when Shekhar was eating, Shashi said, 'I've complained about you to Mother,' and then she left the room. After that, Shekhar had to ask for dal, roti and the rest himself. The next day he said, 'Aunt, I'll eat in the kitchen.'

He went to the kitchen and his aunt said to him, 'Shekhar, Shashi asks that you not call her "Sisterji" any more. She's younger than you.'

'But she doesn't even speak to me.'

'That's why she doesn't talk to you.' Aunt started to laugh.

Shekhar said, 'She could have told me sooner.' After that, whenever he got the chance, he would go right up to Shashi and pointlessly say, 'Sisterji!' And she too refused to speak . . .

And so, when Shekhar wasn't waiting for Savitri, he would be on the lookout for Shashi so that he could tease her. He never knew how much of his study time was spent in studying and how much in waiting for these two . . .

When his thoughts would return to Sharda, he would burn with guilt and anger that he had spent even a moment of his time on anyone other than Sharda . . .

His studies continued in this pattern, and the exams were also over . . .

When it was time for Shekhar to go back, he said goodbye to everyone, except Shashi. He couldn't say it because when he started with 'Sisterji—' Shashi turned around and left.

But she did come to the station to see him off. Once he had found his seat on the train and said his goodbyes to everyone, Shashi came up to his window and just barely touching the tips of her fingers together gave him a half-formed pranam and said, 'You're going to call me Sisterji now, too.'

Shekhar was moved. He blurted out, 'Shashi!'

The train started to move.

Shekhar saw that she had a soft smile on her face. He immediately called out to her, 'Sisterji!'

He couldn't see Shashi in the distance, although Shashi certainly heard his voice.

But once the train left the station, Shekhar forgets all about Savitri, Shashi, his aunt, studies, the results of his exams. There was only one thing on his mind—that he was heading south, and the south was where Sharda was.

This thought so completely overtook his body, head, mind and soul that the material world faded away.

Even when he got back home and learned that there had been a telegram to the effect that his older brother Ishwar was missing from college, the news had no particular effect on him; he didn't understand why his parents were so upset or why his younger brothers were so scared and quiet . . .

It was as if his feet didn't touch the ground, like he was walking at some distinct height from the earth, from which all the power in the world could not pull him down . . . It was as if his body still felt that trembling under the pressure of his hands, as if he could still smell the scent of young berries on a neem tree and it was about to make him faint . . .

Somehow, he went through his first day back at home. As soon as he got up the next morning, he went out to walk. He went to the tree. She wasn't there. Nor was there a reason that she should be. Next he went to the top of his mountain, and from that vantage point he could see the grove of eucalyptus trees in front of him, but he couldn't see the pillar of smoke rising from the chimney of 'Eagle's Nest' over them.

Shekhar raced down the mountain to the eucalyptus grove. When he got to 'Eagle's Nest' he saw that everything was still. There was no one anywhere. The front door had been locked from the outside. He looked in through the windows and saw that everything was gone, the house was completely empty.

She wasn't there either. Shekhar sat down on the steps.

When he got up, the fever of adolescence had broken.

*

Shekhar was sitting in the room next to the kitchen and eating his dinner. Mother was sitting in the kitchen making rotis.

Shekhar's hands and mouth were cooperating to finish the work of eating, but his mind was somewhere else. Wherever it is, it's not clear. He's finished his roti but Shekhar doesn't seem to realize it. Mother calls to him from the kitchen, 'Take the rotis out to everyone,' so he goes to get them.

With two or three pieces of pink paper in his hand, Shekhar's father passes him and goes into the kitchen. The fact that he's there tells Shekhar that something strange has happened, and he forgets about eating his roti and sits there dejectedly trying to listen to what is being said.

They've learned where Ishwardutt is. He's in Bombay and he's trying to join the police force there. When signing up he listed the name of his college correctly, but lied about the name of his father. The college made a few inquiries and then sent the telegram.

There's silence for a while. Shekhar thinks that the matter is settled, but then Mother says—'When he comes back here, get him married.'

Father says, 'Unh, what will a marriage accomplish?'

Then a short silence. Then she says, as if she's talking about someone else entirely, 'He's a strange boy. How could anyone trust someone like him?'

Father makes a soft, partly unconvinced, partly thoughtful sound, 'Hmm.'

Then a silence—pregnant with meaning. Mother says, 'And if you ask me in all honesty'—and then her voice suddenly got soft, but not so soft that Shekhar couldn't hear—'ask me in all honesty, I'll say that I don't trust this one either.'

This one!

Shekhar's jaw drops, his eyes widen, he forgets the world—he falls from somewhere high above. With a fiery, blind instinct, he hugs the wall and looks at his mother's facial expression, the suddenly frozen expression in her eyes and the thumb pointing at Shekhar.

This one!

Shekhar doesn't see anything; he drinks it all in with a blind, deaf and precognitive instinct—like poison!

This one!

He stumbles to his feet and walks out of the room. He doesn't go to the kitchen to wash his hands. Behind him, his mother asks, 'Do you want more roti?' And when she doesn't get a response, she gets irritated and says, 'This devil torments me—I can't understand his ways.' Father was waging a mini-campaign against using the word 'devil' . . .

It was as though he heard all of this with an altered consciousness. Afterwards, a darkness descended inside, outside and all around him . . .

This one!

This one phrase had shaken him from his apathy, which had conquered and ruled over him after Sharda's departure, but where had it thrown him? Where had he fallen—something had broken inside him! Whenever he looked at someone, some 'thing' pointed its thumb at him and said, 'This one!'

'This one! This one! This one!'

It was night. Shekhar had been sitting in his room since the incident, like a statue. He hadn't eaten or drunk anything for which he received insults, but it didn't faze him, even though they were delivered with acrimony and tears. Father shouted at him and left; Mother said her fill, cried-beat-wailed and then fell silent and left.

Everyone was asleep. Shekhar locked the door to his room, turned off the light, sat down on his bed and began to smoulder. There was an inexhaustible feeling inside him. Who knows whether it was anger or dejection or hatred or something else entirely, but it was so intense that he couldn't turn it into a thought; not just his mind but his entire body was being pulled along with it and being trampled upon; the impact of that feeling was so pervasive and numbing that it left no room for any wilful activity (conation);[19] his entire being became a bubble of depression . . . which burst. Shekhar got up in the darkness and unlocked the drawer under the table and removed a notebook and began writing in it in the darkness . . .

Who knows how long! Who knows what he wrote!

The notebook served as Shekhar's diary—a record of all the wrongs and injustices that he had suffered that year (and despite keeping it as secure as he did, he didn't have the courage to write about Sharda in it). There could be so many injustices in just a few months!

When night was over, Shekhar had already stopped writing for a long time, and he stayed there staring out into the darkness, not going to sleep. Of the lines he had written, one of them circled his mind, blowing fiercely like a hot desert wind, ringing in his head:

Better to be a dog, a pig, a rat, a stinking worm than to be a man whom no one trusts . . .[20]

Suddenly Shekhar got up and said to the wall in English (who knows why he couldn't express feelings of hatred in any other language):

'I hate her. I hate her.'[21]

Then, before anyone else was awake, he got dressed and jumped out of the window of his room on to the path outside and went off in some direction.

By the time the sun rose, Shekhar had already walked eight or nine miles. He sat down next to a muddy pond in a large grove. He had thought about many things—from murdering women all the way to suicide, he considered a great many options.

He was never able to determine whether it was the strength of his mental make-up or the principles that he had been taught or the influence of some internal force that saved him from himself that day. Nor could he fathom what end, what tragedy he had barely avoided. But he did know this much, that nothing was impossible for the vengeful demon that awoke inside him, nothing was beneath it; nothing was immoral for it; because that demon was more ancient than good and evil, morality and immorality, than reason . . .

Shekhar took a piece of paper and a pencil out from his pocket and began writing a vow.

I won't do anything that Mother needs doing; never do anything for which she might have to have even the slightest bit of trust in me; I'll stop speaking to her altogether; and if anyone ever asks, I'll tell them that she isn't even my mother.

A voice from out of a novel cries out and repeats, 'She's a stepmother! A stepmother! A stepmother!'

Suddenly, without realizing it, a change overtakes him. Something casts a shadow over him like a colour, like the colour red, like rays of sunlight refracted through glass . . .

He tears up his vow and throws the pieces on the soft, wet earth and grinds them with his big boots, pulverizing them until those pieces of paper are buried under the dirt, until they're invisible . . .

Why should I accept defeat? If someone doesn't trust me, let them not. I am worthy. I'll become worthy and remain worthy. I'll bear this wound in silence, swallow the insult. And I won't let it show. And when I've won the respect and trust of the entire world I'll throw it in her face and say, 'Look! I spit at these things!'

Hiding yet another fire in his evolving soul that transformed him into a quiet revolutionary, he returned home.

*

If Shekhar hadn't sought death it was because his life was in a state worse than death—he didn't live a life worth seeking extinction.

Many have sung paeans to love and loss, but no one has ever praised hatred and lust. But Shekhar's life was possible now only because of those two forces—hatred was the only thing that had given him enough strength to challenge the world despite having lost everything, and lust had goaded him to confront the wound which had afflicted his heart.

Shekhar had lost Father, Mother, Saraswati, Sharda and ultimately even himself. And maimed from all of that as he was, he was unable to think about anything. The energy of these two poisons, though, was slowly reviving him . . . Liquor can make a healthy man crazy, but it is necessary if you want to wake an unconscious man . . .

Poetry and song have become meaningless for Shekhar. Listening to his most cherished records didn't bring him an iota of happiness—but he did find a little bit of peace when he dashed them on the ground and shattered them in a fit of rage . . . He would sit lifelessly in his room, or outdoors, or anywhere really, as every place had become the same for him—and just stay there sitting . . .

If someone said something to him, he never heard it. But if people were having a conversation nearby, he would listen to what they said.

Mother and Father were sitting and talking to each other; Shekhar was sitting apart from them. Suddenly he realized that he had heard what they said and taken in the meaning.

Shekhar's father had just returned from one of his tours. Mother was inspecting the things that he had purchased. While talking about a fine sari from Madura[22] Father said, 'I got it for Saraswati. Didn't you say that we needed to send her one?'

Mother said, 'This? Why should we send this to her? It's so beautiful. We needed to send her a sari out of custom—an ordinary sari will do just as well. Why don't I keep this one for myself?'

Shekhar spent the next several days determined to get hold of that sari somehow so that he could set it on fire, or rip it to shreds, so that Mother couldn't wear it . . . But who knows which trunk she put it in, because it was never taken out again, nor did Mother ever wear it. Shekhar was left holding only his determination.

Shekhar was sitting there aimlessly and softly humming two verses from the *Gita Govinda*—so absent-mindedly that he didn't even realize it:

Lalita-lavang-lata-parisheelan-komal-malaya-sameere
Madhukar-nikar-karambit-kokil-koojit-kunj-kuteere[23]

He had heard his father singing this verse many times. He didn't know what the lines meant, but there was a certain charm in them and he had memorized them the first time he had heard them, and he often used to repeat them.

That's when Father arrived and heard him singing and asked, 'Where did you learn that?'

'I don't remember.'

'Do you remember any more of it?'

'Yes.'

'What?'

Dheer-sameere-yamuna-teere-vasit-vane-vanamalee,
Gopi—[24]

Father objected angrily, 'You've read the *Gita Govinda*?'

'No.'

'Then where did you learn this?'

'You were singing it—I heard you singing it and memorized it.'

Father hadn't beaten Shekhar for days. Perhaps he had begun to think of him as an adult.

But at this moment, he was so angry that he slapped him hard three or four times.

'I don't know what's happened to these boys. All they learn are obscene things.'

Shekhar decided quietly that one way or another, he was definitely going to read the *Gita Govinda*.

He sifted through Father's Sanskrit books and found the *Gita Govinda*—with the commentary. First, he read the entire book, and it was so charming that he had already memorized most of it. Then he wanted to know why Father had become so angry, so he read the commentary to try and understand the meaning of the work. The commentary was in Sanskrit, but understanding some of the original text using some of the commentary and sometimes just guessing, he slowly translated his way through the book . . .

He understood and didn't understand. He was agitated, filled with aversion, and he didn't know why. He would read it and feel disgusted, and the disgust made him read more. He felt hatred for Krishna, and in his hatred he'd put himself in Krishna's place; and his soul continuously asked itself, 'Why? Why? Why?' . . .

Countless images began dancing before his eyes—tiny groupings of countless forgotten things, symbols, light and darkness . . .

Father . . .

Mother . . .

The cook . . .

Atti, the maid . . .

The Kashmiri ayah, Jinniya . . .

Then a scene in Kanhaiya Market in Amritsar . . .

He was going back home after taking his exams. He stopped to see Amritsar on the way—a man from Lahore had been sent with him to show him around Amritsar. After they had seen the Golden Temple, Jallianwala Bagh and other sights, his companion said, 'Now let's see something new,' and he took Shekhar with him to that market.

It was evening. On the ground level of the market were several shops still open—haberdashers, sweet-makers and savoury food stalls—and here and there men selling garlands were sitting and calling out, advertising their wares. But people were attracted to the market for the second storey—lights glowed from up there, and in every window or balcony sat a beauty . . . Shekhar's unaccustomed and naive eyes felt as though he had never seen such vast beauty. He suddenly stopped. A big, smiling face looked down at him. Shekhar was transfixed—he stared back, fixed, unblinking, stunned and drowning in wonder. Such beauty! His innocent eyes nevertheless noticed that there was blue eyeshadow around the eyes, but his mind told him that it was probably from too much mascara, and besides, when had it ever been possible for him to get in his critical comments? That pure, joyful wonder— such beauty! His companion looked at him, laughed a harsh, vulgar laugh, pulled him away and said, 'These damned women even go after the young and the elderly.' And now Shekhar is walking and thinking about what those words mean when the companion starts again, 'I'm responsible for you, otherwise—' And then he's silent.

And then sneaking into Father's collection and finding an image of Chinnamasta[25] whose nether parts were obscured by a strip of paper that Father had placed there, Shekhar removed it and looked . . .

Shekhar trembled. He felt nauseated to the core as if he were being bitten by countless scorpions, though their sting didn't contain poison but honey—it was such a sweet sting . . .

*

Atti was around twenty years old. Like the women of her country and caste she dressed in a single bolt of cloth. She covered her entire body in a multicoloured, chequered sari, but her head was uncovered, and often times, a shoulder was exposed.

She had an ordinary body, wasn't tall or short, wasn't thin or overly fleshy. She was, nevertheless, very healthy. Her vitality shone through her skin. She had thick hair, deep black in colour, a very small head, short arms, too, but black, a small nose somewhat turned up and a chin that was a little recessed. You could say that the only things that were large on her face were her eyes; everything else was small. You wouldn't call her beautiful, but there was a vivacious charm that would appear so that no one would be tempted to go closer and determine whether it was beauty or ugliness.

She was always laughing—about everything, with everyone. Laughing was her work and her rule.

Even when she talked to Shekhar (or when she didn't talk to him, but just looked at him) she would laugh. Sometimes Shekhar felt as if there were something serious in that laugh, some meaning. He couldn't make out what, but whenever he thought about it he felt uneasy and agitated . . .

Sometimes, when he was near Atti, she would be so preoccupied with her chores that she didn't seem to notice that he was there. Then he would watch her and say something to startle her. But Atti was never startled; whenever she heard his exclamation, she would straighten her sari, compose herself, smile at him and keep on working . . .

One day she was sweeping in Shekhar's room when he walked in. Atti's back was towards the wall and she was bent over while sweeping, so the end of her sari had slipped off her back and had stopped at her neck and her back was exposed. Shekhar stood there and stared, and realizing that Atti didn't know that he had entered, he slowly crept up to her.

As he got closer he thought about how he would try to startle her, by the sound he might make or by tickling her back.

Having settled on tickling her, he bent forward only to realize that Atti was holding back a smile—she knew that Shekhar was there . . . He was hurt; he stopped his outstretched hand. Atti quickly stood upright and completely covered her back and her shoulder, and turning her covered shoulder towards Shekhar, she rested her chin upon it and began laughing.

'She knew I was here'—the thought hurt Shekhar but it also gave him a sharp thrill; she knew and that was the reason she had stayed bent over like that. Shekhar stepped forward and caught the end of her sari so that he could pull it and expose her as before. Atti, as if trying to save herself, bent forward in his direction. Her face came very close to Shekhar's mouth . . .

Shekhar immediately released the end of her sari and stumbled back.

Memories of a small head being held by both hands and of the fragrance of the neem blossoms danced in front of him . . .

Shekhar quickly left the room and slammed the door behind him . . .

*

There was another house at a little distance from Shekhar's house, where a girl, probably eighteen or nineteen years old, was usually lying on a lounging chair in front in the sun.

Her name was Shanti. Shekhar had heard that she suffered from tuberculosis and that was why she was always lying there. He had also heard that she wouldn't survive much longer and ever since he heard that he would sneak away and stand on one side of his house and watch Shanti. Sometimes he would feel compassion, sometimes sympathy and sometimes when he was really depressed he envied Shanti as she was going to be free of this existence soon . . .

Sometimes Shanti would look up in his direction, but he would always move out of sight. He was afraid that if she saw him watching her she wouldn't sit there any more . . .

One day Shanti looked over at him and smiled. Shekhar was trying to decide if he should hide or stay there when she beckoned him over with a gesture from her hand, and she may have even called out to him.

Shekhar looked back nervously once towards his home and then went over.

Shanti gestured to the grass spread out next to her chair and said, 'Sit.'

Shekhar sat. When he sat down he realized that he couldn't be seen from his house, that he was being screened by an oleander shrub, and he was able to sit more at ease.

Shanti said, 'Your name is Shekhar, right?'

Shekhar was surprised, 'Yes.'

'I can hear the things going on at your house all the way here— your mother talks quite loudly.'

Shekhar was silent.

After a little while, Shanti spoke again, 'What are you always looking at?'

Shekhar was caught off guard, so he hung his head and started counting the nails on his toes.

Shanti said gently, 'Tell me, what are you always looking at?'

'Nothing.'

'What do you mean, nothing? Then why are you always running away when I look over at you? That's why I don't look over there so often.'

Shekhar was silent.

'Tell me, why are you being so shy?'

'I have a picture—you look just like it,' Shekhar said and then stopped.

'Which picture?'

'I'll get it.' Shekhar said and got up and brought the picture from his house.

'Here, look.'

Shanti took the picture, looked at it and said, 'Arré! I have this one, too.'

'Really?' Shekhar asked as he sat back down in his spot.

The picture was Rossetti's *Beata Beatrix*, which was also known as *The Glory of Death*.[26]

Shanti said, 'Some day this glory[27] will also be mine.' She laughed a melancholic laugh.

Shekhar's heart fell. He said, 'They call it *The Glory of Death* but that's the wrong title! Its real name is *Beata Beatrix*, which means Beatrix in a trance. Rossetti's wife had fallen unconscious once, and Rossetti painted this picture of her.'

Shanti said, 'Really?' as if she were really saying, 'You really know a lot.'

After a little while, Shanti said, 'Tell me something. I lie here alone all the time, so it would be nice if you came over. You can tell me things and I'll listen. I have a lot of patience[28] for listening.'

'I'll come over but I don't know what to talk about.'

'Whatever you want—things that happened to you, or else stories, or some poetry.'

Shekhar thought to himself quietly. She watched him for a while and then said, 'If you can't come up with anything then you can just sit here quietly—I only have a few days left.'

Shocked, 'Why?'

'Yes, it's true! Then I'll be completely alone!'

This saddened Shekhar so much that he just sat there, saying nothing, and went home half an hour later.

Shekhar started going over to see Shanti often. Sometimes he would take a book of short stories or poetry with him and read it to her, sometimes he would take a picture book and sometimes he would just sit there quietly . . . He felt as if he were Shanti's protector, as if she had no body and was merely an infant soul and he was her guardian angel . . . Sometimes when Shanti would close her eyes and rest her head against the back of her chair while listening to him talk, he would stop and look at her pale face, and then start reading again in an anxious voice, as if his reading would keep Shanti's life force fixed in place in order to hear him—as if she would fly away if he stopped reading . . .

One day Shanti said, 'Give it to me! Let me read something today. You can listen.'

Shekhar had brought over a collection of English poems today and he handed them over to Shanti. She flipped through the pages for a while—then she said, 'Yes, I'll read you this one—I have it memorized.' She closed the book and put it on her lap. Then she lay back down and rested her head, closed her eyes and slowly began reciting:

> Break, break, break,
> On thy cold gray stones, O Sea!
> And I would that my tongue could utter
> The thoughts that arise in me.
>
> O well for the fisherman's boy,
> That he shouts for his sister at play!
> O well for the sailor lad,
> That he sings in his boat on the bay![29]

She stopped for a second and then continued:

> And the stately ships go on
> To their haven under the hill . . .

And she stopped again. Shekhar waited for a while expecting her to continue (Shekhar knew the following lines) but she stayed silent, and he couldn't say anything either . . .

Shekhar began to notice Shanti's neck. It was glorious like gleaming white moonlight! And her skin was translucent—Shekhar could clearly see the pulsating blue lines of her veins underneath . . .

There was such indifference to the world in that pulsation—how carefree, so contained within herself!

At that moment, she looked exactly like that picture . . .

Every pulse took her closer to unconsciousness—closer to a trance . . .

Or to the glory of death—*mrityu ka gaurav* . . .

Shanti opened her eyes all of a sudden—Shekhar felt as if the opening of her eyes was so lacking in will as to be involuntary—and a feeble, soft voice said, 'What are you looking at?'

It was unexpected, but it was so soft that Shekhar wasn't surprised. Haltingly, he said, 'Shanti, can I touch you?'

Shanti assented with her eyes and said, 'Come.'

Shekhar went to her respectfully, fearfully putting one hand beneath Shanti's chin, on her neck; he didn't really put but rather grazed it with his fingers.

Shanti moved her head forward and pressed down on his fingers with her chin—with a soft, gentle, grateful pressure . . .

Shekhar stood still.

All of a sudden, a large tear fell on Shekhar's hand, and the hand under the chin shuddered once.

There was no pressure on Shekhar's hand, but he could not free it.

A little while later, Shanti lifted her head and rested it against the chair once again! Shekhar lifted his hand and slowly walked back home—he felt as if nothing else could happen after that.

At night, in his dream, Shekhar saw Sharda stricken with tuberculosis and dying. He goes to her and Sharda says to him, 'You've forgotten all about me, haven't you? Otherwise, would I be dying?' And her large, hot tears are streaming down on Shekhar's hand . . .

Shekhar sat up. He realized that his whole body was trembling. The darkness felt as if it were slicing through him. He quickly lit the lamp and put it on the table; he sat there staring at it, wide-eyed . . .

He didn't go to see Shanti for a week. He stayed locked up in his room all day. He had heard that Shanti's fever had worsened. His mother had even been to see her and offer her sympathies, but he didn't leave his room.

Atti no longer came near him. Nor did he ever come face-to-face with her or try to talk to her. Recently, Shekhar had come to see that even when he did run into Atti she laughed a disrespectful and derisive laugh. To her he was contemptible, a joke.

Which is why, as he sat in his room with the door closed, he wasn't prepared for Atti to enter that day. Atti opened the door and came in loudly and unsympathetically, and mockingly said, 'That Shanti of yours, she's dead.'

At the same time, sounds of wailing could be heard in the distance . . .

Atti turned her nose up at him and walked out.

Three or four months later Shekhar would learn that Atti has returned to her home to get married—that she had been thrown out of this job in disgrace.

*

To Shekhar it seemed clear that if he loved Sharda he shouldn't be thinking about any woman other than Sharda. And it was also clear to him that he was always thinking about them.

Did that mean he didn't love Sharda?

The mere thought of this made his heart rebel—he wanted all the fire of his personality to believe that he loved Sharda and only Sharda . . .

Or perhaps letting yourself think about other people wasn't a sin.

Then why did he feel excited and dejected? What about those fuzzy desires and the disgust they produced in him? Why did he always feel as though he was committing a sin?

But was Shanti's attractiveness a sin? Wasn't it a sin not to go to her in her final hours? He had touched Shanti—had made clear his desire to touch her. Was that betraying Sharda? Or was using Sharda as a pretext not to go to Shanti also unfair to Sharda? What about that dream . . .

Shekhar's mind went blank—he didn't ask any more questions after that. But Shekhar clearly knew that the chain of questions hadn't stopped in his mind, that he was at the edge of a big, important question and he was trying to grab hold of it—he wanted to take a huge step away from the personal and into the universal . . .

But what is chastity—*satitva*?[30]

Shekhar, like always, sought solace in books. He had seen a book, *What All Married People Should Know*,[31] and that was the book that he took down and went out of the house to a secluded spot and read. He knew that the book was not for him, but experience had taught him that the things he wanted to learn were always in the books that were 'not for him'.

Knowledge offers neither satisfaction nor produces disgust, but as he was reading Shekhar felt a disgusting satisfaction and a satisfying disgust. He didn't know the reason for either, but this strange throbbing, this wave of electricity, spread from his shoulders through his arms, from his back to his quivering feet, and an involuntary, uncontrollable pulsation or shudder coursed through his organs . . .

He didn't completely understand all the things that he was reading, but he did understand a lot of it, and he slowly picked up speed as he went on reading . . .

One chapter after another—selection; what to look for in a groom; what to look for in a bride; what shortcomings to avoid; choice in marriage—courtship; wedding; abstinence; and then pregnancy . . .

Then, like a bolt of lightning, in one second the book slipped from Shekhar's hand and the ground slipped from under his feet, and it grew dark before his eyes . . .

The whole world now stood exposed to Shekhar. He understood it all now—all of those vague symbols that he had seen, those strange cries that he had heard, the thrills that he had felt, the stings he had endured—all of them came undone. Mother beating her chest, Father's anger; Jinniya's bare legs as she danced; the prostitutes in Amritsar; the cook's sarcasm; Atti's bare back; the verses from the *Gita Govinda*; the eight-month-old newborn; the image of man and nature beneath Chinnamasta; the pleasures of poetry . . . and yes, Saraswati's embarrassment; Shanti's tears; Savitri's silence; Shashi's insistence; Sharda's trembling—all strung together on a single thread, all became clear, all were understood . . . All of them ran the same course towards that despicable act of sin that his mother and father had committed, that Sharda's mother and father had committed, that every mother and father had committed since the beginning of creation. This is what love was, this is why he longed for Sharda—this unmentionable, despicable, unimaginable depravity . . . It was better to die, Shekhar, better for Sharda to die, better if the whole world dies—if this is what happens, then . . .

This was knowledge; this was truth, fact; this was reality; this was knowledge . . .

*

And beyond this was a screen of darkness. Behind that screen there was movement, commotion, struggle, but that was all such an integral part of the individual that speaking of it, thinking about it was the worst kind of indecency . . .

The tide has ebbed underneath the screen. The day that Shekhar was making his preparations to leave for college, he saw a book with this line from Romain Rolland, 'Truth is for those who have the strength to bear it.' On that day he lifted his head and realized that he had crossed an ocean, that he was complete, was free, and was a man.

Part 4

Man and Circumstance

Loneliness was not a new thing for Shekhar. Ever since he could remember he had become accustomed to being lonely all the time, and one could even say that ever since he had come to depend only on himself. But when he got to a big city like Madras, he suddenly felt that he was extremely lonely.

He was fifteen years old. And in those fifteen years he had never really crossed beyond the shadow that his house cast.[1] The core of an individual, the domain of the soul—there Shekhar had always been alone, had never let anyone in, or at a minimum, no one had ever entered it. So his soul had never felt the need to depend on anyone else. But on the other hand, he had never had to worry about what he would eat, what he would wear, how much to spend and how much to save. He had never had to worry about such 'small' details, he had never had to fend for himself and he had never had even a little bit of money in his life to have ever had to exercise any control over it. He had money only twice in his life—once when he had an eight-anna piece which he happily spent on a ten-paisa whistle and once more when his older brother Ishwar had stolen money to buy cigars and he had been asked to hold on to the money for a little while after his brother had been caught stealing . . .

He had, it's true, gone to Lahore for his exams, but he had his tutor there with him and then also because his aunt, Vidyavati, was there, he never really felt as though he was away from home. Vidyavati wasn't a blood relative, but no one had ever felt the difference. She had this ability to make everyone feel like a relation; and still, more than her mother, Shashi's presence made staying there a pleasurable experience for Shekhar—Shashi who was younger than him and not; who never played with him, but who was slowly becoming his playmate . . .

As he sat in the rickshaw nearing his college, this was what Shekhar was thinking about, and in his heart of hearts he was filled with terror. What would college be like? What about the dormitories? What kinds of boys? And the servants and the cook? How would they eat? What about his room? That day the weather was of no help, either—it was depressing, too. It was June and the sky was littered with clouds. There was neither rain nor wind and the heat was oppressive, and . . . and then, Shekhar was coming from mountainous climes . . .

After he enrolled in college, paid his fees, put his things away in his room and, without even making his bed, Shekhar collapsed on to his cot, let out a long sigh of relief and said, 'Uh-oh.'

From another direction came a voice, 'Rama, looks like we've got another new animal.'

Shekhar didn't realize that they were pointing at him, but he heard the footsteps of two or three people coming towards his room and he waited expectantly.

Three boys entered his room. Shekhar was about to give them an annoyed look when he was hit with a flood of questions:

'Where are you from?'

'Where did you finish your schooling?'

'What class are you in?'

'What's your name?'

Had these questions been asked one at a time, Shekhar still wouldn't have responded to them because first of all he didn't like their tone of voice and second, those kinds of questions carried an air of humiliation about them. He didn't say anything, just kept staring at them.

'Don't know how to speak?'

'He's probably a first year, that's why.'

'It's not as though he's royalty; he's just a man, after all.'

'Well, you hit the nail on the head. Man? Then we'll all have to start calling you a "man", too, won't we?'

Shekhar said, 'I'm tired. Please let me rest. You'll get the answers to all of your questions tomorrow.'

'Oh, so that's it.'

'Let's go, boys. Let's let him rest, he's tired. We'll get the answers to all of our questions tomorrow.'

'It's not as though we were twisting your arms. Go ahead and rest.'

'Some manners. Hey, all we did was ask your name—no one's going to eat you alive.'

Angrily, Shekhar said, 'Get out of my room, all of you!'

One of them said, 'Well!' But when they saw the expression on his face they all left. The criticisms that were on the tip of their tongues were only uttered after they left the room. Shekhar tried not to listen to what they were saying and turned his face towards the wall. But he wasn't able to block their voices . . .

Shekhar became quite depressed. He unconsciously began comparing this welcome to the one that he had received in Lahore. Shashi with her big, innocent eyes, that candle held in one hand, those two hands joined together in greeting, her insistent disobedience and many other things . . .

He started feeling as if his parents had banished him from the house because he was a criminal in their eyes . . . because he had been contemptible since the beginning, because he hated his mother because she didn't trust him, because he had stopped loving his father, because . . . don't know . . . what . . .

Whom did he believe in—no one! Those whom he could find worthy of respect, whom he could admire, they had all become vile criminals for him now, ever since he had read in that book how children are made—through such wile, sinful acts . . . His mother and father, brothers and sister . . . he, himself . . . Shashi . . . and yes, Sharda, too—all of them were products of sinful actions . . .

It was wrong, despicable, loathsome, but . . . Then God made women for—then why were women made? Why?

Shekhar thought that since there were already women in the world, one had to accept them. But why were they?

But . . . Then he remembers, although he has faced many hardships because of the existence of women, still had there not been women, then perhaps he would not be alive . . .

But was it necessary that one only look at women with a singular intention, was there only one question to ask them? He had read somewhere that when a robber meets someone new the first thing he thinks about is whether that new person is a friend or a foe. Will he participate in his crime or will he be an obstacle? Was it necessary that women had to be regarded from a robber's point of view—thinking that either she will be a companion in man's specific sinful act or that she will be an enemy, a terror?

Could man not live without women in a world with women . . .

He was so lonely. In a big city like Madras, in the midst of throngs, he found himself alone for the first time, worn down; there was only opposition and enmity in all directions here; all of the men here were his adversaries, and he wanted—he did not know what he wanted, but he didn't want any women present there, but he wanted . . . wanted . . . don't know what . . .

He began to fall into an anxious sleep . . .

He woke with a start at the sound of a knock.

There was a young man at the door, waiting for permission to enter. He had a courteous smile on his face.

Shekhar said, 'Come in.' He began looking around for a place for him to sit.

The young man went and sat on the trunk next to Shekhar and said, 'Don't worry—I'll be fine here. Your name is Ch. Pandit?'

Shekhar, a little surprised, said, 'Yes.' He scrutinized the young man with curiosity.

The young man had a beautiful face, his eyes were big and bright, blue, constantly laughing, his nose was straight and small, lips that were thin, long and playful. He had long curls on his head, which he had styled well.

He had no hair on his face—it didn't seem as if they had even come in yet. From his height and his build he didn't seem to be older than fifteen or sixteen.

Shekhar was about to ask something when the young man said, 'My name is Kumar. What does Ch. stand for in your name?'

'Chandrashekhar.'

'I see! That's my older brother's name, too. What class are you in?'

'I just enrolled as a first-year student.'

'Oh—well then we'll be in the same class. I'm a first-year, too.'

Shekhar was surprised again—because this boy didn't seem to be the least bit anxious or scared, even though he was just starting college as well. He said, 'That's good.'

The boy asked, 'Have you seen the whole dormitory—introduced yourself to people here?'

'No, I haven't done any of it. Plus, I'm exhausted.'

'All right, we'll leave it for now. If you want I can introduce you. I already know everyone.'

Shekhar wanted to ask, 'How?' but he kept his mouth shut. He thought, 'I'd be facing serious problems if it weren't for his help,' and then this, 'I should show him how grateful I am.' He said, 'If you can wait a little bit, I'll go with you. I know it's an inconvenience for you. I would rather talk to you, and that's why I think that I'll wait until later to meet the others. I'm grateful for your kindness, Mr Kumar.'

'It's no big thing. But why are you calling me "Mr Kumar"? If classmates start calling each other "Mister" we're all in trouble. Just call me "Kumar". That's what everyone calls me.'

Shekhar said, 'All right, Kumar.' He paused for a bit and then said, 'You're the first person here who has been courteous to me . . .'

Kumar laughed.

Shekhar's mind filled with gratitude for this young man. All of a sudden he felt that if Kumar hadn't been in Madras, he might have had to drop out of college and run away . . . Kumar hadn't done anything other than speak to him, but still, in the condition that Shekhar was in, he felt as though his happiness and his life depended on that conversation, and that was what Kumar had given him. Before long, he discovered that he was telling Kumar about his home, his homeschooling, his loneliness, his frustrations, everything. His trusting heart had accepted Kumar as though he were a brother—that inconceivable brother whom he didn't have at home, and whose position couldn't be filled in any way by sisters . . .

Kumar introduced Shekhar to everyone. He went with him and made sure he had dinner and then took him back to his room and made Shekhar promise that whenever he needed anything he would call on Kumar. As he promised, Shekhar asked, 'It seems as though you've lived here a while, haven't you?'

'Yes, I have been here since last year.' Embarrassed, he continued, 'This is my second year being a first-year.'

'Really? You seem quite young.'

'I'm sixteen. What about you?'

'I'm fifteen. But I look older than you,' and then he laughed. 'And I can't believe that I'm younger.'

'That's fine—from now on you can be my older brother— what do you say?'

Shekhar was too grateful to say anything. He took Kumar's hand and gently pressed it.

Kumar left. Shekhar closed the door and sat down on his cot and began to think whom should he thank for this random gift, that in a city as big as Madras, on the first day, without searching, he had found a friend—to which mysterious force . . .

'Shekhar, do you want to go see a film?'

Shekhar responded with a note of indifference, 'Who can watch films every single day? We just went the day before yesterday.'

Kumar said, 'You're right. And it's not as though I can afford to go all the time. But the film today was quite good, and so I thought, I should take Shekhar with me—' He let out a long sigh.

There was a feeling of disappointment in that sigh, and it stung Shekhar's heart. He recalled that one day Kumar had told him that his parents were poor and that it was a real struggle for them to cover the cost of his education. Last year, he didn't have the slightest bit of fun—and it was so bad that he wasn't even able to study properly because he was always worried and, as a result, he failed. Ever since that day, Shekhar had resolved that whenever he could, he'd try to keep Kumar happy, and that at a minimum he wouldn't let him feel any financial hardship. His heart melted today when he remembered that and he felt that it was such a wretched existence to have to depend on someone else for your happiness, and to have reminded Kumar of that fact was worse than a wound on the flesh—it was an unpardonable offence. He quickly said, 'Then let's definitely go, Kumar. But don't ever tell me that you—' he stopped and then spoke again, 'It hurts me deeply.'

Kumar said, 'What's wrong in saying something if it's true? But if you don't want me to, I won't.'

Both of them went out.

A month passed.

One day, Shekhar went to Kumar's room and said, 'Kumar, let's go to the ocean today. I'm sick of going to the movies every day.'

Kumar said, 'All right, let's go.'

They sat on the tram and set off.

Once there, they began walking. Beyond the residential areas they came upon a deserted street. It was almost evening—on the path were the long shadows cast by the trees planted along the sides. It seemed as if someone had painted on the golden slopes of the earth made uneven by the dust . . . Shekhar kept walking silently as he looked at the ground, holding Kumar's hand in his. Who knows what he was thinking? Kumar kept looking at him directly as if he wanted to say something, but he would remain silent when he saw the expression on his face.

By the time they could hear the grave roar of the ocean, evening had fallen, the rosy glow of the sky had grown dense until it was tenebrous. They began walking faster and soon reached the water's edge. They sat down on the flat sand under the cover of a large rock and watched the waves. As they watched, the last light of the evening sky was extinguished.

It was peaceful. The wind wasn't stirring. People had also gradually headed back—that part of the shore was quite far from the residential areas. Looking out at the ocean in the darkness Shekhar felt that he was completely alone with Kumar there and that the ancient roar of the ocean had enveloped them . . .

Because despite the fact that the air was still, there was a deep disquiet in the ocean—foamy waves weren't coming in over great distances, but there was a foamless commotion in the distance that was growing . . . Who knew where that vast, deep thunder arose—more powerful than the voice of the waves, and resolute . . .

There was a full moon out, and on the other side of the ocean, in the east, the moon was about to rise—and to steer it through the sky was a lone cloud, standing on the horizon, laced on all sides with a fringe from the moon, and behind it, just about to manifest, the breaking dawn of some unprecedented treasure of beauty . . .

Shekhar was quiet, and Kumar was quiet because of him.

Shekhar was slowly tousling Kumar's long hair by running his fingers through it. It seemed to Shekhar that Kumar's hair returned his touch with a tremble, just like a dog sometimes shows its gratitude to its master's loving touch . . .

When Shekhar spoke, Kumar was startled. 'Look, Kumar, it's as if there's no one else in this world.'

Kumar didn't respond.

Shekhar bunched up Kumar's hair into his fist, pulled gently and said, 'Why aren't you saying anything?' Even though he didn't think it was particularly necessary for Kumar to say anything . . .

Shekhar spoke again, 'That's all right, too. Everyone's world is only as big as what they understand. Because how could we fathom the existence of those things that are outside of our experiences? I know that I have left several worlds behind, and I am certain that there are many ahead of me, but I don't know, the one and the other seems like a complete lie to me—I feel nothing for it. At this moment the boundaries of my world are that rock behind us, that cloud in front and the moon about to rise behind it, me over here and you over there . . .'

He stopped talking. Kumar still hadn't said anything. Shekhar took his hand out of Kumar's hair and pressed it against the ground and became contemplative.

After a little while, he spoke again, 'Kumar, nothing seems real today, like it's all a dream. Still, the dream that I am a part of at this moment, doesn't it seem lovely? Why do I feel as though you are younger than I am, that I am your protector, your guardian angel[2] (protective goddess),[3] and that you depend on me?'

Kumar responded quickly, 'You're right . . . I do depend on you.'

The response was in line with Shekhar's line of thought, but it felt wrong to him. As if there were some hastiness in it, some aversion, some pretence; as if it were dragging him back to a mean reality from the world of his splendid dream. He said, 'Kumar, it doesn't seem as if you've heard a word I've said.'

Kumar was taken aback, 'How did you come to that conclusion? If I hadn't been listening, how would I have answered you?'

Shekhar became even more serious and said, 'Tell me the truth, what are you thinking about right now?'

'I'll tell you—but you can't get upset.'

'Me—upset with you?'

Kumar hesitated over the words, 'The thing is that my mother was really sick and Father spent his entire income on her treatment—it's likely he even took out a loan. They haven't sent anything for me this month and probably won't be able to next month either. I haven't even been able to pay my fees, and college . . . I'll probably have to . . .'

'Why didn't you tell me this before?'

Even more anxiously than before, 'I ask you for help all the time—who else is there who cares for me? But—I worry sometimes about how much—'

Shekhar was offended, 'Am I just anyone to you?' And then, 'How much money do you need?'

Kumar stumbled over his words, 'I don't know exactly. Maybe fifty—maybe some—probably fifty or sixty . . .'

'Will a hundred be enough?'

Shyly, 'What will I do with a hundred . . .'

'It's settled—now let's talk about something else! Everything will be fine tomorrow. Don't ever think such things again.'

'Shekhar, I am your—'

Shekhar knew what the next word was going to be and so he stopped him—'Enough, now quiet! I've already said there will be no more discussion about this!'

They fell into silence again.

Slowly, the moon rose. Shekhar saw as the tiny cloud that had been adorned with a silvery fringe until now suddenly became dark as soon as the moon emerged.

In the moonlight, in the slipperiness of the sand of the nearby beach, scattered stones became visible, like black stamps. Shekhar looked at Kumar, who was looking at the moon.

Shekhar blurted out—and as soon as he spoke he was surprised at what he said—it had taken so little time to find words for his thoughts and make them manifest—'Kumar, if you ever become someone else's, other than mine, I will choke the life out of you.'

Kumar responded with a note of fear in his voice, 'What are you saying, Shekhar!'

Shekhar pulled Kumar towards him and kissed him on the mouth. But at the same time a doubt welled up in his mind—'Why this fear?' He also felt that whatever he was feeling wasn't being returned; like his own reflection on the surface of a lake, which shudders, not with life, but with illusion. But he suppressed both of these doubts immediately . . .

Kumar said, 'Come, let's go now. It's getting so late.'

It took Shekhar some effort to avert his eyes from the ocean, and he said, 'Come.' He didn't want to leave, but when he thought about the thing that he had just said, and the compulsion which had made him say it, he didn't think he could challenge Kumar's request.

They went back to the hostel. Neither of them said a word.

*

Shekhar gave Kumar 100 rupees. A few days later he gave him twenty more. Of these, fifty rupees had been given to him to save—so that he could use them if the need arose. What remained was his monthly allowance. And having disbursed money in this manner, he wrote a letter home asking for more money.

Two days later a reply to his letter arrived, but money did not. Father had written that Shekhar was wasting his money, the money was for necessary expenses, not to be squandered on friends, and—more things like that . . . And also that next time he should think it over seriously and write how much money he needs and—it would be sent to him.

With wounded pride, Shekhar wrote back that whenever he wrote, he took care to think about what he wrote. He needed that amount of money and he didn't need to think it over again. If his father wanted to send the money, he should, otherwise he shouldn't.

That letter got no response—nor did money arrive. Shekhar stopped leaving his room.

Kumar went to him and said, 'Come on, let's go to the circus today.'

Shekhar said, 'I really don't feel like going today.'

'Why, what happened? You don't go out at all any more. What's the matter?'

'Nothing, just because I don't feel like it.'

'You just have to come today. Your mood is just going to get worse sitting here all day. It's even been ten or fifteen days since you've gone to the cinema.'

Shekhar turned away and said, 'I don't have any money. And it doesn't seem likely that any will arrive soon.'

Kumar waited for a moment and then asked, 'What happened?'

'Father wrote that I was spending money on trivial things and that he wasn't going to send that much money. I wrote back that if he was going to send a lesser amount then he shouldn't send any at all. That's all.'

The two were quiet for a while. Then Kumar got up and said, 'I'm going now. I have something—'

'Come on, sit down! I can't concentrate. Let's just sit and talk this evening. Or let's go to the ocean.'

'No, I just remembered, I have something important to take care of. It's good that we didn't go to the circus, otherwise—' He said it as he was leaving the room.

Shekhar was lying on his back, staring up at the ceiling.

What is poverty? What is wealth? Why is it that one man who is looking for entertainment cannot go to the cinema or the circus, and why is it that another man prevents him from going despite having the ability to allow him to go?

But was entertainment just cinema and theatre? Could a person not be happy without going to those places? There had been days before when he didn't go to the cinema—was he not entertained then? When he had gone to Lahore for his exams, he'd get bored studying all day and want some entertainment, but it was enough for him if Shashi walked by him without saying anything and he could tease her by saying 'Sisterji?' and if not even that, just to be able to hear her laugh from a distance . . . Why couldn't he do that any more?

Had Kumar been there, perhaps he wouldn't have thought such things. Kumar's closeness, Kumar's conversation, Kumar's laughter—all of that would be enough for him . . .

But for Kumar?

But for Shashi?

What is this unexpected accident of love which makes a man dependent on someone else like this, but at the same time also gives him strength, also becomes his protector . . . And what was that unexpected accident which was greater than love, a force greater than love, which made love possible, which created new circumstance, in which love could exist, in which two souls could meet?

But were he and Kumar one? Wasn't there an emptiness in that oneness, somewhere deep down? Did they want the same thing? Did they desire in the same way? Did—

But was it necessary in love for any two people to be sold by one another's own hands and become each other's slave? Was there no love without servitude?

And if so, why was there this condition that love had to exist between two individuals? Was it necessary that one had to have someone to love—was it impossible to separate the feeling of love from some crude, isolated object? Was it necessary that the sentence 'I am in love' was unerringly followed by the question 'With whom?' and did that 'whom' have to be only one? Couldn't all humanity be loved, all love be loved?

He had always brooded; he had never tried to step outside of himself, embrace life, make the world his own, he had never tried making himself the world's. He kept asking for love; he had never known how to give love . . .

But the condition that he found himself in at this moment, was it his fault, or Kumar's, or someone else's? Was the desertion that he was feeling at that moment a result of his incapacity to love or the result of his inability to receive it?

A verse of poetry danced in Shekhar's mind. He got up and started writing:

O Man, O you formless, dense feeling of which I am a part, I want to forget myself, forget my loves, and become only yours; I love you; I love the desire to love you and my ability to . . . O you, give me the strength that I might love only you and that I might endure your love . . .

That night, Shekhar went downstairs to eat dinner and asked the hostel peon, 'Hasn't Kumar come?'

'Now? No, he has gone to the circus.'

'With whom?'

'With Krishnamurthy.'

Shekhar went back upstairs without eating dinner. He sat on the windowsill in his room and watched the various tramcars racing outside, listened to their gears, the horns of the motorcars and the screams of the *rickshaw-wallahs*, but when he found himself unable to observe, hear or understand anything, he began repeating the verse he had written like a meaningless rant—'O you, give me the strength that I might love only you and that I might endure your love . . .'

*

For two days, Shekhar didn't go to class. He sat in his room, waiting for Kumar to come to him and ask for his forgiveness, or at least come clean to him, but Kumar never came.

On the third day, a very bored Shekhar emerged from his room. He had decided that he would go sit by the ocean and clear his muddled head. He wasn't even thinking about Kumar—nor did he have any desire to enter his room and see him.

As he was descending the stairs, he heard two or three voices laughing from a room and when he recognized Kumar's voice among them he stopped in his tracks.

One voice—'Shekhar doesn't leave his room these days. What's the matter?'

'Haven't you heard? His father's cut him off,' Kumar spoke.

'Then it's probably for the best,' and then a loud guffaw.

'That's why Krishnamurthy's so lucky these days, right, Kumar?' and then another chortle.

Then Kumar's voice, 'Come on, man, don't blather on like a fool. Shekhar was an idiot.'

Shekhar leaned on the railing for support as he slowly descended the stairs. At the bottom, he composed a message and gave it to the servant, 'Please give this to Kumar—I'll be waiting here.'

The message read, 'It's true, I am an idiot and a fool. But do you know which day I became a fool? I said to you on the ocean shore, "Kumar, if you ever become someone else's, other than mine, I will choke the life out of you." I was a fool for not understanding my own words . . . Insects belong to no one.'

It didn't take long for Kumar to show up and say, 'What's the meaning of this, Shekhar?'

'Meaning? Didn't I make myself clear enough?'

'I'm your debtor, and it's because of the fact you have that power over me that you've insulted me so deeply, isn't it? If I—'

Shekhar was enraged, 'Debtor?' But he immediately became calm and said, 'It's all right. I won't take offence if this is the only thing that your soul-for-sale can come up with.'

He turned around and walked towards the edge of the ocean in long strides.

It was dark, the sky was thick with clouds. The beach was deserted, desolate. The air was completely still. And the ocean, too, was uncommonly still, still and hushed, although it seemed as though a light were burning somewhere inside it, or veiled lightning were dancing—the early stages of an explosion . . .

Shekhar felt that had the ocean appeared any other way to him, he wouldn't have been able to stay at the water's edge for even a second . . .

*

When Shekhar awoke from that sleep, he began to hear all manner of things being said about him throughout the hostel—a give and take of opinions.

He was a Brahmin, moreover his name was Chandrashekhar Pandit, but where was his topknot? Where was his sacred thread? When and where did he perform his prayers? He may very well have received God's greatest gift—being one of the twice-born— but he had forsaken it with his conduct, he was fallen . . .

The hostel where Shekhar lived was for Brahmins. That's why Shekhar, according to his father's wishes, lived there. Before now, no one had even raised any questions about his Brahmin-hood. Several students lived according to the rules set for Brahmins and practised the rituals, but on the inside, they didn't really have much respect for them. Their dining hall was enclosed on all sides so that their meals wouldn't be polluted by the 'sinful glance' of a passer-by—so that it wouldn't become polluted by being looked at by members of the lower castes. If ever that happened, they treated their food as though it had become as disgusting as if a dog had partaken of it. Although sometimes a dog would wander into the dining hall and it was considered sufficient if it was chased away with a, 'Get!'

It didn't take Shekhar long to figure out the source of these criticisms. But he never had the desire to talk to Kumar or even to look at him. He realized that all the students were looking at him as if he were some alien creature, and it seemed to him that they were all thinking to themselves about what Shekhar would be in his next life—a dog, a crow, an insect—as if they felt pity for his fate. Sensing their 'pity' enraged him, and he thought, 'Even if I go to hell, what's it to them?'

But their 'pity' was never strong enough that they were moved by thoughts of his damnation to forget their future heaven. They had all decided that they wouldn't eat with Shekhar, and one day Shekhar learned that the principal had received a petition from all of the students, which demanded that separate arrangements be made for Shekhar's meals, otherwise they would be forced to leave the hostel.

They also told the people who ran the mess that until they had reached an agreement, Shekhar should be seated apart from the rest.

Shekhar found all of this completely unacceptable. But he didn't want to drag the staff at the mess into this argument; so, he decided that until some kind of agreement was worked out, he would go and eat at a restaurant.

A decision had been made. The principal had decided that the hostel was for Brahmins, and that determinations of Brahmin-hood could only be made by members of one's own clan, since there were a variety of traditions amongst Brahmins; Shekhar had been born a Brahmin and so he would remain there and continue to eat there, and no one could force him to leave.

Shekhar won. The other boys also saw no benefit in continuing the fight. The matter ended there—though the boys never forgave Shekhar his victory, and they never lost an opportunity to remind him that irrespective of what the principal said, they didn't consider him a Brahmin.

This victory gave Shekhar no satisfaction—not even when he thought about it as a victory over Kumar. It no longer meant anything to declare victory over him. He asked for a week off from college, and he took off to explore Malabar. He had money since he had asked his father for forgiveness after the fight with Kumar.

Malabar is an incredibly beautiful region, but Shekhar hadn't gone there to observe the beauty. In college, the stories he had read about untouchability in Malabar—these things were so unbelievable to him that he couldn't consider them to be anything other than stories—were the things that drew him there. The untouchables there—the fifth or the outcastes—could not come too close to a Brahmin—they had to stay a few yards away; there were separate roads for the Brahmins on which the outcastes couldn't walk; the outcastes had to cross the river in a boat because the bridges over the water were reserved for the upper castes; untouchables couldn't buy land next to a Brahmin's; and if ever a Brahmin and an outcaste were to cross paths, the outcaste had to announce himself as an outcaste so that his shadow didn't inadvertently fall on the Brahmin . . . He had heard all of these things, but even after he heard them he couldn't believe them. Since the fight at college had been about the question of his untouchability, after he had won he wanted to go to Malabar to see what it was like there.

When he got there, he settled in at a mission run by the Arya Samaj. He spent some time waiting to find a worker at the mission so that he could talk to them, but all of them had gone out. Finally, when he saw that the rain that had been falling all day had stopped for a while, he quickly changed his clothes, put on a common Madrasi outfit and went out walking barefoot.

Evening had fallen. Aimlessly wandering, Shekhar found himself on a deserted road and was trying to decide which way would be the most convenient to go. The roads for the most part had turned to slush—in some places, they were completely submerged under water, and some of the roads that went into the paddy fields had been lost to the waters that flowed over the embankments. Shekhar hung his head and walked on, deep in thought.

It was twilight, and the reflection of the now hazy sky sparkled in the waters. A coppery red spread out over the foliage of the trees, and over the paddy fields a melodious melancholy slowly condensed like drops of dew. Everything was completely still. The birds were crying out and the frogs croaked interminably in their sharp, cracking voices. It wasn't completely silent, but there was a profound stillness.

Shekhar got off the muddy road he was on and moved on to another path. It was drier—and so Shekhar's feet had turned towards it on their own—but he wasn't sure if this was the shorter way back to where he was staying. Water flowed on both sides of the path.

His concentration was broken by the sounds of someone groaning. He stopped to listen closely and discern where the voice was coming from. A moment later, he heard the groaning again, and Shekhar went over to a bush that covered the small stream flowing on one side of the path and looked: there was a heap of flesh and blood, half covered with a dirty red sari, that once was perhaps a woman—and there was still life in that heap, and it could still feel pain . . .

For just a second, but for many reasons, one of which was the fact that the heap of flesh was a woman, Shekhar hesitated. Then, he somehow got that body on his back and turned around and, going from one path to the next, carried it all the way back to the mission. There the body was treated and bandaged, but by dawn, she was dead. The people at the mission made preparations to cremate her—she was an untouchable.

The police were notified. But Shekhar didn't stay; he packed up his things and immediately left for Madras—he began to feel it was impossible to stay there for even a second longer . . .

On the train, he read in the newspaper that after the body had been examined, it was announced that 'Death was the result of a blow from a blunt instrument; no reason could be found for the murder.' But there was also this bit of reporting, that the body had been found on a 'segregated' road, and that the woman was an untouchable.

Shekhar recalled how that woman's body, her clothes, were dripping with blood and mud—and a shiver ran through his body . . .

She was an untouchable, and he was a Brahmin, and he had been bathed in her blood . . . And her killers had been Brahmins who had probably gone up to her themselves and beaten her to death with stones so that they could avoid being polluted by her coming too close to them . . . Brahmin . . . Shekhar, too, was a Brahmin . . . and untouchable . . . The kind of untouchable that Shekhar had carried on his shoulders . . . And her blood . . .

When he got back to the hostel, Shekhar packed all of his things, called for a rickshaw, loaded his things into it and told the rickshaw-driver where to take his things while he got on to a tram to go to another hostel—one for untouchables, where all of the workers were untouchables as well. At first, everyone there looked at him with suspicion, but quickly the day came when Shekhar knew that all his friends and companions and comrades were untouchables, his brothers were untouchables . . .

And also, the community that he was supposed to be a part of considered him an untouchable, and it couldn't stand the fact that he had an identity separate from it . . .

*

'They say that everything will change eventually; that eventually ignorance will fall away, that this fog that has descended over our souls will dissipate. They say a lot of things, but they are all sitting on their hands, and eons pass in waiting, and nothing happens. The fog can be lifted, the veil, too, can be lifted, but walls can't be lifted, they have to be torn down, they have to be made to fall, otherwise they don't go away . . .'

That was Shekhar speaking. He was naturally a quiet person, but there was something inside him that wouldn't let him stay quiet, something that ceaselessly stabbed at his reluctance and compelled him . . .

Shekhar has begun making friends among these 'untouchables'. And he allows them to see the compulsion inside him, every change in its veils. He's got a few boys together and created a committee, which doesn't have a name or rules but which always convenes in his room, in which ideas and exchanges, tastes, dispositions and feelings are constantly being debated . . .

Shekhar isn't their leader—he doesn't consider himself to be, nor do they—but somehow leadership seems to emanate from him—this formless committee that only runs because of Shekhar.

*

In the middle of the flat wasteland, which the students in the hostel call their 'playground', stands the untouchables' hostel, and four boys are lying on the cement floor of the roof without spreading anything out under them. These are the cadres of Shekhar's nameless committee. All that 'cadre' means in this instance is that all four of them have an inner disquiet, they are awakening and are naturally concerned as they look around them. There are two or three other members of the committee who don't have the tumult, the rapids coursing inside them; for them, the waves only rise up when someone else's hand stirs them, or if someone from afar throws a rock into the peaceful tranquillity that normally reigns over them . . .

Besides Shekhar, the others are Sadashiv, Raghavan and Devadas. Of them, Sadashiv was the shortest in stature but in intellect, he was the brightest. On top of his usually unbuttoned tennis collar was his thin neck, and on account of his tousled hair on top of it, his looking-bigger-than-normal head casts a shadow over his peaceful, egg-shaped face, whose small but usually opened-quite-wide eyes were filled with a feeling of wise compassion, as if his eyes were saying, 'I don't want to trouble you, I just want to take a closer look to understand you'—and when he looked at all of this together, Shekhar recalled a picture of Shelley, so he started calling him 'Shelley'. The name really embarrassed Sadashiv, he felt it was a joke about his self-abnegating love of nature—and that's why the name became permanent.

Raghavan and Devadas were different. They both came from cities in the Madras Presidency, and the influence of the cities on them was considerable. Raghavan's eyes sparkled like flighty fish and Devadas's eyes were always on the lookout for trouble. There was no poison there, all there was was a feeling of love for the human race, but Devadas's love wasn't naturally of that kind, which living in isolation could motivate the self out of its proud silence; he found that kind of 'sentimentalism'[4] obnoxious. He preferred hiding his love in constant fidgeting, conversation, laughing and joking. Whenever someone would accuse him of 'heartlessness' he would laugh and say, 'Brother, there's one kind of love that prostrates itself across a road and another kind which is always tickling and pinching people as it goes. I don't have the first kind of love in me.' This wasn't an excuse; there was truthfulness in it. A natural fault—or a virtue—prevented him from speaking the truth plainly.

Because of his shy yet sharp intellect and because of his love of the generous beauty which grew in the vast greens and blues of Travancore, Sadashiv was quite close to Shekhar. Still, Shekhar knew that life wasn't complete without Devadas and Raghavan, and it made him happy that they were in his committee, too, because the objective of the committee was to find completeness in life.

Lying on the rooftop, Shekhar would intermittently look over at Sadashiv to make sure he wasn't lost in the sunset. He said—'In that book by Stevenson, there's a story of four reformers who sit down to think about how they will change the world. One of them explains all that is wrong about society and says that we should destroy society altogether. The second one revises the ideas of the first and argues that societies are ruined when religion becomes orthodox, religion was the source of all the problems and that was what had to be done away with. The third says that religion was just a set of governing principles set up by culture, and if the culture was wrong then how could the religion it set up be right, and that's why culture was the problem. Ultimately, they come to this conclusion: wherever humans tried to move forward they found culture already there, and so the human race was the original criminal and it had to be destroyed completely! The conclusion makes perfect sense on its own terms. Let's destroy the human race! Then we wouldn't be here discussing reform, nor will Sadashiv lose himself in the setting sun and insult me, nor—'

Sadashiv said, as if to demonstrate his attentiveness, 'Nor will Shekhar be able to abuse someone whose attention he thinks has drifted elsewhere.'

Everyone laughed. Shekhar started again, 'I think that there's a danger in not undertaking a fundamental change like this. I'm not saying that one should only reform superficially—that's foolishness, too. If there's going to be a change, it has to start at the root, but only in those places where the problem can be clearly discerned, not one that only comes to light through reason.'

Raghavan said, 'For instance?'

'Look at that story. Religion is a set of governing principles set up by culture, and so the problems of religion are born in culture, and so culture is the problem. All of this is just a juggling act of the power of reason. If we want to see the problems in culture, then we have to look closely at culture. We can't prove them from afar like this. Otherwise, there isn't anything that's good—all there is are problems, and our restlessness, too, is an emotion that is born out of that problem, that if humans are bad how can they think good things? If you want to get rid of the darkness, then all you can do is find a light; you can't rid the darkness of its dark.'

Sadashiv interrupted him to say, 'But, Shekhar, your thinking is also dangerous. From a political point of view, you are advocating establishing a principle of violence. If we do what you're suggesting, all we will do is destroy real problems, in a theatre of destruction, and according to you, it's foolish to find a way to stop these problems from developing in the first place.'

'Umm, no. Up to a point, what you are saying is right. I don't think of destruction as a bad thing, nor do I think of it as violence.

'It's only violence when the impetus is violent, when there's an attempt to do harm. Murder committed for love is not violence, provided that love is not personal but for all of creation. But it's wrong to say that this doesn't contain room to stop these problems from developing. What I am saying is that attempts to solve these problems can only happen when you understand what the problem is. Which is to say, only when it appears right in front of you will you be able to try to stop it. Your self-preservation instinct will rise with a primitive aggression. Because without that, what will you save yourself from? Organizing a defence against an unknown nothing is like a sword fight with shadows.'

'Hmm, that sounds right. But the first point still doesn't sit well. Do you think that in matters of love it's so difficult for people to deceive themselves? There are people who visit prostitutes in the name of keeping society pure. A man who doesn't go to visit prostitutes could perhaps say with an objective[5] perspective that prostitutes are the invisible mechanisms of social purification. But what right does a man who can be called a slave to his subjective[6] desires have to look at society with an objective perspective? But there are still people who try to convince themselves of this fact and in your estimation these people are blameless. Love and harm—who could possibly adjudicate between personal love and world welfare?' Sadashiv kept talking softly and slowly and was looking out towards the setting sun as if he were asking it his question.

Raghavan said approvingly, 'Hmm, that is the question.'[7]

Shekhar began talking as if he were thinking about something, 'But there shouldn't be a difference between personal welfare and world welfare . . .'

Sadashiv sat down and said, 'That's the same mistake as before—there is no difference only when it's looked at with an objective, universal perspective. But when the observer is a lone individual, and the question is about his welfare, how could he possibly take such a broad view of the matter?'

Devadas said, 'It seems to me that you all are no better than the reformers in that story. All of this arguing that you people are doing may very well increase your self-respect, but it doesn't amount to anything. It is personal welfare, not world welfare, no matter what perspective you take. World welfare takes action. A hundred mistakes made in the course of activity are better than one good deed done by inactivity, because in the course of activity there are opportunities to correct your mistakes, while inactivity can't even establish its own virtues anywhere. So if you want to do something and agitate, set up a programme. If you want to take advantage of this entire argument and use it for world welfare, then don't think of any programme as final and incontrovertible. Humans have a right to uncertainty, but if it doesn't give rise to generosity, it also becomes the curse of humanity.

'That's what Shekhar is always shouting out. Act when there is necessity. Create a programme and make the first project on the list generosity, because that inspires everything else. The oracle has spoken.'[8]

Devadas's words brought the discussion down to earth, where it could wash its hands and feet not in the brackish waters of raw logic but in the sweet nectar of activity. The four reformers got up and moved in close together. Shekhar said, 'All right, tell me, what shall we do first?'

Ultimately, they came to the conclusion that the primary work could only be the awakening of the youth, giving birth to a seriousness within them and providing a purpose to their lives. They realized that the kind of fundamental transformation they sought would have to be of that type and they would definitely avoid any acts of violence. And with Shekhar's love of literature, Sadashiv's love of art, Raghavan's love of science and Devadas's love of history they also concluded that constancy in life doesn't make its purpose stronger, but rather proves deadly for it, just as a wall built on a single brick can never be stable. In order for one's purpose to be firm, for one's activity to be lasting, it's necessary for life to find a piece of earth and plant roots, like a banyan tree, with tongues hanging down in every direction, lapping up sustenance and strength from the earth. They began studying all of these issues seriously and started expounding their ideas to others.

But for Shekhar, this steadily progressing line of work became a burden. Who knows why his disposition was such that he was never happy when he only had a reasonable quantity of work. He wanted so much work, so much work that he wouldn't be able to lift his head, so that a moment's rest could wreck his work, so much that the thoughts, doubts and impossible dreams that shook him to his core, that all of these would wilt and die for lack of opportunity . . . Even from the experience of his meagre sixteen-year-old life he could feel that his pride, his impatient, youthful estimation of his abilities was in reality the mark of his failure, because he wanted faith—and the questions that welled up inside him were there so that they would vanish, would be resolved, when he reached somewhere. The entire course of his life was so that he could reach that 'somewhere' . . . He felt as if the society's programme from its very inception began as if they had already arrived somewhere, and he couldn't bear the idea that the dream of going beyond that point was impossible! One day he set out by himself and the first place he went to was the colony of untouchables about a mile away from the hostel. When he got there he saw that a Hindu middle school had been built with brick and mortar at its entrance, while the other homes were either half or completely made of mud, and next to them and in between them flowed an open sewer.

Evening was about to fall. The water in the sewer glowed like old brass. Except for the stench, it would have been difficult to call the water dirty at that moment. As he stood at its edge, Shekhar suddenly realized that he was alone; there were no children nearby. It was something of a shock to him that there were no children playing outdoors in the evening. Why weren't they outside? And especially because in that untouchable colony no matter where 'inside' was, it was no place for children.

As he pondered new directions appeared to him, as if one more wall was crumbling under his accumulated strength. He remembered the stories from the Bible about Jesus's messenger,

John the Baptist—that young man with those wild eyes, coarse, tousled hair and hardened body clad in deer skin stood in a place just like this and called, 'Come! Let me baptize you with the water of life!' And in a similar rust-stained twilight the members of the rejected lower castes of humanity turned a deaf ear towards him, perhaps said he was crazy, but upon hearing his interminable caterwauling probably came out of their houses to see what this water of life business was all about . . .

Shekhar was pleased with the fact that he had remembered that incident here because what was the water of life anyway? Ganga, Yamuna, Godavari, Krishna, Narmada—the waters of all of these rivers had become lifeless from being washed over and over with religion and devotion. Life, if ancient, life was anywhere it was in an open sewer like this in which the boat of society had been flowing down obliviously from time immemorial, through this colony of untouchables . . . The waters of those so-called 'sin-purifying' rivers were just as dead as the erudition of the pundits; that was why they were so useful for putting out funeral pyres, washing away the remains of the dead . . .

It was now clear to Shekhar that within a week he would open a school for the untouchable children in that neighbourhood and teach them himself. He hadn't worked out yet how the arrangements would be made or where the books would come from or the rest. Having come to a decision he no longer felt the need to wander any farther; he went straight back to the hostel.

On the way, he spotted a middle school building and immediately cried out, 'Guard!'

Exactly five days later, Shekhar's night school opened in that very middle school building. The Hindu patrons of that middle school gave permission for untouchable classes in two of the rooms on the condition that the watchman was given three rupees a month—so that he could get up early and do the extra work of cleaning, sweeping and sprinkling water in those rooms so that the taint of the dirty children would not rub off on the regular students.

There were only two books, both of which were picture books. There were two instructors—Shekhar and Sadashiv. The blackboard was used to teach the alphabet; all other instruction was done orally or through many kinds of games. There were seven students.

*

Those people whose minds are restless, who always enjoy battling new problems all the time, the first problem that seems to arise for them is always the same—the problem of suffering. The first revelation of the world is always a revelation of its afflicted form.

The next problem that comes up is also always the same— the first problem is a sort of preamble for it—and that problem is the condition of women. The second revelation of the world is a revelation of the idol of woman.

Shekhar's mind was very soon standing face-to-face with this second problem.

Shekhar had gone home for the week-long holiday during Dussehra and was returning. In the atmosphere created by the reverberating din of four or five Dravidian mothers in a railway car crammed with throngs of Madrasis, Shekhar's mind was absorbed with matters concerning his night school, his young and adult students and their textbooks. There were now twenty-five students among whom were several adults who could already read. The small gauged railroad engine groaned as it moved forward, struggling to carry the weight of its load. The undulations of its progress comforted Shekhar's thoughts and he could rise above the commotion that had descended around him. Whenever the train stopped, he would stop thinking for a while and watch the crowds getting on and off.

The train stopped at a major station, and Shekhar saw that behind the throngs of men getting on the train through the doors and windows was a woman who was watching the crowd helplessly. She has two bags in each hand, and a coolie stands behind her with a trunk and some bedding. The woman occasionally steels herself to move forward, but then stops. Sometimes she looks over at another car with an even greater crowd and it is now time for the train to leave. The guard has sounded the first whistle, too.

Shekhar got up, stood next to the window and said, 'Here, give me your luggage.' He pulled the bag inside and took the trunk from the coolie and put it on the floor. Then just before the train started moving he went to the door and opened it and pushed the crowd aside and said, 'Please, this way.'

Nervous about being thanked, Shekhar gestured towards his seat and said, 'You can sit there.'

'No, you took great trouble to get me on to the train, that's more than enough. It would be ill-mannered to take your seat after that.'

'I will be fine,' Shekhar said as he sat down on the trunk and bedding and looked out the window so that the woman would see that his attention was in the opposite direction and would sit down on her own.

He guessed right. She sat down. Shekhar turned around to look in her direction and she was about to offer her thanks, but Shekhar immediately turned around as if he hadn't looked over there and she became quiet. After a while, she took out a book and began reading. Shekhar drifted into his thoughts about his school.

But he was suddenly startled. At some distance stood an Anglo-Indian whom Shekhar had stopped from taking the seat next to his because he had come on board the train by pushing a few men out of the way and had even cursed at one. He was now muttering to himself on seeing that woman sitting there. He was saying something in his vulgar British imperialist language about Shekhar having given up his seat. Shekhar saw that the woman turned bright red on hearing that man's mutterings but she hid behind her book and pretended not to hear.

Shekhar also utilized the White imperialist (though a very mild version) language and said as he got up, 'Shut up, you cad!'⁹

It was fuel to the fire. The Anglo-Indian began cursing even more. Shekhar moved towards him and said, 'So you'll have to be made to shut up,' and punched him very hard on the left side of his jaw. He fought back but Shekhar pulled him towards his chest and landed a second punch on his chin which had the effect of making him stare up at the ceiling of the car, and then his back collided with the back of his seat and he collapsed with a thud and didn't get up for a while.

The train slowed; the police arrived when they heard the commotion at the station. But the Punjabi sub-inspector at the station knew Shekhar; he heard the narrative of what happened and said, 'You did the right thing, should have landed a couple more on the scoundrel.' He then took the white man off the train and let the train go on its way.

That should have been the end of the story, but this is actually where the problem began. Shekhar now had a place to sit down, and he even got to know the woman well enough that she told him her name and also told him that she was a teacher in some school, and Shekhar told her that he lived nearby. Then the two fell silent and the schoolteacher began reading again. Shekhar wanted to get lost in his thoughts again but he now realized that people were looking at him with strange, terrified eyes, that he was being assessed in multiple languages, in hushed voices. One of them said that he was Punjabi (because he was dressed as a Madrasi, his Punjabi-ness hadn't been detected until now) and in all that staring and assessing no one had been able to see that Shekhar had upheld common decency in seating that woman on the train and ending the ravings of that white man.

In the eyes of some he was a lustful young man who wanted to use this small matter as a pretext to get closer to that woman; for others he was a stupid youth who would remain trapped in the clutches of modern, educated and immoral women; for others, Shekhar and that women were both immoral and wanted to mask their shameless crimes with this deceitful action . . . All of this was not something that was heard, but their gestures—their glances and their whispers—said it for them. They weren't saying it for

Shekhar's benefit; they were trying to conceal their conversation from him and so it stung Shekhar even more . . .

Shekhar turned away and put his head out the window. The wind from the cloud-covered mountains whirred past his overheated ears and he began to wonder about what was wrong. He had never experienced such deep moral suspicion before. He had seen sin in many places, committed it, too, but the terrible doubt—such certain suspicion—that sin was the root of all of man's desires was never something he had held in his heart. He didn't understand how someone could go on living, how anyone could have peace when worms were writhing around in the vessels around his heart . . . The relationship between man and woman—not the relationship between individuals but between men in general and women in general—appeared before Shekhar for the first time as a form of brutal suspicion; today he realized that even more important than the problem of the suffering in the world was the problem of the suspicion in the world, this very serious matter which humanity has focused on that one individual who Shekhar had until now only understood as being a support—woman! And this thought began choking him as if worms were crawling into his nostrils, his lungs . . .

In his committee, Shekhar's views began slowly acquiring clarity. As important as it was to nurture feelings of grave dissatisfaction and a desire for change in young men, it was equally important to nurture them in women. The self-satisfaction of this male-centred civilization would need to be broken, the falsity of its claims to propriety would have to be exposed, so that we can find the way forward. This mistrust of womankind, this collective conspiracy to view only the feminine as sinful, would have to be destroyed. Crazed by the intoxication of their own virility, our philosophers and thinkers say that understanding women as driven by sin is a relic from the Romantic[10] period; when we start losing confidence in old conventions, old religions, old ways of thinking, old divine laws, the rationale for our new ways of thinking seem insufficient and false, the first time we realize that our previously well-ordered world contains something chaotic, even out of place, that's when we call it a sin; but when we also think of it as sweet, when it draws us to it, we become Romantic and hide the impropriety of our attraction.

We say that beauty is attractive. It shackles us, turns us into slaves of fate and pushes us into an abyss. And if woman isn't the best, the pinnacle, the most powerful symbol of beauty then what is? This is why woman is the root of sinful thought, is a great delusion, is fallen, and in this way we make ourselves content. And we erect the walls of collective mistrust. We will have to fell those walls.

It was Shekhar speaking. Sadashiv occasionally offers praise, but otherwise remains silent. Shekhar understands his silence to be agreement. Devadas laughs but he still diligently performs whatever task is assigned to him. It's only Raghavan whose enthusiasm wanes. As the objectives of the society grow in number, so do the number of its members since they want to attach their dinghies to the steamboat of an extremely clear principle and be dragged along to cross the realm of society. But it didn't seem as if this made any substantial improvement in their work. Rather their detractors now had an easy time finding something that they could oppose.

Still, the steamboat continues to move along, cutting through all kinds of snares and nets, billowing plumes of dark smoke, and its captain, Shekhar, considers himself lucky to have a first mate like Sadashiv.

One day, all of a sudden, Shekhar and his friends had their naming ceremony, 'Antigonon Club'. This is what happened . . .

After much debate, the society came to the decision that their youth group would relate to women in the same way one would relate to a respected guest—even if they were strangers, they would still be respected, would receive help in times of trouble, would get protection in times of danger, and even after all of that they would still be independent and would in no way feel obligated to men. As for himself, Shekhar had also decided not to marry, wouldn't even think about the matter. It was only after coming to that decision that he called for a smallish meeting under a vine that grew on one side of the hostel and that's where he shared his views. And by the time he got to explaining about remaining unmarried and maintaining an emotional distance from women the audience had got bored and began leaving in ones and twos.

The only ones who stayed were his three friends. Shekhar was still going on:

'Look, in our literature, in stories, in novels, in plays, on stage and screen, everywhere you will find that writers create false models of ethics—girls who are enduring the torments of hell will give lengthy, eloquent speeches[11] to demonstrate that they are dying in order to fulfil their marital vows because marriage is their greatest resource, their most important duty, for which hundreds have died, hundreds have performed sati[12] or *jauhar*[13] and immolated themselves, hundreds have been crushed under the feet of elephants[14] . . . A mirage created by men for male spectators! Drunk on his own vaunted image and self-importance, the stupid bull of a man watches, listens, reads and becomes heady . . . why? Because what after all are the marital obligations of the heroine of the story or the play? It's another kind of slavery, even if it is a slavery that is voluntarily accepted, by which she subordinates herself to her husband, or rather to the spectator, to all mankind, and so to an infinite number of spectators! Because by virtue of being a man, the spectator is vicariously[15] the husband, and the disgusting spectacle of the heroine's cruel suffering is all for him, confirming the arrogance of his own personality . . .

'This is ruination, it's the greatest of sins. It is a vast conspiracy to manufacture an original sin and perpetuate it—in order to maintain the privileges of men.'

Sadashiv interrupted, but not out of disagreement, 'But women accept this fact, after all.'

'We beat them into acceptance. That's why women's literature doesn't have the same power. When they write, they do so by chaining themselves to the models set by men, and that's why their prose is always false and lifeless, even when beautiful—like flowers made from paper.'

'But—' Sadashiv started but trailed off into thought.

Devadas said, 'Hmm, your ideas will make life impossible. How are we going to accomplish anything if we try to be idealistic all the time and in everything we do? And what will happen if some woman asks you something? You won't even be able to give her an answer since you'll be stuck thinking about whether or not there's any male chauvinism in your response! I promise you, you'll make a fool of yourself in no time. You won't be able to move.'

Shekhar clutched the vine in his hand. A faint smile crossed his lips as he heard what Devadas said, and then he became serious and said, 'So why should I be afraid of turning into a fool? If you're going to do anything, you'll have to be a fool at some point. Rather I want to be able to be proud of that fact—to wear my embarrassment like this vine bears these red flowers.'

As he finished speaking, he broke off a bunch of flowers and placed them in the buttonhole of silently sitting Raghavan.

In jest, the others also plucked some flowers and fixed them to their buttonholes. The meeting broke up in laughter. The four of them went back to the hostel, when someone spied the flowers of the antigonon vine and said, 'Here comes the Antigonon Club.'

And in an instant, the name became famous, and accepted, too, and as it was accepted the sting of ridicule contained evaporated.

But it wasn't the case that the ridicule itself evaporated.

The membership of the club began to expand. Shekhar began to suspect that the reasons for this growth were not the club's principles but the club's symbol—that antigonon flower. A number of times he had seen that when you called people out in the name of the nation, no one came, but when you waved the national flag around many people would come to stand underneath it, and there would even be a tricolour badge on the lapel of their coats. At the same time, Shekhar didn't have any means to discriminate between them; there was no trial save a trial by fire, and to his mind, fanning the flames just for a test was such a great sin that he even found it impossible to respect the God Ram.[16]

After much deliberation, Shekhar decided to publish a handwritten newsletter that could disseminate the principles of the club. He asked for articles from the members and began writing himself. He assigned Sadashiv the task of illustration—a red antigonon bouquet for the title page, and whatever he wanted on the inside.

The issue was nearly completed and people were anxiously awaiting it. So much, in fact, that a few of the students in the hostel were plotting to snatch the manuscript from Shekhar's room, since it would be passed among the members of the club for several days before they would get a chance to see it. Shekhar was pleased by the fact that there was such interest in the newsletter, but his happiness was also the source of a problem in his work. The editorial piece wasn't finished, and as the expectation grew so did Shekhar's uncertainty, because he wanted there to be an uproar when people read the editorial—that would silence those who had opposed his club, that would make them swallow their ridicule . . .

Then one day something happened.

Raghavan came back from class and began packing his things. When Shekhar asked, he learned that he was going home on ten days' leave.

'What's the matter? Is everything all right? You're leaving so suddenly.'

'Everything is fine—there's some work I have to do.'

'Well, come on, tell me what it is.'

After much interrogation, Raghavan haltingly replied, 'Look, I'm getting married.'

Shekhar was taken aback, 'Huh?'

After a little while he had composed himself and he began asking questions—when, with whom, how was it decided, why and so on. At first Raghavan was quiet, then he began to explain that his father had got him engaged five or six years ago, that the girl was from a wealthy family, that he had never seen her nor did he want to get married, but his father was pressuring him and that the date had already been decided and so he was going.

'How old are you?'

'I'm old enough—twenty years old. But I still—'

Shekhar couldn't contain his rage any longer. 'Aren't you ashamed of yourself, saying you're old enough? You're twenty years old and you still don't have it in you to say no to a forced marriage! If you don't want to get married, then why don't you say you don't want to get married? Does it really take that much courage to say "I won't do what you ask"? Are you some sacrificial lamb with a rope around your neck being dragged to slaughter? You're a man, you hear me, a man! And you keep talking about how we're going to strengthen the resolve of the youth! You became my comrade in this project—we were going to empower women. You—your wife, how will she ever respect a man who couldn't keep himself from being braided into her tresses? Because I don't consider that a marriage. It's only a marriage when you enter into it of your own free will, choose your own mate, and you are willing to fight the entire world in order to attain her. You—'

Raghavan didn't care for this hectoring. Irritated, he said, 'Talk is cheap. How am I supposed to go against the wishes of my parents! They cared for me, raised me, got me an education. Don't I have any obligations towards them? I can't hurt them like this in their old age. You might think this cowardice, but I don't. I'm not heartless like you are nor do I ever want to be.'

'Obligation! They raised you for twenty years so that you would be the kind of person who could stand on his own feet, be independent, or don't you feel any obligation to that fact? Don't you have obligations towards humanity? Imagine, after twenty years your parents now realize that they haven't raised a man but have raised a sheep. Imagine, after being married for twenty years your wife realizes that the only reason the two of you are together is because your father chained her to a sheep. Were I either the unfortunate husband or wife, I would kill myself. Raghavan, you—'

'Look, stop talking to me. I can't do what you're asking. I can't go against them. You'll see for yourself when you have to face such helplessness.'

'Helplessness. Yes, helplessness. Then why blame your parents? They aren't the ones who are helpless; you are. Hidden inside those clothes is the helplessness of a bleating sheep.'

Shekhar stamped his feet as he stormed out of the room. He went to his room and took out his club's newsletter and put the blank page that had been set aside for the editorial in front of him. He picked up his pen and began writing. Until that point, all of the articles had been first composed, then proofed and then rewritten in excellent penmanship, but at this moment, a furnace was blazing inside Shekhar and his thoughts were boiling over like molten lead, spilling and pouring out, with no need for proofing or refining. There was hardly an opportunity to . . .

> . . . in literature, in society, in art, in life, everywhere it's the same captivating beginning, the same captivating course of events and, in the end, the same deep abyss! The bird of life takes flight. It seems as if it will be able to touch the roof of the heavens, but it suddenly breaks and falls, as if it has been destroyed by a bolt of lightning. We make such spectacular structures, put rocks together one by one and erect beautiful temples, but when we go to apply the plaster, the whole thing becomes the dense dust beneath our feet, is ground into the dirt . . . and why? Because our ideals are built on walls of fear, the foundations of our immense buildings are hollow and, just as it is written in the scriptures, the feet of our gods do not reach the surface of the earth . . . We wrap the decaying bones of society in gaudy, red silk and say—Look, our young people . . .

Shekhar still hadn't finished writing, but as it was dark, he got up to turn on a light when he realized that there were large beads of sweat on his forehead and his nose. He went outside to get a bit of fresh air and began to stroll around on the balcony.

A few other boys were going home. He realized that it was the auspicious time of the year for weddings. It would be a few months before there would be any more. He also realized that none of the young men had ever seen their future wives nor did any of them seem in any rush to get married.

Shekhar took a deep breath and went back inside and started writing again.

. . . Each Indian youth regrets his marriage and every one of them blames his own parents. 'I don't want to, but my parents are pressuring me, and the situation is such that . . . and so on.' What this means is that every Indian youth is his parents' slave. And he wants to escape from enslavement to foreign rule, enslavement to society, to escape from the enslavement to ignorance and nature—but he only talks about escaping the enslavement to the Almighty! Those who have been crammed into the dark well of life and who have put family-shaped lids on top and made those dark wells darker and even more deadly . . .

The ink in the pen had run dry. But the editorial was finished. Having completed its last lines by somehow dragging the drying pen, Shekhar put the pen down. Then for a second, he suddenly felt alone and wanted a companion. He put his head down on the pages of his editorial spread open on the table and drew a long breath. Then he got up, he took some money out of his coat pocket and put it in his wallet and descended the staircase in the hostel. Downstairs, Sadashiv was standing in the middle of a few boys outside the 'common room'.[17] Shekhar went up to him and said, '"Antigonon" has been published. It's there on my table. Take it.' And without paying attention to the curiosity that this news awakened, Shekhar went outside.

He plucked a bunch of flowers from that teeming antigonon vine and then set off towards the ocean.

*

Shekhar now saw that he was a fool, and not just the hostel, but the entire class and the whole college also knew that he was a fool. When he went from one classroom to another in the college, it felt to him as if all the people who passed him were staring at him, and that all of those looks were filled with ridicule. Was it because of the antigonon flower? But many of the boys wore them, and no one laughed at them. It was as if people knew that no matter who wore the antigonon flower in his lapel, it was there because of Shekhar. And everyone knew about the club and also its newsletter. Even a few upperclassmen who came from another college would look at him and smile, and from their smiles Shekhar could discern that they, too, knew that he was a fool. Occasionally someone would startle him with a yell, 'Mr Celibacy!' or 'There goes the guru!'[18] If a few boys were walking together, one would speak loudly enough to be overheard, 'Friends, you're all just sheep! Sheep!' And the rest would start bleating like sheep. Shekhar was filled with hurt and dejection, and he thought to himself, 'What do all of these people have against me? So what if I'm a fool? Or if all of them know it, why do they have to remind me of the fact all the time when I can never forget it?'

And to hide his wounded pride he would walk even taller, as if the antigonon blossom in his lapel were glowing an even brighter red, which is when he realized that perhaps the women who studied in the college were also ridiculing him.

But that fact didn't hurt him; it made him furious. He could understand it if men thought him a fool and laughed at him because he was trying to demolish their deeply held beliefs, but these women? If they didn't value their own liberation couldn't they at least forgive him for his good intentions? Sometimes he would think to himself, 'It's men who have made them so petty and vile that there is no generosity left in them.' But for some reason this conclusion seemed false to him, and he would think, 'Even if men had given birth to the pettiness, this mockery was natural to them . . .' He couldn't bear the fact that there was this inherent cruelty in women, in the women of India in whom he could see hope for the future; nor that . . .

But one day a classmate said to him, 'Man, you've thought it all out.'

Shekhar responded with some surprise, 'What?'

'All of this talk about uplift and reform, not getting married, staying away from women, et cetera . . .'

'What do you mean?'

'Yes, it's a fantastic trick, man.'

'What are you trying to say?' Shekhar asked, somewhat annoyed.

'Please, man! There's me who can't get anyone to even look my way, hoping for any attention, and then there's you, whom everyone is talking about all of the time. All of the girls at this college are on the lookout for you, and the girls in your class are absolutely smitten.'

Shekhar became more irritated and even more taken aback. He said, 'You've been fooled. Please, why would they be interested in someone like me? I don't go anywhere near them, nor do I—'

'Stop it, you're not fooling anyone! Do you think girls like those people who chase after them all the time? They don't give men like that a second thought. They consider such men to be slaves they can buy on the cheap. They prefer men whom they can enjoy hunting while winning them over—with a little danger, a little challenge. No one has ever even seen you anywhere near a girl's shadow, so any girl who is able to make you carry her books on your head and drag you behind her will know that she can seriously rival Queen Christina. You can count on that. You can have your cake and . . .'

Shekhar was instantly enraged. But at the same time he remembered that a few days ago a girl from his class had asked him, 'What are your thoughts on society? It's for an essay I want to write about it—' Shekhar said, 'I'll give you my article, you should read that.' But she insisted that she wanted to hear it from Shekhar.

So Shekhar sat with her in the library and explained his views to her with considerable effort and much trouble, and he gave her several books to read. He had said some very harsh things, but when he was leaving it puzzled him that when he folded his hands in farewell a sweet laugh was offered in return . . . And as he recalled this episode he was filled with a doubt that perhaps what his classmate had said was true. Angrily, he said to him, 'You can keep your filthy thoughts to yourself, understand? I am not interested in this nonsense.' But he was overcome with an anxiety that people were looking neither at his ideas nor at his intentions but merely at him . . .

He tried to avoid the girls in class even more than before. As much as possible, he would show up to class at a time when it was impossible to talk to him, and he would leave through the back door before anyone else. In order to dispel attention, he even stopped wearing antigonon blossoms, but it appeared to him that it had the opposite effect. The first day that he arrived without the flower he looked up and saw—there were three or four bouquets of antigonons hanging from the chalkboard, and someone had also put a few flowers on the girls' bench. The next day, someone had written on the board, 'Where are Shekhar's flowers? Ask the back bench.' The back bench was where the girls sat.

He knew there was no place to hide. Sometimes he wanted to run away, and sometimes he wanted to ask a girl, all of them even, what were they thinking, what did they want from him? Was it true that they really were thinking the things that the boys imagined they were, which were expressed by the words the boys had written? And other times he felt that if this were in fact the case, he would be even more foolish for asking . . .

This never-ending dilemma began eating at him. One day he realized that he was always thinking about those girls for no reason—whenever he asked a question in class or answered one of the professor's questions, he found himself thinking about the effect it was going to have on those girls. The first day he became aware of this fact, he was stunned for some time—Have I really lost? Were the Romantics right, and did women become Fate and unconsciously turn men into slaves and take their lives? He couldn't accept that! He wasn't a slave to Fate; he was its antagonist.

At that very moment he got up and walked out of class, wandered around for two or three hours and ultimately, as if defeated, he set out for the ocean.

But on that day, the ocean didn't console him; so he turned back and went to the night school and started talking to the children.

The exams were approaching and Shekhar's college was going to be closed for the study break, and it had been decided that as soon as the break started the night school would also be closed down and restarted when the college reopened. The children were a little upset about the fast-approaching four-month-long break and so they greeted Shekhar with extra enthusiasm, and for a short time Shekhar was able to forget about womankind and his own misfortunes. Amidst those children, he felt protective, even capable, and he forgot that he was an encumbered, exhausted fool named Shekhar who was being set upon by hunters . . .

*

After wandering for the entire afternoon, bare-chested, at the edge of the ocean, in the cloudless heat, Shekhar returned home in the evening. He had gone for a swim, but when even after swimming his mind remained restless he threw his shirt over his shoulder and began roaming on the baking sand; when his skin had been burned from the blistering sun he went for another swim, put his clothes back on and went home.

As he ascended the staircase in the hostel, he saw that two of his students from the night school were standing outside his room. He went to them quickly and asked, 'What's the matter, Shamb?'

Shambshiv quietly extended an envelope towards him. Shekhar opened it and began reading.

It was a card that had been crafted with visible effort and the writing on it was in large, childish letters that said that the students from the night school had organized a farewell party for the teachers that night, and that they hoped that their teacher, Shekhar, would come.

Shekhar's heart was moved by a sweet tenderness. He asked, 'Have you invited the others, too?'

'Yes, sir, everyone's been invited, but except for Sadashiv, no one else is coming.'

'Why?'

The boys didn't answer. So Shekhar asked, 'What has been planned for the party?'

'There will be a celebratory speech.'

'And?'

The two boys looked at each other and stopped. They didn't speak. Shekhar smiled and asked, 'Why, is there a surprise or something? Is there some mischief being planned?'

The boys said, 'We aren't supposed to tell you.' But seeing Shekhar smile opened something up in them and they said, 'Dinner is being prepared.'

'What?' Shekhar said and fell silent. It occurred to him to ask where they had got so much money, but he was so moved by an appreciation of their affection that it seemed insulting to ask that question. He said, 'You two go on ahead. I'll be there in a little while.' The boys left.

Shekhar hadn't learned how to be suspicious, but for some reason today it occurred to him that the people who had rejected the invitation had done so out of fear of having to come to dinner. The hostel was full of students from untouchable families, and even they seemed to worry that the schoolchildren were untouchables, and perhaps also that they were poor and dirty . . . In his own mind, Shekhar decided that next year he wouldn't ask those people to be his associates. Instead, he would refuse to meet with them.

Then he took a bath. Wore fine, white clothes. He took three photographs out of his new album, collected a lot of flowers from the antigonon vine when he came downstairs, and then set off for the night school. Sadashiv had gone out somewhere and was going to go directly to the school.

While they were eating dinner, Shekhar and Sadashiv gently chided the twenty-six or twenty-seven male and female students—three young girls also attended the school—for taking up a collection amongst themselves to pay for dinner without asking them. After dinner, Shekhar distributed the photos and the flowers amongst them. But when their hands were joined together in a gesture of thanks, Shekhar took their hands and said, choking up a little, 'Look, don't be silly!' And after Sadashiv thanked all of them in a few words, the children saw that Shekhar was getting ready to leave. One of them said, 'Brother Shekhar, aren't you going to say anything?'

Having been transformed from 'Teacher Shekhar' to 'Brother Shekhar' he found he couldn't remain silent, but he was already finding it difficult to say anything; moreover, Shekhar only knew enough Tamil to teach the alphabet and get very basic things done. He certainly didn't know how to express his feelings at that moment since he wouldn't have been able to do so in his own language, but on account of all of the innocent eyes that were fixed on him he began to acquire a new language of expression, and constructing a stew of Hindi, English and Tamil this is what came out of his mouth:

'At first I thought that I had come here to help you, that this was my gift to you. But you all have taught me that this was a mistake. We've reached dotage by living in our own arrogance, gnarled like dry pieces of wood. Now we have to learn humility from you, to acquire your gentleness, a new life and a new youthfulness.

'Today, I have on my lips those tiny meaningless letters that we teach you from your primers, but one day your lips will carry the words of a new language which will have meaning, which will have the strength to create a real upheaval and which will destroy both caste and religious difference, will give birth to a new religion, in which all of us will be brothers, will be related by blood. If that day has not come, it is because it has not entered our hearts—but that day will come soon . . .'

Shekhar stopped and looked all around to give his choking voice a rest. Some of the boys understood what he had said, and some had not understood but were looking at him affectionately. This sight made something inside him well up and he called over to Sadashiv, 'Sadashiv, they aren't getting what I'm saying. Will you listen to me and translate it for them?' And he started talking . . .

'The people that I have chosen to live and eat with, all of them are untouchables, unseeables, but let me tell you, I have found friends among them, found brothers. No one consults them, looks at them, goes near them, that's why their hearts are true, vital and filled with fire. No one talks to them, that's why their senses are even sharper. You are those people, you are my only companions and my only friends, you are my only world and you are the source of my strength. I have adopted you, known you, and this has made me happy. But you should not feel gratitude for this. Don't make yourselves smaller by doing that. I don't feel as if I am a Brahmin who is leading you forward. I've only accompanied you. Somewhere inside, I'm an untouchable too, your brother, too. I haven't given myself to you as a bit of charity, I have acquired you . . .'

Shekhar became quiet. Sadashiv stepped forward and began translating his speech. The boys started to listen; the older ones stared at Shekhar with compassion and love. Behind them, Shekhar spotted a boy with two garlands in his hands and all of a sudden, he was overwhelmed. He felt broken and exposed like earth that has been upturned by a plough . . . Before Sadashiv was finished he got up and walked out very quickly. He could tell that there was a commotion behind him and some people had come after him to stop him. He ran . . .

It was wrong to forget; it was impossible to forget; he was encumbered, exhausted, and a fool, and he was surrounded on all four sides . . .

*

Again at the ocean, only today it doesn't look like an ocean to him. Today the gathering clouds inside him have filled up its horizon, advancing to devour him . . . He returns to the hostel, ties up a few clothes, some books and a towel into a bundle and goes to the Adyar River and gets on the night boat headed for Mahabalipuram. The beach in Mahabalipuram is deserted. There are several temples at the edge of the water, and there are tanks behind them, probably covered with lotus petals—perhaps he would find some peace there, be able to study a bit, could prepare for his exams . . .

It's summer. It was impossible to sit inside the boat. There is no room to sit on the roof; the roof is slanted on both sides. The boatsmen lie somehow on the slanted roof, sleeping, too, and Shekhar tries the same after seeing them do it. He links his arms to the highest part of the roof, in the centre, and lies down. He is fine as long as his arms stayed in place. But when he loosens his grip he feels as if he will slip and fall into the river. The danger of falling somehow makes his spot seem more agreeable. Holding on to the roof with one hand, Shekhar moves to the edge and looks out over the river out towards the horizon.

The moon is rising. Small fish rise to the surface of the water by the course of the boat, sparkle in the moonlight and then move aside, as if they are calling. Tiny fish flashing like lightning below the surface dart hither and thither as if they are writing something in green flames. And because of their commotion, the churning waters also sparkle with an unknown light, as if those green flames have caught it as well . . . The boat, too, is washed in moonlight, and this makes its progress seem even more silent. The boatman is quiet, too, because of the heat . . . Mystery, mystery, mystery . . . It was as if Shekhar was slowly leaving his body, opening out, joining up with that vast, mysterious silence and settling into it . . . The boys from the hostel, the girls from college, the people in the city, all began to disappear from his consciousness, and the blows and wounds he had received from them began to wash away like dirt in that pure moonlight . . . His arm is getting tired, so he puts his neck where his hand used to be, and hooking his feet into a knot of the rope attached to the top of the roof he lies flat and realizes he won't slip off, that he can lie down . . . Fatigue overtakes him, a very pleasant fatigue, but his head is filled with those schoolchildren, their captivating eyes, this captivating moonlight, and who knows why today but thoughts of Sharda, too . . . It had been two years since he had last seen Sharda—who knows where she was. Shekhar hadn't kept in touch, but today after all this time, after all this turmoil and bitterness, in this one clean, tranquil, love-filled moment she revealed herself a part of this vast mystery . . .

Sharda . . . Fatigue . . . Moonlight . . . Sharda . . .

If he could only sleep—he could see Sharda in his dreams—sleep . . .

Mahabalipuram is called the land of a thousand temples, and not inaccurately. But the crown jewel of those countless temples is that Shiva temple built on the bank of the ocean, whose door faces the ocean, from whose crude, stone doorway the vastness of the ocean can be seen as well as the dawn of the sun and the moon beyond that . . .

Shekhar saw both of them on the first day. All night long, he lay down on the threshold of that temple and watched the gradual rise of the moon and its concurrent shrinking, as if it were getting farther and farther away. And as he watched it, Sharda's memory drenched him with sweet caresses like dew . . .

On the second day in Mahabalipuram, Shekhar left the temple only after he had watched the sunrise and then went to sleep. He got up at 10 a.m. or 11 a.m., cleaned up and ate breakfast, and then he strolled back to the beach again. He had taken a book with him, even though he knew he wasn't going to read it.

He sat in the shadow of a temple on the beach and looked at a stone column standing in the ocean. That column would have been a part of the tower of a temple, but as the ocean advanced it swallowed the temple and its tower and came up to the Shiva temple. That pillar stood as a memorial, unvanquished like the Shiva temple, unflinchingly suffering the ceaseless attack of the ocean for 200 years . . .

Shekhar felt an overwhelming urge to swim out to that column. The view of the temple from that spot would be so beautiful, and when the sun would set behind the temple, how enchanting would be the play of the golden-crested waves on the temple steps . . . It was 3 p.m. He stayed there for an hour convincing himself he was staying so that he could study, then he took off his clothes, tied them into a bundle and went into the water.

He still hadn't learned how to swim properly. He somehow managed to get out only a short distance. He was panting by the time he had covered half the distance, but the thought that he had just as far to go forward as he did backward kept him moving forward. Finally, when he was completely spent, when it became a challenge to raise even one arm, he somehow found himself next to the column, and with his remaining strength he gripped the flat part of the column and pulled himself up until he was sitting atop it.

But even after sitting there, he couldn't recover his strength. The tide was rising, the waves were coming in faster and the flat part of the column was sinking into the water. In order to maintain his position Shekhar clutched the column while he sat but it was as if every wave lapped at him more angrily in order to shake him loose. It didn't take long before Shekhar realized that the energy it would take for him to stay there would quickly wear him out, and then he would certainly drown.

It dawned on him with a certain detachment that he didn't want to die there, that he was supposed to die in some other way, and that he still had things left to do.

Shekhar let go of the column and began swimming back to shore. There was still time before the sun would set, but the light from the sun was turning reddish and on the shore, the naked children of the fisherfolk had got together and were dancing. Shekhar could hear their voices, but he felt as if they had seen him standing by the column and were calling out to him. And as he swam he began to feel as if he was one of those children . . .

He was exhausted. His hands refused to move and he began to sink under the water. He remembered that one wasn't supposed to panic in situations like this, that one should sink under the surface and then come up for breath. He sank under a wave, came up after a little bit, when the lack of oxygen made his entire body feel like it was being stabbed by needles. He opened his mouth for a huge breath of air . . .

When a wave crashed over him and he couldn't get to the surface, he took in water with the air and then sank again . . .

He came back above the surface, opened his mouth and took a deep breath . . .

And immediately was lost in a wave, stunned, drowning.

Then suddenly he let go of himself. There was no point in holding on. Death stood before him. *I'll come up for air again, my lungs will fill with water, I'll become unconscious and then I'll die without knowing it. Senseless. Why should I breathe? Death is certain—death. I'll finally understand what death is, I will experience it. I shouldn't be afraid now.* Someone had probably said that— don't be afraid . . .

He opened his eyes. The brackish water stung them. A vast, bitter blue. I'll see death. I shouldn't be afraid—death . . .

The commotion of children. Are these angels?

Shekhar tried to get up, but he was only able to panic and force the briny water out from his mouth and nose. His back was killing him, it felt as if there were boulders crushing his chest and his entire body was rattling.

He was dying for sure. But why hadn't he died yet?

He tried to get up again. Opened his eyes.

The children of the fisherfolk had gathered around his flayed body and a man was pressing down on his chest.

The ocean didn't need him. The waves had picked him up and thrown him out.

He got up with a painful effort that burned deep inside.

He wanted to go back to Madras that night. But it was impossible for him even to stand up. The fishermen had taken him back to the rest house; that's where he was lying. His entire body hurt terribly, but he felt as if whatever had happened had happened for the best. Now he could live, could go forward. It was as if he were reborn, and now he was ready to face life again. It had been senseless, had been wrong to try and drown his sorrows in beauty, to save himself from struggle. Beauty was nothing if it wasn't a force, a stimulant. This is what the ocean, that original teacher, that original truth, that original divinity, that original beauty the ocean had taught him! Beauty exists where there is conflict, and only he could see it who had power within him. And he who had seen that primal power even once, had made himself ever capable, he would never stray off course; he could die but would not bow; he could be destroyed but would never crawl through the slush . . .

*

But for some unknown reason, life became a wasteland. Shekhar pulled himself away from any interaction with the people in the hostel and gave up on the Antigonon Club. He shut down the newsletter and dispassionately began poring over his textbooks. He had been over that nothingness again and again until it started to say, you can hide from people, but how will you hide from me? By studying all day or by subjecting yourself to the hard and nearly pointless penance of studying? In the evenings, he would go and sit sad-facedly at the edge of the ocean, sometimes behind a temple built in the middle of a lake some distance from the hostel, where one could hear the sound of the temple bells and the evening prayers, and where one could see the reflection of the oil lamps in the lake, but one would not see the people coming and going. He had been stamped with pain, even though he didn't know what hurt him, couldn't comprehend it. Sometimes he feels as if he desires beauty. Beauty is power but he doesn't want power, he wants beauty. Sometimes he feels that he wants a companion, but that companion isn't Devadas, nor is it Sadashiv, and Sharda—it isn't Sharda either, although . . . He wants something more, something different from these, something greater than these—but what is there that is like that? Frustrated with himself, he asks, 'Do I want a God when gods don't exist, cannot exist?'

One day, Sadashiv said, 'Look, Shekhar, we still have three weeks until the exams, right? We can get a lot of studying done. Why don't you come back home with me? We can study properly in the peace and quiet of Travancore.'

For no rhyme or reason, Shekhar responded unhappily, 'Do you think that I don't study?'

'You do read. But you don't get any studying done. You've always done well in class. But now it seems . . .'

In a sad voice without any sense of confrontation, Shekhar asked, 'I'll pass, won't I?'

Sadashiv didn't respond to that question. He said, 'I was thinking about leaving tomorrow or the day after. It would be good if you came with me. And if we're together, we'll be able to encourage each other. You really should be able to pass with high marks, right Shekhar?'

Shekhar was quiet for a long time. He could tell that Sadashiv's invitation was genuine and that his faith was genuine as well. And Travancore—it was Sharda's birthplace, her childhood playground and perhaps her current residence, too . . . He was suddenly embarrassed at being so abrupt with Sadashiv. But he couldn't bring himself to say 'yes', not even for Sharda. And especially not because of that temptation. The ocean had tossed him back here and this is where he would stay, in this half-dead condition, alone . . .

'No, Sadashiv, I won't go.'

'Why won't you go?'

'No. I'm an ill-tempered man—I'll fight with you and won't let you study. Also I don't even want to pass. I'm finished, and I'll end up taking my anger about that out on you.' Shekhar turned around and started walking.

Sadashiv put his hand on his shoulder and said, 'Shekhar, tell me, what's bothering you?'

Shekhar melted. He wanted to slap that hand off his shoulder, that hand that Sadashiv had used to get so close to him, but he wasn't able to do that. The touch of the hand changed his mind and the coldness of rejection turned into agreement. Limply, Shekhar said, 'All right, I'll come. But I have one condition.'

'What?'

'That we leave today—on the evening train.'

Sadashiv smiled tenderly and said, 'Let's go. Pack your things.'

When they got to Trivandrum Sadashiv set Shekhar up in a separate room in the house and told him that he could have as much privacy as he wanted, and that Sadashiv would only come when called. The servants would come, though, to do their work.

Shekhar turned and looked around the room. He gazed out of the big glass window and looked out at the eucalyptus tree and the canvas lounge chair standing underneath it, and satisfied, he asked, 'Whose room is this?'

'It used to be mine, but now it's yours. It will be good for getting some studying done.'

As if just waking up, Shekhar said, 'Sadashiv, you are a real friend!' He felt embarrassed at the excitement in his voice. Sadashiv left.

The studying was going better. He felt that in addition to Sadashiv, the other people in the house also cared for him. He had decided that he would start joining them for dinner, and for a little while after that he would spend some time in conversation with them—with Sadashiv's elderly and a little crazy but loving mother and with his younger brother. (Sadashiv also had a sister whom his mother loved very much. The painful memory of her death had driven her a little crazy and ever since her mental health hadn't completely improved.) It was only when he went for his evening walks that he couldn't bear anyone's company—he would go alone, wandering who knows where and come back by night, and if ever anyone asked where he had gone, he would say, 'Around, towards the city' or 'Just out, don't know where, all I saw were shops and more shops.'

After six days of studying, he received another shock.

As he walked around, he would generally read the boards on the shops so that he could remember his way, but not very carefully; and generally he would forget them right after he read them. That day, too, he was absent-mindedly looking at the signboards when his heart missed a beat, and reeling from that jolt he read the signboard again—Sharda's father!

He was stunned. He went up close to the board and read the name again. Then he just stood there. He started to go inside but he was so agitated that he couldn't do it. Then slowly, he made his way back.

That evening and the next day he didn't talk to anyone. He went out for a walk in the evening again and went straight there.

He opened the gate and went inside and saw that there was no one there. He went to the porch of the building and knocked on the door.

A servant opened the door and asked for his name. Shekhar told him. After a little while he realized that he was standing in front of Sharda's mother.

Her mother made all manner of small talk. She asked how he was, how he had done in his exams, how his studies were going, whether his parents were well, why had he come and where was he staying, and did he want any tea; Shekhar had only wanted to ask one thing, but he couldn't muster the courage, all he could do was answer question upon question . . . After half an hour, he went back.

When he hadn't been able to get any studying done on the eighth or ninth day, he remembered that Sadashiv had said that they would only be here for ten days. Would they have to return tomorrow?

He quickly put on his clothes and went over there again. As soon as he entered the gate, he saw that Sharda was standing on one side of the balcony. He also noticed that Sharda had seen him as well, recognized him, and without waiting for even an instant, she quickly went back inside . . .

He went inside and sat down. Her mother was there and he began talking with her. He didn't turn down the offer for tea today—that would require a little time after all!

Sharda entered the room, and now it was as if she had seen Shekhar for the first time, and in a surprised voice she said, 'What are you doing here? When did you arrive?'

Before Shekhar had a chance to respond, her mother sweetly asked, 'Daughter, go and have some tea made and sent for him!' Shekhar could tell that the sweetness in her mother's voice was the result of the experiences of decades of civility . . .

He drank the tea and left. He didn't see Sharda again.

When he got home, he asked Sadashiv, 'Do we have to leave tomorrow? Couldn't we stay for two more days?'

'Forget two, we'll stay for three! I take it that your studies are going well?'

'Yes.'

'How many hours are you spending reading? I haven't seen you the whole week. Leave some of it for when we go back to Madras!'

'Hmm,' said Shekhar and he retreated into his solitude.

Shekhar went back there every day, but he didn't go inside the house. He had gathered that there was a polite, sweet, but firm opposition being raised to Sharda meeting him. He stood at some distance from the gate and waited for her . . .

On the third day, Sharda emerged by herself. She held a satin purse in her hand; perhaps she was headed to the market.

Shekhar was standing in the shade of a tree. When Sharda approached close by he emerged and shouted, 'Sharda!'

Sharda's face lit up, but she immediately turned around and cast a terrified glance back at her house.

Shekhar said, 'You're acting as if you've seen a ghost.'

Sharda didn't respond.

'You came to this place and didn't tell me,' Shekhar said with sweet reproach.

'And where did you disappear to without telling me? I had no idea where you were.'

Shekhar observed that they were walking in the direction of a nearby park.

'What are you doing these days?'

'Preparing for the exams! There are only ten or fifteen days left.'

'Matriculation?'

'Yes.'

'My exams are about to happen as well.'

'Intermediate?'

'Yes.'

After a few quiet moments Shekhar said, 'Come to Madras after your exams. You should study at the college there.'

'Why?'

'I'll be there, too . . .'

'And if I don't come?' Sharda smiled a little, perhaps.

'Then I'll take it that I am no one to you.'

'Who are you to me?'

In that dim light, Shekhar couldn't tell if Sharda was smiling or not. He began swinging the gate at the entrance to the park.

But Sharda said, 'No, not now. I'm going. Mother will get upset. I'll come back in the morning.' And she hurried back.

Shekhar also walked back slowly.

They met at the park again in the morning. The conversation began haltingly, but gradually the dam burst open. Sharda revealed that they had returned for her older sister's wedding, and that her father had been transferred there at the same time, and they had been here ever since. She also revealed that after Shekhar had left for his exams, she had cried quite a lot. She had cried so much that it made her ill, and that's when her mother began to surmise what had happened. Ever since then her attitude towards her had changed. She stopped thinking of Sharda as a little girl. Now she treated her politely, like an equal, but there was such discipline lurking beneath that politeness . . . As she was talking, she suddenly burst into a smile and said, 'I'm a grown-up now, no?' Then Shekhar started telling her about himself, how his mother, too, was a strict disciplinarian but there was not even any politeness there, how he made friends in college, stories about his Antigonon League[19] and its principles, his night school, his frustrations, his friend, the ocean, and the temple and the lake and the lotus petals . . . And then he began narrating how he went to Mahabalipuram, how he went swimming in the ocean and drowned . . .

A faint yelp escaped from Sharda's lips, which pleased Shekhar—she was so worried about Shekhar . . . Then he began telling her even more romantic stories—about his running away from home, about falling into the waterfall in Kashmir . . .

Sharda interjected, 'Stop this! I don't want to hear talk like that.'

'Why?'

'Make me a promise.'

'Tell me what first.'

'I want something from you. Promise me that you'll give it.'

'I will.'

'Promise me that you won't treat your life so casually—you won't put it in any danger—'

Shekhar's heart welled up in happiness, and at the same time, a courage coursed through him as well. But his heart was racing so fast that it was about to burst . . . All of a sudden he blurted out—'Sharda, do you love me?'

Sharda didn't answer.

'Tell me, Sharda, do you love me?'

Sharda was agitated and she got up and said, 'I'm going home—it's very late. Mother will be angry. I won't be able to go out again. All this time—'

Gradually, Shekhar's heart stopped racing. He had already started and going forward was not that difficult. Sharda's avoidance of the question discouraged him a little, but he insisted, 'I didn't know what love was, but now I do. I will cherish you, Sharda. Tell me if you love me.'

'And what if I say that I don't?'

'Then . . . then . . .' Shekhar couldn't find the words. He was quiet for a long time. Who knows what he was going over and over in his own mind . . . Then he said, 'Perhaps I shouldn't ask this now, but you will come to Madras, won't you?'

She almost certainly didn't care for this change in the direction of the conversation, but Shekhar didn't notice that. Disappointed, Sharda said, 'And what if I don't come?'

'What do you mean you won't come? You'll have to come,' said Shekhar somewhat angrily and with a little laughter in order to hide his anger from himself.

Gradually the threads became entangled. Sharda said, 'I won't come. I'll study here. There's no point in going there. Besides, where will I live all by myself? And—'

'If you don't come, I'll know it's because you don't care for me at all.'

Even more frustrated, Sharda said, as if repeating what he had said, 'Then it seems as if I will have to give you an opportunity to think that I don't care for you at all.'

'Sharda?'

Sharda, silent.

'Sharda!'

She, still silent.

'Sharda!' This time, his voice trembling, 'Sharda, do you remember those days?' Shekhar rapidly recounted so many of the things that had transpired two years ago—waiting for Sharda on her way back from school, their meeting in a forest of pine trees, sitting together and reading the *Gitanjali*, plucking flowers and finally that moment when he had suddenly got up and covered Sharda's eyes with both hands and hidden his face in her hair, intoxicated by the fragrance . . .

Sharda, too, had turned away and haltingly said in a tormented, trembling voice, 'I don't think that there is any point in remembering those things that shouldn't have happened.'

Shekhar stepped closer and clutched both of Sharda's wrists. There was a desperate plea and a consciously suppressed rage in his sudden movement, in his touch, in his voice, all together. 'Sharda! What's happened to you? You love me. Say that you love me—'

'Let go of my arm!'

'Why won't you say it? Say it—' Shekhar tightened his grip even more.

And then in a voice suddenly straining with rage and tears, 'You? Love? I regret ever having spoken to you!' Sharda jerked her hands free, and worrying the dark marks that Shekhar's fingers had left on her wrists, she ran home!

Shekhar stood there, paralysed, for a long time, trying to understand what had just happened, and then slowly made his way back home.

The next morning and evening, and then the next morning and evening, Shekhar waited for her in the park. Sharda didn't come. Then, suddenly, Shekhar realized that everything was at an end. He wasn't surprised. The ocean hadn't accepted him, the ocean which accepts everything into its blue, it too had rejected him and thrown him out!

He was defiled. If Sharda didn't accept him, what was surprising about that?

Shekhar told Sadashiv, 'We should go back now.'

'You've finished preparing! You—' Sadashiv stopped suddenly and was left speechless, left staring into Shekhar's eyes. After a little while he said in a hurt voice, 'All right, let's go. We'll find out when we get back just how prepared you are.' He started packing.

'Sadashiv, you didn't ask what happened.'

'You're upset. You'll want to be alone while you're upset. You won't like getting close to me.'

'Sadashiv, how did you come to be so wise?'

Softly, Sadashiv said, 'I've learned a lot from my mother's insanity. People who have suffered are qualified to be gurus.'

When they were leaving, Shekhar bowed to pay his respects and Sadashiv's mother said, 'Son, you haven't told me when you're planning on coming back.'

Shekhar was overcome with emotion. He immediately bent down and touched her feet.

With tears in her eyes, she placed her hand on his head and blessed him.

Shekhar noticed—filled with a feeling that was very similar to gratitude—that she didn't give him the regular blessing—'Be well.' She had said, 'Be glorious . . .'

*

For a few more days that meaningless, pointless effort, studying with those eyes that didn't see anything; and then dispiritedly taking the exams; and then even they were over . . . Shekhar knew that he would pass, but he would barely pass and not more than that. He said goodbye to his friends and classmates.

And then to say goodbye to Madras he went to the ocean shore.

He no longer had any attachment to the region around Madras. He knew that he would never come back. Now his struggle with nature, the pageantry of his contamination, would take place on some other battlefront. Farewell to Sharda, farewell to Sharda's land . . .

He watched the tide ebb and flow for a long time, and its unfathomable mysteriousness . . .

VOLUME 2

STRUGGLE

Part 1

Man and Nature

Roaring, the train raced on. Shekhar had already left his mother, father and brothers behind in the land of the Nilgiri mountains, and now Madras was fading in the distance, too. Nilgiri, Madras, Malabar, Travancore—all would be left behind! He was moving on, the train pulling him along as it recklessly raced on northwards, and only stopping for a breath after 1000 miles. And from there another train would leave and drag him another 1000 miles away. Two thousand miles away from all the places he had known . . .

But what were these places that he had known? What did they matter to him? What were the Nilgiri mountains to him except a place where his relatives lived? And what was Mahabalipuram except a place where he had almost drowned? And what was Travancore even, other than the place where Sharda was and where he had managed to fight with her? If he wasn't there, these places didn't really exist . . . These places existed because he had been in them, and now he was running away from all of them, running away from the mark he had left on all of those places, running away from himself . . .

Was any of this real? Were those places real? Was all of that conflict, love and accusation real? Was he even real? The train pulled him along as it raced on, and it seemed to him that nothing was real, perhaps not even the racing of the train . . .

But it couldn't be anything other than real. Shekhar was running away from his failures, running from his pain. He was a fool. He was making a foolhardy attempt at running away from life. And was there any place where he could really hide from life? Those who run from the battlefront, run from their own failures, ultimately finding new battles at each step, and they remain defeated until they realize that they can't run any more, until they hold their ground and fight . . . Running from life? There was only more life ahead. You couldn't stop life; its expanse never ended . . .

Let it be. Madras will be 1000 miles behind and Punjab 1000 miles ahead. There was a new life there; and Vidyavati was there, and Shashi, and . . . The din of the train is like the thunder of the ocean. Ocean . . . but this thunder was leading him away from the ocean, far away . . .

*

The Punjabis were tall and strong in stature, fair-complexioned, attractive and, from the sound of it, well-reputed. Shekhar looked them in the eye—they didn't flinch, neither from fear nor from meaningless courtesy.

And he thought, 'Here is a man. I can work with him; he will fight shoulder to shoulder with me.'

He had run away from the battle and come. He had arrived exhausted, and so he didn't believe himself to be battle-ready, didn't find himself to be alert. It was as if he had loosened his armour and was resting. He wasn't asleep, his eyes were open, but he wasn't holding a sword either. He was simply observing—his eyes held only the vague feeling of an attempt at recognition, with neither the compulsion for friendship nor the hesitation of enmity.

And after seeing the people of this new land two years later he thought, 'Here there are men. I can work with them.'

Two years ago, when he had come here to take his matriculation exams, he hadn't really seen the people. He had come with a head full of thoughts of Sharda, and he left with new markings put there by Shashi, and he hadn't really seen anything special. But now that he had just come from battle, he was measuring them with a warrior's yardstick—although it was one that belonged to a tired and resting warrior.

Shekhar wasn't a partisan—and if he was partial at all, then
it was because there was some justification for Punjab and its
people—and as soon as he arrived, he began trying to become of
one mind and one spirit with them. He tried to talk to the boys
in the hostel to understand their ideas, their principles and their
hopes. When he realized that he was the source of the problem—
since he didn't speak their language, he didn't wear the same
clothes, it was clear that he wasn't one of them—he tried to look
for a solution to this as well. He had a few outfits made—collars,
ties, socks, shoes, comb, brush,[1] cologne, an iron to press his pants,
a hanger to hang his coat and even a khaki sola topi—but not with
any desire to impress. All of the things he bought were ordinary, he
didn't spend an exorbitant amount of money, but he liked things
with a special simplicity so that while his purchases were not
expensive they didn't look cheap. It's necessary for showy things
to look expensive when someone gets up close, but if no one ever
gets too close, an inexpensive, workable thing can pass just as well.
When he put on his clothes and went to meet with his classmates,
he felt that as far as trademarks went, he was worthy of standing in
their ranks. The language problem persisted, though—he couldn't
speak their language well and he didn't understand the idioms at
all. But since he looked and behaved more like them, and because
he was able to understand most of what they were saying, he didn't
appear to be an outsider. And he was gradually granted entrance
into their midst.

The ease with which his clothes opened all kinds of doors
for him should have made him suspicious, but he wasn't in the
right state of mind to be suspicious. Gaining acceptance, being
welcomed, becoming recognized was so nice . . . Shekhar's face
wasn't especially unattractive; nor did his European clothes weigh
him down.

The tongue of a reserved man, an introverted man who is
half-wild and half-ascetic, may very well falter in the constantly
running, contrived, polite small talk of a foreign culture, but he
has no problem or hesitation in putting on the clothes of a foreign
culture or in making them his own. These clothes weren't that

strange to him. English wasn't his mother tongue but it was his father tongue—an American priest had taught him to speak it using his own language . . . Soon, Shekhar discovered that the majority of the students knew who he was, and they didn't know him the way that he was known in Madras . . . He gained some self-confidence, and with that confidence his studies improved. In the first quarterly exam, he learned that he was ranked first in three out of four subjects. So he became even more popular, received more invitations and was introduced to a wider circle . . . Slowly, the admiration he received from all corners spread through him like an intoxicant—he never noticed how or when his expenses more than doubled, how he now had more than three suitcases full of clothes when he only had a trunk before, since he could still never find the right colour tie for the right occasion—and even if you put all of his ties together, they still probably didn't take up more than two inches of space! He knew that people came to ask his advice before they bought new clothes, and that the day after he wore a new tie, he could spot it in several places even though it was no longer around his neck. He even noticed that he had started getting invitations from male and female students who didn't live in his hostel.

His armour was still on, loosely. There was so much happiness in abandoning it, in surrendering himself to each gust of wind. The wind would steal away his fatigue, dry his sweat, replace the blood tainted with exhaustion in his veins, cool it down and revitalize it, alleviate his pain . . . It was good to surrender yourself to the wind, to drift in the breeze . . .

But drifting in the breeze and flitting to and fro meant that the steel armour would pinch . . . As long as he had the armour on, he would have to remain a turtle—or he would have to take it off and throw it away so that it didn't make things worse and injure him. Should Shekhar take it off and throw it away? But he had already cast off and thrown away all of his clothes, those vain pretences which are too heavy to carry on a journey . . . All that remained under the armour was his naked skin, naked and soft and vital . . . And hiding underneath the bone and meat and blood was a small, vulnerable, helpless, trembling life—Shekhar himself . . . So should he put the armour back on?

But it was so pleasant to lie down after taking off one's armour in a boat lying on the edge of a river at some remove from the battle, to rise and fall with each gust of wind as if it were a swing . . .

*

But Shekhar came to find that the entire society that he had just been admitted into was divided into different factions. He didn't detect such cliques amongst the students in the hostel, where people were divided into classes according to wealth or intelligence, but the people he met outside the hostel did things differently. Sometimes it seemed to him that these factions were based on ideologies because he noticed that Plato was revered as an idol in one of them and Schopenhauer in another; another would always be discussing Stoicism while another was debating Hedonism. Sometimes he felt as if all this factionalism was everyone's attempt at differentiating their own particular addictions[2] . . .

Shekhar slowly found himself being drawn towards two factions. The two groups were different from each other temperamentally speaking, but the internal conflict raging inside him drew him towards both simultaneously.

Most of the members of the first group lived with Shekhar in the dormitory. Shekhar had moved into this dormitory from his previous one because he had hoped to meet the best and brightest members of the student body. Generally, this was where the sons of well-to-do families lived, and most of the names that one heard around the college were residents of that dormitory because they played prominent parts in the sports teams—hockey, soccer, tennis, and so on—and took part in the debates that happened in the various clubs, or you could say that special places were reserved in this dormitory for such students . . .

Every evening Shekhar would hear the sound of laughter coming from the room next door, so he went inside one day and that's how he was introduced to this group. The room belonged

to the chief member of this group, Chatursen, whom no one had
heard speaking the vernacular language, and for this reason alone
he was one of the three monitors[3] of the dormitory. His friends—
whom Shekhar had been introduced to as Narendra, Bhupendra
and Moti on the first day, but starting on the second day began
to be called 'Kaalu', 'Bhopu' and 'Puppy'—came regularly. It was
considered taboo to call any member of this group by his full
name; given names were social conventions. Kaalu had said one
day, 'Members of our group are opposed to social conventions—
it's another barrier between men relating to others in an honest
way. We want to know humans as humans, not as social veneers in
the shape of "scarecrows".' Shekhar didn't object to this idea, but
it seemed strange coming from Kaalu's lips as he was the dimmest
member of the group. 'Puppy' had a keen intellect—he ranked
high in the university—but he would laugh a distorted, sarcastic
laugh after anything anyone said, so much so that he even laughed
in constant displeasure at himself. He often talked about the girls
at the college, and he had such intense disrespect and contempt
towards them—towards the whole of womankind—dripping in
everything he said about them . . . Shekhar thought, 'Here's a man
who's dispositionally an ascetic, but his self-restraint has turned
around and become poisonous, and unable to detest the detestable,
he's constantly spitting out venom.'

This fact both attracted him and sometimes filled him
with repulsion and pushed him far away, but his keen intellect
magnetically drew him towards Shekhar slowly and, one day,
strangely, Shekhar learned a lesson from him.

Puppy introduced Shekhar to three sisters named Miss Kaul
who were known in their circle as Rani, Lily and Ruby. The eldest
was getting her MA and the other two were getting their BAs.
One could still see their natural beauty beneath their fashionably
eyebrow-less and colourfully painted eyes and their lipstick-stained
lips, a beauty that they had spared no effort in perfecting. A few
times, after Shekhar had been listening to their war-wearied,
haughty and indifferent banter, he would leave wondering how
they ever managed to put on all that lipstick and make-up through

their indifference, and once he unconsciously asked this question aloud. Puppy asked him, 'Which one of them seems the most indifferent to you?'

Shekhar responded, 'Can't really say. Maybe Ruby.'

'Come on, I can't keep their names straight. I can only tell them apart by the smell of their perfumes.'

Shekhar couldn't keep from smiling. He was now mature enough that he could appreciate such conversation, even if he couldn't participate in it. He said, 'I'm not much of an expert as of yet . . .'

Puppy said, 'It's for the best. You'll never believe what happened the other day. I told Kaalu something similar, and that rascal snuck in and switched their perfumes. We all went to the movies later, and on the way back I couldn't tell who was who.'

Puppy shut up when he saw that Kaalu was coming this way. But Kaalu had already heard what they were talking about and said, 'Hey, tell him the whole story! Why did you stop? The thing is that we were walking back under a canopy of trees. Puppy was taking advantage of the darkness to take Ruby's hand when she snatched it away and said, "How dare you, Puppy!"[4] The poor guy started apologizing. And that's when Lily burst out laughing.'

'Liar! Why don't you tell him about yourself—did you already forget? It's only been two days. After your little joke, Lily was—'

'When was this?' Shekhar smiled as he asked.

'Just the day before yesterday.'

But Kaalu interrupted Puppy in the middle of what he was saying, 'In all honesty, though, it's impossible to tell anyone apart these days. The other day Chatter [that's what Chatursen called himself] thought that he was being really cheeky, said that you can only know who a person is by the taste of her lipstick, but—'

Shekhar was a little vexed. He didn't mind listening to talk about women or jokes about their mannerisms, but it still upset him to listen to jokes about sex which was for him connected to love. 'There's no such thing as love. There's the body and there's the brain—one chooses the body and the other chooses money. That's all that love really is.' Shekhar could never accept that point of view. He left his friends and remembered that the night before last all of them were in the dormitory, and Chatursen had taken attendance himself at 9 p.m., so how did they go to the movies?

He couldn't get this question out of his mind. Without realizing it, he started paying attention to what these fellows were up to after the nightly attendance. On the third night, he saw all four of them descend the back staircase after attendance, and they were followed by a young servant who worked in the dormitory. The servant was about to close the gate after the four had gone out when Shekhar rushed to say, 'I've got to talk to Chatursen,' and he went out as well.

Neither did it escape Shekhar's notice that the servant hid the bottle he had been carrying.

Shekhar returned at 11.30 p.m. The four boys had walked about two miles and then sneaked into a house. Shekhar turned around and went back after he saw that. The gate was open. He quietly climbed up the back staircase, went to his room and went to sleep.

The next day, he set out in the evening to find out whose house that was. He was standing at some distance from it, thinking to himself about whom he could ask, when the mathematics professor from the college emerged, recognized Shekhar and said to him, 'What are you doing here, Shekhar? This is no place for decent men.'

'Why?' asked Shekhar in surprise.

'Can't you see? That's the neighbourhood where the brothels are.'

Shocked and embarrassed, Shekhar left with the professor.

*

In the second circle, Shekhar never heard any talk of women. All of the focus of this group was basically centred on reforming society. When talk of women happened, it was only in the singular— woman was the fulcrum of civilization, woman held the reins of civilization, woman was the centre of this male-dominated society, woman was this and that . . . It's possible that the reason for this was that there was only one woman amongst the members of that group and she was its leader.

Manika was educated in Oxford and Paris. She came back to India after getting her degrees there, but because she was independently wealthy she didn't find it necessary to seek employment.

It was only to pass the time that she had accepted an unpaid job as a lecturer on literature for four or five hours a week at a college, and that was how she maintained her reputation amongst the students. It was well known in all the colleges that any young man of quality from any college would certainly be in Devi Manika's salon. So the boys who fancied they were—and those who didn't—were always trying to gain entrance into her salon.

Shekhar was taken there by a young classmate. That Bengali boy had a flat, Mongol face and thick lenses on his glasses that covered fixed and slightly swollen eyes, all of which dripped with stupidity. But supposedly he had some ability and was considered knowledgeable about certain genres of English literature. Because of an essay he had written on Rossetti and the Pre-Raphaelite poets for his exams, Shekhar was deemed worthy of attending Devi Manika's salon, and that's where the Bengali boy was taking him.

Shekhar was on his way, but he thought the timing was wrong. He was filled with contempt and loathing for all of these cultural organizations. Earlier that day he had been in a fight with Kaalu when he had gone to take a bath—Kaalu had sworn at him when he noticed that Shekhar was taking too long in the bathroom. Shekhar had come out naked and beaten him up—ever since, something had been eating away at him. He didn't want to go to her in his present condition, but when he learned that time had been set aside especially for him, he went.

Devi Manika's drawing room was beautiful, but he never had the chance to admire its beauty.

He certainly did notice for just a moment the three other people sitting in the room. Devi Manika had been reclining on

the sofa when she noticed Shekhar and his companion enter the
room. She fixed on the other boy and said, 'Hello, Cream Puff, is
this your friend?'

Shekhar was a little stunned when he looked at his friend. It
fit him well—Cream Puff. He couldn't suppress a smile at the
sharp tongue on the slight woman reclining on the sofa and the
appropriateness of the name it had chosen. Cream Puff—once you
heard the name, it was impossible to imagine that the man had
ever had another!

Shekhar also noticed that in the time that it took for his
companion to introduce him—'My friend, Chandrashekhar
Pandit, Miss Manika Devi'—Manika had looked him over from
head to toe and decided that he was not an interesting person.

Manika stretched out her arm to gesture him to a chair, 'Sit.
Do you smoke?' With two fingers, she slid an elaborately carved
walnut box in Shekhar's direction.

'No, thanks, I don't smoke.'

Seated to Manika's left was a fat, pink-nosed Anglo-Indian
man who said, 'Miss Manika, not that. Give him the other stuff.
Initiate him.' He placed a glass next to Shekhar and yelled, 'Waiter!'

Shekhar followed his finger to a side table next to Manika and
the tray with two bottles and a few glasses of different sizes on it.

'No, thanks.'

'What—don't you drink? That just doesn't fly here. I can't
stop until I've had a drink. And the rules of civility—'

Manika interrupted drily, 'Well, good sir, at least leave the
rules of civility alone.'

Cream Puff said, 'Matthews always says that the Greek empire
fell because the Greeks stopped drinking—they were fine as long
as they were drinking.'

The waiter brought tea. One of the men who had been quiet
until now spoke, 'Surely, you drink tea, don't you, Mr Pandit?'

'No, thanks, I don't.' There was a hint of condescension in
the question, which angered Shekhar enough to get up. He said,
'Moreover, I find it insulting that you'd even ask the question.
"Surely you drink tea?", "Surely you'll have a cigarette?", "Surely

you'll have a drink?" As if the only test of civility were the answer to the question, "Surely, you'll have some?"'

It was the first time that Manika looked interested. She said, 'Well said, Pandit. It's the first intelligent thing I've heard all day.'

Matthews was hostile, 'Mister Pandit speaks! I thought that he didn't say anything other than "no" and "thanks".'

'Mahatmas don't speak much, but when they do it's always meaningful.'

Shekhar turned to Cream Puff in order to make clear his contempt for these questions lobbed at him and asked, 'Do you also drink?'

Manika smiled, 'Are you trying to test his civility?'

A cackle of laughter erupted. Matthews spoke first, 'Hey, Cream Puff! You're a spongy cream puff soaking up liquor like a sponge,' and he laughed at his own pun.

Shekhar responded, 'I had no idea that the life of a student in Punjab was so disgusting. I had hoped that these able bodies might have something of substance in them, but they are just putrid, rotting masses of flesh.'

What happened to that meeting was not unlike what happens to pet goldfish when a crab is released into the bright waters of their fish tank. Everyone got up and walked out immediately, and finding himself alone with Manika, Shekhar, too, got up in order to take his leave.

As she was getting up, Manika proclaimed, 'It was really nice to meet you' and just as Shekhar was about to respond to her ordinary formalities in kind, she added, 'The people who come to me have intelligence, certainly, but no character, and that saddens me as well. We have big teeth, but we don't have strong intestines— we can take big bites, but we can't digest what we have eaten. You don't seem to take an interest in eating, but your digestive system seems to be in order.' She stopped for a moment and then continued, 'It really was a pleasure to meet you.' This time, her voice didn't carry a note of formality, just honesty.

With the slightest of gratitude, Shekhar replied, 'Goodbye.'

'No, not like—' Manika said as she extended her hand. Shekhar shook her hand and she added, 'You definitely have to come again, John the Baptist.'

Shekhar liked the nickname—'John the Baptist'. It had something of the plain-spoken goodwill of the half-crazed and the prophetic. And the gentle pressure of Manika's hand also felt nice—it felt affectionate, as if it were a man's hand.

*

There was an idiosyncratic compassion in Manika's disposition which made one angry, made one feel sorry and even made one feel a little respect—and that was the reason that Shekhar went back to her house a few more times. Each time he left, he was a little more impressed and substantially more distressed. Manika had a piercing intellect, but she didn't have the resolve to keep it in check; at the same time, she had the pathetic and painful knowledge of her own lack of resolve, and that made it difficult to get angry with her.

After their first meeting, Shekhar received an invitation for tea one afternoon from Manika, in which she had added after the customary words of invitation, 'At that time, there won't be any undesirable people here, don't worry.' And on that day, Shekhar learned how deep Manika's intellect was and how feeble her strength—although intellect is often confused with strength.

A few other times, Shekhar went whenever he had been invited, but he had never seen anyone else present. After that, he was familiar enough with her that he wouldn't hesitate to go over without an invitation.

One day, Shekhar went out for a walk after dinner when he decided that he wanted to see Manika. At her place, European customs were in sway, which meant that there was nothing inappropriate in dropping by for conversation after dinner—this is what Shekhar thought when he arrived at her house.

He ran into Matthews outside. He didn't care—nor was Matthews pleased with their sudden encounter.

Shekhar knocked on the door to the drawing room, knocked again and then went inside. The drawing room was empty, and the other door to the drawing room was open; there were some dirty dishes on the table but there was no one in the room. Shekhar stood there confused for a moment. Then he sat down on a chair in the drawing room and immediately stood back up again. In the opposite corner of the drawing room, in a dim light, on a blue sofa, in a dishevelled sari, was Manika, lying down, a bare arm dangling down to the floor.

Shekhar called out to her, 'What happened? Are you all right?' Then he went to her and asked again, 'What's the matter, Miss Manika?'

Manika's eyes fluttered indecisively and then opened. They stared at Shekhar's face for a moment and then closed again. They opened again—the effort it took to open them was written clearly on her face—and she said, 'Shekhar, oh!' She tried to get up once, admitted defeat and then, as if in desperation, said, 'Shekhar, I am dead drunk![5] That Matthews brought something . . . I've never had a wine so strong . . . I had no idea . . . the scoundrel!'

'Matthews brought something? Why did you drink it?' Shekhar didn't know what else to say.

'Drank! I drank!' Manika laughed. 'I have a wicked laugh, don't I? I know I do. I am feeling stupid, stupid[6] [I am not myself].' She stopped momentarily and said, 'Will you bring me that book, the one with the blue cover? And bring the lamp over here, too.'

Shekhar did exactly that. Manika opened the book, her hands trembling, and pointed to one passage and said, 'Have you read this poem?'

Confused and overwhelmed, Shekhar took the book from her hands and began reading to himself distractedly.

'Read it aloud. I want to hear it.'

Shekhar read it aloud:

My candle burns at both ends
It will not last the night

But ah my foes, and on my friends—
It gives a lovely light!⁷

Shekhar was silent.

'Read on.'

Shekhar said in a hurt voice, 'Forgive me, but I don't want to read any more right now.'

'Don't want to? Why? But you're right. You're feeling sorry for me, aren't you?'

Shekhar didn't answer.

'But I think—' Manika sat up in a fit of emotion '—you're wrong. And why did you come here when you weren't invited? Go away. Who do you think you are to feel sorry for me and disturb my solitude?'

Shekhar had turned around to leave when Manika laughed—'I'm drunk, aren't I? I know I am. I have such a stupid laugh. Yes, you should go. And don't come back unless you're invited, understand?'

Shekhar left.

'I was right before. Burn at both ends,⁸ that's what a body is good for. What it's good for. You're an idiot, an idiot, my John the Baptist.'

Outside, Shekhar recalled that when they had been talking the day before, Manika had asked, 'Do you have any passions?' And he casually replied, 'I like collecting pictures.'

'How uninteresting!⁹ No divine being?'

Shekhar explained that a long time ago he had a great interest in keeping animals and birds as pets and in catching butterflies, but he didn't any longer.

'That's all? I collect men.¹⁰ They're all such strange specimens—but—' when suddenly her voice fell from boredom and exhaustion—'they're all the same under their skins. Uncivilized, uncultured—avaricious beasts!'

*

As he recalled that day's conversation, Shekhar began drawing a connection in his mind, 'They're all the same under their skins—

all men, all women—men and women, women and men . . .' 'We
have big teeth, but we don't have strong intestines—we can take
big bites, but we can't digest what we have eaten . . .'

'They're all the same under their skins—avaricious beasts—'

'John the Baptist—'

'You're an idiot, an idiot—'

Shekhar had made up his mind that with or without an
invitation he wouldn't return to Manika's place; he had been
banned from Chatursen's group after fighting with Kaalu; aloof
from those who were less intelligent than he was out of arrogance;
unhappy with his family after getting letters of rejection to his
repeated requests for more spending money; when Shekhar was
sitting in melancholy isolation in his room like an untamed, proud
horse trampling on the dust of the past, he began wanting to write
formal prose or poetry to give himself solace like he used to, he
realized that a few of the things that Manika had said echoed in
his mind and scattered his thoughts and compelled him to think
about them rather than brush them off easily . . . He didn't want
to do that, but his memory contained a certain compulsion and
it made him helpless. It was all too easy to remove thoughts of
the members of Chatursen's group or the Kaul sisters from his
mind—they were merely the fashionable forms of irrelevant vices;
but Manika—she was the mutilated and corrupt form of power,
depressing, but not contemptible that she couldn't be ignored.
Manika's—her type's—their souls were completely infected, but
it was still a soul, and the infection was not hers alone; it was the
desire of the modern soul . . .

Shekhar gave up the futile quest for solace, and having
dropped the pretence of formal prose or poetry, he began writing
whatever came pouring forth from his brain—students and
teachers . . . fashion[11] and culture, reason and passion, hedonism
and asceticism and obsession . . . Gradually he began to write
faster, as if his mind were being cast in a mould, and in his growing
astonishment he realized that he was automatically composing
prose and poetry, narrative and exposition and so much more; and
although he wasn't experiencing the pleasure of creation, merely

the satisfaction of exertion; and although he wasn't colouring the pages with the sweet colours of his imagination, merely pouring forth the bitter juices of familiar experiences; and once he had written something down he had no desire to go back and read what he had written; he'd pick up the piece of paper and toss it in the large drawer in his cupboard—nevertheless his mind was becoming disciplined and skilled. Slowly he was overtaken with the knowledge or the belief that the people he was writing about, the men and women who had surrounded him and made up his world, were ultimately not all bad; they were pathetic ensembles of good intentions—they possessed noble desires, but their desires weren't strong enough. They were satisfied with setting out to find the virtuous but were ultimately ensnared, trapped and destroyed by the wicked . . . Could a man possibly condemn such people? But wasn't compassion for such as these equally impossible? A lone individual trying to view the whole world with compassion—he had set for himself an immense challenge!—Slowly, without coming to any resolution to this question, the stack of coloured pages began to grow, so much so that he began to stack his filled notebooks in a box and then, when it was no longer possible to divide them into categories, he filled up an entire cupboard . . .

His friends mocked his new-found asceticism. The circle around Chatursen took it as a sign of its complete supremacy, and no matter when Shekhar would leave his room they would greet him with barks and meows, a new sort of tradition to announce their victorious glee; others thought it was just preparations for the exams, a few said that he had been wearing borrowed clothes and shoes, and now that he was no longer getting them, he wasn't out and about as much . . . Everyone scoffed at him, but really they were all burning with curiosity about what he was up to.

It was now the height of summer—examination days were fast approaching. Shekhar read a few books as if intoxicated to prepare, took the exams in a daze and knew that he would still easily score well and then immersed himself in writing. His classmates went back home after the exams, but the remaining students spread all manner of rumours about him when they saw that he was still studying—everything from preparations for the ICS exams to opium dens—but he remained immersed. Finally, the remaining students had gone back to their homes and Shekhar was left all by himself.

Shekhar wasn't prepared for the isolation. Something of the terror of isolation had fallen over him. It was necessary for him to run away from it—from himself—constantly; constantly establishing himself and staying put. Finding himself alone in the hostel, he began to be drawn towards the servants—and suddenly he was interested in their lives. But after two or three days, he had decided that there was nothing more there that could keep him interested— these hill folk smoked their hookahs all day and spoke vulgarly, sang a few songs in the evening and played kabaddi at night, and that was it. And then when he found nothing of interest nearby, he unconsciously started wandering the streets and the alleys. It was terribly hot during the daytime, so he slept through the day, and from evening until midnight he'd be wandering, and after a couple of hours of sleep, he'd be walking again in the early morning.

Those who have not spent any time in such aimless wanderings—in perfect vagabondage—cannot imagine how deep the intoxication is. It took Shekhar a long time to realize that the curiosity which was drawing him to wander each chance he got was slowly destroying him—he was gradually becoming a full-fledged 'loafer',[12] the kind with no curiosity, with no desire, ambition, hope or will, who had no more to his existence than the fact that 'he was'. Unconsciously he was approaching that condition where he might steal in order to eat if he got hungry, without noticing that he had stolen or that he had done it because he was hungry; or that he could steal someone's blanket because he was cold but wouldn't realize it . . .

That was why when he suddenly set out on the same path on which he had followed Chatursen and the others that one time, he wasn't completely at fault, even though he was at the time completely aware and very mindful.

*

As he walked through that hazy neighbourhood, lit by multicoloured lights, his mind grew dim and tired instead of alert and awake. This irritated and frustrated him. It was as if he were shaking his mind trying to wake it up, saying, 'Wake up, Shekhar, do you know where you are? This is the red-light district. They sell flesh here, they sell satisfaction here, they sell happiness here. Get it?' . . . But his mind refused to grasp this. In his growing rage, he began repeating, 'Whores, whores, whores, prostitutes,[13] harlots, get it? Where there are no relations—no shame—no light, no darkness—only colours—faces colourfully painted . . .' But this only made his mind even more tired. It didn't wake it; it refused to come under Shekhar's command and it wasn't prepared to go forward either. It was as if it had no concern for either the one that was going forward or the one that was advising caution . . .

All of a sudden, a woman bumped into him. He realized with some shock that the bump hadn't been accidental; the woman had intentionally, purposefully and indecently shoved him. Shekhar stared at her for a second—without anger, without feeling, and stood off to the side. Astonishingly, the woman cursed at him. Shekhar wanted to ask himself, 'Why did I come here? What did I want to do here? What did I want to get here?' . . . He had perhaps hoped that he would have an exciting time or feel a sharp disgust or get angry; some overwhelming reaction which would stir things up inside him, which would make him tremble—this softly—very softly!—he wasn't prepared for this fatigue—nor for the slightness of the tumult . . .

Two half-naked boys were sitting on a porch. They were sitting together in an obscene pose, their arms around each other's necks, each kissing the other on the mouth, and after each kiss they'd look across to the facing window and laugh a meaningful laugh. Shekhar followed their eyes—in the light from a blue light bulb[14] was a woman sitting wearing a purple sari, and in the coloured light her made-up face looked like—the face of a corpse lying in water . . .

Shekhar moved on.

Four Muslims wearing chequered, jute sarongs were standing under a window and watching a tall mendicant. The mendicant was old, wearing an ascetic's red and yellow, with a string of large rosaries around his neck, looking up at a deformed, middle-aged woman sitting on the balcony above saying, 'What? Aren't you a woman? I may not have any money, I might be a beggar, but—' now beating his chest, '—I'm a man, a man . . .' The woman is staring at him with contempt, and the gathered onlookers are laughing . . .

No. Not this either. Here, too, there was only the same note of alienation, a faint repulsion and the echo of Manika's phrase, '—They're all the same under their skins—avaricious beasts' . . . Man and man, woman and woman . . . man and woman . . . Shekhar moved farther on.

A young girl, half-naked and in rags, pulled at his arm and said, 'Sir, give me some money.'

'I don't have any money; away with you.' Shekhar jerked his arm free; his tone was cruel, too.

The girl clutched on to his legs. She said, 'Give me some money or come with me—you can give me money afterwards.' She stopped speaking and gestured to a small building in the distance where a lantern was glowing . . .

Shekhar didn't even free himself; he walked on with her on his leg. The girl let go.

A voice from the sides, 'Kinno, look—it's one of your countrymen—call to him, won't you?'

Shekhar felt a faint twinge of curiosity. From the name of the person addressed and the revelation that she was a countrywoman, Shekhar couldn't immediately tell what region she was from. But he didn't pause, nor did he turn around to look, even though he heard the loud sound of the kiss that had been aimed in his direction . . .

He turned at the corner when the person coming towards him said—'Flowers for sale!'

No, they weren't garlands of jasmine. Shekhar took one look, staggered backwards as if he had been shot and then, steadying

himself, bent his head and covered his eyes with one hand and
ran—ran . . . In this place—bouquets of lotuses! Lotuses, which
had been for him symbols of purity, which . . .

He ran, and for no apparent reason a meaningless phrase
repeatedly overwhelmed him like a blow from a hammer—God
and Man—God and Man . . .

The conclusion to which those lotus flowers forced the various
streams of thought in his head, and the shackles that were on him
as a result of the decision not to go home for the vacation, became
the reason that Shekhar was filled with a burning desire to go
to Kashmir as soon as possible. The beautiful playground of his
childhood . . . How long had it been since he had seen anything
beautiful, and how deep was the longing in his heart to see such
things—that were beautiful, completely beautiful . . .

But was that real? Was it really the quest for beauty that
had made his life here so tumultuous? Was it the ugliness of his
condition that was wreaking havoc inside him? He wasn't certain,
but war was another name for chasing after possibilities, and life
was merely a protracted struggle to catch the possible . . .

*

There's an ancient Chinese poem which roughly says, 'Should a
man be lulled into a stupor by the desire that his bones be buried
in the same tomb as his father's? Wherever one goes, one can find
rolling hills "dark with the crops of the harvests".'[15]

He turned that poem into a proverb and set out for Kashmir.
On the way, he kept on filling his mind with the reborn memories
of his past, but he couldn't taste their sweetness, the past isn't
made more attractive by having a grave next to it; it only produces
a desire to find a better hill dark with the crops of the harvests than
the first, no matter where one would have to go to find it . . .

He would also laugh at his own quest—a quest for truth, a
quest for knowledge, a quest for freedom, he had heard of all of
these, but he was undoubtedly the first detective on a quest for
beauty.

The past was a lie. There was no hill dark with the crops of the harvests—only graves.

When he got to Srinagar, Shekhar searched in each lane and alley—it had no effect on him. There was nothing special in Srinagar—except for the varieties of smells. He even went to visit the renowned forests outside the city—but all that was there were lines and angles and circles—and the austere serenity and exacting arrangement of the trees only reminded him of the tranquillity of death. The person who had famously written about those forests—'If there was ever a heaven on earth, it was this, it was this, it was this'[16]—was probably a mathematician who caught the craze of forestry . . . Shekhar travelled over rivers and streams and lakes, but the beautiful vistas were wrecked by tourists and the reckless throngs of their smoky boats. That was when he set out on a journey to a certain lake hidden in the perfect whiteness of the Himalayas. He looked at the yellow, red, blue and white flowers blooming in the mountainous foothills on either side of the road with eyes soaring upwards, and he had gone so high that here and there he could see last year's ice hidden under the cover of rocky crags. He broke off a lone blossom of blue poppy flower, which was considered a lucky find, from inside one such crag—how strange was the fortune of that flower which bestowed luck on the one who had it but meant the death of the flower!—but beauty, he wasn't able to find beauty! He climbed higher, while the coolies who accompanied him prepared to rebel because others had been where he was headed, but none had been able to camp—no one had been able to strike a tent there . . . But, 'That's where beauty would be found!' These words convinced them to go as far as the lake; at the edge of the lake, they struck camp and he lay down to think, 'Where to now?'

The lake was wide, and in places in the middle, sheets of ice floated on the surface; above, a flock of cranes flew back and forth, and a gust of wind blew across the surface of the lake as if preparing the glorious path for the arrival of some mountain goddess. Shekhar watched for a while, and then because he was tired and shivering from the cold, he went inside and closed the

tent to think—because the trails stopped here, and they'd have
to go back, but he never paid attention to the trails leading back
down, so how would he go back . . .

Standing in a crevice on one side of the lake, Shekhar
thought he saw, in the cave created by two boulders in front of
him, some goddess clad in white, standing, dipping her feet in
the water. Then he thought, no, she wasn't a goddess, she was
human, and she was someone that Shekhar knew. But who?
It wasn't that either, the face merely resembled someone's—
Sharda? Shashi?

Shekhar woke with a start. He had fallen asleep, and
moonlight streamed in from the crack in the opening of the tent
and spread across his face. His dream had unsettled him, and
he felt something like guilt. He wrapped a blanket around his
shoulders and emerged from his tent.

Outside, clear moonlight was scattered everywhere, so bright
that only a few stars could be seen even in the cloudless sky.
The lake shimmered. Watching the play of colours—the play
of only one colour, white—or rather the play of mere light and
its absence left Shekhar speechless. The sparkling waters of the
lake reflecting the smoky, dark mountains and the distant haze
of the sweet, beloved, brilliant snow-covered range . . . Seeing
this scene on that vast, perfectly still night sent a quickening
wave through his body, as if he were waking from the dream of
this world and entering into some higher plane of reality . . . It
thrilled him. He closed his eyes, as if the only way to preserve
this scene was by closing his eyes, as if open eyes would have
mutilated it . . .

Oh, beauty . . .

Shekhar found himself shivering fiercely. He felt as if there
were some heavy weight on his head and it was necessary to get rid
of it; he slowly returned to his tent.

He went inside and lit a candle, got a pen and some paper
and for a moment fidgeted with his pen indecisively. Then he
wrote, 'The union of beauty and reason can never be binding.' He
stopped for a while and then suddenly decided to put that piece of

paper on his knee, and he bent over and started writing—the very first and most beautiful story of his life . . .

*

He had spent his whole life in cities—in the filth and the crowds of cities, in their strife and commotion, and he had learned to be so quiet and content amidst that that he served no purpose other than to add one more to the ranks of the urban population. He was a part of that filth and crowd, that strife and commotion. His neighbours knew of his stoic disposition. That's why, when they heard about his decision to go to Kashmir, they laughed until their bellies hurt. 'You're going to visit Kashmir?' He couldn't even see the beauty in a buffalo—and Kashmir? He was setting out to understand the beauty that had eluded even the best artists' attempts—this slithering worm of the city's back alleys, eyeless, which couldn't go forward if it wanted without first bunching itself into a ball. The saying was right—the camel, the horse and the buffalo drown and then the ass asks if the water is too deep!

But because he was a stoic individual, none of these words had any effect on him. He had to go, so he went.

He stayed in Srinagar for several days. He wandered around, drifted in search of the beauty that everyone could see and appreciate, but he was the only luckless one who couldn't find it. He was slowly coming around to the belief that beauty might only be imaginary—and as he became more convinced, his quest became increasingly disoriented. He went to see the monuments built by the Mughals—cheap ornamentation and experiments in mathematics—that was all they were! He went to the village first and came back disappointed. Gulmarg made no impression on him. Dal Lake seemed lifeless to him, and Wular Lake was just a pool of dirty water.

Ultimately, he became restless to go back to his town—its filth and crowds, its strife and commotion. There things might not have been beautiful, but they were perceptible, they could be grasped and understood! Should he go back?

But leaving a task halfway through—that was what connoisseurs did—and how could he, one numb to pleasure, abandon his quest in the middle? He went outside his tent to sit and think, 'Am I the only person in the world incapable of experiencing beauty? Am I the only one born with this disability? Or have I not deemed myself worthy yet . . .'

He decided that he would try once—and if he still couldn't experience it, then he would go back to his dirty, crowded and noisy city forever . . . He would know once and for all whether he had lost or won—if he was incapable of pleasure, then he would live with this harsh inability being his truth . . .

He put all of his necessary supplies on two mountain mules and set out with the mules' owner.

He climbed the slopes for four days non-stop—the forests grew thicker, the silence deeper and the air thin, short and cold. For three more days, he and his mountain-dwelling companion kept moving on—crossing over countless tiny mountain streams and waterfalls from gurgling streams, strung together like pearls— past where the cedars and the birches stopped and the vast lowlands spread out all around them, lowlands covered in green, red, blue, yellow, white scentless flowers . . .

They went even farther—past where even the flowers stopped—except for the rare, forgotten blue poppy that one could see, and occasionally a strong-smelling shrub or a misshapen bush with dried leaves . . .

And beyond that even the lucky blue poppies stopped, the shrubs stopped, and all that remained were dull crags and trampled, insensitive, dull grass . . .

A thought occurred to him, that one by one all of the pleasurable things had fallen behind on this impassable trail—the trees had been left behind, the flowers had been left behind, the shrubs had been left behind and even the solitary, meditative blue poppies had been left behind—all that was left were the dull rocks, the dull grass and the dull curious one, himself . . . He should have been able to find beauty on this desolate path—but was beauty even a real thing? Wasn't beauty just a name for an imagined pleasure, the feeling of an imminent experience of attaining pleasure? 'This is just about to make me happy,' thinks the person so overwhelmed by the thought that even before he attains happiness, he perceives pleasures and then says, 'How beautiful!' Isn't beauty the name for the satisfaction acquired by the nectar of desire . . .

Did that mean that he had been separated from his own desires? He knew that wasn't true, that his body could burn with desire, had burned, would burn . . . Did that mean that there was nothing in the world that could bring him happiness, or which would give him the hope of happiness? It was also difficult being that unlucky—even amongst the rocks that lie nearby, one could occasionally spy a green or white coloured vein.

He crossed a mountain pass and suddenly came to a clearing; there was a wide lake before him, surrounded on all sides by peaks—some naked and dark, some veiled in ice . . .

He told the mule driver[17] to set up camp, and in the light drizzle of rain, he went inside, ate a little, and lay down—he was exhausted. He was so tired that he couldn't even sleep—he just lay there thinking.

He was such a fool . . . Had anyone else set out on such a quest for beauty? One had heard about that in stories—some prince went to the island of sapphires where the goddess of beauty lived, or some king said to his minister that he wanted the essence of beauty—but had anyone ever tried to determine whether these stories were true? 'Story' and 'reality'—even a small child was made to learn by rote that these were two different categories . . .

He was the only fool who hadn't understood this—he lived in the real world and wanted to obtain something from a story world . . . Why shouldn't people laugh at him? Or consider him a fool? At home, his wife, surrounded by the crowds and the filth of the city, would also laugh at him, saying that the fool had married but set out on a quest for beauty . . .

He woke with a start. In his dream he had seen a black boulder with two large, round eyes that were fixed on him and it said to him, 'You did very well to set out on this quest for beauty that led you here—to me.' And then all of a sudden it transformed into his wife, who burst into thunderous laughter.

He rose and went outside, taking long steps on his way towards the lake . . .

As if struck by lightning, he stopped in the middle of the path. Some inexpressible thing was gathering speed and welling up towards him—a little cold and frosty, a little awesome, a little thrilling—not just welling up, but shaking every vertebra in his spine and pervading his head . . .

Spread out before him—the light from the moon's rays, shadows, the blanket of ice, sparkling waters, ripples, stars . . .

Beauty, like a deeply felt wound—the sensation coursed through his veins . . .

The dance of the moonbeams on the ripples of the water—the dance of mountain nymphs on a sheet of liquid velvet—and, on the far side, in the shape of a massive column and in a fixed pose, a row of seated ascetics—peaceful and meditative and immovable . . .

He staggered from the force of knowledge—he was lost in the infinite sky—he had attained it, but far beyond his capacity—his mind was left wounded, defeated and shattered in the face of that development . . .

Whoever sees Diana bathing is left blinded—it's impossible to retain the ability to see anything after that sight . . .

A madness overtook him, he began babbling and walking forward with his arms outstretched so that he could embrace the beauty of the lake and the ice and the sky . . . But can one embrace a dream with one's arms, hold it tight . . . ?

He was half-asleep as he was advancing—towards the lake, where the nymphs were dancing on the moonbeams . . .

The next day, when he emerged from his tent by sunrise, the mule[18] driver went inside Shekhar's tent, but he wasn't there. He waited for him for some time and then set out to look for him.

There was nothing to be found—save a few footprints in the snow headed towards the lake that disappeared at the edge of the lake—and there was nothing beyond that, except an impregnable, veiled, ancient beauty—silent, smiling, secretive . . .

*

The very next morning, Shekhar packed up his things, tore down the tent and began his return. Now that he had secured his new feeling, it wasn't necessary for him to stay there—not just unnecessary, it became impossible, too.

Three days later, he reached his first post office, where a letter finally reached him after having been sent from various places. There weren't too many letters, only a few from familiar hands—when he saw one in an unfamiliar handwriting he tore open that envelope first, and the rest of the letters remained unread.

Shashi had written him a three-line letter—her father had died and her mother was suffering from repeated fainting spells.

*

It was evening, dark and silent; when Shekhar didn't see anyone as he entered the house, he breathed a sigh of relief. For some reason, he was anxious that he wouldn't be able to handle his share of the grief that had cast a shadow over this house. Even though he had come here and stayed here while Shashi's father had been ill and had become a part of the household, still he felt that his connection was really only to Aunt Vidyavati and Shashi, and since both were presently racked with grief, he wouldn't be able to go near them, share in their sorrows. It seemed as if he had become impersonal, personal feelings—pain and joy—didn't affect him; and in that condition, it was both impossible for him to offer condolences and cruel for him not to . . .

At the door, on the threshold, in the courtyard, on the stairs—Shekhar saw no one. He quietly put his meagre bedding down in the courtyard and walked softly up the stairs.

On a mat spread out on the ground, Aunt Vidyavati lay unconscious; Shashi sat next to her, one hand on her mother's forehead, the other fanning her.

Shashi's younger sister Gaura was standing nearby with a glass of water, but it was her silent tears rather than drops of water that she sprinkled over her mother.

Involuntarily, 'Shashi—' escaped from Shekhar's lips and he immediately felt embarrassed. Kneeling next to his aunt, he took the glass from Gaura and sprinkled the water himself; Shashi looked over at him once, in a straightforward, general acknowledgement of his presence and kept on fanning; Gaura perhaps went downstairs to look after his things. Aunt gradually opened her eyes, looked at him blankly, recognized him and then closed them again, and then she tried to roll over and gave up; softly, Shashi said, 'She's asleep—it's the first time in three days.' Shekhar looked up at her once, as if to ask, 'Have you been watching her for three days to see whether she's slept or not?'

But he didn't say anything; Shashi got up and left the room, Shekhar followed, and as soon as he left the room, she closed the door and asked, 'When did you get my letter?'

'Five days ago.'

'Where were you?'

'I was in Kashmir—'

'Where in Kashmir? It took you five days to get here?'

'Nowhere, Shashi. I was out of sorts,' he said and then fell silent immediately.

Shashi went to the kitchen and slowly began gathering things for cooking. Shekhar asked, 'Can I help?' She silently pushed the plate of flour towards him and gave him a jug of water. She began chopping vegetables.

Shekhar was struck by this manner of uncontroversial agreement to his offer of help and he stared fixedly at Shashi. That's when he realized that she wasn't there—all that was there was a mechanical human that kept going on only to keep others going, kept going on . . .

He suddenly realized that he wasn't impersonal, that he was drowning in melancholy, that their sorrow was his sorrow—a font of deep sympathy gushed forth inside him . . .

Sorrow generates connections; it's also sublime and redemptive. The connection of sorrow can even make the fallen sublime and pure.

While staying with them, some similar knowledge was breaking out inside Shekhar, which is when he decided that he wouldn't leave and would sojourn in the lap of that sorrow . . .

More than a month had passed since this family suffered deep wounds from the maelstrom of death; the house, at least, seemed to be running as usual from the perspective of regular activity—daily obligations are the only thing keeping the order of the world constant and stable—and Aunt Vidyavati and Shashi were busy all day with some chore or another. Whenever women from the neighbourhood came over to offer their sympathy, they would sit with some work and faithfully remain receptive to collect the fleeting, sometimes fake and more often ritualized sympathy, because that was convention, obligation, even if the deep wounds of fortune became even deeper, burst open and drained the life force in the process . . .

Shekhar would be perfectly still while watching this pervasive, silent faith in duty—standing at a distance, with eyes wide open, he would stare at Aunt Vidyavati and Shashi; whenever they looked at him with a momentary concern, he would leave quickly . . . Sometimes his aunt would call to him to ask, 'What's the matter, Shekhar?' He was never able to respond, and she thought that she shouldn't display her own grief and make him sad—she couldn't imagine that it was her refusal to show her own pain that was creating the tumult inside him, that which immediately transformed her joys and sorrows, scolding and anger, love and indifference into work, which is ready to lead an individual on a rugged path to the highest peak, but will not stop for even a short while to help create a flat, paved street that will help an entire community . . . which has no self-control, which has a command of the physics that go into the flow and diversion of water, but hasn't understood the work of irrigation . . . That's when he would run into an empty room to hide, and he would curse himself for having wasted a long life; he was a dog running around in small circles in the same area chasing his own tail, he hadn't understood, hadn't wanted to understand, hadn't set in motion his ability to understand the pain that others felt, their suffering . . .

Who knows who should get the credit for this, but that day all of a sudden, the dam burst and three of them—Aunt, Shashi and Shekhar—began talking. It made Shekhar very happy to see that his aunt would even smile occasionally at something Shekhar said—although that smile could have brought someone else to tears.

Perhaps Shekhar said something about his future plans and let it slip, 'I won't be able to do that—I don't have the line for it in my palms.'

Shashi asked, 'Do you know how to read palms?'

Before Shekhar could answer, Vidyavati extended her hand and said, 'Really? Look and tell me how long I'm going to live.'

The question startled Shekhar so much that he couldn't respond even in the negative to Shashi's question; he took his aunt's hand in his own, looked at the life line and, as if he were responding to some unspoken doubt, said, 'Why, there is still a lot left—'

'No, no, Shekhar, tell me that it won't be long now!' There was a piercing sharpness to Aunt's response—'Not long, Shekhar, not long!' It was as if he were drifting in a current of pity. His aunt fell silent and drew her hand back . . .

Shekhar's hand remained outstretched and half-opened, just as it had been when holding his aunt's hand—his eyes fixed, as if hurt, on his aunt's and he stared—a glorious light flashed in those bottomless lakes of the soul and then burned itself out—his aunt regained control and composed herself and laughed a false laugh. She said, 'Let it go, it's not as though palmistry is ever accurate . . .'

Is life so cruel, and was a clear purpose indispensable for living? Shekhar didn't know what his purpose in life was . . . He got up to go.

Shashi had finished seventeen years of her life and was starting on the eighteenth. Shekhar could hear talk of this fact from different places in the house—almost as if from the walls—and sometimes from the mouths of the women who had come to offer sympathy, 'Dear God, who will get this one married? Dear God, to have such an old, unmarried girl still living at home!' Still

Vidyavati never mentioned this nor did Shashi ever give it any thought—even though Shekhar could clearly see that there was a huge difference between the Shashi from four years ago and this peaceful, grave idol.

Shekhar's vacations were over; it was time for him to go back to college and enrol in the MA programme. But he didn't want to go. When Vidyavati asked him, 'Shekhar, how many more vacation days do you have left?' he knew that he could still get admitted even after registration had closed, so he said, 'There's still a lot left.' But when Shashi asked him the same question, he said, 'Why?'

'Aren't you going to continue your studies?'

'Yes. But what's the rush in going back?'

'You really should complete your education. You can always come back here—what do people like us have after all? And these days we can't even offer you the slightest bit of happiness—'

'I'm never as much at peace as I am when I'm here—'

'That's just what people say—'

'No, it's true. And this time, there was a special peace in being able to share in your grief—'

'Why?—'

'The pallor of grief is a kind of penance—it redeems the soul.'

'Are you certain?'

Shekhar was a little taken aback; he said, 'Why?'

'Grief only cleanses the soul of one who attempts to drive it away. No one else's.'

'So . . . I don't follow.'

'It's true that you've come and shared in our grief, and it offered us consolation, too, but did you think that your obligation ended there? There is pain everywhere. So, you've decided that pain only lives here and you want to live under its shade, but you're showing no interest in the obligations that you do have. You should go back to college—'

Shekhar was stunned. Shashi had never spoken so many words to him before—and not just so many words, but also deep ones . . . He said softly, 'You're right—I . . .'

'And look, don't you dare ever call me "Aap" again! My name is Shashi and yours is Shekhar.'

Perhaps surprised by her own audacity, Shashi immediately turned around and left; Shekhar was left staring.

*

This time, Shekhar didn't have to do anything extra for his studies, because since he was studying literature for his MA he was already familiar with most of the material included in the syllabus—a few special textbooks—one on literary criticism, one on linguistics, and the rest could even be read afterwards . . .

Shekhar kept himself at a remove from ordinary student life and began digesting the experiences of the last several months—becoming the monitor of a small hostel helped him in establishing his distance. A while later when the National Congress asked for volunteers for its next session, Shekhar signed up with the first group and duly began learning the official drills.[19] It wasn't that he had some political awakening, but he found a kind of comfort in the discipline the drills provided. He also thought that these external rules might provide a discipline in him internally.

After he completed his training, he was given the task of training the group of new recruits. In truth, this was even better as training because along with disciplining the body, one had to have an alert mind to see what someone was lacking and how that would be remedied . . .

It didn't take long for the Congress session to draw near. One day, Shekhar rolled up his bedding, draped it over his uniformed shoulders, got in a lorry and arrived at the camp with the first group of volunteers.

The training was mostly completed, all that remained was the attempt to ready the few latecomers by making them march in formation four times, quickly; but, the volunteer corps still hadn't been organized. There were commanders and volunteers. But the network of junior officers which is necessary to link them to one another didn't exist. Until now, it hadn't been given any special attention, because 'We only have four days. Everyone has to come together and make this work.' But 'come together and make this work' doesn't tell you who gives the orders and who follows them, so one day five head officers—group leaders—were chosen and the next day the remaining five officers were 'elected' during the parade. Other than his strengths and his weaknesses, Shekhar had nothing to recommend him, but he was still made a junior officer—'chief'—and given the job of managing the camp.

There were 1400 volunteers in the camp. Taking care of them shouldn't have required anything special, but amongst the volunteers, there were at least 300 college students who believed that since they had become volunteers and paid for half of their uniforms, there was no reason that they should also be expected to do any work or be prevented from watching the spectacle of the Congress party. They also required three leaves each week so that they could go home—they couldn't be expected to freeze to death in this jungle. Work was done during daylight hours, so whose business was it where they slept? And on top of that, after carrying the heavy burden of voluntary service, they also needed entertainment, and there was no cinema in the Congress encampment; they had to go to the city, all that you could do in the camp was play cards or backgammon, and to make that a little more interesting, sometimes they need to bet a little something.

Then there were those poor souls who had no idea where they should go to relieve themselves; where, how and what they had to do for food; whom they should ask when they didn't have a blanket; and who thought it wrong to ask or 'complain' about these things. Brother, we're working for the Congress, is it really that much of a problem if you have to burden yourself a little . . .

And there were those who, because they had put on uniforms, felt entitled to do all the things they had seen the white soldiers or the police doing and which had made them fill up with hatred and impotent rage—threatening passers-by, suspecting a poor person of something and therefore insulting and harassing him, et cetera . . . According to them, not exercising these entitlements amounted to turning the 'soldier' into a cripple since there would be no reason for him to be here if it was enough just to fold one's hands and flatter someone . . .

Then there were certain visiting delegates (and their entourages) who had paid the rent for the tent and therefore turned the whole group of assembled volunteers into their servants—at all hours of the day, they would say, 'My stomach hurts, I need a volunteer to warm some compresses'; 'I have a fever, I need two volunteers to be by my side all night'; 'I'm having indigestion, send a volunteer to clean the toilet' . . .

Even if such requests were legitimate, they should still have been taken to a doctor who was responsible for the appropriate remedies for any ailment; but upon saying such things, every volunteer—or just Shekhar—would be reminded: a volunteer must make it his religion not to look down upon such requests—'Do you know that while he was in Africa, Mahatma Gandhi cleaned toilets himself? And you're not more important than he is—'

And then there were certain volunteer officers whose worthiness was not based on their abilities, but rather on the influence of their friends; such people had no shortage of things to do, but they still came to the camp though to not engage in dialogue with fools. The fellow who was supposed to relieve the volunteers from their post would go around twice during the day and relieve people, but in the evening, after supper, he found it disagreeable to leave his place and return to camp in the bitter cold of January, so often the volunteer on duty in the evening would be left standing there after dark because no one came to relieve him . . . After 11 p.m. Shekhar would start receiving messages, 'Volunteer so-and-so has been on duty for five hours, no one has come to relieve him', 'Volunteer so-and-so has been out for six hours, he's soaked through in the rain', 'I've been standing here for eight hours, I got someone to stand in for me so I could come here; if you'll send another volunteer, I can show him where to go' . . .

There was a lot of work for Shekhar to do. He would come into his office under the tent at 6 a.m. and sit on a stool. At 2 p.m. and at 10 p.m. his Pathan 'orderly'[20] would have to argue with him until he got him to eat somehow. He'd also bring him his tea once a day. At 12 a.m., Shekhar would leave camp, demoralized from the complaints and think, 'I should go around once to see who has been out and for how long, so that I can sleep worry-free . . .' But there was another problem for him—replacements could only be made by the officer in charge of replacements, Shekhar didn't have the authority, so when the volunteers didn't come by themselves he would send one of the volunteers he was in charge of who had been sent to him to help manage the camp . . .

He would get back to his tent at 2 a.m., and without loosening his uniform or taking off his shoes he would fall down on to his bedding, spread out over straw . . . Not taking off his shoes was for the best since a tent housing eleven men had barely enough space for him to lie down and spread his legs—his heavy shoes and thick socks were his real lifesavers . . .

Discipline—discipline—discipline—one day, exhausted from chasing after discipline night and day, Shekhar sinned gravely against that very discipline.

In the tent for college students, groups of people had been found gambling a few times. The first time, Shekhar merely confiscated the dice and gave them a warning: that this was unseemly behaviour and shouldn't happen again. The second time, in addition to confiscating the cards and the money that had been wagered, he made them perform their drills. The third time, he kicked the three individuals out of the camp and had a notice circulated throughout the camp that gamblers would be removed from the volunteer corps.

The hard workers would complete their assignments—as they never had occasion to gamble—but they were also the ones ground down by the mercy of the assignment officer so that even when they had spare time they could do nothing but collapse on their backs. But the college students didn't do any work, and if they ever fell into the clutches of the assignment officer (and even he didn't disturb their liberties because how could he maintain his own unfettered freedoms once he had upset the group which raised the loudest cry of them all?) and were sent on assignment, they would immediately leave their posts, 'My friend, this is such dreadful work—guarding the streets. Is someone going to come and steal the street?' This group had a lot of free time, so each time Shekhar admonished them, it was fruitless.

The fourth time a group got caught gambling, two of the members of that group turned out to have participated in the previous three incidents, so Shekhar thought it necessary to enact more serious consequences.

The bugle sounded for assembly. The volunteers who were present in the camp stood in formation in the space that had been left empty for the parade drills. From their faces, one could tell that they were surprised to hear the bugle sound in the afternoon because who knew what hardship was about to fall on them all . . .

Shekhar gave the order to stand 'at ease' to the men in formation and stood under the flagpole. He said, 'Volunteers, you have been called here for a necessary announcement. It's an embarrassment to this camp that a group of people have been caught gambling here four times. The first time—' and Shekhar listed in succession the names of the individuals involved in each of the four incidents and the first three punishments delivered. 'The fourth time, three of them were first offenders, and they will be given the same punishment that was given out last time, but for two of them, this is their fourth time being caught gambling. It is clear that the last punishment was not enough for them; rather talk of any punishment appears to be a waste.'

He stopped momentarily. He looked all around. His pause had an effect.

'The only solution is that we regretfully find these volunteers are not worthy of their uniforms.'

Stopping again for a moment, '—Three steps forward—march!'

The two of them stepped forward. Shekhar said to his 'orderly',[21] 'Bring their things out here.'

The orderly brought their things—their bedding, small luggage.

'The two of you need to take off your uniforms. Put your own clothes on.'

The two of them gave Shekhar one look of contempt, but the perfect stillness which had fallen over the entire parade ground made them yield. They quietly changed their clothes.

'Pick up your things—about face! March, leader, show these men out of the camp.'

The footfalls of three pairs of feet—thud, thud, thud—could be heard . . . Shekhar was listening to them but was looking at the remaining volunteers and thinking to himself, 'If they had refused to obey, what would I have done?'

All at once, three men from the ranks stepped forward. All three were college students—Shekhar had seen them before. They knew him, too.

'What is it?'

'You have no right to take away their uniforms. We are opposed to this. You have insulted the students from the college—we're going to protest.'

This was not a time to show indecisiveness. Shekhar said, 'Volunteers, those of you who think that it is an insult to put an end to gambling, please step forward three paces.'

Three individuals stepped forward. It was as if their brazenness spoke for them, 'We despise your rules.'

'All right. You all want to break discipline. You can. All six of you can take your uniforms off. Orderly, gather their uniforms in a pile.'

Their momentary hesitation was a signal to Shekhar that discipline had won. He said, 'Those of you who will follow the rules are welcome to return to their places.'

Four men stepped back.

'And you two—do you still want to break discipline?'

'We want to appeal to the general. We—'

'You only get an appeal after you've been punished. But you definitely can. Return to your places.'

The ranks were dismissed. As he returned to his office quietly, Shekhar thought that he hadn't wanted to escalate the conflict, but what alternative was left? And it wasn't as though he had done anything inappropriate . . .

He had just sat down in his office when he was summoned— the general wanted him.

Shekhar went over, stood at attention, clicked his heels and gave a salute. The general was sitting on a mattress in his tent. There were two high-ranking party workers with him.

'Come, come, sit—don't be so formal.'

Shekhar stood as he was.

'These two have some complaints.'

'Yes, sir.'

'What's all this about?'

In his summary, Shekhar included mention of the four incidents of gambling and the events of that day. He continued, 'These people have an objection to my decision.'

The general turned towards the plaintiffs and said, 'Look, brothers, it's wrong to play dice, so those who play should be punished.'

'We aren't talking about that. But it is completely unacceptable that two college students were publicly humiliated. There are several uneducated rustics amongst the volunteers. What must they be thinking? We didn't come here to be insulted like this. If you won't intervene, then all of us will—'

Now the general turned to Shekhar and said, 'Look, brother, it's only a matter of ten or fifteen days. We've got to come together and get through this. What's the use in getting someone upset? We have to get by.'

Shekhar couldn't let this go. He bit his lip in anger and said, 'Get by? Is that what you want, to get by? Then why all of these uniforms, all of this organization, all of these ranks? Why are you sitting there wearing a uniform with golden epaulettes and a sword attached? Why do we perform these drills? Why do we blow that bugle? The old village councils were better than this. All I know is that you need discipline to have an organization. I don't think that my decision was wrong. You can overturn it— that's up to you.'

The general was unprepared for this outburst. He said, 'You seem very angry.'

'No, I know exactly what I'm doing. I know that if we had the kind of discipline that I want, I'd be suffering the same punishment that I have doled out to these gamblers. But if that were to happen, I wouldn't have had to show up here. You can get by however you please. I couldn't care less about that. I'll take your leave.'

Shekhar was about to leave when a fellow, wearing pure khadi, sitting next to the general, said, 'But this goes against our principle of non-violence.'

Shekhar turned around. Angrily, he said, 'What?'

'To humiliate two men like this and cause them pain is violence. Our volunteer corps is non-violent.'

Shekhar was speechless for a moment. He wanted to burst out laughing and go away. Then, regaining control of himself, he said, 'The answer to your question will also be violence.' And then he left. When he got outside, he happily remembered that a few days ago he was given an opportunity to join the general's security detail on account of his height—the members of that detail didn't have to do any work, except for every two or three days when the honourable general went out somewhere with his entourage, they would have to march in front and behind him carrying spinning wheels on their shoulders as if they were Lewis guns.[22] He had turned down that opportunity then. Had he not done so, would he have been able to forgive himself today? . . .

Nothing came of it. The people who had been kicked out weren't asked to return, although they were given their uniforms back because they had paid for them. Aside from a few officers, who only did paperwork and never showed up, everyone else was opposed to overturning Shekhar's decision.

The student rebellion that was going to happen didn't. To create an unnecessary conflict and cause a commotion and to watch a free spectacle in the confusion—this wasn't their objective!

*

It was almost 9 p.m. By evening a thick fog had descended. It had begun to dissolve because it had started raining. Shekhar had put on an overcoat[23] and was standing at the gate to the camp watching people prepare to go to work and he thought to himself, 'The complaints will start coming in soon—"No one came to relieve of me of my duty"—who knows why the people responsible for the watch can't make adequate arrangements . . .'

To the left, there was a commotion near the statue of the dead leader who was this city's namesake. Shekhar tried very hard to listen; the commotion was getting louder and coming towards him. He took big strides and set off in its direction.

Three or four days ago the police had raided the camp—after searching the entire camp, they had left empty-handed. Ever since then, the mood in the Congress encampment had been a little tense—the volunteers suspected each person who looked strange, wore a black coat, had a long moustache, wore a turban with a plume, wore shoes and socks or held a cane in his hand of being an agent of the secret police. There was no threat from the secret police, nor was there a prohibition. But since the volunteers felt that this was inappropriate meddling, and because exposing spies was a natural human tendency, the volunteers would routinely tussle with such men and sometimes bring them to the camp's headquarters.

Five or six volunteers had just apprehended such an individual and were dragging him back with them. He was cursing at them and kept trying to free himself, but he was dragged along.

Shekhar approached and barked out, 'Who is this? Let him go! What's the problem?'

'He's a CID, CID!'[24]

'He's a thief! A thief! He was trying to get away!'

'Congress rule is no joke, you fool.'

Ignoring all of these replies, Shekhar broke in, 'Let him go!' The volunteers let him go and stood to one side. 'Who apprehended him? What's the problem?'

'He was walking by himself near the statue. I asked him what he was doing there and he told me to mind my own business.

I told him it was my business to guard the statue and that if he didn't have any business here that he should move along. He said, "I know your type, you watchmen." When I told him once again to leave and asked him for his name and address, he cursed at me. We caught him and were bringing him back to camp but more people showed up in the commotion, a couple of men even slapped him.'

Shekhar asked the man who was dusting himself off, 'Is that what happened?'

'I am a CID inspector. The men have disrespected me and have interfered with my work. I am to see each of them punished.'

'If you had just said at the beginning that you were a CID inspector, do you think you would have been insulted? These men are supposed to watch out for thieves or crooks. You have to agree that your behaviour was suspicious. Look, you are free to go. Please accept my apologies for your inconvenience.' Shekhar turned to the volunteers, 'You men have needlessly humiliated a respectable man. Those of you who hit him should apologize and will be punished back at camp. Two of you should take this man out of the camp, respectfully.'

'I don't need these bastards,' he said and then started off in one direction.

'It's for your own protection so that it doesn't happen again.'

Two volunteers followed him.

The guard had changed. Shekhar thought that while he was out, he would make a circuit through the township and see where the guard hadn't been changed so that he could do something about it.

Shekhar was startled to learn that because of the rain, some men had abandoned their posts after completing their shifts without being relieved and had returned to camp to find their replacements to send them to their posts. There was only a day left in the Congress session—only three days left for the camp—which is why he decided that it wasn't worth it to ask too many questions about all this. And besides, the men had enough good sense to go and find and send their replacements. He remembered what the general had said about 'getting by' and smiled.

It began to rain harder. Shekhar sped up.

As he approached the statue, he heard someone singing.

'Where are you, Krishna of the flute . . .'

And then a little haltingly as if he were experimenting with something new.

'Where are you, Mohan my replacement . . .'

The singer stopped when he heard the sound of Shekhar's boots. Shekhar saw the watchman eyeing him intently.

Shekhar asked, 'Is this your first shift?'

'No, sir.'

'How long have you been at it?'

'Since 3 p.m.—'

'Three? And no one came to relieve you at 6?'

'No, sir. The person who was supposed to replace me told me he had to go somewhere and asked me to cover for him. I agreed.'

'And at 9?'

'I don't know about that. Had someone been assigned to replace me, he would have shown up by now.'

Shekhar smiled and asked, 'Is that whom you were serenading?'

Embarrassed, 'I was just trying to ward off the fatigue—'

'Are you very tired?'

'No, but I am soaked through, and my arms hurt—'

Shekhar immediately felt sorry for the fellow who had done the work of two men and was now doing the work of a third—he felt as though he had found the one man in a camp of 14,000 who believed in his idea of discipline—not just believed but also followed it. First of all, it immediately lightened his heart and, second, he wanted to know what it felt like to stand in the rain, alone, for three or four hours. He came to a decision, 'You should go. I'll relieve you.'

'You?'

'Yes. I should see what it's like to be on the night watch, too.'

'But you don't have an umbrella,' said the volunteer as he uncertainly extended his own torn umbrella.

'This overcoat[25] should be enough. Go on, you should get some rest now.'

The volunteer left. Shekhar began pacing, steadily . . .

The night felt long. Shekhar thought about that volunteer for a short while, and then he fell into a conundrum.

It was wrong of them to have beaten up the CID man. But he had identified himself—what would have happened if they hadn't apprehended him? What would the point of keeping guard have been? If a stranger were to show up here, wouldn't I ask him who he was? Perhaps he came just to pick a fight—that's what they do after all. There was a tussle, so he accomplished his task. But how could we have avoided a fight? And if he had begun defacing the statue . . . How much should we put up with? Was the matter finished or were there new blossoms waiting to bloom? We'll have to see.

That volunteer had been on duty since 3 p.m.—he had to be one of the people who caught that man. So why didn't he go back with them? Perhaps he thought it necessary to guard the statue—he was standing there as if it were his only purpose in life . . . Would I be able to do anything with the same kind of devotion? If it's something that I think is important, then I stick to it like a leech, but what about work that has no meaning—work that is only work and more work? . . . Could I lose myself in work, forsaking all worldly distractions?

That's what Shashi had said, that I worry about my own problems and don't fulfil my obligations to the world around me . . . 'Grief only cleanses the soul of one who attempts to drive it away. No one else's.' That's what she had said . . . And 'pain is everywhere'—I had assumed that it was only in one place—and I am wandering around carrying only my own sorrows . . . Redemption does not come from sharing someone else's pain, but only in taking the place of someone in pain.

Is that why I decided to relieve him? I had also wanted to do something mindless—I relieved him for my own pleasure . . . and how could one ever avoid such pleasures? They were everywhere. There was also a pleasure in self-destruction—did that mean that people destroyed themselves for the sake of pleasure? . . .

Truth be told, I should have first called that scoundrel of an appointed officer here, given him a piece of my mind, and told him, 'You should relieve this poor man's duty. Walk and do some rounds in the winter rain, you might lose some weight' . . . *To suffer injustice is to increase it—was it a penance to suffer for the wrong reasons?*

In the distance, the bells rang, marking midnight. It seemed as if the sound of the bells had frozen from being drenched in the rain—it was so faint . . . Shekhar felt as if his overcoat were four times as heavy as before, and if it was once his protection, it had now become his enemy—because of his overcoat, his uniform was also soaked through and small rivulets of water ran down his back, tickling him. The socks on his legs were also soaked through—water filled his boots. The soles of his shoes were 'waterproof'[26]—they wouldn't let water on the outside in, nor would they let water on the inside out . . . Shekhar shivered once and then started walking faster.

It kept getting colder . . . 'Why hadn't the replacement come yet? Would this shift be just like the last?' His body was numb down to his thighs and knees. Now he couldn't even tell if there was water in his shoes or not, whether he had feet or not . . . It felt as if his hands and shoulders were only being held in place by crutches . . . He thought, 'If I stand perfectly still, I'll be stuck here like this statue.'

One . . . The sound from the bell was so faint that had Shekhar not been listening with rapt attention to the silence, it wouldn't have been heard . . .

The appointed officer . . . Everyone had become worked up about discipline—'It's violence.' If that was violence, then it was established on the fundamental violence of duty—of life even. Look at this, the appointed officer should be made to stand outside in the rain all night and that's called violence, but if he makes countless men stand here all night, drenched and exhausted, without a word or a sound, that's not called violence . . . If I were to say anything to anyone about this, he would say, 'What's it to you? You should do your work dispassionately. You should carry the weight of his mistake yourself. That is true penance. Penance is divine merit. Penance is religion. Penance—penance—penance! I am not trying to suggest that penance is bad, but who are you to demand penance? If you can tell me to renounce things, to do my duty selflessly, why can't you also tell him to do his duty one way or another, whether it is selflessly or selfishly . . .'

Two . . . This time Shekhar didn't get angry. An irrelevant smile spread across his face.

Penance . . . Everyone has their stick that they measure penance with—and that stick is a person's own penance or ability for penance . . . He who cannot renounce anything can be found praising renunciation everywhere, all the time—'So-and-so has performed such great penance', 'So-and-so is so sacrificing' . . . His stick is so short that everything appears to be extraordinary to him . . . A person who actually performs penance has no idea that it is a big deal. Giving of himself is only one part of his regular, daily routine, which is not strange, surprising, praiseworthy or exciting, and it does not explode with excessive sentimentality . . .

But would no replacement ever come and would this night never end?

Appointed officer . . . Make him stand on a stage and he would thunder out a speech about penance and make it seem much easier than his appointed post . . . Those obese, cursed people . . . Will only unqualified men ever become officers and honest men only ever servants? Each day I hear, the leader isn't here, the leader isn't here . . . Society will be crushed under the weight of such leaders, never to rise . . . The load that is placed on top of us can only be a burden; it can never help in carrying any weight, the ability to bear the burden will only be possessed by those that rise from beneath—overcoming obstacles, ties, burdens, fetters; with haunches hardened from wounds and hearts steeled through struggle, proud and free . . . We are fighting for freedom, but all of our leaders— those who will us forward, bear our burdens—are like snow falling from soaring clouds; none have grown from this broken earth, none have broken through the tough soil like new shoots . . .

Freedom, liberty, independence—such beautiful words! But where is the tilled, fertilized soil in which they can grow—the people; where can you find the chemical reaction in that soil to fertilize it—the people and the people's leader; and where is—

Three . . .

No, there was no use thinking about the replacement— what would happen now? It was 3 a.m., soon it would be 6 a.m. Then someone would come or he could go and call for someone.

At 6 a.m. the morning bugle would sound, and he would have to take attendance.

Yes, the leaders reproached the people, but was it the fault of the people that those leaders didn't come from within their ranks?

Independence is a natural right—those who desire it should appear automatically, they should grow like weeds. What need of soil or fertilizers or gardening? Then is it right to say that the people are to blame, that there is something wrong with the soil and that we aren't worthy of independence?

But our forests have been felled, our natural streams and springs have dried up, our soil has turned into wastelands. Whether jungles or orchards, we have to cultivate them again, so it is necessary that . . . And our leaders—they aren't necessary—there is no juice in those thorny cacti of the desert sands, nor do they have the ability to catch the rains of life or to break down themselves and make the desert bloom . . .

Shekhar was startled—the sound of footsteps . . . Would he really be relieved? There was no need for him now. The rain had stopped and he was as cold as he could possibly get . . .

But these were more than a single set of footsteps—Shekhar was blinded by the light of four or five flashlights and torches. Someone said, 'This is where it happened—this man is the officer in charge of the volunteers who attacked me.' Shekhar recognized the voice of the CID officer from earlier in the night and saw that a few police officers were standing with him. The officer said, 'Arrest him. Tell the Congress headquarters in the morning.' Two soldiers flanked Shekhar on either side. Shekhar asked, 'Am I a prisoner?' He got a response, 'Yes, you'll have to come to the police station.'

'What's the rush? You can arrest me in the morning. Right now, my legs are stiff from the cold; I can't walk.'

The soldiers caught him under his arms. The CID man who had been beaten said, 'Do you see his arrogance?' The soldiers dragged him along. Suddenly feeling insulted, Shekhar broke free with a jerk and said, 'I'll go where you want to go—I'm not desperate enough to need your help.'

The officer and the spy exchanged glances. The group advanced—and as they walked on Shekhar saw that the volunteers had seen the hubbub and spread the news and that people had begun to gather.

As he sat in the police car he remembered Shashi's words again, 'Pain only cleanses the soul of one who tries to end it. There is no purification in sharing someone else's pain, but only in taking the place of someone else in pain . . .'

Was he merely a vessel? Was a new chapter of his soul about to begin? Was he fully a man—a conqueror—a master of his circumstances?

Part 2

Bondage and Curiosity

Shekhar made his first appearance in court a full twenty-one days after he was locked up. That day he came to learn that he, along with five others, was charged with battery, assault, conspiracy to commit violence, attempted murder of a government official, interfering in the work of a government official and hiding materials in connection with a legal case. That very day he was transferred from police custody to a prison.[1]

Shekhar didn't know that there was a difference between police custody and prison—nor did he know the laws associated with each. Had anyone asked him, 'Do you want to go to prison?' he would have answered completely honestly, 'No.' When he was being sent to prison, he kept thinking, 'Is the case over? No witnesses, no testimony, no ruling. Will I be in prison forever?' He had heard and read about other cases; the process seemed strange to him . . . He wanted to ask his companions, but he was afraid they would laugh at him. At the time, he felt very small, very unlucky, very stupid . . . His companions were sitting in the lorry, laughing, and he thought with some surprise, 'They don't seem worried . . .' Shekhar learned from their conversation that two of them had already been to prison. Was it because they had already been to prison that they were so brave?

'Hey, Chief, how did you end up here?'

Shekhar surprised himself by how easily he narrated the events of his arrest.

The inquirer laughed. 'Did you notice his argument—*this man is the officer in charge of those volunteers who attacked me*—isn't that something? How were you implicated in the attack?' Suddenly the inquirer's face went serious. 'Your arrest was a drama of sorts—we were all picked up the next morning—and since you've been established as the officer in charge, they will place all the responsibility on you. So whose shift did you relieve?'

Shekhar told him.

'He was the one who caught him. We all got there afterwards. When people were caught and brought back to the camp, he said that he would remain on duty; he didn't have anything against any bastard CID agent, but if someone had done something to the statue, he'd deal with them.'

'Yes.'

'Are you planning on offering a defence?'

Shekhar looked at him silently—he didn't know how to answer the question.

'This is your first time, isn't it? Whatever happens, keep asking to stick with us. Co-defendants in the same case have the right to stick together. A lawyer and some arrangements will be made for the trial—then we can all decide together what we want to do.'

'All right.'

'And act really tough. You won't survive in prison if you don't act tough. And you're not a convict yet; you're just an accused. Nobody has the right to lord it over you, right?'

'Yes.' Shekhar smiled. He remembered that he had read somewhere that there was a legal principle that one was innocent until proven guilty. And toughness—he already knew how to do that.

When the lorry stopped inside the gate of the prison, Shekhar got down and noticed that there was a large, iron gate and the handcuff on one of his wrists was joined to a guard at the other end. That is when he understood the meaning of freedom, and he began cursing himself that until now—now that he was twenty years old—he had been uninterested in it. Why hadn't he ever thought about the significance of freedom as a deeply vital thing like hunger or thirst or breath, a matter of life and death . . .

When Shekhar found himself locked in a cell, he saw that his bedding lay in a pit on the right, a grinding wheel on a platform on the left, in the back corner was a plate coated in tar and a small clay jug for answering the call of nature, there was a lattice on the ceiling for light, a picket fence through which he could see an iron gate in front and a gap in the iron gate through which he could see more picket fences, and everywhere, everywhere it stank—and suddenly it became important for him to know his geographic location. *Where am I exactly? What are the boundaries of the prison and the land around me?* It was as if he couldn't breathe without knowing the answers to his questions . . . He knew what side of town the prison was on, that the gate to the prison faced north. He faced that direction and then turned and turned and turned and . . . So his cell faced east, but after that . . .

The matter could only be resolved the next day. In the morning he was allowed out to walk around which was when he realized that his cell was the twelfth in a row, and after that row was another row of perhaps forty cells, and there were two doors on the wall in front . . . The guard who brought him out into the yard to walk told him that one door opened up into a factory and the other to the barracks[2] for the whites . . .

In his mind, Shekhar transposed a map of the world on to the prison and then the location of his current position became clear to him—the gate was the North Pole, the warden's office was the Himalayas to the north, the factory was Japan, the far cells for the condemned was Arabia; and he, where was he? In some Siberian snowy oasis . . . It gave him some peace—wherever he was. Here the only real fear was that he might lose himself . . .

A little later his pride awoke. Had he been in the row facing the other direction, he would have been in India. But that wasn't a good row—the guard had said that the worst offenders were kept there, but it was still India . . . He was taken aback at his love for the shape and the condition of his nation's soil, its name, its map which had sprung up without his knowing . . . It wasn't like that before—there had been picturesque lands, family, but not India. Where was he outside of geography textbooks? He remembered

that while telling stories of Rajputs, rishis and courage, his father
would break into them saying, 'These are the kinds of gems that
burst forth from the land of the Aryans' . . . Shekhar felt that he
wanted to use his keen discerning talents to determine whether
he was one of those gems or not; but that was about some distant,
ancient land—about Aryavarta—while in his mind the Aryavarta
of the great epics had never been identical with the India of today,
which he trampled under his feet . . .

'Act really tough' . . . That toughness was growing inside him
uncontrollably . . . He hadn't committed any crime; but those in
the cells, the ones in 'India' who were completing their sentences,
he would be like them, he would get tough and fight . . .

His time for being out in the yard was up.

A full three days later, he had a chance to ask to be moved
near his 'friends'. The warden had arrived for an inspection.
Contemptuously he said, 'So those are your friends, eh?'

Shekhar ignored the sarcasm. 'We are all defendants in the
same trial. We have the right to meet.'

'Right? Hold on! This is prison, Mister! The only right you
have here is to grind flour at the wheel, understand? It's over
there!' The warden pointed to the platform inside his cell. 'Don't
worry. You'll get it.' He left without responding to his request.

But that evening when Shekhar was taken from his cell, he saw
that ten or twelve cells down was another open cell, and the one
who had advised him to act tough, Vidyabhushan, had emerged
from it, and the three other friends were being led in from the
other direction.

He had never imagined that he would be that happy to see
Vidyabhushan. He jumped up and hugged him, and then quickly
let go and stood back, embarrassed by his excitement.

For a moment the pair sized each other up from head to toe.
Vidyabhushan was a twenty-year-old lad of average height, well
built and fair-skinned. He had dry hair that was combed back, wide
forehead, straight nose, thin lips and a straight and narrow chin—
he looked like the studious and stubborn sort, and he certainly had
the flickering light of gentle mirth in his eyes. Shekhar decided

that the man was like-minded. He asked, 'You've been to prison before, haven't you? What did you do?'

'Yes. I was imprisoned during the non-cooperation movement. I was young then. It was harder then, too. I was charged with shouting out "Hail to the Motherland".[3] These days, political prisoners get fewer beatings.'

Shekhar looked at him from head to toe once again. *No, there was no shame in confessing my ignorance to this serious young man.* He said, 'Are political prisoners different? I don't really understand all this.'

Vidyabhushan smiled. 'It's no big thing—you'll catch on soon enough. Prison is a good college. I was sentenced to caning so when I felt the rod I understood some things very quickly. You get a degree in character here, definitely. But many fail.' His face became serious.

'Hmm.'

Suddenly remembering something, Vidyabhushan said, 'Right. We aren't going to be kept together, but we are going to be allowed to meet during the day. That's what they decided. That should be fine, too.'

'And what about the trial?'

'My brother came to see me today. A lawyer has been hired; he'll meet all of us tomorrow. That's when we can decide what to do next.'

He was suddenly overwhelmed by a hope that someone—not anyone, but Shashi!—might come to see him . . . His brother might come, but if Shashi came—could come . . .

The three other friends had arrived. They met, Shekhar learned their names, looked them over from top to bottom and determined that they didn't measure up to Vidyabhushan; they may very well have been fine volunteers, but there was nothing special about them that would make them emerge from prison improved. And he found it very easy to go on talking while thinking about the possibility of Shashi coming . . . He wasn't too worried about life in prison—the condition of daily life there wasn't as bad as the one he had proposed as punishment for himself during adolescence . . .

The days would pass—his body was tough enough; true, the Fates
were not under his control and they were so unhappy that . . .

*

The charges began to be read out. The lawyer explained to
Shekhar that it was unnecessary to worry, no charges would
really hold up—except possibly for one, the one about interfering
in the work of a government official; and that one not because
of the evening incident, but because of the incident at the night
arrest . . . The policemen could say that they had gone there
for official business when he had stopped them and argued, et
cetera. . . . But even without this reassurance, Shekhar's interest
in the court proceedings waned somewhat. Prison had opened up
a new world of sorts and there were so many questions rearing
up inside him that he couldn't worry about the questions and
answers asked in the courtroom . . . It seemed to him that he was
looking at this prison world from inside a prism;[4] the many forms
and many colours of each scene would appear to him in multiple
directions, and it became impossible to tell which was real, which
was a lie . . . All of the gauges that he had relied upon until now
were rendered useless; he was learning a new and terrible reality,
that everything was real, everything was a lie, everything was good
and everything was bad . . . And even now he could see that all
determinations about aims and plans had to rely on idealism alone,
but that idealism could not remain standing on a foundation of
tired ideals—there needed to be a revolution in the soul within . . .
Seeking out Vidyabhushan's help became a necessity for him. But
during the day Vidyabhushan was focused on the trial—Shekhar
had entrusted his welfare to him—so Shekhar would spend the
mornings confused, in knots, and the days thinking about this web
of a dilemma and unravelling its threads.

It began on the day that Vidyabhushan was saying that
in defending the honour of our nation we need to build an
organization that could keep the arrogance of government officials
and rulers in check, when Shekhar interrupted him to ask, 'So tell

me, did you beat that CID officer or did you just get locked up like me?'

'I hit him. I wouldn't have been able to forgive myself my whole life if he had escaped untouched after such insulting behaviour.'

'Why?'

'What would you do if someone insulted your mother or sister while you were on a walk? Would you let him go even though he was a scoundrel just because he was also an agent of the government?'

'But he was a part of the government—how could any government run? What if you were running the government? Then—'

'A part of the government—so should we hit him if there was no fear of retaliation by the government? If you are talking about violence, isn't it also a kind of violence to fail to defend one's self-respect? Violence against the self is the worst kind of violence, because it breaks the spine of national pride—of the nation itself.'

'So what you are saying is that whenever someone gets angry he should express it, never hold himself in check? That will cause a total breakdown in morality.'

'No, that's not what I'm saying. One kind of anger is a weakness, and another kind of anger is an obligation. If one's nation is insulted, then getting angry about that is an obligation with respect to the nation and the community—that anger is something required of all of us by the nation. Otherwise it would be like being stuffed with rubbish on the inside instead of breath.'

'If it's justifiable to get angry over an insult to the nation, then it's also justifiable to get angry over an insult to the province, the religious sect, the family and ultimately even one's self. Why are those signs of weakness?'

'All right. But the issue is not over the crude object that is the nation or the region or the self. The issue is intention. To say that our national soil is barren can be a plain fact, while saying "Our nation is impotent" is an insult. Anger for one's principles is justified.'

'Then is religious zealotry justified? Religion is an ideal, too.'

Vidyabhushan stammered, 'N-no! You have to draw the line somewhere. But we understand that "devout" and "zealot" are different words with different meanings, which means that there are some elements in zealotry that are bad. What they are, we'll have to find out. The anger of zealotry primarily arises from individual intolerance—I want to show that my religion is superior to your religion because I am better than you. This is obviously unjustifiable and the root arrogance in it has to be dug up.'

'Humph.' Shekhar thought for a long time and said, 'So what did we decide?' He laughed at his own question.

'The anger that is for your principles, that's a religious obligation, we've agreed to that. What remains is determining what principles are, since simple definitions of it are tricky, but we can say that a principle is that feeling which attempts to end the enmity between man and man, that gradually attempts to expand their boundaries and bonds.'

'But when it's a question of man against man, then nationalism can also produce a barrier, no?'

'Definitely! Europe is already facing an era where nationalism is a problem—there national organizations have become impediments to human liberty.'

'Hmm.'

Shekhar's 'hmm' was so pregnant with thoughts that he forgot to be curious any further. He wasn't entirely convinced, but Vidyabhushan had certainly delivered a serious blow to his mind— he was shaken by the challenge posed by such great questions.

*

That pride or arrogance could be a social obligation was a new idea for Shekhar. He had never had any special interest in political matters, and it grieved him to see the pettiness of politics each time he read in the papers about political arguments or proportional electorates. 'Why politics?' The question wasn't about politics but about life, and he could never ward off the magnetic pull of such questions. When his brain had become entangled in this knotty question derived from Vidyabhushan's thesis, the push from this new perspective left him in a daze. He knew that he wasn't completely convinced by Vidyabhushan's words, and he also knew that no one could ever be convinced by explanations that someone else had thought up; arguments became valid when they emerged from one's inner spirit. At most someone else can clear some of the weeds from the fertile soil of the inner spirit.

He was at war with himself over this matter for three or four days. Was pride a social obligation? Three days later the giant demon of curiosity awoke inside him as though it had just overpowered one rival and was preparing for a new battle when its call of 'Battle me!' received a new, terrible question in response—what is government? Isn't it an obstacle to freedom? Can't we live without it? Can we also destroy it? How can we destroy it?

If it was good to move towards liberation—and how could that not be good?—then the existence of state power was bad—or if it wasn't, then it could be. When? And in such moments, which of our principles become a religion for which we must become angry, go to war, become proud?

And rage . . . war . . . violence . . . Was violence justified? If Vidyabhushan's argument was right, then violence was justified and could be a religion. But . . . he believed, wanted to believe, that man hated violence, had a natural aversion towards committing acts of violence . . . And he held that no natural drive could be wrong—if our ethics did not support those drives, then our ethics were wrong—not nature; he had total faith in a natural law grounded in nature. When he couldn't give answers to 'Why? What proof did he have?' the only reply he would offer was that his instinctive desire to believe in it was the proof. Why should a man choose to believe in it? Because in his heart of hearts he was ethical. He wanted to accept as valid the criterion of the morality of creation. And if the main element in human nature was morality, then how could it not be foundational in nature, too?

Nature was moral. Then was violence also moral? If not always, then sometimes, in special circumstances, could it be? Was murder justified sometimes?

324 Shekhar: A Life

And then the practical question—could any good come from it?

Ah, Goddess Curiosity—she is so irrepressible that she seems a demoness.

The question of actions is always smaller than the question of principles, and so much more immediate; the practicality of violence was such a question for Shekhar.

He asked Vidyabhushan, 'Is violence ever justified? Can any good come of it?'

Vidyabhushan smiled and said, 'You've been thinking about it the whole time, haven't you?'

Shekhar bristled, 'Shouldn't I?'

Vidyabhushan laughed. Then he turned serious and said, 'Then listen. Sometimes violence is so extremely necessary that it becomes justified. Or you could say that it becomes so justified that it becomes necessary. In reality, it is then no longer violence. When you get a boil, the treatment is to lance it. If that causes you pain, is that violence? It's not violence because it is for the good of the sufferer; there's no benefit to the doctor. And if an untreated patient is writhing in agony, then it's not violence even if you have to kill him to save him, even though he would lose his life. Or when violence comes in the form of a social obligation. All that remains is the question of its utility— in the examples I gave, the warrant was in its utility. Yes, one has to remember that the warrant cannot be personal gain, only social utility.'

'It worries me to see you come to such conclusions. Do you really think that violence is forgivable if it's social? Can one society commit injury against another society?'

'Don't misunderstand me. By social I don't mean any one society; I am interested in that entire collectivity of which we— humankind—are one part. From the same point of view where murder is non-violent, plucking and throwing away a single shaft of wheat will be violence too because that action does no good for the global community, rather it destroys the possibility of a little bit of good.'

Still unconvinced, Shekhar spoke, 'All right, we'll leave that aside. Let's go back to where we started. What good came or could have come from hitting the CID agent like you did?'

'I've already given you one—it was necessary to defend one's self-respect, and that was impossible without thrashing him. If you think that is too ephemeral a benefit, the second is that it will teach the CID agent a lesson, that insulting a man is not a laughing matter.'

Shekhar smiled and said, 'That's the lesson they wanted to teach you.'

'Yes, but not every CID agent can teach this lesson to everyone all the time. It costs the government 1000 rupees to conduct a single trial. If they had 100 such incidents to deal with, the government would have to find another remedy.'

'In other words, you want the government to be afraid, to tell them that these are men deserving of respect. If I'm not mistaken—I don't know much about these things, after all—then this is the same argument made by people who are called terrorists.'

'Umm—yes. And no one is treated as unjustly as they are. First of all, it's unfair to call them terrorists, although they don't make a point of removing terror from their programme. In this day and age, a person whose political development gets to the question of terrorism and stops is only as mentally developed as a seven-year-old child. The plain truth is that he cannot have the same moral force that everyone knows several so-called terrorists possess.'

'You are testifying as if you were a terrorist yourself.' Seeing Vidyabhushan shake his head, Shekhar said, 'But to me it seems that this is all wrong. Nothing can come from violence. It is destructive. It is pure ruin; it cannot be creative. Take that same example of the lance: the cure for an illness is medicine—that's what makes someone healthy. The lance is a trivial object; one becomes healthy after a month of nursing and recuperation. Similarly, any improvement in our social conditions will only come through natural developments.'

'I can accept that. I accept that the lance is trivial and secondary, but it is still necessary, right? There is also a social medicine that is given to society after acts of violence—you can think of that as more important if you like. But it doesn't eliminate the importance of the first thing.'

This was another large morsel for Shekhar—it would take him a long time to chew it. Shekhar wasn't comforted. He felt, 'There was definitely a mistake in the logic.' Extraordinary circumstances—unavoidable evil—he had heard these arguments before. He had heard the story of Vishwamitra having had to eat dog meat a long time ago—but he felt as though there was a weakness in the principle that was hiding behind sophistry. If one justified even some violent acts, it meant justifying everything; it meant accepting all violence. Even if a person saves himself with recourse to violence, he finds himself living in the shadow of sin for the rest of his life. It was a straightforward matter—violence was either justified or it wasn't, it was completely defensible or completely indefensible. But in either case, the way forward was unclear . . .

*

Shashi came to see him along with his older brother Ishwardutt.

Shekhar had wanted her to but Shashi hadn't come before. He didn't know that there could have been a reason for his hope. No . . . had Shashi been there in the city, then he could have hoped, but she was in a distant village, and alone . . .

But she came. Shekhar was so overwhelmed with emotion that he couldn't even talk to her, and visiting hours were drawing to a close . . . As he was talking to Ishwardutt, he'd stare at her for an instant and then go on talking to his brother . . .

When visiting hours were almost over, Shashi finally asked, 'Shekhar, were you really involved?'

Shekhar looked at her searchingly. He wanted to know what she was thinking—fear, concern, admiration—what . . . He couldn't detect anything. He said with a plain gravity, 'No.'

Shashi didn't say anything. It seemed to Shekhar that she had no further curiosity or demands. So he distanced himself from the storm of his emotions and asked, 'Why, Shashi? Did it give you some comfort?'

'What do you mean, comfort?'

'That I am innocent.'

'Oh . . . Yes, it gave me some.'

'Why? And what if I had been guilty?'

'That would have given me comfort, too. I wanted to know. Just knowing your side of the story gives me solace. It doesn't scare me.'

Shekhar had wanted so much to ask, 'Why, Shashi? Do you have so much faith in me . . .' but the presence of his brother drained his courage. He wasn't sure if he would have been able to ask such a personal question even if they had been alone, but she had deciphered his secret query, which is why as she was leaving she looked him straight in the eyes and said, 'Heroes are never guilty . . .' And she kept walking. Shekhar quivered from the look of affection in her eyes and saluted the pioneering sister who had first coined the word 'hero' for her brother . . . How important it was to receive affection in jail! Love—love was ultimately a passion, and jail was the playground of passions, but affection . . .

The court case became exceedingly boring. Day after day after day after day—listening to the same stories each day from ever-new voices in ever-new tellings, and the tricks and acrobatics the lawyers used to present the real truth in an upside-down manner . . . One day, after much turmoil, Shekhar came up with a way to entertain himself—he wrote a satire about his lawyer's arguments, showed it first to his friends, then sealed it in an envelope and put it in front of the magistrate. At the time the magistrate[5] was paying attention to what the lawyer was saying. Disinterestedly, he asked, 'What is this, an appeal?' and kept listening. But after the afternoon recess when the court reconvened, he looked at Shekhar intensely, with a little bit of mercy and a little bit of irritation, and the faintest of smiles appeared on his lips . . . Shekhar couldn't be certain that he had understood his state of mind, but then he remembered his satire and smiled, too . . . 'My Lord, the witness says a certain thing was above, another thing below . . . But if you were to stand on your head and look—and it's clear that justice cannot be served without looking from this vantage—then the thing that was described as being above is really below, and the thing which was on the right is now indisputably on the left . . . The person who gives such an incorrect answer and false testimony can only be corrupt. I ask you not to give his testimony any weight and ask your permission to cross-examine him.'

But such things couldn't be done all the time. And as he sat in the courtroom, Shekhar often found his thoughts turning to Shashi. He recalled each word she had spoken to him, and it was as if the light in his mind focused on them and kept taking photographs of them; and then surprised, he would think about why this girl was becoming more important to him . . . Wasn't she like a sister to him? Certainly, but why wasn't she like Shekhar's older sister, Saraswati? Saraswati, too, cared deeply for Shekhar— still did—but now that she was married, and had two or three children, she had become a distant object to him. Shekhar had also received a similar, straightforward, honest friendship from Saraswati, but . . . He didn't know what to call the difference, and if he couldn't say it, how could he explain it to himself . . . He couldn't fully understand Shashi the way he could Saraswati— Saraswati simply was. Ever since he had regained his senses, he had seen her near him. But Shashi was this result of his search— he had searched for her in a teeming world of countless lives to fix in the sphere of his life. She was his sister, meaning related, but still new, a little unfamiliar, a little hard to comprehend . . . No, that wasn't it—he couldn't understand it at all . . .

Shashi came to see him again. This time Shekhar found the courage to converse with her, and he told her some things about his friends in jail. She listened quietly, her wide eyes fixed on Shekhar . . . After a long time he suddenly realized that even though her eyes were focused on him her mind was somewhere else, as if she were trying to say something to him while listening to his meaningless chatter.

'What? Do you have something to say?'

Shashi wasn't startled. She smiled.

'Do you know the people who beat up the CID officer?'

'Yes, why?'

'Were they all arrested?'

'No, most of them are still free.'

'Really? And were the rest of them there with you?'

'Yes, they were, although . . . let it go. Those are legal issues.'

'So why were you arrested?'

Shekhar gave her the abridged version of how he was on duty in the place where the incident had happened, and that was how he was caught up in all of this.

'You were on watch—why?'

Shekhar explained the circumstances.

Shashi was quiet for a while. Then she said, 'Are you doing all right?'

Shekhar looked her in the eyes and said, 'I'm happy. I haven't been able to forget what you told me when I was leaving for college.'

Shashi was a little confused, 'Me? What did I say—I don't remember.'

'That's for the best. You should always forget the best gifts, Shashi—'

The question that was in Shashi's eyes slowly vanished. Who knows what Shekhar felt when he looked at her expression—as if the blood from a single artery was coursing through the distant brother and sister, and in that perfect intimacy there was no room left for conversation . . . Was Shashi thinking the same thing? How could he know?

As she started to leave he asked, 'But you didn't tell me—'

'What?'

'You wanted to tell me something—I could tell.'

There was pain in Shashi's smile. Haltingly she said, 'Yes, I did want to. But I couldn't say it—not here. And I couldn't write it—I didn't want to write the kind of common note that gets passed around amongst the guards.'

'I tore one up after writing it, too. So then?'

'We'll see—' she said and then left. If only she had understood
what it meant to get someone in jail all worked up and then leave
them unsatisfied, then . . .

That night Shekhar did what had made him grind his teeth in
irritation when he had heard countless prisoners in jail do it—after
he was locked in his cell, after he had been counted and the locks
and chains had been checked and the cry of 'All is we-ell' had
made a mockery of the terrible fact that 'All is awful' and there was
a little peace and quiet, he caught hold of two bars on the door of
his cell with both hands and began violently shaking the door with
his whole body . . . His body began to tremble, his teeth gnashed
together as if grinding sand, the lock, the bars, the frame all rattled
and the solid iron door across the courtyard let out an expectant
hiss in sympathy . . . And from the shaking of his taut body, his
sensory perception seemed to take the form of the trembling of
the earth, that unbearable, booming racket was like the sound of
the dance of some destructive God . . . He couldn't stand it—and
because he couldn't stand it he shook the door even harder . . .
I want to break these chains, want to be free, because someone
wants to tell me something and I need to know what it is . . .
It's more important than happiness, more important than peace,
more important than life, more important than my strength and
efforts . . . impotent, impotent, impotent vain anger . . . useless,
useless, useless drifting arrogance.

Ultimately, it was this illusion that gave him comfort—
drenched in sweat, reeling with exhaustion and drowning in shame
at the contempt from the other prisoners, he threw himself down
in the pit and stared at the ceiling with still, dry eyes . . .

She wants to say something—I want to know what, I want to
know, I!

He turned over all of a sudden with a shudder—something
like a shudder shook his body. After half an hour the smell of
fresh mud from under the reed mat let him know that he had been
sobbing involuntarily.

*

A stultifying fog descended over Shekhar's brain—a curtain of numb rage. That night after crying like that, he was unable to shake off the weight that was crushing him beneath it . . .

Slowly, a fear came over him—am I losing my mind? Is life in jail breaking me? Am I a coward? . . . A doubt poked at his insides like a stone poking at an internal wound . . . Otherwise why would I cry so helplessly? The powerful, heroes—did they cry? Did they bleat like sheep locked up alone in a cell?

He had read somewhere that those who cannot cry are clearly deceiving themselves. To be able to cry is a sign of being true to yourself—to your heart . . . Perhaps that was right . . . But this—this was something else; this was sheer, completely effete helplessness . . .

But why did he feel very light, clean and, yes, strong after he had cried . . . Defeat didn't feel this way; each time they were defeated men found themselves weaker, a little more fallen . . . Had he fallen—was he falling?

His wounded ego screamed out in protest at this question, but he kept asking questions like a relentless inquisitor—Why, if it was a lie, did it sting? Say it, tell me, are you guilty? Have you fallen?

If he had even the slightest of suspicions that the guards had given him greater liberties because they had seen him in this defeated state, he would have rejected them. No one had said anything to him about these new privileges, but the warden didn't stop him when he walked past his row of cells during exercise time and into the other row—'India'—and would often let him talk to the other prisoners.

It was during one of these walks when Shekhar ended up in the hall outside one cell that the warden said, 'Sir, the inspector will kill me,' but Shekhar could tell from the sound of his voice that the inspector didn't really care; it was the warden himself who wanted to prevent him from going near that particular cell. That prisoner certainly had to be a special man. He ignored the warden and slipped inside.

'You've probably only been here for a short while, haven't you?'

The friendliness of the question and the natural affability of the voice made Shekhar look with a start. A wizened countenance nestled between the bars, whitened, matted locks above and a gleaming beard below hiding a pure smile which greeted him like sunlight dancing on the peaks of the Himalayas . . .

Shekhar said with wonder, 'How did you know?'

'It shows on your face. New faces are always full of questions. They want to understand. Old sinners are always on the lookout for someone who will listen. When one's life is over, there is only one thing left for him—his story!'

Filled with a new wonder, Shekhar asked, 'Who are you?' It was as if all his good manners had slipped away with this man—the question could either be asked in a direct fashion or it wouldn't be asked at all.

'My name is Madansingh. I was arrested in 1909. Been in jail ever since.'

How could this man laugh after being in jail for twenty-one years? Shekhar felt as if he had become a little smaller, or perhaps that the man in front of him had grown taller.

'You've already figured out that I've only just arrived here. I used to be in college. I went from being there to being here.'

'What class were you in?'

'MA. I passed my BA last year.'

'You are a fortunate man. I was completely uneducated when I came here. I learned to read and write here, and I cried and struggled to understand the big ideas they contained that one cannot live without knowing. And you—you've come with an education. There's a heavy vault in front of you, but you possess the key.'

Thoughtfully, Shekhar responded, 'I don't know about that—I feel quite small.'

'Man is quite small, after all! But whether you like what I say or ignore it, it's still true. I made my own key through my own efforts. You've heard the saying that a poor man's breath is like a bellows that helps melt iron? That's what I used . . .' Another sweet laugh rang through the cell.

Shekhar's face clearly showed an expression of disbelief. Despite trying to, he couldn't hide it.

'Oh, I see—you're thinking that this man is making up stories. But believe me, whenever my intellect failed me, I relied on the strength of my tears, yes, in the strength of my tears.' He turned to face the inside of the cell and said, 'Look over there, I have proof. Can you read this?'

On the facing wall where Madansingh was pointing, Shekhar could make out some words written with great pains.

What is slavery? It is not the knowledge of the unpleasant, not even faith in the false; slavery is the condition of being unable to discriminate between fact and fiction; that bondage, that prohibition, which steals away the right to know.

'And look at this.'

Shekhar read, again, with some difficulty:

Civilization is an endless effort at prolonging infancy. It wants protection; manliness demands courage.

'There's more here in the darkness—if you want I can read them to you. But perhaps you plan to go now. Well, the important thing is that to come up with each aphorism I had to cry for hours. It seems to me that sitting still for hours is not penance; penance only begins when one can't sit still.' Suddenly his face lit up. 'Look—I learned something without crying, just by being close to an educated man.'

Shekhar fell silent in embarrassment. Madansingh kept speaking, 'There are a hundred similar aphorisms up here—three years' worth of work—that's when the walls were whitewashed. The ones from before were erased; a few are still visible—' He ducked down in one corner, 'Yes, look here—*The truth of revolution is that tradition is indispensable for it.*'

He stood up straight and looked at Shekhar; he was growing anxious to say something, 'You're thinking that I read all of these in books, right? You have the key to knowledge—I am still learning.'

There was not even the slightest hint of immaturity in that man—his humility seemed to burst forth from some internal spring. Feeling even more inconsequential, Shekhar asked, 'Have you been in this cell for three years?'

'Three? I've been here for nine years. But you've heard the story about the Pathan, haven't you—the one who spent three years in jail and said he was twenty-eight years old?' Seeing Shekhar shake his head, he said, 'When he was released from jail, someone asked him, "Khan, how old are you?" He said, "Twenty-eight." The questioner asked again, "How long were you in jail?" So he answered, "Don't know." "How old were you when you went to jail?" He said, "Twenty-eight." When the questioner doubted his arithmetic, he said, "Why do you count jail? Nothing happened in all that time I was here, so how could I have aged?" That's how I feel. Can't stop my hair from turning white . . .' The slightest trace of sadness passed over his eyes.

Shekhar was seized by a sharp desire to fold his hands and bow down to this grey-haired infant . . . But some false pride spoke to him, 'No, this can't be done.' He thought he would say goodbye and leave.

'You aren't annoyed, are you? You'll come back, won't you? I told you, this foolish old man likes to go on talking, he just needs a real listener!' Then Madansingh smiled.

The inner tension in Shekhar seemed to dissipate. He laughed and said, 'And I am just such a curious one.' And then in a suddenly serious tone, 'I got answers to some of my questions that I didn't have the courage to ask just from listening to you right now. It seems that arrogance is natural, humility must be learned.'

'Have you caught the bug of speaking in aphorisms, too? In jail, all conversation becomes unnatural.'

As he reached the gate to the courtyard, he gathered up all of his courage, turned back and said, 'Last week, I cried a lot, too . . .' And then suddenly filled with gratitude and embarrassment he quickly set off for his own cell . . .

Then one day while walking he reached the end of the row of cells in 'India'. The last four cells perhaps held prisoners condemned to be hanged—the solid gate to their hell was shut, and inside the sentry kept guard with a rifle. Shekhar turned back.

He was walking past a few cells and thinking that he wanted to talk to someone when someone called out, 'Hey, Moulvi!'

Shekhar couldn't imagine that the call was for him, but the warden with him was Sikh and the same voice called out again, 'Hey, Moulvi, come and talk to me.'

Shekhar asked from the courtyard, 'Were you calling me?'

'Yes, who else? You've turned into a real Moulvi—you haven't shaved for days. Don't you have a razor?'

'I do, but no one pays attention here, so I didn't bother.'

'But you're a respectable man. Even if no one else notices, shouldn't it bother you? You should always be ready to return to life outside—then, if they release you or not, it makes no difference!' And he started laughing, exposing his enormous but beautiful and dazzling teeth.

Shekhar couldn't decide how to respond to this simple familiarity. If it had come from a place of self-confidence then it deserved respect, but if it came from a place of mockery, then . . .

'If you're not, then can you send me a blade? I like feeling that I could leave at any time.'

Shekhar laughed, 'All right, I will bring you one tomorrow.'

'You're one of those new political types who are in here for beating up that CID man, aren't you?'

'Yes.'

'All right. Well, shall I keep calling you Moulvi?'

'It's up to you.'

'Moulvis are all hypocrites, but if my Moulvi is a Hindu, then it will work out.'

Shekhar was quiet.

'And listen, I get lonely here. The evenings are the worst. Which cell are you in?'

'In the last row—the twelfth.'

'Hey, that's far! Well, I'll sing for you in the evenings. You don't dislike singing, do you?'

'If it's a song, I won't dislike it.'

He chuckled. 'You can decide if it's a song or not. I'll sing either way. All right, you should go now.'

Shekhar started to leave.

'My name is Mohsin—Mohammad Mohsin. But what will you call me?'

Mischievously, Shekhar replied, 'Pandit.'

'Too good. That works. Then I'll put on a tilak, too, after I shave.'

When he returned, the warden told Shekhar that the young man, Mohsin, was a strange character. He called everyone 'Hey, you'—the subinspector and the gentlemen, too—and he was always making jokes all the time. He was an orphan, had no parents, siblings or relatives, which was why he had fallen apart. He had been raised and educated by a moulvi, but he was a trouble-maker later in school, and he was here on a year-long sentence for spreading treason. He had been there for five months now. He was always up to something and was always receiving extra punishments—he was going to spend tonight in handcuffs.

'Handcuffs at night?'

The warden explained that this was a punishment meted out as per the jail's penal code. The prisoner would be handcuffed at night after being locked in his cell, and they would be taken off in the morning for hard labour. If you were really bad, then your hands were cuffed the other way—behind your back. Then you would have to spend the entire night lying on your stomach. 'But this young man really is a strange and shameless one in that he has been handcuffed behind his back for the last fifteen days and he still doesn't stop misbehaving.'

'What did he do?'

'First of all, he wouldn't do hard labour. He says, "I spread treason and you put me in jail. Why should I do hard labour? I'll grind flour for the king when you grind flour for me." Second, he throws away the work that he has been given. He was given grain to grind and he fed it all to the pigeons. When he was asked, he said, "The pigeons are my brothers—they keep me happy." The warden put him in chains so he used the chains to dig up the grinding wheel. He made a pit with some bricks and filled it with dirt and started watering it. When he was interrogated he said,

"I'm farming—I've planted corn there!" You know what that kid is—? Spawn of the devil!'

Shekhar's curiosity was piqued. He decided to see Mohsin again and went to his cell.

That evening, he was sitting thinking about who knows what when he heard the sound of someone banging on the bars of a door in the distance. He suddenly stiffened—he remembered what it felt like when he had caught hold of the bars and jerked them back and forth . . . He was filled with sympathy—at that moment someone was going through what he had just been through . . . He listened more intently. All of a sudden, the commotion ended, and Shekhar heard something that sounded like someone calling.

Had he heard correctly? The call came again—yes, Mohsin was calling. He filled his lungs with air, raised his chin, cupped his hands around his mouth to amplify his voice, imitating the farmers he had heard in his childhood, and cried out, 'Pandit, Ho-o!'

That time Mohsin heard him. 'Shall I sing?'

'Yes, sing.'

'What were you doing?'

'I was just sitting here.'

'All right, listen.'

Shekhar crossed the distance of eighteen cells in his imagination and focused his attention there. They say that all the senses work independently; Shekhar used the perceptive powers of all five or six senses collectively to listen to Mohsin's song:

'. . . so what if he comes . . .'

Mohsin had a good voice. His voice had intensity and depth. But singing so loudly also made it occasionally harsh—and it cracked sometimes, too—but still the natural vibrato in his melody sent shivers through his listeners—as if the 'da-dum' beating of the silently endured suffering within it found an echo . . .

> When all hopes have vanished, all thoughts vanished, too
> What difference does it make if the postman brings a message then.

The song stopped. Shekhar's tension dissipated somewhat.

'Is it a song?'

'Yes. Quite good, too.'

'Shall I sing some more?'

'Aren't you tired?'

'I don't get tired from singing!'

'All right, sing.'

Mohsin began singing again. But after singing two or three more verses, his voice grew faint and soon it was impossible to hear it. Shekhar didn't want to point this out—he was full of irritation, praise and compassion for that crazy, courageous man . . .

A few minutes later, another cry, 'Moulvi, O-ay!'

'Pandit, Ho!'

'Now go to sleep. I'll sing more tomorrow.'

'All right.'

Silence. Shekhar remembered that since he was still only an accused he was allowed a lantern—he could read and then go to sleep. But Mohsin was a convict—he had no light, just the pitch-black night. Shekhar turned down the light, got up, went to the door of the cell, caught hold of the bars and stood staring at the dark sky.

The clouds had gathered above—untimely clouds—meaningless and random . . .

There were around 1400 prisoners in the jail at present and at least 700 didn't have any light, nor did they have the oblivion-generating darkness of sleep . . .

Silence—the sentries' footsteps, the watchman's 'All is well!' and the hooting and moaning of some owls in the distance all pierced it. Shekhar's unblinking eyes looked out on the invisible, dark sky . . .

Drip-drip—the first raindrops of April . . . Suddenly tired, Shekhar lay down and watched the small, half-blue flame of the lantern and the dark shadows it cast on the ceiling.

Bondage . . .

*

Shekhar received a letter.

He couldn't stand the thought of his own letters being read and censored before being sent out so he had stopped writing them altogether. And he had received very few letters from others, and when they did come they were ones that didn't need responses. But one day the lawyer gave him some papers and said, 'Be careful with these, they are important documents for your court case. When you go home—forgive me, back to jail— read them carefully.' Shekhar took them. When he was locked up in his cell back in the jail and the night had become darker, he took them out and started to read. The papers were merely transcripts of the court proceedings that had notes scribbled in pencil in a few places, but in the middle were a few pages stitched together, pages that had caused Shekhar some surprise when he first saw them—it was a letter from Shashi written in pencil in tiny characters . . .

For a moment, Shekhar forgot everything and stood there impotently—his heart was beating so fast that he felt like he was drowning. Then he began devouring the letter with starving eyes . . .

Shashi was getting married. The groom had been chosen, a date had been set in June, too, and Shashi didn't want to get married—she didn't even want to consider it for a few years.

Had Shekhar been out of jail, she would have asked for his help to delay the discussion, but he was in jail, and . . . and there was no one in the whole wide world who was on her side. There was her mother but she was alone, and how could she stand up against society? At the most she could push things from June until November, but what would that accomplish? She would still have made commitments, so she couldn't do anything else . . .

In a daze it occurred to Shekhar that the letter shouldn't be saved, so he mechanically reread it as if committing it to memory, diligently tore it up into tiny pieces, added water to the plate that normally held the wheat next to the grinding wheel, rubbed the pieces in the water until the writing disappeared, and then wadded up the pieces into a ball and threw it out the window. Then he stamped his feet as he stood up and began pacing in his cell and thinking . . .

What would he do? How would he help Shashi? She really didn't want to get married. She had written in the letter that her unwillingness was not like the fear and the lack of interest of ordinary girls; she was unwilling and unready and also felt like the victim of an injustice . . .

Had I been on the outside, I would definitely have done something. I would have argued and fought, debated. The groom was probably no good, too. He recalled the boys he knew in college who would become civil servants in the future—successful and famous and deemed 'worthy' in the special lexicon of the fathers of unwed girls—could he see his own sister as the wife of one of these men?

If she didn't want to get married, what was making her get married? Who was society to force her? Who were her relatives? Who was I? Who was anyone in the space of that sacred fire in which she offers up her soul as a promise? 'This is offered to Krishna; this is not mine—' No, it was, 'This is offered to the God of Fire; this is not mine . . . Fire . . .'[6] Fire . . . That was the real truth—the soul of a wife was always sacrificed like a martyr's . . .

Could I write to Aunt? But Shashi has already made her unwillingness clear. Could Aunt ignore her feelings? Still, she was pursuing the discussions about the wedding. Had Shashi not pressed her point hard enough?

What would happen if Aunt accepted Shashi's objections and stopped the wedding? First of all, the people who were running around looking for a groom—uncles, cousins, these, those—they'll all say that she had cried when one couldn't be found and now that they've found one she's acting all high and mighty, and if that was the case, then she could take care of her own arrangements; it's of no concern to us. Let them talk, to hell with them. At least Aunt will be free . . . Second, the people on the groom's side will be angry—yes. Third—third—what was third? There would be problems in the future—another husband would be impossible to find. If the race of man found no value in a woman like Shashi, they could go to hell. Shashi wouldn't die if she didn't get married.

Why doesn't Aunt put a stop to this? Doesn't she have any obligations regarding Shashi? Doesn't she feel them? And if she doesn't feel anything, who else will? She must feel something. But she also has an obligation to marry off her daughter. Parents have to do that, too. Whether or not the obligation actually exists, she certainly acknowledges it as does the whole society. That's how culture works—tradition is the same . . . If arranging marriages is a duty, then is it also a duty to arrange marriages well? Was this an example of arranging a marriage 'well'? . . . What does 'well' mean here? He should be educated, wealthy, from a good family, virtuous, upstanding, handsome, well-reputed . . . And what proof is there for all of these? He has a degree, he has a steady job or owns property, he has a relative who is a judge, he speaks with refinement, there is no gossip about him, he is fair-skinned and has nice features, he is praised by his friends and perhaps he has even been mentioned in the newspaper! Did these things make a man? Did these and only these things endow a man with that godlike quality entitling him to put the gains of someone else's lifelong sacrifices in his ledger? . . . Shekhar's mind turned again to several of his college friends—ugh! All of these things didn't guarantee[7] that the man-God of one's dreams wasn't actually a prayer-destroying demon . . .

The real question came down to this: whose obligation was marriage? The parents' or the bride's and groom's? And which obligation was paramount—that a person become a householder or that parents become in-laws? The parents' job was to assist, not to legislate . . . Should Shashi have been the one to put a stop to all this?

And what would have been the consequence? The relatives would certainly be angry. Her mother, too, perhaps. There would be gossip—'That girl has a bad character' . . . 'Her mother has spoiled her' . . . And the girls who had been deemed characterless, how long did it take to find proof of their characterlessness? And then? The ones that were called 'dangerous for society', society would become immediately dangerous for them . . . 'The girl hasn't been married. Why hasn't she? She must be too independent-minded' . . . 'Can such a girl keep on ignoring men now that she is twenty years old? Impossible!' And a slandering society will come together to enjoy the spectacle of the slandered—cruel demons!

Shekhar's brain was in knots and he couldn't think any further . . . He began pacing in rapid circles, and at each step he clenched his fists and asked, 'What do I do? What do I do? What do I do? . . .' His pace quickened and it only took him three steps instead of five until he had to turn around, and he had to turn around so often that it made him dizzy—he rubbed his forehead with both hands, then filled both of his fists with clumps of hair and clenched them . . . He was pulling his hair out as the ache descended over his head, but the question . . . What do I do? . . . What do I do? . . .

'Hey, Moulvi—O, hey!'

Mohsin was calling. Shekhar had no desire to respond to him. At that moment, he didn't want to think about anything other than Shashi's situation and his plans—he didn't want to know that anything else existed! Just his situation and Shashi's . . .

'Moulvi—O, hey! Hey, Moulvi!'

Who knows why, but Mohsin hadn't called him earlier that evening. Now he just kept on yelling, and his voice was getting louder and louder . . .

'Moulvi—O, hey! Are you dead? Hey, Moulvi!'

No, he wasn't going to leave him alone. Shekhar yelled, 'Pandit—hey!'

'What were you doing?'

'Nothing.'

'Why didn't you answer?'

'Wasn't paying attention.'

'Are you crying?'

'No—'

'All right, go to sleep. I'll stop calling you.'

Could he feel his pain from that far away? And could he tell from Shekhar's voice that he was upset? He felt guilty. He gathered himself up and yelled back, 'Pandit! Ho!'

'Yes, hey!'

'Will you sing for me?'

'Really? You're not up for it.'

'No, sing!'

'All right.'

Mohsin sang . . .

Shekhar only paid attention to a few verses before he started thinking, 'Why did Mohsin think of that song just then? Was he singing it for me?' But soon his mind wandered and he forgot to listen to the song.

He had asked, 'Are you crying?' How did he know? He had cried before probably—but Mohsin? Impossible. Had he felt like crying, he would have just fought with someone, that's all! Baba Madansingh had said that crying was a good thing—that crying brought clarity. A hundred times in three years—thirty-three times a year—about three times a month . . . Had Baba cried that much? How pure his laugh was! Could anyone imagine that that man had cried? And me—

In one quick motion Shekhar wiped the large tears that had formed in his eyes. Then he sat down.

I won't cry—fool! Who cares about clarity? I don't want clarity if it means crying. I'll burn my own blood to find clarity . . . Tears of blood—tears of blood—what does that mean? Is crying the same as burning one's blood? Nonsense. It's an excuse born out of weakness.

And me—I'm the kind of person whom Mohsin could tell had been crying even from afar . . . It would be better if I could just cry it all out—

No, I have to find answers. I have to find a way out for Shashi.

He got up and caught hold of the grates on the ceiling and looked up at the sky. There were a few stars scattered here and there. Unconsciously his body stiffened. His hands had become raw from gripping the bars—he let go in surprise.

No, I won't let the ferment in my soul dissipate; I won't ask anyone for help; I will find a way myself, for me and for Shashi, for Shashi and for me . . .

He began pacing again—one, two, three, four, five—one, two, three, four, five . . .

And the night rolled on—11 p.m. and all is well! 12 a.m. and all is well! 1 a.m. and all is well! 2 a.m. and all is well! . . . Nothing, fog, nothing . . . Afterwards, Shekhar regained consciousness when he realized the sunlight was on his face, it was 8 a.m., and he was exhausted and lying in the pit.

What had happened? A wave of memory crashed—Shashi.

He knew what he would write to her.

*

Shekhar felt as if he had awakened from a long sleep after he had written the letter; suddenly the world around him came into focus and all of his curiosities came alive; occasionally his thoughts even turned to the trial. Who knew why but the court dates kept being pushed further and further back. Perhaps the evidence was acknowledged to be weak and the government was coming up with a new strategy. Sometimes while listening to the testimony in court, Shekhar would think about which side was benefiting from its effects. But more often his attention would be on matters of principle and behaviour that had no bearing on daily life—the kind of questions that rose up repeatedly after butting heads with Vidyabhushan . . .

It had been a few days since he had been to see Baba Madansingh. One day, Shekhar suddenly got it into his head that he would ask Baba the questions that he normally asked Vidyabhushan—Baba's words left him with the feeling that even though the answers that he provided may or may not have been studied, they would definitely have the force of serious thought behind them . . .

The second time he met Baba Madansingh, he was as pleasantly surprised and welcoming as before; but he almost immediately became serious and asked, 'You look worried—what's the matter?'

It wasn't hard to talk to Baba, to ask him questions! Shekhar gave him a summary of the debate between himself and

Vidyabhushan and then asked, 'I want to know what you think. Take the question of violence first. Is violence justified? Can it be beneficial?'

Baba Madansingh looked over at the gate in the courtyard and asked, 'Are you alone?'

For a few days now, the guard had become more lax in his duties—the only thing he never forgot was lock-up time. The rest of the time he left Shekhar alone. 'Sir, you are an intelligent man, don't get a poor man like me into trouble.'

Baba Madansingh said, 'Look, I've told you already that I am not an educated man. If there is any substance in the things I say, it's because I've tried to understand things that I didn't understand by reading, by suffering through them. I've also told you that men don't live or think naturally in jail; it has a strange logic. So what do my words matter? I have a few aphorisms that I've created to comfort myself. One of these sayings is that each person should make his own path for himself. You probably have that aphorism in your books, no?'

Shekhar said, 'I'm in jail, too—in unnatural conditions. That's why these questions have become so important for me—do such matters come up in ordinary life? Out there you have to survive using your five senses, but here the sixth won't leave me alone. So what's wrong if the solution is also unnatural? I feel that your ideas will be more valid because you will also explain their shortcomings.'

'I'll tell you since you're asking. But after I tell you, forget what I have said, don't take it to heart. But if you ever find yourself in here, you'll work it all out yourself—and you are an educated man, too—and then you can recall the things that I said and determine if there are differences.'

'All right.'

'These aphorisms won't make you feel better—let's start with you. I consider nature to be of paramount importance. I also believe that its rules have been built on a very great wisdom, a great intelligence, and I have great faith in the future of humanity. I say these things intentionally—you will find them irrelevant right now.' He stopped momentarily and continued, 'You believe that violence is nihilistic, it causes total havoc and it cannot be creative. Completely fine. But how have you come to the conclusion that a thing that is not generative must also be wrong? And how did you come to believe that you alone are capable of acts of creation?'

Shekhar didn't say anything. His expressions revealed that he hadn't understood what Baba was driving at.

'You've probably read in books that when you want fresh air to flow through a house, you only need to make way for the air to exit. It enters on its own. When you breathe, you concentrate on breathing out; the lungs fill up by themselves. The scientists have turned it into an aphorism: nature abhors a vacuum. Good, it appears that you remember this aphorism. I have an aphorism, too, and it's that the most important God is the God of destruction—there is no question about the necessity or the lack of necessity when it comes to the God of creation. We will have to compose new terms of destruction; the things that are creative in your words—creation, birth—are assumed to be given. Compensations for imbalances are cyclical processes. That is why even in this age of devastation I have faith in the future of humanity—the future is the compensation for the present, which is why it is cyclical, and there is no escape from it.'

Baba stopped and looked at Shekhar. He seemed a little pleased and said, 'This argument perhaps hits hard at our egos. If destruction and creation are the ebb and flow of nature, then where does that leave us? Are we merely the means by which nature fulfils its objectives and nothing more? Have our destinies been ordained? Is free will a lie? There are no answers for such questions because these questions don't arise for everyone. And those for whom they do arise should come to their own conclusions.'

He stopped again for a while.

'I don't agree with the argument about lancing and treatment. I think that it's wrong to pose the question "Is it violence or not?" The question is, what is non-violence? Because I agree with you that we have a natural distaste for violence in us and there should be a reason for that. This aphorism of yours,' a smile spreading across his face, 'is very meaningful. All right, so what is non-violence?

It is clear that it is not passivity. Passivity and cowardice are the worst, most loathsome forms of violence. So then what is non-violence? If selflessness and self-sacrifice are non-violence, then it leads me to the conclusion that bloodshed can also be "non-violent". So how we can accept this last point and still continue calling all bloodshed violence?'

Baba Madansingh fixed his gaze on Shekhar once again.

'This is not a compelling argument. I'll say it before you do. If I am proposing it, it is only so that you will consider another point—that bloodshed can become a social obligation. And if that is the case, then bloodshed is not unjustified and it can be non-violent. My meaning is that if self-destruction can be non-violent, then the test of whether or not bloodshed is violent is its—let's say spiritual—necessity. Not whether the blood spilled is mine or someone else's. My blood is no less red than anyone else's.'

Shekhar's mind was unsettled. He didn't like Baba's arguments, nor what they implied, but he needed time to think. He said, 'That's enough for today. Let me chew on this and then we'll see about the rest. If there are any pits left after I'm doing chewing, I will bring them to you to help me crack them open.' He laughed.

'That's fine. I'll crack open your pits for myself. Today you should cut and eat your own fruit. I'm just offering a sample of my harvest.' Baba laughed, too. Then he started again, 'If you're going to have me crack open the pits, then you should take some more fruit. I told you that the elderly are always looking for someone who will listen.'

'Go on.'

'I contend that non-violence is good but only when it is defined correctly. That's also the only way it can succeed. It seems to me that non-violence will only be useful when it is aggressive—meaning when it is non-violent in name only. Like a boycott—a boycott is only useful when it is turned into a weapon against a particular individual or group. So even if India enacts an economic boycott against the whole world, it will be both impossible and useless, because it won't be felt by Britain and won't get us independence either. It will only succeed when it is focused against

Britain, meaning when it becomes an instrument of aggression. It's clear that this non-violence is only nominally so because non-violence shouldn't contain the feeling of aggression, not even for self-defence, isn't that so?'

In reply, Shekhar gave an indecisive, 'Hmm,' as if he were unable at present to give any kind of response.

'And if you want to fight about definitions, then "true" non-violence is self-inflicted suffering which is the ultimate violence. So let's stop these useless word games and turn to meaningful issues. I've already said that non-violence will only be successful when it's "aggressive", meaning non-violence in name only; even if there is no offensive violence from the other side, even if it is only self-defensive, it can succeed. This point should be so clear that it requires no elaboration. You know that the law makes an exception for self-defensive violence. So the conclusion is that self-defensive violence can also be successful—meaning only nominal violence, because how can it be violence if there is no aggression? Now it's not my job to draw a distinction between the definition of non-violence and the definition of violence—that's the job of fools.'

Baba Madansingh grew quiet. Shekhar waited for a long time hoping that he would continue, and when he didn't speak, Shekhar thoughtfully said, 'So what conclusion did we come to?'

'Conclusion?' Baba laughed loudly. 'I said what I had to say. Now you need to turn it into an aphorism.'

Shekhar was about to say something when he heard the sound of footsteps approaching—perhaps the guard had come to fetch him. He suddenly had an idea to startle him, so he said loudly, 'That's too much. Then what did the sahib say?'

Baba looked at him once and then smiled to say, 'You've caught on quickly—is this self-defensive violence or a lie? So yes—' looking at the guard standing at the door, '—what could the sahib say! He walked off embarrassed.'

The warden said, 'Sir, you're here? But I was—'

Shekhar pretended not to hear him and said, 'But we've ignored the other topic altogether. Well, I'll come back to hear the rest some other day.'

The warden finished his thought, 'I was going crazy looking all over for you. Please come now.'

Shekhar went with him.

Once outside, the warden asked him, 'Was Baba telling you all about his fight?'

'Why?'

'He likes to tell everyone about it. He got into it with the previous warden. The old guy really laid into him.'

'Hmm.'

As if recalling history, the warden said, 'The old fellow was probably a real wildcat in his heyday. But he is a saint of a man, the poor fellow, and his health is just terrible.'

'Hmm.'

Shekhar was locked in. Just as the warden shut his door, rattled the chains and left, Shekhar let out a quiet laugh—the sweetest chuckle.

*

A man who is used to living life will find it intolerable if he can only get the leftover scraps of life, its half-eaten morsels—but this had become the law for imprisoned Shekhar . . . The sheer thought was unbearable to him, but it reared up again and again, and each time it was as if one of the iron bars on the doors that locked him in had already sated itself on his spirit and was driving deeper into his heart . . .

He had one connection left to the outside world—to Shashi—lifeless pieces of paper and the words and letters scrawled on them by a lifeless pen . . . Language is immortal, pain is immortal, but can their life outlast the knowledge that presents itself so clearly today, that the last time it had a vital pulse was three days, or seven days, or ten days ago . . .

When Shekhar got Shashi's letter, it didn't occur to him when he saw the date on top that the nine days that had elapsed for the letter to reach him had swallowed up a whole section of his life in a single gulp. With growing anguish, he read the letter once, then read it again—yes, there was much anguish, but not enough to tear him apart, make him numb. That came later, when he started counting the days and realized that fourteen minus nine was five . . .

This time Shashi's letter was brief. She agreed with Shekhar that everyone had to find their own path in life; we couldn't show someone else the way, nor could we shine the light for them. All we can do is massage the weary feet of the traveller, tighten his armour and, if he has a lamp, we can lengthen its wick. And that was why she was doubly grateful for Shekhar because he had done all that and even more: he was filling her lamp with love . . . 'I don't know what the future holds; and the path that I've set for myself doesn't even concern itself with whether there is a future or not. It's so well-lit, but I say this much to you today, that I will never forget what you have given me. You wrote that the decision is mine, but that yours was to honour it; you wrote that in one choice I had your eternal blessing, love and good wishes and in the other choice I had your support and protection, and if necessary the strength of your hands and the bread earned by the sweat of your brow. Your respect has already given me both, and now that I have to choose, I choose your blessings. I've told Mother that I have absolutely no interest in such matters and her decision would be acceptable to me.'

Hard and bitter and hidebound, just like a woman, was Shashi's decision . . . hard, bitter and hidebound this decision of hers to sacrifice herself . . . hard, bitter and hidebound this pride of womankind that since society will not respect her, she will show her contempt for it by being destroyed at its hands, ripped to shreds, ruined . . . Blessing? What kind of a blessing was a wretch of a husband for such a woman? That you become a martyr, that your light burn bright, and fragrant, and pure! Shekhar beat his chest with his fist in shame, anger and dejection . . .

Had he not offered Shashi his support? Had he not told her that sacrificing herself on the altar of society was a cruel irony for both herself and for society? Why hadn't he said to her that society was simply an aggregation of its isolated individuals, and that the neglect of the individual meant the neglect of society? Why hadn't he said that suffering injustice was to take part in it? Why had he given her the freedom to make her own decision? Why had he offered to be sympathetic to both choices?

He recalled what he had written . . . That the matter was Shashi's, and no one else's other than Shashi's, and none had advice that was appropriate for it, neither her mother, nor Shekhar . . . Shashi, terribly isolated Shashi, should struggle with the issue and come to some conclusion, and all that the rest could do was to look on sympathetically, to pray with their heart of hearts that she reach the right decision and offer her the assurance that whatever decision she settled on, they would be with her . . . 'And I am with you, Shashi, if you should get married, if you should dissolve your future in someone else's future, even then all of my strength will be with you so that you can be firm on the path that you've chosen; and if you don't do that, if you chose not to erase yourself for another person and instead to take on society head-on, I will still be with you. Even if they ostracize you, if your family abandons you, you will still have my meagre resources; if I have to earn your bread from the labour of my own hands, then that will only be a source of pride for me . . . I know that I can never repay the value of what you have taught me, and that I can only do this much to show my gratitude: that I can keep following what you have taught me, or perhaps die trying to follow! I am not so bad that I cannot offer up even this much gratitude—even if I was before, now I wear the crown of your teachings and am no longer. I am with you, and no matter which direction you travel, where you go, may your inner light guide you . . .'

Shashi had picked her path. 'Exactly two weeks after today, on this day, I—oh, Shekhar, why can't this remain unsaid!' And the letter was dated nine days ago—only five days left!

Why? What thing had compelled Shashi to make this decision? Was it her intellect? Her conscience? Or was it fear? Ignorance? Was it her heart? Her desire? Her spirit? Her pride?

'I know that I am completely averse to this. But do I have the right to my aversion, to the refusal that would follow my aversion?

I am a part of society, I have obligations towards it, but I can ignore that because it has no real concern for me, and then again its principles keep changing and will change. But Mother—Mother is eternal, Mother is forever, and I have obligations to her, too . . .

'Mother is a widow and so she has her inbred principles. What effect my refusal towards society will have on her, I can't say at the moment, but I know that it will crush her before my eyes. She won't say anything, I'm certain; but it's not as though I won't be able to see. Her silence will be proof of her distress and it will kill me each moment . . . I can fight my own battles, but what right do I have to make her fight them, too? . . . And if someone has to burn in silence, why can't that be me? I'll be leaving home after I get married, neither Mother nor anyone else will see my sacrifice—no one other than me will see it! This is the only way that this pain can be taken beyond the reach of my relatives . . . This is what I've decided, Shekhar, so give me your blessings that I might follow through with pride . . .'

Was Shashi right? Was what she wrote wrong?

One thing she was definitely right about was that someone was certainly going to be hurt. The question was who would step forward to bear the burden on his shoulders; who could draw upon such a vast reserve of pride to bear it so that it could be borne easily . . .

He recalled a few lines of verse that he had composed, which had remained lifeless until now, but which had now brightened with a vital spark—

I have burned in solitude
And burning has brought its own solace
In more quenchless burning . . .[8]

Was this the meaning of suffering in proxy—that he had read in a book somewhere but ignored it as irrelevant—that one's suffering could be used to redeem the sins of others? That each individual was the salvation of another, could bear someone else's cross? Was this what suffering was, the first and last ray of light in this torment of hell . . .

A wave of anguish overcame Shekhar . . .

It didn't take as long for the second letter to arrive—but the time that it did take was too long. Shashi had written, 'This is the last day of my freedom in which I have any connections beyond my relatives . . . Surrounded by my sisterly affections—you! From tomorrow onwards, I will first be known as Mrs So-and-so, and all other relations will come second to that . . . I don't know when you will get this letter, but whenever you do, bless this Shashi who was until today your sister and was nothing more to anyone else; but tomorrow that won't be the case, and so I greet you for the last time from this role . . .'

Shashi had touched Shekhar's gentle heart—the hurt was so great that he could not even let out a cry . . . 'greet you for the last time' . . . 'surrounded by my sisterly affections' . . . 'nothing more to anyone else' . . .

This was the truth—dear God, what truth!—that Shashi had raised that 'nothing' to the dignity of kinship, and she had done so like no one had ever done before—not even his two real sisters . . . She had given his life meaning and purpose and something so valuable that living, fighting and dying for its dignity was a purely manly honour . . . Then was it also true that today was the last day he served as guardian to that treasure? And why today, it had already been two days since Shashi had been delivered to her new protectors! Was the thing which had never even begun ending today?

Pain . . . Something inside him says, she wasn't a relative, wasn't your sister . . . What happened was supposed to happen . . . He had no right to this pain . . . Yes, no right, because if he had the right, why would he be in pain? Her pain is the gift of my love, just as her gift of love to me is her sisterly affection! She isn't related to me; she is my twin; one split soul born in two different places . . . That's why . . . That's why . . . Shekhar considers himself and doesn't understand where he was sliced—still a sharp ache rises suddenly and the notes of helplessness take over the rest of his body . . .

But he still had a duty that remained . . . Mechanically, Shekhar picked up his pen and paper, wrote a brief note of blessing, sealed it in an envelope, wrote the address on it, called the warden and had it sent to the office. There was no other way—and at any rate, it took a long time to send a letter.

Then Shekhar, severely wounded, empty, lifeless, braced his head against the grinding wheel and stood up. Something burst forth from his dense pain, piercing through his insides like light . . .

Burn, ever-ascending, burn, sacrificial flame, burn! Burn wildly, bright and fragrant, ashless and smokeless, burn invincibly! This is the blessing that I, a wretch, can offer you! Then the tears came, big and fast . . .

*

A fog descended over Shekhar's life. But this time it didn't bring up feelings of hostility. He wasn't disturbed by his tears, nor did he have the desire to challenge the knowledge that he had been defeated. It was as if he had descended to some lower plane of existence. Life had grown lax, and laxity seemed to be the natural order.

Shekhar asked the 'Sir' for permission to be moved into a cell in the first row. Surprised, 'Sir' asked him his reasons and when he learned that Shekhar wanted to be alone, he gave his permission with a smile. 'It's up to you if you want to restrict your own freedom. Over there you'll have to follow the rules that are set up for that row—and you'll have to remain in lock-up. Yes, and if the number of men condemned to be hanged grows, you will have to move back.' Shekhar nodded in silent agreement.

The cells on death row were clean and well kept. The floors were made of cement, there was no grinding wheel and there was a type of toilet made in the corner next to the door where water would flow out, so there was no stench in the cell. Shekhar would remain locked up during the day, would be allowed out for a walk in the morning and the evening and, after being searched, would be locked up again. He didn't like these rules, but it was as if he were not in his own skin, and so they didn't put him out. He spent his days half-numbed—like an addict unable to get his hands on opium. Except in the evenings and mornings when he woke up from his sleep—then he could tell he was alive.

From dawn until the time they opened the door for exercise in the yard and after the evening walk until the end of day—who knew why these two occasions were special enough to make a life that had been wilting all day suddenly bloom—he would wake up around 4 or 4.30 a.m. when he would turn and face the door, look up at the sky and walk imaginary circles in his mind; if it rained, he would walk with the sound of raindrops providing the rhythm . . .

With the first light of dawn, and with the last ray of light before dusk, one question bore into Shekhar's heart like a spear: 'Is she happy now that she's sacrificed herself?' He hadn't received another reply from her; and Shekhar had no means of getting any news about her save his imagination—what useless imagination!—and his compassion—what worthless compassion!

Why hadn't she written? Was it because she was suffering? Or was it because she was happy?

Sometimes he'd work himself into such a frenzy that he would grind his teeth, clench his fists and strike the floor or the iron bars on the door, once, twice, three times . . . until his knuckles were bloodied—then he'd wipe the blood across his forehead, and the red trace it left would offer him some peace! Sometimes he'd scare himself with what he had done and ask himself, 'Have I lost my mind?' But the next day, the primary question would displace this secondary question, and it was as if the kind of punishment that emerged from this temporary amnesia was even greater . . .

But during the day he never had that much strength; he was caught up in a low-grade worry all day: 'Was that self-sacrifice the right thing to do?' . . . Who could say? No one knew—the only one who could know, who could say, who could decide was Shashi! This question was her question . . . Baba Madansingh had also said that everyone had to find their own path . . .

Sometimes he even doubted that. Was this really a personal question? Is there no social responsibility in any of this? Whether a person saved himself or sacrificed himself, whether it was for a good cause or a bad one, was the individual the only decision maker about these questions, and did society have no right to speak on these matters? His mind began to wander . . . This was the previous question about violence and non-violence . . .

Either because he had an overwhelming desire to get an answer to his question, or only because he wanted to go for a walk, Shekhar went to see Baba Madansingh. And no one could say why, but his old curiosities began to bubble forth; the question about Shashi got tangled up in this, and Shekhar sat down again to discuss violence and non-violence and social responsibility.

Baba spoke. 'Look, I don't know why I'm so distressed these days. Perhaps I'm on the verge of a new aphorism, or maybe it's just old age. That's why I'll answer you in aphorisms—in old aphorisms. The question is definitely also a social question. It seems to me that Indian life and thought is introverted and individualistic—for instance, we believe that the path to salvation requires us to separate ourselves from society as much as possible and know thy self.[9] The consequence of this individualism is that we also believe that sin and merit are also individual things. That's why our holy men also consider it a good deed to offer milk to snakes. From a social perspective, this should be a sin. The life and thought of the West is the complete opposite of ours. They are extroverted and socialist. Their norms are different, and they believe that spiritual contortionism and cowardice define us. We can call them uninhibited materialists and they can call us empty spiritualists. But even this exchange of insults can't hide the fact that neither of us can forget the other's ideals. But more importantly, our ideals are in need of reform because we are behind them.' He was quiet for a while. Then he smiled and said, 'If we live like a herd of sheep, then we have to walk the way that sheep walk. The civilized name for the way sheep walk is culture.'

Shekhar was quiet for a while. When two drops fell on his face at the same time, he was jolted out of his thoughts. He looked up. The thick clouds of the monsoon had covered the sky, and on the northern horizon, a dusty patch was swirling quickly as it advanced—and from its inside, it was as if a light were bursting forth somehow.

'A dust storm is coming.'

'It's for the best. I've been needing one these days.' A cloud spread over Baba's eyes. 'In the story, when the Pathan is released from jail, he didn't count the days of his sentence, but for me "nothing happening" has become a permanent condition. These twenty-one years weigh heavily on me. So, dust storms and thunderstorms give me a little release.'

Shekhar looked at him quizzically, and it was the first time that Baba had seemed old to him—his eyes had grown old, so much older than his white hair and his white beard! As if the curse of the cursed first man shone through him—'You will live only on your own pain.'

Frightened, he slowly went back.

On his way back to his cell, Shekhar was suddenly overcome with a feeling of disgust. It was utterly shameful that he was mired in irrelevant intellectual puzzles when who knew what Shashi was facing at that very moment . . . Psychological torment, perhaps physical suffering—he stopped while walking—who knew what condition Shashi was in at that very moment!

What was her condition? What was he afraid of? What was that nameless fear inside him?

It was as if the wind, in answering his question, blew a gust through countless bars, iron doors and windows and groaned as it left—that groan got louder and then quiet, and grew louder again, turning into the scream of a wounded, unearthly life form, and its agonized breath pushed Shekhar backwards—the first whirlwind of the dust storm had also swept him up . . .

He started walking again . . . But how could it be stopped by thinking—not by thinking—how could it be stopped by asking the right question? And where did the questions end? One doesn't take sips of curiosity; it is a wildly flowing, unstoppable river, irrepressible like life itself . . .

Madansingh had said that pain was penance, but real penance was curiosity—since it was the worst kind of pain . . .

He arrived at his cell. The sentry was already there, and as soon as Shekhar went inside, he locked the door and went out past

the courtyard and stood in the docks that had been constructed at
some distance outside. Large raindrops began falling in the middle
of the dust storm . . .

Curiosity . . . curiosity . . . this unnameable affliction . . .

But I want to know . . . I want to know how Shashi is . . . Is
she happy?

. . . 'It is the definition of delusion to suffer pain over things
we cannot control.' Where had he landed? This? Or was this one
of Madansingh's aphorisms, arrived at in the throes of pain? There
was no knowledge without suffering, which is why knowledge
was divine—it couldn't be achieved by human growth; it could
only be glimpsed through pain, through penance. It wasn't nectar
that could be made from churning the ocean of life; it was some
limitless idea that descended . . . That must have been the way the
ancient sages received their wisdom in the form of verses that we
now call the Vedas—they were 'revealed', emerging suddenly from
some internal light—and they, too, must have awakened suddenly
from their penance of pain, bristled with the burden of the people
and said, 'Divine!' . . .

A dazzling light ripped the gathering darkness of the night
apart, a terrible rumble shook the iron and the stones in the jail,
as if the heavy curtain of the sky tore under its own weight, and
it began to rain torrentially; something brushed against Shekhar's
feet and when he looked down he saw that it was a large hailstone.
He went and stood next to the iron bars. Trembling from the cold,
he stood, scared out of his wits by the deep roar of the clouds and
the crackling lightning, bearing the cruel punishment of the dust
storm and the rain . . . How pleasant it was to bear these blows
head-on, how pleasant it was to remain standing while being
beaten, as opposed to helplessly swallowing the blows from that
nameless, formless enemy . . .

But it didn't provide salvation, did it? It wasn't as though his
spirit had calmed in this tumult of the natural elements . . . There
were others in jail, too. What were they doing right now? . . . He
remembered, one day on a June afternoon, he had seen a prisoner
drenched in the rain and shivering, hunched, squatting like a

monkey, under the iron grate in his cell; and his eyes, like crystal beads, were fixed on the white sky expectantly . . . Was that life! It was as if his life had been delayed, his existence, too, had been suspended; at that moment he was considering the eons-old inert substance inside him which, according to evolution, had perhaps been dust before the first forms of life . . . Baba Madansingh's story about the Pathan had been right—man did not live in jail, didn't develop . . . But he certainly grows old—the body dries up, the hair thins . . .

And in the desolate interior of a suspended life, the only support one had was this wretched intellect. Curiosity was one's only means of support . . . That was life's surrogate . . .

Shekhar trembled once, and then he sat down to write. 'Yes, . . .'

*

God set about creation.

There was only a formless emptiness in all directions and a dark pallor spread across the endless sky. God said, 'Let there be light.' And there was light. God broke up its radiance into countless pieces and attached a star to each of them. Then he created the solar system, made the earth. And he was pleased with his creation.

Then he made the plants, trees, bushes and shrubs, fruits and flowers; planted vines; created bumblebees and butterflies to flutter over them; and crickets to sing, too.

Then he made the animals. And he was pleased with his creation.

But it didn't bring him peace. And then to provide some variety in life, he made day and night, storm and rain, clouds, heat and shade, and the like; and then insects, spiders, mosquitoes, scorpions and, in the end, even snakes!

But that didn't bring him satisfaction either. Then he opened his (third) eye of knowledge and looked into the distant future.[10] In the darkness, there is a disturbance in the lifeless mist that has descended over the earth and the solar system, and slowly a shape forms in the disturbance, a body that possesses nothing extraordinary but still has potential; a soul which despite being formed is not bound by its body, keeps growing; a life that each time it touches anything becomes anew, becomes even more vital and grows . . .

God understood that this future organism was human. Then he sliced through the mist that covered the earth and picked up a fistful of dust and bringing it up to his heart, blew a breath of his glorious spirit on it—and humanity was created.

God said, 'Go, the greatest of my creations, the jewel of my creations.'

But God still received no pleasure from his creation; the artist within still remained unsatisfied.

Because the earth was standing still, as were the stars. The sun didn't blaze because its rays were stopped from radiating outwards. There was no motion in this wide, beautiful world.

Lying at a distance, the primordial snake laughed. He knew why Creation wasn't moving. And he kept this knowledge to himself, hidden in his coils.

Once more, God opened his (third) eye of knowledge and then took two teardrops from man and created woman.

Man quietly accepted this gift. He was content before, and now he was doubly content. In that placid life, God still found no satisfaction and Creation still didn't move.

And that primordial snake kept his secret hidden in his coils and kept laughing.

*

The snake said, 'Fool, don't be satisfied with your life. There's still so much that you haven't achieved, haven't seen, haven't known. Look at this. I hold knowledge. That's why I'm equal to God, and ancient.'

But man looked at him once absent-mindedly, and then hid his face in the woman's tresses. He had no curiosity—he was at peace.

It went on like that for a long time. It becomes bright and then fades, man and woman look at each other amorously, and they sleep, embraced by the darkness.

And God remained invisible and the snake kept laughing.

Then one day, when dawn broke, the woman lowered her eyes; she didn't look at the man. The man tried to look her in the eyes, when he realized that not only was she not looking at him, she wasn't looking at anything else either; it was as if her gaze had turned inwards, looking at something inside herself, and that gaze contained an ineffable concentration . . . And then it grew dark, and she lay down with him in that same connected feeling, but without looking at him, with her face turned away from him, keeping him at a distance . . .

The man got up. He closed his eyes and prayed to God. He didn't have the words, didn't have the feelings, didn't know the rituals. But the prayers that are beyond words, feelings and customs, the prayers that depend on relevant verses, those prayers began to burst forth from his lips . . .

But the world remained unchanged; it didn't move . . .

The woman began to cry. A twinge of pain sliced through her somewhere inside. She began to scream, 'What is happening to me? I am being undone! I will be ground into dirt . . .'

The man could do nothing in his powerlessness; his prayers became increasingly desperate, frenzied, agitated, and when he could no longer bear the sight of the woman's pain, he closed his eyes tightly . . .

In the pitch-black darkness of night, the woman screamed, 'Dear God—my husband—look at this!'

The man went to look, groped around and then was quiet for a moment. Inside his soul, he was shaken by a tremor of shock and fear. He gently lifted her head and placed it on his lap . . .

In the gentle light of dawn he saw that the woman was hugging his chest, very lovingly, affectionately, and sleeping. His heart welled up with enormous surprise, unbearable joy, and a question erupted from within him, 'God, what is this creation that is not yours?'

God didn't respond. Then man asked the snake, 'Serpent, you guardian of knowledge, tell me what is it? Who is it that has made you and God into equals—one creator? Tell me, I want to know.'

As soon as he asked the question, the impossible happened. The earth began to rotate, the stars began to shine, the sun rose and shone, the clouds thundered, lightning struck . . . the world moved!

The snake said, 'I have lost. God has stolen knowledge from me.' And his coils slowly uncoiled.

God said, 'My creation has succeeded, but the success belongs to man. I am all-knowing, infinite. I want for nothing. Man possesses curiosity and therefore he makes the world run, makes it move . . .'

But man was still unsettled; there was still the matter of existence. He screamed and screamed, 'I want to know!'

And the more he repeated the question the brighter the sun shone, the quicker the earth spun, the faster the world moved. And man's heart began to race.

Even today, when man asks questions, impossible things begin to happen.

*

Another letter from Shashi—she writes that perhaps her life will work out. There may not be any happiness in it, but there was also no sorrow; there was absolutely nothing noteworthy happening, only a slight nuisance, like a headache from being tired, that followed her around all the time . . . 'Sometimes I wonder if this is how my life will be spent? Only to grow like carrots or turnips and then plucked? But then I remember that many live like this for dozens of years . . . And everyone seems acclimated to a mechanical life . . . No one is even interested enough in me to insult me . . . This isn't the life that I had imagined, but perhaps I can learn from everyone else's example and become like them and not hate my lot in life, and live my life in peace, contentment, dispassionately.

I have no sorrows at all now . . .' And then suddenly changing directions, 'When are you coming?'

When would he come? The court case seemed like it would never end! The witnesses had been exhausted and the lawyer had said that there was no evidence against Shekhar, and they had asked for permission to call new witnesses and the court had even called them in . . .

But now it didn't make a difference whether he went or not. Shashi was now married and he was no longer in her thoughts, just as he was no longer at home. And now she was living contentedly, asking nothing from life nor receiving any pain. He was resigned, too; was nothing; the inside and the outside of jail were the same.

September . . . October . . . November . . . It becomes bright and then fades. The 1400 men in the jail all count the passing of one more day; people think that their train of life has moved on to the next station; everyone thinks that they are alive . . . Three months pass in this way—Shekhar listens and watches, but his life, too, is suspended . . .

The warden is consistently angry with Mohsin. He gets punished for the crime of shaving, he's put in chains and no one knows how, but every Monday at drill time he is clean-shaven and smooth again, and he pulls out an old razor blade from somewhere and presents it to the warden. Such blatant insubordination is not tolerated—the warden keeps increasing the punishments—chains, then a rod and chains, then standing in handcuffs, then handcuffs at night, then two or three punishments at the same time—hands cuffed behind at night and then rods and chains all day and night, then 'punishment rations' which meant instead of food he gets flour mixed with water . . . Then one day he was sentenced to lashes. The warden caught him and led him out before Shekhar's cell. Mohsin looked at him, laughed and said, 'Look, Moulvi, I'm going on Haj!' Fifteen minutes later he came back the other way, wincing—but this time completely naked and bloodied to his waist. He saw Shekhar and said, 'Moulvi, they're moving me next to you. Now you'll be able to hear me sing!' And he walked on—or rather was dragged on . . . The warden explained to a stunned Shekhar that the lashes were his punishment, not one from the courts—meaning because the crime was committed in jail the punishment would be delivered by the guards, and so the lash was soaked in oil and used with an executioner's force . . . After Mohsin had suffered thirty lashes and was taken down from the stockade, he looked at the warden and said, 'Is that all? Now I've become a caliph. Nothing else matters!' And when he saw the junior officers in jail smiling, the warden was beside himself; Mohsin received a new punishment—a uniform of jute! He had already been asked to strip for the lashes, and afterwards he was given a pair of shorts made of jute to wear which he refused to put on and so he was sent back to his cell naked—and his cell had been moved so that he could be watched more closely. He was moved to the eastern wing, the one for the condemned men . . .

But inexplicably, Mohsin could not be broken. At the next drill, his chin was again clean-shaven, and he stood unabashedly naked before the warden . . .

After that, the warden found it impossible to bear this daily effrontery and so he stopped bringing Mohsin out for drills, and he was moved from the condemned cells to another cell which was known throughout the jail as 'the cemetery'—it was usually reserved for prisoners with terrible, infectious diseases or for recidivists. And when there were no such people, it was left empty. Mohsin didn't stop shaving nor did he put on the jute uniform. The warden had hoped that the onset of winter would make him admit defeat—if he would put on the uniform, that would be a defeat. But November had come and Mohsin still hadn't changed except for the fact that the bones in his emaciated body protruded more; his dried-out skin became more sallow . . . Then one day Shekhar heard that a few boils had erupted on his body and that the doctor had said he had consumption . . .

One day, the undefeated Mohsin was called into the office where he was given his own clothes to wear. Five minutes later he was seated in the police lorry and sent off. Later, it was learned that his release date was quickly approaching, and so he was sent to a jail in the district he was from . . .

Baba Madansingh had also fallen ill. More recently, Shekhar had been to see him each day and he could tell that there was no change in his extremely wizened face, but those parts that were still young were quickly moving down the road to elderliness—Baba's eyes . . . As if the darkness of a life held in suspension for nineteen or twenty years suddenly wanted to drain the light from his sparkling eyes . . . Shekhar had come to hold this imprisoned sage in deep regard, and ever since he had heard that Baba had developed dysentery he was racked with concern all the time. He was worried all day, and each morning and evening he would religiously go to see him—this had become his daily routine.

And that was how September passed, October passed and November passed. Then suddenly one day, Shekhar's suspended life was jolted out of its reverie, and it seemed to him that nothing was in suspense, that his heart was protected by a thin sheath which could be ripped to shreds at any moment and leave his heart unprotected from any injury . . .

There were four cells in the condemned wing that Shekhar was in. The inmates there changed regularly. Shekhar was in one of the cells, but there had been eleven different men in the three other cells since he had been there. A few had been released since; the rest had been executed.

One October evening, a new man was brought in. Shekhar observed him with curiosity—a twenty-three or twenty-four-year-old young Jat lad, handsome and well built, fair-skinned, a thin, twisted moustache and clear and courageous eyes. Shekhar couldn't believe that this man was a murderer. After the warden had placed him in the cell next to Shekhar's and left, he asked the guard on duty about him and learned that he was a murderer and that he had confessed.

His name was Ramji. This was something Shekhar had learned on the first day. The next day when Shekhar was being let out for exercise, he called him over and they introduced themselves.

'Excuse me, Babuji!'

Shekhar went up to his cell.

'How did you end up on this stage of beauty?'

'What do you mean?'

'Have you been sentenced to death as well?'

Shekhar explained that he had only been charged and that he was in the cell voluntarily.

'So you can get things from the outside? Then can you get me a couple of cigarettes now and then—it's a terrible habit, sir, but since I'm going to be hanged I may as well smoke. You smoke, too, don't you?'

'No, but I'll ask for some. Come by later and get them.'

'You don't think it is a bad thing to show kindness to a murderer, do you? Otherwise—'

'Why is this a question of kindness—' Shekhar stopped; he had a question on the tip of his tongue that he didn't want to ask.

'Why did you stop? You wanted to ask me something—it was why I killed someone, right?'

'Yes.'

'And on top of that, a woman. You knew that, right?'

'No.'

'You asked, so I'll tell you the whole story. I've already told the court everything.' He stopped and then started again. 'We own some land in our village—it's my older brother's and mine. But my brother doesn't care for farming, so he left my sister-in-law at home and went to look for work in the city. He found a job and every other month he would send her twenty or twenty-five rupees.

'But my sister-in-law had other ideas. She told me about one of the neighbours who used to come to ask after my brother; he used to come to see her when I wasn't there. I had no idea; I learned about it accidentally one day. One evening in September, I told her that I would have to spend the night in the fields. Why? You won't find it interesting. There was some work in the fields. I ate dinner, took some leftovers and left.

'It had been raining all day, at any rate, but at night there was a torrential downpour and it even started to hail, so I left my work and went home. When I got home, no one opened the door even after I had knocked for a long time, even after I had shouted for a while. Then I got angry and started banging on the door when my sister-in-law came and opened the door and stood to one side slowly. I saw that neighbour in front of me. His clothes and shoes were dry which meant that he had been there for a long time.'

Ramji went quiet. Then he drew a long breath, 'Babuji, if you had been in my shoes, what would you have done?'

Shekhar couldn't give him an answer. He stood there quietly. Ramji started talking. 'Well, I've done what I've done. I asked my sister-in-law, "Who is this, why is he here?" She didn't respond. I asked that man and he didn't respond either. Then I threatened and asked my sister-in-law if he had been here before. After much threatening, she said, "He has been here many times." I asked, "Do you love him?" She didn't respond. I asked the man, and he didn't respond either. Then I said, "If you both love each other, then you should get married. I won't stand in your way. I'll take care of everything that happens. I'll even explain things to my brother. So tell me, are you ready?" My sister-in-law didn't say anything. I asked that man, and he said, "Who are you to interfere?"

'I was getting angry, but I didn't want to be unjust to my sister-in-law. She wasn't my sister-in-law any more, but I had to have some respect for the three years she had spent with my brother. I asked again, "Tell me, are you prepared to marry him?" He said, "I'm married with children. Why should I take on this problem?" I asked, "Then why did you even come here?" He said, "She called me over." It was becoming difficult to contain my rage at his vulgarity. But somehow, I managed to say, "I don't know about all that. Either the two of you get married tomorrow morning or I'll do what I need to do."

'He threw curses at me. I asked my sister-in-law, "Are you willing? If you are, then I will come to terms with it and drop the issue," but she still didn't say anything. Then I saw blood. I cut them both down with an axe.'

He stopped for a while so that he could breathe and see what kind of effect the story had on Shekhar. 'Then I immediately went to the police station and confessed—after killing my sister-in-law

I didn't feel like staying in the world. A murderer should be killed. Whatever happens next happens!'

There was a long silence. Then Ramji volunteered, 'Babuji, I won't ask you whether you think what I did was right or not. I'm not ashamed, and I'll die well. That's why I haven't filed an appeal.'[11]

Shekhar thought quietly as he went away. After that, they got to know each other quite quickly—Shekhar felt warmly towards this half-wild and completely honourable man.

One day in October, he heard that Ramji's appeal had been denied and that he would be hanged in four days. He hadn't filed the appeal but the officials in jail had nevertheless petitioned the high court themselves.

Shekhar was saddened. But it was as though Ramji wasn't affected at all, as if nothing new had happened.

In the evening, Ramji called for Shekhar, 'Babu Sahib!'

Shekhar caught hold of the bars and spoke, 'What is it?'

'Have you ever seen a hanging?'

'No.'

'You're a writer, aren't you? You should see everything.'

'. . .'

'Why don't you ask the warden to let you watch my hanging? That way, I won't feel alone—otherwise in my last moments all I will have are the faces of the executioners.'

Dumbfounded, Shekhar couldn't speak. Could he request to see Ramji's execution!

'Babuji, why are you quiet? There's nothing wrong in this— you're helping out a helpless person. And I will know that I have a friend there when I die.'

Trembling, Shekhar said, 'All right.'

But he didn't get permission. When Shekhar sadly told Ramji, it depressed him, too. He said, 'Bastard executioners!' And then he was silent.

That day Shekhar didn't leave his cell, nor did he say a word. Ramji repeatedly tried to talk to him, but Shekhar couldn't manage more than, 'Uh-huh.' Finally, that evening, Ramji said, 'Babuji, you aren't saying anything and you seem sad. Did you get bad news from home? So, here, I will sing something to make you feel better—when will we have another opportunity?'

Shekhar burned with embarrassment.

Ramji sang through half the night. Who knows when Shekhar fell asleep . . .

Another day, too, passed somehow. Night fell, and Ramji began singing again. He became tired somewhere around midnight and said, 'Babuji, now you sing something. I'm tired. I'll fall asleep listening to you.'

Shekhar couldn't sing. But for Ramji he tried to sing something. He wasn't successful. Ramji teased him sweetly, 'Babuji, are you singing for me?' Then Shekhar started telling him stories . . . Some from the Puranas; some from foreign literature; some from things that had happened in his own life . . . Ramji's 'uh-huhs' began to become fainter and then stopped altogether. Shekhar asked the warden and learned that he had fallen asleep.

But Shekhar couldn't sleep. The night passed on with the rhythm of the jail's announcements. 'All is well!' . . . All of a sudden, Shekhar awoke from his sleep; dawn had broken. The doctor had come to examine Ramji.

'Doctor, you're going to hang me anyway, so why the check-up?'

'Brother, it's my duty, so I have to do it. You should pray to God—'

The doctor left. As soon as the day broke, the warden, the inspector, the magistrate, the chief warder and the army of guards—all appeared.

Shekhar looked out through the iron bars to see what he could see, and he tried to hear the rest.

Ramji was being searched—his hands were bound—he was being taken outside—

'Do you have any last words? Do you need to tell anyone anything?'

'Can I speak to the gentleman next door for two minutes?'

Three seconds later the warden responded, 'No, I can't let you do that.'

'Then let's go.'

A little fear, a little uneasiness, a little speed . . .

Suddenly at the gate near the courtyard, Ramji spoke, 'All right, Babuji, we'll meet again some other time. On the other side—' A flash of a smile—then the procession moved on.

And Shekhar, tightly gripping the bars, slowly realizes that his grip has slackened, his arms have gone limp, his head is hanging . . .

Six days later, when Shekhar had for the first time considered leaving his cell, something happened that prolonged his nightmare for a few more days. He received a letter from Shashi that said she was in serious trouble, and she prayed to be freed from her life quickly . . . Why, what the trouble was, she hadn't explained at all; she had left it for the demon of his imagination to provide its own colouration to his nightmare . . .

Shekhar thought, life does stand still in jail! And what was it that had thrown him down and stepped on his throat and said, 'Me? Standing still? Then look, handle my weight and suffer the wounds of my speed.' Oh, he couldn't stand it . . . It couldn't be borne . . . Life couldn't be borne . . . Bondage couldn't be borne . . .

Why couldn't it be borne? Weak, coward, liar! In front of his eyes, each day, the most insignificant men without any talent, wealth, status, relatives or education faced life and passed, and he, proud, cried that he couldn't bear it . . . Cowardly hypocrite . . . There is pain . . . There is sympathy . . . What is it about sympathy that lightens life's burdens or makes one think and be grateful for life? He says goodbye to sympathy and fears life! Soulless . . .

Burning with affection and insult, Shekhar sat up slowly like a crazed bull, lowering his shoulders, ready to clash with the pressure of life . . . He drew a breath through flared nostrils and stomped on the earth as he left his cell to stroll around, meet everyone, and let no one see that life was standing still for him, or rather that it was moving twice as fast . . .

Baba Madansingh was sitting up in the pit, leaning on the wall for support. Shekhar looked at his face once, and the question that came to his lips never left them. Baba's health had worsened.

Baba didn't get up, nor did he smile. Shekhar saw that even
the skin beneath his hair and beard had become white. It was
now only his eyes that had any colour, and today it wasn't merely
colour, they had a light, too—they were on fire . . .

'You came . . . Where have you been for so long?'

'I haven't been myself. My neighbour was hanged.'

'I haven't been myself, either, Shekhar. The body is gone, and
the mind is really broken.'

'Why, Baba?'

'Nothing—weakness! Whenever I get news from the outside,
I become depressed.'

'What kind of news?'

'Have you read about what happened at Chittagong?'

'Yes.'

'Not about the shoot-out that happened, but about what
happened afterwards?'

Shekhar had read in the papers that much violence was
happening there, many things were being prohibited, and he also
read that news from there was being censored and that letters were
stopped.

'And?'

'I don't know any more than that.'

'Shekhar, I've heard that the soldiers are doing whatever they
want—they beat the villagers repeatedly and force them to salute,
the women are raped and . . . and—' Baba's throat suddenly seized
up and he couldn't say any more. He stood up in a frenzy . . .

'Where did you hear this?'

'I got a letter.'

'But when there's no news, how did the letter writer learn any
of this?'

'He didn't learn—he heard. You want to say that this is a
rumour, and that rumours happen all the time, that it's a lie, that
there is no proof, that it is wrong to say anything until we have
all the information? I have thought similar things a thousand
times! But that's all stupid. I'm not angry because I have no proof,
I'm angry because I don't have proof. You don't understand how

terrible our situation is, how helpless we are that we can't investigate these serious allegations; we can't make any inquiries about the evidence or the conclusions. I'm not saying that the allegations are definitely true. But these allegations are being made, and we don't have the resources to investigate them. It's our right to acquire those resources, and we aren't getting our rights . . .'

Baba came up to the bars. He raised a clenched fist to Shekhar's face and said, 'Slavery—absolutely contemptible servitude—if this isn't the definition, then what is? Not the knowledge of the unpleasant, not faith in the false, slavery is the condition of being unable to discriminate between the true and the false. Slavery is that bondage, that prohibition, that steals our right to know . . .'

He suddenly stopped. 'I've probably said all this before— it's been a year since I've come to this realization.' He laughed a hollow laugh. 'Something realized a year ago stings today when it has become a truth, and I'm locked up.' Baba's breathing became laboured. He drew a few long breaths and said, 'Shekhar, Chittagong is a stain on our national reputation. To me, this is the warrant of revolution—it needs pride and so it has to instil pride at the same time—and what is more important than that? We need pride and so we need revolution! Revolution! And I'm locked in chains . . .'

Baba went back to the pit. Drily, he said, 'Shekhar, you should go. I am not well. I wanted you to see me happy—the world to see me happy—but it still pains me even more than my ego does. That's what I'm learning today—it's good that I'm feeling this sharp pain. Go!'

Shekhar went quietly back to his cell, afraid and trembling.

Three days later, in the evening, Baba's health worsened. The doctor wanted to take him to the hospital, but Baba said, 'I won't go for just one day. I have spent the greatest part of my life in this cell; I won't go somewhere else now to spend my most important day.' Had it been anyone else, they would have forced him to go, but nobody had the courage to force Baba. The doctor ordered a guard to stay on duty near him and left; he even came once during the night to check on him.

Shekhar got the news after he was locked in his cell. That's when he discovered just how respected Baba was in jail. He had never seen the jail as silent as he had that night—news of Baba's illness had spread to every corner of the jail, and even the night watchman's call of 'All is well' was quieter than usual.

'For just one day' . . . 'most important day' . . . truly? Shekhar felt a strong desire to pray rise up inside him . . .

In the morning, the cell was empty.

When the cells were opened, Baba's body had already been moved. When Shekhar noticed that the cells were opened later than usual, he asked the warden, 'Is someone being hanged today?' Because it was on such days that the cells were opened late.

'No—' The warden hesitated and stopped.

'Then?' and then suddenly glimpsing the light through his fear, 'Is Baba . . .'

The warden didn't answer.

Shekhar ran to Baba's cell like a devotee running to a temple that has been devastated by an earthquake . . .

Someone was speaking, 'He got up in the night and cried for an hour. He used the wall to help him stand up and then went and lay down and said, "Let's go now!" That's all.'

It was the guard who had been posted for the night. Restlessly Shekhar went inside the cell. Yes, he had guessed right, there was a new aphorism written in an unsteady hand on the wall . . .

'Final verse—pain is greater than pride, but faith is greater than pain . . .'

Shekhar believed that it was beneath him to touch Baba's feet. He cursed himself now for feeling such things and bowed his forehead to that final verse. Then he unashamedly displayed the two large tears that had formed in his eyes to the guards and went to his cell.

Faith is greater than pain . . .

*

Mean days . . .

The court case was over. The effect of so much preparation of evidence was that suddenly it became pointless to present it. When the prosecution's case is weak, it doesn't benefit the defence to argue. It can actually make things worse. Witnesses were only produced for Vidyabhushan, and they all finished testifying in one day since there was no cross-examination . . . And the lawyers finished pointing fingers at each other which, it seems, passed for argument.

'Now, all that remains is my decision—we'll fix a date for delivering it, but for now I will put something down as a placeholder.' And the judge extended the case for thirteen more days . . .

Those days wouldn't pass. It wasn't that there was any major worry or anxiety about the outcome, but to be suspended in mid-air like that . . . The proceedings had been completed. The things that were necessary for the verdict had all been presented, and it was likely that the judge already knew what his decision would be. And now all they were waiting for was news, and they had to wait thirteen days for that! No, in thirteen days they would learn when the verdict would be read . . .

Finally, the thirteenth day came . . . But it was already afternoon and he still hadn't been called to court. Shekhar guessed that the judge had set a date without calling them to court and that they would learn it in time. He lay down to think and fell asleep while thinking . . .

'Babuji! Babuji! You've been called to the office.'

Shekhar got up confused. 'Who is calling me?'

'The inspector.'

'For questioning?'

'No, he's called you to the office. The verdict is out.'

When he got to the office he learned that the verdict had been given. The magistrate ruled that the testimony against Shekhar wasn't strong enough that he be sentenced, but there was still substantial doubt. Even if the evidence had been stronger, the time that he had already served in jail would be sufficient to cover it, so he was being released.

Lifelessly, the inspector said, 'Congratulations! You are now free. You can get your things from the office.'

'And the others? Can you tell me the entire verdict?'

'Vidyabhushan got one year; Santaram and Kevalram got six months each; Hansraj has been released.'

'Can I speak to them?'

The inspector laughed out loud. 'Haven't you heard what they say about friends in jail? Who meets with convicts?'

'So you won't let me see them?'

'They are convicts now. They get one visit every three months. You can make a request, but if you meet with them they won't be able to meet anyone else for the next three months. They might not appreciate you for that.'

'And Hansraj?'

'He was released an hour ago.'

Shekhar went to the office quietly.

Ten months wasted . . .

After he dejectedly finished up in the office, Shekhar stood waiting for the doors of the front gate to open. No one had come to get him—no one had received the news. The lawyer had probably heard, but he was probably busy with other work. He would leave this place, alone, alone and dejected—having wasted ten important months of his life . . .

Wasted? Baba Madansingh had spent twenty-one years there, and even after that he had written that faith was greater than pain . . . It redeemed the ten months spent to have learned that— and he had known Baba Madansingh, known Mohsin, known Ramji, and even learned about himself . . . Wasted? Thankless Shekhar . . .

Ten long, life-consuming months . . . An end to this bondage— an end to curiosity—life, only life, wide and unobstructed life . . .

But when the gate creaked open, and he saw the view of the outside world right in front of him, without bars in the way, he suddenly doubted his own ideas. An end to bondage? An end to curiosity? Shekhar recalled two lines of a poem he had read a long time ago:

Peace, peace, such a small lamp
Illumines, on this highway,
So dimly, so few steps in front of my feet . . .[12]

There was still everything to learn about, everything to cut down and fell . . .

And Shashi?

He had only one small thing to lean on—but Baba had written his final verse . . . Was it his last or mankind's last? . . .

The gate closed behind him. He was free.

'Pain is greater than pride, but faith is greater than pain . . .'

Part 3

Shashi and Shekhar

Is this Baba Madansingh's voice that is ringing in my ears? Did this deep, booming voice belong to the same man whose own voice transformed his weakness into dignity?

> Don't let your thoughts wander to things beyond these walls. Thinking about your relatives will neither help in lessening their sorrows, nor in bringing them any happiness. Instead, by dwelling on their pain you are only digging up the foundation of your determination.

Was this right? No, this couldn't be Baba's voice—his wisdom was greater than this! Then what was this? Was it my arrogance?

The past didn't diminish my determination, it improved it, since the more I've thought about it, the more I've realized the essence it contained—I know the reason that this 'ghost' remains is because it was once the future—certain destiny . . . I realize that I will have to fight, we'll have to go on fighting, because giving up on account of the pain that comes with fighting means making that pain and injustice and tragedy, which were present before, permanent . . .

I wager the deep voice also agrees with me—it booms in a frenzy, 'Prisoner, a day will come when you will be willing to give your right arm for the honour of this suffering—that's how great this honour is—'

Why? Am I not ready even now? Am I still unprepared to sacrifice an arm or even my own head?

377

The voice laughs. 'Head? Your head's already been sacrificed!'

But was this voice right? Wasn't this just a trick of an instinctive self-preservation? Was suffering really an honour? Wasn't the real honour the memory of a certain someone, the mere thought of whom frightens me into making excuses? If I had been an 'ordinary' man, I wouldn't have been the plaything of newspapers and bureaucrats and soldiers and imperial power. Would it really diminish my honour much if I found 'someone' to love and be loved by in the plain, poor traditions of living, surviving and dying?

Shashi, I don't know whether your leaving was also destined, but you did indeed leave; and I am not embarrassed to admit that if you hadn't gone, then—then—

But no, how could there be sorrow? Had you been here, why would there be any need to be sad about anything!

*

Standing outside the gate, Shekhar was stupefied for a few moments. For a moment he felt like he wanted to go back to jail, that he didn't want to be on the outside. Then he ordered his feet to move forward. As he passed each building, he reminded himself to keep moving, 'You've passed the cells', 'That's the mortuary you just passed', 'That was the blacksmith's workshop', 'These are the bars on the exterior and the gate, and now you're on the street' and 'That's the bend in the street.'

He stopped once more at the bend; then a scrape of doubt, of aversion, sliced his heart. At the same time, he realized that his aversion was not a desire to return; it was a fear of advancing to the place where he was headed.

Where should he go? College? A dreamy scene appeared before him—a crowd of students surrounds Shekhar, and a few want to hoist him on to their shoulders and there's a big commotion—'Long live Shekhar! Revolution!' And immediately after that another scene—a naked Mohsin tied to the docks, his backside sliced and dripping with blood. No, there was no place for him in college—and after ten months it was unlikely that his name was still in the registry.

Fearfully, his mind turned towards the source of his aversion—Shashi's home? 'Bless this Shashi who was your sister until today . . . I greet you for the last time from this role . . .' Wouldn't she have changed, wouldn't she have moved? Hadn't the same situation as 'after the wedding, Rama went to live with her husband' become as irrepressibly true as it had once before in Shekhar's life?

No, no, no! I am being despicable!

To reassure himself, Shekhar forced himself to recite one of Baba's sayings—'Faith is greater than pain.'—Do I lack faith?

He moved forward. But the effort it took to raise his feet also brought him the knowledge that he wasn't going towards Shashi's house.

He didn't understand why his feet had brought him to his professor's house. He never had a special relationship with Professor Heath, and there was no reason that he should now be drawn there. Professor Heath was English and fitted the sketch that Shekhar had drawn of the English middle class from reading novels. Hiding beneath his social aloofness, conservative beliefs and customs and etiquette was an embarrassed emotionality—Shekhar held that Professor Heath possessed all of these traits in sufficient quantity.

It would take him substantial effort to gather his scattered thoughts to meet with him at this moment—perhaps he would be unable to and be a fool . . . But wasn't he going there to be compelled into decisiveness? To be compelled into decisiveness meant being compelled into a social struggle, and his scared soul wanted to run from that fight . . .

He ran into the professor as he was coming down the stairs. Professor Heath's first expression of surprise quickly turned into happiness, 'Hello, Shekhar! What are you doing here?' And before he could say anything, 'You're totally free, right—there's no trouble left, right?'

Shekhar withdrew his hand from his grasp, but he kept smiling.

'Yes, sir, there is no trouble left. Everything—has been taken care of.' A shadow fell across the screen of his mind—really? And Shashi . . .

'Good! So you'll come inside and visit, right? I have to give a lecture—it's another headache I've got to deal with—You'll have tea here, won't you?—You'll have to drink some with me.—There are plenty of books inside—and pictures—'

'Thank you, but I only came to visit. We'll meet again—'

'No, you'll have to have some tea'—and then noticing the fidgety expression on Shekhar's face—'Do you have other obligations? Then come back at teatime—Oh, and when were you released?'

Slowly, Shekhar said, 'I came straight here after being released.'

'Oh—really? Then you still have your friends to meet. I'm being unfair. Go and meet them. Make sure to come back for tea—'

He came down the steps with the professor and stayed behind with a fake smile on his face. When the professor repeated the invitation and left after coming downstairs, Shekhar's smile burst into a cackle—'friends to meet!' Shekhar made a face as though he had just eaten something very bitter.

Shekhar's uncle lived on the third floor. He had no shortage of weariness at the thought of climbing those steps, but it took so long to climb those narrow steps that he reached the uppermost limits of his weariness . . . Shekhar's resolve—no, the compulsion that comes from a lack of resolve—wilted as he got to the top. He stopped for a moment, his hand on the lock of the closed door.

What is the connection, the similarity, between this post-office inspector uncle and me? Shekhar remembered that one day in the summer when his aunt had heard from his uncle that he was sick, she sent over some tamarind so that he could drink a sherbet made of it . . . Had Shekhar been a letter instead of a man, perhaps his uncle might have taken a special interest in him—as it was, Shekhar was like a foreign object in his life . . . His hand lifted from the lock and he quietly went down the stairs.

Shashi's house shouldn't be that far from here—Shekhar estimated as he recalled her address, but there was no going there—and—

Why had Shekhar torn up all of Shashi's letters? He desperately needed them now—their intimacy, their love, their closeness which sent a 'final greeting'! Oh, if he still had those letters, Shekhar could reproduce that lost feeling—

As if letters could ever take the place of love!

Idiot!

*

Shekhar hadn't arrived too early. The door opened as he knocked on it and Professor Heath placed a hand on his shoulder and said, 'Shekhar, I have a surprise[1] for you.'

Shekhar looked up. There was no need for introductions: seated in front of him was the magistrate who presided over Shekhar's case.

Mister Barnes said, 'Congratulations on your release!'

Shekhar responded immediately, 'Congratulations on your verdict—at least on this part of your verdict!' The atmosphere became a little tense. Shekhar sat down and they made small talk. Professor Heath explained that he had invited Barnes for tea so that the conversation would be more interesting, and he could voice his real opinions face-to-face.

Tea was served. In the course of the conversation, the professor told Barnes that Shekhar was a writer. 'What do you write—' Barnes had merely started the question when the professor interjected, 'Shekhar generally writes fiction, sometimes a few—'

'That's what I had guessed earlier.' . . .

Shekhar asked eagerly, 'Why?'

'Because your testimony during the trial was an excellent example of fiction!' Barnes laughed mirthfully at his own joke.

The images of Mohsin's naked backside and Baba's last days danced before his eyes. The insult stung him twice as hard, but he became rebellious and laughed and said, 'Too bad I can't agree with your literary assessments.' He told himself that he would get even.

Perhaps trying to defuse the conversation, Professor Heath said, 'Shekhar, I thought that if the two of you came here, you would have an excellent opportunity to get to know each other better. Generally, in India, relations between Indians and the English remain limited to formalities. Mister Barnes has excellent taste in literature. He is a chess player, too. Barnes, you'll have to invite Shekhar to your place sometime—' He looked at Barnes; he said, 'Certainly—' The professor continued, 'And Shekhar, you definitely have to go to his place. Mrs Barnes is a very gentle lady and an exceptional woman by some standards.'

Shekhar found his angle. His face lit up a little and he said, 'That's what I had guessed earlier.'

Barnes was taken aback, but the question on his mind appeared on the professor's lips—'Why?'

'Because in court, whenever I saw Mister Barnes, I used to think to myself that this man was probably the husband of an exceptional woman.' Satisfied, Shekhar leaned back and relaxed. In order to release some of the tension in the air, the professor bobbed and weaved, 'Shekhar, why don't you write in English?'

Thoughtfully, Shekhar said, 'In English . . . ?'

'Yes, people from abroad who have been here for some time are starting to become very interested in India. If a picture of Indian life told in the form of stories could be presented to British tourists, they would certainly be well liked.' As he spoke, the professor looked at Barnes for support.

'Hmm—There's a great demand for such things in America, but I don't think that we as a people are terribly drawn to them. Personally, I like them quite a bit, but we British don't particularly care for them.'

Professor Heath tried to demonstrate his agreement, 'Yes, they don't have any meaning for us—'

Shekhar turned to the Professor and asked, 'What is your opinion—I mean, personally, what do you think? Do you enjoy them?'

'Yes, certainly. I like them quite a bit—'

Shekhar stood up. So wasn't that something! Both of these men enjoy something, but they still claim that as a people we don't find it interesting, we don't find them meaningful, we don't really care for them—we are one country, one nation, one unit, we who are us, we were, we will be . . .

He felt as if someone had slapped him. His teeth clenched tightly, two half-formed tears burned in his eyes. He forced himself to drink a few more sips and took his leave. He went out quickly and went down the stairs.

Did our countrymen say similar things—could they? Alas, India! Alas, us! Alas, us!

*

In the hazy, slick, pale-blue light on the street, just before the lamps were lit, he felt as if he had become worked up over nothing; the energy of the first day out of jail was erupting in mysterious ways . . . Did we not possess a single culture, wasn't this country—fifty times as diverse and ten times as populous—more firmly culturally unified than Britain? And here too there were disagreements between the tastes of a lone individual and the preferences of the whole—'I' like Eliot and Ezra Pound while 'we' prefer Shadowist (Chayyavad) poetry . . . I'm becoming hysterical[2] for no reason . . .

But he wasn't convinced. He felt like he was contorting himself into that conclusion. Even if that were the case, we didn't possess that feeling—forget the pride of unity, we didn't even possess a living, breathing knowledge of it. It was a truth that had died, and so was a lie . . .

The anguish settled over his brain. Whenever a monkey sitting in the rain, drenched, becomes resigned to his fate, that's when hailstones begin to fall, and Shekhar felt as insignificant as that monkey must feel, and he was being kicked onwards, being pulled by the collar of his dejection . . .

Suddenly the lamps were lit. He paused. There was an aluminium sign in the spot he was looking at.

Shashi's house was in front of Shekhar.

*

'There is a permanent divide between the suffering individual and the creative artist. The deeper that division, the greater the artist!'

But am I an artist? Do I really want to be an artist when I can live a life that exists because you are connected to it? Why be infatuated with isolation, why love neutrality, when I don't want to be separated from a single atom; when each atom gets its life from you! Artists are greater than me, will always be; I am penitent, still, waiting, and I know that your hand is raised in blessing above me . . .

*

Shekhar trembled slightly, but no doubt was big enough to turn him away now that he had arrived at her door. He drew two long breaths as someone would take before jumping into a lake. Along with those breaths, Shekhar drank in several emotions—among them was the feeling that Shashi was a stranger—not just a stranger, but one who had become unfamiliar forever, because she had left the grasp of familiarity.

He raised his hand to knock on the door, but he immediately felt that it was an excuse to stay down here a little longer, so he drew his hand back and went up the stairs to the second floor.

There were three or four chairs in the sitting room. A man dressed in a suit was sitting on one, eating some fruit; on the small table in front of him was a used saucer and cup. Hearing the sound of Shekhar's arrival, the man turned to look, and his eyes suddenly clouded with unfamiliarity. In that instant, Shekhar noticed two things—that the suit fit him well and that his eyebrows were thick and met in the middle. Then he said, 'My name is Chandrashekhar—'

'Come in, come in—when did you arrive? This is a very good day . . .' The man quickly got up and moved forward but then stopped and said, 'Come in, come in, please sit down—' Shekhar could tell that the natural feeling in the first words gradually became hidden behind a screen of politeness, as if that man wanted to assess something before he said what he wanted to say . . .

'You are all Shashi ever talks about. We were thinking about coming there to visit you, but . . . the work has piled up—' and then suddenly shouting, 'Shashi, look who it is—your brother!'

So this was Shashi's husband, Rameshwar. After a few moments of anticipation, Shashi entered through a curtained door in the back room. As soon as she set foot on the threshold she asked, 'What are you doing here?' And then she stopped.

Not even a smile—there was no glimmer of any feeling on her face. But was the affectionate surprise in her eyes and the natural familiarity of the question a lie? But Shekhar got no chance to be disappointed.

Rameshwar said, 'I told Shashi that we should have at least gone to see you on the day of the verdict, but she didn't show any particular interest—' Shekhar looked over at Shashi for confirmation, but her blank expression gave him no answers '—so I stayed here, too. I always say that only the very fortunate get to see such heroic men. You are a renunciate, a mahatma.'

No, that couldn't be true. Whom was this false flattery for, for him or for Shashi? He secretly but piercingly looked over at Rameshwar who was staring fixedly at Shashi. Shashi was silent and was still standing with one foot on the threshold.

'And you're a fine sister—no greetings, no words, nor have you asked him to sit! Please go and bring some tea for him—and please, have some fruit until then—'

Before Shekhar could make his apologies, Shashi turned and went inside, and a minute later, she emerged with a cup of tea.

'Oh, not like—' Rameshwar hesitatingly glanced in the direction of the kettle, the milk and the other items on the table.

Quickly Shekhar said, 'It's fine, it's fine. Truth be told, I don't even drink tea—' And to put an end to the matter, he picked up the cup. Shashi sat on the reed mat on the floor and put some fruits on a plate.

Rameshwar laughed, 'Your sister has a curious disposition.' There was no power in that laugh; its only intention was to make his remarks not seem like criticism, but merely an observation.

Shekhar laughed a little, too, and said, 'In fact our entire family is curious—'

Shashi gave Shekhar a quick, angry glance and then went back to her work. Rameshwar faked surprise, 'Really?' Shekhar could tell that there was a note of sarcasm in his smile. But why, he couldn't tell.

Shekhar wanted to change topics immediately, but he couldn't figure out how. In the meantime, Shashi took the plate of fruit and put it in front of him. He wanted to ask, 'Why aren't you eating?' but then he thought that every family has different ways of doing things and perhaps she didn't eat in front of her husband, so he picked up the plate and asked Rameshwar, 'Won't you have some, too?'

'Please have some—' he said as picked up a slice of orange. 'We aren't even doing anything for you. Didn't you just get released recently? Oh, I didn't even ask you about the verdict!'

Shekhar narrated the details of all the places he had been to since he was released.

'And where are you staying?'

Shekhar laughed a little, 'I'm not staying anywhere yet—I'm still travelling!'

'Oh, then you should stay here! A sister's home is one's own home, after all. You must stay here; it would make me very happy, and of course, Shashi, too. She talks about you all the time—'

Shekhar recalled faintly that this fact was being repeated. He looked over at Shashi, but it was as if she were indifferent to his invitation. Rameshwar followed Shekhar's gaze and said, 'You should tell him to stay, too. He's probably being shy with me—'

Shashi lowered her eyes, 'I'm the younger one.'

This answer seemed enigmatic, not only to Rameshwar, but also to Shekhar.

'So what?' He stopped a little, and then as if a new stratagem occurred to him, 'I hope you're not thinking that you can't stay at your little sister's house. Come on—' and he laughed loudly. 'You can consider this a hotel and pay a fee! But these days—'

Rameshwar laughed deeply.

But after the laugh died down there was an emptiness—the feeling of intimacy or at least familiarity between two people that should accompany laughter didn't develop. The dance of politeness began again. Rameshwar asked, 'You'll have dinner, won't you? Shashi, how long until dinner?'

'It's ready now—'

'No, dinner will—'

'Whoa, how can we let that happen? I take my tea late, which is why I asked you to have tea. But it is dinner time. Come, we can go for a walk and eat when we come back.'

'No, I'm not hungry at all, and I've already eaten as it is. This fruit. And—'

'Come, let's walk around a little, you'll be hungry by the time you get back—'

Shekhar said, 'I'm tired from all the walking I've done. I should go—I should go to the college and find out what happens now.'

'You can do all of that tomorrow. But if you're tired, then you should sit. I am going to the club for a bit. I have something to take care of. I'll be back soon.' And then turning towards Shashi, 'He's going to stay here. Don't let him leave—do whatever it takes to keep him here.'

Without giving Shekhar a chance to say anything, Rameshwar went downstairs.

No one said anything for five or six very long seconds. Then Shashi asked, 'Where will you stay?'

Shekhar knew that he wouldn't stay at Shashi's. But he found it odd that she didn't ask him to either, not even in adherence to what her husband had said. But in order to hide his disappointment, he quickly came up with a lie, 'I think I'll stay in the hostel. I'll find out at the college whether I'll be able to finish my studies or not. Otherwise, I'll have to come up with something else.'

'Aren't you going home? Your mother is sick.'

'Really? But I won't go now—'

'Will you have dinner?'

'No, it wouldn't be right.'

There was silence for a while. Then Shashi asked, 'How did you find jail?'

Shekhar couldn't wrap his head around that sudden question. He asked, 'Why?'

'Many people sour after their time in jail—they find that they can't trust anyone. That hasn't happened to you, has it?'

In his mind's eye, he could see Madansingh's image.

'Umm—no. I learned quite a bit in jail—much of it was bitter, but I don't think that I've become bitter—'

Shashi took a long look into Shekhar's eyes. He liked the feeling of encouragement and contentment that he saw in her eyes. Her curious behaviour transformed the feeling of toughness that was growing within him into tenderness.

'You need to decide what you are going to do very quickly. Wandering around aimlessly like this isn't right. The next time you come here, I will ask you about what you've decided to do—not next time, you'll be here tomorrow. You'll come, won't you? He's already said you should.'

Shekhar looked at Shashi, a little taken aback. What was that mysterious note in what she was saying? He suddenly realized that everything she had said from the beginning, beneath every distinct word was profound and deep meaning—but what? He thought about what Rameshwar had said—there was also something in his words that—

There was something mysterious here—which Rameshwar and Shashi shared—and I am not a part of it. What is it? Is it that there is a deep intimacy that comes from the relationship between a husband and wife that needs to remain deep, because it is intimacy, and which it is sinful to want to see ruined? But that intimacy is related to love, and love produces joy—was Shashi happy? No, I don't think that the immovable curtain that stands between Shashi and me—Shashi and Rameshwar and me—is a curtain that happy people hide behind. Happiness is a thin film that encases an individual and separates him from everyone else, and having given his life for others, he does not meet with others, lives separately from them . . . Was that the distance that Shashi had found?

No. Shashi has left my world. Not because of happiness, just because. We've become strangers. The new relationship that would develop would have to go through Rameshwar, and what was the similarity between him and Rameshwar? My vices are different and my virtues—I have no virtues . . . Shashi isn't happy, but I am not anyone to know what her pain is, now that I am a stranger—

'What were you thinking?'

Shekhar was surprised. 'Nothing, really. I'm going to go now.' He got up. A powerful restlessness surged within him, and it was the reason he didn't want to stay.

Shashi said, 'Sit for now—' But then she looked at his face and quietly stood up. She went with him to the door at the top of the stairs. When he got there, he stopped and turned to face her, 'All right, so I'll be going now—'

Quickly, Shashi asked, 'So now you've seen my house, haven't you?'

As if in a wave, Shekhar realized that if there was something being concealed it wasn't of Shashi's making, and feeling the absolute pettiness of his previous suspicions, he said with an honest, loving, natural affection, 'I've seen it, Shashi, I've seen everything—' He went downstairs.

A question came from behind him, 'When will you come again?' Shekhar knew the questioner and because of this familiarity he knew that the question didn't come from curiosity, rather it was an announcement that she would be expecting him.

*

Where will I go with all of this unallocated energy, what will I do?

'You need to decide what you are going to do very quickly . . .'

What should I decide? What decisions have I ever made? Or if I have, what decision can I say that I have taken . . . Has the unobstructed flow of life not tossed me hither and thither

like an empty tin floating on the water—and if I hit a rock
somewhere, I echoed with a 'clang', an echo that was not the
cry of life's revolt, just of an internal emptiness, of the air that
filled the hollow—sometimes rising and sometimes submerged
under, and even that was not the result of an internal power, but
of the streams of influence of the passing waves . . . What do
I have that can be called strength? An internal hollowness that
has kept me afloat, prevented me from drowning! Can I fight
life's battle with this mere luggage, these meagre provisions, on
life's thorny road—

Poetry-wallower; bombast!

But in this state of mind, thinking didn't settle anything. It's
possible that the greatest thing one can do is to submit to this
wave of life—but that doesn't sit well with my disposition . . . Or
perhaps it's also the case that I have not been worn down enough
to be able to find that conclusion agreeable—there's still some
struggle that I think is urging me on—even if it's a mistake . . .
The ego is prideful, it's true, but until that ego is sated how will
one ever achieve disinterestedness, or how will it seem to be true?

'The next time you come here, I will ask you about what you've
decided to do—'

As he wandered on the streets, Shekhar looked up at the sky.
The dust from the streets that had flown up and dimmed the light
from the lamps had also turned the sky grey. Shekhar thought that
the stars in the water were brighter than those in the city—and
he smiled to himself. Then he was struck by a memory of Baba
Madansingh and the question about plans was in front of him
again . . .

What should I do?

'Can you give the truth that you have discovered within
yourself to another?'

Shekhar knew that the words were Baba's. It didn't surprise
him because he knew that Baba had left a heavy footprint on his
thoughts. It was as if he were talking to Baba's imaginary voice.

'Can that be a life's purpose? But when did I discover truth?—
All I have ever discovered is doubt and more doubt.'

'That's true, too. Some former truths are no longer clear today, that's also a truth in the negative.'

'Can you use a truth in the negative to—'

'Shekhar, take a look deep inside yourself. Are there no positive reserves, no faith in there, merely debts and more debts?'

'Faith . . . "Faith is greater than pain" . . . might be. Faith in one's self—that means pride. Can that be life's purpose?'

'Can you see nothing that you might be able to do—not for yourself, but for something greater than your self—meaning some work that will connect you to something greater?'

'If I am proud, then what can be greater than me! That something greater is me, right?—'

'Don't dodge—you know that you are avoiding the question, you know that you have glimpsed something greater than you—everyone does—'

Shekhar looked up at the sky again. The atmosphere was just as dusty as it was before, but the colour of the sky had deepened and so the stars seemed a little less dim. He thought that he could see a few colours sparkle in the twinkling of one of the stars and the colours were distinguishable—blue, red, white . . .

He recalled that if he was going to spend the night at someone's place, he had to let that person know that he was coming. He set out for the hostel where he could find at least one boy with whom he could stay . . .

*

Rameshwar wasn't home when Shekhar visited Shashi next. Partly for this reason, and partly because Shekhar had sketched an outline of his future plans, he could present himself to her in a more contented demeanour and chat with her. All the incidents that could be narrated were abridged: his feelings about Congress and jail, his memories of Baba Madansingh, some of his aphorisms, his magnificent death, Ramji and Mohsin. Shashi listened rapturously. But once Shekhar had told her everything and when it seemed as though he had been speaking continuously for a long time, she suddenly asked the question that she had been wanting to ask for a long time, 'What about you?'

Shekhar was taken aback, 'What?'

'You've only told me about other people. You haven't told me anything about you. I want to hear about that, too.'

'Oh, me . . .' Shekhar blushed. How could he tell Shashi about that private life which depended so much on the gifts that she had given him?

'No, I will definitely make you tell me. It's fine if it's not today, but I'm not going to let this go. You can be a stranger if you want, but I won't be one, and I'm not afraid of you.'

Shekhar was shocked; he kept hanging his head in embarrassment.

'All right, so have you decided what you are going to do?'

'Yes.'

Shashi was silent in anticipation; but when she saw Shekhar was not volunteering an answer, she asked, 'What?'

Shekhar felt that he wanted to say that he could only tell her if he could make fun of it at the same time, otherwise the plan would sound conceited . . . He laughed as he said, 'I am going to do something that we call revolution. I will turn everything upside down, and if some things get broken I will say that they were old and rotten.'

Shashi intentionally and seriously said, 'Hmm. And?'

'What else? Baba used to say, destruction is the only religious obligation; creation happens by itself. So if my tooth falls out—why should it fall out, you should pull it out—a dentist appears by himself. This is the law of science—nature abhors a vacuum.'

With that same unchanged seriousness, Shashi asked, 'This is your plan? What are you going to do to achieve this?'

'What will I do? I won't have a hammer, and teeth don't fall out from being hit by pebbles, so I'll hang a stone from a rope tied to a tooth of every person—so that the tooth will pull itself out. I saw an old woman in Kashmir with a stone hanging from her tooth—she had a toothache.'

Seeing Shashi getting more annoyed, Shekhar laughed a little and said, 'Which is to say, I am going to write. I won't tie stones but rather stacks of my books to people's teeth. After all, they will be heavy enough at some point to—'

This time Shashi smiled a little. She said, 'So you want to be a writer? Good.' Suddenly her eyes lit up. 'And your writing will have one purpose—to destroy so that you can completely rebuild.' Then she calmed down and said, 'But, Shekhar, not everything that's written like that is good, not everything becomes literature. Will you betray literature or your purpose?'

Shekhar knew that he didn't have the ability to say what he meant under the cover of sarcasm. He suddenly turned serious and said, 'I won't betray either. Betrayal is the tooth that must be extracted. But to do that requires a strategy—everything I write is written when I am worked into a frenzy; afterwards I think that it isn't so good. Moreover, sometimes I feel that there is no purpose in what I've written, because it is only frenzy and more frenzy, and a purpose requires a map and self-control.'

Both fell silent. All of a sudden, Shashi stood up and said, 'I have to make tea—'

Shekhar said goodbye and left.

*

Shekhar rented a room and a half on the top floor of a four-storeyed building near Gawalmandi for twelve rupees a month. The larger room was in one corner of the building. Because of the enclosure constructed for the stairs, the half-room wasn't regularly shaped; it was in the shape of the letter L. The larger part of the L faced east–west, and that's where Shekhar set up a sitting room. The other part faced north–south and he furnished it with a cot. There was also a small closet, and beyond the closet was a courtyard connected to the stairs. There was a faucet for water on one side of the courtyard and the remnants of the whitewash for a makeshift kitchen left by a previous tenant. On the first day, it made Shekhar happy to think that he could make one room do

the work of two; on the second day he was amazed that people
with wives and children could make do in such a small space; and
after three days he decided that it wasn't the job of respectable
people to think too much about their homes. And then, that the
size of his 'home' was at least twice the size of the cell that Baba
Madansingh had spent eighteen years of his life in . . . And one
didn't have to have a bathroom in one's room; there was one
downstairs . . .

No servants; meals would be ordered from the restaurant
(there would be the matter of the bill, but that would be settled
later). So there was little work to do and plenty of free time.

Shekhar was pacing in his bigger—meaning only—room. He
was thinking about how, in this room, he would write the literature
that would catalyse the revolution . . . It suddenly dawned on him
that this was the first time where he had his own place and was
standing on his own two feet—since he was not a small part of a
family or a clan, he could be the head of his own family—and why
just the head, he could be the whole family, because there was no
one before or after him! He was an independent unit of the very
society he wanted to transform . . . This wasn't an extraordinary
idea, but as Shekhar's entire focus was on the individual unit
and not on society, it seemed new to him. To be independent,
to be whole, to no longer see oneself as a fragment, a sliver, an
insignificant part of existence but as a whole—perhaps an isolated
part, but complete, whose actual, visual form was a separate Big
Band of a tiny existence . . . He hadn't done anything yet, but this
thought gave him confidence, comfort and a little bit of pleasure
which helped him to see the illuminated path his life would
take . . .

He remembered that he had read something which detailed
the benefits of living on the top floor of a building. He had
forgotten what the various benefits that had been enumerated
were, but he could come up with his own list. Fresh air, privacy,
distance from the commotion of the street, a stance of neutrality
towards the people . . . In his childhood, he used to believe that
people who lived on mountains were closer to God . . . Shekhar

laughed to himself. Then he started to think, now that he had this elevated position in life what would he write which could be his donation . . .

Literature—the kind of literature which would catalyse the revolution . . . And revolution? Not a one-dimensional but a multifaceted revolution! A revolution that only moves in a singular direction after closing all other roads is no revolution. The only reason we cannot move forward after such upheaval is because we are trying to wash progress down artificial gutters. Restraint is necessary, but this is not restraint. It made Shekhar think of a slimy insect similar to an earthworm that had to go in another direction in order to move forward; when it goes as far as it can in one direction, only then can it move in the right direction. Several of our leaders are like this, too. Some have chosen the field of economics, others social reform, some have chosen politics and others religion, but in each instance every one of them has limited themselves in another field of their own existence at some level substantially lower than the heights of their own upheaval . . .

Is this evil perhaps an unavoidable part of organization? Every organization has a mission, and then it has an established programme, which means that in order to advance it they withdraw from other activities . . .

But can anything be accomplished without an organization?

Yes. Revolutions have an organized aspect but they also have an important individualistic aspect. Even without organization—especially without organization—an individual can sow the seeds of a multidirectional transformation . . . And perhaps this is the only thing an individual who chooses literature as his vocation can do, since he is first an individual and only second a member of an organization! It's his special calling to plough and seed the ground for a multifaceted revolution, to water and nourish the seed of revolution . . .

The third time Shekhar went to see Shashi, there was such a glow of happiness on his face that she asked, 'Have you written something?'

'I haven't written anything, but things have started to become clear after a lot of contemplation. There isn't a lot of housework, so I spent most of the time thinking and sketching; now I'll write.'

Rameshwar was there, too. He said, 'So you want to be a writer? You've decided to quit college?'

'That happened by itself. I can't sit for the exams after being absent for ten months, and I don't have the patience to start all over and take another two years. And then, it's not like I am looking for a job that requires an MA!'

'Getting a job isn't a bad thing. You don't have to be a civil servant like me but becoming a professor is a good idea. You'd be respected, the work isn't too taxing and there are long vacations. And then you get to be around knowledge all the time—a man can spend his time reading and writing and can disseminate good ideas. It would be the best profession for you.'

Shekhar said, 'That's true. But I've developed some bad habits, and I don't think I could ever work as someone's subordinate.'

'Oh, so that's the issue. You're an idealist.' Shekhar couldn't tell how much of this was sarcastic. 'So what are you up to these days? You must be reading a lot? I—well, Shashi reads. She is constantly reading. She doesn't care for fun and games. I am always tired from all of the work that I do, so entertainment is very necessary'. . .

*

All of Shekhar's attempts to write came to naught. He didn't know why, but whenever he sat down to write, all of his ideas would disappear; sometimes it seemed to him that he was turning writing into a profession, which was draining the quality from it. But he still hadn't written anything. It was still a ways off until his writing earned him any money, so how was it a profession? But professionalization was a matter of perspective, when literature is not an aspiration, but an accomplishment . . .

Yes, there would be an accomplishment, but what was it that was accomplished? Was his mission inadequate? Literature was for the sake of literature, it was self-satisfying, but wasn't the accomplishment of a mission self-satisfying? A mission shouldn't be a special influence; the only mission should be beauty, because beauty disappears in the pursuit of an influence. But why? Was it only by finding beauty in them that other objects could find the means to be composed into a mission? Could beauty even exist without the feeling of social welfare? All of a sudden, he remembered Shashi's question, 'Will you betray literature or your purpose?' He wouldn't betray either, because as long as he examined his purpose with a clear and dispassionate single-mindedness, then all he would see would be an unsullied beauty; if one didn't have convictions, how could one's plan be clear?

But this couldn't be accomplished by thoughts alone. It required action. Whether he was right or wrong would only be determined by what he wrote. But he couldn't write a thing . . . Why couldn't he just write down his thoughts?

His room was filled with light from the afternoon sun, save for a corner of the room next to the closet that it did not reach. That's where he sat, with his legs extended into the sun, thinking about what he would write.

The sun hadn't moved off his feet when a boy ran up from downstairs and asked, 'Look, is this letter for you?' And he gave him an envelope.

Shekhar said, 'Yes,' and took the envelope. He examined the handwritten address with some surprise . . . It was a letter from Aunt Vidyavati. She had written that Shashi had written that he had rented a room to stay in and that he wanted to do something for the world of literature, and that she should pick out the best books from Shashi's collection and send them to him. She had sent the books in a trunk, whose receipt was enclosed in the letter. She had also sent her best wishes now that he was out of jail. Also included was ten rupees for good luck and some sweets packed in the trunk—she hoped that he wouldn't be upset that she had sent him the money. Many blessings, too, and if he ever got a vacation that he should come see her . . . Aunt Vidyavati.

When Shekhar finally got up a long time later, the sun had vanished. In the multicoloured light of the evening, the room felt bigger. But a spectacular glow of an affectionate joy encircled him—because he had finished writing a long poem and a short story . . .

He wanted to run to Shashi at that very instant and tell her, 'Look, I've written something . . .' But then he quickly thought, 'If she could write to Aunt without telling me, then I can send her my poem and story in the mail without telling her.' He made up his mind and put the handwritten pages into the empty cabinet in the room. That's when he remembered that his own books had been left behind in the hostel. He decided that he would go to his previous roommate, collect his books and bring them here, too, and keep on studying . . .

*

After he searched and found his roommate's new room and learned from him that his books had been taken by 'people' and that his collection of pictures had been stolen, Shekhar returned with the remaining stack of books—even though more than half had been lost, the ones left were more than enough. There were fewer textbooks amongst those, and all of them were books that Shekhar especially liked. It was night by that time. He just left them as they were in the room. In the morning, he cleaned out his cabinet and put some paper down on the shelves and organized the books carefully. Then he went and got the package of Shashi's books and spent a little time arranging them, too. There were five shelves in the cabinet—the top four, which had glass cabinet doors, were now full of books; on the bottom shelf, Shekhar placed his stack of notebooks on one side and the sweets that his aunt had sent on the other side. And then he closed the cabinet doors and admired the fruits of his labour from a distance for a while.

The sight of a cabinet full of books thrilled him. How beautiful his room had become with these books in it—half of which had been collected by him one by one and the rest by Shashi! Shekhar knew that Shashi had bought the majority of these books over many years with the pocket change that she received as a monthly allowance; just as he had by setting aside some money saved (or which was saved by itself) from his monthly expenses. It seemed to him that she was looking at his room with her kind, bright and tender eyes from two of the shelves of that cabinet, and that her gaze had warmed the atmosphere of the room. Suddenly he was filled with gratitude, and a desire overcame his heart: to show his gratitude to Shashi . . . But he stopped himself from going there at this time. He decided to go in the evening when she would be done with her housework and Rameshwar would also be free (he had half the day off that day). And there was something else that was important—by that time Shashi would have received the letter that he had put in the mail last night—she would have read his story and the poem . . .

Rameshwar was sitting on a chair with his legs extended on another, smoking a cigarette. Shashi was sitting on a reed mat on the floor doing some sewing. When Shekhar arrived, she put her sewing down on her lap and looked up at him calmly and gently. Then she straightened her neck slightly and returned to her sewing. Rameshwar said loudly, 'Come in, come in. It's good you've come!' He smiled through a cloud of smoke. 'Tell me, what are you writing these days?'

'Nothing. These days I can't seem to make myself write.' Shekhar looked over at Shashi as he said this to see if she would say something or laugh, because she would have received his poem and story earlier that day. But she continued to work on her sewing.

'That is the best part of being a writer. Writing, writing, then not writing, months without writing. And when you don't have to earn a living by writing, then there's no telling. Whereas I don't get to eat until I finish all of my wretched files. If you slack off a little, you have to take the remaining files home with you—all of my work has to be completed the same day.'

This time there was no room for doubt—the sarcasm in Rameshwar's words was clear: that being a writer was an excellent excuse to be a loafer! Shekhar didn't respond. He turned to Shashi and said, 'Aunt sent me a trunk full of books.'

'Hmm.'

'She sent a letter, too. She sent her best wishes on getting out of jail and some things for luck.'

Shashi smiled a little. It was clear from her face that she liked what her mother had done.

Rameshwar asked, 'What books?'

'Shashi's books were just sitting there. She sent those.'

Rameshwar held back his curiosity and asked, 'Did you tell her to send them?'

'Yes.'

'Oh—All right.' Then to Shekhar, 'Do you read much? Of course, how else would you pass the time? They must be fine books—your sister has a very refined taste.'[3]

And then a glimpse of the same unclear thing—was something hiding under that claim? But the words were spoken in a straightforward way.

Shekhar said, 'I had left many of my books behind, too. I went and got those as well. I think that I am going to study regularly again.'

'Definitely, definitely.'

Someone knocked on the door downstairs. A voice called at the same time, 'It's the postman, sir!'

Shekhar was the closest to the stairs. Before Rameshwar could get up, Shekhar went and grabbed the mail from the postman. Shekhar was suddenly stunned. There were two letters—one was the one he had sent!

Shekhar was temporarily thrown into a dilemma. He gave both letters to Rameshwar and quickly said, 'All right, I must take your leave. I have some things to take care of—'

Rameshwar was about to look at the letters, but he stopped and said, 'So soon? Please sit, you can go after you have had some tea—'

'No, thank you. I'll come some other time—' Shekhar said and left. He could hear behind him, 'Here, this letter is for you.'

'For me?'

'Yes, who is it from?' It was said in that same tone of repressed accusation, as if wanting to appear as if it wasn't expression of authority but mere curiosity.

'The handwriting seems to be Shekhar's—'

Shashi's gentle surprise—

Shekhar laughed to himself as he descended the stairs. When Shashi sees what's in the letter, she'll be astounded . . .

*

When he got back home, Shekhar started going through his old notebooks. He began to open the bundle of papers from the days when he used to visit Manika's place and started to read. Today, he was pleased, as if the disorganized thoughts that had once occupied his mind were being strung together in a chain . . . It was unclear, but he could see, in a form that was gradually gathering clarity, that all the things that he had seen and thought in the last two or two and a half years contained in essence the developed conclusions that would be the foundation of his ideas about his society; and on the basis of these conclusions, he could raise an accusation against the current condition of society and could demand that society be transformed . . . He could see the scattered argument in that bundle of papers which could be organized into a book, the 'grammar' of the reconstruction that Shekhar had imagined . . . He had also decided on a name for the book—'Our Society' . . . Because only by calling it 'society' could the theoretical ideas of society be brought out; if one used 'traditional' or other such adjectives, then it wouldn't be clear that the subject of the book was contemporary society . . .

No, writing wasn't his profession; it was his accomplishment, because he had something to say and because he had a burning desire—a desire, and an ability, too . . .

After five or six days of writing, when the shape of the book had become clearer and the first few parts were in their final form, Shekhar realized suddenly that he had gone that day to show Shashi his gratitude! He hadn't done that, nor had he learned what she thought of his poem and story! And the real issue was that he wanted to bring her here to show her his crooked room and how beautiful and overflowing his cabinet full of books (and full of notebooks!) looked—because that would be the best way he could display his gratitude. Otherwise, he would have to open his mouth wide to say, 'Shashi, I am grateful for the books that you've sent,' and she would half-close her eyes and raise her eyebrows to respond, 'Is this even something worth mentioning?' No, he couldn't stand formality.

He took the outlined pages of his incomplete novel and went to Shashi's in order to invite Shashi and Rameshwar over. After he had come to this decision, he hesitated for a moment about what he would be able to offer Rameshwar when he came, and then he remembered that the money his aunt had sent was still in the cabinet. It didn't matter that he had already finished the sweets; he would get a tea set, a stove, some coal and the like, which could be of use to him afterwards, too—because the cold weather had already begun as well . . .

Rameshwar wasn't at home. Seeing the bundle of papers in Shekhar's arms, Shashi asked, 'What have you brought?'

Excited, Shekhar said, 'It's the outline of my book. Do you want to see?'

'Yes, give it to me . . .'

Shashi didn't mention the poem or the story. Did she not like them? Then she should have said so. Why should she keep quiet? Proudly he said, 'Why should I show you? Are you even interested?'

'Why? What do you mean?'

'You haven't read my story or my poem—'

Shashi's face suddenly went serious. She calmly asked, 'Why did you send them by mail?'

'Why didn't you tell me that you had written to my aunt? I thought it would be a surprise—' Suddenly Shekhar realized that Shashi's face wasn't serious, it was grave; her voice wasn't calm, it was lifeless. He asked nervously, 'Why Shashi? What's wrong?'

'Nothing. Why surprise me—you could have showed me yourself—'

'No, Shashi, there is something—tell me now!' Shekhar said with a terrified urgency.

'Nothing. After you left, he asked, "Who's it from?" I told him. He was taken aback and said, "He was just here, why a letter?" I told him that it was a story and a poem. He said, "Good, then let me read it, too." I gave them both to him, but I could tell by the way he was flipping the pages that he had no real interest in poetry or fiction. Then he said, "Well, I don't know anything about poetry-shmoetry; only artists understand such things" and then returned the pages. After a long time he said, "So why did he have to run away so quickly?" At first, I didn't understand what he was talking about, then I remembered. I didn't feel like saying anything to him about it.'

Shekhar sat down in silence. After a very long time he said, 'Should I explain it to him?'

'No, that will make things worse. Let it go, it's done. What are you writing now?'

Shekhar quietly accepted this obvious attempt at changing topics. He said, 'I am taking things that I had written earlier and reorganizing them into an essay—a critique of our society.' But his voice no longer possessed its previous excitement.

'Our society! How much have you written? And what have you titled it?'

'Exactly that—"Our Society!" I will finish it very soon.' Just then, Rameshwar arrived.

'It's been several days since your last visit.'

'Yes, I've been working on something.'

'What have you brought with you? Have you written something else? Your poem and story were beautiful. I read them on Shashi's insistence. But this time I won't need a recommendation before I read it—you are a beautiful writer.'

Internally, Shekhar praised this man whose lips could produce words perfectly by themselves, whether he believed in them or not. He was the one who couldn't say anything.

'Come, let me have a look—'

Shekhar wanted to say it now. This unfinished manuscript felt like such a part of his own personality that he didn't want to show it to Rameshwar . . . But he stopped himself from saying so.

If he had, Rameshwar would have thought it meant something else entirely. Forcefully repressing his antipathy he handed the notebook over to Rameshwar.

When Rameshwar began absent-mindedly fingering its pages, and when Shekhar began to think that the fingers were not merely moving absent-mindedly but also critically, he felt humiliated. He stood up to leave. When Rameshwar asked him to sit, he said, 'Truth is, I hate sitting while watching someone read my work'— and to himself he thought that this would serve as the absent explanation for the other day, too.

Rameshwar looked at Shashi and said, 'Well, how can you hate it? It's going to be printed, right?' And then suddenly, 'Or if you want, you could send this by mail, too—' He guffawed loudly. 'But it would be expensive to send such a thick notebook by mail—'

How could one deliver an invitation in this situation? Somehow, he got up and left.

*

Shekhar didn't leave his house for the next four or five days. He also had no desire to write anything; he would blankly sit in front of the window and sometimes, if it was too cold, close it and pace in his room. A few times, he tried to read, but his distracted eyes would sometimes register nothing, and then he would shake himself and think, 'If you wanted to waste time, then why the self-deception?' Sometimes in the mornings he would lie in bed and read a few verses of poetry and hope that they would colour the rest of his day with their influence.

About a week later, one evening, Shashi showed up. At first, she knocked on the door nervously, but when she saw it was Shekhar and was reassured that she hadn't made a mistake, her face lit up. 'I finally found your place! None of the people downstairs even know your name!'

Delighted, Shekhar said, 'Why didn't you ask them where the hermit lives? All of them are very curious about what I do in my room all day.'

'So why don't you go outside?'

Shekhar gave her a long look.

Shashi lifted the corner of his bedding and sat down on the cot and said, 'I've brought your book. I read all of it—as much as you gave me—and I've come to tell you that you have to finish it quickly.'

'I haven't been able to write anything else.'

'Why? What did you do all this time?'

'Nothing. My heart wasn't in it. I've been wondering whether my writing will make any difference!'

With a concerned intensity, she said, 'Hmm.'

'Yes, of course. If I finish writing it, it won't get printed. If it gets printed, people will make fun of me. I could even be content with being made a fool—but for what?'

'Shekhar, isn't there any satisfaction in bearing a little strife for one's ideals? I consider it to be a great consolation. Otherwise I wouldn't have—'

'There is. But—I don't know what. Sometimes I think that an ideal that takes the form of a revolution in name only isn't enough. It has ideals, but perhaps ideals aren't enough for satisfaction; perhaps one needs the exemplar of the ideal.'

'Really?'

'Yes, that's what I think.'

'So you want to find an exemplar of your ideals so that your efforts towards it will bring you satisfaction?'

Shekhar thought about it and said, 'Yes.'

'Yes,' Shashi mocked him and said, 'You say it like a child—"Yes."' And then she paused. 'What kind of exemplar, a certain object or a certain—person?'

Shekhar did not seem to be paying attention. Till then, he had been leaning on the windowsill; now he started looking outside.

Shashi stood up. She faced the opposite direction from Shekhar and said, 'Shekhar, can you write something for me?'

With a start, Shekhar said, 'What?'

'I asked, can you write something for me? I didn't think that I would have to say it myself, but there's no harm in saying it.'

Shekhar went and stood next to Shashi. After a moment of indecision, he grabbed her by the shoulder and turned her around. Shashi's eyes were on his chin. She didn't look up. He removed his hands from her shoulders and then returned to his spot and said, 'No, Shashi, I am unlucky. Everything I touch turns to rubbish. Nothing I write will be worthy enough to—'

Shashi spoke again, 'I asked you, can you write for me? And listen, the better you write, the greater will be the rejection from everyone else. But you will find peace inside yourself. It will sound terrible if I say it, but your exemplar could be composed of not just that peace but also that rejection.'

'Shashi!'

Shashi looked up and took in her fill of him. This time Shekhar lowered his eyes—he could not hold the gaze of that proud anguish.

Shashi said, 'Well, show me what you've written beyond this.'

Shashi's words changed the mood. Shekhar said, 'What did I write? I have some notes that you can see if you like.' He took some papers out of the cabinet and gave them to her.

'And what are all those bundles?'

'Random things, things I wrote while I was in college—'

'I want to read those, too. From now on, you will have to give me every little piece of writing, understand?'

Shashi began to read the pages that Shekhar gave her. He asked, 'Doesn't the room look better with these books in it?'

Shashi smiled as she read.

'Have you read all these books?'

Without lifting her head, Shashi said, 'Hmm—wait. Let me finish reading these.'

Shekhar went back to stand next to the window. As he looked outside, he began to feel grateful for Shashi in his heart—she who came here without being asked and fulfilled his unspoken desire . . .

'Yes, so when are you going to finish this?' Shashi had finished reading all the pages.

'We'll see.'

'No seeing, you have to finish!' Shashi laughed. Then turning serious, she said, 'You haven't invited him here yet.'

Guiltily, Shekhar said, 'I had come to invite him last time.'

Shashi put the pages in the cabinet and said, 'All right, I'm going now. When you come next time, be sure to invite him.' And then spying the ten rupees in the cabinet, 'Where did these come from?'

'A gift for luck.'

'They're still here? Couldn't you use them?'

'They are most useful when they are lying right there.' Shekhar started laughing.

'What do you eat?'

'Why? I order food from the restaurant. Is that funny?'

'Food from the restaurant!' Shashi said in disbelief. Then composing herself, she asked, 'Can I hear the name of the restaurant?'

Shekhar bristled, rolled his eyes and, deliberately pronouncing every letter, said, 'Chintpurni Devi Consecrated and Pure Restaurant—the name is enough to fill your belly.' And he started laughing.

Shashi furrowed her brows in fake anger, 'Don't laugh like that with me! All right, I'm going.'

She began to descend the stairs. 'Wait, I'll see you off,' he said and ran downstairs after her.

*

Shashi and Rameshwar had been to Shekhar's a few times already. The cabinet placed in the closet next to the sitting room now contained a tea set, some pots, utensils, a few tins, a bottle of honey, a packet of biscuits and another of matches—all of these things had been purchased. In exchange, the gifted ten rupees in the other cabinet had disappeared. Shekhar hadn't written anything special; if the papers in his cabinet had grown, it was because of a few letters—a couple from his aunt, one from Gaura and one from his father. Shekhar's father was partly angry at his son's idleness and partly secretly proud of his having been to jail; and along with that, was the news that his mother was very sick and he should come immediately to see her; that his younger brother Ravidutt was going to be taking his BA exams this year; and that Sadashiv had written from Madras that he would be a doctor next year and that he had asked where Shekhar was and what he was doing. He had heard the news that Shekhar had been to jail.

It had been a month since Shekhar had moved into his home. It suddenly occurred to him that he would have to pay rent next month and also pay the restaurant bill—and he didn't have anything! The rent could be paid late because it was hardly necessary to pay it on time every month, but it had been a month since he had received the restaurant bill, and being late with that bill meant not getting anything to eat . . .

He was a little worried. Then he thought, 'The book is almost ready. I can get a little something for it from some publisher.' It was fine if it wasn't a lot, a little would work for now, but altogether his monthly expenses were twenty-five rupees, so the book would be able to earn him enough for a year . . . He didn't know how much publishers offered for a book . . . But he didn't think that 300 rupees was excessive for one book.

'Our Society' . . . Is for sale—our society is for sale for 300 rupees—any takers? Shekhar laughed to himself—our society doesn't sell for cheap; it goes for 300 rupees!

Shekhar decided to inquire with a few of the best publishers in the city. He worked continuously for four days and finished his manuscript and then wrapped it in a large handkerchief and went to see the managing editor of Vani Niketan Publishers. When he finished explaining his project to the manager after placing the manuscript in front of him, the manager looked carefully at Shekhar from head to toe instead of at the manuscript. After a little while he said, 'Sir, we only publish things from established writers here. As you know, we are the best publishers in town, and we would like to keep our reputation. How can we take responsibility for publishing an entirely new and unknown writer?'

Shekhar insisted, 'But you should evaluate the thing, too. Is fame the only criteria you use? Even the most famous writers were unknowns at some point.'

'Of course. But at that point, their books weren't being published with us. We only took them once the importance of their work had been established. That's when we offered them much better terms compared to other publishers. The ones whose books didn't sell, we don't take.'

'But that's like stealing food from someone else's mouth—'

'You can think that way if you like. But it's the mark of intelligence to learn from the mistakes of others. We don't print things by people who are or could be unsuccessful.'

The managing editor of Saraswati Kunj Publishers sent Shekhar to his literary editor. After Shekhar found his address in a lane in the city and arrived there, the editor looked at the title and said, 'Is it a novel?'

'No. It's a collection of critical essays. I created a picture of contemporary society and tried to demonstrate that—'

'Oh, so you tried to demonstrate something? But, Sir, first of all, no one reads essays. Moreover, definitely not essays that are just critique and more critique. Why don't you write literary essays?'

'What do you mean?'

'There are hundreds of topics—like . . . like . . . "the images of women in Chayyavad [Shadowist] poetry", "the depiction of women by female poets" or "sexism amongst Sanskrit and Hindi poets". These are also modern topics—it's the age of comparative studies these days.'

Shekhar asked, 'Does anyone read such essays?'

'Well, not by themselves, but they can be published in literature textbooks. So it's publishable.'

Shekhar was quiet for a while. Then the editor said, 'You probably didn't like my advice much; I only said it for your benefit—'

Dejectedly, Shekhar replied, 'No, I'm grateful for your recommendations. But I'm only interested in society and social issues—'

'All right, then pick a topic that fits that—"is the beloved of the mystical poet masculine or feminine?" There is a popular opinion these days that the mystical poets displayed their love only for embodied beings—It's already accepted about Farsi poetry that the wine-bearer or the beloved is not imaginary, but the new opinion is that the wine-bearer and the beloved are neither masculine nor feminine, but neuter. This study will also give you a good opportunity to investigate medieval society. I really believe that it is the prime moment for this topic.'

Shekhar was silenced. After a little while, he said, 'So you don't think this book is publishable?'

'No, no, I didn't say that. Everything is publishable. But only the things that will sell get published; otherwise who will take on the risk? But I've always advised the people at Saraswati Kunj to promote innovative new writers—even if that is a little risky. Otherwise how can there be a new literature? And they even listen to me.'

Shekhar felt a flutter of hope. He said, 'So will you read this and tell me? I am hoping that quickly—'

'You should talk to the managing editor. I will advise him to publish your book at your expense, and as quickly as possible. New writers should get opportunities—it's a publisher's duty.'

Shekhar was disappointed again. He slowly wrapped his bundle, said goodbye and left.

Shekhar made the rounds of second-tiered publishers, too, and then went to a bookseller and got a complete directory of publishers and began to look at the remaining ones from top to bottom.

Another week passed. Ultimately, the managing editor of New Age Books decided to publish his book on the condition that Shekhar would bear the costs of the printing and the paper. He would not have to pay anything up front, rather the publisher would print and sell the books and use the proceeds to cover their investment first, and then he would get a fourth of the profits from the books sold after that. After ten days of frustrated wandering, Shekhar didn't have the patience to sit and do the accounting of what he would get and when; he thought that the manager was doing him a great favour by not asking for payment . . . He had also forgotten that he had set out to sell the book so that he could pay his bill—and the demand for immediate payment had already arrived.

That day Shekhar didn't leave with his bundle. He didn't believe that he would need it! He promised the managing editor that he would be back in three days—he left a delay of two days so that the publisher wouldn't think that he was overeager!—and went back home.

When he got home, he lay down on the bed, exhausted and sad. He had a fleeting notion that he would go and tell Shashi about all this, but he couldn't make himself do it. And what was there to tell? He stared unblinkingly at the ceiling; he suddenly felt that it was exactly the same for all these days and the realization depressed him. He turned to face the window.

Who knew when the book would be printed, or how it would be reviewed? . . . Would anything come of it? When? How much would it cost? The paper probably cost 200 rupees. Another 100 or 150 on top. And if the book sold for one rupee, then . . . Shekhar gave up doing the math. 'Our Society'—cost: one rupee. And I get a fourth of the profits after covering the costs! . . . A cold, dry line of a smile spread across Shekhar's face—who knows when he fell asleep.

It was pitch-black when he woke up. It was past midnight, and the square in Gawalmandi was perfectly quiet. Shekhar was shivering from the December cold . . . He was also hungry. Since the start of the month, he had resolved to eat only one meal a day from the restaurant. He had told the restaurant staff that he would make his own dinner from now on . . . One day he purchased rice, lentils and flour and made a rice and lentil porridge and ate it.

Should he make dinner now? He wasn't that hungry. No, he was hungry, but it wasn't right to let hunger have so much control over him. He straightened his bed and wrapped himself in his blanket and tried to sleep. He was shivering so hard that he couldn't get warm. So he got up and began quickly pacing in his room to warm himself up.

Suddenly, his feelings of total failure in all of his efforts, which he had repressed after last talking with Shashi, welled up inside him. The failure not only of his efforts but also of all efforts . . . What was to be gained by setting foot in the bubbling swamp of life after all—? No matter how you entered, you would sink into it . . . I will write a book—a book, ha! As if no one had written a book until now. As if no one had tried to reform society until now. As if—

Shekhar began walking even faster. Was there no release from this deadly circle of cause and effect? Couldn't one escape it?

A thought rose like a bubble from the chasm of his emotional torment—he hadn't ever believed in something so deeply that he was willing to sacrifice himself completely for it—not even for a moment had Shekhar been able to erase from his mind the idea that he was Shekhar. Was it only a matter of time? Was it really not his fault? Hadn't he been hoarding himself like a miser, even though he dreamed of turning the world upside down so that he could converse with it! Forget about everyone else, but so many women had come into his life, and he had been unable to get very close to any of them. He had kept himself from living! Manika's way of life was much better than his—she had the audacity to throw life around like dust! 'My life's candle burns at both ends! It won't burn all night long, but my friends and my enemies, how beautiful is its light!' Did he have the ability to illuminate the heavens with that kind of light? Manika hadn't chosen the right path, but she had the real substance in her that the gods hide away from humans . . .

He remembered a saying he had read in a book that Manika had given him—'What is abstinence? It is the miscarriage of the strongest lust!' Then he remembered a story about a Pathan—he couldn't remember where he had heard it, perhaps it was in jail—a moulvi was explaining to a Pathan why he should be celibate (abstinent),[4] but the Pathan didn't understand that word. The moulvi began to explain that a celibate man kept his eyes down, didn't chase after women or go with women. Suddenly the Pathan interrupted to say, 'Oh, now I understand—in our language we call him a eunuch.'

Shekhar stopped. He felt that there was certainly something wrong with the direction that his thoughts were streaming. As with all thoughts, this one had some partial truth in it, but it wasn't the whole truth. Absolutely not. Because when had his circumstances ever handed him any advantages, what big opportunity had he ever let slip through his fingers? Even if no extraordinary obstacle had ever fallen in his path, still some . . . The life of others, too, was a mixture of advantages and obstacles . . .

Was it only that he was hungry right now? Were all rebellions here clouds of unsatisfied desires? Would these desires keep building until there was an explosion and then nothing?

Then all of this—is hysteria![5]

He could tell that his energies were being directed internally and would gradually destroy him unless there was a radical revolution which turned them outwards, externally . . . And it needed to happen, because only an extroverted force could produce a revolution, not an introverted one. Even if his introversion made him into a special kind of poet, it would completely obliterate everything that he wanted to accomplish . . .

Shekhar sat down on his bed and wrapped himself in his blanket. In a vague way, he wanted not merely to write but to do some other work that might bring him into contact with other people, but what kind and how, he couldn't figure out. He lay down after having resolved to ask Shashi for her advice.

With the first light of day Shekhar got a telegram stating that his mother had passed away.

Shekhar had got up with a strange feeling of exhaustion. Even after he read the telegram, the feeling didn't dissipate; he couldn't make sense of what he had just read. He put the telegram down and picked up his toothbrush and towel and went to the faucet to clean himself up. Then he came back inside and went and took some papers from the cabinet. Suddenly the four words of the telegram flashed in his brain like lightning—Mother has passed away!

A strange feeling of anguish came over him, which was different from sorrow. He didn't feel sorrow, and he felt a little ashamed at himself because of that . . . But he wanted to cry just once—to cry simply like an ordinary man who had lost his mother! But his eyes were drying out, with a burning sensation.

Shekhar stared blankly at the papers and sat there for a long time. Slowly, many memories of his childhood passed before him—but there was not a single element of emotion in those memories, as if his emotional capacity had degenerated and only his vision was working. After a while he realized that these images had finished spinning around and were finally focusing on a single point—Shekhar was eating dinner, and from the adjoining room Mother's voice says, 'I don't have any faith in this one.' But there was no residue of that terrible anger which had been previously tied to that image . . . Why? Had he forgiven his mother? He didn't recall ever having come to that decision deliberately. Perhaps he had unconsciously realized that it was stupid to hoard his anger, or perhaps he had just now decided that it was a sin to think ill of the dead. He had tried to imagine a picture of his mother's face before, but he was usually unsuccessful. But today he could see it clearly—it wasn't a beautiful face, but there weren't those lines across her face that he usually saw, even though he knew that they weren't always there—the face was peaceful, and there was nothing in it that would contradict its relationship to motherhood . . . All mothers have their own faces, but motherhood has its own special countenance—or rather, it should have . . .

But why couldn't Shekhar cry?

His mind went completely blank asking himself this question. After a while, he got up all of a sudden so that if nothing else he would at least do his daily chores. He cleaned his room, washed and put away his dishes, fixed his bed. And then he took one look at the bare walls of his room. Had there been a picture on any of his walls—he hated hanging photographs—but at that moment if he had a photograph of his mother, he might have hung it on the wall and tried to know that face anew, that face which had become so unfamiliar . . .

For no reason, he thought of Shanti—wearing that expression of hers and looking like a picture by Rossetti—'The Glory of Death'[6] . . . Was death always glorious . . . ? Now Mother is no more—

He remembered, too, the poem that Shanti had recited to him, but it didn't hold any meaning for him right now, and so his mind went to a different poem by Tennyson:

The sounds of the twilight and evening bells
And a clear call to me;
Let there be no sadness of farewell then,
When I lift my anchor and set out for the open sea[7]

. . . They say that this was Tennyson's last poem, written when he was eighty-two . . .

For no apparent reason, Shekhar went out to the bank of the Ravi River that afternoon. He had never seen a crematorium, and he knew that if he didn't see the final rites of a body he would never understand the reality of death.

A few bodies were burning in the cremation grounds. They had been burning for a while. The bodies inside the pyres were unrecognizable and no one else was there. Shekhar was alone if one didn't count a few dogs . . .

But glorious? Shekhar thought the scene was closer to ridiculous—what a vulgar end! He believed that fire could give anything a nobility and a majesty, but there was none of that here. Rather, from the surroundings here, fire itself had become cheapened. Bitterly, Shekhar wondered if perhaps people alleviated their grief by joining the fate of their ancestors to this cheap place . . .

It was evening by the time he got back. Inside, he realized the oil had run out in his lamp. It was for just such an event that he had purchased a few candles; he lit two of them at the same time, placed them on the shelf and sat on his cot.

All of a sudden, the light from the candles flickered, and then after a teer-teer-teer sound they came back to light. Shekhar saw the moth, bigger than a butterfly, which had often circled the lamp, now burned after having clashed with the flame of the candle.

Suddenly, an image of life as mere existence flashed before him; existence, which is a mere event . . . Had the lamp been lit today, the moth would have still been circling it—but because of an event, of the lack of oil—'teer-teer-teer'—and—nirvana!

The news from that morning's telegram flashed before his eyes. Mother is no more!

Shekhar got up and kneeled in front of the shelf as if in a pose of prayer and, placing his forehead against the shelf, began to cry, first dry-eyed, and then with a sobbing that shook his entire frame and then slowly with tears . . .

He still hadn't stopped crying when suddenly from behind him, Shashi's pain-filled voice said, 'Shekhar?' He lifted his head with a start. Shashi said, softly, 'So you've heard the news.' He nodded. Then he wiped his eyes with his fingers and stood up. Shashi went over and placed her hands on his shoulders and gently manoeuvred him to his cot. She still didn't move; she gently caressed his shoulders with one hand, in a soft, comforting touch.

Shekhar thought that if she kept on, his embarrassment from crying would dissipate and he would burst into tears again. He said, 'I want to be alone for a while—'

'Then I'll leave you alone—'

'No, you should sit. I'll be back.' And without giving Shashi a chance to say anything, he went out.

Shekhar came back after about an hour. Shashi was sitting worried on the edge of his cot. When he arrived, she said, 'Now I should go—it's late. I just got word this evening, so I came right over to see you. Take care, my brother! I'll come back tomorrow.'

Shashi left but Shekhar kept looking at the stairs for a while . . . Then he noticed that there was a light coming from the smaller closet. He took a candle from the room and went over to look. He was surprised to see a covered plate had been left there.

In Shekhar's absence, Shashi had made some gram flour cakes and put out some pickle and honey next to it—what else was there in his house!

Shekhar didn't want to eat. But when he looked at the plate, he felt he wasn't free to make up his own mind in the matter.

*

Shashi came back once more, and two days later, she came again with Rameshwar. Christmas vacation was starting that day, and Shashi and Rameshwar were leaving town. Without prodding, Rameshwar offered, 'I keep saying to her that she should stay here, but she won't hear of it. I thought that if she stayed here, it might help you feel better—being alone in a time of sadness makes it worse.'

Shekhar said, 'No, it's not a problem. I'm only used to living alone.'

As they were leaving, Shashi said, 'If you had gone home once it would have been good. You should go and see your father.'

Ambivalently, Shekhar remained quiet.

A week later, he received word from his father that he was coming. His father planned to go to Haridwar, and pass through Lahore on his way back home. He was there four days later. Shekhar went to get him at the train station. Seeing the deep lines of exhaustion, sadness and hurt on his father's face, Shekhar was stunned. He had never before imagined that that mature, unselfconscious face could ever look aged, but now his face and eyes were clearly afflicted with the kind of fatigue that gradually manifests after passing several milestones on the difficult road of life.

Before he had followed him up to his room, his father asked once at the stairs, 'What kind of neighbourhood have you chosen to live in?' He had the luggage on one side and then saw the tonga-wallah off. Then his father asked him, 'Is this where you live?'

The question was unnecessary, but it was said to make clear the note of disbelief it contained. Shekhar said, 'Yes, sir.'

'Are there any servants?'

'No, sir.'

'What do you do for food?'

'Once a day I get a meal from the restaurant.'

'And the other times?'

Shekhar was silent.

His father said while thinking it over, 'You probably make something tip-top[8] yourself.'

The question made room for the possibility that there need not be an answer. Shekhar didn't want to lie, but he also didn't want to tell the truth.

'And the cleaning—the dishes?'

'It's a small room. It doesn't take long to clean up.'

After a period of silence, his father spoke again, 'Aren't you embarrassed living like this?' His voice wasn't full of anger as much as wounded pride.

Shekhar kept his mouth shut.

His father began pacing in the room. Shekhar began running around to make the necessary arrangements—he took things out from the closet, borrowed a bucket from a neighbour and placed it in the room after filling it with water, placed his father's attaché case on the shelf and hung his dhoti and towel from the window. His father hectored only once, 'Leave it be. I'll do it myself.' But when Shekhar kept doing what he was doing, his father watched silently.

When his father was leaving to take a bath, Shekhar said, 'I'll go to the restaurant and be back—'

'All right. And get my medicine from the store, too.'

His father told him the name of the store and gave him two ten-rupee notes. Shekhar asked him, 'How much does it cost?'

'That should cover it. And buy a box of biscuits, too—to have with evening tea—I don't like plain tea very much.'

When Shekhar purchased the medicine and the bill was one rupee and some change, he suspected that there was another reason that his father had given him twenty rupees. When he went back, his father had finished bathing and was writing something in his

notebook. Shekhar put the medicine down in front of him and
began counting out the remaining rupees.

His father said, 'Keep it for now—I will need more things—'
Shekhar's suspicions were confirmed.

Dinner arrived a little bit later. Every other day, the boy
would drop the food off and leave and come back later to get
the dishes. But today, Shekhar stopped him to ask him to do
something.

His father looked at each item on the plate carefully, ate five
or six bites and then pushed the plate away.

Shekhar had never spoken of such things with his father before,
and moreover he always felt it strange to hear other people talk of
such things, but today partly because he felt somehow responsible
and partly because he could tell that his father couldn't terrorize
him as he had before, Shekhar steeled himself and said, 'But you
didn't eat anything—'

His father answered in an uncharacteristic fashion, 'What's
the point of eating now?—My interest in food went with her—'
and he immediately got up. Shekhar was silent. He also pushed
his plate away and gestured to the boy to bring some water so that
they could wash up . . .

Nothing much happened in the next few days; occasionally
something would happen to remind his father of Shekhar's
mother and the atmosphere would become heavy with sadness
and dejection, but then a little while later things would go on as
before. At first, Shekhar and his father didn't chit-chat much, and
when it did happen it would be one-sided; but now Shekhar was
noticing a change in his father and began to feel a little more like
his equal, and because of that the ratio of chit to chat in their chit-
chats became more even, although it still wasn't entirely equal; the
conversations would start abruptly and suddenly break off in the
middle . . .

'How long will you live like this?'

'. . .'

'Aren't you going to do anything? What will come of eating
restaurant food all day? Is this any way to live?'

'I am doing something. Actually, I've never worked as hard as I am—'

Full of disbelief—'Maybe you are, but what good is hard work without a purpose? Do you think anything comes of sheer effort? Life needs a plan to make effort meaningful. The first thing that you need is to live properly—all you've done is spread out your wares like a gypsy!'

'I have my plan right in front of me. It's fine if you don't approve of it, but all of my hard work has a purpose.'

'What plan? You've given up your education. Why don't you keep studying? At least get your MA. If you work hard, you'll even pass with high marks—you'll even get a scholarship.' Or if you don't want to study here, you can go to England.'

'I don't have any interest in studying. What will an MA accomplish—everyone has an MA these days, and not all of them are undeserving. I'm not anything special.'

'Don't get an MA if you don't want to; pick something else to pursue. Didn't you once talk about becoming a lawyer or an engineer? These professions can be of use in social reform work— Or if you are really bent on doing social service, you can try education. Service is not a bad thing—'

'I have come to think that those sorts of things speak to the ideals of other people, not my own. And if your heart isn't in something, all of your hard work goes to waste.'

'So you must have some ideas—'

'I've picked literature.'

'Picked! What will literature accomplish? Life doesn't run on literature! And you can do literature at the same time as other things; can't doctors or lawyers or engineers be writers? Every writer I read in Hindi has a "Professor" in front of his name. These people must all be teachers somewhere. It's good work, it's also service, and there's some stability in life, and there's literature, too. That's the best of everything. And—'

'But that's not true of all writers. The best writers have—'

'Leave them out of it. Not everyone can be a Shelley or a Keats. And didn't Kalidasa serve his time in court? Or are you talking about ascetics like Surdas or Tulsidas—those were special men. Not everyone can follow their example.'

'Look, either I possess genius or I don't. If I don't possess it, then what makes you think that I will be any better after I pass my MA than all the other fools who have their MAs? And if I do possess it, then who knows, I could do something important in literature—'

'Hmm, that's spurious logic!'

The matter was closed.

A long time after that, suddenly, 'What will you write in, Hindi?'

'Yes.'

'Hmm. What's so special about Hindi? If you write in English, it may even make you famous. Even if you don't earn a lot, a man can at least get some satisfaction from his fame. What will Hindi get you?'

'But there should be a purpose to the writing. One doesn't write for mere fame, does one? Only a few people will be able to read books in English—Hindi will reach millions—' (and then suddenly remembering that even if there were millions of Hindi speakers, there were substantially fewer readers!)—'or at a minimum thousands will be able to read it.'

'But what class of readers? Who values Hindi in this day and age?'

With a note of pride, Shekhar said, 'Hindi is the language of the people. The spirits of millions of people speak it.' And then, thinking that this line of argument would please his father, he said with deliberate mischief (although it was not as though he didn't believe in this argument at all), 'And our caste traditions are all in Hindi—our entire past is bound to this language.'

'It may be. But when something isn't useful for a man's future, what good is there in holding on to it as a symbol of his past?'

'I can only see the future in Hindi—if we lose Hindi, then it makes no difference whether there is a future or not.'

'Of course you can see it—you have to contradict everything I say, after all. Your mother thought about you a lot. But you turned out to be so useless that you didn't even come to see her. Even if the parents are rotten, no one acts like that.'

Shekhar was silent.

'She thought about you until the very end. She had decided that when you were released from jail, she would get you married. She was even looking for brides for you.'

A memory struck Shekhar like an arrow, 'Next time, when he comes back, marry him off!' When his older brother Ishwardutt had run off, that's what his mother had decided to do . . . Suddenly he felt as though all of his efforts—mental and physical—had been reduced to one spot in a respectable fantasy of life which had been set from time immemorial as a solution for all such efforts—when he gets back, marry him off! As if all of his thoughts were a familiar disease—with a clear remedy—formula number such-and-such! Shekhar wanted to reply, 'Will each brother get the same medicine?' But instead restrainedly, he said, 'Why me? I don't want to get married. And besides, I have older brothers.'

'This has nothing to do with what you want. Marriages don't happen because the children want them to. It's a social obligation. A boy, a girl, the parents, the caste, everyone is involved. Yes, you're right that your older brothers should be married first. But Ishwar is already engaged, and Prabhu's will happen soon enough. Nothing happens anyway until there is an engagement; the engagement will happen when a suitable girl is found. And—'

Shekhar could tell that this issue was coming to a close too easily. He was emphatic, 'I don't want to get married now, so—'

'Why? Prabhu is still studying; it will take him two years to become an engineer. You've abandoned your studies. You need to live properly. You need to think about the future. Make a home, earn a living, live a stable, separate life. If you can find a wife from a respectable home, she can make do with a meagre income. After all, half of what you need for running the home will come in the dowry. And I haven't remarried, so whatever I've earned, I've spent on you all; and then whatever else there is left, I'll leave to you as inheritance. I don't need any of it after I'm gone—I will give to you as my father gave to me. If I can get you married, I'll know that I've fulfilled one of your mother's unfulfilled desires. The poor woman had no happiness in her life. We're not talking about how wives used to be in the past—wives used to do so much back then—' His father became distracted.

Shekhar said, 'Look, I don't have the slightest desire to get married. And I'm not ready to—I don't earn anything, and I don't have a degree with any promise of earning more in the future. I could get thirty or forty from being a clerk, but I would never do that. It would be wrong to pursue a relationship in such circumstances, and foolish. And then—' He stopped for a moment and then pleadingly said, 'And I've chosen a mission[10] for myself, so why would I intentionally put up roadblocks?'

'What mission? What kind of mission?'

'I don't want to earn a lot of money. I want to write, but not for money. It will be only to achieve an ideal—I am vowing to change the condition of my society, of the lives of the people around me—you have to agree that a major transformation is necessary. And if you don't, then at least you agree that the country has to be free, no?'

Partly from irritation and partly from a paternal pride, his father said, 'Look at how much you've learned!' He laughed a little. 'Let me tell you about my life—I've never told you these things, but there's no point in hiding them now. You're all grown up now.' His eyes seemed very distant now and he started talking in a deeper voice, 'When I finished my studies, a few of us took similar vows. We had studied in a traditional Hindu school, so when we left we all promised each other that we would spend all of the years between then until we turned twenty-five—I was eighteen at the time—in accordance with our vow, because one was supposed to be a *brahmacharya* [celibate] only until twenty-five. Our only possessions would be the clothes on our backs, a pitcher and a bag with a few books in it. You're talking about changing conditions; our plan was very straightforward. To kick the British out and to organize a Hindu nation and finally establish a pure Aryan tradition . . . For four years, we wandered around, propagandizing and begging for food. We went to such wild regions that you can't even dream of, let alone ever go to. And'—hesitating and laughing in embarrassment—'the poisonous things that we did against the British would make today's terrorists squirm! But in the end'— his eyebrows and shoulders gave away the end of the sentence— 'everything was in vain.'

His father looked at Shekhar. Seeing the clear look of curiosity on his face, he started, 'We stayed together for a year. Then we went our separate ways. Our duty was so clear before us that if we ever saw a random Englishman along the way, we would beat them up. I—' his nostrils flared from pride—'was pretty well built—and my face would get so red! It's not like now. I wasn't a gentleman.'

For a little while, his gaze turned inwards, as if he were digging up a repressed memory and bringing it back up . . . 'But it didn't end well. Two of my friends were picked up along with a terrorist cell and were hanged. We never learned how the third one died— we only learned later that some missionaries had become angry with him and slipped him poison. The fourth—I was the fourth. After four years of this work, I began to feel that I was doing useless work—not only because the work was exceptionally slow, but primarily because propagandizing hate can never have a good result . . . Then one day something happened which completely opened my eyes and'—and then suddenly changing the topic— 'and this was the preaching of hate. What will you do? You will also propagandize about the destruction of things that are wrong, won't you?'

'Not only that, but also about what we want—'

'Yes, yes. But the nature of the resentment will compel you to focus on destruction. I've seen that all propaganda is the propaganda of hate; because there is power in hate, there is none in love. Just like there is in poison. When wars are fought, when jihad is conducted, it is all on a foundation of hate . . . And hate really is a poison. It kills others, and it doesn't spare us, either. And if it is unable to kill others, it attacks us so fast that . . .'

He suddenly became quiet. Shekhar wanted to argue with him, and he even wanted to ask him about what had happened, but he was scared that if he asked him it might alter his father's mood. Because he had never talked about his past before. In all honesty, Shekhar had never dared to imagine that his father had been such a youth. So he stood quietly. After a while, his father spoke again, 'It will make you go mad, too.' And then he seemed lost. And then, as if to wake himself up, 'In three or four years, I lost all faith in my work. Then it seemed absolutely necessary for me to seek someone else's advice. But who was there to ask! Then someone told me that there was a holy man who lived in a cave near Tehri in the Himalayas and that I could get excellent counsel from him. We had grown up with the idea that truly holy and wise men lived in the caves of the Himalayas, so I set out for there. After wandering for several months, one day, after passing through the forests, I decided to rest on a clear hill. At the foot of the hill flowed a mountain stream; its topmost part played recklessly with the stony ground as it flowed on, but the bottom part seemed to get trapped in a grassy pit where it was turning into a mire.'

His father drew a long breath and said, 'A while later, I saw a terrible figure approach. A tall, glistening, black form, with matted locks, a lion's mane, wearing a loincloth. He would sit down wherever the ground bubbled and dig up large clumps of mud with his hands and shape them into a mound. After he had gathered up a large amount of mud, he would pat it down for some unknown reason. I was quite a way away, and in order not to startle him, I went around the other side of the mound so that I could get closer, and I stood under the cover of a tree a little below the spot where he was sitting and watched him. What I saw left me stunned.

'He had made a cannon out of mud. He would bend down to take aim and then light the cannon with a stick in his hand and then scream a word—"Bang!" Then the jungle echoed back a peal of laughter and echoed him . . .'

His father stopped to see what effect this was having on Shekhar. Then he said, 'I watched, infatuated, for a long time. Then I noticed that all around that spot were several more mud cannons whose mud had dried and broken off . . . Two hours later, I got up and left.'

Now Shekhar couldn't keep himself from asking, 'Then?'

'I asked around and found out that he was one of the rebel soldiers of 1857, who had run here to hide after the British began taking revenge barbarically. Ever since, this was his daily routine— he had been firing mud cannons for forty years!'

Shekhar remained quiet for a long time.

'That event exposed the uselessness of my endeavours to me clearly. I abandoned the search for holy men and came back and registered at another ashram. This happened thirty-five years ago. I don't think that I made a mistake.' He stopped for a minute to think. 'Hatred always ends the same way. It's the only possible end it can have. Madness.' And feeling that no objection could possibly be raised to this, he looked at Shekhar knowingly.

Dozens of objections immediately came to Shekhar's lips. He said, 'How can you say that? First of all, you don't know that he went mad from hate—or that hate was the reason for his failures. The real reason that he was in the jungle firing mud cannons was that he was afraid—he was hiding and firing cannons, which is why they were made of mud. The rebellion was powerless—and powerlessness is self-reproducing—so the rebellion was a failure. If he hadn't hidden, if he had fought and died, then would hatred still be seen as failure? Let's say that the reason he went crazy was because of the rebellion. But how can you say that his life was less meaningful? Everyone is crazy. But his madness had an extraordinary intensity—isn't that really all that we've established?'

His father was annoyed, 'Forget about going mad, you are already crazy.'

His father said, 'Security is very important.'

Shekhar couldn't think of what to say in response.

'You won't understand its significance now. Security[11] is very important in life. Even if you get a little money from writing, you won't be able to depend on it. Income turns into wealth when it comes regularly and altogether, even if it's not substantial. That's why I'm telling you, set up a home, earn a living, live comfortably. A man only knows where he is standing when his life has some solidity.'

Again, Shekhar was quiet. His father said, 'Why aren't you saying anything?'

'I don't understand what I should say.'

'What is there to understand? Is there anyone who doesn't want to be secure in life? Why else would we have established institutions like insurance, provident funds and pensions?[12] These days, people ask about whether there is a provident fund or a pension before taking a job. What do you think? Am I right or not?'

'It's right. But I don't want to be secure. You're talking about starting a home, earning an income and being secure. To me, these things sound like life's illnesses—I'm trying to avoid these things. A comfortable life, a feeling of safety, the absence of day-to-day challenges—these are all termites that devour a life's force. I want the opposite of these things. I want a world of endless instability and challenges so that I am always compelled to fight—to be able to tear it down with my own hands and destroy it and build it anew with my own hands.'

'You will keep arguing for the sake of pointless argument. If you truly live like this for two days, you'll have a nervous breakdown![13] One walks a challenging road when it comes along, but who asks for one? You like to make a show of your learning—isn't it the course of the development of civilization that man ceaselessly advances towards a state of increasing prosperity?'

'Civilization! This civilization is a fraud. What security, safety and prosperity all really amount to is the prolongation of man's childhood. The more civilized someone is, the longer is his childhood. Civilization is another word for dependency. An animal's childhood lasts a year, two years at the most. It probably lasts ten or twelve years with savages in the jungles. We've become so civilized that children remain children for thirty years or so, and they don't stand on their own feet. Some people die before they escape childhood.'

'What do you mean?'

'I'm twenty-one years old now. And today, you don't think that I am ready to get my own place and live in a safe city like

Lahore. It seems to me that you are saying that everything that you have taught me for the last twenty years or so is rubbish because it hasn't prepared me for this. I think that we have become more civilized than necessary. And who knows what goes on in our joint families! Isn't this the way that people are forced into dependency, their true personalities and internal strength laid to rest? Is the meaning of civilization supposed to be turning a deaf ear to the provocation of life, to grind out the strength to stand up and take it on? Tell me this, if the first Aryans were simply seeking comfort, would their culture have spread as far as Java, Cambay and China? Would they even be Aryans—they were only called Aryans when they went to new countries and settled there.'

Irritatedly but in admiration, his father looked at Shekhar, 'Are these things you've read somewhere or are they your own ideas?'

Shekhar suddenly thought of Baba Madansingh. 'You have to search your pain for your own aphorisms' . . . His thoughts perhaps bore the imprint of Baba Madansingh's ideas, but was it so deep that Shekhar was merely repeating these things like a parrot? Did the corresponding feelings to everything that he had said not course through his veins?

He became dejected and fell silent . . .

His father butted heads with Shekhar for a few more days. In between, he walked through town and met his friends a few times, and a few of them even came there to visit. Three days later, Rameshwar came with Shashi for a visit—they had just come back to Lahore that day. When his father's heart melted from all of the words of sympathy and he began to think about Shekhar's mother, Shekhar quietly got up and left the room. He knew that in his absence Shashi would be able to offer him comforting words more naturally, something that he was completely incapable of doing—he didn't know if he could console anyone else or not, but he got tongue-tied when he tried to do it with his father.

That night, Shekhar woke suddenly with a start. He hadn't been dreaming. He didn't understand why he had woken up so fearfully. His fear and unbearable restlessness were extremely discernible. He turned to look at his father and was startled again—he was awake, too, and sitting up. Suddenly a strange sound emerged from his father's constricted throat which was neither a moan nor a shriek—and Shekhar realized that it was this sound which had woken him up in confusion . . . He trembled slightly. Perhaps his father had figured out that he was awake, so he got up quickly, put on his shoes and went outside into the courtyard.

Shekhar had never seen his father cry—and crying so desperately . . . He felt a deep pain somewhere inside, and a wordless sympathy overtook him. He didn't know that his father could feel so much pain; nor had he imagined that no matter who, when or where, everyone pays the price for the daily toughness and meanness in private—that a father who was a tough disciplinarian with his children could also display a natural, human tenderness sometimes . . .

Outside in the courtyard he heard the hesitating sounds of someone sobbing and then the sound of someone clearing his nose . . . Then the sound of slippers told him that his father had come back inside; he quickly covered his face and lay down. He tried to breathe more regularly to hide the rapidity of his heartbeat . . .

A little while later, his father came and sat on the cot, drew a long but broken sigh and gently lay down.

Shekhar stayed up for a long time wondering if his father had gone to sleep or not. Eventually he fell asleep himself.

The next day, his father had to head back. After washing up in the morning and getting his things together, at teatime, he drily asked, 'So what have you decided to do?'

Because the memory of last night was still fresh in his mind, Shekhar didn't want to let anything slip that might upset his father. He made his voice appropriately submissive, 'Just what I've already told you. I've already sent a book off to be printed.' This entire time, Shekhar still hadn't gone to deliver his manuscript.

'Really? What is the book about?'

'It's titled "Our Society". In it—'

'So you're bent on raising cudgels against society. Do whatever you want, son. It's not as though you are going to listen to reason.' And then he relaxed a little, 'I didn't listen either. There's something about the blood of youth. No one listens until they've actually been pushed around.'

Shekhar thought to himself—'That's how it should be.' But he didn't say anything out loud.

Just then, Shashi showed up. His father looked at her and said—'Why don't you make him understand? I've heard that he really listens to you.'

Shekhar asked, 'Who told you that?'

'Someone or another. Why? Did I get it wrong?'

Shashi said—'He's never listened to me—he just scolds me all the time.'

'Who is he to be scolding you? Why do you pay that any attention?'

Shekhar was close to laughing at Shashi's false accusation. He got up and went to the closet on the pretence of getting something and went past it and into the courtyard; he paced back and forth there for a long time. He was a little dismayed that no one had come looking for him. It was a mystery how Shashi talked to his father without any hesitation—and he, too, spoke to her adoringly without any trace of authority. The two of them could have an uninterrupted, natural conversation, but Shekhar and his father would start arguing in the middle, or there would be long, tense silences.

Suddenly Shekhar remembered that he still had his father's money and hadn't returned the change. He went back inside just as his father was calling him, 'Shekhar!'

Shekhar took the notes and coins from his pocket, held them out for his father and said, 'This is the rest of it; I've written down the expenses on a piece of paper.'

In a mild reproach, his father said, 'All right, all right, just keep it. Big shot here trying to settle accounts with me!'

Shekhar was in a momentary dilemma. Then noticing that Shashi was giving him a sign to drop the subject immediately, he put the money back in his pocket.

The tonga arrived later. Shashi bowed respectfully and said goodbye. Shekhar went with his father to the railway station.

*

After delivering the handwritten manuscript of 'Our Society', Shekhar felt as if he had climbed one rung higher on the ladder to the goal he had set for himself. It gave him great satisfaction and he began trying to work more religiously. This time, he had decided to conduct a comparative study of the rights of men and women from various communities throughout the world. The thesis that he was developing was that very few of the beams which governed the relationships between men and women and the powers that they exercised over each other were built on foundations of logic, or rather, that the traditions which lay behind them were basically economic arrangements, economic arrangements that lacked notes of currency and so traded in lives instead. Moreover, he also wanted to establish that the prevailing argument amongst reformers—that the traditions of some past society were right because they were appropriate for the conditions of that time, but are no longer appropriate for today's conditions—was fallacious, because many of the aspects of those beliefs were hardly necessary in any condition of the past or present—or more precisely, the logical consequences of those conventions bore no relation to the conditions of the past. Their real source was a complete blind faith or the irrational practices of magic and superstition. Many of these outmoded superstitious practices continue today, and we constantly try to create logical justifications for them. These attempts are like trying to fix new brass bottoms on to newly discovered ancient clay pots—and we perform such ridiculous endeavours daily.

Shekhar wanted to say that this was also the reason that the reformers were unsuccessful. They affirmed human arrogance by

trying to justify these traditions of past societies—and they say
with even more enthusiasm, 'Dear Sir, all of these old customs
were established by the sages—and you know that they were all
historically specific!' And from there, they easily move one step
higher when they realize that many of our contemporary practices
are not logical. Then they say, 'Sir, they were sages. The things that
they established were not only specific to the past, but are right for
all time, because they were omniscient—if they could prescribe
logical rules for their own time, couldn't they also make rules for
the future?' And then that was that, no reformist argument stood
a chance against that line of thought—it was the impenetrable
armour of tradition.

Shekhar wanted his book to be proof of clear principles, and the
arguments that he would develop would be based on a mountain
of evidence from history, psychology, biology and especially
anthropology as that would make each argument unassailable. He
knew that his previous studies were not sufficient for this. He had
been majoring in science in college. Even then he had read several
books on various subjects, and the ten months in jail had allowed
him to read much which had piqued his interest in sociology
and anthropology; but he knew well that human knowledge was
advancing at an incredibly rapid pace and it was difficult to keep up
with it, especially for a man who had no guidance from an expert
in the field. He wanted to become a member of the best public
library in the city so that he could get hold of the necessary reading
materials. After he had used the money his father had given him
to pay off the restaurant bill, he still had twelve rupees or so left,
but the annual subscription to the library cost eight rupees, and
the books on the subjects that he wanted required an additional
deposit of twenty rupees . . .

One day while he was sitting, he realized that while he had
definitely lost many of his books he still had many of them. What
was the point in displaying the books he had already read like some
millionaire? They were very important to him, he even considered
them to be a greater part of himself or more precisely his social
persona, but why should knowledge be any less important? And

how could knowledge be acquired without effort?—Knowledge was not an after-dinner mint that one could eat for free!

Shekhar went to his cabinet and began perusing his books. After he had looked at them all once or twice, he took out two or three of the most expensive ones; then he scanned his books again and put two back and took another one out; then he put them all back and started pacing . . . Then he removed one large book of a two-volume set—Wells's *A Short History of the World*.[14] He quickly flipped through its pages and thought to himself, 'This is a reference book and I rarely need to make use of it—I've read it twice, too.' He put it to the side. He walked back and forth twice and then took out an even bigger book—*The Collected Paintings of Chughtai* . . . He looked at a few of the images and, as if speaking aloud to the book, thought to himself, 'When I don't have the other volumes, what good will a single one do? And it's not as though Chughtai is the world's greatest painter—and then, a man should only have paintings when he has a proper place to put them. There could be moths here at any time.' And he reminded himself that bugs had devoured his first creation and that a cow had eaten his second . . . But his mind was racing like a thief; he was completely indecisive . . .

Shekhar opened all three volumes once more. He had won these books as prizes in college, and the associated certificates had been affixed inside the covers. He looked at the certificates for a moment, then all of a sudden, with a steady hand, grabbed them at their corners and ripped them out. He wrapped the books in old newspapers and set out.

The books were worth approximately forty-eight rupees, but he couldn't get anyone to offer more than eighteen in the bazaar. He asked around and then sold Wells's history at a second-hand bookseller's for fifteen and a half—this was a fair price for it. No one was willing to give more than four rupees for the second book, because, as Shekhar learned, despite being worth seventeen rupees, new copies of the book were being sold at a 50 per cent discount in the market for eight and a half. So Shekhar took it to a college student whom he knew who was also interested in

painting. Somehow, Shekhar stuck him with the book and got
eight rupees for it—although he could clearly tell that the buyer
was putting as much pressure on him as he was . . .

After he joined the library, on his first trip he checked out
Frazer's *The Golden Bough*, Crawley's *The Mystic Rose* . . . and
got a commentary on the *Manusmriti* and a clear, critical edition.
The feeling of depression lifted from his brain, and he became
completely absorbed in reading these books whose pages he read
over and over as his enthusiasm grew. He set aside his reading and
put his books in the cabinet and felt as if they were not strangers
to him; they had become encircled by his soul . . .

One day while Shekhar was writing, he was shocked to
discover that someone was standing at his door waiting for him to
lift his head and give him permission to enter. Shekhar stammered,
'Come in—come in—' and gathered up the pieces of paper that
were scattered everywhere and cleared a place on the cot.

The newcomer forced a smile. 'My name is Amolak Roy and I
am the president of the local Hindu Reform Society.'

Shekhar said, 'What can I do for you?'

'I've heard that you want to make social reform work your
life's mission. You are also very educated—I can see that clearly
for myself. Truth be told, the first demand of social reform is
devotion. I—'

Shekhar was a little taken aback, 'Where did you hear all this?'

'You can't hide brilliance . . . No matter how modest you are—'

This couldn't be—there had to be something amiss. Drily,
Shekhar said, 'To what do I owe this visit?'

'I came just to admire you. Very few people take a real interest
in social service work—and you know how young people are these
days—they aren't interested in anything—they are allergic to the
word "service".—I have great hopes for you—'

'Tell me, what can I do?—'

'There is much that you can do. You have drive, dedication
and the strength of the young. You should come to one of our
meetings and see for yourself. Once you see our projects you will
see for yourself how helpful you can be.'

Shekhar's interest was piqued, 'I will definitely come. But could you give me a general idea?—'

'Yes, yes. There are many things that we want to reform, but we have decided to focus on the family as we feel that the family is the foundation of society, and society can be reformed only when family life is reformed.'

'Very good—'

'And the foundation of the family is marriage, so we want to reform marriage practices first.'

'This is very important work. What is your programme?'

'If it was just one thing, I would have told you, right? But such matters require a multifaceted approach. We require the cooperation of young men and young women and their parents; journalism is also important; then there is keeping political and religious leaders happy—'

'Why?'

'Because what's the point of creating unnecessary antagonism? It's best to get your job done with as little opposition as possible, don't you think?' Lala Amolak Roy laughed a little.

'I suppose. All right, I will definitely come to your meeting. When is it?'

'Don't just come, you will also have to speak—'

Squeamishly, Shekhar said, 'But I'm not good at public speaking at all. I can be more useful in conversation—'

'Well, how about that? How can you run away from society and still hope to do social reform work? It's not going to be a very large meeting—there will only be a few men who are interested in the work. You could say that it will be a meeting of our core members—all of our real work happens outside the meetings; the meetings are for an exchange of ideas—'

Ultimately, they agreed that Shekhar would come to the meeting and would say something and take part in the intellectual exchange. Lala Amolak Roy left.

Even though Shekhar had been very calm when he told Shashi about the invitation, and had very calmly also accepted her approval, on the inside his disquiet grew rapidly—on the one

hand he had the excited feeling of new responsibility and finding
a direction for his efforts, and on the other hand there was the
fear and anxiety of participating in his first ideological debate—
In college and particularly in the 'Antigonon Club', he would
defend his positions with substantial flair, but that was completely
different—there, he knew everyone or they were friends, and he
was just one of the many leaders of the club; here he would be
an outsider and bound by the formalities of being invited, and
amongst the experienced social reformers he would be a neophyte
'amateur'[15] . . .

He immediately began preparing very diligently—and in the
process of writing 'points' for his speech he managed to finish
an entire article . . . He made full use of the things that he was
currently reading and the examples they used—while discussing
the reform of familial tradition, he examined the origins of the
family and its development—He determined that there was no
connection between that development and economics and that it
was foolish to search for the economic bases of ancient familial
structures. But gradually these traditions escaped the realm of
magic and superstition and began to be influenced by economic
conditions, and now they underwent substantial changes side by
side with economic development. By quoting from the *Manusmriti*
he proved that at the time of the composition of the smritis,[16]
ideas about the family were connected to contemporary economic
theories—so not only the traditional logic of the *Manusmriti*, but
also its style and its examples were dependent on the particular
conditions of an agrarian civilization. That was why whenever the
rights of woman were laid out they were established by making
use of examples comparing her to cows, horses, camels, slaves
and buffaloes—man was considered the 'breadwinner', and all of
these and women were considered commodities to be bought and
sold—and in the manner of agriculturists, all of their offspring
were considered the property of the 'breadwinner', and all of their
wealth, the wealth of the master. And even to determine paternity,
the allegory of master, land and produce became customary
practice. But saying all of this wasn't meant to show contempt for

the smritis—as long as the rules of society developed alongside the current form of civilization, society was fine; the rot inside it did not grow.

But (as Shekhar was arguing) in more recent ages this correlation was destroyed—the condition of our lives began to change with great speed but society stopped developing. Undeniably, one of the reasons for this was that foreign rule had established new and harsh laws—to maintain order in society, they collected together social customs from different places, created an aggregate from them, and made everyone bow down to it as law—all the while forgetting that customs have always undergone change and continue to change. The conditions in which those customs were accumulated became even more impermanent, indeterminate and fluid! When ice suddenly forms on a flowing stream—how would a new seed sprout and grow under that icy sheet? But this external cause was only one of the causes— the other cause that was incredibly important for our purposes was the weakness and paralysis in our society—that dynamism which is life's crucial religion . . . After these ordinary ideological arguments, he evaluated the main parts of family life and offered necessary reforms so that equality could be established to the condition of life in other civilizations.

With each day the meeting drew closer, Shekhar grew more excited—he wasn't as anxious after finishing 'Our Society' as he was for this meeting . . .

A smoky, slate-blue evening—the smoke from a city's December crept in through an open window of a lonely corner room of a four-storeyed building, cold, heavy, with a sting like poison, slick like dead and discoloured snakeskin. Piercing through the shroud of smoke, an unwelcome commotion rose like a ghost from the invisible city that spread out below and around, but its silent heaviness seemed to magnify the room's stony silence. Shekhar is huddled in the corner of his bed and forcing his eyes open, blind from the smoke and even drier from the burning, he hazily feels that the picture outside is an excellent imitation of his internal state of being . . .

Shekhar has been back from that meeting for an hour already. He wants to convince himself that he has forgotten all about that meeting, but in the same way that the paralysis induced by the poisons unleashed by a stroke is the first indication that they have spread, Shekhar's numbness repeated the sensations from that meeting . . .

When he saw that there were more than a hundred people at the meeting, Shekhar was shocked and thought, 'Were there really this many social reform activists in the city?' A new-found hope coursed through him, and his growing curiosity about organizational matters made him forget his anxiety about his speech. The meeting started haphazardly—Shekhar listened attentively, but gradually his attention drifted and after a little while he was completely turned off. He completely ignored the speaker and began studying the expressions of each individual member of the audience. Several were listening attentively—or rather they were so entranced that they moved their hands and nodded, changed the shape of their lips and brows not only as proof of their agreement but also as if they were translating the speaker's incorporeal thoughts into physical actions. Shekhar suddenly couldn't believe his eyes—because he was completely incapable of focusing on anything and was getting irritated with the speaker. He had a hazy sense that the speech had taken the form of a resolution—the sense of the resolution was that the increasing lack of Brahmin grooms was creating a grave crisis for unmarried daughters, so to help them and to relieve their parents the reform society would create a committee called Committee for the Arrangement of Marriages of Brahmin Bachelors, whose most important task would be to create and publish a complete registry of all eligible Brahmin bachelors, which would enable any father in need to locate a suitable husband for his daughter. It would have all the relevant information—age, income, lineage, character, father's income, rank, height, physical attributes, hobbies, what kind of wife he's looking for, future plans, et cetera . . .

How convenient would things be with such a list, how much frenzy, trouble and waste could be avoided! The resolution was also put forward, and it was passed without any discussion . . . Shekhar breathed a long sigh of relief and waited for the next speaker whom Lala Amolak Roy had stepped up to introduce. He was shocked to realize that the person who was being described with such words of praise was Shekhar himself! He became even more depressed; but he somehow gathered up his courage (at that moment, gathering his courage meant dispelling the feelings that the meeting had stamped on him!) and went forward and began speaking according to his previous plan. Immediately after he started, he heard a few men whispering and then someone saying to Lala Amolak Roy, 'The young man seems like a good catch, Lalaji. Congratulations!' and he became confident and anxious, but like a newcomer virtuously steeling himself against all temptations, Shekhar similarly remained glued to his script . . .

But the willed blindness of ascetic meditation eventually dissipates—not from seeing the celestial nymphs Urvashi and Tilotamma sent by the gods, but by seeing the yawning, gaping mouths and the furrowing, angry brows multiplying from boredom! Eventually, Shekhar came to a point when he could no longer ignore the collective disapproval of the audience—not even by doubling the pace of his speech . . . His mind, then, began working on several fronts at the same time, and his memory, too, lost control over the order of things and he began confusing facts and events with one another . . .

After the meeting was over, Shekhar was lost, sitting in his room, unable to untangle the threads of this dilemma—he couldn't decide what had happened first, what happened next. All at once he hears himself quoting from the *Manusmriti* and then someone speaks (or some people speak?), 'If the groom agrees and the bride's father agrees, then, man, why should we meddle? Get married or don't get married, but why are you insulting us? Panditji, you can keep your ideas to yourself—he's insulting the *Manusmriti*! The less foreign education one has the better! After all, if Christians are doing the teaching, how will anyone retain respect for Hinduism—they didn't come to preach Hinduism, after all. This can't be what Lalaji had in mind! A Kshatriya youth will marry a Brahmin girl, a Brahmin boy will insult the *Manusmriti*! It was a fine gambit, Lalaji, but Brahmin daughters still have good futures.' Shekhar was citing examples from Malinowski but he heard Amolak Roy's name; or was he citing examples from Amolak Roy and hearing talk of Malinowski's daughter; or both or neither—he couldn't make sense of any of it. He had a vague inkling that he had lost himself in that meeting, but actually he was standing on the stage and speaking, or was it that the stage was missing and he was in the audience, or were both the audience and the stage missing—and then suddenly a flaming arrow pierces the armour of his consciousness and he understands everything— Amolak Roy's daughter was of marriageable age, and they are Kshatriyas, but they'd be all too pleased to find a Brahmin son-in-law; and what could be better than a social reformer father-in-law finding a social reformer son-in-law—the union of the like, the improvement of reform! And he's standing in front of this audience that knows everything to announce, 'Look, I, Shekhar, am being made a fool and the proof can be found by citing the *Manusmriti*, by citing Malinowski . . .'

The smoke is good, the sting of poison is good, the dead, discoloured, cold slickness of snakeskin is good, let it all into this fourth-floor grave—social reformer Shekhar!

In that devastated state, Shekhar was prepared for anything like a slave, but he wasn't prepared for what happened next— someone knocked on the door and entered without waiting for a response—stumbling to his feet, Shekhar saw a stranger standing with someone—Lala Amolak Roy!

Natural courtesy demanded that he light a candle, but Shekhar felt that courtesy would be an injustice to himself. He said, 'What can I do for you?'

Lala Amolak Roy was a little wounded when he responded, 'You seem very upset.'

'I'm not upset—'

'You seem exhausted—give the candles to me, I'll light them—'

Shekhar quickly lit the candle and put it to one side and said, 'Sit.'

Lala said, 'This is Swami Hariharanand. We have come to talk to you about the meeting—'

Shekhar saw that the newcomer was wearing saffron robes, and because his shiny head was turned, his oily hair seemed to balloon. He made an incomplete gesture of greeting and asked, 'What is there to talk about the meeting? The meeting has happened—'

The swami said, 'An action is never complete in itself—it has effects. The furore that the meeting has caused—' and then he stopped as if it were necessary to chew this morsel of information.

Lala said, 'Your speech created a commotion. I had invited you with great hopes that—'

Shekhar was steaming, 'Hopes? You made a fine fool of me. If that's what you had planned, then—'

'What plan—which plan—I took you there with the best intentions. People will blather—'

The swami said, 'Yes, son, it's their habit. They were burning with envy.'

Drily, Shekhar said, 'Fine, let it go. It's all over now—'

'Let's talk about something other than the meeting. So now that you know who I am, we should develop this relationship—'

'That's up to you. I'm a savage, I'm accustomed to living alone—knowing me doesn't help you in any way—'

'Every individual is obligated to live in society; moreover, how can anyone survive without society?—'

'It's living in society that I find impossible—just as impossible as living in a vacuum-sealed tin. It's easy to live alone—have lived and will keep on living!'

'I knew that you were an abnormal individual. But that you were also an abnormal man—'

The swami interrupted, 'Why abnormal? It won't work to cry "abnormal" all the time. I tell you, all men are normal and should be normal.'

Shekhar said, 'I never claimed to be abnormal. I am normal and want to remain normal. You are the ones heaping accusations of abnormality on me and making my life difficult—'

The swami repeated, 'Everyone is normal. Does the fact that someone does not possess something special mean that they cannot survive? You have a long nose. Does that mean you don't go to the bathroom? Even if a man loses his nose, he can still live; he can't live without going to the bathroom. That's why everyone is normal.'

Shekhar couldn't tolerate this man, his arguments, his way of repeating things. In order to end the conversation he said, 'What you say is right.'

'That's why I say society is necessary. If you enter society, your nose will still be long.' (Shekhar wanted to tell the swami that he should revise his phrase, 'Even if you go to the bathroom, you still won't have a nose,' but he kept quiet.) 'Don't you agree?'

Shekhar didn't say anything. He wanted the conversation to end by any means necessary and them to go.

'You aren't answering my question. You are probably thinking, let him blather on. Everyone is afflicted by the same youthful pride. I had it too—and you can see the consequences—'

This time Shekhar looked with some interest at Hariharanand.

'I'm an ascetic, wearing saffron robes. You know what it means to be an ascetic. But I'm not an ascetic because I've renounced everything, but because everything has been taken from me. And all because of my pride. Pride was my vow, but that was broken, too. I go around preaching, but these saffron robes are not a banner; they are a shroud. The colour of dirt—the dirt that covers everything. Everyone is normal—'

The clarity of the swami's confession touched Shekhar. A little more gently, he said, 'I wasn't quiet out of pride; I was quiet because I had nothing to say. I know how poor I am. But the argument that because I am poor I should cut off my own leg doesn't make any sense to me.'

'Lalaji is a supporter of yours. The things he is saying are right. You shouldn't become a fame monster. Everyone is normal, which is why marriage is appropriate.'

'When have I ever said that it wasn't appropriate? But I don't want to yet, and I won't because someone tells me to. It's not even that I don't want to, even if I wanted to I wouldn't be ready.'

'Why?' Lala asked hopefully.

'There are fifty reasons. But never mind them—'

'Tell us something, at least—'

'No, leave it be. To speak of marriage now is to court disaster.'

Suddenly Hariharanand became excited and said, 'Fine, it's courting disaster. Do you have it in you—to step up and face disaster head-on?'

Shekhar took one careful look at Hariharanand and said, 'Forgive me but I'm tired. This debate will never end, and I've already told you all I have to say.'

Shekhar saw Lalaji's seat shift and breathed a sigh of relief . . .

*

When he saw Shashi next, he told her everything about the meeting and about the conversation with Amolak Roy and Hariharanand after the meeting. At first Shashi listened quietly, but then she burst out laughing. Then she became somewhat serious and said, 'Were you very upset?'

Shekhar stammered out, 'I was pretty unnerved when it happened. Now I wonder why I couldn't laugh the way you just did—'

Shashi started laughing again.

Then she asked, 'Are they coming back?'

'There is a chance, but I've put them completely out of my mind.'

'Completely? Well, can I ask you one thing, Shekhar? Did you find anything of use in what they said?'

'Of use? Not one bit—in what they said—'

'The one about "Step up and face disaster head-on"—'

Shekhar looked at Shashi stonily for a moment. Then he said, 'Some of their arguments were well-suited for someone like me, but—' suddenly choking a little—'Shashi, what are you trying to say?'

Shashi remained silent. Shekhar spoke again, 'Are you also worried about the future of this Brahmin bachelor?'

'Yes, honestly, I am a little. Why won't you get married—'
'Shashi!'

There was complete silence for a while. Then Shashi started speaking, 'Your father told me that I should convince you. Convincing you isn't that difficult. But it doesn't seem to me that a man can be useful very long when he has isolated himself off from the world the way that you have. You will lose your grip on reality—'

'My grip on reality—or its grip on me?'

'Aren't they the same thing? Or if you prefer, the connection between you and reality will break down—'

Shekhar gathered up all of his courage to say, 'Look, Shashi, we've never talked about these kinds of things before, but tell me the truth, have you got anything out of your marriage?' Then seeing a slight trace of pain on Shashi's face—'I don't want to hurt you, but—'

Drained, Shashi said, 'No, I understand. But you can't use me as an example—my marriage had a completely different basis. I didn't get married; I was married off. It was never a question of my getting anything out of the marriage; getting something—' She didn't finish the sentence.

A little later, Shekhar said, 'But why is my situation any different? For me, too, it's also a—Or, if the only thing one gets is pain, then—'

'No, that's not what I'm saying. You need to find a companion who can walk with you as an equal; who can bear pain with you and enjoy happiness with you, too. Pain and sorrow are not the important things; the important thing is the companionship—the ability to enter into and sustain a relationship.'

'What proof is there that all that will happen if I get married? And especially as a Brahmin bachelor—'

'I know that there is no proof. And I'm also not saying that you should get married like that. All I am saying is that if you find a suitable companion—'

To end the discussion, Shekhar said, 'Let's talk about something else—if such a person is found, then we'll see. It's clear that searching for such a person won't reveal him—her. If I find her along the way, then I find her; and then I'll get down on one knee, all right?'

He suddenly realized that Shashi was not only not paying attention to what he was saying but that her wide eyes had grown even wider looking at some scene on a distant road—as if her soul had expectantly opened its door to welcome the significance of that distant scene . . . Shekhar was similarly wandering and a little curious when he said, 'And if while walking now I come across a pearl I won't ask any questions, won't have any misgivings, won't make any demands. If the gods give—'

Shashi didn't hear a word. Shekhar was intentionally trying to shock her when he said, 'If the gods give, then why do the sacred texts need to be asked to bear witness?'

Shashi was startled into attention, 'What?'

Their eyes met and were glued to each other. Shekhar forced himself to wish his eyes to move, but he kept on looking at the light behind those open windows, and the pain inside that light, and the resounding echoes linked together inside that pain—'asked to bear witness . . . asked to bear witness . . .'

*

An odd calm had descended over him, and he began reading and writing intently. The completion of the article for the Reform Society, two new essays, two stories—when he paused to take a breath after finishing all of this, two weeks had passed since the incident at the Society; and ten days since he had seen Shashi—and in those ten days, Shekhar had seen no one other than the boy from the restaurant; except for one day when the two children of the woman from the third floor came to him with some inexplicable, easy, childlike faith and asked, 'Do you know how to make kites?' When Shekhar said yes, they said, 'When we get some money, we'll go buy the paper—you'll have to make us a kite, for sure!' Shekhar laughed and gave his word. He also calculated how much money they would be getting, how much the string and the winder would cost and how much to glue the powdered glass to the string—in sum, if they didn't buy the paper and make the kites themselves, they would only have enough for one kite and what good would one kite be for the kite festival (Vasant Panchami).

The kite festival . . . What if Shekhar bought all of the materials for the children himself and saved them their time and effort? The kite festival . . . But he didn't have the money. And there was still the restaurant bill and household expenses . . .

Shekhar decided that he would send everything he had written off to magazines and ask each of them for an advance—someone would offer him something . . . But all of his pieces were returned. There were letters of recommendation along with each of them. At first, Shekhar didn't understand this contradiction, but eventually he gleaned from a vague line in a letter from an editor that it wasn't the case that things that were good when free were also entitled to payment . . . He decided to try again, but he didn't have the resources to gamble on postage; once he even thought about cutting out the address on a used envelope and sending it, but it didn't seem wise to acknowledge on the cover of the new letter that his work had already been rejected somewhere else . . . Ultimately, he decided to take his stories himself and knock on the doors of local editors.

It was a repetition of the drama that happened with 'Our Society', this time with other explanations, and less consequential . . . Only one editor of a weekly asked him for a story or a poem about the kite festival because a special edition of the magazine was going to be published. Shekhar recalled his previous decision never to produce commissioned literature, but then he thought that there was no obligation to call something that was commissioned 'literature' and that in order to keep literature out of the vulgar market it was necessary to have another means to earn a living . . . He agreed to write the story and received the following as an assurance of payment: 'It will be settled after it has been written, and whatever is offered, a leaf, a flower—'[17]

But producing something under those conditions wasn't easy. Even after battling himself for hours, Shekhar was unable to produce a story about the kite festival, and repeatedly, his beaten and frustrated mind returned to the children from the third floor and their demand for a kite . . . Spring festival . . . Kite festival . . . He imagines bringing home a kite, string, winder, crushed glass and glue, and the children are jumping and squealing with delight on the roof; and he is teaching them how to fly a kite—it isn't that he knows, but with those children, he's an 'expert' . . . And then the string breaks on the kite in his dream, and he spins a lonely winder back in reality and thinks, 'Kite festival, story, and the restaurant bill' . . . All of a sudden he realizes, 'Why not turn that into a story?' The idea seemed ludicrous to him, and a little bit like a betrayal of the children, but such things were daily published in Hindi and what was the harm as long as he didn't pretend that it was literature? It was commissioned work; what was wrong with earning his bread by the sweat of his brow like a labourer, detachedly . . . This argument didn't convince him, but he still wrote the story—he called it 'The Kite Festival'.

The editor looked once at the title and then once at Shekhar and said, 'You are a very enthusiastic young man.'

Nervously, Shekhar said, 'Yes, sir.'

The editor put his work to the side, then he looked at Shekhar as if he were done using something and his sense of order couldn't tolerate it lying around in the middle of things.

In an intentionally abrupt tone, Shekhar said, 'And my payment?'

Displaying enormous surprise, the editor said, 'Payment? Oh—yes. But we offer payment at the end of every quarter—and we haven't even determined how much—'

Suppressing his rage, Shekhar said, 'So why don't you determine now?'

Calmly and smoothly, the editor said, 'Literature requires a great deal of devotion—'

Suddenly Shekhar felt that politeness was pointless, or rather wouldn't bear fruit; and for a labourer, the fruits of one's labour were all that mattered. He said, 'If it is literature then it would require it. But even if you are going to make the mistake of thinking this to be literary, I won't. When I write literature, I will also be patiently devoted. But now, I am selling myself. I want its worth in cash.'

The editor looked him over this time with care and a new bewilderment and said, 'Look, I've explained our policies to you already. You wrote this story at my request, so it's clear that I should pay you.' Then turning out his pockets, 'But you already know the state of things here . . . I can only pay you in leaves and fruits . . .'[18]

Dejectedly, Shekhar said, 'Thank you!' and went back home . . .

On his next trip, when Shekhar went back out in the direction of New Age Books, he thought he would ask about how 'Our Society' was doing. The managing editor was there himself. Upon seeing Shekhar, he said, 'It's good that you've come—I was thinking of sending someone to see you—'

'Why? Was there anything important—'

'No, just because—' He looked long with half-closed eyes at Shekhar, and then said, 'The thing is that—in truth—I've shown your book to a couple of experts and they recommend—There are some necessary revisions—'

Meekly, Shekhar said, 'It's possible. I am only a student, not an expert. What are the revisions that they've recommended?—'

'Look, I can't recall all of them, but basically, they didn't like the concluding chapter, and recommended that it should be changed—'

'But that's a fundamental alteration. An alteration like that would mean the writer—'

'I think that if you make all the revisions and get his permission to use his name it will be for the best. If the book is printed with his editorial signature on it, it will definitely sell, and—'

'Who is this gentleman?'

Not answering the question, the editor started again, 'It won't take you long to revise the conclusion—'

'But the conclusion grows out of the facts, and how could I change those? The conclusion—'

'A conclusion is a matter of one's opinions. A single fact can produce five different conclusions, it's all a matter of perspective. And when the conclusion is revised, then the facts—'

Insistently, Shekhar said, 'Do conclusions come from facts or do facts come from conclusions? You can't unsee a fact once it's been presented—'

'But what is a fact? Everything that exists is a fact. And things that don't exist are also facts—their non-existence is a fact. A man chooses facts according to his preferences; then he draws conclusions from those facts, ergo, conclusions are also predicated on preferences, right?'

'Fine, let's say that's true. Then the book I've written is based on choosing facts and conclusions that are to my tastes. So why does it need revising? Still, I think that facts are facts, and the conclusion that I have drawn from them is the necessary one.'

More firmly, the editor said, 'You are being stubborn. Everyone has their own tastes, but tastes can also be evaluated. The criticism of society is a matter of great responsibility—I always take the advice of the experts. It's a good opportunity for you—if there is a famous editor associated with the book, then it will sell and open doors for you in the future—you should be grateful that he's taken the pains and made these edits—'

Shekhar choked on his words, 'Made these edits? But shouldn't you have asked me first? At least tell me who this expert is!'

'He's a very experienced intellectual and he's deeply committed to social service—'

'At least tell me his name.'

'Lala Amolak Roy.'

Haltingly and emphasizing each word, Shekhar said, 'My book will be published as is—I will be responsible for my own argument and opinions.'

'But opposing the advice of experts—You must understand that this is a matter of a publisher's responsibility—I am working in your interests—'

Shekhar asked, 'Do you mean to say that you won't print the book without the revisions?'

'Look—My hands are tied—There is no need to get overly emotional—'

'Then please give me back my manuscript—'

'Please think it over—'

Firmly, Shekhar said, 'Please give me back my manuscript immediately—'

'Why won't you listen to reason? I am very disappointed—'

Shekhar repeated, 'If you will please give me back my manuscript, I can leave—'

The editor called out, 'Orderly!' A lifeless statue came and stood before them.

'Go to Lala Amolak Roy's place and bring back the papers—tell him to give you the pages of "Our Society"—You'll remember the name, right—"Our Society"?'

'Yes, sir. "Our Society".'

'Yes.'

Shekhar asked, 'How long will it take?'

'It will be here in an hour to an hour and a half—'

Shekhar didn't want to stay there. He said, 'All right, I will be back in two hours.' And he got up and left.

Shekhar didn't want to go back home while his brain was in revolt, and he had no business out in the street, so Shekhar began aimlessly wandering through the streets and alleys. He only stopped once in front of a shop when he saw a potter's wheel hanging out front. He stopped for a little while to study the potter's wheel and the shapes of a few pots and a heap of kites barely visible in the darkness inside the shop, and then he walked on. When he saw a fruit stall farther along, he recalled that he had read a book about nutrition while in jail and had thought about becoming a frugivore. He walked up and asked the owner about the price of Kandahari pomegranates. The owner told him that they were a rupee and a quarter for a kilogram and a single pomegranate was roughly fourteen annas. After that he didn't stop again. He got back to New Age Books around 4.30 p.m., took his manuscript and, without saying a word, bowed quickly to the editor and went home . . . The days had become very short, and it was also so cloudy that at 4.30 p.m. it seemed as if the day was over . . .

When he got home, Shekhar flung the manuscript on the floor and lay down on the cot. Then he got up all of a sudden, picked up the manuscript and began flipping through the pages . . . Several pages of the conclusion had been removed and replaced with new ones, written in someone else's hand—it was clear from the handwriting that the writer was a novice and probably a girl . . . Shekhar pulled those pages out, tore them in half and threw them away. Then he noticed that sections of his prose had been crossed out on several pages and there was something new written in the margins. He tore these pages out as well—he already had the original, unedited version of the manuscript!—and tore them in half and threw them away just as before. He looked at the remaining sections backwards and forwards, and then, with a lassitudinous 'hmm,' he threw the manuscript on the floor and scattered the pages with his feet.

He looked all around once and then lay face down on the cot, hiding his face in his pillow.

The tickling darkness of the cotton filling of the pillow—welcome, darkness! You are not insignificant and insubstantial; you have a shape, weight and density, so welcome even more! . . . Shekhar felt that if only he could melt into the darkness—then—then . . .

He got up in a blind haze and slowly went downstairs and out on to the street. As he shivered and huddled, he was struck by the emptiness of the day, but even without that there was more than enough darkness inside Shekhar . . . Darkness and loneliness—an unsullied nothingness—discrete, exilic darkness . . . There was no meaning in anything; everything was merely an effect whose original cause had been lost . . . Cause produces effect, but there was no plan in either cause or effect—anarchy had become the truth . . . Anarchy, confusion, nomadic . . .

What was he doing—where was he going—and what was the point even if he was going and doing? There was still some fog ahead, and if the deepening darkness stung his eyes then what was the point of trying to see . . . When people get lost in the jungle, they automatically start walking in circles, and the walking in circles gets them killed. He didn't want to go anywhere, nor did he want to walk in circles. Like a mountain goat blinded by the ice, he staggered, head lowered, as he walked on, walked on. He began to realize that there was a plan hidden in his planlessness, that his plan was total planlessness, a desire to be snuffed out . . .

A car horn sounds behind him. He pretends not to hear, and the car barely misses him. Another horn sounds. Shekhar ignores it again and keeps on walking in the middle of the street. The horn sounds again, sounds louder, sounds bold, sounds taunting, sounds threatening—

He walks on in the middle of the street, planless, planless—

Suddenly someone grabs his arm with both hands and pulls him forcefully; a cry drowns out the screeching brakes, 'Sir!' Shekhar looked up—it was a woman. She wasn't young, wasn't beautiful. The car brushed Shekhar as it hissed on; the unsteadiness from the slamming of the brakes had dissipated and it disappeared in a flash of shimmering chrome.

Extremely annoyed, Shekhar asked, 'What is it to you?'

What was it to anyone?—whether he lived, or died, was hit by the car, drowned in the ocean, burned in a flame, what did it matter to anyone?

With wounded surprise, the woman said, 'Sir, I just—' and then she was silent.

Shekhar's eyes met hers. No, she wasn't young. She wasn't beautiful. But her eyes possessed a fierce will, a motherly fear . . .

Shekhar responded in an insensate voice, 'Forgive me, sister—' and he quickly turned around and headed back home. But his footsteps went on repeating that meaningless taunt, 'What was it to anyone, what was it to anyone . . .'

He climbed up the steps but suddenly stopped when he got to the threshold of his room. The room was just as he had left it, but a candle was burning and Shashi, sitting on one edge of the cot, was staring directly at him.

*

No one knew how much time had passed while no one spoke, nor moved. Then Shashi said, 'Where were you, Shekhar? I've been sitting here waiting for you for a long time—and what is all this?' And then suddenly jumping up towards him, she grabbed both of his shoulders and, in a voice filled with panic, 'Shekhar! Shekhar! What happened—'

Shekhar grabbed both of Shashi's wrists and gently pushed her back to the cot; with the same gentle pressure, he sat her down on the cot. Slowly freeing his shoulders, he crossed the room, trampling over the scattered pages, and stood on the other side, and after a moment, he sat down on the ground in the middle of those pieces of paper.

'Nothing, Shashi. What could have happened—'

Shashi got up again and went to Shekhar.

'Tell me, Shekhar! What were you planning on doing? And—and what all have you done?'

He remained silent. His eyes were fixed on Shashi's feet.

'Speak, Shekhar! While I waited for you, you have no idea what I—'

She left the thought unfinished and was silent. No one knew how long both of them were quiet, still. Then the sound of paper crackling somewhere made Shekhar stand with a start, but Shashi's back was to the lamp, her face in the darkness . . . Shekhar looked at her intently and wanted to grab her by the shoulders and turn her around, but when he touched her, her body went stiff and she didn't move . . . Shekhar immediately let go of her shoulders. He went to the cot, sat down with a thud and then lay down. As his mind dimmed he realized that there was no going forward—his unblinking eyes stared at the ceiling—planlessness, planlessness, cold planlessness—

Shashi went and stood by the head of the cot. Indecisively, she said, 'Shekhar?' She leaned over him slightly—a drop fell on Shekhar with a plop—

Suddenly, Shekhar extended his arms and made her lean in closer. He buried his head in her chest and burst into tears . . . His body shook uncontrollably, his fists clenched atop Shashi's shoulders. Shashi didn't utter a single word as she remained leaning over him . . . like a shady saptaparni tree leaning over a mountain stream . . .

The trembling breeze passes through the shade of the saptaparni, a mysterious slackening overtakes its limbs, and everything gradually becomes peaceful under the diaphanous touch of its shade. A silky touch cobs through Shekhar's hair and asks, 'Will you tell me now?'

No, if there was no plan in life, then there was no point in remaining quiet, in hiding; if the thing couldn't touch him, then neither could its loving reaction . . . Shekhar said, 'I didn't know when I left, but while I was walking I realized that I was looking for a way to commit suicide.'

A gentle shudder went through the saptaparni.

'Why, Shekhar?'

'Just because; I realized that it wasn't necessary to have a reason to die. You need a reason to live. For a person without a clear plan, death is the natural conclusion.'

A voice filled with worry and objection—'Shekhar!'

'Don't live to get something, live to give something. I accept that. But what do I have to give? Planless, purposeless, meaningless suffering? Why should I give that, for whom should I offer that? If accomplishment is one source of happiness for people, then giving is another form of happiness—otherwise nothing matters, everything is a lie. And I know that in eighteen or nineteen waking years I have—' Another sobbing shudder shook his limp frame.

'I haven't given anyone happiness; my entire life has been based on conceit and all I've done is bring people pain—'

'How do you know, Shekhar?'

'The only thing I know is that I don't know. I've brought no happiness even to the people I've loved. I haven't asked them; but shouldn't love give one enough wisdom to tell you whether a person that you have loved has also received happiness or not?'

Slowly getting up, Shashi said, 'Perhaps it doesn't. Otherwise you'd be able to see—' She slowly walked over to the window, and for a while, she looked out the window, her hand resting on the windowsill—suddenly raindrops began to fall and, for a moment, they sparkled as they hit the pale light encircled by the window—dissolving from one nothingness into another . . . She turned around in the same spot and said, 'And Shekhar, isn't love its own gift—a gift greater than happiness?'

'It is, it is a very great gift—but only because it is also great happiness. If love doesn't bring happiness, if it only consumes one, then it's better for it to burn away—'

Shashi quickly returned to her spot; she sat down at the head of Shekhar's cot and yelled at him, 'Be quiet, Shekhar. You have no idea what you are saying.'

Shekhar was quiet. He remained lying there, but he lifted his eyes to look up at Shashi. Shashi wasn't looking anywhere, her gaze was fixed straight ahead, but she definitely knew that wrinkles had formed on Shekhar's forehead from looking up, because she gently brushed them with one hand, like someone removing wrinkles from silk. When this attempt failed, she extended her fingers and forcibly closed Shekhar's eyes—and they stayed there, didn't move from his eyes.

In very hushed tones, Shekhar said, 'Listen, Shashi!'

Shashi again leaned in over him.

'Shashi, I haven't been able to figure out what you are—'

Firmly, 'Why, Shekhar?'

'I've always called you sister, but you aren't as close to me as sisters are, and yet you aren't as distant from me—as much—as much as a sister would be.' Suddenly, he forcefully pressed Shashi's fingers with both of his hands on to his eyes, as if opening his eyes would mean some great calamity . . .

It was as if Shekhar could hear the incessant pounding of the rain outside in Shashi's quivering voice, 'What are you trying to say, Shekhar?'

Shekhar lifted both of his hands again, gently grabbed Shashi on both sides of her face, drew her towards him and said, 'I don't know what I'm trying to say. I only know you, and I know that all of the dreams that I have dreamt vanish into you—'

There was neither consent nor opposition in Shashi's leaning form; she was bent over, but was still and speechless . . .

The same stillness had also filled Shekhar's veins. It seemed to him that everything had been restored to its prior tranquillity because there was nothing else to come; everything had reached the point of unity with the absolute because it was nirvana . . . Although, somewhere in the distance, the clouds rumbled and the rain hissed, and there was a flash of lightning which revealed nothing and made the darkness that followed even darker.

Hovering over Shekhar was the shade from a young saptaparni sapling that trembled from some distant, drifting gust, a wind from the distant south, because it possessed a loving warmth and in the meantime, it had filled Shekhar's nostrils with a fragrance— the same fragrance that comes from the first, all-consuming scent of sandalwood . . .

There is a line beyond which silence becomes is its own answer, and all questions are dissolved into it because it is the ultimate non-question . . . No one knew when the external calm around Shekhar seeped into his insides and he fell asleep. Later, he woke, startled by the sound of thunder crackling, but that wakefulness never went beyond a soporific confusion, and he became completely absorbed by the fragrant, protective cover of the saptaparni's shade . . . Only once, as if hard facts meant to strike a blow to his liquid condition, Shekhar jumped and said, 'Shashi, it's very late. You have to go back—' He tried to get up, but Shashi didn't move. In her motionlessness, the icy rains of December answered for her, that it was already too late to go back home, and then Shekhar said, 'You'll exhaust yourself, Shashi,' and he tried to get up again so that Shashi could sit properly; but she stayed his efforts with a silent hand, and he realized that the resolve in his mind and the strength of his limbs had been bound by a completely agreeable bondage; then that drowsiness completely enveloped everything, and in the shade of the saptaparni, existence slumbered . . .

This is definitely from a rose-tinted dream—the atmosphere has a crystalline cold clarity, but with an affectionate colour. Shekhar lifts his head slightly to touch the shady saptaparni sapling above him—would his head be able to see the vessels that coursed life inside of the saptaparni tree—could it feel the pulsing of its heart?

The soul of the saptaparni tree speaks—how gentle is the voice of the soul!—'Are you awake, Shekhar?'

'Hmm—'

'Do you remember everything that you said?'

'Yes—'

'Do you know what it all means?'

The silence said, 'Yes, I understand.'

'There's no shame in what you have given me. I can say without any embarrassment that it is a boon. And one does not have the option of declining a boon.'

'. . .'

'I am a married woman. I have given myself voluntarily; I have made a vow of myself, of my world—turned them into sacrifices. And what I have given is not mine any longer, so I cannot speak for it; I cannot accept anything nor oppose anything, and—I can't give anything.' She fell silent; for a long time no one spoke, only the crystalline atmosphere began to feel a little colder—

'I haven't been miserly in giving up my selfhood—I gave it openly—I made a sacrifice of it and watched it all burn—turned to ash. I never thought that I was tricked, I knew that this was going to happen.'

There can be so much anguish in peace, and such cold-studded defeat in the crystalline redness of dreams . . . This was the end of everything, the end of dreams, too—

The soul of the saptaparni regained its strength once again—like a sacrificial fire rising up after a new offering!—and said, 'But that part of my life, which is me, which is my "I", is inside of you.'

Then a respite . . .

'And it's no less true, no less alive, just because it is intangible. Shekhar, don't think of me as your sister, mother, brother, son or anything else because I—now—am nothing. I am a shadow.' Then filled with an internal brilliance, 'And despite being intangible, I—I am a part of you that you will not name.'

Again, silence—the red crystal trembles within it—

'Shashi, is this—for you—an achievement—a sense of fulfilment?'

'Achievement? Hardly! My life was neither that much soil nor that much—air. There is no achievement or fulfilment; but I am content, Shekhar, and the happiness of this contentment is your boon to me.'

The crystal fades into redness. The cold did not belong to the dream, but to the break of a rain-washed December dawn . . . Shekhar withdrew from under the shade of the saptaparni tree suddenly and sat up, a flickering light in his consciousness suddenly gave him a fleeting glimpse of the events of the last ten hours; and then quickly filled with the feeling that today he would look at Shashi in a different form with the light from the first rays of dawn and then, enveloped by the feeling of faith from the Vedic songs—some of which he had recited as a child and now read from a new reprint—he looked straight at Shashi and said, 'Let my eyes be pure—'

Shashi's distant voice fully embraced his mood, 'And my vigil—'

Shashi got up. With one hand, she straightened out the wrinkles in the bedding on the cot from where she had sat all night, and then she went and stood by the window. Leaning against the sill, she spread both arms outside.

The sight of this slender, flexible but upturned sapling unexpectedly filled Shekhar's heart with a grateful feeling of benediction. His gaze touched the averted form attached to the windowsill from head to toe, and he made a silent prayer to himself and waited expectantly for the first rays of light to illuminate Shashi's outline in gold . . .

The reality of the reassuring rays of dawn never happened, merely a dull glow formed—as the day broke, the clouds thickened overhead. Who knows what mirthful desire prompted Shekhar to sit on the majority of the pages of 'Our Society' that had been scattered below; Shashi was still standing at the window, but now she faced him.

'Shashi, do you still sing?'

An inward-looking, sad Shashi said, 'Humph!' which seemed to say, 'Singing? Now?' Then she said out loud, 'I'm going back now.'

Shekhar made a gesture of tying up the pages of the scattered manuscript into a bundle and said, 'Our entire society is waiting—' (Torn, scattered scraps of a society—and Lala Amolak Roy's edited-by-reform society . . .)

Shashi said, 'It's been a year since I last sang—' There wasn't an objection in it, just an acknowledgment of insistence, 'I won't sing now. I can only recite—'

Gradually the room began to reverberate with the waves of her voice becoming more distinct:

> May air's mid-region give us peace and safety, safety may both
> these, Heaven and Earth, afford us.
> Security be ours from west, from eastward, from north and
> south may we be free from danger.
> Safety be ours from friend and from the unfriendly, safety from
> what we know and what we know not.
> Safety be ours by night and in the day-time! Friendly to me be
> all my hopes and wishes![19]

But then Shashi turned herself around and stood facing the window and, after humming for a moment, began to sing in an unwavering but echoing voice—with a powerful and steady rhythm, like blood in a healthy vein . . .

> Why has the sound of murmuring leaves arisen today.
> From bloom to bloom
> Waves of air quiver.
> Who is the beggar knocking at my door
> Needing my heart and my possessions.
> My heart knows him,
> Knows the flowers blossoming in his song.
> The stranger's footsteps echo in my heart today.
> Waking me, suddenly.[20]

Shekhar's mind wandered far away, listening to that voice and watching that composed back produce a rising and falling vibrato. That moment seemed so remote when he used to hide to try and listen to the waves of Shashi's radiant songs, when he would stand perfectly still to listen to her singing—remote not only from himself, but also from Shashi . . . She was happy then—happy in her flawless happiness, she who didn't understand her own condition; and today—today she knows that she isn't even happy in her happiness, only content—content meaning patient—she believes this destruction of her personality, this decimation, to be a kind of dignity and owns it . . .

But if this is the case, even if Shashi is content in this moment, then isn't this the most important moment in Shekhar's life since he cannot give Shashi any greater joy than this? And—and since this moment between yesterday and today has completely changed his life—

He recalled that when he was saved last night by an unknown woman he had been furious with her and had come home thinking what was it to anyone—what was it to anyone . . . Today—today he was something to someone—and he knew that he was something to someone . . .

Wasn't this the right moment—this very second—to do what he had set out to do yesterday? To be snuffed out by the happiness of an accomplishment and a satisfaction, given and received—and what an accomplishment! . . . If he were to slip away quietly now, disappear with Shashi's song ringing permanently in his ears—

He slinked his way over to the door slowly, and stood up straight when he got to the threshold—

She suddenly stopped singing and said, 'Shekhar, where are you?'

He stood still. Shashi turned around and asked, 'Where were you going?'

Shekhar didn't say anything.

'Are you still feeling guilty? Shekhar, I'm telling you, you won't go anywhere.' And then with the same resolute but completely altered voice, 'Look at me, Shekhar—look into my eyes. Can you be that wilful—are you absolutely alone?'

Shekhar lowered his eyes. Defeated, he returned to the room. 'Tell me what I should do, what do you think—'

Shashi gestured a sweet slap with her hand and said, 'There's so much time for telling and listening. I'm going now—it's morning already. But if you do anything crazy this time, then—' She raised one finger and left the sentence unfinished.

Shekhar said, 'Something is wrong with my brain—I'm completely crazy.' There was a note of weariness and shame in his voice.

With the serious voice of an intellectual, but full of laughter, Shashi said, 'Crazy—not crazy. But a very big kid!' And she went down the stairs. Shekhar began gathering the scattered pages of 'Our Society'.

Suddenly the morning's feelings rose within him again, and he was surprised and asked himself how quickly Shashi's mind reflected his own emotion. This curiosity made him even stronger. Gratefully he said again, 'Let my eyes be pure . . .'

And Shashi joined in, 'And my vigil—' But the vigil was mine, Shashi, the vigil was mine—I remain in vigil for the consequences of your good deeds . . .

Part 4

Threads, Ropes and Nets

Cloudy and cold, but the day's breath is beautiful—beautiful and tender, freshly bathed . . . Had he been a singer, he would have drawn the soul of the day with the paintbrush of his voice—had he been a painter, he would have painted it; had he been a sculptor, he would have caught its breath in crystalline shape and chiselled it—not immortal, it was already immortal, but he would have drawn its form into a physical halo . . . Because joy has a definite shape that can be felt by the intellect's fingers—and since there isn't a given, physical form, the artist gains an interpretive freedom—imagery and desire become handmaidens to that form—

Shekhar would write. If it was possible, he would write poetry, but he would definitely write something, because he could never remember his mind being as clear as it was today, and who knew if this wave of life, which he had found after waiting for ages, would ever crest again . . .

Was there nothing that was beyond writing, that was so vast, so deep, that could not be contained because it was itself the container?

There was. But no one dared to try and capture it. The shade of the saptaparni covers me, everything else is gone, but I can take in the rustling in her breath and melt into it. I can even hum the melody . . .

Creation is first and foremost an act of appreciation . . .

Shekhar began to write.

*

463

Nine, ten, eleven, eleven-thirty—

In jail, Shekhar learned to tell a person's mood from the sound of their footsteps, which is why he was startled by the sound of footsteps coming up the stairs. Such aversion, such weariness in dragging one's self through the snares of the muck and weeds of life! Who was this poor soul on this unsullied day, who—

But the weak feet stopped at the threshold, and there, with one arm and one elbow leaning on the door frame and the shoulder leaning on the hand, with a pallid complexion and cloudy, glassy eyes that stared out into nothing, was Shashi.

He stumbled to his feet and said, 'Hey, what are you doing here—' and then when he saw Shashi's face he rushed to help her.

'I'm here, that's all—I won't be going back there—no, don't touch me, I'll be gone soon enough—'

'Hey, what are you saying, Shashi—'

'He's kicked me out of the house.'

'What—why?' He was stunned, 'Come inside, Shashi. Let's sit and talk—'

'No, Shekhar; I've been abandoned by my husband, I'm a fallen woman, I'm not fit to be anywhere. Don't ask me to come inside—'

When he saw Shashi bending down to sit by the threshold, Shekhar, wounded, started to say, 'Shashi—' but then he suddenly realized that she wasn't sitting down intentionally, but that Shashi was sitting down because she couldn't stand any longer. He rushed to grab her by the arm to support her and then led her inside.

'Yes, I was saying. Think it over, Shekhar. There's still time. There is no reason for you to invite me or let me come inside. I haven't come to stay for long—I can't bear the thought of causing someone else trouble—and you—definitely—never . . .' Her voice broke, and in a voice full of strain, 'And what you have given me—'

Shekhar closed her mouth with his other hand and led her to the cot; he made her sit and then gently tried to get her to lie down—

Suppressing a groan, Shashi said, 'No, let me sit—'

Shekhar moved aside slightly and said, 'Why did he kick you out, Shashi?' And then immediately, 'If it's too hard to say, then don't worry—'

'I will tell you. I have to be going soon, after all. He said that I am a harlot, a sinner.'

And after a moment's silence, 'Why?'

'I was out all night—'

'What? Didn't you tell him that you were here—with me?'

Shashi didn't seem to be saying anything, but she still turned her face away. She didn't speak.

'Why didn't you tell him? I will go right now—'

Flaring up, 'No, no! Don't go there—'

'Why—'

'No, Shekhar, no! I—'

'You didn't tell him?'

Somehow Shashi managed to say, 'He—he knew.'

'So?'

Just as the banks of a river slowly collapse in a flood, Shashi's patience was breaking down. Gradually becoming more agitated, she said, 'Don't ask me to tell you, Shekhar; I can't repeat those words to you—'

'Do we keep secrets from each other, Shashi?'

'Oh, you don't understand, you don't understand at all! He thinks—you have no idea what he thinks—he thinks—that I spent the night here—that I am fallen—oh, no, no, Shekhar!'

As her voice became even more upset, it began to sound like a hiccup; and then silence descended and it swished as it flowed on . . .

A little later, Shekhar said, 'I understand, Shashi! Enough'—then stopping and repeating—'I understand everything . . .'

His voice became so calm and steady that Shashi's unsettled gaze focused on him, and nervously she asked, 'What will you do, Shekhar?'

Thoughtfully, 'No, I won't do that again, Shashi. I won't do anything.' Then, 'And you, Shashi?'

'What about me?'

'What will you do?'

Shashi laughed a weak, hollow laugh—'Me!' And then seriously, 'Shekhar, if you just say the word, I'll leave. I will really go away. I will really go away. Just say it!'

Wounded, Shekhar threatened, 'What should I say? What do you—'

'It's not because it would make things simpler for you; it would also help me, Shekhar—'

Shekhar went to the window. He said, 'They say there is something attractive about heights—a terrible attraction.' And then to make his meaning clear, 'One person could jump from a four-storeyed window, two people could jump. That's one way.'

A trembling admonition, 'Shekhar!'

'No, I can't say that that way should be taken. There must be—another way.'

'Another way! What?'

Shekhar spun around and said, 'Shashi, promise me that you won't do anything, won't go anywhere—'

'I—where would I go—not go anywhere?'

'Don't stall, Shashi; say it: you won't go anywhere—'

' . . . '

'Say it, Shashi, promise me—'

'Is that what you want, Shekhar? Is that what you wholeheartedly want—'

'Shashi, will you trust me this much—'

Slowly, and curiously, as if testing to see how these words sounded, Shashi said, 'I won't go. Perhaps not going—is giving— is paying debts—' Then coolly, as if neither side had anything left to say or hear in the conversation, she closed her eyes . . .

Shekhar began pacing back and forth in his room, trying to understand and accept all that was said completely . . . The promise of intimacy that was established last night—had been made, there was no doubt in his mind about that—Shashi was unquestionably and inescapably a part of his world; and the ethics of the duty he had sworn to stand by Shashi—a deeply held, and considered his privilege, ethics—were just as unquestionable. But wasn't acknowledging this certainty merely seeing the certainty of the situation; wasn't avoiding the situation just as likely a certainty? . . . He realized that the insistence that 'there has to be another way' was not the reassurance of 'there is another way'. That reassurance—

Shashi got up and staggered towards the door—

Shekhar moved towards her to help her, 'Yes, Shashi—'

'No, stay here. I am going out for a bit—'

Worried, Shekhar said, 'Shashi, you promised—'

'Shekhar, I will be right back; stay here in the room—' Then with a thin smile that disappeared with the emotion, she said, 'Don't worry.'

Shekhar stood lifeless in the middle of the room, but there was a vigilance in that lifelessness—from just outside, he heard the noise of water being sprinkled and then a breathy moan; then the sound of a faucet running . . .

'Shekhar—'

He raced outside. Shashi was bent over, using the faucet for support, reaching out towards him. Shekhar helped her back inside and asked, 'What's wrong, Shashi? What happened—'

'Nothing, nothing—'

Why the unnecessary insistence? Concerned, Shekhar asked, 'Should I call the doctor?'

'No, it's nothing, Shekhar—' But as soon as she lay down on the cot, Shashi immediately curled up and half-sat up; and then painfully changing positions, she became still, one arm slowly rising and then resting on her forehead, her fingers moving towards her hair, three nails disappearing in her tresses—suddenly Shekhar can see that although Shashi's eyes are open, she neither sees or understands anything, not even that Shekhar is there—or that he even is . . .

Was the power of unity the power of death?—Was the only reward for understanding one another not having anything to say to the other, nothing to exchange between vacant, unblinking eyes on one side and on the other, a confused, dumb stone? And then the implication of the whole affair—Rameshwar's attack,

Shashi's injury, cruelty—fell like a hammer blow on the mirror of
Shekhar's consciousness; he was outraged. A tension overtook his
entire body and welled up in his soul, and for a moment, he made
an offering with his gaze fixed on Shashi; then he slowly freed
the blanket from under Shashi's feet and covered her with it. He
wrapped an old shawl around his shoulders and headed outside.

'Where are you going?'

Shekhar was caught off guard, but without stopping, he said,
'I—I'll be back, Shashi. You should stay here—' and he quickly
went downstairs. He didn't have a clear plan in his mind, except
that he knew that he was going to see Rameshwar face-to-face.

Rameshwar was sitting in front of the doorway; Shekhar saw
him a second before he did; but in that second, Rameshwar's
composed, sparkling face contorted and bristled; two brows, dense
and already connected, became entangled like a milk hedge—

'How dare you—what are you doing here—'

Ignoring Rameshwar's bark and pushing him to one side,
Shekhar said, 'What I am doing—that will be settled here. But
what have you done—are you out of your mind?'

'Shameless! You've come to prosecute me—she went to you
with her charges, didn't she—get out of my house—what was
she to you anyway—' Rameshwar's face was extremely contorted
with rage and revenge. His nostrils and lips were flared; Shekhar
realized his rancour had gone so far past the point of logic that
if he didn't speak slowly, he would start stammering like a child!
But what entitled him to such anger—had he been grievously
wronged? That cruel, blind, murderousness! Sternly, Shekhar said,
'I didn't come here to give you answers, I came to demand them—'

For a few moments Rameshwar kept spitting out 'you-you-
you', as if Shekhar's challenge had rendered the astonishment that
had flashed across his face incoherent and speechless. Shekhar
took advantage of the opportunity to speak directly and quickly,
'Shashi was at my place. I came home late. I was suicidal—' and
then stopping for a second, 'She stopped to comfort me, and then
the rain—' and then realizing that he was giving answers, and even
then incoherently, he bit his lip and left the sentence unfinished.

'You are making such a big mistake, you don't even realize it. Shashi—you aren't even fit to touch her feet, and you, sir—' He was surprised that some lingering sense of responsibility to Shashi compelled him to address this man as 'sir'.

There is a sound that a scythe makes when sawing through broken bamboo, and a sound just like that was being made by someone speaking from the door to the room behind Rameshwar, 'So go and kiss her feet, you—maybe having you lick them will cool her down—'

Shekhar was startled to see that behind Rameshwar was a woman's face, from whose countless, dark wrinkles emerged a rotting reflection of Rameshwar; there were the same dense brows, but in the sockets below them were two, thick clumps of mould where the eyes should have been . . . Was this Rameshwar's mother? Shekhar hadn't seen her before and didn't know when or why she had come.

'She stayed to comfort him. Did you get so much comfort last night that you became this audacious—you villainous scoundrel!' He spit at Shekhar like a cobra with its hood flared, as if he discovered a new reserve of anger, and Shekhar saw an old face with quivering, mottled whiskers had appeared next to him.

'He's shown his true colours now—goes around town calling himself a communist. He's just got out after a year in jail—no respectable home should let him enter. Communists consider women to be common property—atheists! It's their job to mislead young women and turn them into whores. They're all worthless, they have no money, so this is their cheap trick. First "sister", then "comrade", then "whore". What's it to them if someone's family is destroyed—they get a new whore—a girl from a respectable home, and for free!' Filled with the feeling that the crimes of this class of people were indescribable, he poured all of the venom inside of him into a single word which those mottled whiskers paused over for a second and then released, 'Communist!'

Shekhar felt as though he were on another planet; some planet of slimy white ooze and black pits filled with poisonous vapour—shocked and stunned, he couldn't even be angry at this vulgar assault, merely speechless. But the stallion of Rameshwar's anger broke through its bit after being whipped a second time and raced on—Rameshwar suddenly stepped up to Shekhar and slapped him across the face.

This was definitely another planet, where nothing happened with thought or deliberation—or even intention—everything happened automatically, willed into existence by some damned, demonic power inside the event itself—the flash of the event decides for itself . . . The faint outline of a slap is on Shekhar's face; with an automatic reflex, Shekhar's hand went up and grabbed the assailant's wrist, and the grip gradually tightens and the wrist is bent backwards—the violent impulse has gone dead in the wrist which begins to shake under the pressure of that grip. A fuzzy thought, that the grip might become so tight that Rameshwar's bones might begin to crack—that the wrist was Rameshwar's, that if it hadn't been Rameshwar's wrist, but his throat, then—if it had been . . .

But why was it a wrist, and why wasn't it a throat? It definitely was a throat; but a throat could be crushed the same way that a wrist could be, because the grip has no intention, no desire, it is only a grip, a demonic force that runs on its own, even though it is blind—

A touch on Shekhar's shoulder tore through the veil of that other planet, and Shashi said, 'Shekhar!'

The grip slackened, but the hand remained in the exact same spot. Then Shekhar suddenly felt as if his hand had been gripping some gelatinous piece of filth, he spread out his fingers and then his hand swung down immediately.

In the silence, the course of that demonic force continued unabated for a long while . . .

Then Shashi said, 'I was afraid that you would do exactly this. Why did you come here?'

Shekhar's complete rebellion peeked out from his silence.

'You should leave—'

Shekhar's stare bored straight into Shashi's. After a few moments, he said, 'And you? You should leave, too—'

'Go away. Go away because I'm telling you to.' Her voice had the pride of command that knew that it had authority not just over the people nearby, because it also directed the ground on which she stood, because that, too, was her subject.

Shekhar silently began descending the stairs; his entire being cried out in protest at his expulsion, but not a single word escaped his lips, and if there was one thought that was clear in his mind it was that all the devotion, the faith, the love that not one but fifty Shekhars could give to that queen had all in the manner of an instant been shamed and stripped naked.

He didn't turn around to look, but he understood what was happening behind him by means of a sixth sense . . . For stunned figures, Shashi's eyes made a circle from the first to the second, from the second to the third, where they stopped and remained fixed. No one had the ability to read that gaze, not even the one on whom it was now fixed and would not leave, who would quickly turn inwards in shame!

Suddenly the door slammed shut and then came the clicking noises of the lock being locked. It was only then that Shekhar turned around to look; six or seven steps above him, Shashi stood like a stone column outside that closed door. He didn't say anything. He just stayed there and then slowly began descending the stairs. That's when he noticed that there were sounds of someone else's slow and hushed footsteps following him.

When Shashi had followed him down to the street below, from the window above, a moustache-strained voice spoke, 'She's gone—'

Then the grating voice of a scythe sawing through broken bamboo raised a taunt.

'Take him into your lap, shamefaced whore—bitch!'

Shekhar figured out that the lack of any mention of him in these cries was the result of his responsibility. He didn't turn around, but he did pause so that Shashi could walk next to him . . .

*

In the double isolation of the room, there was so much to learn, so much to ask, which Shekhar still hadn't understood and hadn't asked; he had never asked, and who knows when he understood, there had been no opportunity to ask in between the momentary flashes of the tiniest, disconnected, wilful waves of anger, Shekhar had gathered that something more important was happening behind and inside of everything that he had seen, had kept happening, but where was the time to gather and disentangle the meaning of those feelings when there were so many immediate matters that had to be considered and demanded resolution . . .

Shashi wasn't lying on the cot, she had collapsed into it, her body gathered into a question mark, her eyes involuntarily closed and opened a little late. Shekhar knew those eyelids were hiding a hurt . . .

It was important to settle some questions immediately before it became dark. The evening meal came from the restaurant, but the restaurant had to be informed—this time, he would cook something himself—when he got back; first of all, bedclothes and another blanket for cover . . .

Shekhar took out a new change of clothes and started to go outside to change. Lifelessly, Shashi asked, 'Where are you going now?'

'I'm going to the college for a bit. I will be back in an hour.' And then taking one step backwards, 'Shashi, don't be afraid. I won't do anything. And you—you should stay here. Don't go out.'

After he had changed his clothes, he went to Shashi and stood watching her for a while. Then he said, 'You should go to sleep now, you're very tired. You were up all night, and this morning—'

In agreement, Shashi said, 'All right, I will go to sleep.'

*

Half an hour later, when he returned from the hostel with three blankets, a thin mattress and a rug under his arm and ten rupees he had borrowed in his pocket and the expression of recent success

on his face, Shashi was sitting perfectly still next to the tap, and
the water was running . . .

Shekhar gathered up his bedclothes and took out a new bed
sheet and spread it over the cot for Shashi, and having decided
to make his bed in the other part of the L-shaped room, he took
his bundle of remaining bedclothes and put them there. Then
he brought Shashi back to the cot; a crust of ice had formed on
the surface of his mind and he couldn't bring himself to ask her
anything; he put her to bed and when he went to the cupboard to
get things for dinner, he saw that the stove had been lit, pots and
pans had been scattered about, dishes of lentils and boiled potatoes
had been set aside, and a few rotis had also been prepared, but it
was as if the work had been abandoned in the middle, the flour
hadn't even been put away, and there were two sparrows sitting
in the window to the closet waiting to fill their beaks—there were
a few signs that the birds had already been in the flour . . . He
went back to the room and loudly said, 'Shashi, you—you are just
terrible.'

Shashi smiled like the accused and said, 'What could I do? I
didn't get a chance to clean up the pots and pans. I can clean it all
up now—'

In fake irritation, Shekhar said, 'Is that what I was saying?
Why did you all of this work—all right, now you have to enjoy
the fruits of your mischief. You should sit up. I'll make a plate
for you.'

'I didn't make it for me. You should eat—'

'It's your punishment. You eat first. I will wash the dishes and
then I will eat.'

'No, that's not right—you have to eat.' Then—unwillingly,
'Even if you won't let me do the dishes—'

'All right, all is forgiven. I will fix a plate for me, too.'

Drained, Shashi said, 'No Shekhar, I won't eat.'

'What? On your first day here, you are going to cook and
feed me but go hungry yourself? What must you think of me? I—
absolutely won't eat.' And then to lighten the mood, he made sure
that Shashi could tell he was playing when he jauntily used the

expression 'Sisterji,' and he imitated his father, 'I am the offspring of the ever-hospitable Aryans—'

Shashi smiled a little to acknowledge his efforts, 'I came this morning as a guest—but you didn't let me remain a guest. And now I—' and then suddenly changing her tone, 'yes, and now even if I want to be a guest, I—' Shashi stopped again when she saw Shekhar's face. She said, 'I won't say it, there! I don't want to hurt you, Shekhar, I would certainly eat, but I—can't eat.'

Shekhar was struck with worry, 'Why Shashi? What's the matter—are you—hurt somewhere?'

'Me—my—I'm not feeling well.'

Shekhar could tell that this was not an admission, but a deflection; but he knew Shashi; if she didn't want to reveal something, she wouldn't. Insistence was futile.

'So you won't eat at all—not even a little bit?'

'No, Shekhar. Bring your plate here. If you eat in front of me, it will be like I've eaten, too—'

'. . .'

'I won't take no for an answer—otherwise I will take it to mean that you find the food that I've cooked unworthy—'

Shekhar quietly went to the cupboard.

Who knew if it took more self-will or not to swallow down balls of mud even when one wasn't hungry. But Shekhar had a vague sense that a flooding stream of love was flowing towards him from Shashi, and the love inside him was growing only for her, like a waterfall that gushes forth to admire the eager, foamy splash at the bottom of the cliff . . . And the seed of affection that sprouted in this manure of pain and stigma was a manifestation of mankind's biggest, visible miracle . . .

*

There really were many things that I didn't understand at the time, and before, I didn't even have the ability to imagine I could understand. But I gradually learned. But I couldn't draw a clear line between not knowing and knowing; I can't clearly recall when

I was told the full history behind these events. I definitely was told, because it was like a separate account in the treasury of my consciousness, which was never separated from that treasury, had always been a part of it—a part of my being. And it was such an inseparable part of me that when I recall it, it feels like they were all my feelings; not the imaginary associated images I created upon hearing Shashi's feelings. In my memory, I become Shashi, I remember her memories, I suffer her traumas, her silences, her matchless, unbroken pride fills me . . . Shashi is no longer, but I am Shashi; so I am no longer, as well—just was. But right now I am more hurt by her pain than by my own, taller from her pride, and therefore she lives . . .

They say that those events that are experienced with very intense emotions are like indelible lines drawn in stone on the slab of consciousness, and recalling them is like recalling an entire picture, not the mere memory of this or that line or shape. Which is to say that when these events are recalled, they are done in a necessary, unchanging sequence, in which the pen of the one recollecting has no independence, it is bound to follow the sequence of events . . . There is another line of thought that says that the consciousness tries to erase experiences born out of trauma, and it gradually wraps them in so many veils of repression that its outline becomes completely concealed; it becomes completely erased from a person's memory. But in my experience, these intensely experienced events are neither erased from the slab of memory nor are they permanent and unchanging like histories written in stone. I have seen that some scenes are brilliant like flashes of lightning, and there are others which have been snuffed out and the connective thread between events has been broken; not just broken, but tangled up; which means that I can't even see those bright events in the proper temporal sequence—they come lit up in a wilful order and then leave, and I can't say with any confidence which was first, which was second, all I can say is that they all happened; which is not to say that this is all that happened or that it happened in this way . . .

Or is it that in waiting for the final verdict, the accused suppresses his resignation and places the judgemental wisdom of the creator upon the stallion of his memory? Have I, in my last days, fallen under the deluded notion that I have actually succeeded in my plan to search for the meaning, for the purpose of my life, searching for accomplishment and success—that I have merely flinched from the cruelty of real evaluation and settled for the laziness of fabrication?

But isn't fabrication the greatest cruelty, the greatest activity, since it makes a gift of its life to its creation?

And is the truth of an event the greatest truth, and is its sequential order the necessary sequence of life? Isn't the sequence imposed by life more important for one who has resigned himself? Isn't it an even greater resignation to negate the opposition between both internal and external time?

When he comes back inside, Shekhar sees his aunt, Vidyavati, sitting on the rug next to Shashi's cot. His hearts skips a beat; it was as if he had ignored the fact that there were others in the world beyond the triangle of Shashi, Shekhar and Rameshwar. He didn't doubt that there was a society outside this small circle; but he was also certain that his aunt was in no way outside the circle, either; and in the middle of this embarrassing dilemma was Aunt—

Shekhar made a formal greeting and said, 'Aunt, why are you sitting on the floor—'

His aunt made a gesture of blessing with her hand, but didn't say anything. Shekhar saw that her complexion was completely sallow and that there were lines beneath the two dark half-moons under her eyes which touched the corners of her mouth and were stretching down to reach her chin; and that Shashi's face was turned towards hers but her eyes were fixed on the frame of the cot—

Shashi said, 'Shekhar, you should go out for a while.' He paused and then left. His trust in Shashi was now greater than his trust in himself. When he went into the courtyard, he even closed the door behind him, and he began pacing in the courtyard. Then he suddenly went to the cupboard and began turning everything over and completely cleaned out the shelves and then began replacing everything properly . . .

Shekhar and the doctor are talking. To the right, behind the cover of a screen, lies Shashi; and between the doctor and the screen stands his aunt, with one hand left holding on to the screen, as if stuck in a dilemma about whether she should have been behind the screen or on the outside.

'There are definitely several injuries to her abdomen. We will have to be very careful. It isn't very serious, but you know that there is a risk that internal injuries can become septic.[1] I am prescribing some medicines, and complete bed rest is absolutely necessary, and she shouldn't eat any solid food.'

'Yes, sir.'

The doctor bends down to write the prescription; from behind the screen come the sounds of the rustling of the bed as Shashi gets up—

His aunt asks, 'And her back pain—'

'That will get better on its own—the fall has caused spasms—' Then after a little thought, 'Where does it hurt?' and he stands up straight; Shekhar is the only one left looking at the screen.

'Here? Here? And if you can bend over a little—' And then in a different tone, 'Oh . . .'

The scene returns to its prior arrangement, his aunt's hand is on the screen like before, the doctor is standing in front of Shekhar, but there is a different face.

'Well, doctor—'

The doctor looks at Shekhar gravely and says, 'Are you the husband?'

'No, she's my sister.'

'Oh, please forgive me. And is this the mother?'

Turning to face his aunt, 'Madam, does she live with you?'

Shekhar answers, 'No, she lives with her in-laws. We just brought her to you for an examination—why, what's the matter?'

The doctor goes quiet. After a while, as if he's thinking something, deciding something, he says, 'Madam, the injury to her back is not an injury from falling.'

'And?'

The doctor's silence seems to say, 'I have many children of my own. I know what you must be going through—'

His aunt turns around to ask, 'Shashi, don't you remember how you got this injury?'

Shashi doesn't speak; as if deciphering her silence, the doctor says, 'I'll give you an ointment for this injury; apply it gently with a warm compress.' Then after a moment of hesitation, to Shekhar in English, 'It's not accidental; it's a deliberate blow. The kidney is fractured.'[2]

Shekhar also asks in English, 'Is it dangerous?'

'No, but irreparable.'

'What treatment would you advise?'

'Rest and endurance—and courage. Chiefly courage.'

The doctor realizes that continuous conversation in English isn't reassuring, so he turns to Aunt Vidyavati and says, 'Complete rest is absolutely necessary—get this prescription filled at the dispensary—it will be necessary to see her again in two or three days—' as if he were advising that instead of bringing the patient in that he could be called out—

Rameshwar's flat was on the second floor, Shashi's body was taut like a bowstring from the reverberating insult, readied like a bow; Rameshwar's face in front, an inanimate wall about to break and fall after its foundation has been shaken, and two more walls behind it that won't fall because they are already ruined and have become heaps of rubble from years of mould . . .

Wiping the ashes that her mother-in-law has thrown into her eyes, Shashi says, 'If this is the final decision that you all have come to, then—'

She folds her hands and bows her head slightly, a few particles of ash cascade down from her head, brush her hands, and fall to the floor, she turns around, one step ahead of her are the stairs, she takes one step down—

The scythe shrieks, 'Look at this shamelessness—'

The wall falls to pieces from the grating of the scythe. Rameshwar leaps forward and a sandal-clad kick lands on Shashi's back, 'Whore!'

The bow is stretched again and in reaction, the echo of warning grows louder, 'I won't accept my last gift from you with my back turned, you can give it to me now—' and another wall rises in front of the crumbling wall, a wall which is supple like the bow and will therefore never crumble—

The scythe grinds its teeth frenetically, 'Hit her, hit her one more time—'

When the kick strikes her in the stomach, Shashi lets out a 'Unh!' but stays there. The scene goes dark in front of her eyes. Bracing herself against the wall, she turns around to leave now that she has had her initial meeting—

Aunt's voice comes from the back of the buggy, 'What was the doctor saying in English—'

Turning, 'Nothing much. He said that she really needs her rest. She needs to lie there quietly, otherwise things will get worse—'

Aunt asks Shashi, 'How did you get hurt? Really, from falling—'

Shekhar turns farther around, 'Aunt, does anyone ever injure their abdomen when they fall forward? And there's nothing on her hands or face—'

Quietly, Shashi, 'Let's get home first—'

In the silence, only the driver's clucking noises with his tongue or the occasional, 'Coooo-ming through!'

Everything in the cupboard has been straightened up, actually everything has been reorganized twice already. Will Shashi and Aunt never finish their conversation, and would he have to stay outside forever?

And Shashi, who has penetrated his life like a truth—and he who has roared into Shashi's life like a comet, would his aunt tolerate all of this—would she be able to tolerate it? The thing that Shashi was trying to save Aunt from by sacrificing herself, that thing was still near his aunt—

Shekhar turns the faucet on and takes the pots and pans and puts them under it. The splashes of cold water are a sort of comfort—

Eventually, his aunt calls to him from inside, 'Shekhar!' Shekhar wants to be able to decipher whether he has been found guilty, or was being called to give testimony or was acquitted altogether—and he now stands next to his aunt. His aunt looks up towards him, her expression is of a confused pain, and nothing else—'Sit down.'

Shekhar sits down on the floor next to her.

'What do you say about all of this?'

Unaware of what the issue is, Shekhar doesn't speak.

'I have been raised to believe that a woman's husband is everything to her. A wife is also something to her husband, I know that, but I never learned to demand my rights the same way I learned to give them over, and now I'm old and can't learn new things.' There is no objection, accusation or command in her voice, merely a feeling of explanation—

'Shashi says that there is no going back now. It's not a question of wanting to or not, it's a question of can or cannot. I went to see them before I came here.'

Shekhar was surprised, 'How?'

'They had sent a telegram and told me to come, which is why I'm here. They said that Shashi is dead to them, and that we were never a part of their lives. Her mother-in-law said that if she were to—forget it, what's the use in repeating it—'

Shashi says, 'Mother, they didn't insult you, did they—what did they say—'

'Why would people who kicked you out of the house leave any stone unturned in insulting me? They said they would rather eat cow's flesh than let you into their home, home-wrecker, sigh—'

'And then—'

'And then what! There's no going back there. But I don't think it's true that one has to go back to one's in-laws to accept that your husband is still supreme. You can still honour your obligations without travelling on the path that your husband has closed for you.' She was quiet for a while, then, 'Shashi says that she won't go back with me, and if she wants to go somewhere—'

Shekhar looks at Shashi without saying a word.

'Mother, please don't take it badly. I'm doing the right thing—'

'Shashi says I should go back, and that I should do what her in-laws do and consider her dead—if not in my mind, then at least in my actions.'

'Why?'

Shashi gives the response. 'Because why should Mother have to suffer for what I do? She's already suffered greatly. Now she needs to live separately, she's given me up after she's married me off, so why should she be responsible for what happens now? And why should I let her—'

'Aunt, I'm the worst one at fault here, I crashed into everything like a meteor and hurt everyone deeply—I—'

'No, Shekhar, don't try to be responsible for everything that was going to happen anyway—' Then as if returning to the main issue, 'Shashi thinks that I should stay out of it, and that she should suffer the punishment that she received at the hands of society by herself.' She looks at Shekhar and doesn't get a response, so she starts speaking again, 'But how can I stay out of it? Wouldn't it kill me, too, to cut off and throw away with my own hands that which I have created in my own body, which I have fed with my own blood? How can I ignore that—'

'Mother, it won't work to think like that. You've already agreed that I can't go back—' It's the first time in the conversation that Shashi has got worked up. She says, 'And to go back home with you and let you bear the hardships to come would not only be unbearable for me, but it makes everything I have done by getting beaten up so completely pointless that—' And then composing herself, 'And it's not as if you will escape any problems that way.' Then pausing for a while, 'Yes, if you say that I shouldn't live here, then—'

Shekhar speaks, 'I should also have to pay for my mistakes. Whatever Shashi has to endure from society—'

'I am not stopping her from staying here. If she's not coming back with me, then this is the only other place she has. People used to say things to me, but I told them that the two of you were connected by a single vein—I've never thought of you as separate, Shekhar, even if according to society our relationship is next to nothing. If she stays here, it is just as good as if she stays with me—except for the fact that I am abandoning my child—not just Shashi, but both of you—'

Shekhar's eyes begin to water. He wants to burst into tears, 'Aunt, Aunt—Mother—'

'Mother, if love comes from the heart, then abandonment comes from the heart, too. If you don't abandon me—us—in your heart, then why should this cause you any pain? And—we, too—will never forget that—'

His aunt faces and looks at Shekhar and says, 'And your father—what will I say to him—' Her voice suddenly breaks. She puts her head down on the frame of the cot right in front of Shashi. Shashi hugs her shoulder with one arm and half hides herself in the extra length of her sari. Seeing his aunt's thin frame shaking from some invisible dust storm, Shekhar starts crying without moving, too—then a new wisdom, rising from the ashes of memory and freshly bathed in the waters of the Ganges, announces that Shashi has not been defeated—

'Take this, Shekhar—'

His aunt extends a single 100-rupee note. 'I will send more later—'

'Aunt, I—'

'It's not for you. It's for Shashi—she's still not well and—'

Embarrassed, 'Aunt, this isn't right—I will figure something out and then—'

Wounded, his aunt says, 'Shekhar, I have been defeated by those who were to defeat me; I have been broken by those who were to break me—let me have something—'

'Don't be proud, Shekhar. Listen to me and take it—'

Shekhar slowly extends his hand, as if straightening up, and says, 'When Shashi gets better, then no more—' and to himself he thinks no more in any case—

'God willing, that will happen very soon. There is no great joy ahead in the future, but her body needs the strength to endure sorrows—'

'Mother, I'm doing well—'

Shekhar wants to say, 'I will be with her—'

The sound of Aunt descending the stairwell interrupts this conversation. She is following Shekhar down the steps on her way to the train station.

'Aunt, don't worry—'

'All right, Shekhar. Let's see what God does.' Turning towards Shashi, 'Shashi, did I give birth to you so that this would happen?' her voice trembles again . . . Suddenly, 'Shekhar, did you really try and commit suicide?'

An embarrassed silence . . .

'She was just a little girl when you smashed her forehead with a jug while you were both taking a bath. She lied then, too, to save you and said that she hurt herself—the naughty little imp has been taking your side since the beginning—' There was such pride, such sweetness, in the pain-filled strain in her voice—but he hadn't heard about this before, so he asks, 'When, Aunt?' And he thinks that he's avoided the matter of his suicide—

Aunt begins to narrate, 'When you were very young, the first time—'

The calm of evening, when the cold, accumulating smoke seeps into the soul by way of the eyes; in the room, the light of the lamp glows from where the lantern usually is, and Shekhar is quickly closing all the windows so that the cloudy, moist mass doesn't settle in the room—Shashi is lying there quietly, her eyes are calm; she goes along with Shekhar effortlessly, and he knows—

'Shashi, you are an awful liar.'

'Why?'

'Such a big lie? You didn't tell me a single thing, but you told Aunt that you fell—such a lie! And what was the need—'

Confidently, Shashi says, 'I don't lie.'

'But that wasn't the truth, either—you kept your mouth shut with me, but—'

'Shekhar, I believe that an unnecessary hurt is the greatest lie—what was the point in hurting your aunt even more? And when it comes to them—I don't hold anything against them any more; they don't even matter—'

'And me—'

'You! What do you—you slowly figure things out so why should I have to tell you?'

'You still haven't told me. Tell me honestly, how did you get hurt? Did someone hurt you?'

'I wouldn't have told your aunt either, but when she saw that I couldn't sit up straight and that there was blood in my mouth, I had to tell her—'

'Blood?'

Shashi's tiny laugh was an admission of guilt, 'Getting up and moving around made me vomit and there was blood—'

He suddenly unravels the mystery behind her sitting by the faucet. Completely stupefied, he says, 'And you still stubbornly kept on working'—and then deeply offended—'And you made me eat. Would I have died if I hadn't eaten then—'

Shashi speaks in a voice to calm not only herself but others, too, 'You told me that Baba said that there is a faith that is greater than pain—'

'Yes, why?'

'There is a helplessness that is greater than pain—as big as pain—otherwise life would always lose out in the face of pain.'

The truth of this claim slowly dawns on Shekhar. Thinking it over, he says, 'Yes, I know—' And then insistently and with a little disbelief, 'You are such a liar—a master liar!'

'Are you any less of a liar?'

'Why, what did I do—'

'I understand English, too, Shekhar. I don't know much, but I what I do know, I know well. 'Not dangerous, but irreparable!' She smiles.

Shekhar is stunned into silence . . .

'But Shekhar, I'm not scared. I have the medicines that the doctor prescribed—I have plenty of them—'

'What—'

'Endurance—and courage. Chiefly courage. Shekhar, I will get better and I'll prove it when I can walk outside with you.'

The carriage is racing on. His aunt is headed to the station; Shekhar is going to see her off and is sitting beside her. He doesn't understand it, but his heart overflows with affection for his aunt and he doesn't know how to express it; he wants to hold his aunt's hand until they reach the station—

'Shekhar, will Shashi get better now?'

'Why, Aunt? Why are you afraid—'

'I'm not afraid, Shekhar, I'm asking because you know her mind better than I do. And this is a question of her will—if she has the determination in her mind to get better, she will, and if not, then never. I know her—Shekhar, I have no problem in losing at the hands of my daughter!'

'I have faith that she will get better soon—'

'God willing—Shekhar, you won't do anything stupid again, will you—'

'What do you mean?'

'You've accepted a very important responsibility. You no longer have the right to consider suicide. You never did—life is always given to one as a promise and throwing it away is a betrayal—'

'Aunt, I now have something that I have to do—'

'You always did, Shekhar! You just didn't see it—'

Shekhar becomes depressed all of a sudden and says, 'If I really hadn't come back home that day, then—none of this would have happened!'

'You can't blame yourself like that, Shekhar! And who knows if something even worse might have happened? Shashi might have still waited all night for you—and what happened the next morning would have still happened—because that was going to happen anyway, there was no way to avoid that; Rameshwar told me that—' and suddenly she stopped!

'What did he say, tell me—'

'He said that—it's nothing new, it was just news to have it confirmed, and the marriage was just an excuse to—Shekhar, I've heard and seen so much in these last three days!'

At the station, his aunt says, 'You should go now, Shekhar. You don't have to stay until the train leaves. I've found my seat. I will get back fine—'

'No, Aunt, tell me what happened—'

'You have to get back before it gets dark, that's what I'm trying
to tell you. Don't leave Shashi alone in the dark of evening—it's
a very sad time of day, especially in winter—' Her hand starts
patting Shekhar on the shoulder. Shekhar obeys and bows down
in farewell, and his aunt brushes his hair with her fingers—'Go,
son—' She chokes on her words and Shekhar knows that her
compassionate blessings are not only for him, but for Shashi as
well . . .

*

Evening and morning, morning and evening—if there is any
constant truth in this passing of time it is that Shashi and Shekhar
are together, strung together on the same chain, with the same
plan, the same goal in life, in their work, where encouragement is
the only spring that bursts out into the open—there is definitely
something that has to be done—many things—for Shashi and for
his goals.

'Reformer, you are paying too little attention to society and
too much attention to cooking—decide for yourself, are you a
reformer first or a chef?'

'Why? Like everything else, our culinary arts are also in need
of reform—that is also a tradition—'

'And it is also an opportunity for creative expression—why
not? But the question is which medium you are better suited for—
paper-and-pen or flour-and-rolling pin?'

'When you put it that way, it seems to me that they are exactly
the same. The cook makes the bread, the guest eats it and the head
of the house gets all the praise. The writer writes the book, the
public enjoys it and the publisher gets the profit!'

'I can tell that a little physical discomfort has made your wit
sharper. So are you going to get to work on something or not? I
am not going to let you do any of my chores—'

'I'm going to write. I mean, I have a lot that I have already
written.' Shekhar says this quickly, because although Shashi
appears to be better, she is still not well enough that she could

swear to it! 'But it's not an issue to write about; you know this, the issue is whether anything comes from writing! It's easy enough to make bread, but what happens when no guests come to the untouchable's home?'

'I keep on telling you that religion's power only extends as far as it is still meaningful—otherwise whatever is meaningful wins! If only Brahmins are able to cook good food, that's one thing, but since that's not the case—'

'But there is a conflict between what's tasty and what's healthy, and if—'

'You can't keep thinking such backward things—what is healthy can also be tasty, we will have to strive for that—'

'Shashi, do you think it's worth it if I finish up that article that I wrote for the Reform Society?'

'Definitely, you should finish it. As long as you have the means to, you should write as much as you can—because as long as you are worried about finishing it, it will be a barrier to the rest of your writing—'

'But I will still be worried! Since—'

'Since what? You have three months to write without any worry—you'll be able to finish a book at least—'

'Three months? And what will we eat—rejection slips?'[3] And then, when he suddenly realized Shashi's implication, 'Look, Shashi, I don't want to talk about this. The money that Aunt gave you for your treatment will only be spent on your treatment, not on food for me, and—not for your food either, understand? Work of this sort has a crumbling foundation.'

Tenderly Shashi looks at Shekhar. 'Fine, don't take Aunt's money. Will you take mine?'

Sharply, 'What?'

Shashi gingerly caressed the gold chain around her neck.

'That's all there is—I've left the rest back there. And this is the only piece, so you won't have to say "no" again.'

Shekhar tried to deflect the discussion, 'Fine, if there's nothing left to eat, I'll take it—you can hold on to it as our savings. I'll try and earn something from the things that I've already written.'

But the thought kept nagging at him that it wouldn't be enough, that he would have to write much more if that necklace was to remain where it was, and the necklace was, after all, a gift to Shashi from her mother . . .

He sits next to Shashi on the ground, using the frame of the cot to support his back, and puts the paper on his raised knees in readiness to write . . . Not even worry produced that sense of intensity whose acrid taste makes one dip one's pen and start critiquing; his mind is a shadow screen of experiences, experiences which despite being sweet have become separated from their emotional elements, because Shekhar has become indifferent to himself . . . He sits down to write . . . He wants to write something more creative than criticism; and underneath his incomplete satisfaction are enough remnants of bitter experiences that his creation will come to life, be powerful . . .

And the knowledge: that although Shashi would be completely unsuccessful in offering him any assistance in his concentration, still there would be two eyes staring from above his shoulders on to a blank piece of paper on to which Shekhar would spread his most intimate details . . . Did he have any right to complain about a writer's bitter future when he had already obtained a writer's greatest reward—a discriminating reader who was reading even before anything had been written—and was sending him the strength from her confidence.

But this knowledge was a hindrance—how could he write like that?

Gradually that happiness will also break away, Shekhar; then it will only give you strength if you write . . .

Slowly the isolation came—tenderly but completely . . .

The light became faint; Shekhar began leaning farther down, but when the light grew so dim that it became impossible to see even when he was leaning over, he relaxed his knees and sat up straight by pushing his shoulders and his head back—

He could hear Shashi's breathing clearly, and he became aware that he could feel her warm breath on his shoulders . . . His isolation was swept away in the darkness. Shekhar was overwhelmed by Shashi's proximity and a little embarrassed, 'Have you been reading everything?'

'Shekhar, I won't be around one day, and by then you'll be a famous man and typesetters will stand by your table so that they can snatch your finished pages and take them away. And then I will still be standing behind you and reading—and you won't know it. But if you don't write well I will scream in your ears—'

Shekhar got up to light a candle.

'Shashi, will you sing a song in the darkness, then I will write a little more later, and in the meantime, dinner will be here.' Shashi still isn't eating anything. She drinks a little cold milk and some chemical solution which the doctor prescribed—

He cleaned out the glass case for the candle when the flickering mood in the room became garrulous—

Glow candlelight!
Amble near the mysterious life of the night!

Then abruptly stopping, Shashi said, 'Not today, Shekhar. I will sing tomorrow—'

Shekhar understood, but he didn't want to mention pain then, and he began softly humming the words to Shashi's song. Then he said, 'This isn't a song—'

'Then what is it?'

'It's poetry—Shashi, are these your words?'

'Me—a poet?'

Shekhar lifted the lamp as if he were searching for a place to put it; and he looked at Shashi's face in the fullest brightness that it offered.

That was when the children from the third floor came in and said, 'We got some money today—we'll get paper tomorrow—you will make us kites for sure, won't you?' The boy began looking at Shekhar's face with deep concern.

Shekhar was silent for a moment—it seemed like such a long time ago that he made that promise . . . Then he asked, 'How much money have you got?'

'Four annas—'

'And I have two annas—Father says that girls don't fly kites—so I got a colourful scarf.'

'Don't fly kites?' Then demonstrating that he remembered why, 'Yes, it's true, girls have balloons.'

'Do you know how to make balloons float?' the girl asks in despair.

'Yes, I do—'

In disbelief, the boy says, 'Hmm—don't boys also play with balloons?'

Shekhar laughs. 'If they wear brightly coloured scarves they can.'

Shashi calls the girl over and asks her, 'What is your name?'

'Kusum. And my brother's name is Ved.'

'Vedkumar Nanda—' he says as if he is defending his honour.

'Good, so come and see me before you go out to get your paper tomorrow—'

Shekhar sees the children off to the stairs and then begins pacing around. The kite festival was the day after tomorrow—morning—morning—morning . . .

The special issue on the kite festival had been published, but the editor was not in the office; Shekhar somehow found out where he was and got a hold of him. At first, he didn't recognize him, but after he was reminded he said, 'Were you ever in the military—'

'No—'

'You're very punctual[4]—'

Shekhar swallowed that.

'Whatever leaves-and-flowers we can offer, we always offer promptly—you know, of course, that immediate rewards are extremely miraculous—'

Stiffly, 'Yes, sir.'

'But we'll have to go to the office to settle everything—'

'So I will come with you—'

The editor shrugged his shoulders, 'Let's go then. No time like the present.'

He vacantly flipped through the pages of a notebook and read aloud, 'Sri Chandrashekhar, leaves-and-flowers . . . here you go.' He slowly opened his drawer and extended his hand to show Shekhar—two rupees. And then turning out his pockets, 'At your service—'

For a moment, Shekhar looked at him in disbelief, then he grabbed the money from the editor's hand, and brashly said, 'Thank you.'

When he got to the door he turned around and said, 'Do you write leaves-and-flowers in your ledger?'

'Yes. Why?'

But it wasn't right to insult the editor, so he would need to think calmly . . . With a great deal of restraint, Shekhar said, 'Just because,' and to himself, he repeated the reply that he had wanted to give, 'If you had just put "water" instead, you would have saved a few letters.'

A vessel of water.[5]

When she saw the kites and balloons, Shashi asked, 'Are these for the children?'

'Yes.'

'And did you get anything for yourself?'

'For me? I'm not a child—'

'Go and buy some dye; I will dye a handkerchief for you—you refuse to wear a turban.'

'And what about you?' Shekhar asked this irrepressible question and then shut up. He thought that he would go out in the morning and get some lotus flowers as a gift for Shashi.

'Do you need to bring me up each time?'

'All right. I will get some in the afternoon. No need to get your hands wet in this cold.'

When it was afternoon and the children still hadn't come, Shekhar called out to them, 'Ved! Vedkumar! Kusum!'

A while later, Ved came up wearing a serious expression and stopped at the door to the room.

Shekhar asked, 'Why won't you come inside—don't you want me to make your kites?'

In a pathetic voice, Ved said, 'Mother says I can't.'

'Why—what did she say you couldn't do—'

'She said, "Don't go over there."' Then he looked over at Shashi and said, 'She said boys from respectable homes don't go to such places.'

Shekhar remained speechless. He looked at Shashi from the corner of his eyes and then looked straight ahead.

Ved turned and left slowly.

'Wait, Ved—take this with you.' Shekhar gave him all six kites, the string, the crushed glass and the balloons and said, 'You should give these to Kusum—they will float if you light a candle under them.'

Ved's face lit up for a moment and then deflated. 'Mother won't let me—'

'No. Take them and put them on the roof; buy a few more with your own money and fly them all. Your mother won't say anything if you don't come up here, right?'

Ved left.

Shekhar kept moving around, back and forth, in the room, as if he had something to do.

Shashi said, 'Shekhar, forget about the dye; it would be a waste of time. Sit and write—or come, dictate to me; you can dictate and I will write.'

Shekhar quietly sat down behind her, even though he knew he wouldn't be able to write then; all he could think about was that bouquet of lotus blossoms that he wouldn't buy tomorrow morning . . .

Were Shashi's eyes still over my shoulder at my paper today—even now—as I am filling it with ink and reading just how well I'm doing by the dim light of this lantern in my jail cell? . . . I, who didn't become a famous man, am now standing at the edge of possibility staring into the chasm of non-existence . . . Shashi, I've never heard the sound of your screams in my ears—and I have never been tricked into thinking I heard your voice, not even by a whisper . . . Coming from above my shoulders, I continue to hear the sound of your steady breathing escaping from its source with a delicate, thrilling touch; and I have never written a lie . . .

*

The people whom children from respectable homes are forbidden to visit, those same children carefully watch each step those people take . . . When the sun had fully risen and the sunlight had reached the inner courtyard, Shashi sat at the threshold so that she could look up at the sky and listen to the peals of laughter from the children on the roof, and Shekhar stood leaning against the wall near her. But it suddenly occurred to him that a pair of eyes were watching them from above, and those eyes had the same cold, unblinking, scrutinizing quality that stones or cold-blooded animals had . . . When he stared hard up above, a few hands went up and drew back the hem of a sari or the edge of a scarf; the stony eyes moved away from him and fixed themselves on Shashi. Just once, Ved looked down into the courtyard and then gave a confused look straight ahead and moved away. Shekhar went back into his room and began pacing slowly; a little later, Shashi went inside, too, and lay down.

Much later—well into the afternoon—Shekhar heard Kusum wailing and he went into the courtyard to see. Later a threat quieted the wails, and then Kusum's face appeared above the wall of the balcony and her lips were still trembling from her sobbing, but her unblinking eyes stared down below.

The balloons had been torn up . . .

There were several benefits to living on the fourth floor. The fourth floor could keep the world at bay, but the fourth floor also had a ceiling, and in the winter's sun the ripples from the world down below rose higher and higher . . . Shekhar began to feel that the room which had once been a refuge had now become a prison, and they couldn't stay there any longer. He knew that Shashi felt the same way, but they both acted as if they didn't see it . . .

They couldn't stay there any longer, but could they find any place to live in Lahore—Wouldn't each place be the same—already was the same? But where else—and how?

In his list of potentials, Shekhar had a completely finished manuscript of 'Our Society', 'The History of the Family', 'Society and Politics', a few more essays, three or four stories, his two hands, his determination and—Shashi's loving blessing—the shade of the saptaparni tree.

Again, the same circuit, of publisher after publisher . . . And this time with the mandatory celerity and without the crutch of his principles! That somehow, on whatever conditions, 'Our Society' and 'The History of the Family' bear fruit—not because he wanted the fruit, but because this was the means that he had chosen for that end . . .

But there were far more connective ties in society than he had imagined—wherever he went, he found publishers who were not only familiar with him but also with the history of both books and their faces had a thin, deformed smile which said they knew not only the creation but also their creator . . .

With the last bit of hope in his despair, he went back to the same editor who had given him 'water' and called it 'leaves-and-flowers'—he had decided that getting 'water' was still a big thing!

The editor looked him over from head to toe as if he were assessing an impending disaster and readying himself for it.

'I've brought a few things for you to consider—'

'Well, you've done me a great favour—you can leave them here, and I—'

'Look, it's best to speak plainly. Do you want publishable things or not? I need something in return. And—'

With a suppressed disagreement, 'You must be aware, our newsletter is a newsletter for families—it goes to their homes—'

'So?'

'Our subscribers are middle class.'

'I understand, but—'

'Which is why we also have to pay attention to which writers' names are printed in our newsletter.'

It was no longer possible for Shekhar to take this as merely another indication that he was exposed! He said, 'I understand. You spoke plainly, so thank you. But I am not insisting that you use my name. You can leave it unsigned, use another name, whatever you like.'

A little relieved and a little surprised, 'Oh—good.'

'And if it makes things easier, don't take the stories and poems, just take the articles—these days articles are signed with pseudonyms or are printed anonymously because they are written by the editor himself—'

'Oh—so you want me to take a beating—'

Laughing a little, Shekhar said, 'If something I wrote gets attributed to you, then there is definitely a chance that you might take a beating—'

'Nor does it help me if it gets out that you were the author—'

'Right. But I am giving you complete authority. You can do whatever you want to the manuscript—'

Ultimately, it was decided that the manuscript of 'Our Society' would be turned over to the editor; after revising it, it would be published in parts, and if it appeared that the audience approved, it would be printed as a book—the book would carry the editor's name, not the writer's. The editor had complete freedom to add or subtract, change, publish or not publish. And in exchange for relinquishing all authority, Shekhar would either get 100 rupees two months after the book was printed or sixty rupees immediately; but if he wanted the money immediately, he would have to sign a contract in which all of this would be spelled out.

Witnesses were also deemed necessary for that; finally, the contract was prepared at the place where Shekhar first met the editor, and Shekhar placed his signature on it. When the editor took out the money and began to pay Shekhar, he said, 'You fully understand the implication of the conditions that you have just agreed to, right? You cannot complain later if you disagree with the editorial decisions. I am doing all of this in good faith; you should take some satisfaction from the fact that at least your ideas will be partially published if not in full.'

Shekhar swallowed this bitter pill. The editor continued, 'These days no one works on good faith any more. If tomorrow you begin to wonder why you handed your book over—'

Shekhar couldn't take any more. He said, 'If you're worried that I will want to claim my authorship of the book later, then let me tell you that this is a baseless fear. I don't believe that there will be anything left in the book after it is published that I will want to claim or for which I will be responsible. I've basically thrown the book down a well—and picked up the sixty rupees which were left there.'

The editor kept looking silently at Shekhar's face. One of the two witnesses was a young man, and Shekhar thought that he could see anxiety mixed with sympathy in his face . . . Shekhar folded his hands in farewell and left.

Suddenly a voice called out to him from behind, 'Excuse me—'

Shekhar turned around to look and saw the young man stumbling over himself to talk to him.

The young man looked all around and said, 'My name is Ramakrishna. You remember Vidyabhushan—'

'Which Vidyabhushan? The one who was in jail? He—'

'Yes, that's the one. We went to school together. He wrote to me about you, but why did you sell your manuscript?'

Succinctly, Shekhar said, 'Because it was necessary. But what did Vidyabhushan write to you?'

'You did the right thing. Your words have strength. Vidyabhushan wrote to me that you were very high-minded and that you had talent and determination. The nation has need of genius like yours.'

Shekhar laughed drily and said, 'A very desperate need! And I, of money—'

Ramakrishna said, 'If you were able to help us—'

'In doing what?'

'There are dozens of things. That's why Vidyabhushan wrote about you. He said that because you have an interest in literature, you would be able to assist us in writing and publishing; so I found out where you live because I have connections to people in publishing. But if I have your permission, perhaps I could come to your place to talk—'

'My place is in Gawalmandi on the fourth floor. Please come any time—'

Shekhar gave him his address and explained how to get there.

Ramakrishna spoke again, 'You made a mistake giving up your book. If it was only a question of getting sixty rupees, then perhaps I—we—'

A little curious and a little hesitatingly, Shekhar said, 'Who are "we"? Who are these benefactors who—'

'We have an organization—we help all of our members as much as we are capable of—'

Seeing the light suddenly, Shekhar asked, 'Are you a member of some revolutionary group?'

'You could say that. We are social activists and among ourselves we consider it our duty to help each other—'

'I have never known social activists to be providers of assistance. Where do you find the resources?'

'From somewhere or another—but let's talk more freely at your place—I can come, can't I?'

'Yes, whenever you like.'

'Good. I will come by in a few days—'

Shekhar said goodbye.

Sixty rupees . . . was a significant thing because it could become the means to freedom . . . A means to freedom from the curse of imprisonment in a house where from all four sides—or rather, from every direction—came the coolness of the neighbours and even worse, the bitter cold!—because how could there be freedom without repaying debts or making arrangements for moving on! That tiny corner apartment which easily became a home when it found the shade of the saptaparni tree, shrank just as easily, because it had only known shade and more shade so far, and not suffocation of roots. The books were moved into a chest; the clothes, into a trunk—Shashi didn't have very much yet!—and after he had returned the borrowed bedclothes, he brought back two thick, coarse blankets which could work as a bedroll . . . He had made all the other arrangements; the only thing that remained were the two mattresses because no decision had been reached about where they would go . . . The thought kept nagging at Shekhar that if they were going to move anyway, why not move so far away that the strings of the web all around them here couldn't

reach them; where things could be done peacefully, where Shashi
could get some rest and get better, and where they could find some
meaning to their lives . . . They didn't have any wealth. They were
prepared to start over from nothing. Why start over under the
burden of debt? But he was also afraid at the same time that going
too far might be dangerous for Shashi. A gentle feeling reminded
him that a tree couldn't flourish for long away from its natural
habitat . . . Shashi was determined and she had forbearance,
certainly, but . . . Sometimes he would think that when his nature
and Shashi's circumstances had thrown them into this cyclone
where there was nothing other than spinning around and around,
wandering, and struggle, then why not forget everything and the
two of them could jump head first into this crazy, daring world;
but then his worry about Shashi's health made him reconsider.
And so, withdrawing completely from the outside world, the
friendliness between two lives continued to flourish in the two
parts of the corner room.

Ramakrishna came two days later; he brought someone else
with him. Shekhar took them to the sitting room part of his room
and Shashi hid behind the corner.

Ramakrishna said, 'We wanted to talk to you alone—'

Catching his drift, Shekhar said, 'My sister is more trustworthy
than I am—and she will help me as much as she can—'

'Oh—then we will have to recruit her—we have a shortage of
female volunteers—'

They started talking about work. Shekhar wanted to know so
much about the organization, but at the time the demand to do
something was substantially greater than the need for answers to
his questions in his emotional condition, and when Ramakrishna
said that they wanted to spread disaffection towards the British
within the soldiers of the army so that the soldiers would mutiny
and attempt to liberate India, he immediately agreed to write a
forceful article that would help do that—and he was so excited
that the words were already echoing in his mind's ear . . .

Shashi gave her assent; the appeal was written in a day, and
Ramakrishna came the following day and took it. At the same

time, he gave Shekhar a few old leaflets and the party's programme to read and said, 'Please keep these in a safe place—' meaning, these were proscribed materials.

And so Shekhar stayed on for two more days, and then two more, and then two more—and on the seventh day he went with Ramakrishna for four or five hours to use the duplicator in a house in a narrow alley in the city to get three or four thousand copies of the leaflet he had written.

Afterwards, they decided that Shekhar should stay for a few more days, and if it was impossible for them to live where they were, then Ramakrishna would make other arrangements somewhere in the city. Shekhar thought to himself, 'This is all well and good, but how will we move after the money runs out?' But he couldn't say anything out loud . . .

*

Writing an autobiography is a kind of—it is full of arrogance: that there is something worth narrating, something giftable, worth preserving, memorable . . . It's possible that that's true, but who is an individual to claim this about himself? The mound of straw does not say about itself that there is life-giving grain in its womb—the grain says it when it gives strength to another body . . .

But am I simply writing an autobiography? Is this self-promotion? Doesn't my heart still say, 'You should hide that which is yours, which is essential, which nourished and anointed you!' Don't I still want the things which have given my life importance, because—perhaps—they could be gifts or need protection, to remain my own and take them with me, keep them secret; because publishing means distributing, which can be a share in prosperity, but how can I make shares of myself . . . And still I bare myself enthusiastically, because this is not an autobiography, it is merely an acceptance, a witness, a witness to my soul. 'I belong to myself, but only as much as it means or shares the same grammar of I belong to so-and-so, and so-and-so, and so-and-so'—My worth is in acknowledging this debt, otherwise I am nothing, an accidental aggregate of atoms without reason or consequence!

Shekhar was not a renter in his new 'home', just a guest. Ramakrishna had explained that he couldn't find separate accommodations despite much searching, and moreover it wasn't appropriate to live in places where they might ask too many questions, because that was the most worrying part of their work, so their organization had decided that Shekhar would be given accommodations with a supporter, Shashi and he would both live there, and the food would be prepared at home, and if they wanted, they could eat in their rooms, otherwise they could eat their meals with the family. And they wouldn't have to pay rent for the room; the supporters had given it as their donation to the organization. All Shekhar would have to do was come up with thirty rupees a month for their food . . .

Shekhar gradually realized that he was beginning a new life. His rebellious attitude towards society was just as radical, but because he had been so separate from society it was taking on a new form—a shapeless feeling was transforming into a rebellion—a feeling which he had vaguely felt before, but had become clearer over the ten months spent in jail and had now suddenly become solid having found a relationship with these new comrades—so solid and clear as if it were taking shape . . . Sometimes a terrifying doubt would well up within him that he was becoming a fool again because unconsciously his intellectual hatred was taking on a completely anti-intellectual and crude character which would crush his spirit and reduce it to a substance that would only produce poison, not fire . . . And then sometimes he would think that his completely passionate life had been unfolding on an airy background and would now become solid on a new, firm foundation and would find with truth a greater peace . . .

And so the days passed, and he grew increasingly entangled in the net cast by the underground movement. That entanglement brought satisfaction, contentment and also a secret pride that it was voluntarily careening into the abyss. There was a hope that taking on a danger like that also erased mistakes and so gave life

significance. It was wrong to gamble, but when one knew that the
dice were made of fire and that touching them would burn one's
hands and one still played, then didn't that give some evidence in
support of a person? Shekhar knew that a zealous revolutionary
outlook could be very dangerous because it had the same foundation
supporting it as a sky vine, whose roots were nowhere to be found
and so it has to cannibalize itself—but he also held on to the hope
that because he realized this basic weakness, he wouldn't fall victim
to it, and that his intellect would help him as much as possible and
would fix itself to an empty rampart and fortify it . . .

There was one reality inside this illusory enclave of unreality
that he held on to with unwavering hands—Shashi's love. Beneath
whose suppressed expression was Shekhar's undeterred faith that
her love was unknowable, greater than experience . . . This faith
and this knowledge became such powerful realities that they were
ungraspable—if Shekhar ever started thinking about them, he
would immediately realize that it was the biggest unreality that
was making even the earthly extraterrestrial . . .

Love is like a flowing river—it lacks the quality of constancy.
Just as a river either breaks through any barriers with its internal
force and picks up speed as it flows or creates a new course from
the sediment it is carrying and goes around the barrier, so too does
love either grind down or move forward—or begins to change—
like the flow of a river . . .

And while floating in this profound unreality, Shekhar
gradually understood that there were either barriers or fetters there,
there was something lacking in that unfathomable infinity . . . He
had immersed himself in new work; and he could see that Shashi
was assisting him, that she was continually reading and compiling
the sociological materials that he had abandoned midway through
his studies and advancing them; he took that to mean that both
of them were completely absorbed by what they were doing and
were finding a significance to their lives, and the cement that
would strengthen their significance was their propinquity, their
cooperation and intimacy, their enormous love—this was the
biggest truth in Shekhar's life . . . But sometimes when their eyes

suddenly met, Shekhar felt a vague discontent and irritation and
would look away and the mental picture he had created would
evaporate, and then suddenly he would get exasperated with
himself because he was creating a breach and a doubt in their
perfect existence . . . In order to wash his doubt away, he would
try to get closer to Shashi, and in a few moments of extraordinary
intimacy he would be overtaken by a concern for Shashi's health
and realize that she was still in pain on the inside and that she
was ignoring her injuries because she didn't want to see anything
other than Shekhar, because there was an ever-present danger in
her concentration that if she looked at anything else, everything
would be scattered to the wind—like that cursed female prisoner
of the tower who had to continuously weave (and unweave and
reweave!) to stay alive, and if she ever looked at the reflection of
the outside world in her mirror everything would go dark, dense
and black and be destroyed[6] . . . And as soon as he realized it,
a fiery doubt awoke inside him; and its whiplike sting made his
already confused love even more agitated. He felt as though he
wanted to get even closer to Shashi than would have been possible,
couldn't have been possible, was unthinkable, because it was even
closer than a nerve is to pain . . . the pain of love, or the love of
pain—'Beloved, I cannot bear the pain of your love . . .'

There wasn't too much work involved in writing leaflets and
pamphlets; Shekhar had more than enough time. Gradually he
began to understand that the organization's work didn't stop at
propaganda. Their various activities included weapon gathering,
preparing bombs and all sorts of chemical research, the organization
of secret societies and many more activities . . . The breadth of his
knowledge of the organization's activities was gradually growing,
or was allowed to grow; he went from being a volunteer in the
publishing operation to being something of a co-director, and as a
consequence his knowledge about various areas of work, was seen
as natural for that work . . . And for the work at the heart of
the propaganda, which was the spreading of consciousness and
political discontent among women and students, it was seen as
so natural to ask Shashi to help him, that he never even thought

about it needing a decision; he just did it . . . She began writing a little, too, and helped with the typesetting. A few times she even secretly distributed the leaflets . . . But then (and who knows whose opinion it was) it was decided that such games of hide-and-seek could be played by others, and therefore, as much as possible, Shashi should continue to do only legal work and enter the societies of male and female students to do so . . .

That's exactly what started happening. Shekhar would sometimes go to the societies of male students, because in order to produce effective propaganda, it was important to know something about the intellectual make-up of the people the propaganda was designed to reach, although he wouldn't take part in any of the business. He would do something else. Shashi would go to the meetings of the female students or the women, and upon returning she would tell Shekhar everything that happened, who said what and who gave what response . . . Sometimes her eyes would suddenly glow with enthusiasm, and she would begin to elaborate on the speeches that were made during the meeting; she would be so fully engaged in it that Shekhar was overjoyed and thought that Shashi was happy and content, that she felt no shortage of significance in her life . . . Sometimes he was surprised to learn that Shashi had gone further with her natural, refined intellect than he had gone with his reading, logic and deliberation. And then he would stop and stare at her in bewilderment, and Shashi's ideas and words would echo in the illuminated cavern of his mind . . .

'Our morality is a territorial morality—north India is on this side of the Vindhyas, and on the other side is the southern peninsula—our moral lines are the same. One side is the truth, and on the other side is the wrong . . . And that's why our morals are lifeless; their ultimate standard is not some living truth, but a mere line, a dead and beaten custom . . .

'At the root of these morals is a prohibition, and so they are only negative morals. Let us conduct a review of all of the sacred smritis in the world; let us set aside those parts that are idiosyncratic or different as secondary, and then we will be left with three common aphorisms as our universal ethics—that we be content, speak the

truth and avoid incest. If we go deeper, what do these tell us? They
are three great prohibitions—the first is a prohibition on man's
natural avarice, the second is a prohibition against his natural fear,
and the third is a prohibition against his natural sexual desires!
Why is prohibition the root of all ethics—why can't our morals
be greater, why not instead of repressing our natural tendencies,
make use of them—drink them in, devour them?'

The echo gradually dissipates, and in the stillness after the
echo a hollow sound emerges, and suddenly a tight knot chokes
Shekhar's heart and tells him that all of his moral conclusions have
been based on ignoring a fundamental truth and are therefore
pointless—pointless and inconsequential is the intellect which
leaves no room for the love of pleasure!

Receiving encouragement from Shekhar, Shashi gradually
began attending ever-larger assemblies, in place of the meetings
of the female students, Shashi went to the assemblies of both male
and female students in the college, and then in addition to the
students, the assemblies of the larger public, too. Shekhar wouldn't
go himself; he would wait for the return of an excited Shashi, and
when she did return, the sight of her glowing face would make
him so happy that it was as if he had returned with the spoils
of victory himself . . . In her excitement he found no indication
that would have let him know whether the red, warm glow on
her face was glowing as a result of victory and joy or whether it
was the result of some hidden turmoil; and in his excitement he
didn't take care to notice that the tension in Shashi's voice was
not directly related to the meeting or the significance of the issue
discussed . . . Evening fell and the darkness grew thick. The
isolating feeling of the two rooms was like the suffocating clutches
of gnarled roots, and because of the unusual quiet from Shashi's
room, Shekhar got up and peeped inside and saw Shashi lying
and staring unblinkingly at the ceiling . . . Sometimes he still did
not understand what was happening; and other times he would
be filled with the dread that Shashi was still unwell and that she
might suddenly leave his side and go away—but he could never
think past this point—the hypnotic charms of his work and also of

his love dimmed his ability to see beyond the limits of a particular boundary . . .

In this spellbound foolishness, Shekhar prepared Shashi for a public rally in which there would be several speakers. The current wave of the Non-Cooperation Movement was at its height, and no matter where or what kind of assembly it was, political issues were certain to come up; that was why members of underground organizations began taking part in these assemblies and were able through them to enlarge their circle of influence and increase their membership. Shekhar prepared Shashi to speak about the primary topic of this particular assembly, 'Equal Rights for Women', and decided to go with her, too, because new, related issues could be addressed through the assembly and relationships could be established with like-minded fellow travellers . . .

Shekhar was sitting in one of the back rows on one side of the stage in the assembly, and his mind seemed to be separated into two different planes of existence—one was listening to the speakers and the other was gauging the pulse of the collective audience— the pulse of its collective form as well as the differentiated individuals within it, measuring the extent of its agreement and disagreement . . .

Shashi rose to speak—she slowly moved forward, standing up with a gentle push of the fingers of one hand on the table, and took in the gathered crowd with a quick scan, and then Shashi began speaking.

Shekhar observed everything with a redoubled vigilance and he could tell that as soon as Shashi stepped forward a current of interest and excitement went through the crowd, as if its collective consciousness leaned forward, and at the same time, Shashi shrank in direct proportion and took a few steps back, and her helplessness at having to say something necessary produced a look of dread on her face . . . A slight feeling of pride welled up within him; Shashi was so far above them all despite being surrounded by them, so unattainable! Those whose inner lives are fulfilling, and expansive, can remain detached and aloof from external concerns . . . And

wasn't it this expectation of external fulfilment that was taunting
the audience, wasn't that the attractive force that was drawing
them closer, wasn't it . . .

Shekhar was so absorbed by reading each individual face in
the assembly that he forgot to listen; the waves of Shashi's voice—
strong, calm, but affected by some internal vibration—lapped at
his insides even though he wasn't paying attention, and as long as
the voice continued in that way, Shekhar was reassured and didn't
feel the need to understand the content—

But what was this slightest of tremors in her voice, its heaviness
begins to dissipate, and where had this sharp rebellion come from
to undermine her calm—

'It's easy to take pride in exemplars, the Hindu ideal of
marriage, the obligations of householders, the Hindu ideal of the
faithful wife—but is the water beneath our mossy pride still vital
or has it turned fetid? There are two sides to domestic duties; but
in today's world the man gives nothing, forget companionship,
not even compassion, and woman has become a mere instrument
of man's pleasure; woman is a thing, which can be destroyed in
the fire of his lust whenever he wants, however he wants, wherever
he wants! And there is no appeal[7] for this situation, because if the
woman ever makes a complaint, she gets a firm answer, "Why do
you think people get married?" This is not an ideal, it is the death
of an ideal, a heap of lifeless bones in skin that has been dead
for ages—'

Shekhar thinks Shashi is distant from this assembly but
she is absolutely not distant from her own words—other people
speak from outside the topic or from above it, but it was like a
fire burning inside her—should she have been speaking with such
intensity? But if not, then what was the value of speaking about
it—if you didn't have light to offer, the rest was darkness—

He is startled back into noticing the crowd—the people
weren't listening, they were smirking—and the determination in
Shashi's eyes was scanning the fickle audience—to find somewhere,
something on which it could settle—suddenly, a cackle breaks
out in the audience somewhere and then the whole crowd erupts

in laughter, and the roar is provoked by either a few whistles or Shashi's screaming voice, 'It's fine. This is all that you have to offer. Your ideals, this heartless, stupid insult—'

What had happened to the assembly? And was that really Shashi? No, Shashi, no, there was no point to fighting with the audience, confronting the audience's stupidity was totally stupid, it would only—

When Shekhar saw Shashi's fully flushed face, he jumped on to the stage and began pulling her to get her away from the middle of the uproarious disorder in all directions, but it was as if Shashi didn't recognize him at all and only recognized the audience and her wounded, embarrassed womanhood . . . Somehow, Shekhar pulled her backwards, off the stage, and took her to a room in the back, where he forced her to sit on a chair while he slammed the door facing the stage shut, and when the cacophonous din died down Shashi stood back up, but Shekhar took her outside; he caught a passing tonga and seated Shashi in it and then got in himself. 'Let's go—' he said and answered the 'Where to, mister?' he heard and noticed that Shashi's body was still trembling, just like a bowstring after releasing an arrow . . . he sat perfectly still, and only after they got to their destination and he had paid the tonga-wallah and he had given Shashi his arm for support did he say with gentle concern, 'Shashi—'

It was as if something had broken inside Shashi, she stumbled and Shekhar's supporting arm realized that she had fallen unconscious . . .

As he laid her down in the room, Shekhar could not have imagined that unconsciousness might be a gift from the gods, that they shower down flowers of forgetfulness as their gift of relief from unbearable tension, that the enfeebled body of an individual gets rest in that magic-drenched sleep and on waking, is renewed; as he sprinkled drops of water on Shashi and fanned her face with a notebook, Shekhar couldn't think at all, the external wave of fear suddenly grew into a total panic . . . The empty grip of his fingers seemed to be massaging the bones of nothingness . . .

Shashi suddenly opened her lost eyes; she recognized him and stiffened and said, 'Do you know why they were laughing, Shekhar?' And she lost consciousness again.

That external wave grew until it devoured him. His arms began to flail about in a vain, destructive flurry, the empty grip of his fingers seemed to be grinding the bones of nothingness . . . Shekhar left a glass of water next to Shashi, loosened the clothes that she was wearing, and placed a sheet over her; then he took one look around and went outside—back towards the meeting . . . The audacity of those barbaric animals—they dare to laugh at Shashi, at Shashi, at Shashi's life and all of her efforts . . . How dare they laugh at her right in front of my face—

But when he got back to the meeting place it was already empty. The assembly had dispersed . . . He stood there for a while before he went back; when he got to the street outside, he suddenly heard the sound of someone laughing. When he turned around to look, he saw two suited young gentlemen walking and laughing. He didn't know why or what about, but their laughter stung him; he walked towards them and intentionally shoved them as he walked between them.

'Hey—what do you think you're doing—'

That's all that Shekhar needed! He snapped back a response, 'What about it?' and punched one of the gentlemen. In an instant the two of them were locked in a fight; the gentleman's friend looked on in shock. But when he realized that his friend wouldn't win on his own, he got ready to get involved, but by then a crowd had gathered; the fight didn't continue. People pulled the two apart, and while the two gentlemen started explaining all that had happened, Shekhar stepped back and stared everyone down before he walked away . . . Gradually it dawned on him that he had just done something foolish, but at the same time he felt relaxed, the tension had dissolved . . . He quickened his pace back home, because as the stress of the tension lifted it was replaced by a concern for Shashi.

Shashi had regained consciousness, but when Shekhar touched her he felt her burning up with fever. He placed one hand on Shashi's forehead and sat down by the head of the cot.

'Forgive me, Shekhar—'

'. . .'

'I don't know what happened to me—this must be what they call hysteria.'[8]

'No, hysteria is what I had.' Shekhar laughs a weak laugh. 'I just fought with two gentlemen.'

'When?'

'Just now. While you were—sleeping.'

'Why?'

'If I knew why, it wouldn't be hysteria, right? It's called hysteria because you don't know why. But Shashi, Shashi, Shashi—' Shekhar was at a loss for words. He began caressing Shashi's hair, and when Shashi placed her hand on his he became perfectly still . . .

'I won't make this mistake again, Shashi; it was a false pride that made me want to show off my fortune to other people; without realizing that it's only fortune when a person is complete despite not having anything to show off . . . May your days be pure, Shashi, each moment be pure; Shashi . . .'

*

Delhi . . .

Sometimes on the right, through the curtain of smoke, the bridge across the Yamuna River shimmers, and other times even farther on the right, a tower and the walls of the fort; and sometimes when the fog is thinner, one can see the thin, dark body of the Yamuna wrapped in long robes of sand, and as soon as you cross over, the trees, and an unfinished dome covering a well . . . Shekhar places a pillow under Shashi to lift her up so that she can see the scene outside the window and then stands behind her, waiting for the first break of dawn. Everything that could be seen between the smoke and the fog was new and unfamiliar, but a feeling of amiability arose within him towards that newness, because none of this was Lahore, they had escaped a poisonous circle, and behind the fog there was certainly a new personality that was a friend, a comrade—even if it took a few days to recognize him . . .

There was a history behind their arrival here. What Shekhar had learned about the lives of conspiratorial agents became the basis for a novella that he had just completed that was short on art; its primary purpose was to present that life in a glowing light for society and use that as the foundation to spread critical, revolutionary ideas. The novella was so 'hot' that it couldn't be set to type openly, so it did not even get as far as finding a publisher; but Ramakrishna took the manuscript from him and showed it to a few people and then told Shekhar that they were going to find a way to print and sell it illegally, and a 'sympathizer'[9] had given a substantial sum of money for this very purpose; and also that the book would have to be printed in Lahore so it was best if Shekhar left town just as he wanted to do; and in order to facilitate this, the organization decided that Shekhar should be given 250 rupees from the sum that the sympathizer had given so that he could go elsewhere and find appropriate accommodations. Shekhar decided to go to Delhi because there was a greater possibility that they could live peacefully in a big city, and it would be possible to find a way to earn a living without drawing too much attention to oneself, and on top of that, there was much that he could continue to do for the organization . . . So that Shashi wouldn't have to endure travelling at night, they set out in the morning and reached Delhi by evening; one of the members of the organization had found a house with two and a half rooms at a cheap rent near the Yamuna, and they moved in that night. And the rays of the breaking dawn awakened two visitors and showed them a foggy scene of Delhi and tried to make them intimates . . .

The bank of the Yamuna in Delhi, a fully furnished house with two and a half rooms, 250 rupees in their pockets, an unfamiliar and, therefore, liberal atmosphere, and—the shade of the saptaparni tree . . . If there were gods, then they deserved to be thanked for making this possible, that he could stand in Shashi's loving shade and that he could lose himself in its love . . . and that the growing stain which threatened to wipe out that love had been left behind, and that there was a new atmosphere around them which was sympathetic because it wasn't familiar, and that Shekhar now had an unobstructed chance to resurrect, or at least make her forget the pain of, that part of her life that Shashi had amputated in sacrificing herself . . . . He didn't think he could ever be free of his debt to Shashi, but he still didn't have the freedom to accept humbly whatever was left to be had, and now he would be with Shashi and he would care for her . . .

Shekhar hadn't come to Delhi with any definite plans. There was no worry about finding employment immediately. Although he had made a vague promise that he would definitely maintain some means of steady income, and that as much as possible this work should not bring him into contact (meaning struggle!) with members of his own class, let intellectuals be the kind of people who earn their living by virtue of their intellects and nothing else! He would only make do with the labour his body could perform so that he wouldn't have to bridle the horse of his intellect to the carriage of another's purpose—wouldn't have to kill it.

But what work could he do? Studying in college hadn't prepared him for any manual labour! If he had any skills, then it wasn't because of college, but because he never could completely be collegiate! After much thought and meeting with a few people from the organization, he decided that he would work as a signboard painter[10]—this would allow him to maintain his independence, and it wouldn't take too much upfront capital, and it would allow him to display a little artistic talent, and—if the work got under way, then an income could be made somehow. It was the organization's intention that two or three other individuals could make use of the place, too—they would stay somewhere else at night, and would while away the days at Shekhar's 'workshop' so that no one where they were staying would be suspicious, since they would believe that they went to the workshop during the day and that's how they spent their entire days. If there was no work, they could work on something for the organization; the property for the workshop would be bought at the organization's expense, but Shekhar would have to make arrangements for all the other materials.

Ultimately, they found a room on the top floor of a building on New Street for eighteen rupees a month. Shekhar made a large, colourful sign for the eaves in front of the building and hung it up; and with three more employees, the workshop started working. There wasn't any work, but to keep up the pretence of work, three or four half-painted signboards were scattered throughout the room, a canvas made of thin sacking material was dyed and put up, and canisters and tins of various sizes were strewn about the room. It was winter so it wasn't necessary to get there early in the morning; Shekhar would get there around 11 a.m. and with all of the mannerisms of one who was very busy he would set himself up to paint and make something; his 'employees' would get there a little earlier and would busy themselves with some reading or writing, but then whenever they would hear footsteps, they would abandon their books and notebooks and busy themselves with some 'work' or start smoking a cigarette—but when the footsteps were finally attributed to a sweeper or a wandering ascetic or the man with the tape, then all of them would look at each other from the corner of their eyes and smile, since they had been such fools!

Shekhar would head back home excitedly at 4 or 5 p.m., and would find Shashi, despite having been warned, up and busy doing some chore, and he would stick his nose into anything she was doing and make it impossible for her to get anything done so that she would give up. They had come to an agreement, that each day Shashi would cook a vegetable dish and some bread, and Shekhar would take care of the cleaning and the dishes, but they had an argument about it each day, because Shashi would argue that cooking and cleaning were her jobs, and Shekhar knew that she was a better cook. And then the thick fog rolled in, and then their entire house became separated from the rest of the world, separated by a great distance, still, calm and loving . . . But one could sense a deep sadness in that love, and an insufficient love in that sadness, because of which the two of them felt very close to one another but some unknown hesitation kept pulling them back . . . Shekhar thinks that the cool shade of the saptaparni tree is the answer to that insufficiency, and he doesn't want anything beyond that; but as he thinks this the same insufficiency pricks from the inside and he knows that he wants something which he cannot name, cannot put into words . . . Sometimes Shashi interjects, 'Shekhar, you can't just sit around all day—why don't you start writing again?' And instead of answering her, he would think that was this what Shashi really wanted or did she want to save him from the emptiness she saw in his idleness? He was empty, so although he couldn't see it, couldn't recognize it, couldn't measure it—he couldn't fill himself up . . .

As the day broke, the wilting leaves realized that they had grown too yellow, and a heavy push made them wobble and fall to the earth . . . An absent-minded gust of wind shook the branches and set about shaking the remaining leaves off. The wind wasn't any less cold, but it left one with the mistaken impression that one felt in its fleecy touch the false promise of springtime; the fog lifted, the demon of darkness daily grew slack when it locked claws with the day's energy . . . And customers began appearing at Shekhar's workshop! One day, when they got three orders at the same time, Shekhar set out to work with his three colleagues. On his way home that evening, he bought a piece of cheese and a few tomatoes with his dwindling savings, and as soon as he got home he excitedly went to work cooking—the doctor had said that Shashi should eat tomatoes, fruit and green, leafy vegetables, and that she should avoid getting cold and being damp . . . The next day he would come home with six or seven rupees that he had earned, and that hope had given him the strength to give Shashi the good news today—Shashi was gradually becoming more pliable, and she began accepting everything that he said without any argument, so much so that he would become shocked by her displays of total obedience!—So who knows why he felt that Shashi was sad . . . It wasn't anything new. The tender sadness on Shashi's face was just as peaceful as it was before. Perhaps it was the effect of the mottled colours of the evening in the northern months of January and February . . . But Shekhar quickly learned that Shashi was sad, and she was sad because she kept thinking about him . . . Which is why he suddenly said, 'Shashi, congratulate me! There's finally work in the workshop today.'

Shashi laughed, 'Well, now that is a cause for great celebration. What kind of work is it?'

'Three large signboards—there's some new company opening up, it's advertising for their oils and soaps, and one fifteen-foot board with their name on it.'

'Well done, monsieur painter! This must be your lucky day—brilliant!' Then Shashi's eyes trembled and she stopped and stared at her plate.

'Why, Shashi, what's wrong?'

'Aren't you going to write any more, Shekhar?'

Shekhar stopped dead in his tracks . . . It was true, the colours of a signboard were not the colours of the revolution . . . And the calming atmosphere had given him no impetus and had put him to sleep instead—he wasn't doing anything, had become a mere signboard painter, and an unsuccessful one at that . . .

Embarrassed, he said, 'Why won't I write? I haven't forgotten, Shashi; I will write—'

'No, Shekhar, you aren't doing anything. You are cooking and cleaning and painting signs about oil and soap for me, how have you been able to go on like that for so long?'

Shekhar let down his guard and spoke what was on his mind, 'Shashi, I don't know what I should write about. It used to be that all of the pressure around me made it difficult; to write, but at least that gave me something to write about; and now everything is so peaceful around us, but—tell me, what do you think I should write? There's nothing happening nearby—'

'Shekhar, then why don't you say that there's nothing to write about? And are the events that happen around you the only important things, isn't there anything real in your experiences?'

'What is real about my experiences? All I've ever experienced has been lie after lie—and my experiences are only—'

Shashi pressed on, 'I can't accept that, Shekhar, that you have any shortage of material to write about. You haven't forgotten, you're avoiding it. Is there nothing in what Baba Madansingh said that is worth writing about? Did you learn nothing from Mohsin that you could pass on to others? Was Ramji unworthy, too? There can be bigger experiences than your own, definitely, but I think that if you write about the truths that you have seen, that you have felt in your blood, they will definitely be worth writing down. They don't have to be important things, but the feelings behind the things have to be important, man's ability to comprehend has to be vast—the determination and the courage to take control of the matter. The heat is not in the wood, but in the flame, and if you write about the truth inside you it will certainly have the flame in it—the kind of flame which nothing will be able to withstand and which will wash away the sin of our relationship!'

Shekhar was taken aback by her last words and wanted to object, but Shashi's eyes lit up with a glow that silenced him.

'I can tell that I am becoming an obstacle along your path. But I don't think that this is unavoidable. The day that I can tell that it has become unavoidable, I will—I will—' Suddenly stopping, 'No, Shekhar, forget about everyone else and write about your own personal truth, whatever that is—'

He could tell from the way that Shashi was talking that the matter had gone well beyond the mere issue of his writing. Shekhar tried to laugh it off and said, 'Then I should write your story—a personal truth—'

Shashi didn't even smile, but rather became even more serious and said, 'Yes, when it becomes such a truth, mere truth, which you can look upon dispassionately, then you should write my story—' Suddenly glowing again, 'And it won't be as bad a story, Shekhar!'

Shekhar was dumbfounded.

Shashi got up to wash her hands. Shekhar also got up from the kitchen, crossed the room, went to the balcony facing the Yamuna River and stood and stared at the river—the river's water was hidden under the smoke, but his eyes were fixed on the very spot that would open up in the middle of the smoke just where he should have been!

Shashi also went to the balcony and stood apart from Shekhar.

Shashi was right. When had she ever been wrong? Because everything that she said was gold forged through her own suffering—just like the things that Baba said . . . Shashi was the same age as he was, but she possessed such deep foresight, such unequalled sympathy and such clear intelligence—wisdom! Why didn't Shashi become a leader herself, why was she settling for playing a secondary, supporting and subordinate role in Shekhar's life, and why was she sacrificing and continually erasing herself so that he could move forward? Could he accept such an enormous self-sacrifice? What guarantee was there that whatever came from such great sacrifice would be worthy of it in return? And even if it was, how could he take such valuable things from her . . .

Shekhar turned to look at Shashi. He couldn't make her out in the darkness, all he could see were her unblinking eyes fixed on the Yamuna. Without any explanation, he said, 'Shashi, it won't do to have you keep destroying yourself and for me to go on accepting it without any sense of shame. However important I am, you are fifty times greater—a hundred times greater—and I can't take your sacrifice, I can't, I can't.'

Shashi stared at him in disbelief and then went to him and said, 'Hmm, what are you saying, Shekhar?'

Shekhar took a deep breath and then said, 'I am saying that I am extremely grateful to you, Shashi. I can't tell you how much, and that is why I cannot insult you like this. You want to show me something, but you are wiser than I am, you are cleverer than I am, are more compassionate than I am, and you are throwing it all away—for me?'

Shashi came closer. 'You're asking so I will tell you. Listen. Woman has always sacrificed herself. She possesses wisdom, just as the earth possesses consciousness. But when a seed sprouts, it does so by breaking through the earth; the earth cannot be fruitful on its own. I might be mistaken, but I don't think of it as an insult that women are the means by which the totality of men advance— we are the only means. The earth is the earth, but it is also like the creator. Is there anything wrong if that requires suffering and pain instead of a creative thrill and passion?'

Everything went silent. A silent whir rose from the fog that covered the Yamuna . . .

'I am not wiping myself away—I will have played an equal part in creating the Shekhar that I see before me, which is why there is no question of debts and repayments; it is only your gratitude and your nervousness that are insulting.'

A thicker silence, and then an even more silent whir's even wilder flight—and the bounded waves of sudden light in between the growing whirs and Shashi's closeness, her deep understanding of selflessness—impulsively Shekhar moved forward and kissed Shashi's forehead at the point where her hair met her skin, and then with a touch as delicate as breath, her lips . . .

'No, Shekhar, no, not that—' Her voice suddenly breaking, 'They have already been used!' Shashi quickly moved back as if she had been stung, and when he heard her violent sobbing, he understood what had just happened . . . And that knowledge was like being slapped and losing consciousness, and even when he saw her standing and crying he couldn't move, couldn't speak, he just kept staring unblinkingly at Shashi's blurred face.

'Shekhar—'

'. . .'

'Shekhar, forgive me—but not that . . . You don't realize that there is a part of my life that has already been tainted, and from the touch of a certain man—whose—shadow even I wanted—to save you from . . .'

Very softly, as if he were embarrassed by his own voice, 'Shashi . . .'

'I'm telling you the truth, you don't understand . . . If I could cut it out and throw it away from my life, I would—but I can't . . . I endured him—my marriage as both important and true . . . And I was prepared for the fact that he might erase me, destroy me; but he didn't destroy me, he just amputated me, left me spoiled and threw me away . . . and now . . .'

Shekhar gathered his courage and put one hand on Shashi's shoulder and then he felt her shoulder pull away, but he still managed to say, 'Shashi, don't cry . . .'

Shashi kept on sobbing. Shekhar spoke again, 'You are making yourself upset for no reason—he's not worth it, Shashi . . . He's out of your life—there's no need for remorse—crying over him is—'

Suddenly crying even harder and angrier, Shashi said, 'When did I ever cry over him—I am crying because I loved him . . .'

Night is the incarnation of compassion, the darkness is God's quick cure, capable of dissolving the hurt of all pain . . .

Shashi and Shekhar lay quietly wrapped in the darkness and in their doubled solitude, watching each other's tremors of anguish, not watching but still clearly knowing and therefore comforted in not having watched. Shashi gradually stopped sobbing and slowly groped her way back inside. A little later, Shekhar also went back inside and put out the candle in the kitchen and went and lay down on his blanket . . .

He couldn't see anything in the darkness, but he could clearly see Shashi's suffering . . . He could always see it, but in the darkness he could see more of it than he had ever seen before . . . There was the saptaparni tree, was the shadow of the Coral Jasmine[11] tree, which didn't offer mere solace, it offered energy, fragrance, pleasure, revelation, not merely the past, but the quivering present and the sleepy future, too—which is also why there was a big emptiness inside it that still hadn't been filled . . .

Shekhar saw with unblinking eyes and unmoving gaze . . . Saw . . . Let the gods be shocked if the gods are shocked—but why did that love have to be spoken aloud?

Shekhar, why didn't you realize your destiny right from the beginning?

*

One more thing about dawn in the winter—the same morning fog that gradually went from grey, coppery-red, red and then white, and then a sourceless brightness, and then the lazy first rays of dawn . . . But Shekhar had woken up before the first rays and gone to the window to Shashi's room and with a finger, he cleaned off the dew that had accumulated on it and looked in.

Shashi was still sleeping—from the position she was in, you could tell that she had been up all night and had just recently gone to sleep; her body had curled up like the touch-me-not, but her face leaning on one side of the pillow seemed to be looking up, her lips were slightly opened, and the lock of hair which fell across her face gently swayed with each inhalation and exhalation . . .

Shekhar stood still for a long time and watched her face—he caressed her ever so tenderly with his gaze, just as Shashi's breath touched the loose strands of hair . . . Shashi's eyelids seemed to be transparent, he had realized that before, but now it seemed as if her whole face were transparent—as if quietly suffering all her torments had further cleansed her already pure skin and had given her an internal lustre . . . Shashi's face was not the face of infirmity, and definitely not in this moment of tranquillity—but by looking at her, it was certain that the knowledge of an all-encompassing, bright pain would come quickly—a suffering that would bathe and tremble you like moonlight . . .

'No, no, Shekhar, they have already been used—' Was there anything out there that could use up her face let alone touch it—this glowing face, scrubbed clean by suffering, was untouchable just as no one could touch metal heated to the point of being white-hot—until something just as bright touched it—

But had Shashi's penance really taken her so far away—so impassably, immeasurably far—had her purifying pain become a crystal barrier around her—through which everything could be seen bright and clear, but which made it impossible to touch?

The light inside the fog grew and turned into rays of sunlight; Shekhar drew in a deep breath which immediately transformed into a blessing for Shashi, then he quietly snuck out of the room and readied himself to go to work . . . It was for the best that Shashi was still sleeping and getting her rest and—because who knew, if when she woke up that same thick panic would arise again . . .

The group of painters kept busy working for the majority of the day; the boards were ready. They hadn't even finished drying when the customers came for them that evening, two had already been picked up that day and the third was waiting to be picked up tomorrow—two had already been paid for. Shekhar divided up the money into two portions—one was his and the other was the organization's—the organization had all kinds of expenses for which each member had to make some contribution or another . . . it was customary to give between a fifth to a half of one's earnings . . .

Shekhar returned home with seven rupees in his pocket. This was literally the income from his sweat—it was manual labour, and he was finally able to give something back to the organization, and he was headed home—headed to Shashi—with the fruits of his labour . . . Whom he always loved, but who—but who—Shekhar couldn't find the words, he could only imagine that Shashi had taken the shape of some godhood that contained all of the wonder of life within . . .

But for some reason, he wasn't as excited today coming home with the fruits of his labour as he had been yesterday coming home with the mere prospect of work. And as he got closer to home, he was gripped by some unknown doubt, a vague hesitation . . . Without a doubt, Shashi would be happy, but he was afraid that her joy would depress him, and that Shashi would recognize his dejection and retreat to some impregnable distance . . . And this was the divine form of love—unflinching divinity and unflinching love . . .

He stopped for a moment outside his home and was stunned. Shashi was singing inside—a Punjabi folk song—in the melody of the mountain folk, the kind of melody that captures the desolate emptiness of the mountains, their incomprehensible heights and impassable depths, and which because of the echoing fluidity of Shashi's voice became even more unbearable, as if it were the melody of some cruel, endless separation . . .

Two leaves of a pomegranate tree
They will understand our sorrow
Two stones on a mountainside!
My robe is tattered—

Return, just once,
And see the plight of your fakir!

Shekhar recalled a Greek verse[12] in which the dripping sounds of the tears of a certain sad forest nymph turned into a waterfall whose crashing waters sounded like a pitiable shriek to each passer-by and left them feeling a twinge of her pain—then he slowly went inside . . .

Shashi stopped singing as soon as she heard footsteps; the silence seemed so heavy to Shekhar that he immediately said something to break it, 'Look, I've finally earned my keep today.'

'Really? How much—' Shashi tries to laugh.

'Take it, there's a lot—I didn't keep track. Give me your hand—'

Shekhar takes out the rupees one at a time and puts them in Shashi's hand. When all seven rupees were handed over and he stopped, Shashi teasingly asked, 'And?'

'And what? It was only one day's income.'

Laughing mischievously, 'Is that all? Is that worth asking me to give you my hand?'

A little hurt but still laughing, Shekhar said, 'And, what else—I handed you everything that I had—' And then he choked on the secret meaning of what he had said and stood perfectly still and silent!

His silence betrayed his secret to Shashi. Her face became serious and the hand which she had held out fell to her side, and she slowly turned and went back inside. Shekhar heard the clinking sounds of the money being put down, and then he went to the balcony, too.

Then a desolate feeling filled his mind—his eyes went dark . . . and in that emptiness Shashi's words began to hum slowly—

They will understand our sorrow
Two stones on a mountainside!—
Two stones on a mountainside . . .

What did stones understand of pain—perhaps what this meant was that no one understood pain . . . Two stones on a mountainside . . . But the stones are from the mountains, and they have seen the summits eroded by the unrequited love of endless ice storms, seen the outcry of the wind being frustrated in trying to touch even the smallest shoot of green life on a naked cliff with its blind fingers, which soars ever higher like vanity and crashes to the ground like pride—perhaps stones on a mountainside really could understand pain . . . They will understand our sorrow, two stones on a mountainside . . .

Shashi again stood next to him quietly. Shekhar remembered the evening before; and for an instant he wondered whether the events of that evening would repeat themselves day after day, year after year—inconsequential repetition . . . He still couldn't ask for anything, because the two of them shared a single artery, whether that sharing was the result of a curse of oneness, or whether it was a gift . . .

Shashi had said that he was a creation, and she was an equal partner in that creation . . . But he was a structure, a composition—an endless campaign on life's completed path to nowhere?

'Shekhar, should I go back?'

'Yes—'

'Back—to the place that I was given to—'

Shocked and hurt, Shekhar asked, 'What are you saying, Shashi—Back there! Is that even possible now?'

'Yes. He—had he known how to love, then perhaps it might not be possible, but still, perhaps—it's possible. Gradually—'

'That's not what I asked, Shashi, I am asking you—can you do this now—do you now want to—'

'Oh, me . . . Shekhar, I can see that I am getting in your way, dragging you down. And I won't ever let that happen—it's much easier for me to go back—'

'No, you can't talk like that, Shashi! Forget about me for now—how can you even think about going back?'

'Why? If it helps you, makes things easier for you, then—'

'And does your own soul mean nothing to you? I can't let anything happen which will injure your soul—'

'This won't kill my soul, Shekhar. I can survive there—can live—because I will be saving you—helping you move forward. . . . I am going away from you, Shekhar, because I've been injured, not because I don't know the meaning of love. No woman understands love who cannot give a sister's, wife's, and mother's love at the same time—and I will be able to go on living after I go back because—I will be able to raise you like a mother—you have no idea how necessary that belief is for me—now and always! . . . I will certainly survive. It might be the life of an insect, but a woman can be a firefly, whose stomach contains an endless flame . . .'

Agitatedly, Shekhar said, 'I won't hear a word of this, Shashi. You've lost your mind—you've become a mental case.[13] You—' and then finding the word and filling out its absence with emotion, 'have become a wretched Hindu—a suffering-and-calling-it-penance Hindu! But I can't let you destroy your soul—and besides, such foolishness can be committed by two people, too.'

Shekhar noticed that Shashi was crying quietly. Becoming stern for some reason, Shekhar said, 'Shashi, should your suffering help me become something, then I say to hell with that! Your—'

'You don't understand, Shekhar. You think that I am prolonging my agony. Do you think that I want to go back there? But I am not speaking of love, because—I can't speak its name—more love than you can imagine, Shekhar!'

Shashi went back inside, leaving him there wounded and speechless, and after a little while Shekhar could hear the muffled sounds of her sobbing . . .

Was Shashi right? And if Shashi was dragging him down then what else could lift him up, that might save him from descending into the seventh circle of hell? And then the matter of being an amputee—wasn't it the cold heartlessness inside Shashi that made her an amputee, which had tied her own life into a knot and never allowed it to be untied—was it one's duty to quietly accept that knot, wasn't one obligated to untie it, release the bound life within and rebel? If life was a gift—if life had any meaning, then it was one's duty to keep it floating, to accept its drowning by virtue of

a submissive fatalism was to be indifferent to life and to commit a
sin . . . Defeat was a lie, the defeated were the only lies, for where is
the blemish on the spirit of the undefeated? Shashi is wounded, but
isn't the depression that tells her that her life has been despoiled
the same depression that is proof that her life hasn't given up its
fight yet—and therefore also hasn't been despoiled, is unhurt and
unbowed. No, Shashi's defeat is not to be borne, it won't do to let
her waste away like that—if she won't fight for herself, she will
have to be fought for—

Shekhar went to Shashi and said, 'Listen, I need to tell you
something.'

Shashi turned her tear-stained face towards him to look at
him once and said, 'No.'

Shekhar held her head with both hands and stared directly
into her eyes, and slowly emphasizing each word he said, 'You will
not go anywhere, and—you won't be defeated, and—you won't
be afraid.' And then without loosening his grip, he bent forward
and touched Shashi's lips with his own. Shashi's head pulled back,
her entire body was shaking, and her eyes were closed. Lifting her
head, Shekhar looked at Shashi's closed, wet, trembling eyelids
and leaned in once again and kissed her on the lips. Her lips were
trembling, salty from her tears . . .

Then Shekhar let go of her head and left Shashi's room. He
lit a candle, went into the kitchen, and began cleaning up the
pots and pans . . . The porridge of rice and lentils was ready in a
short time, the milk that had arrived earlier had been heated up,
and then he went in front of the door to Shashi's room and said,
'Shashi, get up. Dinner's ready. Wash up.'

A steady, controlled voice from inside said, 'I'm coming.'

The calmness of the voice reassured Shekhar. Perhaps life
hadn't become impossible yet . . .

They say that lust is transient and that love is immortal. I can't
say whether there has been inversion of meaning between the two,
but if this is what they say, then they are completely wrong! Love
only lives once; it only comes once and when it dies it dies forever,
it is not reborn. Lust is immortal, it can die from being frustrated,

or from being sated, like the slain-but-unslain demon Raktabeej[14] that finds a new life and rises again . . .

Education, civilization, tradition . . . We raise all of them above us; we remove them from the bounds of our personalities and establish them on a plane of a higher, greater existence, from the smallest plane to the plane of universal feelings.

But tradition and education are such enormous knots in human lives! Because anyone who is educated, who can detect the tiniest tremor in a life of refinement (those tremors that are deeper than those of common civility), they immediately realize in the most important moments in life—in moments of love or of great emotional upheaval—that they are incomplete, lacking an engrossing, encircling movement, that they only possess a strange, disconnected indifference—a kind of separation from their own feelings, that makes of the doer a spectator and a critic—meaning, it exiles one from one's own personality . . . We create an image in our imaginations that there is a lover (or a beloved) whose heart beats (or can beat) with the great pulse of our very souls; who can be a companion not just for our physical and social existences, but can also share in our vulnerabilities and our extremely personal, unique feelings—share with us in art, in poetry, in song, and even in our experiences of joy and sorrow . . . But in reality, we find that love means that no matter where and no matter when, we are only unable to dissolve ourselves into one or another or any other person . . . There can be intimacy, there can be a relationship, a relationship of incredible unity, but we always discover that the relationship is a kind of subservience, a dependence on something external to our beings—to an image, to an idea, to a poem, to a song, to a sound, to a sweet dream, which despite being our own can never really belong to us because we are not alone, we are the sloughed-off skin, crowned with education, and refined and civilized, of that original and endless 'we' . . .

The days were peerless and the flowing fragrance of the acacia blossoms gave the wind a tenderness in which various other scents yawned and stretched their limbs . . . The violent torment that had plagued Shashi previously had quieted down; she was calm, and Shekhar felt that there was nothing else in the world except their intimacy—or rather nothing valuable, and that intimacy was both prosperity and happiness . . . But if you cut this plane of consciousness at an angle, you could see a cross section which said there is work to do, that the individual owes a debt to the collective, that there was failure and frustration and therefore rebellions, that there were entanglements and knots and ropes and chains and therefore revolutions; and there was a third cross section in which he was a miser who wanted nothing more than to hoard his wealth, which was fading away by itself, in which Shashi was calm but was being washed away, and one day would be completely gone . . . And the various torments of life that had been divided up between these various planes, suddenly burst within him, all the chains begin to bite into him, he wants nothing more than for all the entanglements to be sundered, even if that means cutting off a part of himself with it . . . Then he thinks, these agonies are the consequence of the dissatisfactions within him; then he prays for that rebellious spirit to be snuffed out, torn to shreds, so that he can let himself become a tamed prisoner—not just bound and obedient, but willingly and dispassionately bound—so that he could forget the incessant, fiery, stirring, impatient explosion of rebelliousness . . . It is the flame's duty to reach higher, but that knowledge gives it no satisfaction when it can neither destroy everything nor devour everything . . .

Had he been an illiterate yokel, had he been an animal—had he been anything where he could have found completion, could have drowned, unhesitatingly, completely . . .

*

Work steadily came into the 'painters' workshop', and there was some improvement in income, too. The way Shekhar was living, he could easily manage his expenses within his income—or rather with the half of the income that was his. He had decided before coming to Delhi that he would become a hermit rather than meet with people, because he didn't want Shashi to be insulted again and have to leave town; and because of the political unrest these days, the two of them remained even more aloof socially—the members of the organization had stopped coming by to meet them as much as was possible and even then, they only met with a select few 'sympathizers'; contact was made through them as was the passing on of a few confidential documents and donations would be sent back through these very people. That was why Shekhar never had to spend anything on 'social expenses'. He also didn't have any special hobbies and when it came to entertainment, he never did care much for the cinema or the theatre—neither did Shashi.

But on the other hand, Shashi's health worsened. She didn't say anything, but Shekhar could see it on her face that she was suffering terribly. He would try as much as possible to follow and make Shashi follow the doctor's orders, and he didn't have much trouble doing that, because surprisingly Shashi was becoming increasingly agreeable and obedient. But still her body was gradually getting weaker, and sometimes the pain would be so great that she would suddenly close her eyes and become so still that Shekhar wondered whether she became unconscious each time it happened. He took Shashi to see a very famous doctor. He examined her and asked her about her medical history; he repeated the previous instructions and then said that they had to be very careful because of her kidneys, and he also advised them to get an X-ray of her abdomen. He prescribed three or four medicines, too . . . They took the X-ray despite Shashi's objections and had it sent to the doctor; when Shekhar took Shashi back to see the doctor, he stared at the plates of the X-ray for a long time and then said, gravely, 'Hmm, I am still worried . . . but let's see—' and he began to explain why it was so important to keep her back from getting cold or damp, and complete rest, and psychological calm, and fruits and soft vegetables, and the avoidance of any kind of stress . . .

All of these things were expensive . . . So that Shashi wouldn't have to worry about any of it, he would get up early every morning, make the necessary arrangements, and go for a walk to clear his

mind and let go of his worries, so that when he got home his
mind would be refreshed . . . He would walk up and down Bela
Road near the edge of the river, and sometimes he would turn
into the fields. One day while crossing through a field he picked
a few tomatoes from an especially large plant and brought them
home with him; the next day, without thinking of a special plan,
he wrapped himself in a shawl when he set out for his walk . . .
He walked along the edges of fields of vegetables, and each day
he would pick something from a new spot, sometimes he'd pick
tomatoes, sometimes a nice head of cabbage or dig up a few turnips
and hide them under his shawl, and he'd keep on walking; then
when he got home, he'd cook the vegetables for Shashi and after
feeding her, he would eat and leave for work . . . He never thought
about the fact that this was stealing; it was enough for him to think
that Shashi got her vegetables and whatever money was saved this
way could be spent on getting her medicines. Except for one day,
after he had picked a head of cabbage and had hidden it in his
shawl, he heard the sound of footsteps and it startled him and
scared him a little; when he thought about that fear he realized
that he knew he was doing something immoral; but how much
damage could he possibly be doing to anyone? The birds and the
wandering cattle would probably have eaten just as much—and
what could the loss of a few heads of cabbage mean to such a large
farm, and the tomatoes would have become bruised on the way to
market anyway—he placated his conscience with such ridiculous
arguments.

But there was no significant change in Shashi's condition; the
doctor advised a diet of only fruit juices, and Shashi's translucent
skin became even more clean and lustrous, and her eyes seemed
bigger; each day, when Shekhar came home from work, Shashi
was becoming increasingly agitated to see him . . . When he would
come home, Shekhar's heart would immediately melt from this
eager expectation and such a loving welcome—Shashi's mere
presence changed the world so greatly . . . Along with the painting
jobs at the workshop, Shekhar was handed even more work—his
organization had decided to expand its influence during these days

of political unrest, and so Shekhar was asked to write an 'appeal'[15] or a pamphlet on something or another each day. He also discovered that his colleagues were hatching a plan to free some of their more important comrades by storming the jail, and he was given a job to write as part of that plan. He was soon given a pistol, too. All of these things made him constantly nervous and his mind would race with all sorts of questions, doubts and worries; but as soon as he went home and saw Shashi's face, these unnecessary, worthless and trivial dried-up leaves would fall from their branches and all that would remain was the cool, jasmine-scented sky—the sky of Shashi's eyes . . .

Sometimes he couldn't speak. He would put a sitting-up Shashi to bed and sit near the head of the cot and gently pat her forehead. He would get annoyed with the burden of having to get up to do the chores, light the fire and do the cooking; he would start to wonder whether it was necessary to eat; for Shashi, making fruit juice or warming up milk took very little time, but he would manage without or would eat leftovers—from now on, he would only cook once a day . . . Sometimes Shashi would say, 'Shekhar, you don't seem happy. What's the matter?' and then he would be secretly moved . . . As he patted Shashi's forehead, it was as if the beat made her breath echo with the sound of some melancholy tune. Shekhar's mind would again be full of those same entanglements and worries, and sometimes these thoughts would come to his lips, and Shekhar would softly begin to tell Shashi what was on his mind and she would quietly listen . . .

One day Shekhar suddenly received word that one of his 'colleagues' had run away from a town in Uttar Pradesh and was a conspirator with a reward on his head. He had been identified by the police in the city, and so it was possible that the police traced him back to the 'workshop' and so he had to remain extremely vigilant. That was the day when the collaboration of the three colleagues ended—two of them left for somewhere that very day—Shekhar later learned that they had gone to Kanpur—and the third, who had been recognized in the city, was going to stay with Shekhar for a few days since it was decided that it wasn't possible or good for him to leave immediately but that he would leave town as soon as it was possible. Shekhar came home early that afternoon—he had been told that a guest would arrive sometime around 3 p.m. so that he didn't have to cross the city with him.

Shashi would be pleased that he was coming home early—the presence of the guest for two or three days would pose a problem for their closeness. When Shekhar came home with these two opposing ideas in his head, Shashi was surprised and quickly gathered up the pages that were scattered in front of her. She asked, 'Why so early today—'

'What were you writing—are you writing a book in secret? I didn't even know—'

'It's nothing. I was writing a letter—'

'Such a long letter? On whom are you showering so much affection—'

Shekhar had wanted to tease her, but when he saw the nervous expression on her face he fell silent. He also noticed that Shashi's face was unusually sallow, and she clearly looked exhausted . . . An idea flashed across his mind like a shadow, and he thought that she might have been writing a letter to Rameshwar—because if it were a letter to her mother why would she have hidden it; but who knows, she might have been hiding it because she was writing about Shekhar—whatever it was . . . He said, 'Things just fell into place so that I could come home earlier. We're going to have a guest.'

'A guest—here? Who?'

'It's someone. And Shashi, he's a very nervous character—he didn't come with me. He said that I should go and check with you first, otherwise he would be worried, and that he would be embarrassed if I introduced you to him face-to-face for the first time.'

'Then of course not. But tell me who he is? If he's that worried you can put him up on the ledge above the stairs—then he won't have to see me face-to-face!'

Shekhar burst into laughter. Then he told Shashi the whole story.

Concerned, Shashi asked, 'He's a suspect—so the police could come here, too, couldn't they?'

'Yes. I don't expect them to, but it is possible—why, are you afraid?'

Shrugging it off, Shashi said, 'No, what's there to be afraid of—' But then Shekhar's mind turned to the possibility that if the police really did come, they might arrest him along with their guest, and then Shashi would be alone . . . This concern gave the whole issue of hospitality a new twist. Shekhar fell silent. Then after a little while, he said, 'Shashi, let's not think about it—hurry up and let's get things readied.'

'What do we need to get ready?'

'First you need to lie down and then you can be impressed by how skilled I am at everything around here!'

After they finished their discussion, they decided that the guest and Shekhar would both sleep on the floor in Shekhar's room—if the guest wouldn't agree to taking Shekhar's cot and letting Shekhar sleep on the floor by himself. Shashi insisted that she could sleep on the floor and that they could take her cot, but she didn't really press the issue. The guest would bring his own bedding—if he didn't, they would borrow some from someone. They would work out details about food after he arrived—it was possible that he would eat elsewhere. After they had decided all of these things, Shashi laughed and asked, 'So what do we need to get ready?'

It turned out that there was only one thing to arrange, and that was to move the books and notebooks from Shekhar's room into Shashi's, and to take a small table from there and move it into Shekhar's room where it would do the work of a table, a place to have tea and a desk . . .

The guest arrived and settled in. He brought bedding for himself, but he had no other luggage. They learned that he would eat dinner with them, but they shouldn't wait for him during daytime; he would be wandering around town making arrangements to leave Delhi and would eat whenever he got a chance . . .

He went to bed very early after dinner. The next day, when Shekhar woke up, he saw him ready to go out. He said that he would be back in the evening and then left. As he was leaving, Shashi quickly said, 'Look, if you are staying out all day because you are worried that I am here all by myself, then let me reassure you that I have no problem with that; you can stay here throughout the day. I won't be able to host you properly, for which I am definitely sorry. But I don't have Shekhar's permission—'

Shekhar added, 'Yes, it isn't really because of that is it—'

The guest quickly blurted out, 'I was a little anxious, but—' and then he looked at Shashi, 'I'm grateful to you. If it makes sense for me to come back here, then I won't hesitate any more.'

Shekhar was alone in the workshop. He became busy with the job as soon as he received it, but his mind was not in it; the image of Shashi's exhausted, yellowish face appeared to him, and again and again he would think that both Shashi's problem and his were merely internal, but also external, not merely about spiritual love, but also about worldly life; and not only that, but also that the problem was not merely theirs, but belonged to the whole collectivity of life that knew them . . . And going further, that it wasn't just their love, but all love—mere love—was basically one problem and it didn't end with two individuals . . . There were so many sayings—durable and flimsy, crude and nuanced, straightforward and indirect—that were tangled up in this problem and made it overwhelming . . . The real problem was compatibility; love is an attraction, a force, that moves life out of its inertia, and it is this movement that is the source of the problem because it is pervasive, and fundamental, on the edge of life's dagger—on countless edges!—it upsets an established balance . . . The problem persists as long as an equally compatible object is not found . . . It is a problem and an accomplishment, and a penance . . . And after getting this far in his investigation of the problem, his mind would return to Shashi's jaundiced face and there would immediately be smaller issues to attach to the knot of this very large issue . . .

He hurriedly closed up shop a few minutes before 5 p.m. and went home. The days had grown quite long. By the time he got home these days, it was already time to put out the mat and the pillow on the balcony for Shashi, bring her out and stand next to her waiting for the water of the Yamuna to turn red . . .

When he was still at some distance from his home, he saw Shashi standing at the door, watching the road and waiting for him. When she recognized him, she immediately went back inside and sat down on the cot. Shekhar came in and asked her, 'What's the matter, Shashi?'

'Nothing—'

'Is something bothering you?'

'Not at all; I'm quite well.'

'You were standing outside just a moment ago—I saw you—'

'Oh, that was just because. I was wondering when you were going to come and whether it might be very late—'

'Why?' As soon as he said it, Shekhar realized that she was worried because the guest was in the house. After a while, he said, 'I will start coming home earlier from now on—'

'No, you have work to do. Unless you would be coming home to write something—'

As if revealing a secret, Shekhar said, 'I've been writing a little at the workshop—I didn't have anything else to do—'

Shashi became slightly excited, 'Really—you didn't tell me!' She paused. 'Why don't you bring it back here—you could finish it up quickly—'

'No, Shashi. I won't write here any more. I don't want to do anything when I am with you—not even write. I can't concentrate—'

Quietly, Shashi said—'Crazy!' And then she was silent.

The guest arrived a short while later. He came inside and carefully closed the door. Then he looked at Shekhar and said, 'It's good that you're here.'

He went into the room, took out a couple of bundles[16] from underneath his coat, put them on the cot and then sat down. He said to Shekhar, 'I think that you should lock the door.' After Shekhar had done so, he slowly began to unpack the bundles. At the same time, he said, 'I've almost completed the arrangements to leave town. I will leave in the morning the day after tomorrow—if nothing happens in the meantime. But there's something important that I have to do tomorrow—and I will need your help. I have to evaluate these—'

Shekhar looked. There were three pistols in one of the bundles, and two revolvers of different sizes in the other, and the third had bullets of various calibres. Taken aback, Shekhar managed, 'What will I have to do—'

Caressing one of the revolvers with his hand, the guest said, 'This is my faithful companion—I know this one well. The rest are new. They have to be tested. We'll find some place near the bank of the Yamuna to do it. It will be safer there. But we will still need a "lookout",[17] so—'

Shekhar understood. 'When will we leave?'

'Can you come in the afternoon?'

'Fine.'

After dinner, the guest excused himself and went to bed early. Shekhar lay down but was distracted and wide awake, and then when he found it impossible to sleep he got up to see if Shashi hadn't gone to sleep so that he could sit with her. But there was a light on in Shashi's room—he went inside. Shashi was lying down quietly, staring at the ceiling. Next to her cot were an inkwell and a pen, and next to the head of the cot were a few pieces of paper—

'Were you going to write something? Let me write for you—'

'No, they are just there in case I remember something—I have become very forgetful.'

Shekhar looked at her critically, and asked, 'Are you sleepy? Can I sit with you for a while—'

Shashi gathered up the blanket on one side of the cot to clear a space.

'I'll sit here, by the head of the cot,' Shekhar said and then moved towards the pillow.

'No, I can't see you there. Sit in front.'

Shekhar sat down near her arm.

He had come looking for company, and he had certainly found it, but it was a mute companionship! He didn't say anything and neither did Shashi, and now she had even closed her eyes.

'Are you going to sleep?'

'No, I can't with the light on—' And then silence . . .

To continue the conversation, Shekhar said, 'There's no news from Aunt—who knows how she's doing or what she's been thinking . . .'

'We haven't written to her either—does she have our address?'

'We've only given her the address to the post office. I've contacted the post office and given them our information, but we haven't received any mail.'

'It's probably right. What would she write, anyway—I've broken her . . .'

Shekhar gently put one hand on her arm.

'I've been thinking that I should write to Gaura and ask her to send us news regularly. She could do it—she's older now and understands things.' And then as if following up on some unspoken thought, 'She idolizes you.'

'Me—why?'

'Ever since you went to jail. She doesn't say anything, but she thinks a lot.' And then silence descends. Suddenly Shashi asks, 'What were you doing in there behind locked doors?'

'Nothing—he's leaving the day after tomorrow.'

'Is that why you locked the door? Keeping secrets in your room? And there are still two days to go—'

He paused for a moment and then told her everything. 'Shashi, he's probably thinking about keeping you safe—he's hiding pistols and the like.'

'Why did he bring pistols?'

'He keeps them with him—he could have need for them.'

After a little while, 'When is he leaving the day after tomorrow?'

'At dawn.'

'How?'

'I don't know—he'll leave from here. It didn't seem right to ask Brother—the fewer insignificant details we know the better—'

'Hmm.'

The conversation topic ended.

'Shekhar, do you ever carry a pistol when you are in trouble?'

'. . .'

'It doesn't seem right to me that one should be prepared to kill someone at any time just because one could be in danger . . .'

'Those are the rules of war—'

'Is war a good thing? But there's also a difference—war is an exceptional thing, and a person knows that as soon as it is over he will return to an ordinary, peaceful life. But this is a matter of daily life in the city—for everyone to be armed and ready to kill anyone at any moment—'

'Why—only our enemies have something to fear—it's not like you or I are in any serious danger? And if you want to talk about exceptional times—'

'That's fine. I'm not saying that they will kill anyone, but it must have a damaging effect on someone's psyche—it can't be good for any man.'

'Perhaps he would say that he pays the price for his plans with his life. If it's an expensive transaction, then it's one that only he has to pay, and he's willing to pay it.'

'All right, let it go—when are you going tomorrow?'

'Where—to the workshop? Same time—'

There was silence again and it lasted for a long time. Shekhar began getting up very slowly but it made Shashi suddenly open her eyes. Before she could say anything, Shekhar said, 'No, I won't leave yet—' He got up and blew out the candle and then came back and sat by her head. He put one hand on Shashi's forehead. Shashi closed her eyes.

From a distance came the muffled cry of a man guarding a field somewhere. A little later, the laughter of jackals and from the north the barking of dogs, and then the violent screams of some aquatic animal twice or thrice, and then a silence in which the internal quiet of the darkness echoed . . .

Shashi had perhaps fallen asleep—she never slept straight, always turned to one side or another with her legs pulled in. She was sleeping like that now. Shekhar's hand wasn't on her forehead, but just above her ear, and the hand above her ear could feel the gentle pulse of Shashi's veins . . .

Suddenly, Shashi called out, 'Shekhar!' She took his hand—Shekhar responded calmingly, 'What is it, you've woken up—' Shashi didn't respond. She kept a hold of his hand and pulled it over her mouth and she slowly moved his fingers across her perfectly still lips . . . After a while, she let go of his hand and said, 'Shekhar, you should go to sleep now. It's late. I just woke up for no reason. I'll go back to sleep soon.'

Then she became perfectly still, which is when Shekhar got up. He leaned down close to Shashi's face as if to smell Shashi's hair and then walking softly, he returned to his room.

The first thing in the morning, a young man came and asked, 'Where is Brother—'

'Brother who?' Shekhar said drily. In the meantime, the guest entered and said, 'Oh—good. Shekhar, he's come for me.'

Brother kept his revolver and bullets and gave the remaining firearms to the young man and gave him some instructions and then sent him off. Then he left, too, but as he was leaving he said to Shekhar, 'Be ready this afternoon—'

At first Shekhar had thought that he wouldn't say anything to Shashi, but she would ask questions if he came home early that afternoon and then left again, and it was better to explain things sooner rather than later. He came to that decision and told Shashi that he would be back in the afternoon because he had to go somewhere with Brother.

'Where? To do what?'

'Somewhere on the other side of the Yamuna. I don't know why.'

'You mean, you didn't ask?'

'No, Shashi; I really don't know what he wants me to do.'

Shekhar came home earlier than necessary that afternoon and waited for Brother.

Brother didn't come. Around 3 p.m., the young man from the morning arrived and said, 'Brother wants you to come to him. He can't come here now.'

Shekhar quietly got ready and went with him. As he was leaving, Shashi asked, 'When will you be back?'

Shekhar estimated, 'I'll be back before it gets dark—don't worry.' And he left.

Both of them crossed the bridge and stood on the other bank of the river. After they passed one village and had walked a mile, they found Brother in a thicket of reeds. As soon as he saw them, he asked the young man, 'All clear?'[18]

'I believe that we are fine. I saw someone on the bridge, but everything seems to be fine here.'

Beyond the thicket was a sandy slope that made something of a dry trench, and beyond that was higher ground. In the trench, a person could remain unseen from all directions, and it was as if the sandy walls on both sides had been especially made for target practice. The thin course of the Yamuna was on one side—and it shocked Shekhar to realize that his house was directly across on the other side of the river.

Shekhar was given the task of keeping watch on one side; the young man on the other. Brother went into the trench. A little later they heard gunfire; and then at short intervals, the sounds of single and double rounds, some loud and crackling, some serious . . .

Brother returned in a little while; he said, 'Everything works. But some of the cartridges are old—they might let us down.'

The three headed back. But when they got to the road, Brother stopped unexpectedly. Shekhar saw a khaki-coloured truck coming from the bridge carrying several police officers. The truck didn't stop, it was slowly moving towards Shahadara, but Brother said, 'Something smells fishy,' and they made a big loop and came back to the clearing. Shekhar and the young man followed behind.

There was another path out of the clearing. That's the one that Brother took.

'Where does this go?'

'It must go back towards some settlement or another—it's not as though we can wait here until evening.'

Shekhar wanted to ask why they had to wait until evening, and what would happen next, but he left everything to Brother and remained quiet. After they had gone about three miles, they came to a village; the sun was about to set, so Brother felt it pointless to go into the village and they went around it.

'Shekhar, do you know how to swim?'

'Yes, more or less. Why?'

'We'll cross the Yamuna from over here somewhere—the bridge will be dangerous.'

'All right, the river shouldn't be too high now—perhaps we won't even have to swim—'

'That would be great, but if we have to—and we have to protect these things from the water, now, don't we—but I will take care of that. I know how to swim with my hands above water. How far do you think the river is?'

'About a mile—two miles by road.'

'Why bother with the road. We'll cut straight through here—'

'It looks like there are canals in between—it will be muddy—'

A doubting 'hmm' from Brother who turned and walked around a field.

From the edge of the field in front of them, a young peasant girl was walking towards them; she had a bundle on her head that she held one arm up to support but her arm didn't touch the bundle; it swayed with her gait, and the girl was gently humming a song.

Brother stopped for a moment to ask, 'How far is the Yamuna?'

The girl was taken aback. 'Eh—Jamanaji? Turn around and walk straight in the other direction. It will be about two or three miles. Why are you going this way—'

'Can't we get there this way?'

'No.'

Shekhar asked, 'Can't we go this way—if we can save some time—'

The girl looked at Shekhar once and then once again, carefully observing Brother from head to toe. Then she turned to face Shekhar and said, 'It's muddy. And there are some steep hills. You'll be fine, but I don't know about fatso over here.'

Shekhar was stunned. Brother was definitely heavyset, but Shekhar didn't know if he had ever had anyone so frankly critique his body before. He graciously smiled at her sidelong glance and said, 'Daughter, time makes everything possible, watch—' and he walked on.

As the girl walked on, she said, 'You'll get stuck!' and she burst out laughing as if she were imagining the situation.

The three of them walked towards the canals. When the sand began to give under their feet they took off their shoes and held them in their hands. The mud really was as bad as a swamp . . . The sun had set; the embankments of the canal in front of them were barely visible and the evening wind made the tamarisk bushes rustle . . .

When the embankment was directly in front of them, Brother thoughtfully said, 'I walked more than sixty miles at one stretch and the girl calls me fatso!'—then laughing a little,—'I have indeed become a little fat.' And as if to challenge the stigma the girl had given him, he began climbing first . . .

From the top, they could see the Yamuna; lamps had been lit on the other side. Shekhar suddenly became very worried about Shashi . . . Even after they crossed the river, he still had another two miles to go . . .

Brother said, 'Shekhar, I'm going to take a detour through somewhere and be back,' and when he gave him permission to go straight back home, Shekhar was not only happy, he was grateful—because now he could walk faster and get home sooner, and he could ask for Shashi's forgiveness before anyone else arrived . . .

Shekhar didn't look up as he began walking faster—whenever he found an empty stretch of road, he would run for a little while and then walk again . . . As soon as he set foot on the threshold of his home he lifted his head because someone was standing still in the darkness—Shashi . . . She had lifted the edge of her sari to cover her mouth and nose and all one could see were her eyes . . .

Shekhar's heart began pounding. Without saying a word, he encircled Shashi with one arm and pushed until he got her back inside—Shashi was trembling from the cold . . . Just as he was sitting her down on the bed, it seemed to him that Shashi cried two tears—there was no lamp lit inside the house—embarrassedly, worriedly and lovingly, he said, 'Shashi—'

That was all it took. Shashi spoke, her voice breaking, 'You've come back—' and then she burst into tears . . .

Shekhar was overcome with shame. He couldn't say a word . . . Then he quickly remembered his responsibilities, so he wrapped Shashi in the blanket and got up to light the stove. While he was blowing very hard to get the coals to light quickly, he heard the muffled sounds of Shashi's sobbing. That sound felt like a dull knife stabbing him somewhere deep inside . . . When he got the fire going, he took the stove into Shashi's room, set it down and gently tried to get Shashi to lie down. He said, 'Child, why did you let yourself catch cold—why were you so worried—'

Shashi held herself up stiffly. Pushing his hand off her shoulder she said, 'Move—'

Shekhar stood there meekly for a while. Then he repeated, 'Shashi, child, lie down and cover yourself with the blanket—why are you punishing yourself for my mistakes—'

Shashi didn't say anything, or move. Shekhar kept standing there desperately.

After a little while, Shashi drew a long breath and then lay down by herself—curling up her hands and feet, looking at the burning coals in the stove with unmoving eyes—

'Shashi, I wasn't late on purpose. We had to take the long way across the river—that's why I'm so late—'

Those same eyes now pierced through him, 'Why, what happened—'

'Nothing. When we were heading back, Brother saw a truck carrying policemen and said that we couldn't cross back over the bridge. So we walked about five or six extra miles and then crossed the river.'

'What were you doing there?'

Shekhar was silent. After a while, Shashi said, 'Well, at least you're back—'

'Why, Shashi, why were you so afraid—'

Shashi laughed a forced laugh as she kept staring at the coals. 'Hmm—why was I afraid. What do you know about fear . . . I thought that you weren't—you weren't coming back—'

'Why, Shashi? What made you think like that—'

As if looking inside herself thoughtfully, Shashi said, 'You went to the other side of the river, that much I knew. After you left, I was standing outside when I heard sounds of gunfire from the other side of the river. I never specially worry about you—I had thought that if you were hurt I'd feel it somehow; but for some reason today I felt like I would never see you again—that you were gone now . . . And perhaps gone now because—I am leaving, too.'

'What, Shashi—'

'Yes, Shekhar. Fear is a terrible thing; but sometimes it gives you extraordinary insight. Watching what happened to you—not you, but rather waiting to hear any news of you—I've seen quite a bit in the meantime which I hadn't seen before—or at least not as clearly.'

'What was it, Shashi?'

'Many things . . . I read in some foreign novel that love is an art, and that art is another name for discipline. And the intent of the novel was to say that no one should love another person so much that they have no room for any other purpose—that life is an independent unit and if it becomes completely dependent then it is no longer an art because it is beneath art's ideals. Then, I didn't understand what all of that meant . . .'

Shekhar also stared at the fire.

'I still haven't fully accepted it—but I've understood what it means finally . . . I—have moved beyond art . . . And—I've seen that this was the right thing to do—the right thing for me. I don't need room in my life for another purpose—because—I don't have life left to live.'

Shekhar was hurt, 'Shashi, you're only talking this way because you've been hurt badly—'

'No, Shekhar, no. The things that I have realized about you today, I might have got completely wrong, but about this—no. I've done all that I had to do . . .'

Shashi's voice was so definitive that Shekhar was unable to raise an objection. He had been standing, but now he sat down on Shashi's cot. His dumbstruck mind was trying to understand the full import of what Shashi was saying—but he couldn't get any further than the thought that she was saying that she wasn't going to live much longer . . .

Shashi slowly closed her eyes. Shekhar kept his eyes glued to the fire. Much time had elapsed—there was a layer of ash on the coals . . . He was going to get up to shake the stove when he noticed that Shashi was breathing quite rapidly. He quietly called out to her, 'Shashi—' and then he put his hand on her forehead and immediately drew it back. Shashi had a fever . . .

Shashi said, 'It seems as though it's getting worse.'

Shekhar took a blanket off his bed and wrapped her in it, relit the fire in the stove, and then began pacing in the room . . .

Brother gave a single warning knock and opened the locked doors and entered. Shekhar left Shashi's room to greet him and all at once he remembered a thousand responsibilities that he had as a host—

But Brother said, 'Take this. It's for both of you. I've just bought some dinner from the bazaar—it's very late—'

Shekhar was silent and grateful.

'Is Shashiji feeling all right?'

'Umm, no, she has a fever.'

Brother went into Shekhar's room and began putting his materials away. Shekhar stepped forward to get the plates.

*

Brother explained that he would be leaving early the next day—he would be out of Delhi before it was light out and would get on a train at some smaller station.[19] Shekhar wouldn't have to get up to see him off, he would just leave quietly, and it would be wonderful if they were to meet again, but if not—'If not, then whatever will be!'

After he had lain down to sleep and had started breathing regularly, Shekhar quietly walked out and went to Shashi's room.

He felt Shashi's forehead—it was still feverish. Shashi wasn't asleep, she was lying there exhausted . . . He stroked her head for a while and then left, he put some more coals in the stove and increased the flame and put it in Shashi's room. He put a glass of water on the table near her head; softly, he said to Shashi, 'Shashi, call me if you need anything—don't get up for just any reason . . .' He stood there indecisively for a moment and then went to his room and lay down.

He didn't think that he would be able to sleep the whole night, that he would be up thinking—but somehow, he was worn out from the day's wandering and he fell asleep. When he woke up, he was startled and looked at the radium watch on Brother's table, it was 4 a.m. . . . He knew that this was usually the coldest time of night so he thought that he should relight the stove and put it in Shashi's room again, but when he got up he noticed that there was a lamp burning brightly there even though he had dimmed it earlier . . . When he hurried over he saw Shashi lying down, supporting herself on one elbow and writing—not was, but was still writing, and now it seemed as if she was hanging her head and resting from exhaustion, the pen was still in her hand. His first instinct was to read what she had written, but he suppressed that urge and when he moved to lay Shashi down so that she could rest, she woke up. When she sat up, she straightened out her tired arms and began collecting her papers.

Shekhar's voice scolded Shashi deeply, 'Shashi . . .'

Shashi spoke plainly, 'Enough. Now I'm done writing—' But when she saw Shekhar looking so hurt she was embarrassed and said, 'It was important for me to write all this—I won't do any more mischief—Shekhar, I've become very obedient these days—'

Shekhar was disarmed. He picked up the stove and went to relight it.

The noise woke Brother. He got up, went outside, and asked, 'I was going to leave quietly, but you're up before me!'

Shekhar was still lighting the stove so he washed up and got ready. 'All right, Shekhar, I'll be leaving now. I'm sure that we will meet again—the two of us still have much to do!' Laughing a little,

'Give my regards to Shashiji. I am grateful to her—although all I've been able to give her in gratitude has been trouble and more trouble . . . All right—'

Shekhar quickly washed his blackened hands so that he could see him off at the door, but unaccustomed to goodbyes, Brother didn't wait. He flashed him a racing smile and left.

Shekhar slowly closed the door. He went back inside, took the stove and puffed away at it as he took it to Shashi's room.

He put the stove down and locked the door to the room, only the window was open a crack. And then he sat down as if thinking about what he would do next—

Shashi moved. She let her body go slack and stretched out as she drew a long breath. She pulled the blanket up to her chin and began looking at Shekhar. Shekhar asked, 'Shashi, are you comfortable? It gets really cold this time of day; the stove—' and then he stopped. Shashi wasn't listening; her vacant expression was washed out by the thinnest of smiles and she had closed her eyes. Shekhar quietly observed her face. Suddenly Shashi opened her eyes. She fixed her gaze firmly on Shekhar and kept staring at him. Her long, piercing stare made Shekhar's soul swoon; he saw—an ultimate truth; boundless; omnipresent . . .

'Shekhar, come here.'

Shekhar moved towards the cot.

'Sit next to me.'

Moved by a feeling he couldn't name, Shekhar sat at the foot of her cot—Shashi seemed so far away, other-worldly, dreamy, disembodied, as if touching her would scatter her to the wind—

'No'—what was the secret speaking through her voice?—'Not there, come closer!'

Spellbound, Shekhar shifted towards her.

Then without saying another word, Shashi lifts up her chin; her eyes are half-closed and her mouth is half-opened, and that unchanging expression reveals nothing—

Shekhar doesn't understand what is happening for a moment. Then a dam bursts inside him, and he bends down towards those half-opened lips—and as he bends down, his own flood of desire

holds him back, a loving tenderness takes its place and tells him
that half-opened jasmine blossoms should only be touched with
the most loving of caresses, and as he gets closer and closer to her
lips he bends his neck and touches Shashi's lips with his earlobe.
Her lips are tight—from the fever; that downy touch makes
a shudder run through his head, and then compelled by a new
wave in his consciousness he bends down again and kisses Shashi's
loving, fixed but unflinching lips . . . an unopposed, bestowed,
interminable kiss . . .

Shashi drew a deep breath and closed her eyes; bewildered
and unmoving, Shekhar takes a silent breath and sits down. He
can hear his pulse in the silence, then he doubts that the pulse
is his, but is rather Shashi's heartbeat—and then he thinks that
it is neither of theirs, but is the beat of the internal, ever-present
silence of dawn . . .

The dusty blanket of night melted into the rosiness of
dawn . . .

'Shekhar?'

'Hmm—'

'You used to make me sing for you; if I ask you now will you
do so for me—'

'Me? . . .'

'Yes, but you don't have to sing, just read,' and gesturing to
the cabinet with her eyes, Shashi says, 'There's a black notebook
in there—on the bottom shelf—'

Shekhar found the notebook.

'Let me have it—'

Shashi opened the notebook. She flipped through the pages
using one hand and her chin and then finding her place, she said,
'Here—read from here—'

Shekhar took the notebook and was surprised—it contained
poems copied in Shashi's hand—Hindi, English, Bengali—

'And don't just read them to yourself—read them out—'

Shekhar was about to start, he read half of a verse and then
stopped. Then he looked at Shashi's face once and continued
reading slowly.

I want to die while you love me
While yet you hold me fair,
While laughter lies upon my lips
And lights are in my hair,
I want to die while you love me.
Oh who would care to live
Till love has nothing more to ask
And nothing more to give?
I want to die—[20]

He stops suddenly and said, 'No, Shashi, I won't read this—' And the mysterious, instructive intention of the poem and of Shashi's making him read it just then pierced his soul. . . . I want to die while you love me[21] . . . 'No, absolutely not!'

'Why are you scared, Shekhar? It's an old poem—my laughter died a long time ago—No, Shekhar, I don't want to hurt you. Don't look at me like that—I realized things too late—just last night—yesterday in the evening, when you had gone to the other side of the Yamuna—'

Shekhar closed the notebook. He put it to one side, and he extended one hand and grabbed both of Shashi's hands tightly . . .

After a while, Shashi said, 'Let go. It's not as if I am dying right now—' And she smiled. And then changing her tone, 'Shekhar, if you need to go to work, you should go. I am going to sleep.'

Shekhar looked up at the day. He wanted to say that he didn't have any work any more. He thought that if she could get some rest he would be doing her a favour, and he quietly got up and walked out, although he had decided that he wouldn't go to the workshop today . . .

After he did his daily chores, he lit the stove, heated some milk, made a porridge and juiced three oranges; then he quietly started keeping an eye on Shashi's room. He peeped in through the window and saw that Shashi was sleeping peacefully . . .

Why had Shashi made him read that poem now? I want to die while you love me . . . Shashi never talked about mere sentimentality—so what was this—was it a message? Or was it only a possibility? . . . or a feeling—a gratitude for love . . . Or—pure—information . . .

He went to his room and wrote out a letter to his aunt that said that the two of them had been worried as they hadn't received any news from her, that everything was going well, that Shashi was getting worse, and that if it were possible, she should send some money. At one point his hand stopped in wonder at where his former pride had gone, but he couldn't see the reality of his pride clearly in his mind at that moment . . . He wrote the address on the envelope, took one more look at Shashi, and then went outside quietly to drop the letter into a letter box around the corner.

Shashi hadn't got up yet. There were beads of perspiration on her forehead . . . Her fever was breaking . . . Shekhar crept into her room quietly and sat down on the ground near Shashi's head. There were several things that he had to take care of away from the house, and there was nothing to do in the room as long as Shashi was sleeping. But Shekhar had so many things to say at that very moment to that sleeping face . . .

*

Why is it that whenever I recall these most intense days of my life I am left perplexed about what actually happened, and about what didn't happen and was only imagined? My external and internal worlds had become so entangled that it was impossible to separate them—perhaps the force of my internal world had become so intense that it ripped the physical boundaries of the external to shreds and burst forth—even when it didn't exist, the intensity was the truth, was real—is real . . .

'Listen, Shashi. There's much I have to tell you. Don't wake up, keep sleeping. Even while you are asleep you will hear the things that I want to say to you—because I am not speaking to your ears, I am speaking to your lips—lips that hesitated with me today, lips which I will never hesitate to speak my mind to—and especially not when they are asleep . . .

'Shashi, you have given me love—you've granted me a boon . . . But before you gave me this book, why didn't you test me? You need to test me—to see whether I am worthy or not . . .

'Shashi, I have always had a power in me, but I never recognized it. I've been a rebel my entire life, but I've always been uselessly squandering my rebellious energies . . . That's what your face taught me one day—it taught me that fighting is not an end of itself, to fight for the sake of fighting is inconsequential, and that a rebel has to rebel against something—God, society, illness, falsehood, mother, father, one's self, love, it could be anything that a rebel rebels against . . . That's when my rebellion found an edge—it became an opposition . . . I became an oppositionist . . .

'But that was really only partially understood, and so my rebellion was also only partial . . . Then—then you taught me that it wasn't enough just to fight against something . . . I learned that everything was polluted, was in ruins, was in decline—that it wasn't just one society, but all life that had been corrupted from its very roots—God, man, everything . . . corrupted from the roots— was corrupted and rotten, there was nothing left to fight with! Or maybe everything could be made use of, which was saying the same thing—clay can be cut, but a marsh cannot—you can only sink deeper and deeper into it . . . It isn't enough to fight against something; one also needed to fight for something . . .

'To fight for something . . . but for what? When everything was rotten, what was there to fight for . . .'

'So what did you decide, Shekhar?'

'I never needed to—you showed up again—you came into my life—I never knew what I should fight for, but you were with me; I started fighting for you—or I planned to start fighting. Shashi, I've been struggling continuously for my whole life—I've even fought with you, but now I acknowledge that I have loved you, too. I've given the best of myself in fighting, because I was doing it for you. Sometime in the middle I feared that all of my ideals were ignoble, but that vanished, because you were no less than a pure ideal . . . But then a hunger grew inside me and that brought with it a new fear . . . Shashi, have I sinned?'

'Shekhar, I have only ever loved you. I have never committed a sin.'
. . . Two disconnected sentences . . . Shekhar only gradually
absorbed their meaning . . . But when he fully realized them, then—

'And Shashi—now that I have found a goal to fight for—
Shashi, Shashi, are you really going to leave me, Shashi—'

Suddenly, Shekhar took Shashi's head forcefully . . . Shashi
woke up, his fingers kept tracing patterns on Shashi's hand—

'Shashi, will you really leave me—will my life really never have
any meaning—'

Shashi patted his hand and said, 'It will, Shekhar, it does. It
will after I'm gone, too. You won't be defeated—never defeated—
for me, Shekhar, for me . . .'

'I know, Shashi . . . I cannot stop—you've never let me. But
I don't know how I will go on—I can't see how—for whom . . .
Or whether I go on just for you—I go on, without seeing, without
understanding, somehow, for you, only for you, Shashi . . .'

Shashi's forehead was cool, her face gentle and peaceful, so
calm, so still that Shekhar, terrified . . . panicked, said, 'Shashi,
have you—gone?' Then feeling embarrassed, alarmed at the
stupidity of his question . . . But Shashi isn't alarmed, her fingers
reach out for Shekhar's hand again—

Had the atmosphere changed? Could the sun and the shade
trick someone? Why did tiny shadows dance on Shashi's face and
then disappear when her unblinking eyes were still bright and
her lips are still and gentle? Why did the fingers of her left hand
sometimes curl into a fist while lying on her chest even though the
rise-and-fall of her breasts was regular?

'Shashi, are you in pain?'

The blinking of her eyes says no.

But why did it seem to him that underneath his hand, Shashi's
cool forehead would be struck with a pain that then lingered, why
did it seem as though Shashi was trembling?

'Tell me, Shashi, why, what is happening? What is
happening . . .'

Shashi takes his hair and pulls his head towards her and says,
'Joy, Shekhar, joy . . .'

Day, afternoon, evening, night, morning, day, afternoon, evening, night, dawn . . . Fever, sweat, exhaustion, a slight ache, shivering, fever, loving-yet-limp hands, fever, sweat, cold . . . The air smelled of Holi, gentle and cool; the incessant falling of leaves, round, white clouds like scattered cotton, nomadic, carefree, aloof; dusty grey, whirlwind . . . Doctor, a wash basin filled with ash, charts and bottles, fruit juice . . . A letter from Aunt written in Gaura's handwriting—'Mother's eyes are seriously troubling her which is why she isn't writing herself. She sends both of you her best blessings, and she says that you should write very soon about Shashi's condition, it isn't good to wait so long between letters. God willing she will get better soon . . . She sends 100 rupees . . .' And then from Gaura, herself, 'Aunt wanted me to send the money by money order, but I'm putting them with the letter and sending them by registered mail because you might not accept a money order sent from here. I am very worried about Shashi's health, would you even write if we weren't worried? Shall I come to help nurse Shashi to health? I haven't asked Mother, but if you say so, I will definitely come, no matter what happens—write to us soon about everything . . .' Gaura had become very wise—such a slight girl . . . Commotion, the racing and roar of cars, white caps, red shirts, 'Black Laws', 'Bhagat Singh has been hanged', 'Gandhi's pleas unheeded!' . . .

Afternoon, evening, night; and everything is unreal, a lie, a delusion—a distant mirage . . . There were only two big, starry eyes nearby, the shimmering sparkle of stars which hides fear, alarm, worry, panic . . .

*

I am writing Shekhar's story, because I am trying to find the answer to life's questions in it, but there comes a point after which I cannot maintain the separation between Shekhar and myself—the one who suffered that day and the one who narrates today become the same, because ultimately the meaning of his life is the same as the meaning of my life; and I am not neutral towards the answers that I have to find, have to search for, I am not!

If this means that the ultimate victory is the historian's, then so be it. History means nothing to me; the succession of events also means nothing. Life is ultimately redeemed by life—the best aspect of our lives is that wondrous creation, human being—and the pride of an individual's life is his love—his ability to dilate himself, to sacrifice himself, beyond himself . . . The import of the story is not for me, its meaning is for the character that I have been narrating; and so that I can acknowledge it, bear witness to it, before I pass on . . . When I will no longer be, then this work can stand as a memorial to him! Had the circumstances of his life been different, then his future would have been as well—perhaps he would have been the head of a household and all of those lives would have been blessed with that gift-like, affectionate, pure love which is the offering of every expansive soul . . . But that is not what happened. I am the only one who has seen that expansive soul close up, I, who became the cause of its destruction . . .

But I am not offering testimony, making a confession, to wash away my crimes or as atonement. Even crimes could have drowned in that love, as expansive as it was . . . I won't minimize Shekhar's crimes, because his commitment to love lay behind them, that Shekhar who is me . . .

Worry, worry, fear . . . Decision . . . Perhaps Shashi already knows, but one day suddenly Shekhar realized . . . To make the ignored visible is perhaps both proper and necessary; one cannot aim for ignorance . . . He had stopped going in to the workshop for a few days now. Now he had given up leaving Shashi's side, he had moved his bed into her room, he would sleep two hours at night and an hour or so whenever he found the opportunity, otherwise he would remain in constant vigil by Shashi's bed; when she would wake, he would caress her forehead or the hand that lay across her chest; when she was falling asleep, he would curl up and be perfectly still so as not to disturb her, and if she slept peacefully he would immediately watch her face—and such opportunities for watching gradually increased . . . Or sometimes when Shashi would tell him to get some rest, he would lie on his stomach on his cot, balancing on his elbows, his head on his chin, he would keep watching her . . .

Nursing a patient is a science. It depends on the intellect; there is no place for emotion in it. People who have been colonized by western civilization laugh at the Indian mother who won't take her sick child to see a doctor, clutching it instead to her chest all night paralysed with fear . . . Mere, instinctive love—the unreasoned agitation of a maternal animal for her wounded infant—this is not scientific nursing; but one animal's cry is also a medicine for another animal, not only a medicine but also a necessity . . . And for those instances where science acknowledges its impotence, there is the power of this basic instinct which is not powerless—not even in the face of death because death is first and foremost a fear of death, and that fear cannot touch an individual enveloped in a cloud of love . . .

The doctor came twice a day, and he would leave medicines or have them sent. Two young men from Shekhar's organization would leave meals and ask after them, sometimes they would tell them of the happenings in the world which even when he heard them would not remain in Shekhar's mind, because there was no room for them there . . .

Shekhar spoke very little, and Shashi almost never spoke, and only when she gave Shekhar a reassuring message with her eyes . . . After each new attack of illness—a full cycle of tremors followed by fever, and fever followed by sweats and cooling off—when Shashi's aching hand would be trembling on her breast, and her fingers would curl up and then open fully, and the lids would tighten over her already closed eyes and then fully open, that was when Shekhar realized that entertaining conversation was necessary to keep Shashi happy and to keep her mind off the pain. He would try to start such a conversation, but his mind would go blank, and he could think of nothing distracting to talk about. Then he would reach for Shashi's hand and softly say, 'Shashi, don't be afraid. I'm here with you—' Shashi would open her eyes and look once at him; that gaze had the slightest, laughing compassion in it. 'Am I afraid? You should not be afraid, I am with you . . .'

And in this way the wick of the lamp would burn out, but Shekhar sat and watched the light . . .

The night was long, but it kept moving; the stove had gone out, Shekhar was awake . . .

Shashi gently called out, 'Shekhar—'

Shekhar bent down towards her so that he could hear Shashi well, so that she wouldn't have to repeat herself.

'Shekhar—in the cabinet—a letter.'

Shekhar understood her words. He opened the cabinet and took out a few folded pages on the bottom shelf and asked, 'Do you want to send this letter somewhere or to give it to someone?'

The blinking of her eyes meant yes.

'Someone—I'll send it—'

Her eyes were fixed on Shekhar; her mouth opened slowly, 'Read it.'

He didn't know to whom Shashi had written the letter— should he read it? He is still racked with doubt when he opens the pages, he haltingly reads the first paragraph (Had Shashi written to Rameshwar—How could she write to him—) when a flash of lightning strikes him; how could he have been so blind . . . Shashi had written to him, to Shekhar—to Shekhar!

Shekhar stopped at that realization. His hands trembled; unable to read any further, he stares at Shashi—

'No, not later, now—'

He reads the whole thing in one breath—it wasn't the case that by reading it so quickly he didn't understand its meaning, its words—sentence after sentence branded his consciousness like a hot iron and continued to ring in his ears . . . And things began to happen at the same time, things that Shekhar was fully and consciously party to, but that ringing was also present, as if two lives were being lived at the same time, one that was intense because it was life in its immediacy, and the other which was even more intense because it happened before the immediate and was trying to lay siege to the present.

'. . . You were only gone for a few hours, you even came back; but I lost you and found you so many times in those hours, sent

you away and then propped you back up with my own hands . . .
But I never forgot about your love for even a moment, Shekhar,
but when the headiness of the moment passed I saw something
greater than your love—your future. I say that it is bigger than
love because love will be a part of it . . . I am grateful for that
moment . . .

'I am writing this letter to you so that you can read it after I'm
gone—when you read it later, perhaps you will ask why Shashi
didn't tell you these things earlier when they wouldn't have
felt like such a vile curse—but it was for the best, Shekhar . . .
If I had a long life to live, things might have been different,
but in that clear moment I also realized that I only had a few
days left . . . Which is why I won't write about my love in this
letter, either—the love of one who has passed can only produce
anguish, and anguish should not speak . . . I will only talk about
your love . . .

'Love can also be an art, Shekhar; it is not a wicked thought,
I consider it to be an auspicious one; but to me it's become more
intimate and necessary than even art—I don't say that out of
conceit, I consider it my failing . . . The joy of art is a controlled
joy; and just once, I poured my entire being, my entire world, into
the sacrificial flame—that wasn't controlled, so perhaps—it wasn't
joy either—but it caused so much pain that we can't even really call
it a tragedy[22] . . .

'Once, I said to you out of vanity, "Can you write something
for me?" You had said that ideals weren't enough, that you needed
a tangible symbol of those ideas; and I had come to you hoping to
be your symbol . . . Shekhar, I didn't do that out of conceit—I do
not claim that I was the alpha and the omega of your life—I am
not audacious enough to claim to be the ultimate conclusion . . .
All I wanted, all that I had asked for, in exchange for destroying
my life—sacrificing it, reducing it to ashes—was that it be useful
for you, that it find its meaning in you. You became my symbol,
a symbol for me and my life—a symbol of my place in the sea of
trembling failure and idiocy and frustration and ruin all around us,
a symbol of my crossing over . . . That's why I asked you to write

for me—not to give your life hope, but for me to find hope from you . . .

'What you have given me I have gratefully accepted—as a boon, not as a right; I never imagined that I would be able to keep it tied up forever. I need you because the wreckage of my life finds its expression through you—through you, and from the dream that I dream for you; but I know, I realize that you are not wrecked, and that is why I have decided that as long as I have any say in the matter, my love won't be the kind that tries to hold you back . . . Shekhar, my love for you knows no bounds, but I want you to know that I have not tied you down, am not tying you down—not now while I am still here and not—after . . .

'You have your own future, Shekhar; my future was you and only you. If in your quest for your future you ever—'

Shekhar looked at Shashi to see whether it was necessary to read all of this in front of her or—but he realizes that Shashi's eyes are telling him something more immediate than the letter. He comes very close to Shashi; her lips want to say something, but they are speechless, perhaps they want to say something speechlessly— Shekhar puts his lips over them and they stop quivering. He looks into Shashi's eyes and slowly gets up—he knows that he has heard what she had to say, those lips still had the ability to be kissed left in them—and then there were no more words, just a nervous flutter which, it seemed, her will had tried to control but had gradually given up in frustration—in one ultimate deliverance all of the tension and strain and pressure—

'If in the quest for your future you ever think of me, don't blame yourself that you are able to go on without me; you can go on. That won't be my defeat; it will be my greatest victory . . .'

Shashi's entire body, except her eyes, became lifeless matter—

'Everyone can be fortunate enough to be an ideal for a while, a day, a moment; but no one is an eternal ideal, cannot be. That is why one who is "eternally" true to one's lover is always certainly failing in the face of the ideal, and the one who is faithful to the ideal will always certainly let his lover go on . . . An ordinary man and an artist—that's what is different about a rebel . . . I don't want you to be less of a man, Shekhar, but if you have it in you to be more than that, I happily give you permission—freedom to . . .'

Shashi's eyes didn't die; seeing the expansive, fearless, bright kindling inside them having burned out, they retreated inside themselves . . .

'The two of us, you and me, have been building a mansion for years in which neither you nor I will live . . . But will it be any less beautiful just because neither of us lives in it . . .'

In this tranquillity, in this dwindling light, could there be any weeping, any wailing? The mechanical form of Shekhar's numb body moved over to the window, the window opened, and the light from the day flooded inside . . . He turned around to see Shashi's face, bathed in rosy rays, sparkling with the colours of life . . .

Shekhar remained stunned—paralysed, both in the knowledge of some superhuman, cosmic presence, the long-awaited dawn of some inner truth . . .

A sudden revelation . . .

*

But there's no story after this. No sequence of events. Life has lost all meaning, lost all reality, order, motion, everything. Even mere existence—the continuous addition of one moment to the next— had been erased. I am a shade, a dream, a spectral resentment, a parting, a mystery . . . A thought that wanders from feeling to feeling—setting fire to everything, itself scorched in the light, burning higher—continuously rising, rising, not dwindling, not dying . . .

Death, you are also a shadow—devour this shadow, if you have the strength in you—if you have the courage . . . Break the torch, snuff it out, tear it to pieces—the body is a torch and one day it too will burn and be destroyed, but its flame reaches higher— there, and there, and there—evading your clutches, daring you, imperishable, free . . .

Devour it, touch it if you have the power in you, if you have the courage . . .

A young man showed up.

Brother had sent him a hand-delivered letter appealing to Shekhar to come to Lahore if at all possible—some of the organization's members who were in prison were going to be sent to the prison colonies in the Andaman and Nicobar Islands; if the independence struggle were going to be kept alive, then it was necessary to save them from this living tomb, and in order to accomplish this, Shekhar's participation was necessary . . . He didn't know how Shashi's health was, but he was completely prepared to make arrangements for her care and treatment—

The young man spoke compassionately, 'Brother didn't know when he sent the letter . . . You've been deeply hurt . . . But you should come, the work will give you some comfort, and the job requires much effort . . . If sister Shashi were still alive, that's what she would tell you, too—and I have faith that even now her soul will find some peace from it—'

Shekhar wasn't listening at first, but he heard the last sentence; he wanted to slap this young man across his face for speaking so easily; but then all he said was, 'Someone will have to look after all of this—and the workshop—'

*

Hail, Yamuna; hail to the East; hail to the blooming acacias and dhaks of spring; hail to the sad rustling of the tamarisk and whirlwinds of dust; hail to the sandy riverbanks traversed thousands of times by these two feet; hail to the handful of ash that has floated away . . . I used to think that if something else had happened instead of this, or something else, or something else, then . . . But today I think, no, today all I am asking for is for everything to happen just as it did; shadow, you and I should be just as we are—separate but locked in perpetual, active, ordinary competition to see who would lead the other, but in reality, bound together in unbreakable faith, of a single artery . . .

Shadow, I am not leaving to abandon you, you should come with me—first to see Aunt and Gaura and then—onwards; there is no forgetfulness in action, Shashi, there is only you, an eternal urging: eternal because free and—liberating . . .

Notes

Author's Introduction

1. Vision is in English in the original. No Hindi word is given.
2. Vision is in English in the original. No Hindi word is given.
3. 'Intensity' is the translation that Agyeya offers for '*tivrata*'.
4. Agyeya translates '*hetuvaad*' as 'rationalization', but I have used 'sophistry' to maintain consistency.
5. Agyeya seems to be referring to a line from T.S. Eliot's 'Tradition and the Individual Talent', but he has misquoted it: 'The mind of the poet is the shred of platinum. It may partly or exclusively operate upon the experience of the man himself; but, the more perfect the artist, the more completely separate in him will be the man who suffers and the mind which creates; the more perfectly will the mind digest and transmute the passions which are its material.'
6. Agyeya's translation.
7. In English in the original.
8. Agyeya's translation.
9. Luigi Pirandello (1867–1936) was an Italian dramatist, poet, novelist and short story writer. He won the Nobel Prize for Literature in 1934.
10. The third part was never published. See Translator's Note.

Prologue

1. Banda Singh Bahadur (1670–1716).
2. In Nagari-English in the original.
3. Arthur W. Ryder, 'Shakuntala', in *Kalidasa: Translations of Shakuntala and Other Works* (London: J.M. Dent & Sons, 1912).
4. In retaliation for a practical joke, Narad cursed Vishnu to endure separation from his beloved when he took birth on the earth (the basis of the Ramayana).
5. Kalidasa, *The Dynasty of Raghu*, trans. Robert Antoine (Calcutta: Writers Workshop, 1972), p. 94. The original lines are from Kalidasa's *Raghuvansh*, canto 8, verse 46. This can be compared to a more literal translation of the lines: 'If this garland of flowers had killed her all of a sudden why does it not kill me though I have placed it for a long time on my breast?' from Gopal Lallanji, ed., *Kalidasa's Raghuvansham: An Account of the Family of Raghu* (Varanasi: Indological Book House, 1992), p. 112.
6. A translation of '*satyam shivam sundaram*'.
7. Alfred, Lord Tennyson, 'Maud', part 2, 5.1.239–46.
8. Alfred, Lord Tennyson, 'Maud', part 2, 5.1.247.
9. In Nagari-English in the original; Agyeya supplies a Hindi translation.
10. In English in the original.
11. Bal Gangadhar 'Lokmanya' Tilak (1856–1920) was an important Indian nationalist and social reformer.
12. Jatindranath Das (1904–29) was an independence activist and revolutionary; he died while on hunger strike in Lahore jail.
13. In Nagari-English in the original.
14. Rabindranath Tagore, 'Nirjhorer Shopno Bhongo'.
15. Dante Gabriel Rossetti (1828–82), 'Pride of Youth' (1880). Most editions have these lines rendered differently: 'Alas for all / The loves that from his hand proud Youth lets fall, / Even as the beads of a told rosary!'

16. Agyeya glosses 'love' in the Rossetti poem as *'pranay'*; to retain consistency, I've used 'love' wherever Agyeya uses 'pranay'.
17. Agyeya offers 'impersonal' as his gloss for *'akartrik'*.
18. Rabindranath Tagore, *Balaka*, verse 8.
19. In English in the original.

Volume 1: Development

Part 1: Dawn and Divinity

1. In Nagari-English in the original.
2. The naming ceremony usually happens ten days after birth in most Hindu traditions; it is believed that the first ten days after the birth are unlucky.
3. In Nagari-English in the original.
4. In Nagari-English in the original.
5. In Nagari-English in the original.
6. A common way to refer to all parrots.
7. In English in the original.
8. The misspelt English is in the original text. It is followed by a translation in correctly spelled Hindi.
9. In English in the original.
10. A temple dedicated to the goddess Bhawani. It is located fourteen miles east of Srinagar. Kheer means rice pudding, which is offered to the goddess every spring. It has now been attached to the name of the temple.
11. A bridge that connects the two halves of Srinagar, built in the eighteenth century.
12. Zeb-un-Nissa (1638–1702) was the oldest child of Aurangzeb (1618–1707).

Part 2: Seeds and Sprouts

1. Dante Gabriel Rossetti, from the sonnet sequence 'The House of Life' (1881). This is from the sonnet 'Known in

Vain'. Most versions are slightly different: 'Ah! who shall dare to search through what sad maze / Thenceforth their incommunicable ways / Follow the desultory feet of Death?'

2.   Also known as 'gulkand'.
3.   Also known as 'chyawanprash'.

Part 3: Nature and Man

1.   See 'The Homecoming', *Rabindranath Tagore Omnibus*, vol. 1 (Delhi: Rupa & Co., 2004), pp. 891–2.
2.   The actual poem is simply called 'Oenone'. I assume he added 'The Death of' to make it clear that it was a narrative poem and not some strange word which might not have been clear in translation.
3.   Most editions of the Tennyson poem capitalize 'Autumn'.
4.   Most editions of Rossetti's 'Last Confession' use 'growing'.
5.   Caroline Elizabeth Sarah Norton (Lady Stirling-Maxwell) (1808–77).

I Do Not Love Thee!

I do not love thee!—no! I do not love thee!
And yet when thou art absent I am sad;
And envy even the bright blue sky above thee,
Whose quiet stars may see thee and be glad.

I do not love thee!—yet, I know not why,
Whate'er thou dost seems still well done, to me:
And often in my solitude I sigh
That those I do love are not more like thee!

I do not love thee!—yet when thou art gone,
I hate the sound (though those who speak be dear)
Which breaks the lingering echo of the tone
Thy voice of music leaves upon my ear.

I do not love thee!—yet thy speaking eyes,
With their deep, bright, and most expressive blue,
Between me and the midnight heaven arise,
Oftener than any eyes I ever knew.

I do not love thee! yet, alas!
Others will scarcely trust my candid heart;
And oft I catch them smiling as they pass,
Because they see me gazing where thou art.

6. Kalidasa, *The Dynasty of Raghu*, trans. Robert Antoine (Calcutta: Writers Workshop, 1972), p. 94. The original lines are from Kalidasa's *Raghuvansh*, canto 8, verse 46. This can be compared to a more literal translation of the lines: 'If this garland of flowers had killed her all of a sudden why does it not kill me though I have placed it for a long time on my breast?' from Gopal Lallanji, ed., *Kalidasa's Raghuvansham: An Account of the Family of Raghu* (Varanasi: Indological Book House, 1992), p. 112.

7. Most versions of Rossetti's 'The Song of the Bower' have 'illumes' whereas Agyeya uses 'illumines'.

8. Most editions of Frances Pilkington's *Madrigals* have 'fall'n' whereas Agyeya uses 'fallen'.

9. Most editions of Frances Pilkington's *Madrigals* have 'cannot tell' whereas Agyeya uses 'knows not'.

10. Transliterated into Hindi in the original.

11. While Madrasi is no longer politically correct, it is preserved here to mark the text's social context.

12. Alfred, Lord Tennyson (1809–92). Agyeya changes the order of Tennyson's lines.

Come into the Garden, Maud

Come into the garden, Maud,
For the black bat, Night, has flown,
Come into the garden, Maud,

> I am here at the gate alone;
> And the woodbine spices are wafted abroad,
> And the musk of the roses blown.

13. Veene Sheshanna (1852–1926) was a talented veena player with a background in classical Carnatic music. He was patronized by the princely state of Mysore.
14. Tagore, 'Life of my life, I shall ever try'.
15. Tagore, 'Fruit-Gathering', verse LXXI.
16. Rabindranath Tagore, 'The Lotus'.
17. Formal greeting.
18. Later on the same page, the girl's name is Savitri. This is most likely a typographical error, but it is there in both the Mayur and Saraswati editions.
19. Agyeya provides the translation in English.
20. In English in the original.
21. In English in the original.
22. It was called Madura under the British; it is now known as Madurai.
23. Jayadeva's *Gita Govinda*, ashtapad 3–1. Lee Siegel renders it thus: 'When winsome westerly winds caress comely creeping cloves, As bumblebees' buzz-buzzing and cuckoos' coo-cooing resound in huts, in groves.'
24. Jayadeva's *Gita Govinda*, ashtapad 11–1. Agyeya has inverted the lines; the line beginning 'Gopi' comes first, but since it is the 'objectionable' line, the inversion works in the interest of the drama. Reprise: *dheer sameere* = in gentle, wind (breezy); *yamuna teere* = on Yamuna, riverbank; *vasit vane* = located in (lingering in), garden; *vanamalee* = one who wears leafy garland, Krishna.
25. A self-decapitated tantric goddess.
26. In Nagari-English in the original. Dante Gabriel Rossetti, *Beata Beatrix* (ca 1864–70).
27. In Nagari-English in the original.
28. In Nagari-English in the original.

29. Alfred, Lord Tennyson, 'Break, Break, Break' (1842). Both Mayur and Saraswati have errors (using 'crag' for 'stones' and 'day' for 'bay'). These errors have been corrected, as there was no good reason to retain Agyeya's mistakes.
30. Agyeya offers a translation in English, so I preserved the Hindi.
31. In English in the original.

Part 4: Man and Circumstance

1. This has to be hyperbole since we encounter Shekhar running away from home earlier.
2. In Nagari-English in the original.
3. Agyeya offers this as a translation of 'guardian angel'.
4. In Nagari-English in the original.
5. In Nagari-English in the original.
6. In Nagari-English in the original.
7. In Nagari-English in the original.
8. 'The oracle has spoken' is written in Nagari-English in the original.
9. In Nagari-English in the original.
10. In Nagari-English in the original.
11. In Nagari-English in the original.
12. Immolation of widows on the funeral pyre.
13. Self-immolation, especially by Rajput women evading capture by invading armies.
14. Perhaps a reference to the Mughal practice of execution by elephant.
15. Translation provided by Agyeya in both Saraswati and Mayur.
16. In the Ramayana, Ram asks Sita to prove her fidelity by walking on a fire.
17. In Nagari-English in the original.
18. Agyeya has 'professor'; I chose 'guru' to retain the sense of religious instruction from the previous line.
19. Agyeya uses club, society and league to describe the same group.

Volume 2: Struggle

Part 1: Man and Nature

1. The list up to this point is in Nagari-English in the original.
2. All the philosophical references are in Nagari in the original. 'Stoic' is added in parentheses in both Mayur and Saraswati.
3. In Nagari-English in the original.
4. I've used Agyeya's offered translation.
5. In English and then translated.
6. In English and then translated. Here, the translation in Hindi differs slightly from the English, so I've offered them both.
7. Edna St Vincent Millay (1892–1950), 'First Fig' from *A Few Figs from Thistles* (1920).
8. In English in the original.
9. In English in the original.
10. In English in the original.
11. In Nagari-English in the original.
12. In Nagari-English in the original.
13. In Nagari-English in the original.
14. Literally, 'egg of electricity'.
15. Agyeya uses '*shasya-shamala*', which is lifted from Bankim Chandra's 'Vande Mataram'. I have used Aurobindo's translation of the phrase, which has been recognized as the official translation of the poem by the Indian government.
16. In Persian-Nagari in the original. A couplet sometimes attributed to Amir Khusro (1253–1325).
17. Both Mayur and Saraswati have used 'horse'; I changed it to 'mule' to retain consistency with the earlier prose.
18. Mayur and Saraswati both have 'horse'.
19. In Nagari-English in the original.
20. In Nagari-English in the original.
21. In Nagari-English in the original.
22. In Nagari-English in the original.
23. In Nagari-English in the original.

24. Criminal Investigation Division of the colonial police.
25. In Nagari-English in the original.
26. In Nagari-English in the original.

Part 2: Bondage and Curiosity

1. Agyeya uses 'jail' but it is clear that he means 'prison'.
2. In Nagari-English in the original.
3. 'Vande Mataram' by Bankim Chandra Chatterjee.
4. In English in the original.
5. Agyeya switches between 'hakim' and 'magistrate' for this person.
6. In Sanskrit. Mantras said while offering sacrifices to the fire during a Hindu wedding.
7. In Nagari-English in the original.
8. In English in the original. Agyeya offers his own translation in Hindi.
9. Likely from *Avadhuta Gita* 1:12: '*Aatmanam satatam vidhi sarvatrekam nirantaram.*'
10. Agyeya seems to be moving between Hindu and Christian traditions here.
11. In Nagari-English in the original.
12. Dante Gabriel Rossetti (1828–82), 'The Song of the Bower'. Most editions of this poem have 'illumes' where Agyeya has 'illumines'.

Part 3: Shashi and Shekhar

1. In Nagari-English in the original.
2. In Nagari-English in the original.
3. In Nagari-English in the original.
4. Agyeya translates the Urdu '*afeef*' as '*sanyam*'.
5. In Nagari-English in the original.
6. Probably Rossetti's *Beata Beatrix*.
7. Agyeya takes some liberties with Tennyson's poem 'Crossing the Bar' (1889):

Sunset and evening star
And one clear call for me!
And may there be no moaning of the bar,
When I put out to sea,
But such a tide as moving seems asleep,
Too full for sound and foam,
When that which drew from out the boundless deep
Turns again home.

Twilight and evening bell,
And after that the dark!
And may there be no sadness of farewell,
When I embark;

For though from out our bourne of Time and Place
The flood may bear me far,
I hope to see my Pilot face to face
When I have crossed the bar.

8.   In Nagari-English in the original.
9.   In Nagari-English in the original.
10. In Nagari-English in the original.
11. In Nagari-English in the original.
12. In Nagari-English in the original.
13. In Nagari-English in the original.
14. Agyeya has translated this title as 'A Sketch of History'; I've
     used the original title.
15. In Nagari-English in the original.
16. The smritis are sacred Hindu texts composed of truths
     revealed to the Brahmins.
17. Agyeya seems to be quoting the first part of the *Bhagavad
     Gita*, sloka 9–26.
18. A reference again to the *Bhagavad Gita*, sloka 9–26.
19. Atharva Veda, Book 19, hymn 15, verses 5–6. The translation
     comes from Ralph T. Griffith, *Hymns of the Atharva-veda*
     (Varanasi: Master Khelari Lal, 1962).
20. Rabindranath Tagore's 'Aaji Marmara Dhwani'. Agyeya
     misremembers some of the lines, perhaps because of the

conditions under which he was writing. The original version has been translated here. Importantly, the song was in Bengali and rendered into Devanagari by Agyeya.

Part 4: Threads, Ropes and Nets

1. 'Serious' and 'septic' are in Nagari-English in the original.
2. In Nagari-English in the original.
3. In Nagari-English in the original.
4. In Nagari-English in the original.
5. Agyeya appears to be misquoting from the *Bhagavad Gita* 9–26. He has substituted 'vessel' for 'fruit' most likely because he is recalling the verse from memory, rather than referencing the text.
6. Most likely a reference to Alfred, Lord Tennyson's 'The Lady of Shalott' quoted earlier in the novel.
7. In Nagari-English in the original.
8. In Nagari-English in the original.
9. In Nagari-English in the original.
10. In Nagari-English in the original.
11. Parijat—a tree from Hindu mythology.
12. Referring to the myth of Niobe.
13. In Nagari-English in the original.
14. Raktabeej (from *rakta*—blood, and *beej*—seed) was a demon who was granted a boon according to which each drop of blood he lost in battle would reproduce another one of him—until he was finally slain by a devi.
15. In Nagari-English in the original.
16. In Nagari-English in the original.
17. In Nagari-English in the original.
18. In Nagari-English in the original.
19. In Nagari-English in the original.
20. Georgia Johnson (1880–1966), 'I want to die while you love me'. Agyeya has taken the first and third stanzas and omitted the second and fourth stanzas. Quoted in English in the original.
21. In English in the original.
22. In Nagari-English in the original.